Once upon a time...

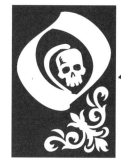

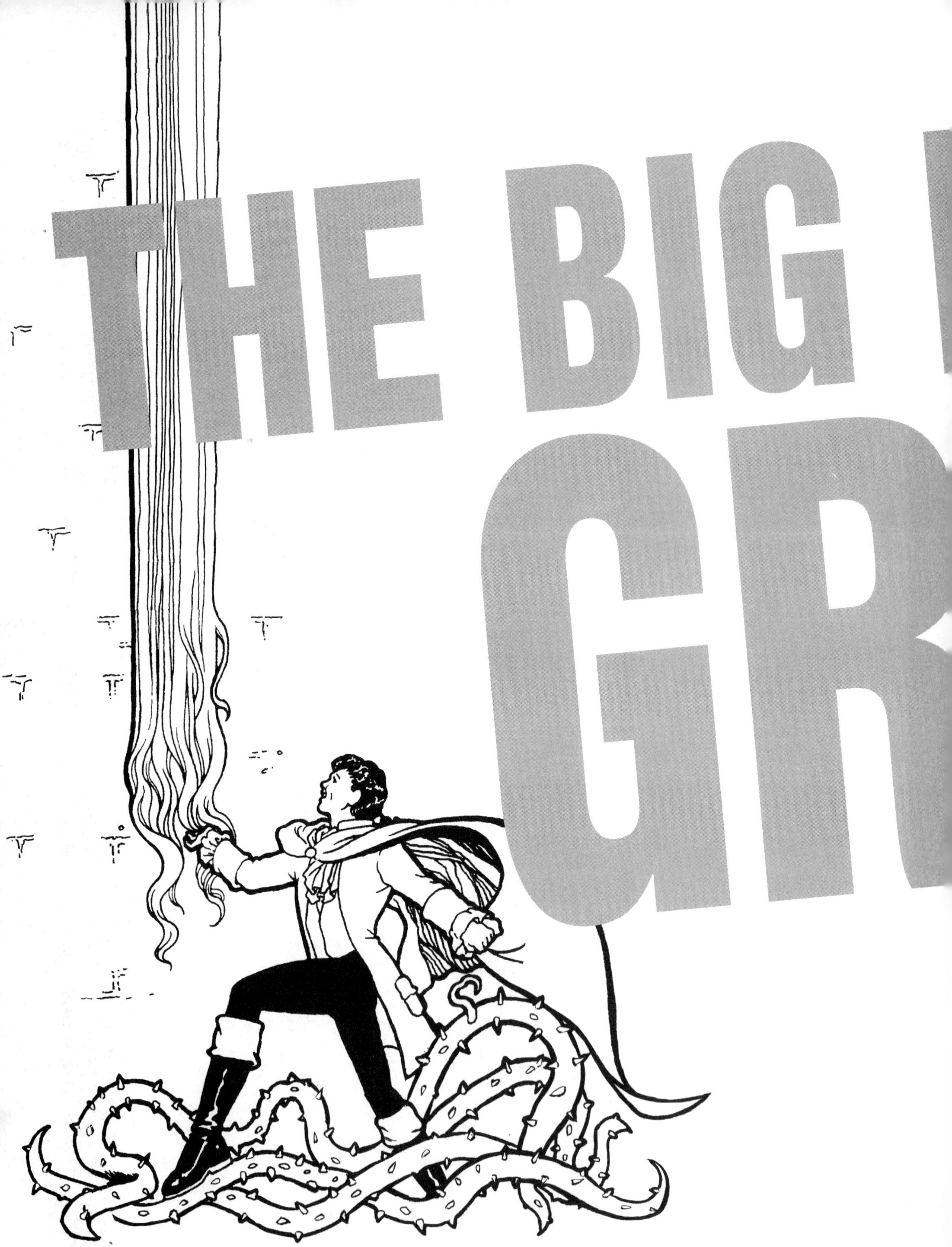
THE BIG
GR

BOOK OF GRIMM

BY
THE BROTHERS GRIMM
AS CHANNELED BY JONATHAN VANKIN
& OVER 50 TOP COMIC ARTISTS!

PARADOX PRESS
NEW YORK

THE BIG BOOK OF GRIMM.
Published by Paradox Press. Cover and compilation
Copyright © 1999 Paradox Press. All Rights Reserved.
Factoid, Paradox Press and related logo are trademarks
of DC Comics. Paradox Press is an imprint of
DC Comics, 1700 Broadway, New York, NY 10019. A division
of Warner Bros. - A Time Warner Entertainment Company.

Printed in Canada. First Printing.

See page 191 for individual copyright holders.

Front and back cover designed by Steve Vance.

Front cover art by John Cebollero.

Title page illustration by Colleen Doran.

Page 187 illustration by Cliff Chiang.

Publication design by Brian Pearce.

Principal Letterers: Kurt Hathaway and Bob Lappan.

Additional Lettering: Jason Little and artists who lettered
their own stories.

TABLE OF CONTENTS

WRITER:
Jonathan Vankin

1 FAMILY HELL

2 PRISONERS OF CHILDHOOD

3 NUPTIAL NIGHTMARES

4 MAGICAL STRANGERS

5 LESSONS LEARNED — THE HARD WAY

CHAPTER ONE

FAMILY HELL

You want family values? Go back to the good old days. Men were men, women were mommies and kids spoke only when spoken to. You know, the traditional family structure. No high school massacres, crack smokers, gangbangers or heavy metal music in the old days. But were the old days REALLY that good? In the following tales compiled by Jacob and Wilhelm Grimm, the central horror in society is — the family. Fathers lust after their daughters. Obnoxious children give their well-meaning parents grief even from beyond the grave. Parents starve and beat and torture their children. And those are just the natural parents! In these stories, collected and edited like the others by the Grimms between 1812 and 1857, the only thing worse than being a cruel natural parent is to be — *a stepmother*. The archetypal wicked stepmother — interloper in the once-secure patriarchal family (it's never a stepfather who's the problem) — crops up again and again, in stories such as "Aschenputtel," "The Juniper Tree" and "The Mother-in-Law." Real mothers in the tales are usually "pure," "beautiful" — and dead. While the stepmother is, obviously, a symbol of family breakdown, one can only wonder if there was some self-censorship involved. Could the Grimms or the storytellers from whom they collected their tales have found the idea of mothers torturing, killing and eating their offspring a tad too horrifying to handle and consequently turned "mother" into the more easily scapegoated "stepmother"?

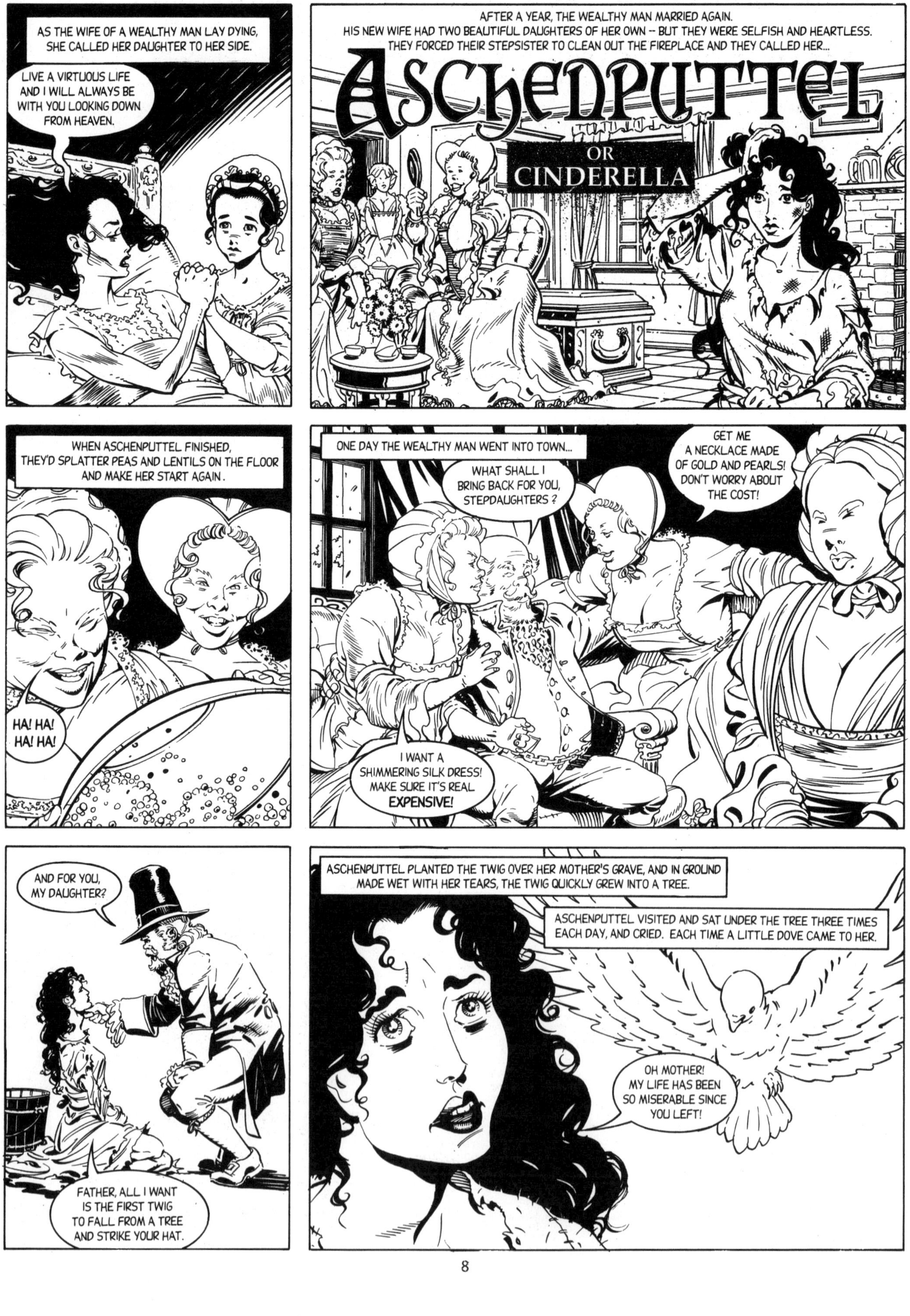

AS THE WIFE OF A WEALTHY MAN LAY DYING, SHE CALLED HER DAUGHTER TO HER SIDE.
LIVE A VIRTUOUS LIFE AND I WILL ALWAYS BE WITH YOU LOOKING DOWN FROM HEAVEN.
AFTER A YEAR, THE WEALTHY MAN MARRIED AGAIN. HIS NEW WIFE HAD TWO BEAUTIFUL DAUGHTERS OF HER OWN -- BUT THEY WERE SELFISH AND HEARTLESS. THEY FORCED THEIR STEPSISTER TO CLEAN OUT THE FIREPLACE AND THEY CALLED HER...
ASCHENPUTTEL
OR CINDERELLA
WHEN ASCHENPUTTEL FINISHED, THEY'D SPLATTER PEAS AND LENTILS ON THE FLOOR AND MAKE HER START AGAIN.
HA! HA! HA! HA!
ONE DAY THE WEALTHY MAN WENT INTO TOWN...
WHAT SHALL I BRING BACK FOR YOU, STEPDAUGHTERS?
GET ME A NECKLACE MADE OF GOLD AND PEARLS! DON'T WORRY ABOUT THE COST!
I WANT A SHIMMERING SILK DRESS! MAKE SURE IT'S REAL EXPENSIVE!
AND FOR YOU, MY DAUGHTER?
FATHER, ALL I WANT IS THE FIRST TWIG TO FALL FROM A TREE AND STRIKE YOUR HAT.
ASCHENPUTTEL PLANTED THE TWIG OVER HER MOTHER'S GRAVE, AND IN GROUND MADE WET WITH HER TEARS, THE TWIG QUICKLY GREW INTO A TREE.
ASCHENPUTTEL VISITED AND SAT UNDER THE TREE THREE TIMES EACH DAY, AND CRIED. EACH TIME A LITTLE DOVE CAME TO HER.
OH MOTHER! MY LIFE HAS BEEN SO MISERABLE SINCE YOU LEFT!

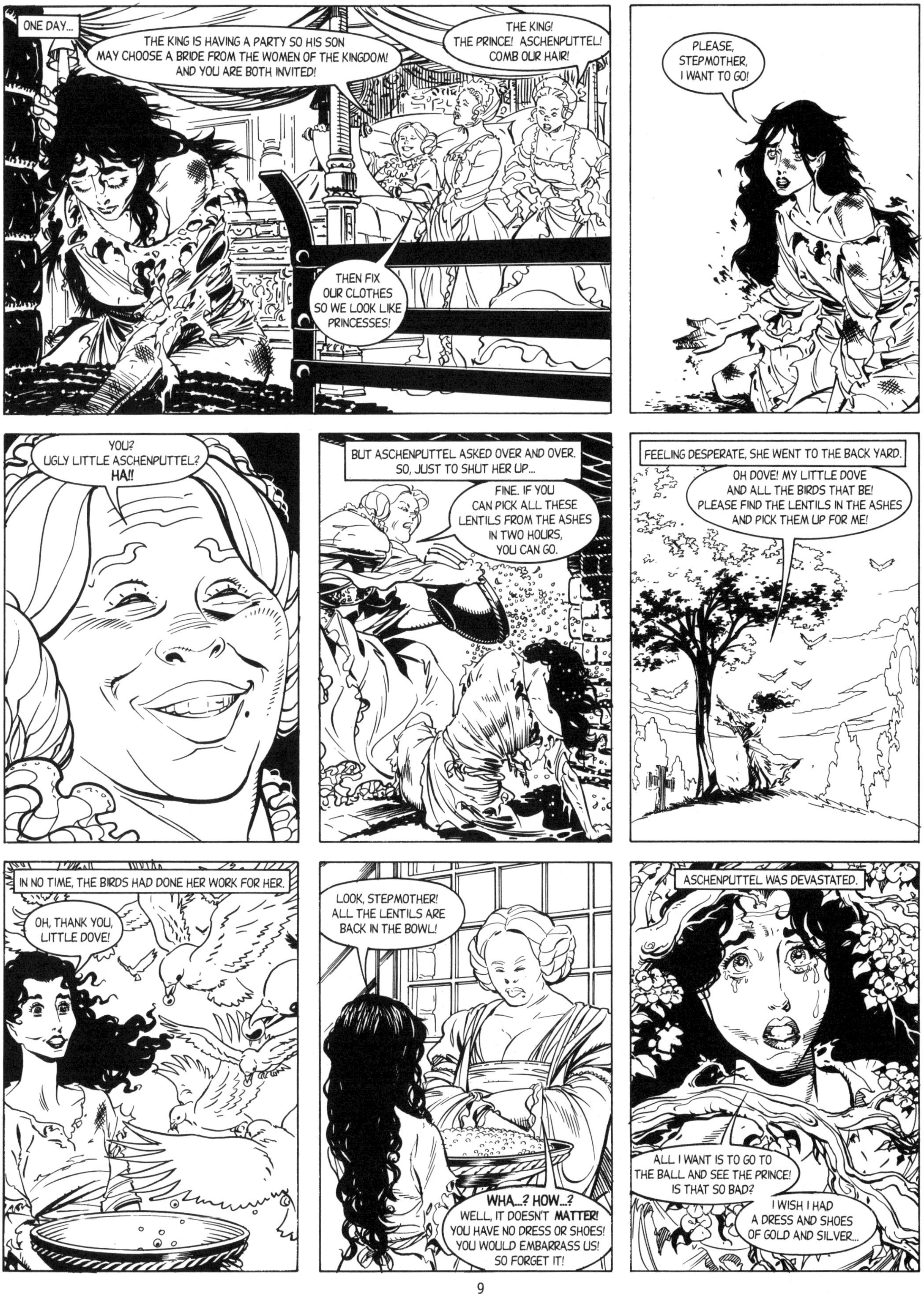
ONE DAY...
THE KING IS HAVING A PARTY SO HIS SON MAY CHOOSE A BRIDE FROM THE WOMEN OF THE KINGDOM! AND YOU ARE BOTH INVITED!
THE KING! THE PRINCE! ASCHENPUTTEL! COMB OUR HAIR!
THEN FIX OUR CLOTHES SO WE LOOK LIKE PRINCESSES!
PLEASE, STEPMOTHER, I WANT TO GO!
YOU? UGLY LITTLE ASCHENPUTTEL? HA!!
BUT ASCHENPUTTEL ASKED OVER AND OVER. SO, JUST TO SHUT HER UP...
FINE. IF YOU CAN PICK ALL THESE LENTILS FROM THE ASHES IN TWO HOURS, YOU CAN GO.
FEELING DESPERATE, SHE WENT TO THE BACK YARD.
OH DOVE! MY LITTLE DOVE AND ALL THE BIRDS THAT BE! PLEASE FIND THE LENTILS IN THE ASHES AND PICK THEM UP FOR ME!
IN NO TIME, THE BIRDS HAD DONE HER WORK FOR HER.
OH, THANK YOU, LITTLE DOVE!
LOOK, STEPMOTHER! ALL THE LENTILS ARE BACK IN THE BOWL!
WHA...? HOW...? WELL, IT DOESN'T MATTER! YOU HAVE NO DRESS OR SHOES! YOU WOULD EMBARRASS US! SO FORGET IT!
ASCHENPUTTEL WAS DEVASTATED.
ALL I WANT IS TO GO TO THE BALL AND SEE THE PRINCE! IS THAT SO BAD?
I WISH I HAD A DRESS AND SHOES OF GOLD AND SILVER...

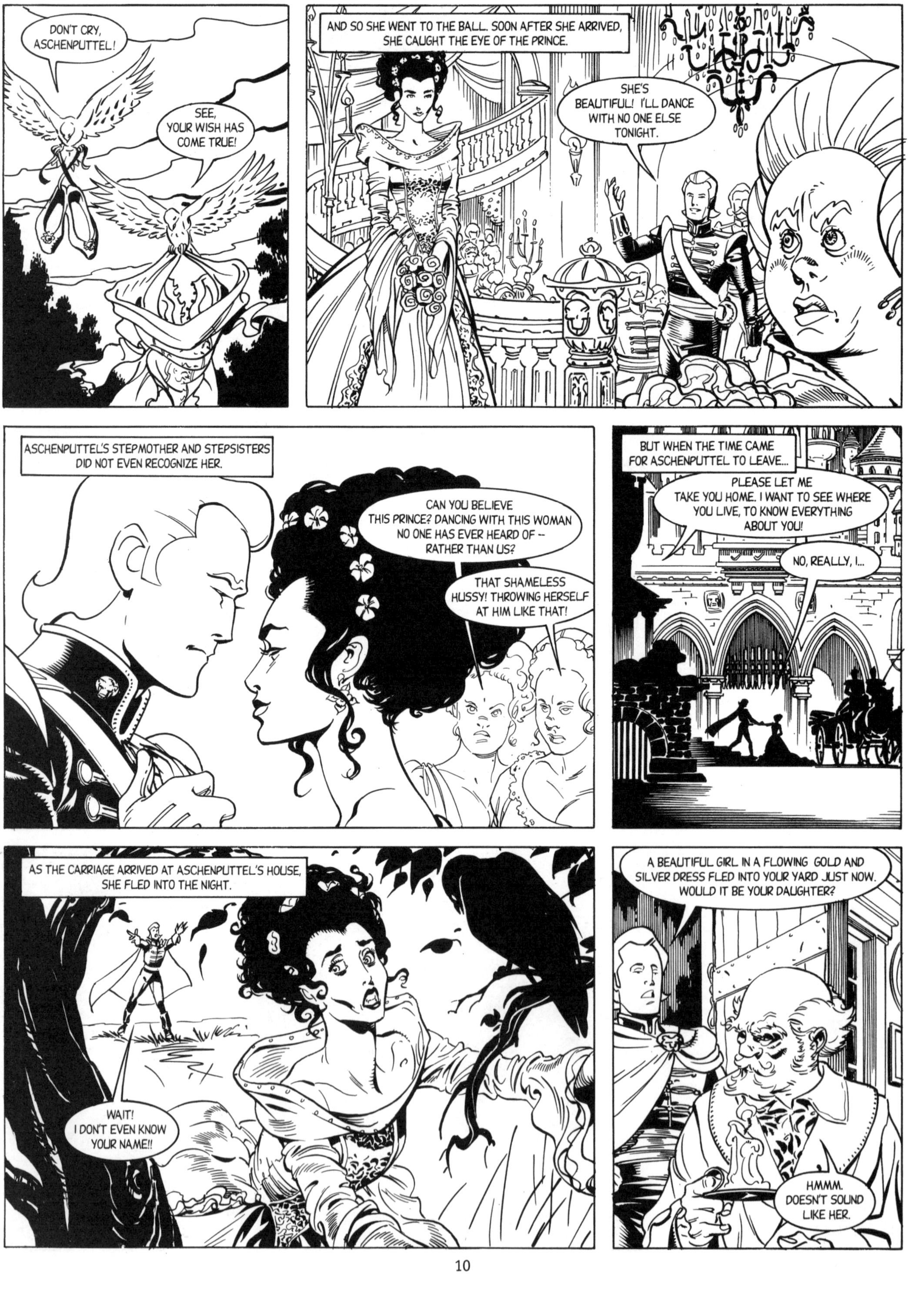
DON'T CRY, ASCHENPUTTEL!
SEE, YOUR WISH HAS COME TRUE!
AND SO SHE WENT TO THE BALL. SOON AFTER SHE ARRIVED, SHE CAUGHT THE EYE OF THE PRINCE.
SHE'S BEAUTIFUL! I'LL DANCE WITH NO ONE ELSE TONIGHT.
ASCHENPUTTEL'S STEPMOTHER AND STEPSISTERS DID NOT EVEN RECOGNIZE HER.
CAN YOU BELIEVE THIS PRINCE? DANCING WITH THIS WOMAN NO ONE HAS EVER HEARD OF -- RATHER THAN US?
THAT SHAMELESS HUSSY! THROWING HERSELF AT HIM LIKE THAT!
BUT WHEN THE TIME CAME FOR ASCHENPUTTEL TO LEAVE...
PLEASE LET ME TAKE YOU HOME. I WANT TO SEE WHERE YOU LIVE, TO KNOW EVERYTHING ABOUT YOU!
NO, REALLY, I...
AS THE CARRIAGE ARRIVED AT ASCHENPUTTEL'S HOUSE, SHE FLED INTO THE NIGHT.
WAIT! I DON'T EVEN KNOW YOUR NAME!!
A BEAUTIFUL GIRL IN A FLOWING GOLD AND SILVER DRESS FLED INTO YOUR YARD JUST NOW. WOULD IT BE YOUR DAUGHTER?
HMMM. DOESN'T SOUND LIKE HER.

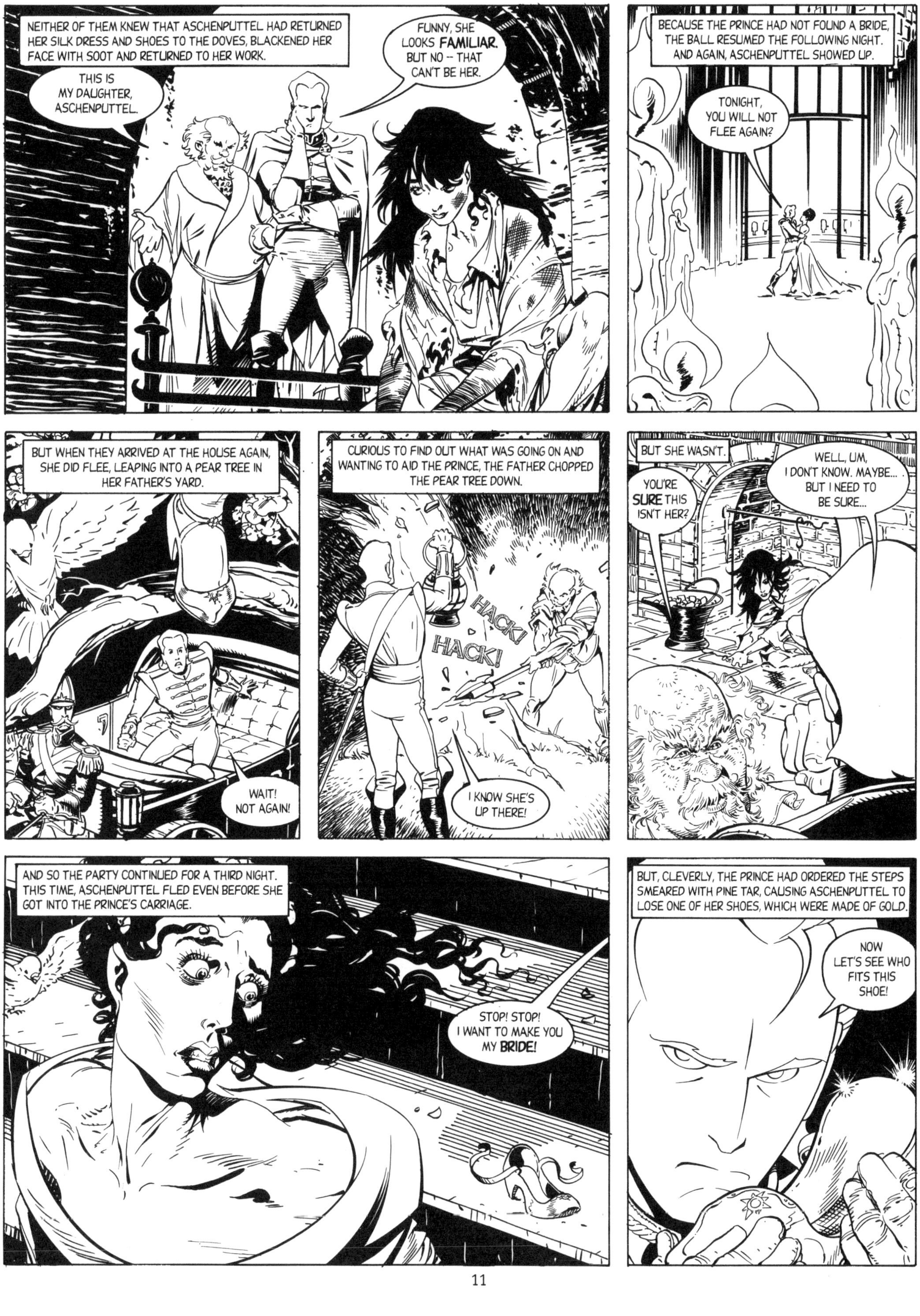

NEITHER OF THEM KNEW THAT ASCHENPUTTEL HAD RETURNED HER SILK DRESS AND SHOES TO THE DOVES, BLACKENED HER FACE WITH SOOT AND RETURNED TO HER WORK.
THIS IS MY DAUGHTER, ASCHENPUTTEL.
FUNNY, SHE LOOKS FAMILIAR. BUT NO -- THAT CAN'T BE HER.
BECAUSE THE PRINCE HAD NOT FOUND A BRIDE, THE BALL RESUMED THE FOLLOWING NIGHT. AND AGAIN, ASCHENPUTTEL SHOWED UP.
TONIGHT, YOU WILL NOT FLEE AGAIN?
BUT WHEN THEY ARRIVED AT THE HOUSE AGAIN, SHE DID FLEE, LEAPING INTO A PEAR TREE IN HER FATHER'S YARD.
WAIT! NOT AGAIN!
CURIOUS TO FIND OUT WHAT WAS GOING ON AND WANTING TO AID THE PRINCE, THE FATHER CHOPPED THE PEAR TREE DOWN.
HACK!
HACK!
I KNOW SHE'S UP THERE!
BUT SHE WASN'T.
YOU'RE SURE THIS ISN'T HER?
WELL, UM, I DON'T KNOW. MAYBE... BUT I NEED TO BE SURE...
AND SO THE PARTY CONTINUED FOR A THIRD NIGHT. THIS TIME, ASCHENPUTTEL FLED EVEN BEFORE SHE GOT INTO THE PRINCE'S CARRIAGE.
STOP! STOP! I WANT TO MAKE YOU MY BRIDE!
BUT, CLEVERLY, THE PRINCE HAD ORDERED THE STEPS SMEARED WITH PINE TAR, CAUSING ASCHENPUTTEL TO LOSE ONE OF HER SHOES, WHICH WERE MADE OF GOLD.
NOW LET'S SEE WHO FITS THIS SHOE!

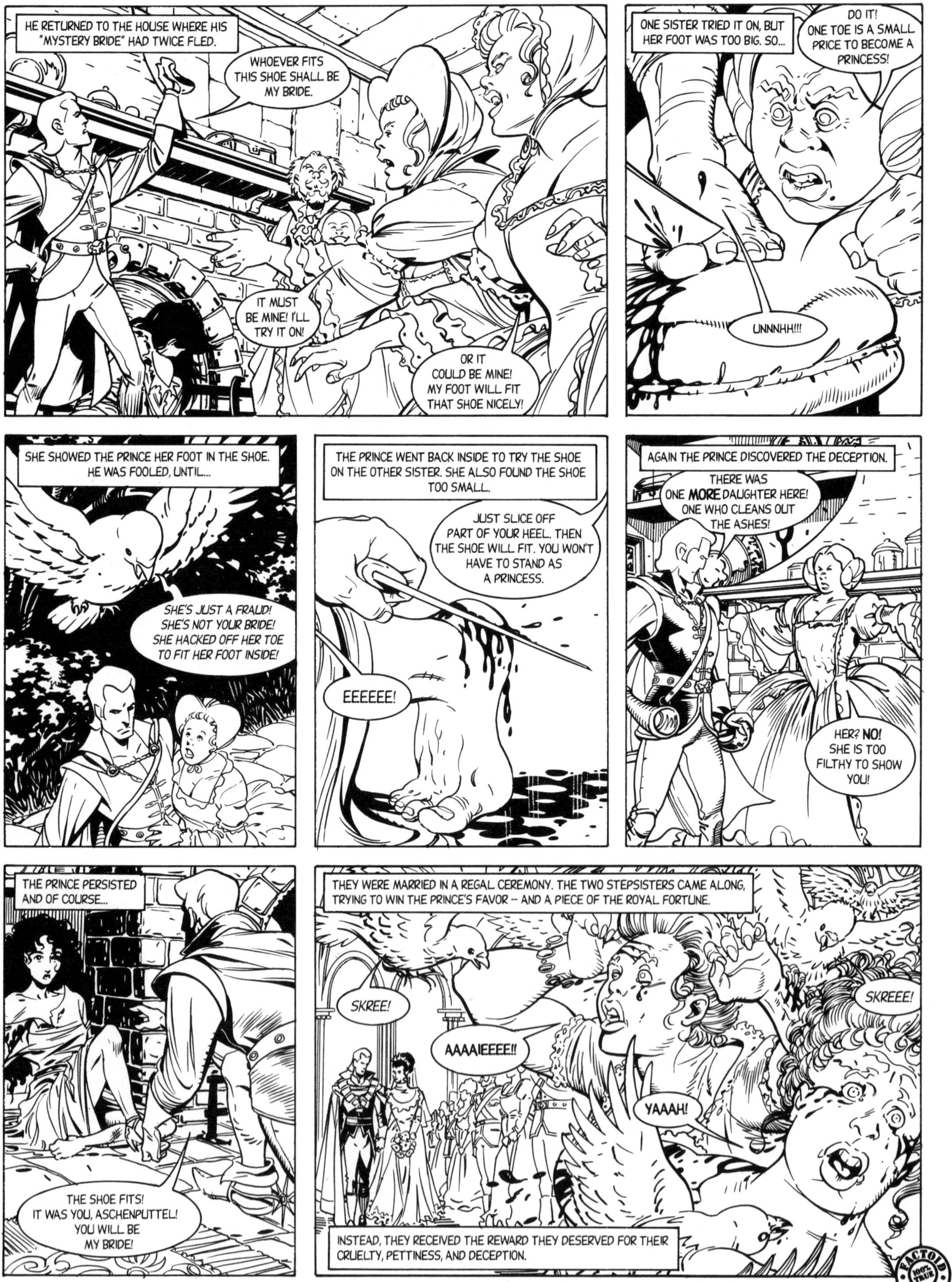
HE RETURNED TO THE HOUSE WHERE HIS "MYSTERY BRIDE" HAD TWICE FLED.
WHOEVER FITS THIS SHOE SHALL BE MY BRIDE.
IT MUST BE MINE! I'LL TRY IT ON!
OR IT COULD BE MINE! MY FOOT WILL FIT THAT SHOE NICELY!
ONE SISTER TRIED IT ON, BUT HER FOOT WAS TOO BIG. SO...
DO IT! ONE TOE IS A SMALL PRICE TO BECOME A PRINCESS!
UNNNHH!!!
SHE SHOWED THE PRINCE HER FOOT IN THE SHOE. HE WAS FOOLED, UNTIL...
SHE'S JUST A FRAUD! SHE'S NOT YOUR BRIDE! SHE HACKED OFF HER TOE TO FIT HER FOOT INSIDE!
THE PRINCE WENT BACK INSIDE TO TRY THE SHOE ON THE OTHER SISTER. SHE ALSO FOUND THE SHOE TOO SMALL.
JUST SLICE OFF PART OF YOUR HEEL. THEN THE SHOE WILL FIT. YOU WON'T HAVE TO STAND AS A PRINCESS.
EEEEEE!
AGAIN THE PRINCE DISCOVERED THE DECEPTION.
THERE WAS ONE MORE DAUGHTER HERE! ONE WHO CLEANS OUT THE ASHES!
HER? NO! SHE IS TOO FILTHY TO SHOW YOU!
THE PRINCE PERSISTED AND OF COURSE...
THE SHOE FITS! IT WAS YOU, ASCHENPUTTEL! YOU WILL BE MY BRIDE!
THEY WERE MARRIED IN A REGAL CEREMONY. THE TWO STEPSISTERS CAME ALONG, TRYING TO WIN THE PRINCE'S FAVOR -- AND A PIECE OF THE ROYAL FORTUNE.
SKREE!
AAAAIEEEE!!
SKREEE!
YAAAH!
INSTEAD, THEY RECEIVED THE REWARD THEY DESERVED FOR THEIR CRUELTY, PETTINESS, AND DECEPTION.
FACTOID BOOKS 100% TRUE

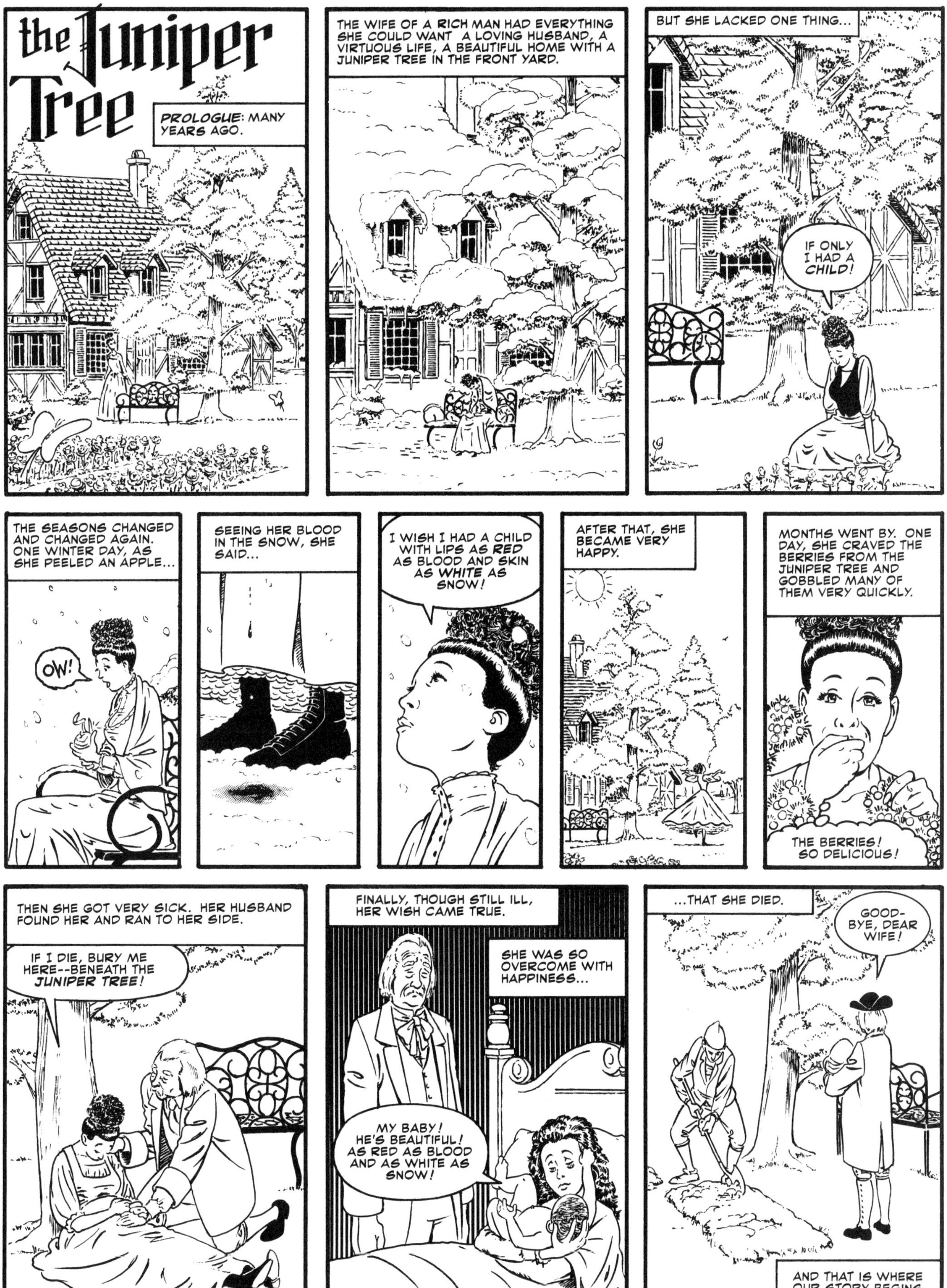
the Juniper Tree
PROLOGUE: MANY YEARS AGO.
THE WIFE OF A RICH MAN HAD EVERYTHING SHE COULD WANT A LOVING HUSBAND, A VIRTUOUS LIFE, A BEAUTIFUL HOME WITH A JUNIPER TREE IN THE FRONT YARD.
BUT SHE LACKED ONE THING...
IF ONLY I HAD A CHILD!
THE SEASONS CHANGED AND CHANGED AGAIN. ONE WINTER DAY, AS SHE PEELED AN APPLE...
OW!
SEEING HER BLOOD IN THE SNOW, SHE SAID...
I WISH I HAD A CHILD WITH LIPS AS RED AS BLOOD AND SKIN AS WHITE AS SNOW!
AFTER THAT, SHE BECAME VERY HAPPY.
MONTHS WENT BY. ONE DAY, SHE CRAVED THE BERRIES FROM THE JUNIPER TREE AND GOBBLED MANY OF THEM VERY QUICKLY.
THE BERRIES! SO DELICIOUS!
THEN SHE GOT VERY SICK. HER HUSBAND FOUND HER AND RAN TO HER SIDE.
IF I DIE, BURY ME HERE--BENEATH THE JUNIPER TREE!
FINALLY, THOUGH STILL ILL, HER WISH CAME TRUE.
SHE WAS SO OVERCOME WITH HAPPINESS...
MY BABY! HE'S BEAUTIFUL! AS RED AS BLOOD AND AS WHITE AS SNOW!
...THAT SHE DIED.
GOOD-BYE, DEAR WIFE!
AND THAT IS WHERE OUR STORY BEGINS.

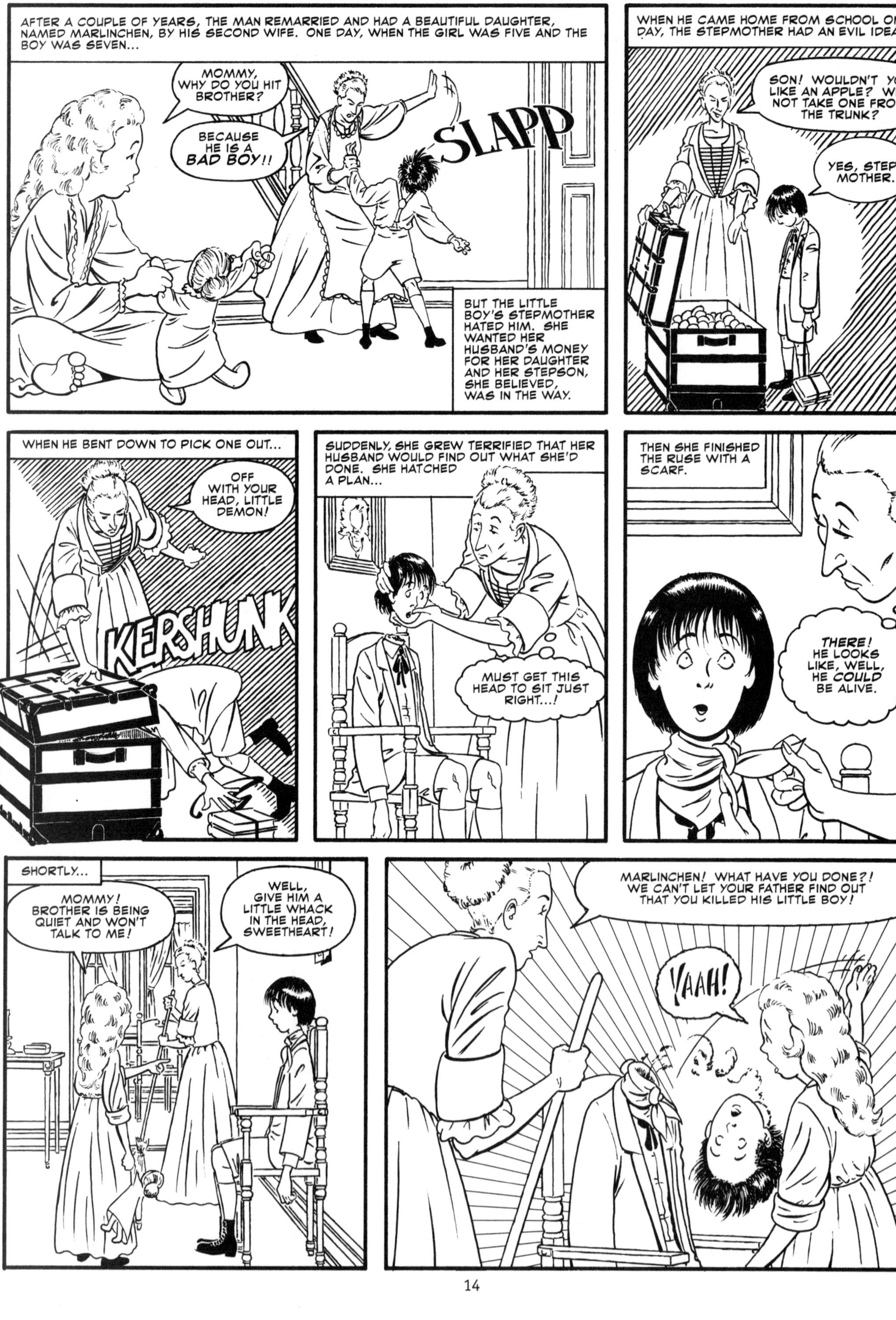
AFTER A COUPLE OF YEARS, THE MAN REMARRIED AND HAD A BEAUTIFUL DAUGHTER, NAMED MARLINCHEN, BY HIS SECOND WIFE. ONE DAY, WHEN THE GIRL WAS FIVE AND THE BOY WAS SEVEN...
MOMMY, WHY DO YOU HIT BROTHER?
BECAUSE HE IS A BAD BOY!!
SLAPP
BUT THE LITTLE BOY'S STEPMOTHER HATED HIM. SHE WANTED HER HUSBAND'S MONEY FOR HER DAUGHTER AND HER STEPSON, SHE BELIEVED, WAS IN THE WAY.
WHEN HE CAME HOME FROM SCHOOL ONE DAY, THE STEPMOTHER HAD AN EVIL IDEA.
SON! WOULDN'T YOU LIKE AN APPLE? WHY NOT TAKE ONE FROM THE TRUNK?
YES, STEP-MOTHER.
WHEN HE BENT DOWN TO PICK ONE OUT...
OFF WITH YOUR HEAD, LITTLE DEMON!
KERSHUNK
SUDDENLY, SHE GREW TERRIFIED THAT HER HUSBAND WOULD FIND OUT WHAT SHE'D DONE. SHE HATCHED A PLAN...
MUST GET THIS HEAD TO SIT JUST RIGHT...!
THEN SHE FINISHED THE RUSE WITH A SCARF.
THERE! HE LOOKS LIKE, WELL, HE COULD BE ALIVE.
SHORTLY...
MOMMY! BROTHER IS BEING QUIET AND WON'T TALK TO ME!
WELL, GIVE HIM A LITTLE WHACK IN THE HEAD, SWEETHEART!
MARLINCHEN! WHAT HAVE YOU DONE?! WE CAN'T LET YOUR FATHER FIND OUT THAT YOU KILLED HIS LITTLE BOY!
YAAH!

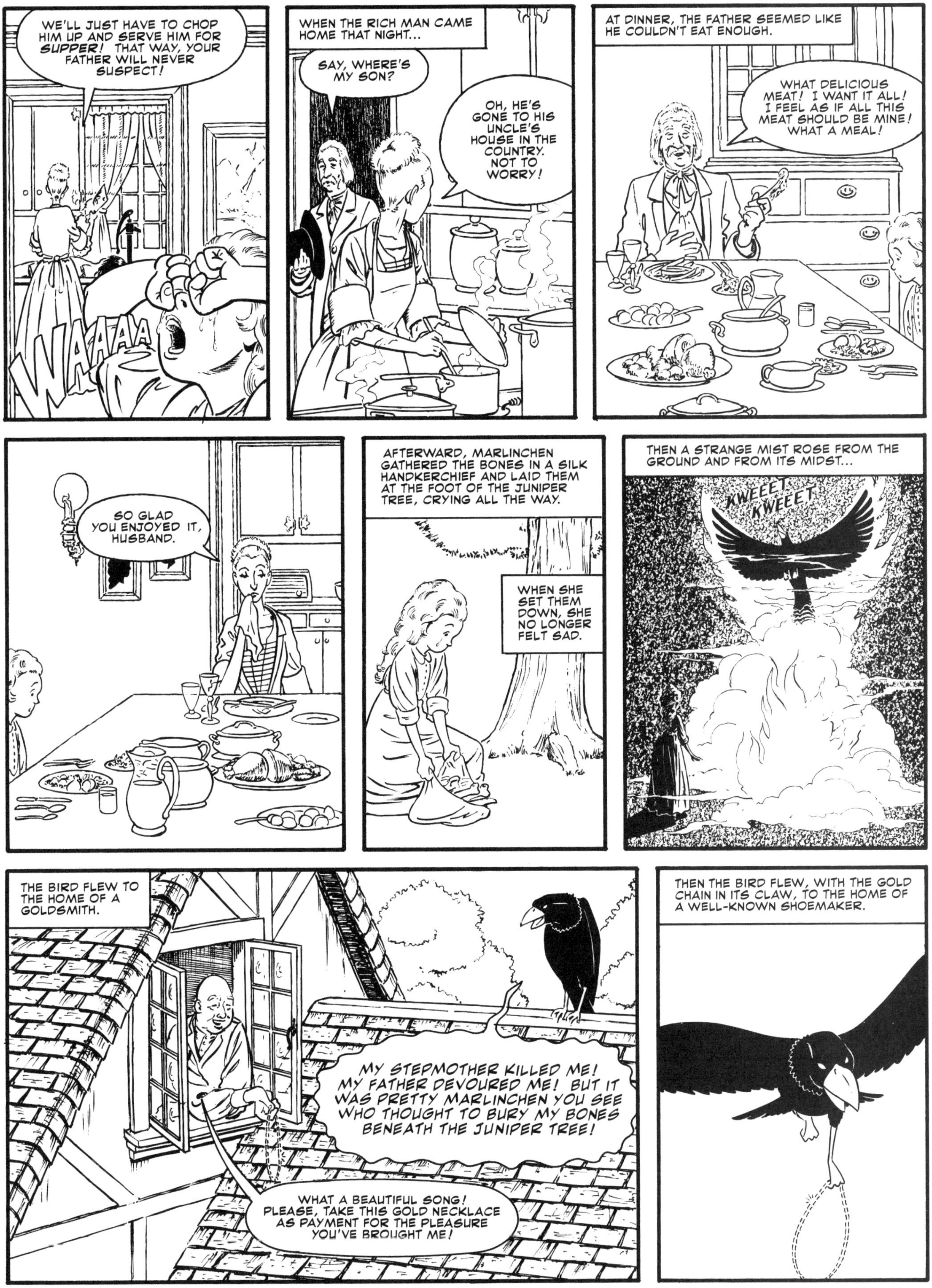
WE'LL JUST HAVE TO CHOP HIM UP AND SERVE HIM FOR SUPPER! THAT WAY, YOUR FATHER WILL NEVER SUSPECT!
WAAAAA
WHEN THE RICH MAN CAME HOME THAT NIGHT...
SAY, WHERE'S MY SON?
OH, HE'S GONE TO HIS UNCLE'S HOUSE IN THE COUNTRY. NOT TO WORRY!
AT DINNER, THE FATHER SEEMED LIKE HE COULDN'T EAT ENOUGH.
WHAT DELICIOUS MEAT! I WANT IT ALL! I FEEL AS IF ALL THIS MEAT SHOULD BE MINE! WHAT A MEAL!
SO GLAD YOU ENJOYED IT, HUSBAND.
AFTERWARD, MARLINCHEN GATHERED THE BONES IN A SILK HANDKERCHIEF AND LAID THEM AT THE FOOT OF THE JUNIPER TREE, CRYING ALL THE WAY.
WHEN SHE SET THEM DOWN, SHE NO LONGER FELT SAD.
THEN A STRANGE MIST ROSE FROM THE GROUND AND FROM ITS MIDST...
KWEEET KWEEET
THE BIRD FLEW TO THE HOME OF A GOLDSMITH.
MY STEPMOTHER KILLED ME! MY FATHER DEVOURED ME! BUT IT WAS PRETTY MARLINCHEN YOU SEE WHO THOUGHT TO BURY MY BONES BENEATH THE JUNIPER TREE!
WHAT A BEAUTIFUL SONG! PLEASE, TAKE THIS GOLD NECKLACE AS PAYMENT FOR THE PLEASURE YOU'VE BROUGHT ME!
THEN THE BIRD FLEW, WITH THE GOLD CHAIN IN ITS CLAW, TO THE HOME OF A WELL-KNOWN SHOEMAKER.

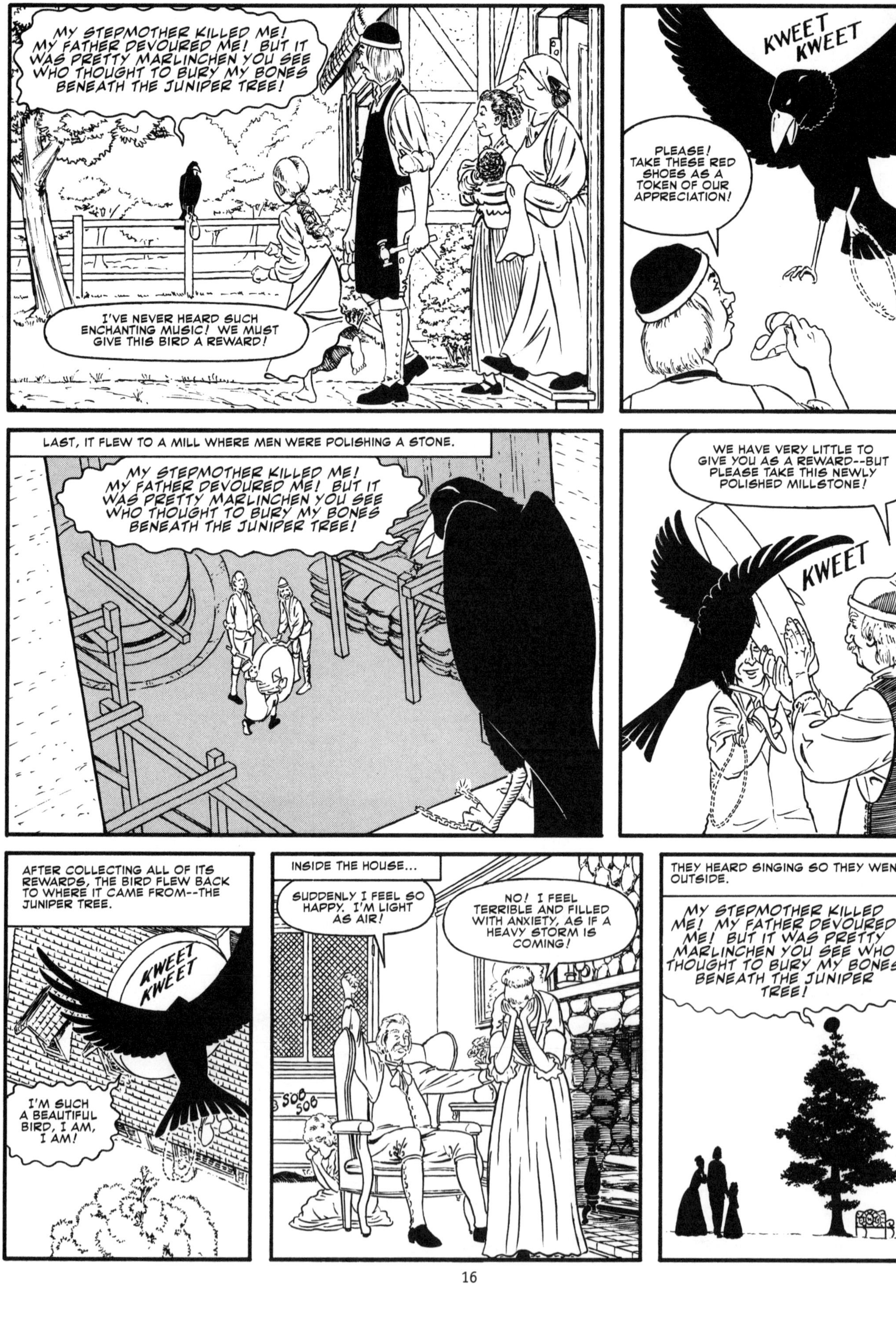
MY STEPMOTHER KILLED ME! MY FATHER DEVOURED ME! BUT IT WAS PRETTY MARLINCHEN YOU SEE WHO THOUGHT TO BURY MY BONES BENEATH THE JUNIPER TREE!
I'VE NEVER HEARD SUCH ENCHANTING MUSIC! WE MUST GIVE THIS BIRD A REWARD!
KWEET KWEET
PLEASE! TAKE THESE RED SHOES AS A TOKEN OF OUR APPRECIATION!
LAST, IT FLEW TO A MILL WHERE MEN WERE POLISHING A STONE.
MY STEPMOTHER KILLED ME! MY FATHER DEVOURED ME! BUT IT WAS PRETTY MARLINCHEN YOU SEE WHO THOUGHT TO BURY MY BONES BENEATH THE JUNIPER TREE!
WE HAVE VERY LITTLE TO GIVE YOU AS A REWARD--BUT PLEASE TAKE THIS NEWLY POLISHED MILLSTONE!
KWEET
AFTER COLLECTING ALL OF ITS REWARDS, THE BIRD FLEW BACK TO WHERE IT CAME FROM--THE JUNIPER TREE.
KWEET KWEET
I'M SUCH A BEAUTIFUL BIRD, I AM, I AM!
INSIDE THE HOUSE...
SUDDENLY I FEEL SO HAPPY. I'M LIGHT AS AIR!
NO! I FEEL TERRIBLE AND FILLED WITH ANXIETY, AS IF A HEAVY STORM IS COMING!
SOB SOB
THEY HEARD SINGING SO THEY WENT OUTSIDE.
MY STEPMOTHER KILLED ME! MY FATHER DEVOURED ME! BUT IT WAS PRETTY MARLINCHEN YOU SEE WHO THOUGHT TO BURY MY BONES BENEATH THE JUNIPER TREE!

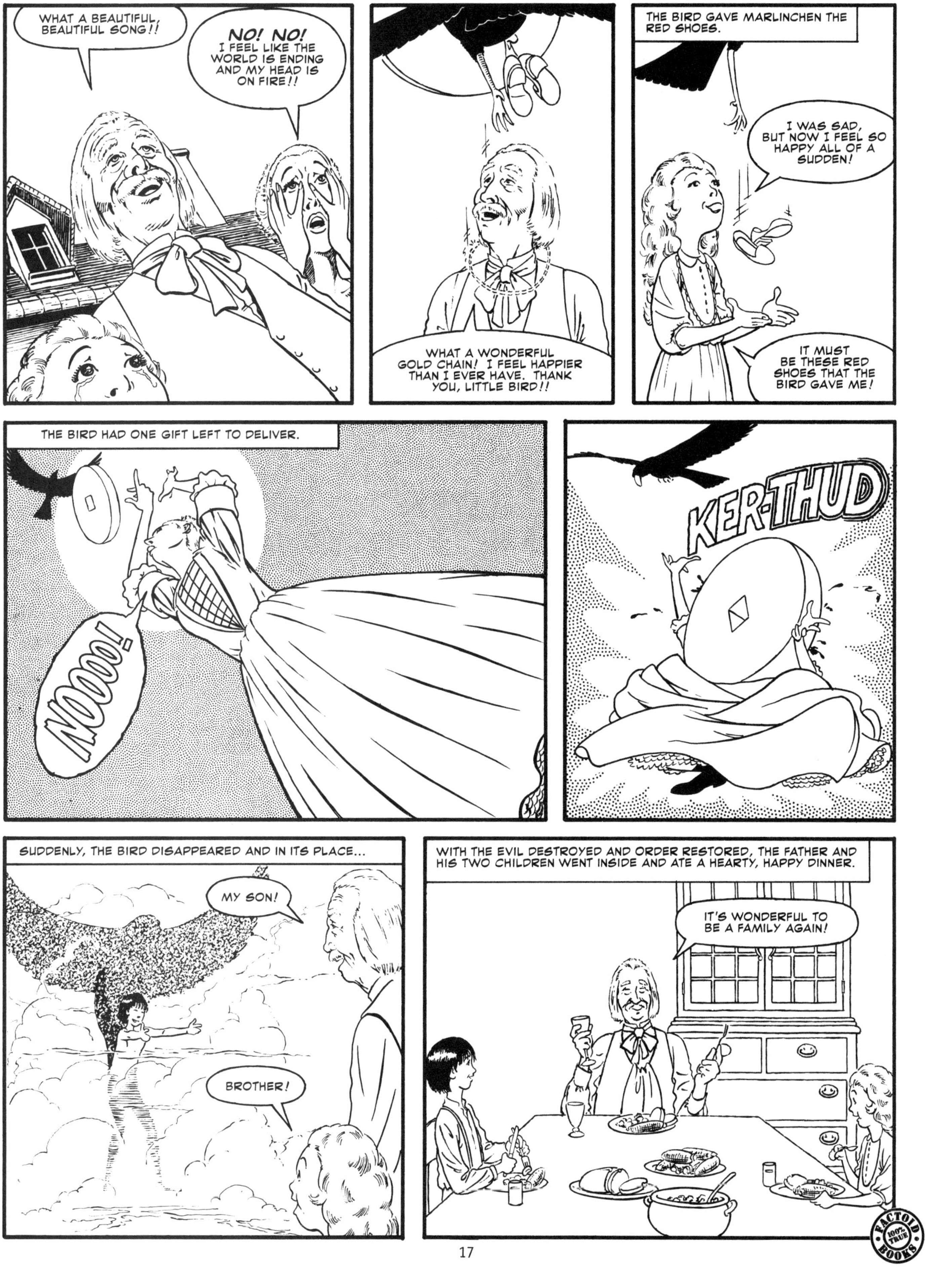
WHAT A BEAUTIFUL, BEAUTIFUL SONG!!
NO! NO! I FEEL LIKE THE WORLD IS ENDING AND MY HEAD IS ON FIRE!!
WHAT A WONDERFUL GOLD CHAIN! I FEEL HAPPIER THAN I EVER HAVE. THANK YOU, LITTLE BIRD!!
THE BIRD GAVE MARLINCHEN THE RED SHOES.
I WAS SAD, BUT NOW I FEEL SO HAPPY ALL OF A SUDDEN!
IT MUST BE THESE RED SHOES THAT THE BIRD GAVE ME!
THE BIRD HAD ONE GIFT LEFT TO DELIVER.
NOOOO!
KER-THUD
SUDDENLY, THE BIRD DISAPPEARED AND IN ITS PLACE...
MY SON!
BROTHER!
WITH THE EVIL DESTROYED AND ORDER RESTORED, THE FATHER AND HIS TWO CHILDREN WENT INSIDE AND ATE A HEARTY, HAPPY DINNER.
IT'S WONDERFUL TO BE A FAMILY AGAIN!

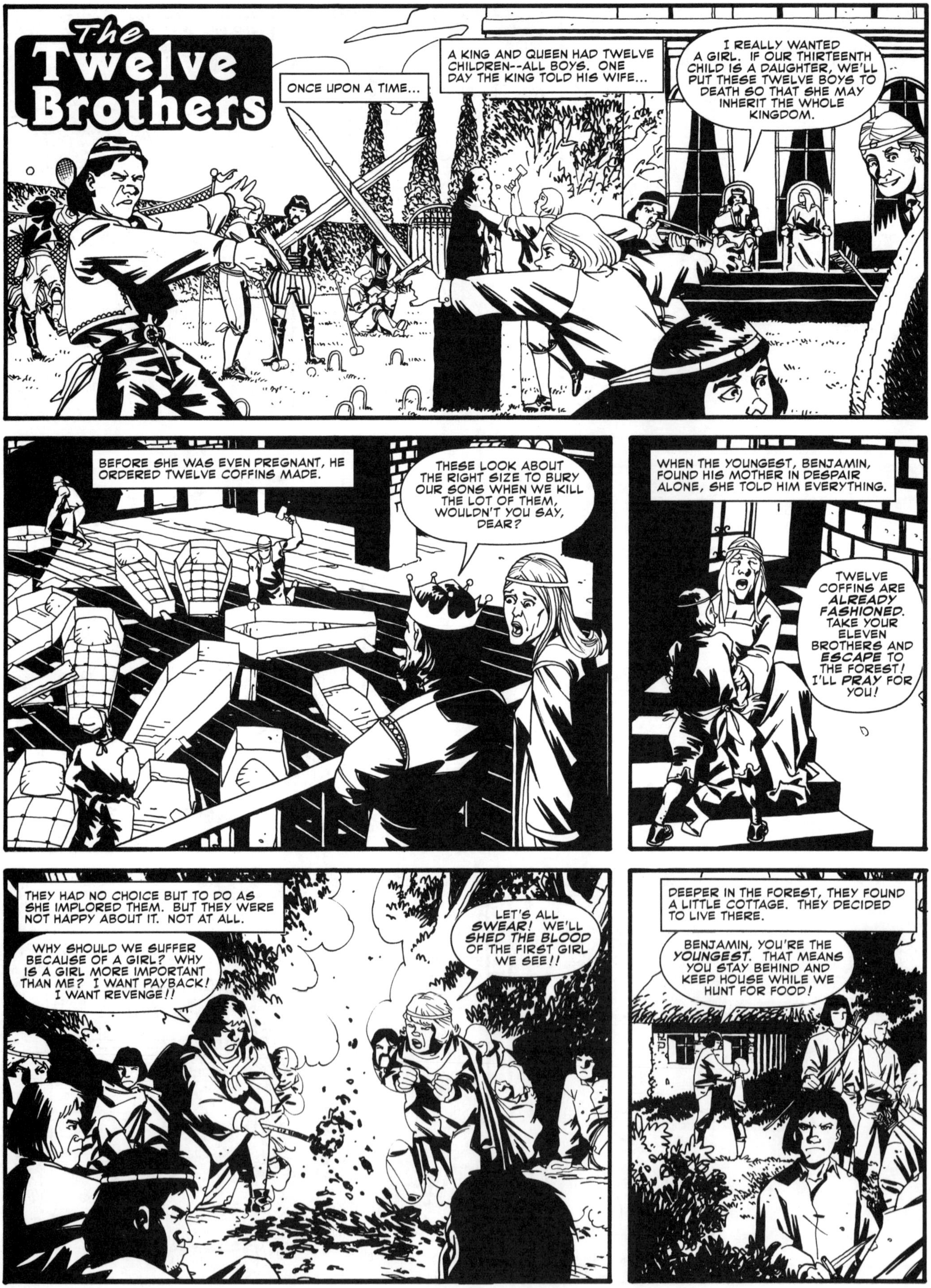

The Twelve Brothers
ONCE UPON A TIME...
A KING AND QUEEN HAD TWELVE CHILDREN--ALL BOYS. ONE DAY THE KING TOLD HIS WIFE...
I REALLY WANTED A GIRL. IF OUR THIRTEENTH CHILD IS A DAUGHTER, WE'LL PUT THESE TWELVE BOYS TO DEATH SO THAT SHE MAY INHERIT THE WHOLE KINGDOM.
BEFORE SHE WAS EVEN PREGNANT, HE ORDERED TWELVE COFFINS MADE.
THESE LOOK ABOUT THE RIGHT SIZE TO BURY OUR SONS WHEN WE KILL THE LOT OF THEM, WOULDN'T YOU SAY, DEAR?
WHEN THE YOUNGEST, BENJAMIN, FOUND HIS MOTHER IN DESPAIR ALONE, SHE TOLD HIM EVERYTHING.
TWELVE COFFINS ARE ALREADY FASHIONED. TAKE YOUR ELEVEN BROTHERS AND ESCAPE TO THE FOREST! I'LL PRAY FOR YOU!
THEY HAD NO CHOICE BUT TO DO AS SHE IMPLORED THEM. BUT THEY WERE NOT HAPPY ABOUT IT. NOT AT ALL.
WHY SHOULD WE SUFFER BECAUSE OF A GIRL? WHY IS A GIRL MORE IMPORTANT THAN ME? I WANT PAYBACK! I WANT REVENGE!!
LET'S ALL SWEAR! WE'LL SHED THE BLOOD OF THE FIRST GIRL WE SEE!!
DEEPER IN THE FOREST, THEY FOUND A LITTLE COTTAGE. THEY DECIDED TO LIVE THERE.
BENJAMIN, YOU'RE THE YOUNGEST. THAT MEANS YOU STAY BEHIND AND KEEP HOUSE WHILE WE HUNT FOR FOOD!

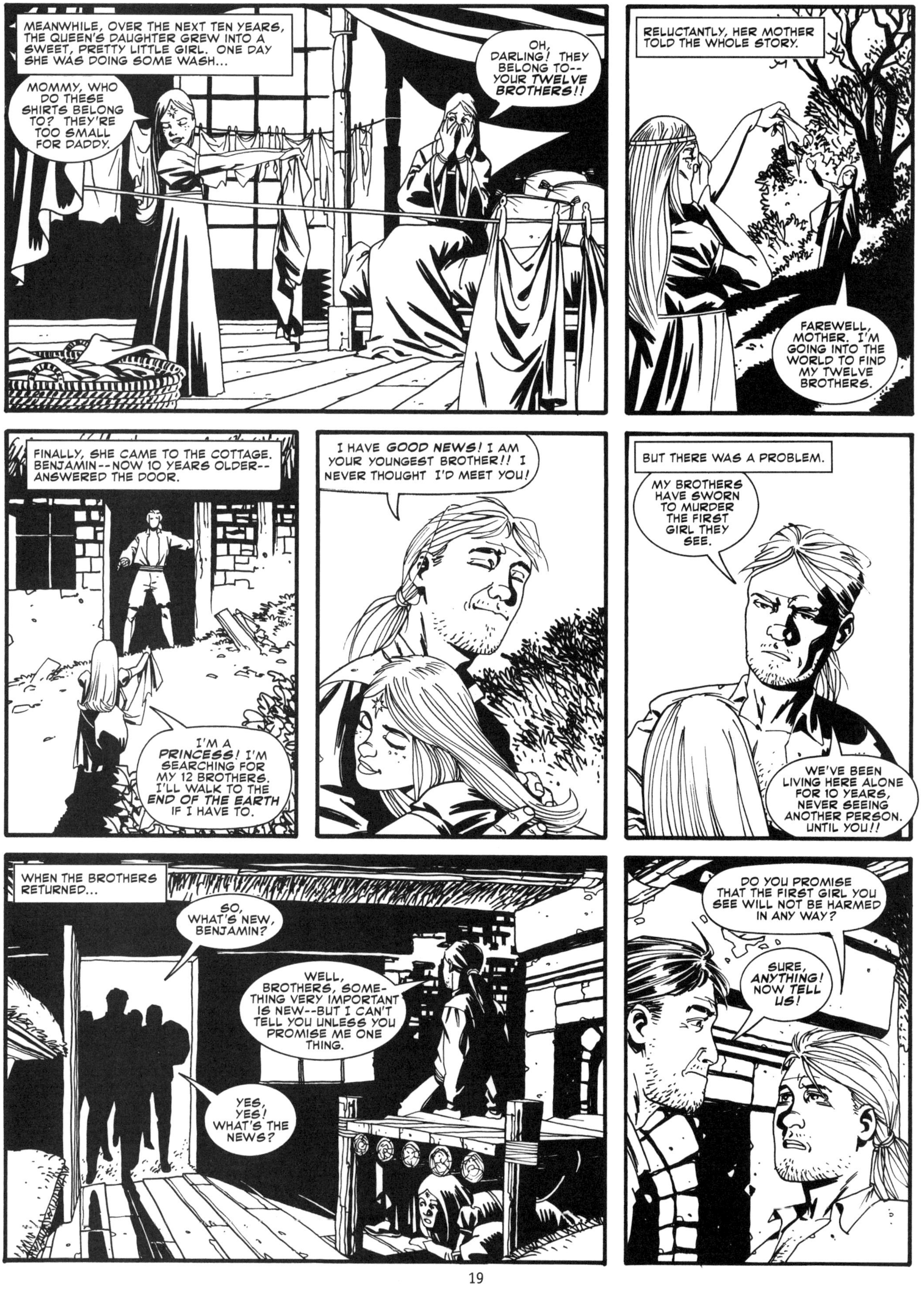
MEANWHILE, OVER THE NEXT TEN YEARS, THE QUEEN'S DAUGHTER GREW INTO A SWEET, PRETTY LITTLE GIRL. ONE DAY SHE WAS DOING SOME WASH...
MOMMY, WHO DO THESE SHIRTS BELONG TO? THEY'RE TOO SMALL FOR DADDY.
OH, DARLING! THEY BELONG TO-- YOUR TWELVE BROTHERS!!
RELUCTANTLY, HER MOTHER TOLD THE WHOLE STORY.
FAREWELL, MOTHER. I'M GOING INTO THE WORLD TO FIND MY TWELVE BROTHERS.
FINALLY, SHE CAME TO THE COTTAGE. BENJAMIN--NOW 10 YEARS OLDER--ANSWERED THE DOOR.
I'M A PRINCESS! I'M SEARCHING FOR MY 12 BROTHERS. I'LL WALK TO THE END OF THE EARTH IF I HAVE TO.
I HAVE GOOD NEWS! I AM YOUR YOUNGEST BROTHER!! I NEVER THOUGHT I'D MEET YOU!
BUT THERE WAS A PROBLEM.
MY BROTHERS HAVE SWORN TO MURDER THE FIRST GIRL THEY SEE.
WE'VE BEEN LIVING HERE ALONE FOR 10 YEARS, NEVER SEEING ANOTHER PERSON. UNTIL YOU!!
WHEN THE BROTHERS RETURNED...
SO, WHAT'S NEW, BENJAMIN?
WELL, BROTHERS, SOMETHING VERY IMPORTANT IS NEW--BUT I CAN'T TELL YOU UNLESS YOU PROMISE ME ONE THING.
YES, YES! WHAT'S THE NEWS?
DO YOU PROMISE THAT THE FIRST GIRL YOU SEE WILL NOT BE HARMED IN ANY WAY?
SURE, ANYTHING! NOW TELL US!

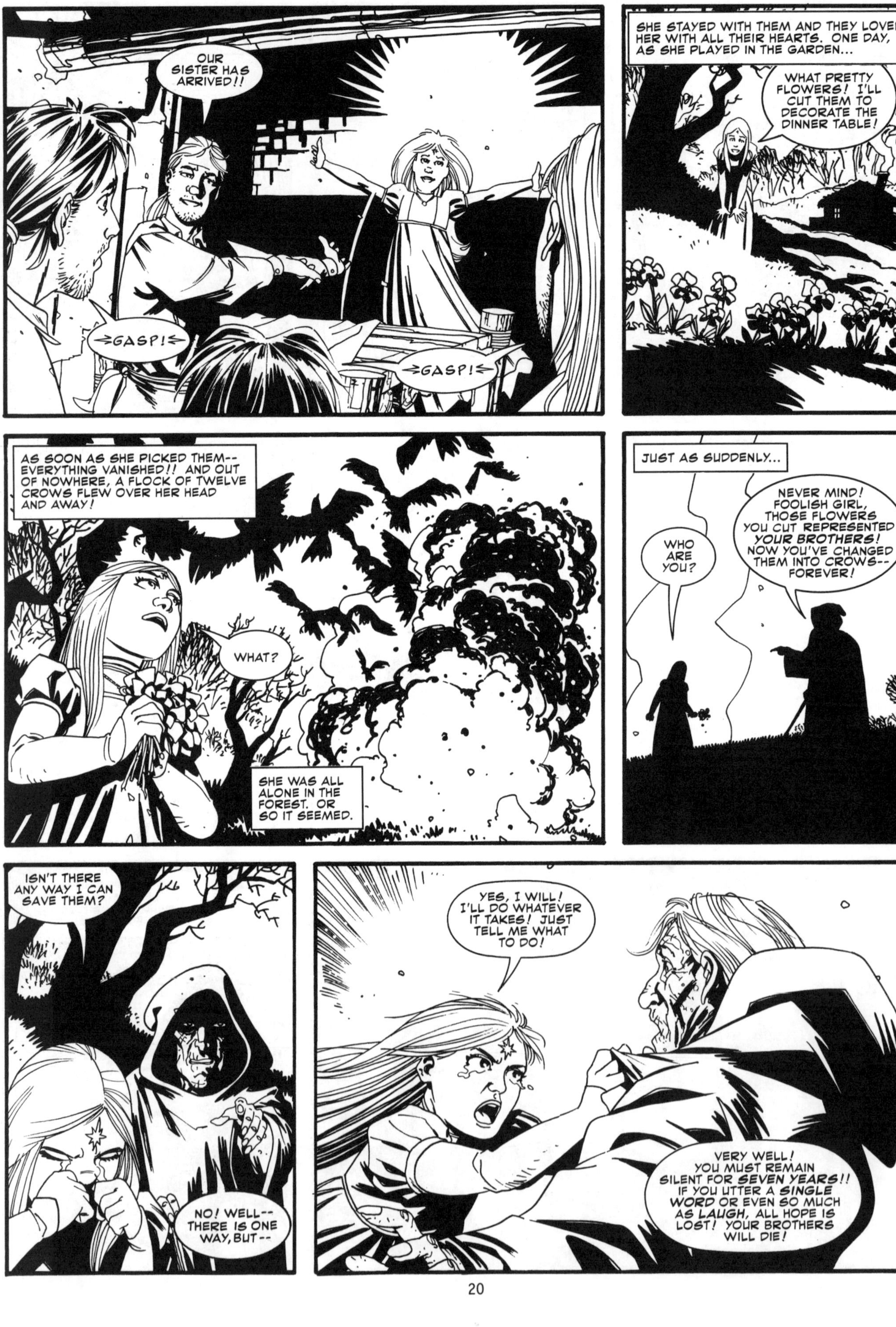

OUR SISTER HAS ARRIVED!!
GASP!
GASP!
SHE STAYED WITH THEM AND THEY LOVED HER WITH ALL THEIR HEARTS. ONE DAY, AS SHE PLAYED IN THE GARDEN...
WHAT PRETTY FLOWERS! I'LL CUT THEM TO DECORATE THE DINNER TABLE!
AS SOON AS SHE PICKED THEM--EVERYTHING VANISHED!! AND OUT OF NOWHERE, A FLOCK OF TWELVE CROWS FLEW OVER HER HEAD AND AWAY!
WHAT?
SHE WAS ALL ALONE IN THE FOREST. OR SO IT SEEMED.
JUST AS SUDDENLY...
WHO ARE YOU?
NEVER MIND! FOOLISH GIRL, THOSE FLOWERS YOU CUT REPRESENTED YOUR BROTHERS! NOW YOU'VE CHANGED THEM INTO CROWS--FOREVER!
ISN'T THERE ANY WAY I CAN SAVE THEM?
NO! WELL--THERE IS ONE WAY, BUT--
YES, I WILL! I'LL DO WHATEVER IT TAKES! JUST TELL ME WHAT TO DO!
VERY WELL! YOU MUST REMAIN SILENT FOR SEVEN YEARS!! IF YOU UTTER A SINGLE WORD OR EVEN SO MUCH AS LAUGH, ALL HOPE IS LOST! YOUR BROTHERS WILL DIE!

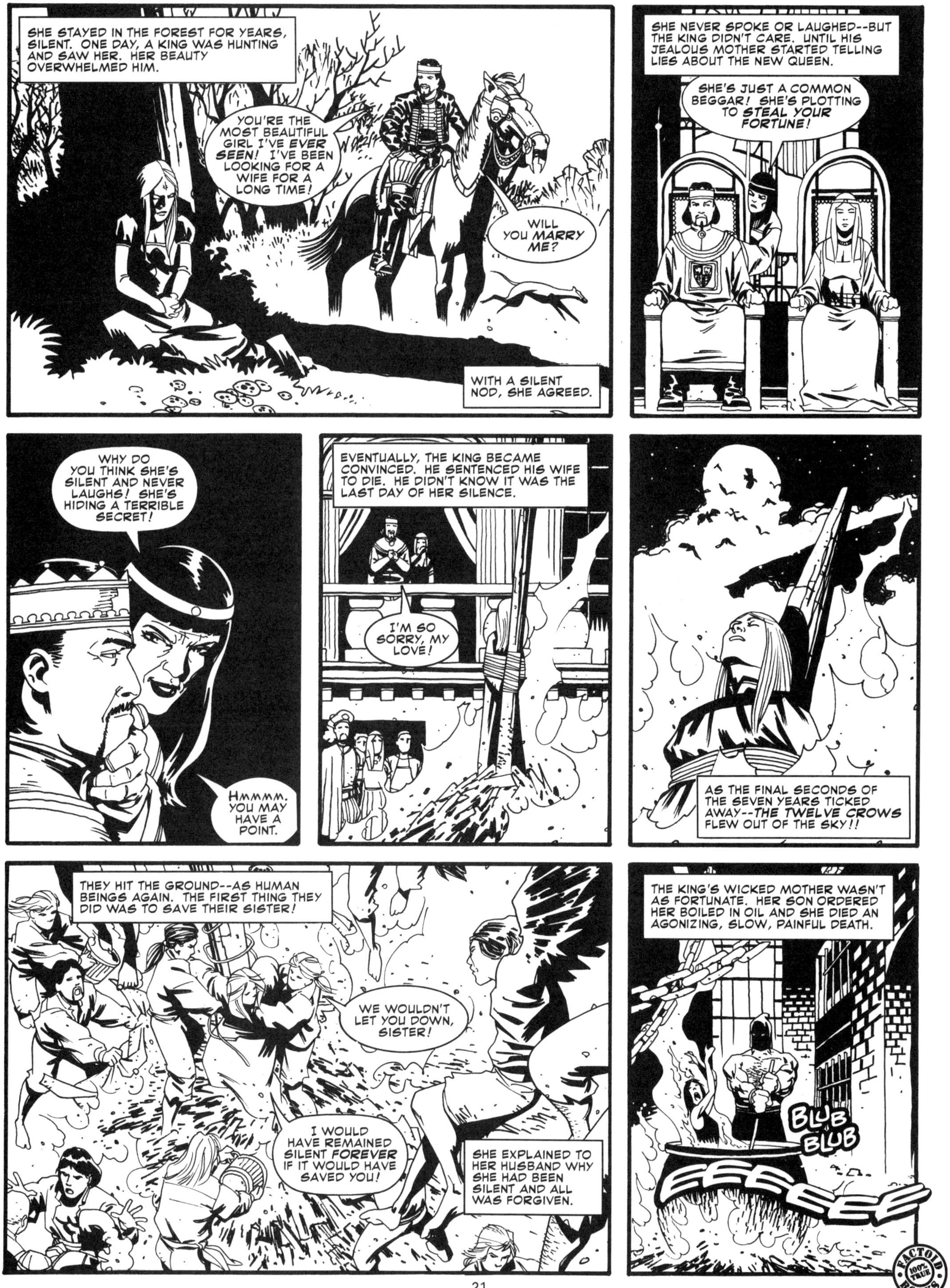

SHE STAYED IN THE FOREST FOR YEARS, SILENT. ONE DAY, A KING WAS HUNTING AND SAW HER. HER BEAUTY OVERWHELMED HIM.
YOU'RE THE MOST BEAUTIFUL GIRL I'VE EVER SEEN! I'VE BEEN LOOKING FOR A WIFE FOR A LONG TIME!
WILL YOU MARRY ME?
WITH A SILENT NOD, SHE AGREED.
SHE NEVER SPOKE OR LAUGHED--BUT THE KING DIDN'T CARE. UNTIL HIS JEALOUS MOTHER STARTED TELLING LIES ABOUT THE NEW QUEEN.
SHE'S JUST A COMMON BEGGAR! SHE'S PLOTTING TO STEAL YOUR FORTUNE!
WHY DO YOU THINK SHE'S SILENT AND NEVER LAUGHS! SHE'S HIDING A TERRIBLE SECRET!
HMMMM. YOU MAY HAVE A POINT.
EVENTUALLY, THE KING BECAME CONVINCED. HE SENTENCED HIS WIFE TO DIE. HE DIDN'T KNOW IT WAS THE LAST DAY OF HER SILENCE.
I'M SO SORRY, MY LOVE!
AS THE FINAL SECONDS OF THE SEVEN YEARS TICKED AWAY--THE TWELVE CROWS FLEW OUT OF THE SKY!!
THEY HIT THE GROUND--AS HUMAN BEINGS AGAIN. THE FIRST THING THEY DID WAS TO SAVE THEIR SISTER!
WE WOULDN'T LET YOU DOWN, SISTER!
I WOULD HAVE REMAINED SILENT FOREVER IF IT WOULD HAVE SAVED YOU!
SHE EXPLAINED TO HER HUSBAND WHY SHE HAD BEEN SILENT AND ALL WAS FORGIVEN.
THE KING'S WICKED MOTHER WASN'T AS FORTUNATE. HER SON ORDERED HER BOILED IN OIL AND SHE DIED AN AGONIZING, SLOW, PAINFUL DEATH.
BLUB BLUB
EEEEEEE

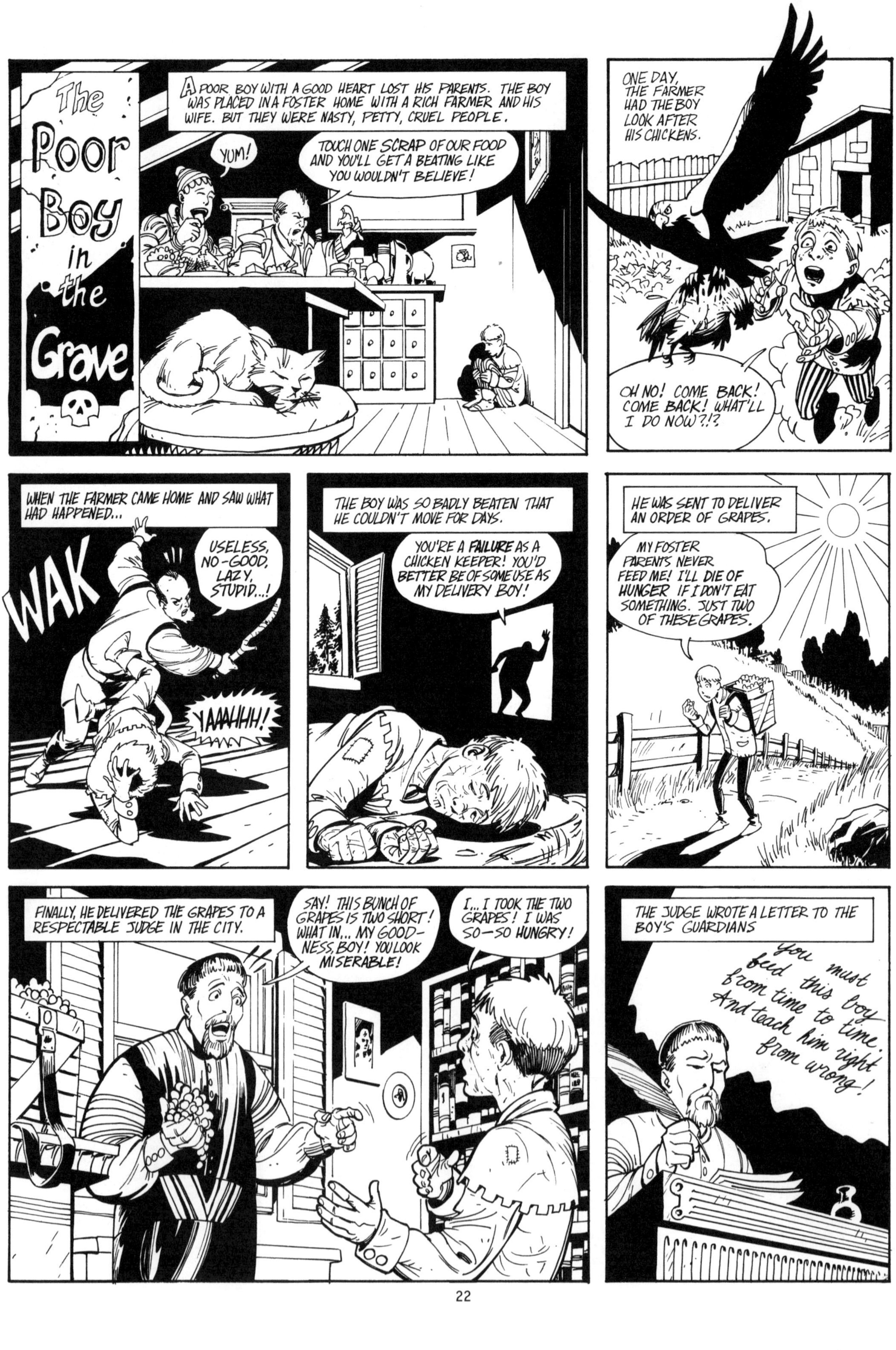
The Poor Boy in the Grave
A POOR BOY WITH A GOOD HEART LOST HIS PARENTS. THE BOY WAS PLACED IN A FOSTER HOME WITH A RICH FARMER AND HIS WIFE. BUT THEY WERE NASTY, PETTY, CRUEL PEOPLE.
YUM!
TOUCH ONE SCRAP OF OUR FOOD AND YOU'LL GET A BEATING LIKE YOU WOULDN'T BELIEVE!
ONE DAY, THE FARMER HAD THE BOY LOOK AFTER HIS CHICKENS.
OH NO! COME BACK! COME BACK! WHAT'LL I DO NOW?!?
WHEN THE FARMER CAME HOME AND SAW WHAT HAD HAPPENED...
USELESS, NO-GOOD, LAZY, STUPID...!
WAK
YAAAHHH!
THE BOY WAS SO BADLY BEATEN THAT HE COULDN'T MOVE FOR DAYS.
YOU'RE A FAILURE AS A CHICKEN KEEPER! YOU'D BETTER BE OF SOME USE AS MY DELIVERY BOY!
HE WAS SENT TO DELIVER AN ORDER OF GRAPES.
MY FOSTER PARENTS NEVER FEED ME! I'LL DIE OF HUNGER IF I DON'T EAT SOMETHING. JUST TWO OF THESE GRAPES.
FINALLY, HE DELIVERED THE GRAPES TO A RESPECTABLE JUDGE IN THE CITY.
SAY! THIS BUNCH OF GRAPES IS TWO SHORT! WHAT IN... MY GOODNESS, BOY! YOU LOOK MISERABLE!
I... I TOOK THE TWO GRAPES! I WAS SO-SO HUNGRY!
THE JUDGE WROTE A LETTER TO THE BOY'S GUARDIANS
You must feed this boy from time to time. And teach him right from wrong!

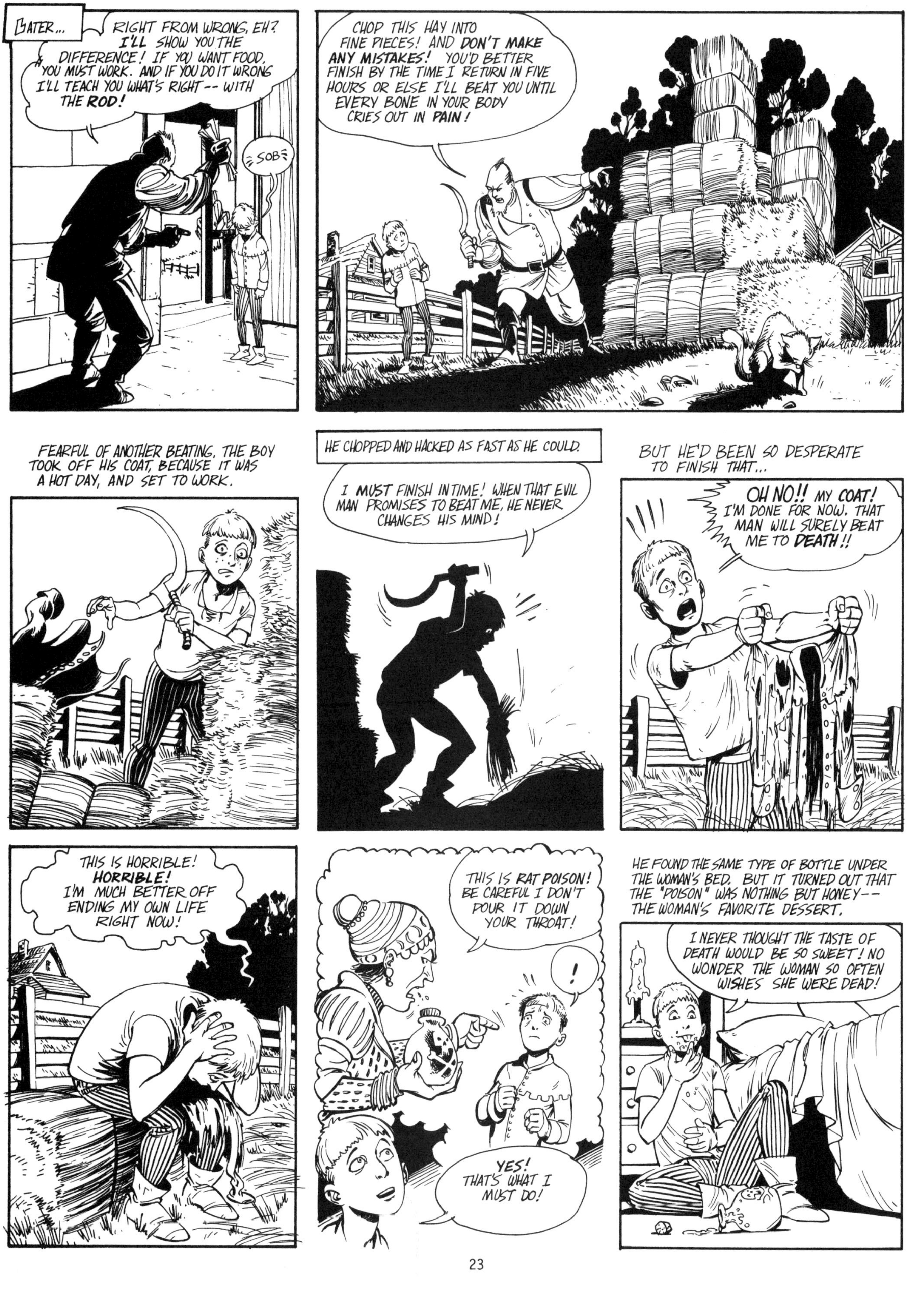
LATER...
RIGHT FROM WRONG, EH? I'LL SHOW YOU THE DIFFERENCE! IF YOU WANT FOOD, YOU MUST WORK. AND IF YOU DO IT WRONG I'LL TEACH YOU WHAT'S RIGHT -- WITH THE ROD!
SOB
CHOP THIS HAY INTO FINE PIECES! AND DON'T MAKE ANY MISTAKES! YOU'D BETTER FINISH BY THE TIME I RETURN IN FIVE HOURS OR ELSE I'LL BEAT YOU UNTIL EVERY BONE IN YOUR BODY CRIES OUT IN PAIN!
FEARFUL OF ANOTHER BEATING, THE BOY TOOK OFF HIS COAT, BECAUSE IT WAS A HOT DAY, AND SET TO WORK.
HE CHOPPED AND HACKED AS FAST AS HE COULD.
I MUST FINISH IN TIME! WHEN THAT EVIL MAN PROMISES TO BEAT ME, HE NEVER CHANGES HIS MIND!
BUT HE'D BEEN SO DESPERATE TO FINISH THAT...
OH NO!! MY COAT! I'M DONE FOR NOW. THAT MAN WILL SURELY BEAT ME TO DEATH!!
THIS IS HORRIBLE! HORRIBLE! I'M MUCH BETTER OFF ENDING MY OWN LIFE RIGHT NOW!
THIS IS RAT POISON! BE CAREFUL I DON'T POUR IT DOWN YOUR THROAT!
!
YES! THAT'S WHAT I MUST DO!
HE FOUND THE SAME TYPE OF BOTTLE UNDER THE WOMAN'S BED. BUT IT TURNED OUT THAT THE "POISON" WAS NOTHING BUT HONEY-- THE WOMAN'S FAVORITE DESSERT.
I NEVER THOUGHT THE TASTE OF DEATH WOULD BE SO SWEET! NO WONDER THE WOMAN SO OFTEN WISHES SHE WERE DEAD!

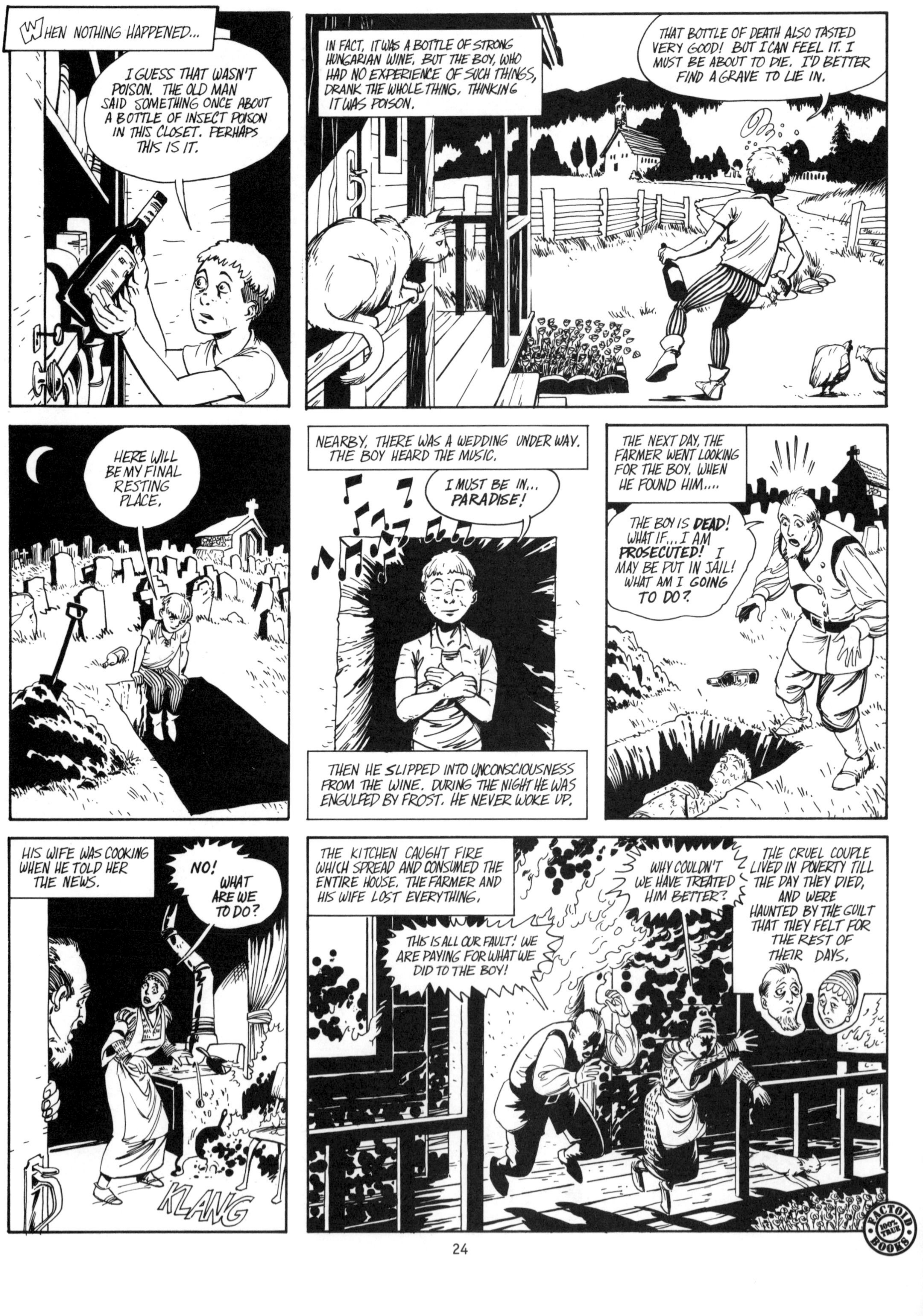
WHEN NOTHING HAPPENED...
I GUESS THAT WASN'T POISON. THE OLD MAN SAID SOMETHING ONCE ABOUT A BOTTLE OF INSECT POISON IN THIS CLOSET. PERHAPS THIS IS IT.
IN FACT, IT WAS A BOTTLE OF STRONG HUNGARIAN WINE, BUT THE BOY, WHO HAD NO EXPERIENCE OF SUCH THINGS, DRANK THE WHOLE THING, THINKING IT WAS POISON.
THAT BOTTLE OF DEATH ALSO TASTED VERY GOOD! BUT I CAN FEEL IT. I MUST BE ABOUT TO DIE. I'D BETTER FIND A GRAVE TO LIE IN.
HERE WILL BE MY FINAL RESTING PLACE.
NEARBY, THERE WAS A WEDDING UNDER WAY. THE BOY HEARD THE MUSIC.
I MUST BE IN... PARADISE!
THEN HE SLIPPED INTO UNCONSCIOUSNESS FROM THE WINE. DURING THE NIGHT HE WAS ENGULFED BY FROST. HE NEVER WOKE UP.
THE NEXT DAY, THE FARMER WENT LOOKING FOR THE BOY. WHEN HE FOUND HIM....
THE BOY IS DEAD! WHAT IF... I AM PROSECUTED! I MAY BE PUT IN JAIL! WHAT AM I GOING TO DO?
HIS WIFE WAS COOKING WHEN HE TOLD HER THE NEWS.
NO! WHAT ARE WE TO DO?
KLANG
THE KITCHEN CAUGHT FIRE WHICH SPREAD AND CONSUMED THE ENTIRE HOUSE. THE FARMER AND HIS WIFE LOST EVERYTHING.
THIS IS ALL OUR FAULT! WE ARE PAYING FOR WHAT WE DID TO THE BOY!
WHY COULDN'T WE HAVE TREATED HIM BETTER?
THE CRUEL COUPLE LIVED IN POVERTY TILL THE DAY THEY DIED, AND WERE HAUNTED BY THE GUILT THAT THEY FELT FOR THE REST OF THEIR DAYS.

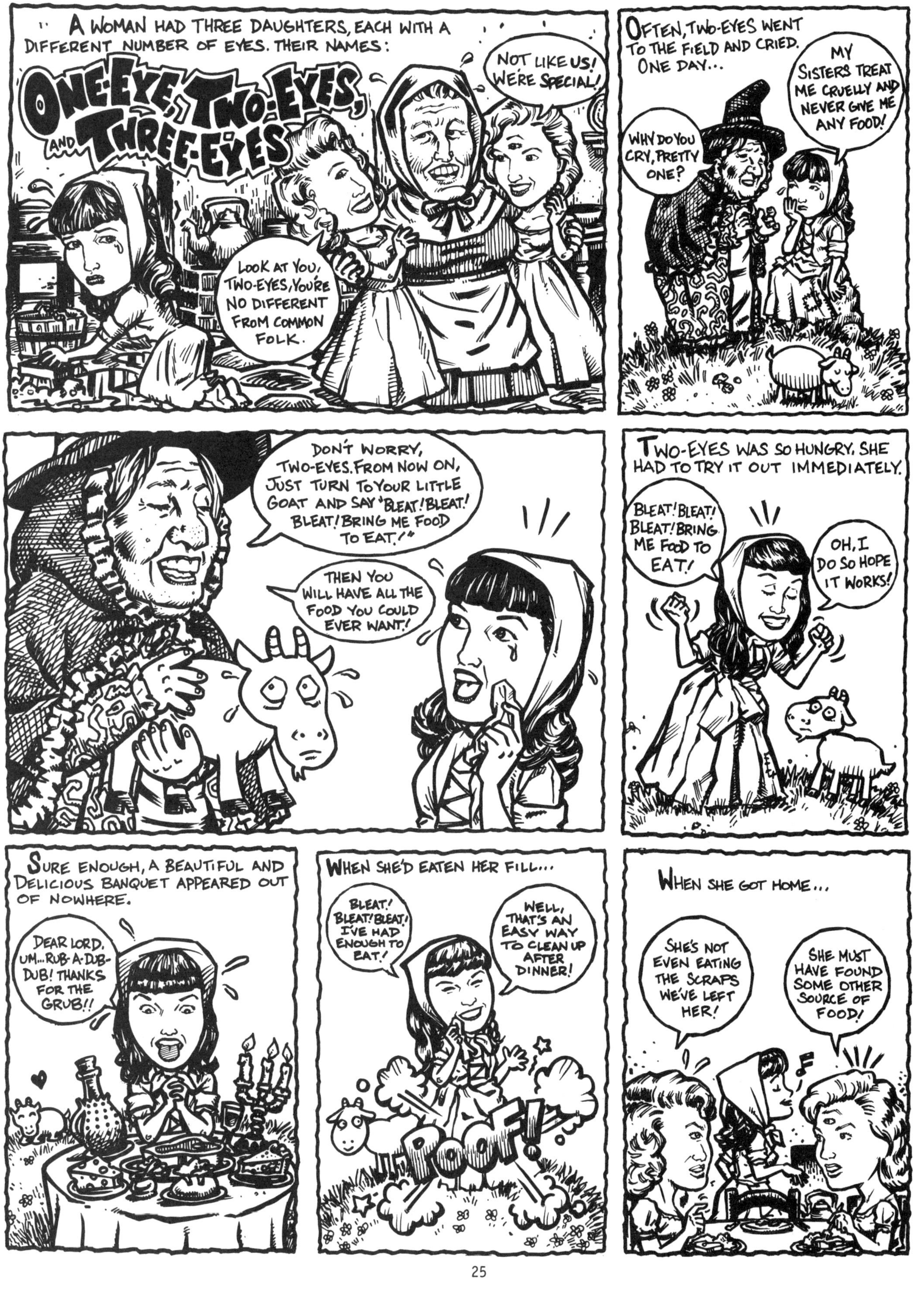
A WOMAN HAD THREE DAUGHTERS, EACH WITH A DIFFERENT NUMBER OF EYES. THEIR NAMES:
ONE-EYE, TWO-EYES, AND THREE-EYES
NOT LIKE US! WE'RE SPECIAL!
LOOK AT YOU, TWO-EYES, YOU'RE NO DIFFERENT FROM COMMON FOLK.
OFTEN, TWO-EYES WENT TO THE FIELD AND CRIED. ONE DAY...
WHY DO YOU CRY, PRETTY ONE?
MY SISTERS TREAT ME CRUELLY AND NEVER GIVE ME ANY FOOD!
DON'T WORRY, TWO-EYES. FROM NOW ON, JUST TURN TO YOUR LITTLE GOAT AND SAY "BLEAT! BLEAT! BLEAT! BRING ME FOOD TO EAT!"
THEN YOU WILL HAVE ALL THE FOOD YOU COULD EVER WANT!
TWO-EYES WAS SO HUNGRY, SHE HAD TO TRY IT OUT IMMEDIATELY.
BLEAT! BLEAT! BLEAT! BRING ME FOOD TO EAT!
OH, I DO SO HOPE IT WORKS!
SURE ENOUGH, A BEAUTIFUL AND DELICIOUS BANQUET APPEARED OUT OF NOWHERE.
DEAR LORD, UM...RUB-A-DUB-DUB! THANKS FOR THE GRUB!!
WHEN SHE'D EATEN HER FILL...
BLEAT! BLEAT! BLEAT! I'VE HAD ENOUGH TO EAT!
WELL, THAT'S AN EASY WAY TO CLEAN UP AFTER DINNER!
POOF!
WHEN SHE GOT HOME...
SHE'S NOT EVEN EATING THE SCRAPS WE'VE LEFT HER!
SHE MUST HAVE FOUND SOME OTHER SOURCE OF FOOD!

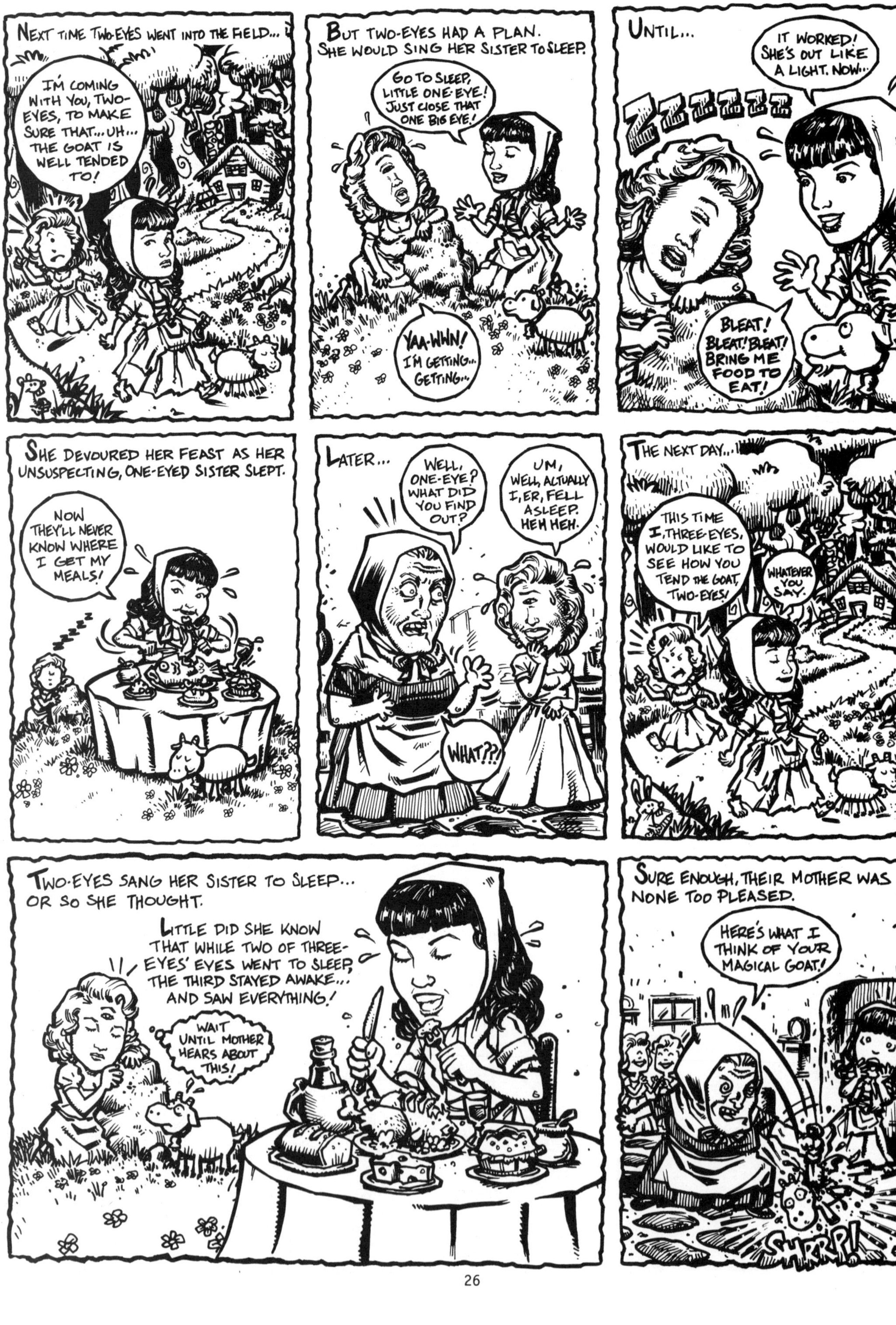

NEXT TIME TWO-EYES WENT INTO THE FIELD...
I'M COMING WITH YOU, TWO-EYES, TO MAKE SURE THAT...UH... THE GOAT IS WELL TENDED TO!
BUT TWO-EYES HAD A PLAN. SHE WOULD SING HER SISTER TO SLEEP.
GO TO SLEEP, LITTLE ONE-EYE! JUST CLOSE THAT ONE BIG EYE!
YAA-WWN! I'M GETTING... GETTING...
UNTIL...
IT WORKED! SHE'S OUT LIKE A LIGHT. NOW...
ZZZZZZ
BLEAT! BLEAT! BLEAT! BRING ME FOOD TO EAT!
SHE DEVOURED HER FEAST AS HER UNSUSPECTING, ONE-EYED SISTER SLEPT.
NOW THEY'LL NEVER KNOW WHERE I GET MY MEALS!
LATER...
WELL, ONE-EYE? WHAT DID YOU FIND OUT?
UM, WELL, ACTUALLY I, ER, FELL ASLEEP. HEH HEH.
WHAT??!
THE NEXT DAY...
THIS TIME I, THREE-EYES, WOULD LIKE TO SEE HOW YOU TEND THE GOAT, TWO-EYES!
WHATEVER YOU SAY.
TWO-EYES SANG HER SISTER TO SLEEP... OR SO SHE THOUGHT.
LITTLE DID SHE KNOW THAT WHILE TWO OF THREE-EYES' EYES WENT TO SLEEP, THE THIRD STAYED AWAKE... AND SAW EVERYTHING!
WAIT UNTIL MOTHER HEARS ABOUT THIS!
SURE ENOUGH, THEIR MOTHER WAS NONE TOO PLEASED.
HERE'S WHAT I THINK OF YOUR MAGICAL GOAT!
SHRRP!!

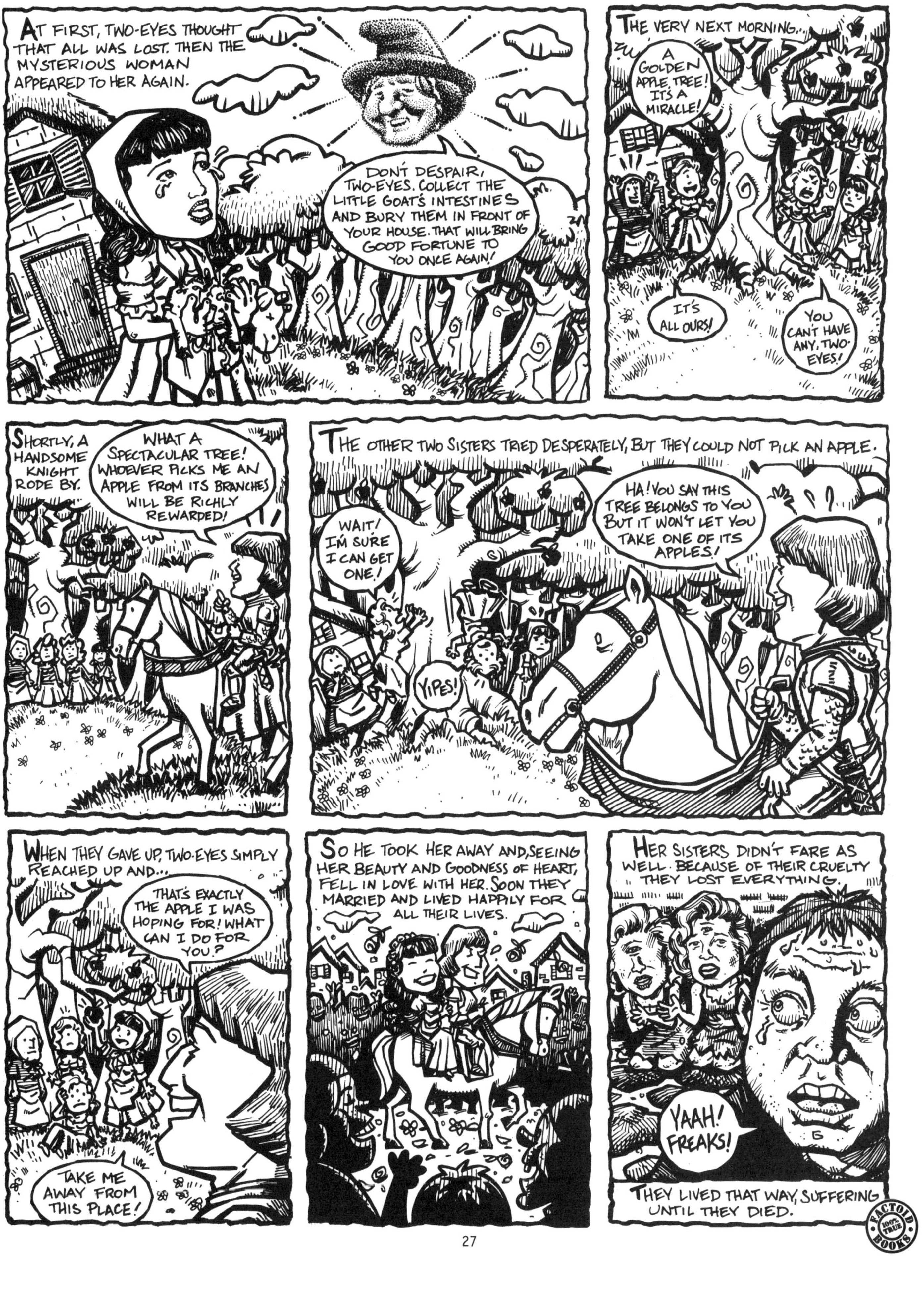
AT FIRST, TWO-EYES THOUGHT THAT ALL WAS LOST. THEN THE MYSTERIOUS WOMAN APPEARED TO HER AGAIN.
DON'T DESPAIR, TWO-EYES. COLLECT THE LITTLE GOAT'S INTESTINES AND BURY THEM IN FRONT OF YOUR HOUSE. THAT WILL BRING GOOD FORTUNE TO YOU ONCE AGAIN!
THE VERY NEXT MORNING...
A GOLDEN APPLE TREE! IT'S A MIRACLE!
IT'S ALL OURS!
YOU CAN'T HAVE ANY, TWO-EYES!
SHORTLY, A HANDSOME KNIGHT RODE BY.
WHAT A SPECTACULAR TREE! WHOEVER PICKS ME AN APPLE FROM ITS BRANCHES WILL BE RICHLY REWARDED!
THE OTHER TWO SISTERS TRIED DESPERATELY, BUT THEY COULD NOT PICK AN APPLE.
WAIT! I'M SURE I CAN GET ONE!
HA! YOU SAY THIS TREE BELONGS TO YOU BUT IT WON'T LET YOU TAKE ONE OF ITS APPLES!
YIPES!
WHEN THEY GAVE UP, TWO-EYES SIMPLY REACHED UP AND...
THAT'S EXACTLY THE APPLE I WAS HOPING FOR! WHAT CAN I DO FOR YOU?
TAKE ME AWAY FROM THIS PLACE!
SO HE TOOK HER AWAY AND, SEEING HER BEAUTY AND GOODNESS OF HEART, FELL IN LOVE WITH HER. SOON THEY MARRIED AND LIVED HAPPILY FOR ALL THEIR LIVES.
HER SISTERS DIDN'T FARE AS WELL. BECAUSE OF THEIR CRUELTY THEY LOST EVERYTHING.
YAAH! FREAKS!
THEY LIVED THAT WAY, SUFFERING UNTIL THEY DIED.
FACTOID BOOKS 100% TRUE

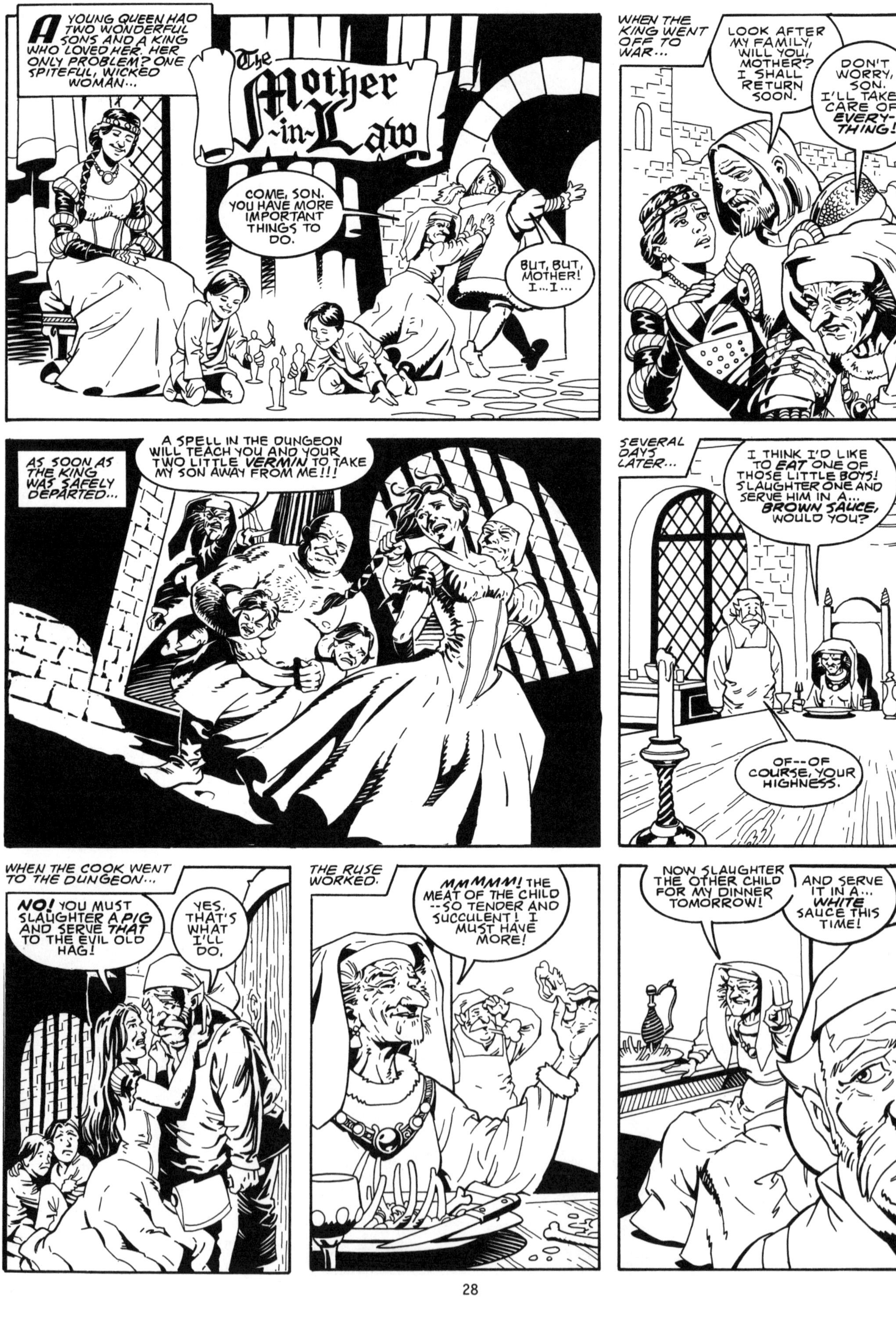
A YOUNG QUEEN HAD TWO WONDERFUL SONS AND A KING WHO LOVED HER. HER ONLY PROBLEM? ONE SPITEFUL, WICKED WOMAN...
The Mother-in-Law
COME, SON. YOU HAVE MORE IMPORTANT THINGS TO DO.
BUT, BUT, MOTHER! I...I...
WHEN THE KING WENT OFF TO WAR...
LOOK AFTER MY FAMILY, WILL YOU, MOTHER? I SHALL RETURN SOON.
DON'T WORRY, SON. I'LL TAKE CARE OF EVERYTHING!
AS SOON AS THE KING WAS SAFELY DEPARTED...
A SPELL IN THE DUNGEON WILL TEACH YOU AND YOUR TWO LITTLE VERMIN TO TAKE MY SON AWAY FROM ME!!!
SEVERAL DAYS LATER...
I THINK I'D LIKE TO EAT ONE OF THOSE LITTLE BOYS! SLAUGHTER ONE AND SERVE HIM IN A... BROWN SAUCE, WOULD YOU?
OF--OF COURSE, YOUR HIGHNESS.
WHEN THE COOK WENT TO THE DUNGEON...
NO! YOU MUST SLAUGHTER A PIG AND SERVE THAT TO THE EVIL OLD HAG!
YES. THAT'S WHAT I'LL DO.
THE RUSE WORKED.
MMMMM! THE MEAT OF THE CHILD --SO TENDER AND SUCCULENT! I MUST HAVE MORE!
NOW SLAUGHTER THE OTHER CHILD FOR MY DINNER TOMORROW!
AND SERVE IT IN A... WHITE SAUCE THIS TIME!

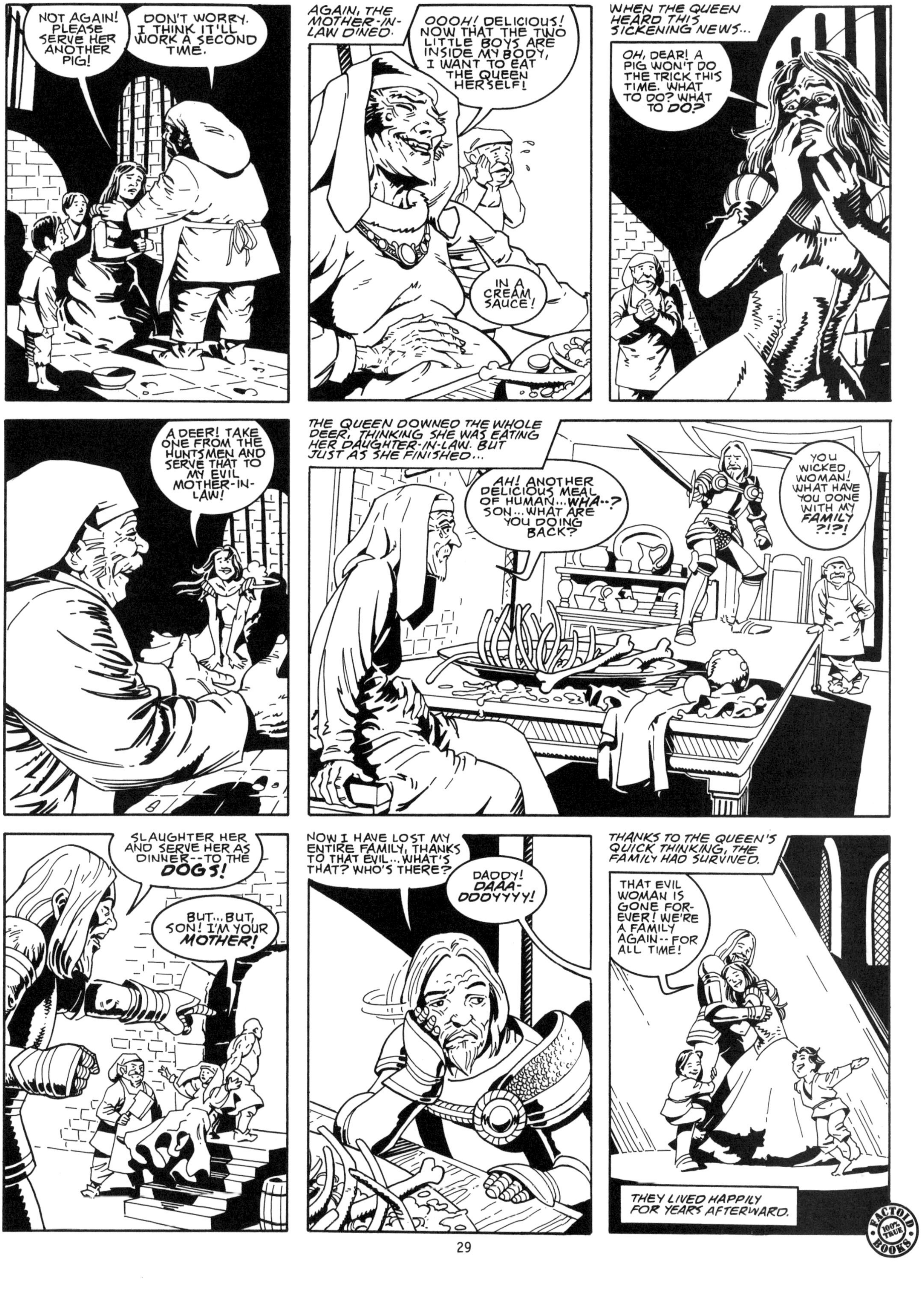
NOT AGAIN! PLEASE SERVE HER ANOTHER PIG!
DON'T WORRY. I THINK IT'LL WORK A SECOND TIME.
AGAIN, THE MOTHER-IN-LAW DINED.
OOOH! DELICIOUS! NOW THAT THE TWO LITTLE BOYS ARE INSIDE MY BODY, I WANT TO EAT THE QUEEN HERSELF!
IN A CREAM SAUCE!
WHEN THE QUEEN HEARD THIS SICKENING NEWS...
OH, DEAR! A PIG WON'T DO THE TRICK THIS TIME. WHAT TO DO? WHAT TO DO?
A DEER! TAKE ONE FROM THE HUNTSMEN AND SERVE THAT TO MY EVIL MOTHER-IN-LAW!
THE QUEEN DOWNED THE WHOLE DEER, THINKING SHE WAS EATING HER DAUGHTER-IN-LAW. BUT JUST AS SHE FINISHED...
AH! ANOTHER DELICIOUS MEAL OF HUMAN... WHA--? SON... WHAT ARE YOU DOING BACK?
YOU WICKED WOMAN! WHAT HAVE YOU DONE WITH MY FAMILY ?!?!
SLAUGHTER HER AND SERVE HER AS DINNER--TO THE DOGS!
BUT... BUT, SON! I'M YOUR MOTHER!
NOW I HAVE LOST MY ENTIRE FAMILY, THANKS TO THAT EVIL... WHAT'S THAT? WHO'S THERE?
DADDY! DAAA-DDDYYYY!
THANKS TO THE QUEEN'S QUICK THINKING, THE FAMILY HAD SURVIVED.
THAT EVIL WOMAN IS GONE FOREVER! WE'RE A FAMILY AGAIN--FOR ALL TIME!
THEY LIVED HAPPILY FOR YEARS AFTERWARD.
FACTOID BOOKS 100% TRUE

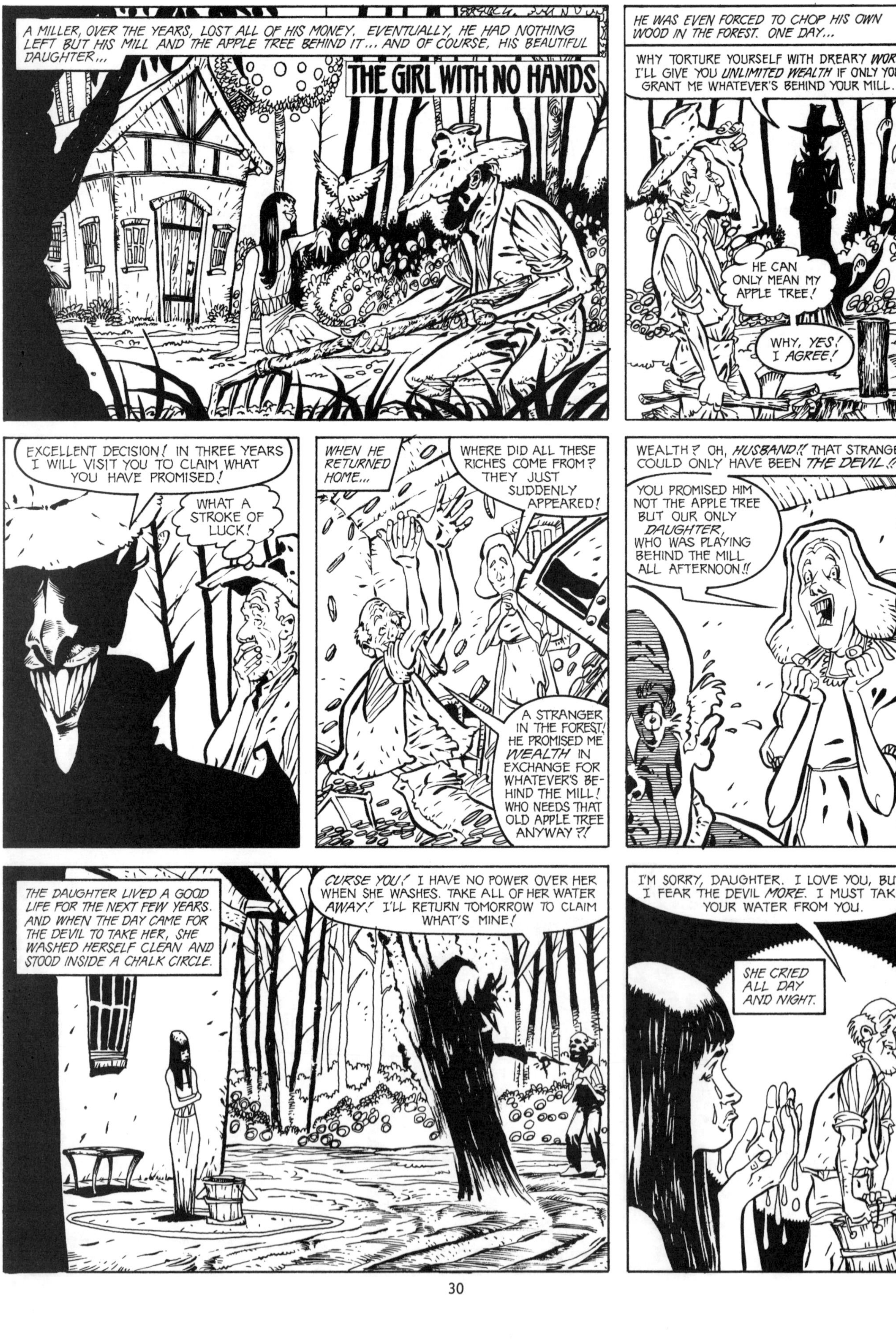

A MILLER, OVER THE YEARS, LOST ALL OF HIS MONEY. EVENTUALLY, HE HAD NOTHING LEFT BUT HIS MILL AND THE APPLE TREE BEHIND IT... AND OF COURSE, HIS BEAUTIFUL DAUGHTER...
THE GIRL WITH NO HANDS
HE WAS EVEN FORCED TO CHOP HIS OWN WOOD IN THE FOREST. ONE DAY...
WHY TORTURE YOURSELF WITH DREARY WORK? I'LL GIVE YOU UNLIMITED WEALTH IF ONLY YOU'LL GRANT ME WHATEVER'S BEHIND YOUR MILL.
HE CAN ONLY MEAN MY APPLE TREE!
WHY, YES! I AGREE!
EXCELLENT DECISION! IN THREE YEARS I WILL VISIT YOU TO CLAIM WHAT YOU HAVE PROMISED!
WHAT A STROKE OF LUCK!
WHEN HE RETURNED HOME...
WHERE DID ALL THESE RICHES COME FROM? THEY JUST SUDDENLY APPEARED!
A STRANGER IN THE FOREST! HE PROMISED ME WEALTH IN EXCHANGE FOR WHATEVER'S BEHIND THE MILL! WHO NEEDS THAT OLD APPLE TREE ANYWAY?!
WEALTH? OH, HUSBAND!! THAT STRANGER COULD ONLY HAVE BEEN THE DEVIL!!
YOU PROMISED HIM NOT THE APPLE TREE BUT OUR ONLY DAUGHTER, WHO WAS PLAYING BEHIND THE MILL ALL AFTERNOON!!
THE DAUGHTER LIVED A GOOD LIFE FOR THE NEXT FEW YEARS. AND WHEN THE DAY CAME FOR THE DEVIL TO TAKE HER, SHE WASHED HERSELF CLEAN AND STOOD INSIDE A CHALK CIRCLE.
CURSE YOU! I HAVE NO POWER OVER HER WHEN SHE WASHES. TAKE ALL OF HER WATER AWAY! I'LL RETURN TOMORROW TO CLAIM WHAT'S MINE!
I'M SORRY, DAUGHTER. I LOVE YOU, BUT I FEAR THE DEVIL MORE. I MUST TAKE YOUR WATER FROM YOU.
SHE CRIED ALL DAY AND NIGHT.

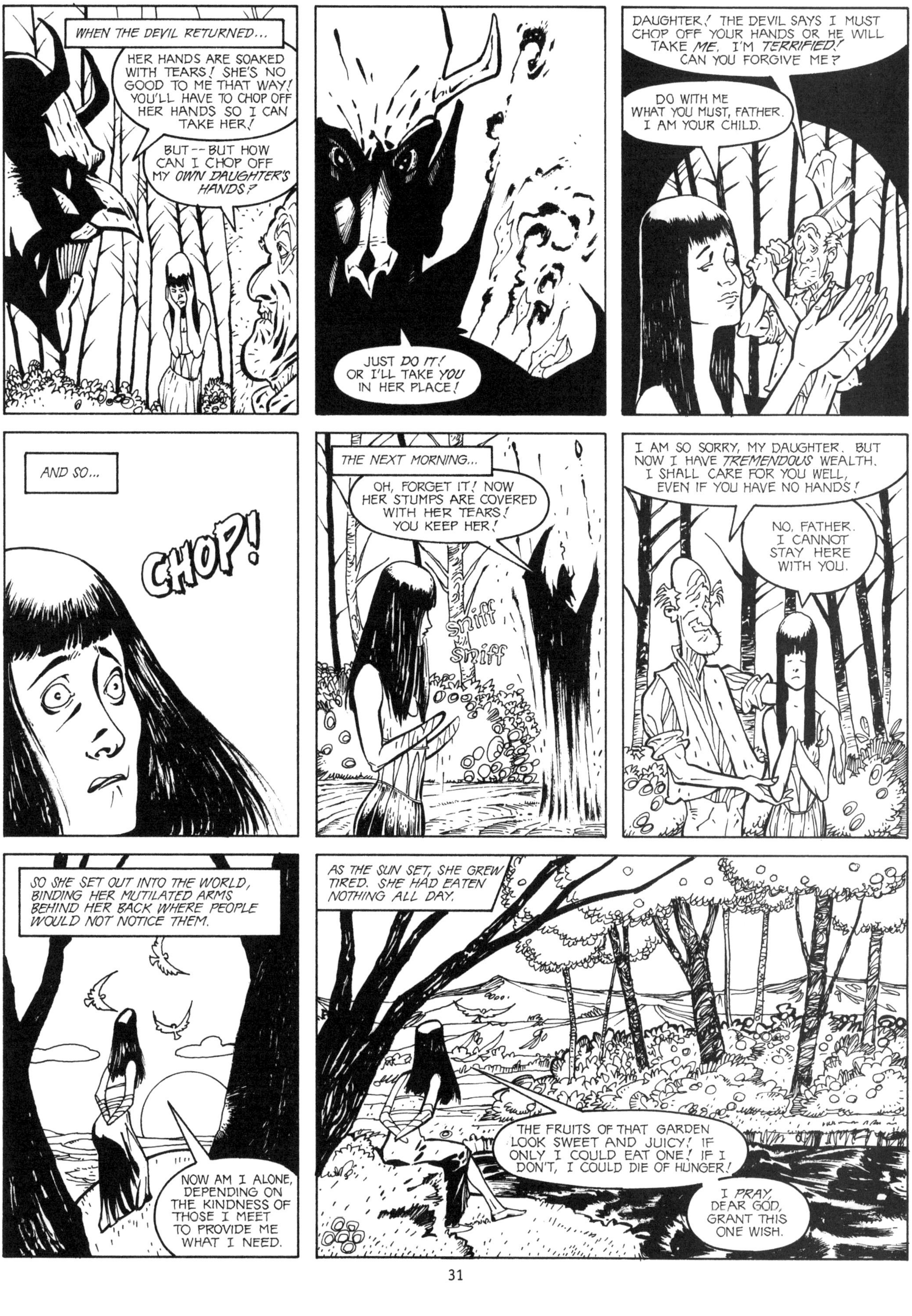
WHEN THE DEVIL RETURNED...
HER HANDS ARE SOAKED WITH TEARS! SHE'S NO GOOD TO ME THAT WAY! YOU'LL HAVE TO CHOP OFF HER HANDS SO I CAN TAKE HER!
BUT -- BUT HOW CAN I CHOP OFF MY OWN DAUGHTER'S HANDS?
JUST DO IT! OR I'LL TAKE YOU IN HER PLACE!
DAUGHTER! THE DEVIL SAYS I MUST CHOP OFF YOUR HANDS OR HE WILL TAKE ME. I'M TERRIFIED! CAN YOU FORGIVE ME?
DO WITH ME WHAT YOU MUST, FATHER. I AM YOUR CHILD.
AND SO...
CHOP!
THE NEXT MORNING...
OH, FORGET IT! NOW HER STUMPS ARE COVERED WITH HER TEARS! YOU KEEP HER!
sniff
sniff
I AM SO SORRY, MY DAUGHTER. BUT NOW I HAVE TREMENDOUS WEALTH. I SHALL CARE FOR YOU WELL, EVEN IF YOU HAVE NO HANDS!
NO, FATHER. I CANNOT STAY HERE WITH YOU.
SO SHE SET OUT INTO THE WORLD, BINDING HER MUTILATED ARMS BEHIND HER BACK WHERE PEOPLE WOULD NOT NOTICE THEM.
NOW AM I ALONE, DEPENDING ON THE KINDNESS OF THOSE I MEET TO PROVIDE ME WHAT I NEED.
AS THE SUN SET, SHE GREW TIRED. SHE HAD EATEN NOTHING ALL DAY.
THE FRUITS OF THAT GARDEN LOOK SWEET AND JUICY! IF ONLY I COULD EAT ONE! IF I DON'T, I COULD DIE OF HUNGER!
I PRAY, DEAR GOD, GRANT THIS ONE WISH.

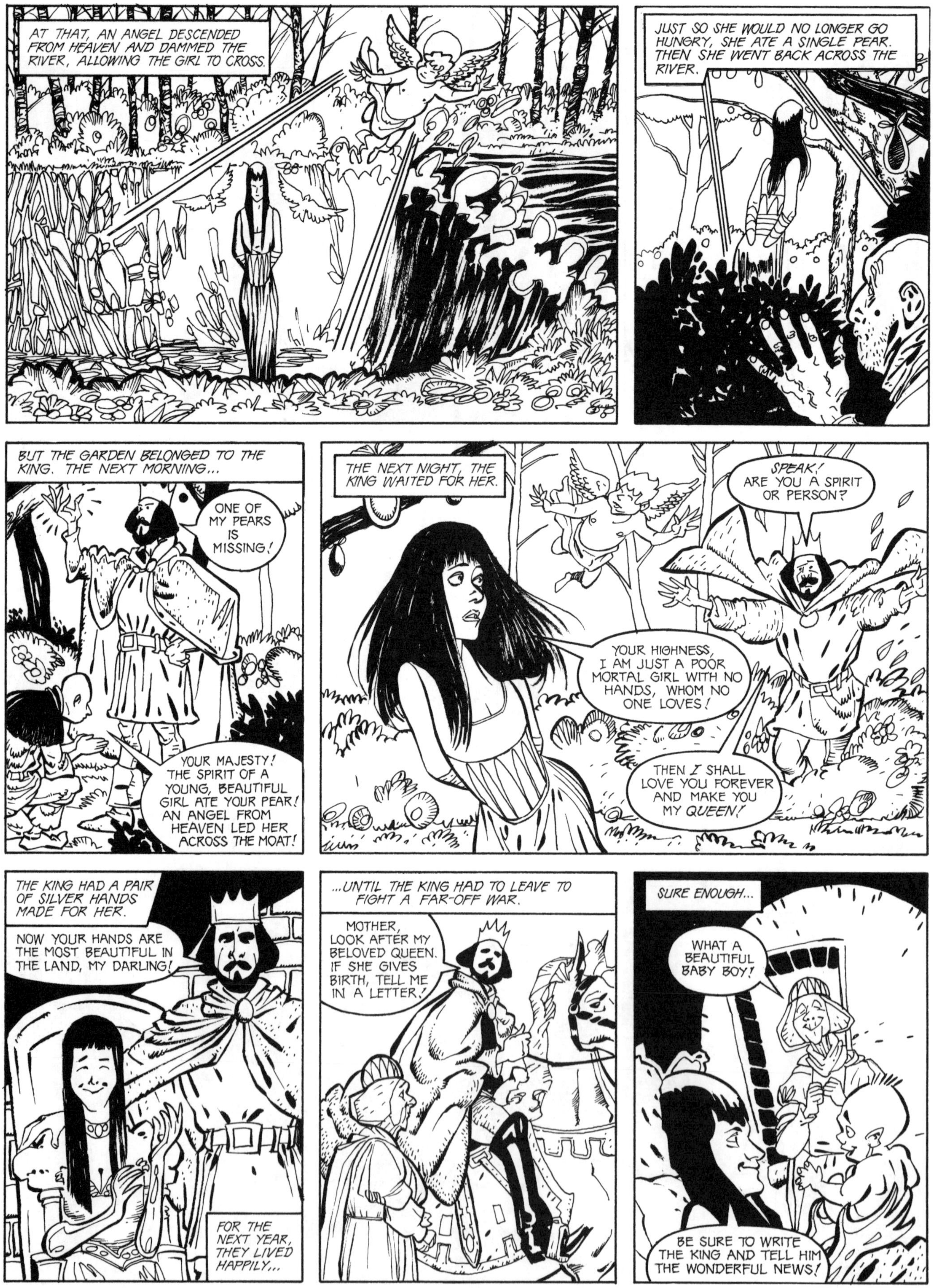
AT THAT, AN ANGEL DESCENDED FROM HEAVEN AND DAMMED THE RIVER, ALLOWING THE GIRL TO CROSS.
JUST SO SHE WOULD NO LONGER GO HUNGRY, SHE ATE A SINGLE PEAR. THEN SHE WENT BACK ACROSS THE RIVER.
BUT THE GARDEN BELONGED TO THE KING. THE NEXT MORNING...
ONE OF MY PEARS IS MISSING!
YOUR MAJESTY! THE SPIRIT OF A YOUNG, BEAUTIFUL GIRL ATE YOUR PEAR! AN ANGEL FROM HEAVEN LED HER ACROSS THE MOAT!
THE NEXT NIGHT, THE KING WAITED FOR HER.
SPEAK! ARE YOU A SPIRIT OR PERSON?
YOUR HIGHNESS, I AM JUST A POOR MORTAL GIRL WITH NO HANDS, WHOM NO ONE LOVES!
THEN I SHALL LOVE YOU FOREVER AND MAKE YOU MY QUEEN!
THE KING HAD A PAIR OF SILVER HANDS MADE FOR HER.
NOW YOUR HANDS ARE THE MOST BEAUTIFUL IN THE LAND, MY DARLING!
FOR THE NEXT YEAR, THEY LIVED HAPPILY...
...UNTIL THE KING HAD TO LEAVE TO FIGHT A FAR-OFF WAR.
MOTHER, LOOK AFTER MY BELOVED QUEEN. IF SHE GIVES BIRTH, TELL ME IN A LETTER!
SURE ENOUGH...
WHAT A BEAUTIFUL BABY BOY!
BE SURE TO WRITE THE KING AND TELL HIM THE WONDERFUL NEWS!

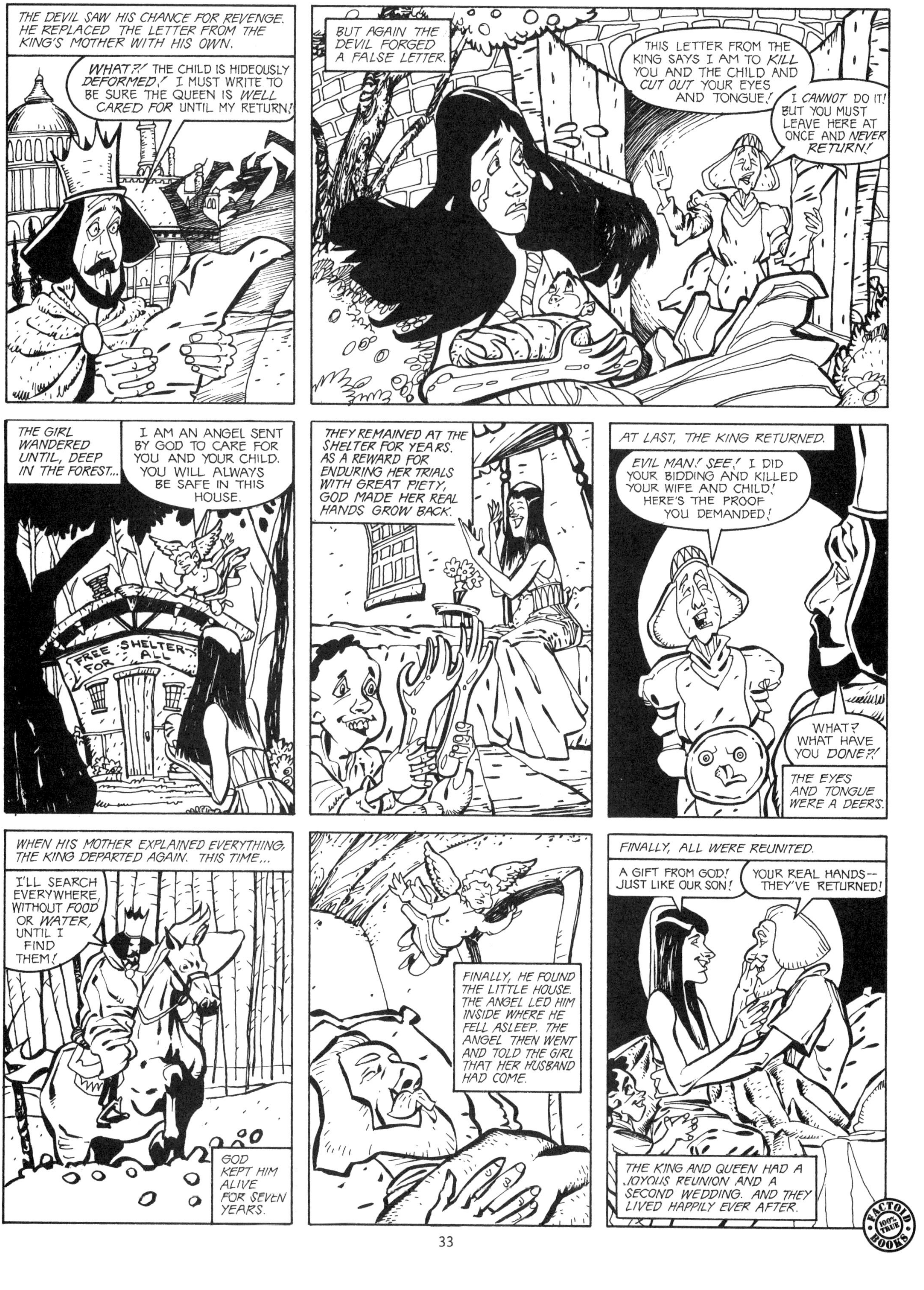
THE DEVIL SAW HIS CHANCE FOR REVENGE. HE REPLACED THE LETTER FROM THE KING'S MOTHER WITH HIS OWN.
WHAT?! THE CHILD IS HIDEOUSLY DEFORMED! I MUST WRITE TO BE SURE THE QUEEN IS WELL CARED FOR UNTIL MY RETURN!
BUT AGAIN THE DEVIL FORGED A FALSE LETTER.
THIS LETTER FROM THE KING SAYS I AM TO KILL YOU AND THE CHILD AND CUT OUT YOUR EYES AND TONGUE!
I CANNOT DO IT! BUT YOU MUST LEAVE HERE AT ONCE AND NEVER RETURN!
THE GIRL WANDERED UNTIL, DEEP IN THE FOREST...
I AM AN ANGEL SENT BY GOD TO CARE FOR YOU AND YOUR CHILD. YOU WILL ALWAYS BE SAFE IN THIS HOUSE.
FREE SHELTER FOR ALL
THEY REMAINED AT THE SHELTER FOR YEARS. AS A REWARD FOR ENDURING HER TRIALS WITH GREAT PIETY, GOD MADE HER REAL HANDS GROW BACK.
AT LAST, THE KING RETURNED.
EVIL MAN! SEE! I DID YOUR BIDDING AND KILLED YOUR WIFE AND CHILD! HERE'S THE PROOF YOU DEMANDED!
WHAT? WHAT HAVE YOU DONE?!
THE EYES AND TONGUE WERE A DEER'S.
WHEN HIS MOTHER EXPLAINED EVERYTHING, THE KING DEPARTED AGAIN. THIS TIME...
I'LL SEARCH EVERYWHERE, WITHOUT FOOD OR WATER, UNTIL I FIND THEM!
GOD KEPT HIM ALIVE FOR SEVEN YEARS.
FINALLY, HE FOUND THE LITTLE HOUSE. THE ANGEL LED HIM INSIDE WHERE HE FELL ASLEEP. THE ANGEL THEN WENT AND TOLD THE GIRL THAT HER HUSBAND HAD COME.
FINALLY, ALL WERE REUNITED.
A GIFT FROM GOD! JUST LIKE OUR SON!
YOUR REAL HANDS-- THEY'VE RETURNED!
THE KING AND QUEEN HAD A JOYOUS REUNION AND A SECOND WEDDING. AND THEY LIVED HAPPILY EVER AFTER.

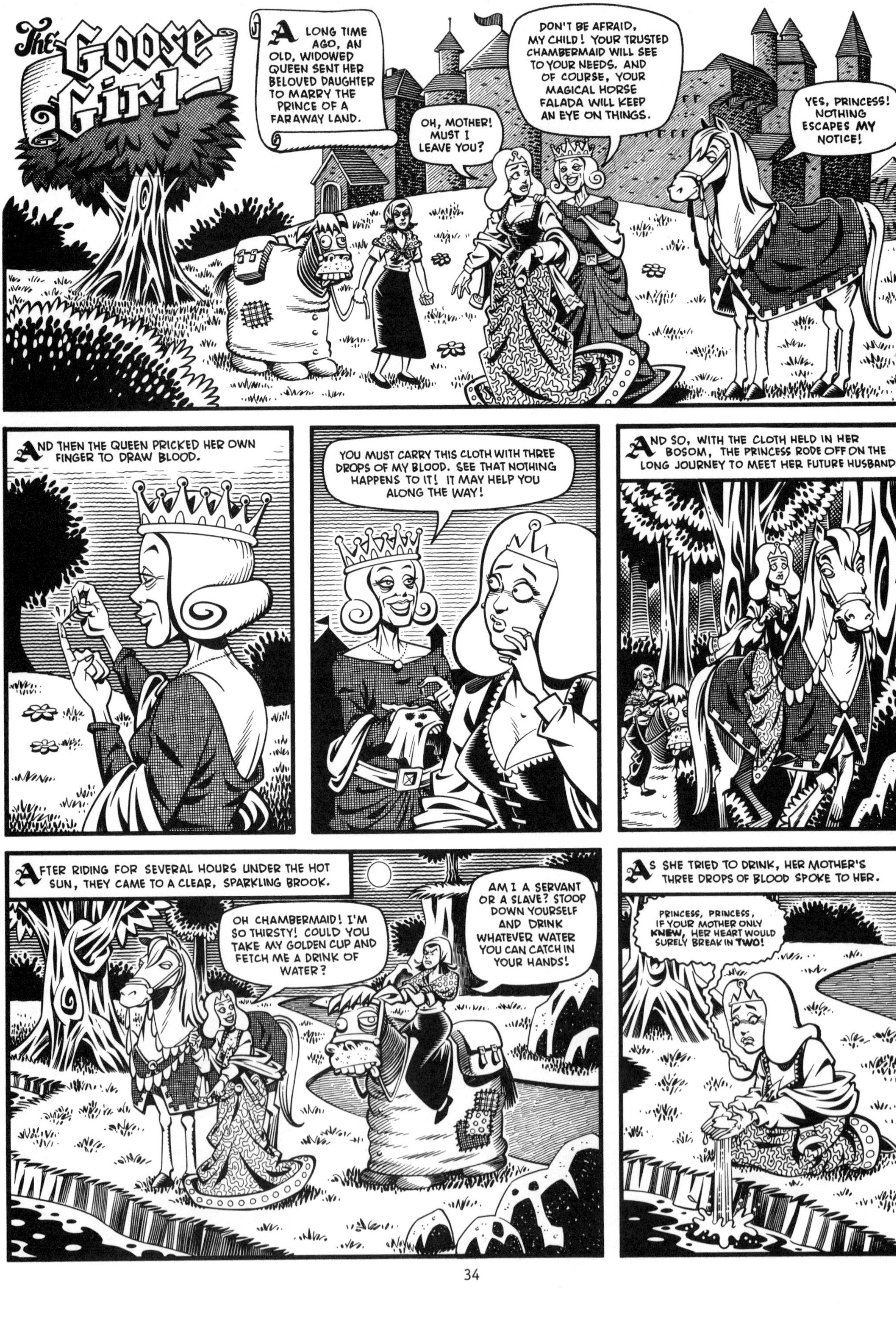

The Goose Girl
A LONG TIME AGO, AN OLD, WIDOWED QUEEN SENT HER BELOVED DAUGHTER TO MARRY THE PRINCE OF A FARAWAY LAND.
OH, MOTHER! MUST I LEAVE YOU?
DON'T BE AFRAID, MY CHILD! YOUR TRUSTED CHAMBERMAID WILL SEE TO YOUR NEEDS. AND OF COURSE, YOUR MAGICAL HORSE FALADA WILL KEEP AN EYE ON THINGS.
YES, PRINCESS! NOTHING ESCAPES MY NOTICE!
AND THEN THE QUEEN PRICKED HER OWN FINGER TO DRAW BLOOD.
YOU MUST CARRY THIS CLOTH WITH THREE DROPS OF MY BLOOD. SEE THAT NOTHING HAPPENS TO IT! IT MAY HELP YOU ALONG THE WAY!
AND SO, WITH THE CLOTH HELD IN HER BOSOM, THE PRINCESS RODE OFF ON THE LONG JOURNEY TO MEET HER FUTURE HUSBAND.
AFTER RIDING FOR SEVERAL HOURS UNDER THE HOT SUN, THEY CAME TO A CLEAR, SPARKLING BROOK.
OH CHAMBERMAID! I'M SO THIRSTY! COULD YOU TAKE MY GOLDEN CUP AND FETCH ME A DRINK OF WATER?
AM I A SERVANT OR A SLAVE? STOOP DOWN YOURSELF AND DRINK WHATEVER WATER YOU CAN CATCH IN YOUR HANDS!
AS SHE TRIED TO DRINK, HER MOTHER'S THREE DROPS OF BLOOD SPOKE TO HER.
PRINCESS, PRINCESS, IF YOUR MOTHER ONLY KNEW, HER HEART WOULD SURELY BREAK IN TWO!

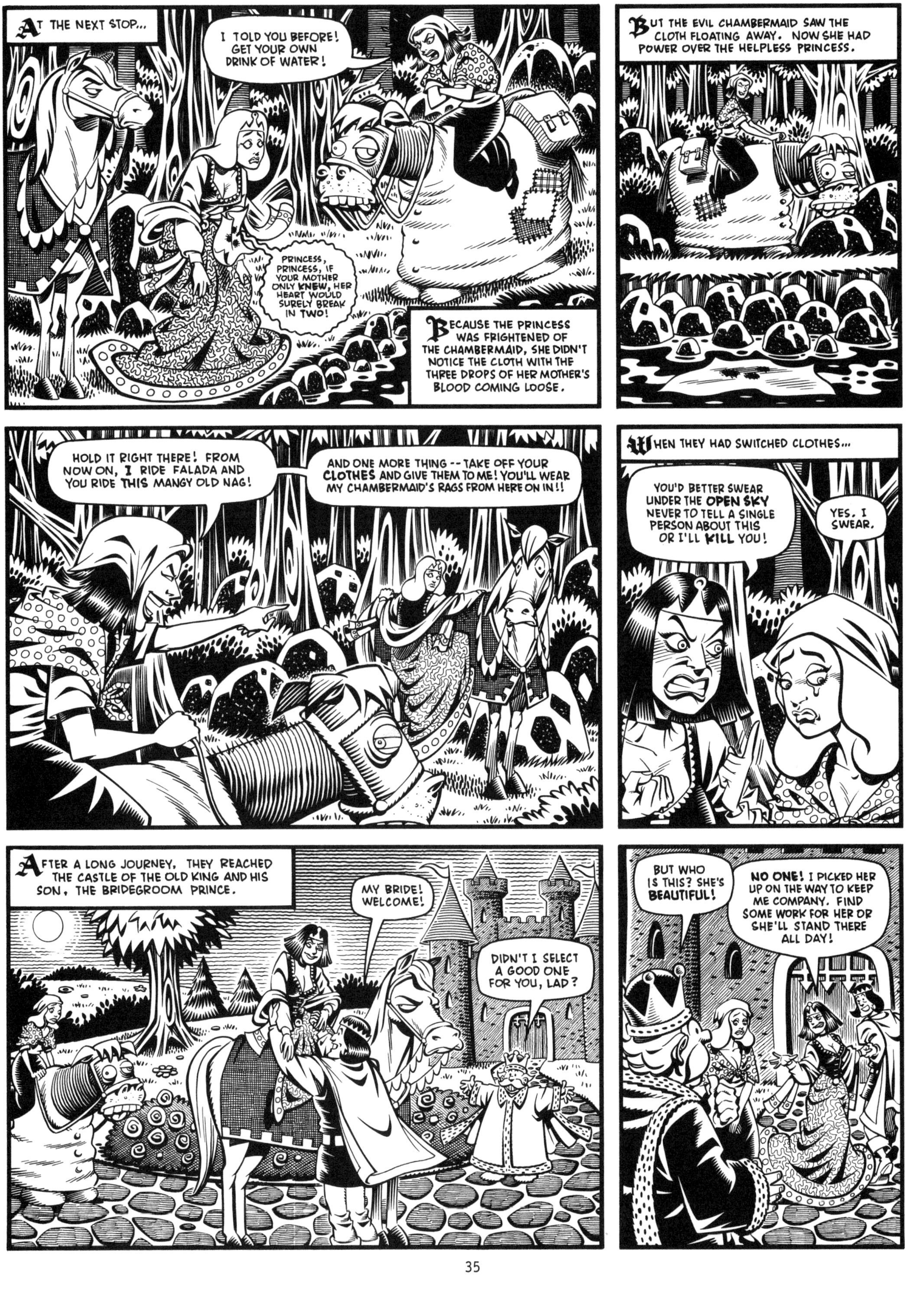
At the next stop...
I told you before! Get your own drink of water!
Princess, princess, if your mother only knew, her heart would surely break in two!
Because the princess was frightened of the chambermaid, she didn't notice the cloth with the three drops of her mother's blood coming loose.
But the evil chambermaid saw the cloth floating away. Now she had power over the helpless princess.
Hold it right there! From now on, I ride Falada and you ride this mangy old nag!
And one more thing -- take off your clothes and give them to me! You'll wear my chambermaid's rags from here on in!!
When they had switched clothes...
You'd better swear under the open sky never to tell a single person about this or I'll kill you!
Yes. I swear.
After a long journey, they reached the castle of the old king and his son, the bridegroom prince.
My bride! Welcome!
Didn't I select a good one for you, lad?
But who is this? She's beautiful!
No one! I picked her up on the way to keep me company. Find some work for her or she'll stand there all day!

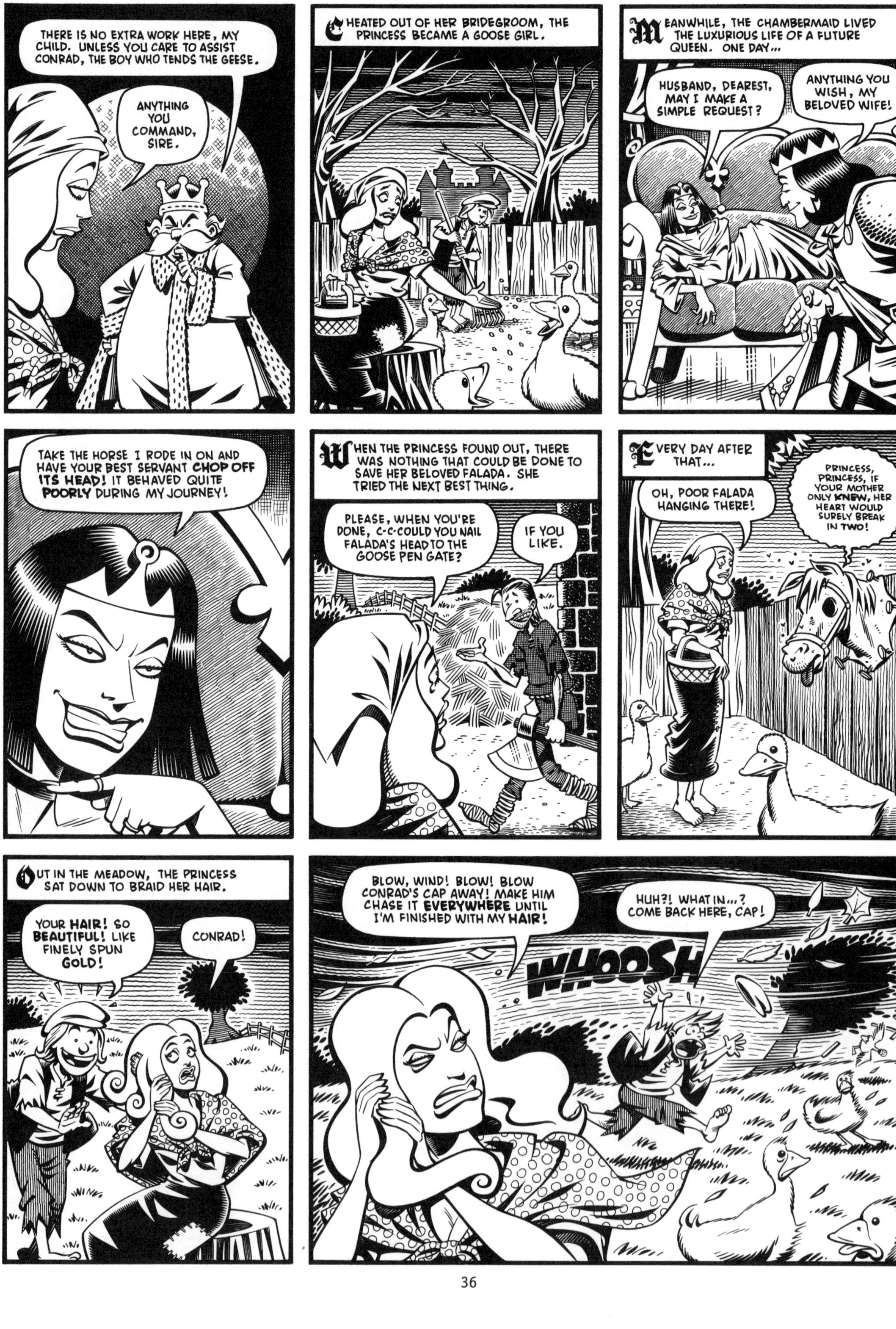
THERE IS NO EXTRA WORK HERE, MY CHILD. UNLESS YOU CARE TO ASSIST CONRAD, THE BOY WHO TENDS THE GEESE.
ANYTHING YOU COMMAND, SIRE.
CHEATED OUT OF HER BRIDEGROOM, THE PRINCESS BECAME A GOOSE GIRL.
MEANWHILE, THE CHAMBERMAID LIVED THE LUXURIOUS LIFE OF A FUTURE QUEEN. ONE DAY...
HUSBAND, DEAREST, MAY I MAKE A SIMPLE REQUEST?
ANYTHING YOU WISH, MY BELOVED WIFE!
TAKE THE HORSE I RODE IN ON AND HAVE YOUR BEST SERVANT CHOP OFF ITS HEAD! IT BEHAVED QUITE POORLY DURING MY JOURNEY!
WHEN THE PRINCESS FOUND OUT, THERE WAS NOTHING THAT COULD BE DONE TO SAVE HER BELOVED FALADA. SHE TRIED THE NEXT BEST THING.
PLEASE, WHEN YOU'RE DONE, C-C-COULD YOU NAIL FALADA'S HEAD TO THE GOOSE PEN GATE?
IF YOU LIKE.
EVERY DAY AFTER THAT...
OH, POOR FALADA HANGING THERE!
PRINCESS, PRINCESS, IF YOUR MOTHER ONLY KNEW, HER HEART WOULD SURELY BREAK IN TWO!
OUT IN THE MEADOW, THE PRINCESS SAT DOWN TO BRAID HER HAIR.
YOUR HAIR! SO BEAUTIFUL! LIKE FINELY SPUN GOLD!
CONRAD!
BLOW, WIND! BLOW! BLOW CONRAD'S CAP AWAY! MAKE HIM CHASE IT EVERYWHERE UNTIL I'M FINISHED WITH MY HAIR!
HUH?! WHAT IN...? COME BACK HERE, CAP!
WHOOSH

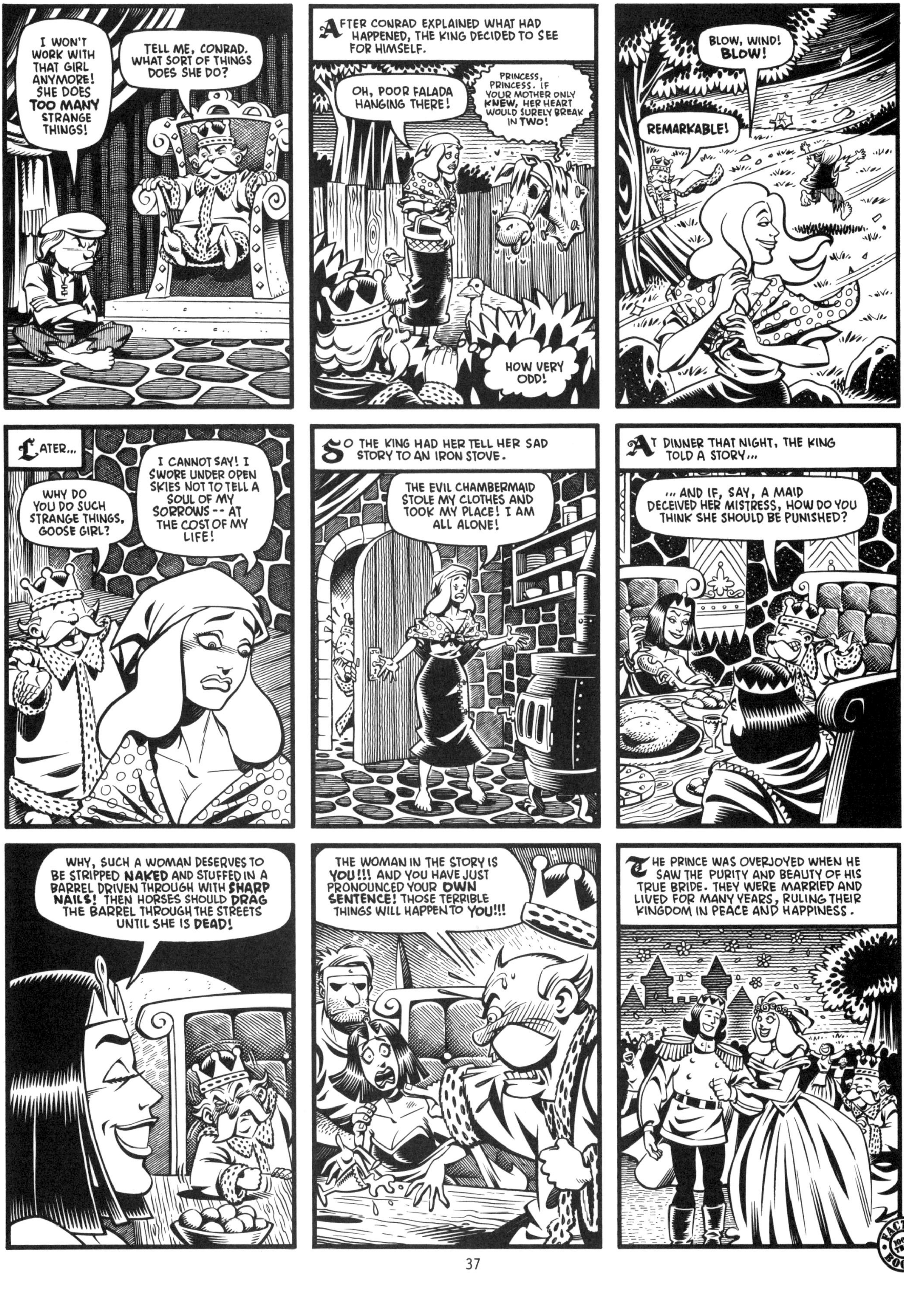
I WON'T WORK WITH THAT GIRL ANYMORE! SHE DOES TOO MANY STRANGE THINGS!
TELL ME, CONRAD. WHAT SORT OF THINGS DOES SHE DO?
AFTER CONRAD EXPLAINED WHAT HAD HAPPENED, THE KING DECIDED TO SEE FOR HIMSELF.
OH, POOR FALADA HANGING THERE!
PRINCESS, PRINCESS. IF YOUR MOTHER ONLY KNEW, HER HEART WOULD SURELY BREAK IN TWO!
HOW VERY ODD!
BLOW, WIND! BLOW!
REMARKABLE!
LATER...
WHY DO YOU DO SUCH STRANGE THINGS, GOOSE GIRL?
I CANNOT SAY! I SWORE UNDER OPEN SKIES NOT TO TELL A SOUL OF MY SORROWS -- AT THE COST OF MY LIFE!
SO THE KING HAD HER TELL HER SAD STORY TO AN IRON STOVE.
THE EVIL CHAMBERMAID STOLE MY CLOTHES AND TOOK MY PLACE! I AM ALL ALONE!
AT DINNER THAT NIGHT, THE KING TOLD A STORY...
...AND IF, SAY, A MAID DECEIVED HER MISTRESS, HOW DO YOU THINK SHE SHOULD BE PUNISHED?
WHY, SUCH A WOMAN DESERVES TO BE STRIPPED NAKED AND STUFFED IN A BARREL DRIVEN THROUGH WITH SHARP NAILS! THEN HORSES SHOULD DRAG THE BARREL THROUGH THE STREETS UNTIL SHE IS DEAD!
THE WOMAN IN THE STORY IS YOU!!! AND YOU HAVE JUST PRONOUNCED YOUR OWN SENTENCE! THOSE TERRIBLE THINGS WILL HAPPEN TO YOU!!!
THE PRINCE WAS OVERJOYED WHEN HE SAW THE PURITY AND BEAUTY OF HIS TRUE BRIDE. THEY WERE MARRIED AND LIVED FOR MANY YEARS, RULING THEIR KINGDOM IN PEACE AND HAPPINESS.

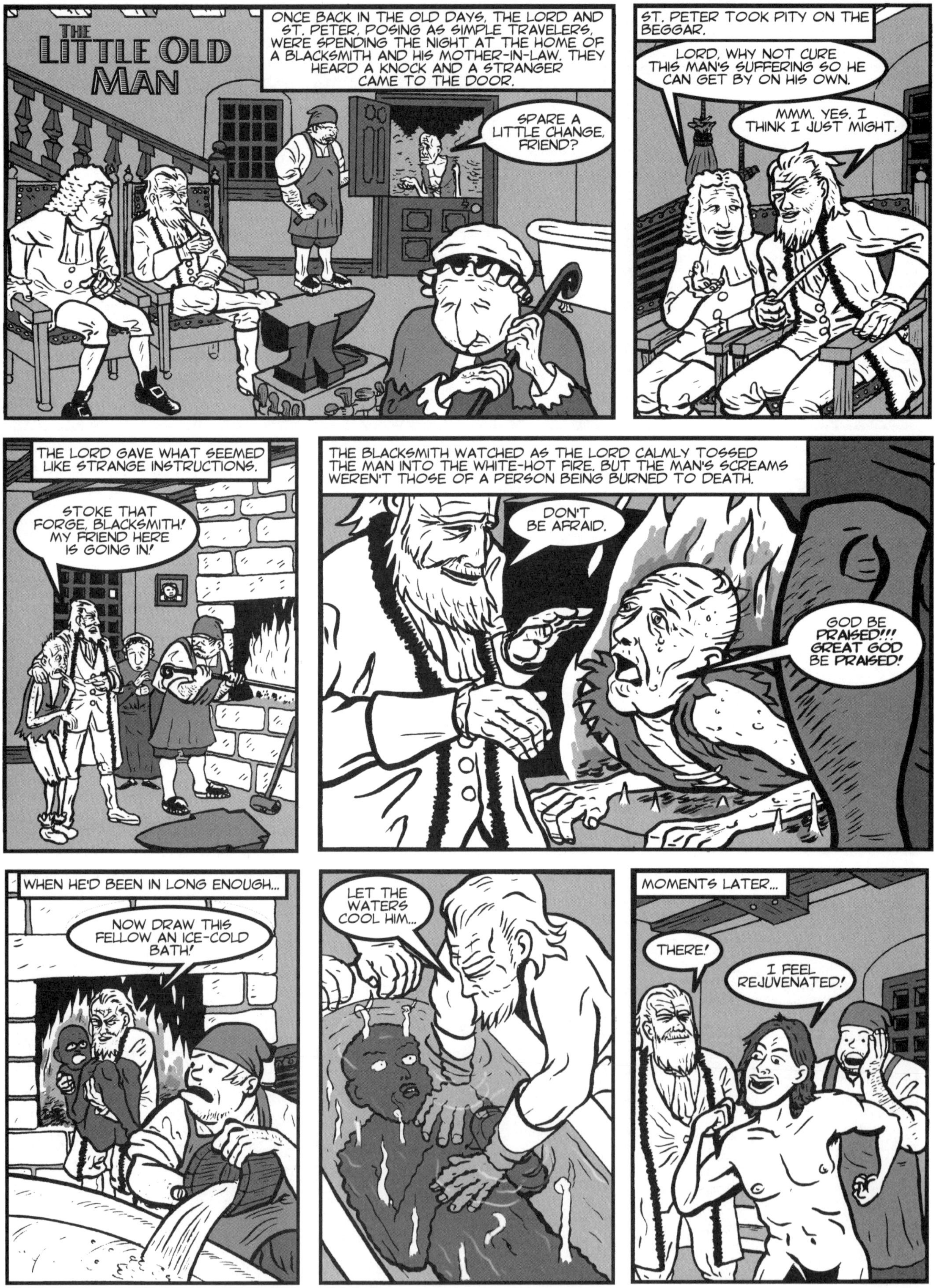

THE LITTLE OLD MAN
ONCE BACK IN THE OLD DAYS, THE LORD AND ST. PETER, POSING AS SIMPLE TRAVELERS, WERE SPENDING THE NIGHT AT THE HOME OF A BLACKSMITH AND HIS MOTHER-IN-LAW. THEY HEARD A KNOCK AND A STRANGER CAME TO THE DOOR.
SPARE A LITTLE CHANGE, FRIEND?
ST. PETER TOOK PITY ON THE BEGGAR.
LORD, WHY NOT CURE THIS MAN'S SUFFERING SO HE CAN GET BY ON HIS OWN.
MMM. YES. I THINK I JUST MIGHT.
THE LORD GAVE WHAT SEEMED LIKE STRANGE INSTRUCTIONS.
STOKE THAT FORGE, BLACKSMITH! MY FRIEND HERE IS GOING IN!
THE BLACKSMITH WATCHED AS THE LORD CALMLY TOSSED THE MAN INTO THE WHITE-HOT FIRE. BUT THE MAN'S SCREAMS WEREN'T THOSE OF A PERSON BEING BURNED TO DEATH.
DON'T BE AFRAID.
GOD BE PRAISED!!! GREAT GOD BE PRAISED!
WHEN HE'D BEEN IN LONG ENOUGH...
NOW DRAW THIS FELLOW AN ICE-COLD BATH!
LET THE WATERS COOL HIM...
MOMENTS LATER...
THERE!
I FEEL REJUVENATED!

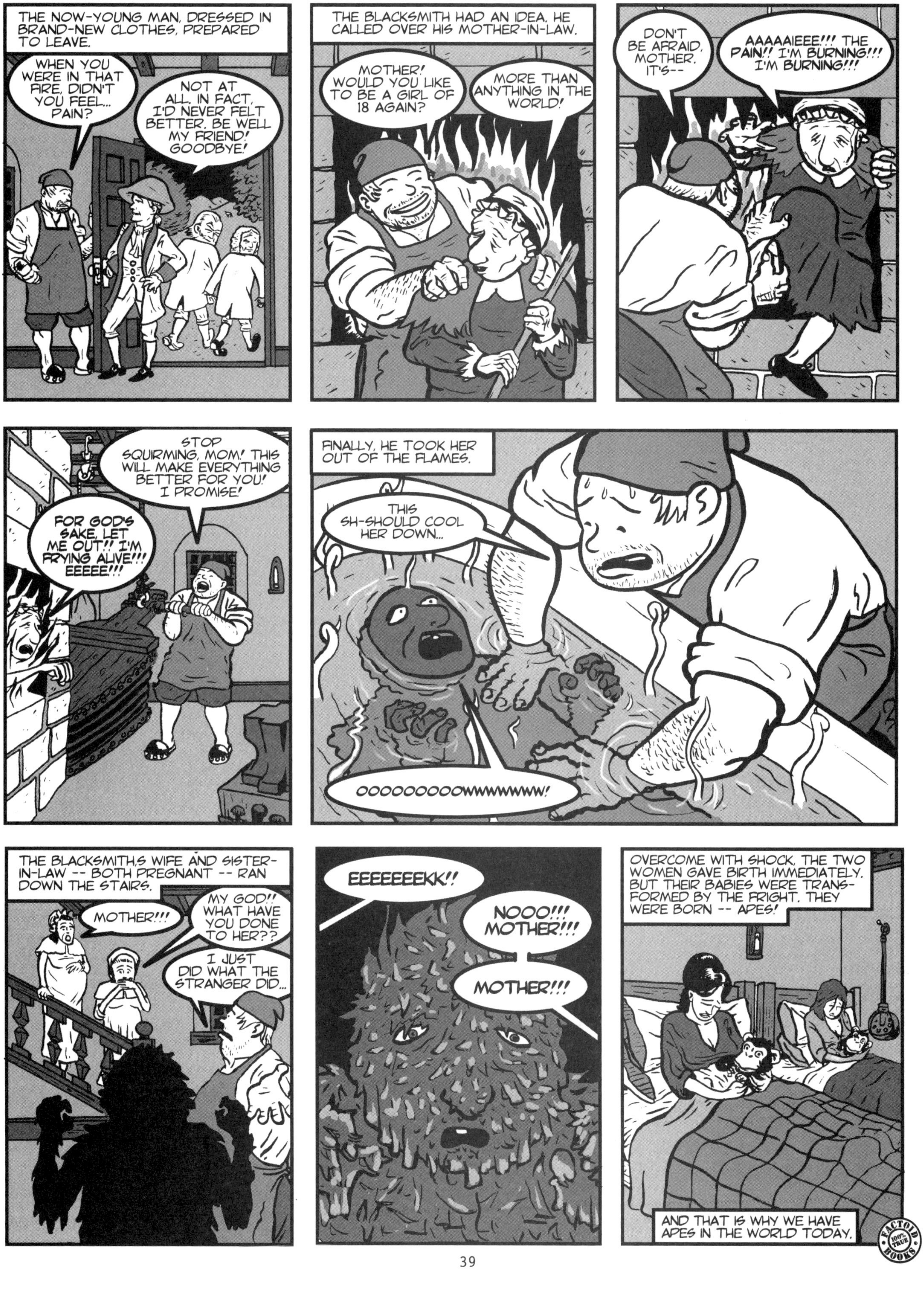
THE NOW-YOUNG MAN, DRESSED IN BRAND-NEW CLOTHES, PREPARED TO LEAVE.
WHEN YOU WERE IN THAT FIRE, DIDN'T YOU FEEL... PAIN?
NOT AT ALL. IN FACT, I'D NEVER FELT BETTER. BE WELL MY FRIEND! GOODBYE!
THE BLACKSMITH HAD AN IDEA. HE CALLED OVER HIS MOTHER-IN-LAW.
MOTHER! WOULD YOU LIKE TO BE A GIRL OF 18 AGAIN?
MORE THAN ANYTHING IN THE WORLD!
DON'T BE AFRAID, MOTHER. IT'S--
AAAAAIEEE!!! THE PAIN!! I'M BURNING!!! I'M BURNING!!!
STOP SQUIRMING, MOM! THIS WILL MAKE EVERYTHING BETTER FOR YOU! I PROMISE!
FOR GOD'S SAKE, LET ME OUT!! I'M FRYING ALIVE!!! EEEEE!!!
FINALLY, HE TOOK HER OUT OF THE FLAMES.
THIS SH-SHOULD COOL HER DOWN...
OOOOOOOOOWWWWWWW!
THE BLACKSMITH,S WIFE AND SISTER-IN-LAW -- BOTH PREGNANT -- RAN DOWN THE STAIRS.
MOTHER!!!
MY GOD!! WHAT HAVE YOU DONE TO HER??
I JUST DID WHAT THE STRANGER DID...
EEEEEEEKK!!
NOOO!!! MOTHER!!!
MOTHER!!!
OVERCOME WITH SHOCK, THE TWO WOMEN GAVE BIRTH IMMEDIATELY. BUT THEIR BABIES WERE TRANSFORMED BY THE FRIGHT. THEY WERE BORN -- APES!
AND THAT IS WHY WE HAVE APES IN THE WORLD TODAY.

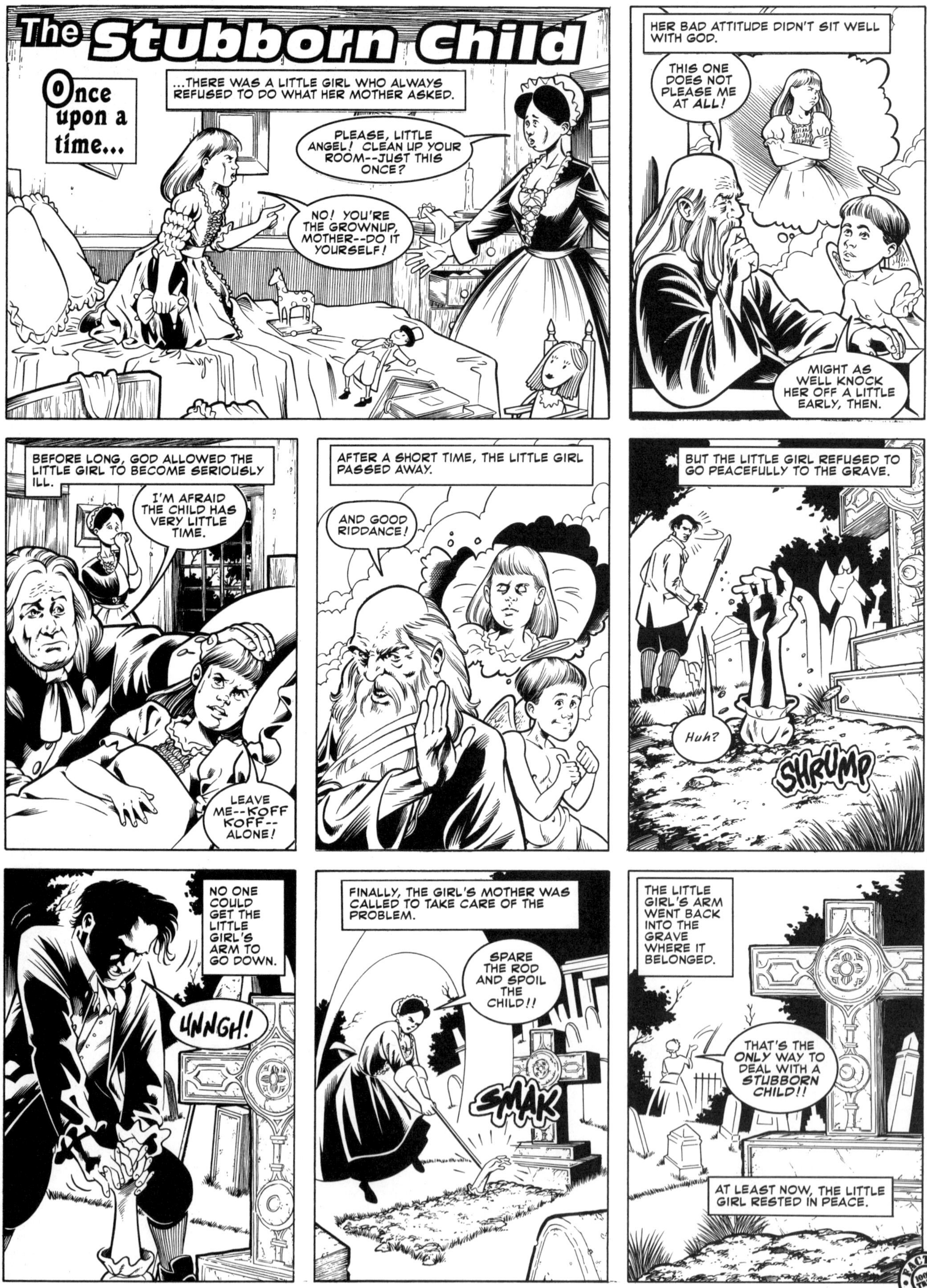
The Stubborn Child
Once upon a time...
...THERE WAS A LITTLE GIRL WHO ALWAYS REFUSED TO DO WHAT HER MOTHER ASKED.
PLEASE, LITTLE ANGEL! CLEAN UP YOUR ROOM--JUST THIS ONCE?
NO! YOU'RE THE GROWNUP, MOTHER--DO IT YOURSELF!
HER BAD ATTITUDE DIDN'T SIT WELL WITH GOD.
THIS ONE DOES NOT PLEASE ME AT ALL!
MIGHT AS WELL KNOCK HER OFF A LITTLE EARLY, THEN.
BEFORE LONG, GOD ALLOWED THE LITTLE GIRL TO BECOME SERIOUSLY ILL.
I'M AFRAID THE CHILD HAS VERY LITTLE TIME.
LEAVE ME--KOFF KOFF--ALONE!
AFTER A SHORT TIME, THE LITTLE GIRL PASSED AWAY.
AND GOOD RIDDANCE!
BUT THE LITTLE GIRL REFUSED TO GO PEACEFULLY TO THE GRAVE.
Huh?
SHRUMP
NO ONE COULD GET THE LITTLE GIRL'S ARM TO GO DOWN.
UNNGH!
FINALLY, THE GIRL'S MOTHER WAS CALLED TO TAKE CARE OF THE PROBLEM.
SPARE THE ROD AND SPOIL THE CHILD!!
SMAK
THE LITTLE GIRL'S ARM WENT BACK INTO THE GRAVE WHERE IT BELONGED.
THAT'S THE ONLY WAY TO DEAL WITH A STUBBORN CHILD!!
AT LEAST NOW, THE LITTLE GIRL RESTED IN PEACE.

CHAPTER TWO

PRISONERS OF CHILDHOOD

Most children's tales come with a built-in moral. We don't seem to be comfortable just entertaining our kids. We always feel the neurotic need to teach them things. In the Grimm brothers' tales, the lesson was always a simple one: Watch out! Or in the parlance of Generation X-Files, trust no one. Certainly not your parents. If you're Hansel and Gretel, they're plotting to get rid of you anyway, because you're eating too much of their food. If you have halfway decent parents — as did Little Red Cap, Tom Thumb or the Boy Who Learned How to Shudder — it still won't matter. Because at every turn, wolves, witches and who knows what else are waiting to eat you alive.

We'll leave it to the psychoanalysts to dig out the hidden, sexual subtext of these tales, though in some cases, as in "Little Red Cap" (a.k.a. "Little Red Riding Hood") it's pretty obvious. A young girl tries to "stay on the path" but is lured astray by a predatory wolf. Nothing's more horrifying to adults, in the Grimms' time or today, than the emerging sexuality of their children. But there are other interpretations of the tales that may be equally valid. Maybe the storytellers that the Grimms and their associates (who went out and collected tales from various townspeople) spoke to were recalling their own childhood, a time that many grown-ups prefer to remember as idyllic and innocent. These stories remind us that our early years are often the most terrifying era of our lives.

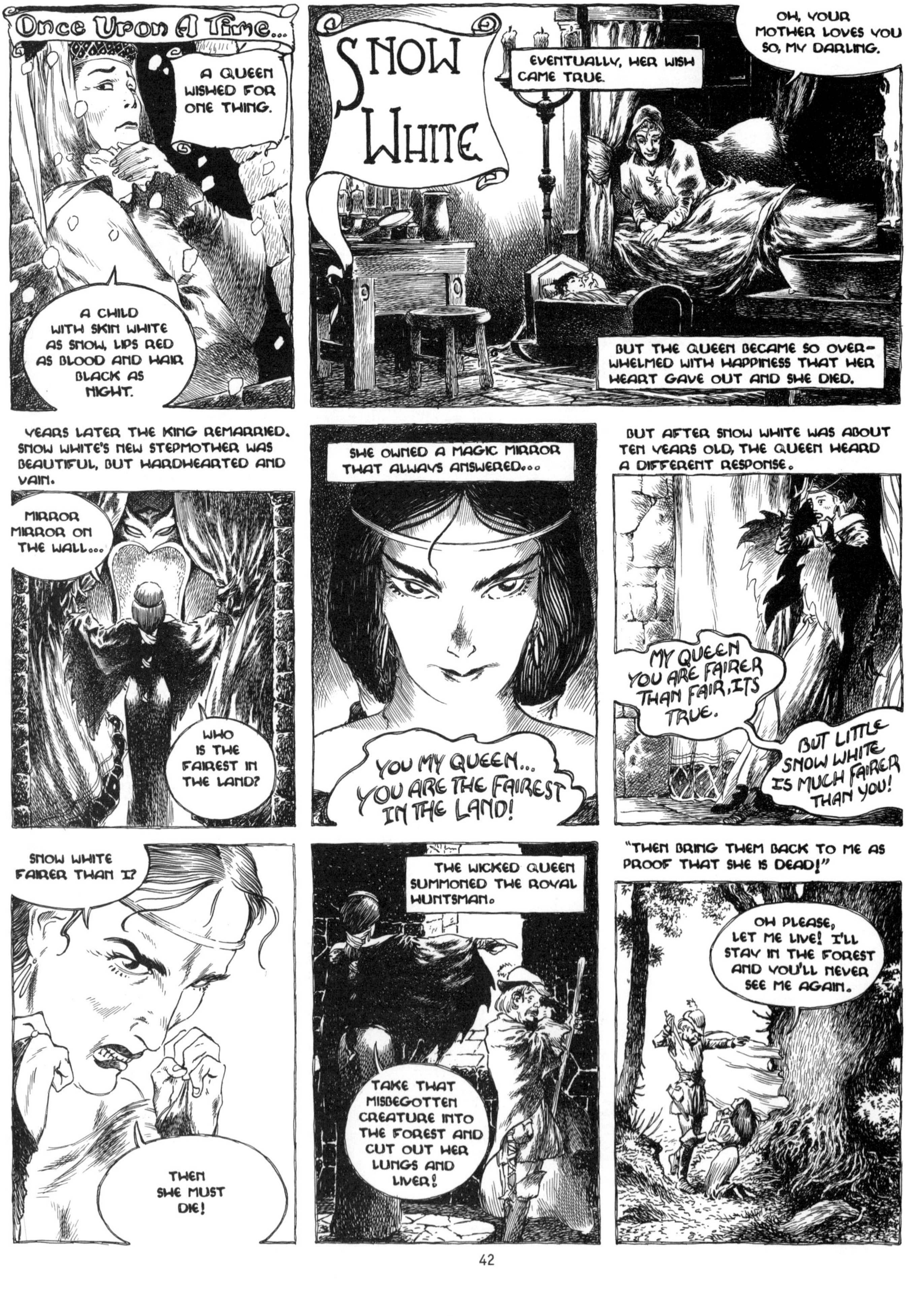

Once Upon A Time...
A QUEEN WISHED FOR ONE THING.
A CHILD WITH SKIN WHITE AS SNOW, LIPS RED AS BLOOD AND HAIR BLACK AS NIGHT.
SNOW WHITE
EVENTUALLY, HER WISH CAME TRUE.
OH, YOUR MOTHER LOVES YOU SO, MY DARLING.
BUT THE QUEEN BECAME SO OVER-WHELMED WITH HAPPINESS THAT HER HEART GAVE OUT AND SHE DIED.
YEARS LATER THE KING REMARRIED. SNOW WHITE'S NEW STEPMOTHER WAS BEAUTIFUL, BUT HARDHEARTED AND VAIN.
MIRROR MIRROR ON THE WALL...
WHO IS THE FAIREST IN THE LAND?
SHE OWNED A MAGIC MIRROR THAT ALWAYS ANSWERED...
YOU MY QUEEN... YOU ARE THE FAIREST IN THE LAND!
BUT AFTER SNOW WHITE WAS ABOUT TEN YEARS OLD, THE QUEEN HEARD A DIFFERENT RESPONSE.
MY QUEEN YOU ARE FAIRER THAN FAIR, ITS TRUE.
BUT LITTLE SNOW WHITE IS MUCH FAIRER THAN YOU!
SNOW WHITE FAIRER THAN I?
THEN SHE MUST DIE!
THE WICKED QUEEN SUMMONED THE ROYAL HUNTSMAN.
TAKE THAT MISBEGOTTEN CREATURE INTO THE FOREST AND CUT OUT HER LUNGS AND LIVER!
"THEN BRING THEM BACK TO ME AS PROOF THAT SHE IS DEAD!"
OH PLEASE, LET ME LIVE! I'LL STAY IN THE FOREST AND YOU'LL NEVER SEE ME AGAIN.

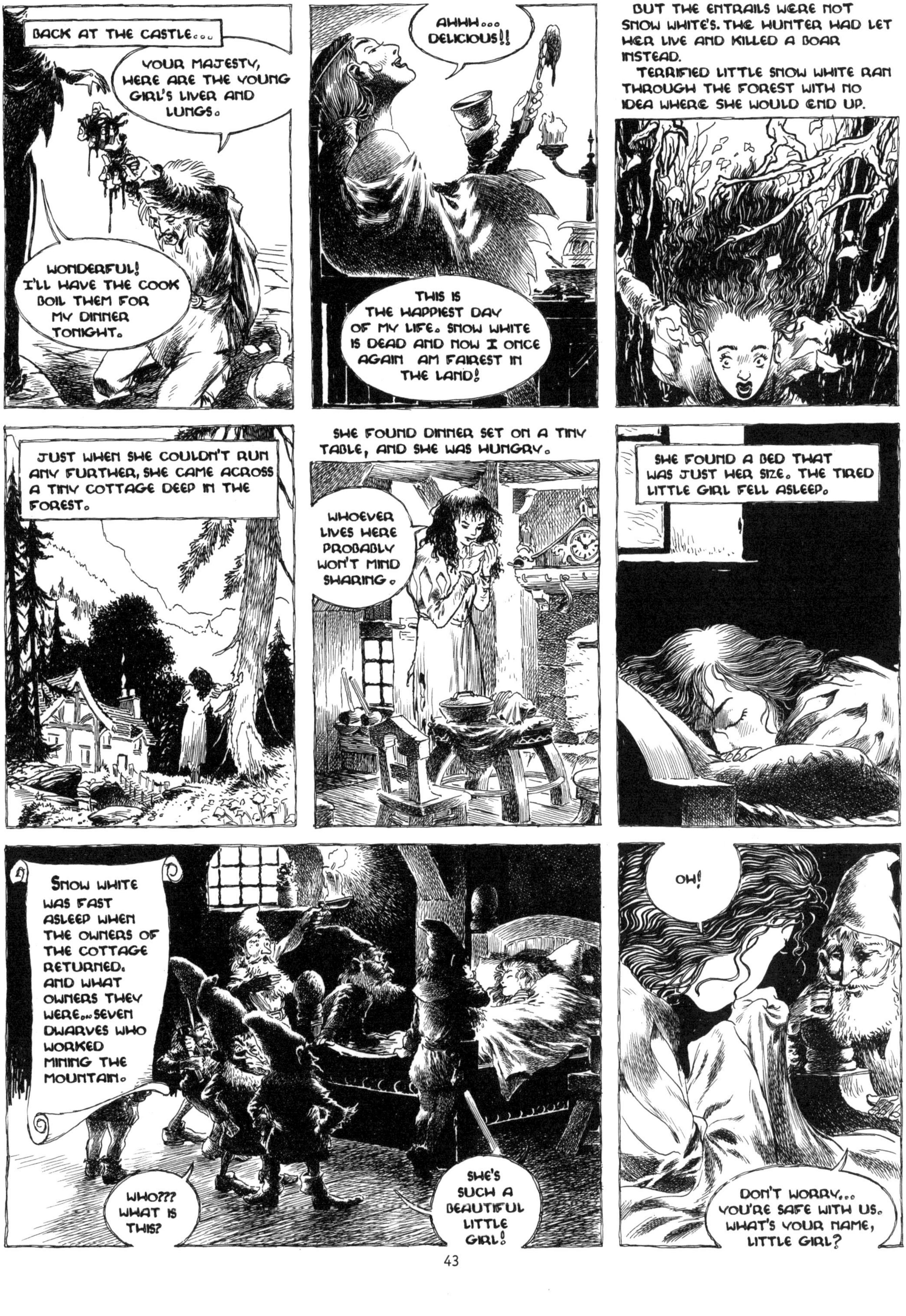
BACK AT THE CASTLE...
YOUR MAJESTY, HERE ARE THE YOUNG GIRL'S LIVER AND LUNGS.
WONDERFUL! I'LL HAVE THE COOK BOIL THEM FOR MY DINNER TONIGHT.
AHHH... DELICIOUS!!
THIS IS THE HAPPIEST DAY OF MY LIFE. SNOW WHITE IS DEAD AND NOW I ONCE AGAIN AM FAIREST IN THE LAND!
BUT THE ENTRAILS WERE NOT SNOW WHITE'S. THE HUNTER HAD LET HER LIVE AND KILLED A BOAR INSTEAD.
TERRIFIED LITTLE SNOW WHITE RAN THROUGH THE FOREST WITH NO IDEA WHERE SHE WOULD END UP.
JUST WHEN SHE COULDN'T RUN ANY FURTHER, SHE CAME ACROSS A TINY COTTAGE DEEP IN THE FOREST.
SHE FOUND DINNER SET ON A TINY TABLE, AND SHE WAS HUNGRY.
WHOEVER LIVES HERE PROBABLY WON'T MIND SHARING.
SHE FOUND A BED THAT WAS JUST HER SIZE. THE TIRED LITTLE GIRL FELL ASLEEP.
SNOW WHITE WAS FAST ASLEEP WHEN THE OWNERS OF THE COTTAGE RETURNED. AND WHAT OWNERS THEY WERE... SEVEN DWARVES WHO WORKED MINING THE MOUNTAIN.
WHO??? WHAT IS THIS?
SHE'S SUCH A BEAUTIFUL LITTLE GIRL!
OH!
DON'T WORRY... YOU'RE SAFE WITH US. WHAT'S YOUR NAME, LITTLE GIRL?

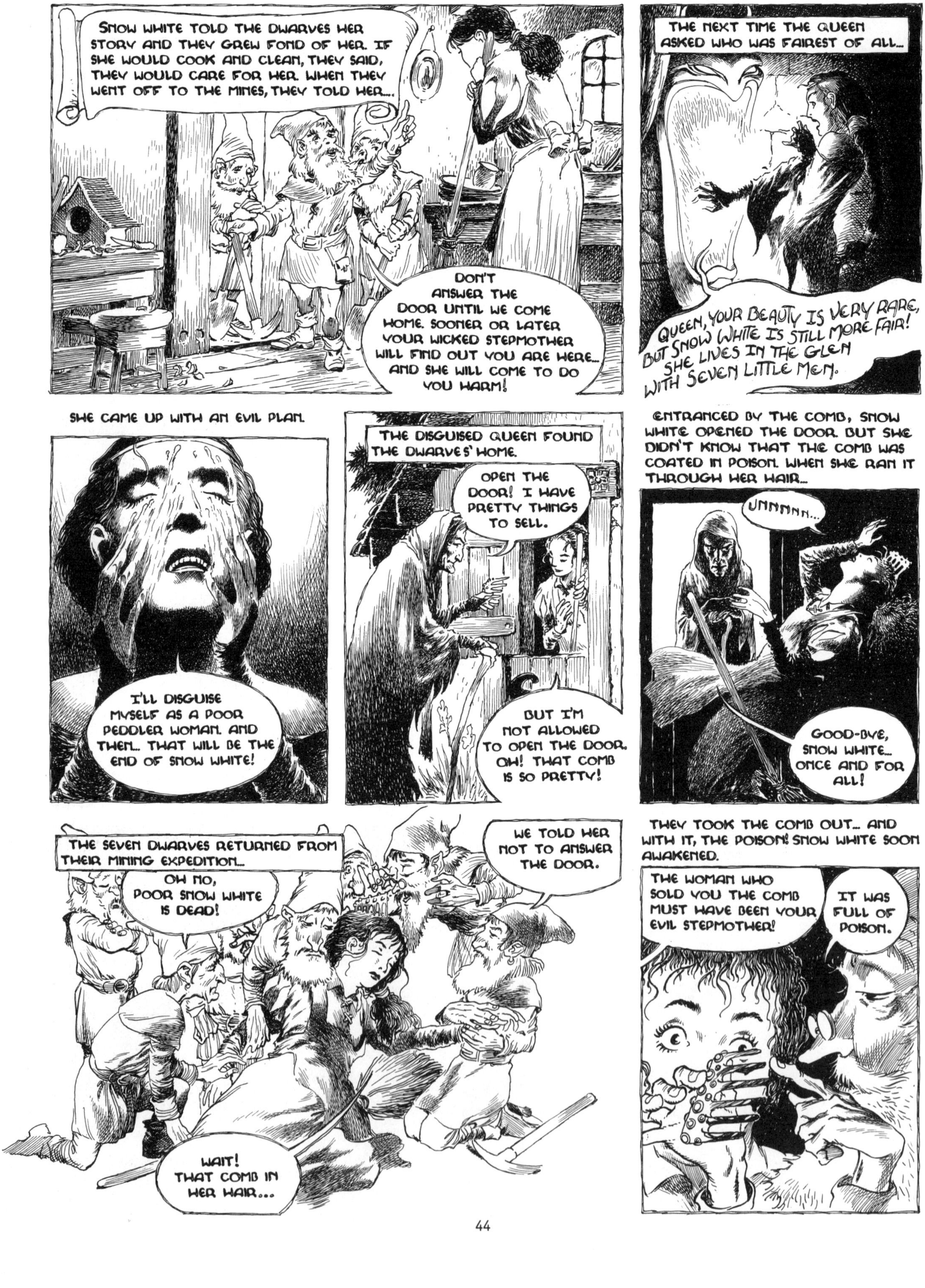
SNOW WHITE TOLD THE DWARVES HER STORY AND THEY GREW FOND OF HER. IF SHE WOULD COOK AND CLEAN, THEY SAID, THEY WOULD CARE FOR HER. WHEN THEY WENT OFF TO THE MINES, THEY TOLD HER...
DON'T ANSWER THE DOOR UNTIL WE COME HOME. SOONER OR LATER YOUR WICKED STEPMOTHER WILL FIND OUT YOU ARE HERE... AND SHE WILL COME TO DO YOU HARM!
THE NEXT TIME THE QUEEN ASKED WHO WAS FAIREST OF ALL...
QUEEN, YOUR BEAUTY IS VERY RARE, BUT SNOW WHITE IS STILL MORE FAIR! SHE LIVES IN THE GLEN WITH SEVEN LITTLE MEN.
SHE CAME UP WITH AN EVIL PLAN.
I'LL DISGUISE MYSELF AS A POOR PEDDLER WOMAN. AND THEN... THAT WILL BE THE END OF SNOW WHITE!
THE DISGUISED QUEEN FOUND THE DWARVES' HOME.
OPEN THE DOOR! I HAVE PRETTY THINGS TO SELL.
BUT I'M NOT ALLOWED TO OPEN THE DOOR. OH! THAT COMB IS SO PRETTY!
ENTRANCED BY THE COMB, SNOW WHITE OPENED THE DOOR. BUT SHE DIDN'T KNOW THAT THE COMB WAS COATED IN POISON. WHEN SHE RAN IT THROUGH HER HAIR...
UNNNNN...
GOOD-BYE, SNOW WHITE... ONCE AND FOR ALL!
THE SEVEN DWARVES RETURNED FROM THEIR MINING EXPEDITION...
OH NO, POOR SNOW WHITE IS DEAD!
WE TOLD HER NOT TO ANSWER THE DOOR.
WAIT! THAT COMB IN HER HAIR...
THEY TOOK THE COMB OUT... AND WITH IT, THE POISON! SNOW WHITE SOON AWAKENED.
THE WOMAN WHO SOLD YOU THE COMB MUST HAVE BEEN YOUR EVIL STEPMOTHER!
IT WAS FULL OF POISON.

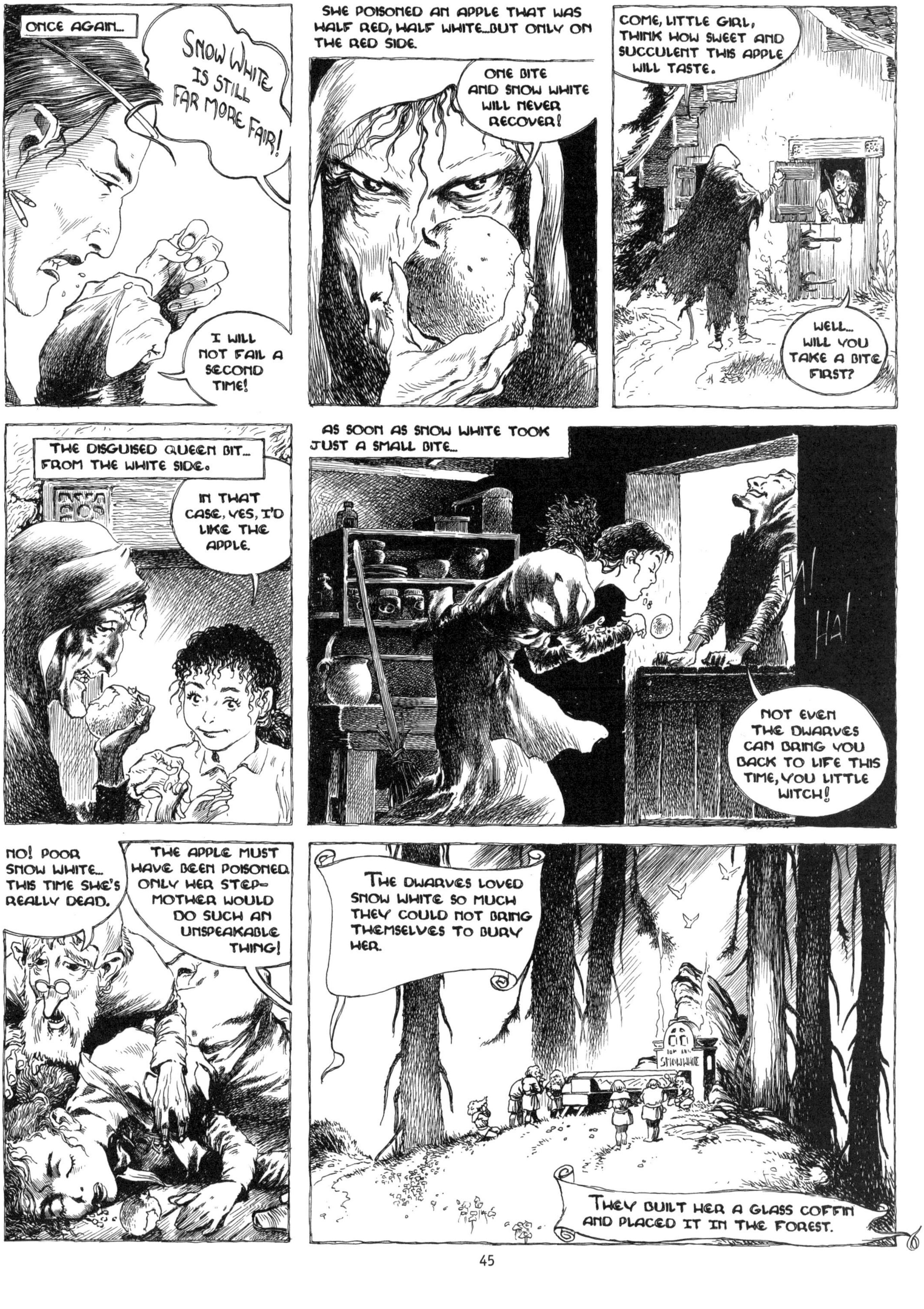
ONCE AGAIN...
SNOW WHITE IS STILL FAR MORE FAIR!
I WILL NOT FAIL A SECOND TIME!
SHE POISONED AN APPLE THAT WAS HALF RED, HALF WHITE...BUT ONLY ON THE RED SIDE.
ONE BITE AND SNOW WHITE WILL NEVER RECOVER!
COME, LITTLE GIRL, THINK HOW SWEET AND SUCCULENT THIS APPLE WILL TASTE.
WELL... WILL YOU TAKE A BITE FIRST?
THE DISGUISED QUEEN BIT... FROM THE WHITE SIDE.
IN THAT CASE, YES, I'D LIKE THE APPLE.
AS SOON AS SNOW WHITE TOOK JUST A SMALL BITE...
HA! HA!
NOT EVEN THE DWARVES CAN BRING YOU BACK TO LIFE THIS TIME, YOU LITTLE WITCH!
NO! POOR SNOW WHITE... THIS TIME SHE'S REALLY DEAD.
THE APPLE MUST HAVE BEEN POISONED. ONLY HER STEP-MOTHER WOULD DO SUCH AN UNSPEAKABLE THING!
THE DWARVES LOVED SNOW WHITE SO MUCH THEY COULD NOT BRING THEMSELVES TO BURY HER.
SNOW WHITE
THEY BUILT HER A GLASS COFFIN AND PLACED IT IN THE FOREST.

BACK IN THE QUEEN'S CHAMBERS.

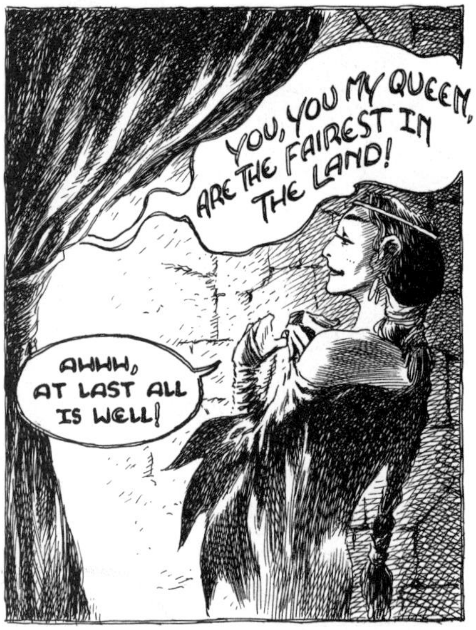
YOU, YOU MY QUEEN, ARE THE FAIREST IN THE LAND!
AHHH, AT LAST ALL IS WELL!

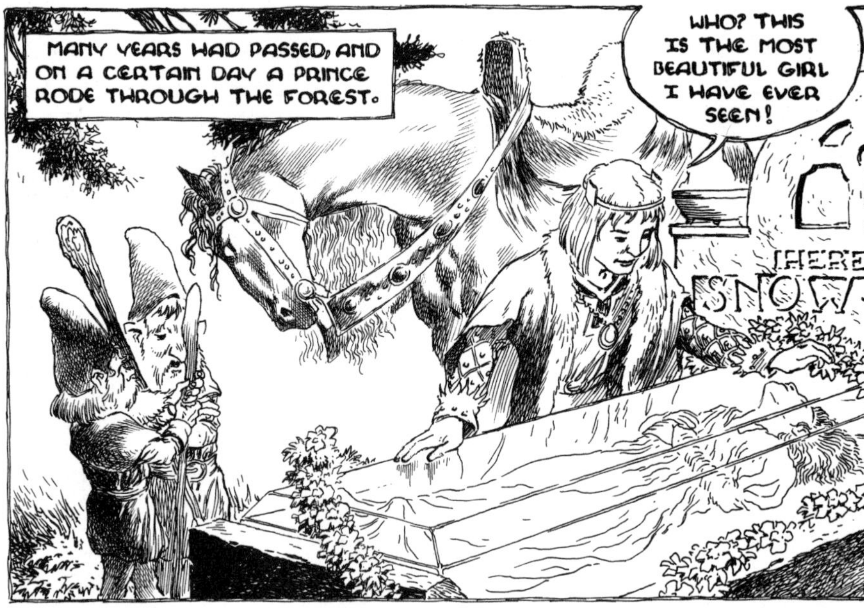
MANY YEARS HAD PASSED, AND ON A CERTAIN DAY A PRINCE RODE THROUGH THE FOREST.
WHO? THIS IS THE MOST BEAUTIFUL GIRL I HAVE EVER SEEN!

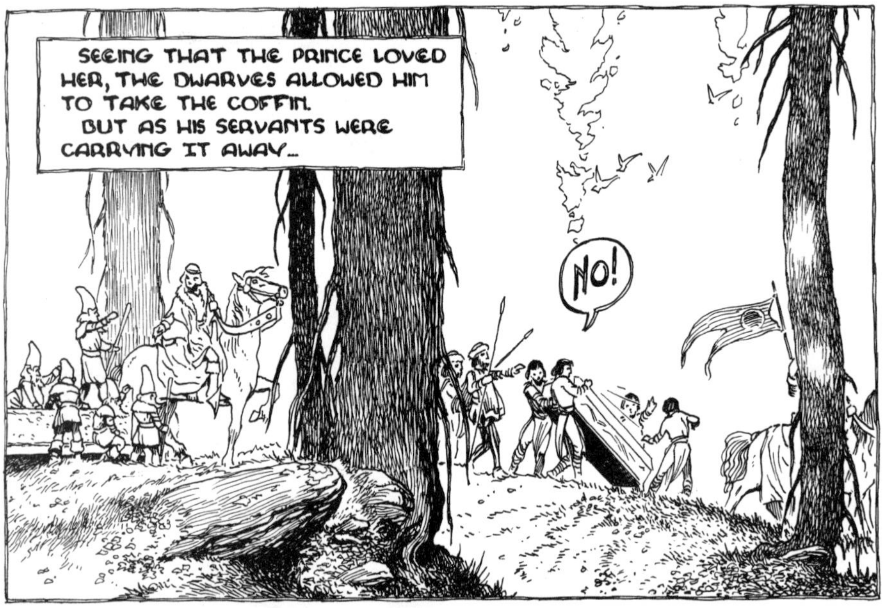
SEEING THAT THE PRINCE LOVED HER, THE DWARVES ALLOWED HIM TO TAKE THE COFFIN.
BUT AS HIS SERVANTS WERE CARRYING IT AWAY...
NO!

THE FALL KNOCKED THE BIT OF POISON APPLE FROM SNOW WHITE'S THROAT.

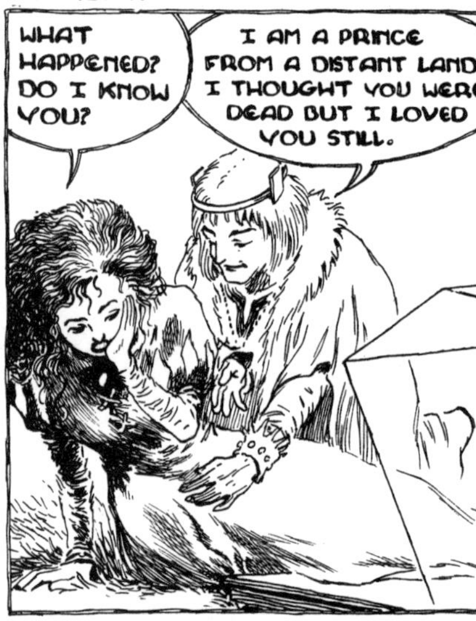
WHAT HAPPENED? DO I KNOW YOU?
I AM A PRINCE FROM A DISTANT LAND. I THOUGHT YOU WERE DEAD BUT I LOVED YOU STILL.

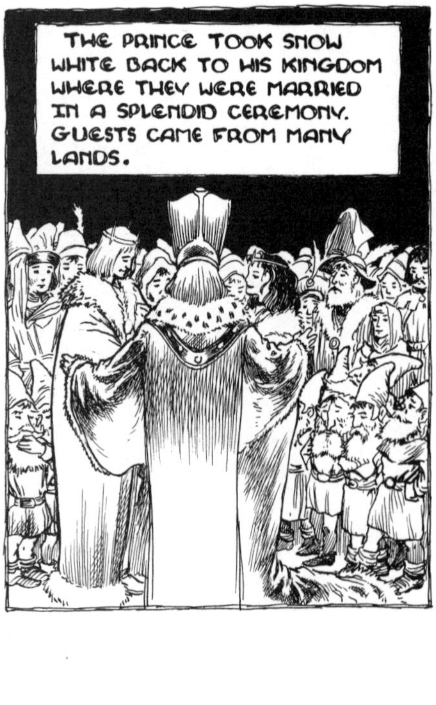
THE PRINCE TOOK SNOW WHITE BACK TO HIS KINGDOM WHERE THEY WERE MARRIED IN A SPLENDID CEREMONY. GUESTS CAME FROM MANY LANDS.

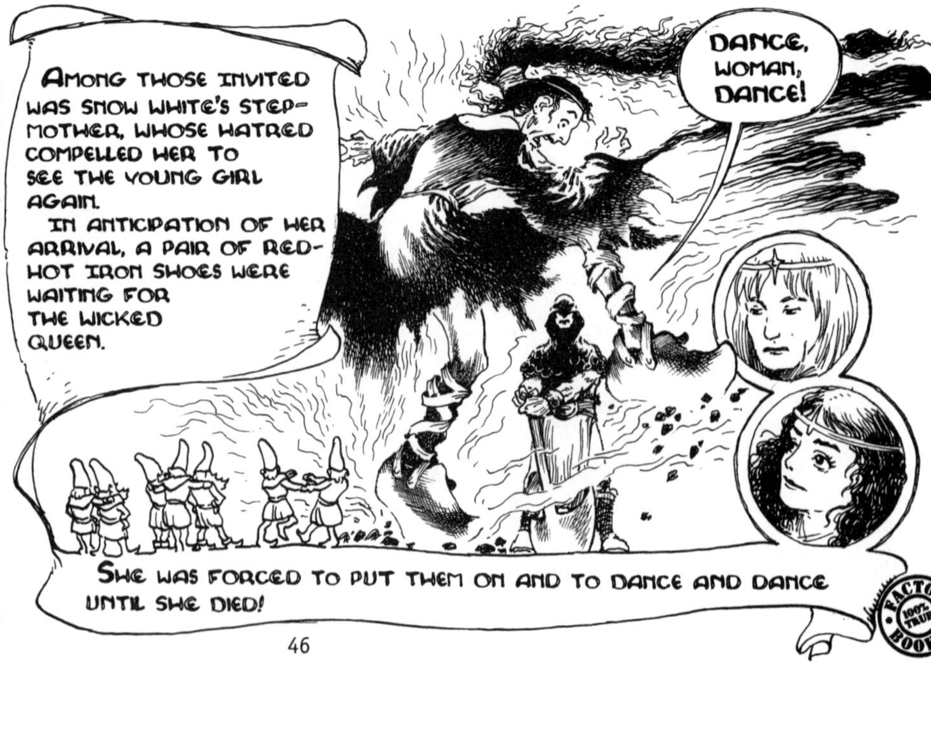
AMONG THOSE INVITED WAS SNOW WHITE'S STEP-MOTHER, WHOSE HATRED COMPELLED HER TO SEE THE YOUNG GIRL AGAIN.
IN ANTICIPATION OF HER ARRIVAL, A PAIR OF RED-HOT IRON SHOES WERE WAITING FOR THE WICKED QUEEN.
DANCE, WOMAN, DANCE!
SHE WAS FORCED TO PUT THEM ON AND TO DANCE AND DANCE UNTIL SHE DIED!

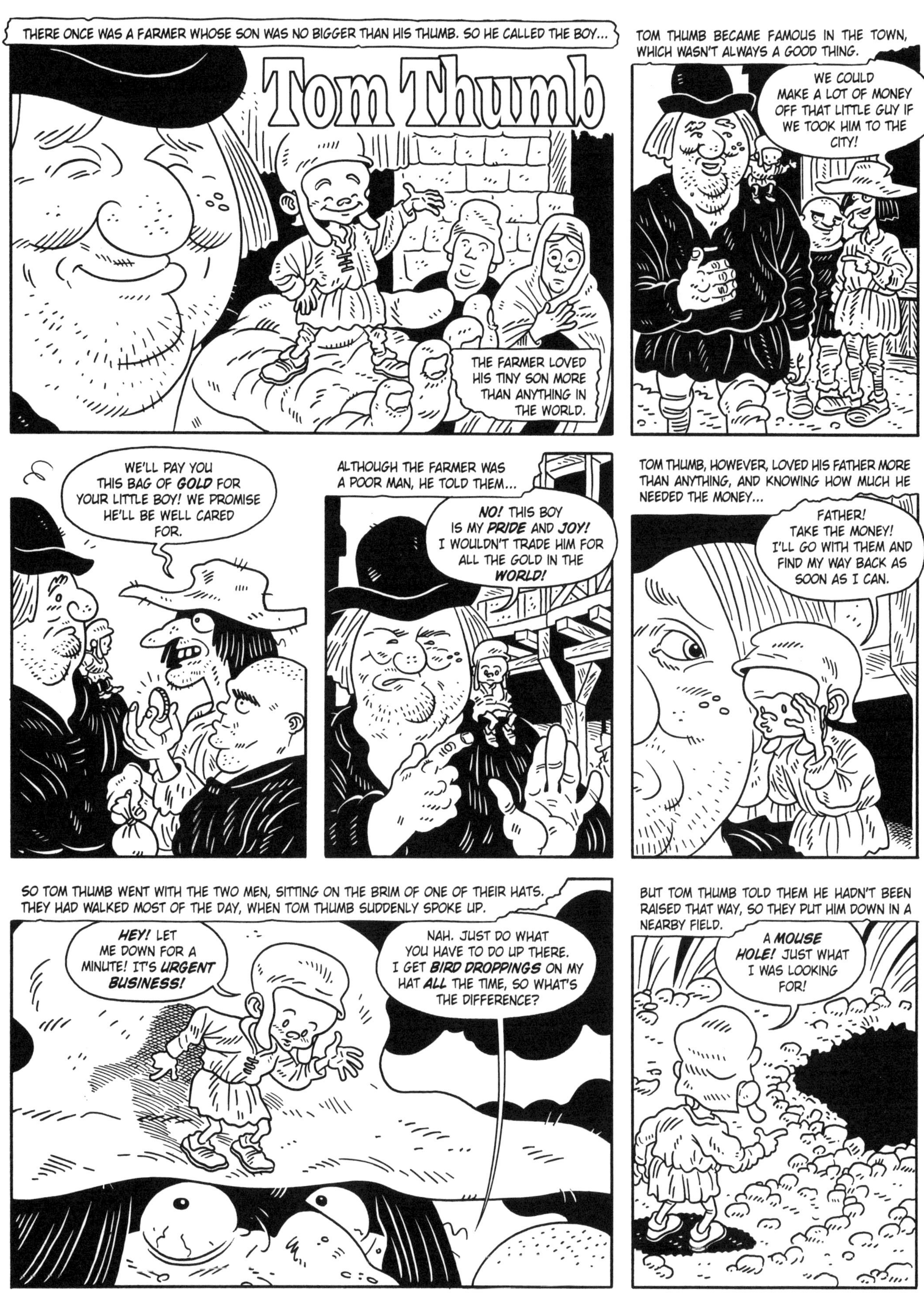
THERE ONCE WAS A FARMER WHOSE SON WAS NO BIGGER THAN HIS THUMB. SO HE CALLED THE BOY...
Tom Thumb
THE FARMER LOVED HIS TINY SON MORE THAN ANYTHING IN THE WORLD.
TOM THUMB BECAME FAMOUS IN THE TOWN, WHICH WASN'T ALWAYS A GOOD THING.
WE COULD MAKE A LOT OF MONEY OFF THAT LITTLE GUY IF WE TOOK HIM TO THE CITY!
WE'LL PAY YOU THIS BAG OF GOLD FOR YOUR LITTLE BOY! WE PROMISE HE'LL BE WELL CARED FOR.
ALTHOUGH THE FARMER WAS A POOR MAN, HE TOLD THEM...
NO! THIS BOY IS MY PRIDE AND JOY! I WOULDN'T TRADE HIM FOR ALL THE GOLD IN THE WORLD!
TOM THUMB, HOWEVER, LOVED HIS FATHER MORE THAN ANYTHING, AND KNOWING HOW MUCH HE NEEDED THE MONEY...
FATHER! TAKE THE MONEY! I'LL GO WITH THEM AND FIND MY WAY BACK AS SOON AS I CAN.
SO TOM THUMB WENT WITH THE TWO MEN, SITTING ON THE BRIM OF ONE OF THEIR HATS. THEY HAD WALKED MOST OF THE DAY, WHEN TOM THUMB SUDDENLY SPOKE UP.
HEY! LET ME DOWN FOR A MINUTE! IT'S URGENT BUSINESS!
NAH. JUST DO WHAT YOU HAVE TO DO UP THERE. I GET BIRD DROPPINGS ON MY HAT ALL THE TIME, SO WHAT'S THE DIFFERENCE?
BUT TOM THUMB TOLD THEM HE HADN'T BEEN RAISED THAT WAY, SO THEY PUT HIM DOWN IN A NEARBY FIELD.
A MOUSE HOLE! JUST WHAT I WAS LOOKING FOR!

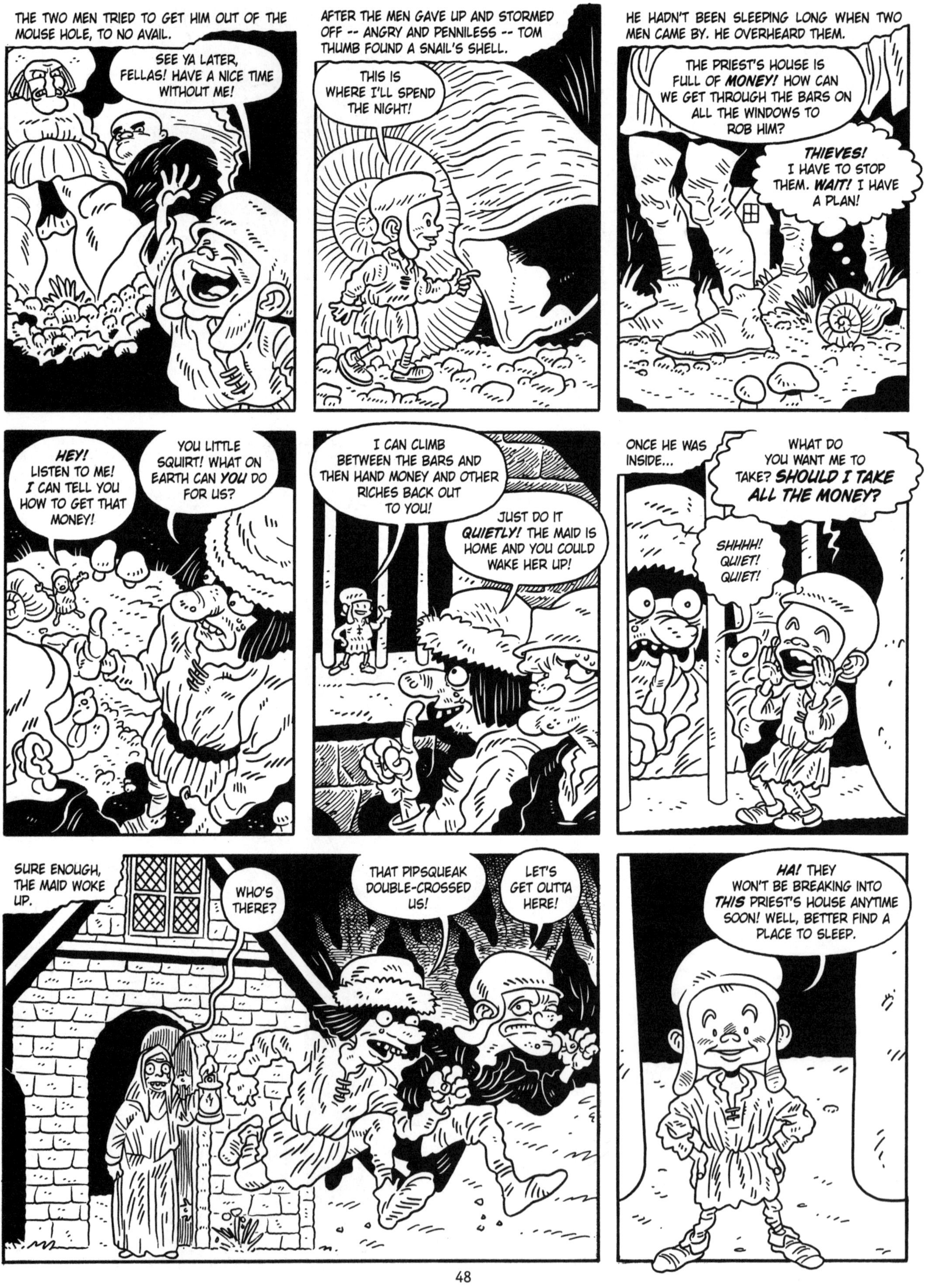
THE TWO MEN TRIED TO GET HIM OUT OF THE MOUSE HOLE, TO NO AVAIL.
SEE YA LATER, FELLAS! HAVE A NICE TIME WITHOUT ME!
AFTER THE MEN GAVE UP AND STORMED OFF -- ANGRY AND PENNILESS -- TOM THUMB FOUND A SNAIL'S SHELL.
THIS IS WHERE I'LL SPEND THE NIGHT!
HE HADN'T BEEN SLEEPING LONG WHEN TWO MEN CAME BY. HE OVERHEARD THEM.
THE PRIEST'S HOUSE IS FULL OF MONEY! HOW CAN WE GET THROUGH THE BARS ON ALL THE WINDOWS TO ROB HIM?
THIEVES! I HAVE TO STOP THEM. WAIT! I HAVE A PLAN!
HEY! LISTEN TO ME! I CAN TELL YOU HOW TO GET THAT MONEY!
YOU LITTLE SQUIRT! WHAT ON EARTH CAN YOU DO FOR US?
I CAN CLIMB BETWEEN THE BARS AND THEN HAND MONEY AND OTHER RICHES BACK OUT TO YOU!
JUST DO IT QUIETLY! THE MAID IS HOME AND YOU COULD WAKE HER UP!
ONCE HE WAS INSIDE...
WHAT DO YOU WANT ME TO TAKE? SHOULD I TAKE ALL THE MONEY?
SHHHH! QUIET! QUIET!
SURE ENOUGH, THE MAID WOKE UP.
WHO'S THERE?
THAT PIPSQUEAK DOUBLE-CROSSED US!
LET'S GET OUTTA HERE!
HA! THEY WON'T BE BREAKING INTO THIS PRIEST'S HOUSE ANYTIME SOON! WELL, BETTER FIND A PLACE TO SLEEP.

HE FOUND A COMFORTABLE SPOT IN THE BARN.

THIS HAY MAKES A COZY BED! I'LL GET A GOOD NIGHT'S SLEEP, THEN MAKE MY WAY BACK TO MY FATHER'S HOUSE TOMORROW.

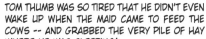

TOM THUMB WAS SO TIRED THAT HE DIDN'T EVEN WAKE UP WHEN THE MAID CAME TO FEED THE COWS -- AND GRABBED THE VERY PILE OF HAY WHERE HE WAS SLEEPING!

ZZZZZZZ!

HE WOKE UP TO FIND HIMSELF SURROUNDED BY TEETH...

HEY! WHAT...??

DOWN HE SLID INTO THE COW'S STOMACH.

WHOA!!

SPOOSH!

HE DIDN'T FIND HIS NEW HOME VERY APPEALING.

THIS PLACE DOESN'T SEEM TO GET MUCH SUN! AND IT SURE IS DAMP! THEY REALLY NEED TO BRING SOMEONE IN TO CLEAN UP AROUND HERE!

HE DECIDED TO VOICE HIS COMPLAINTS.

HEY, CAN A FELLOW GET A LITTLE SERVICE IN THIS PLACE?!

YIPES! THE COW IS TALKING! THE COW IS TALKING!

THE PRIEST CAME TO INVESTIGATE.

SAY, WHAT'S GOING ON AROUND HERE?

THIS COW CAN ONLY BE POSSESSED! HAVE IT SLAUGHTERED IMMEDIATELY!

SO THE COW WAS KILLED AND ITS STOMACH RIPPED OUT...

?

SPLISH!

GLUP!

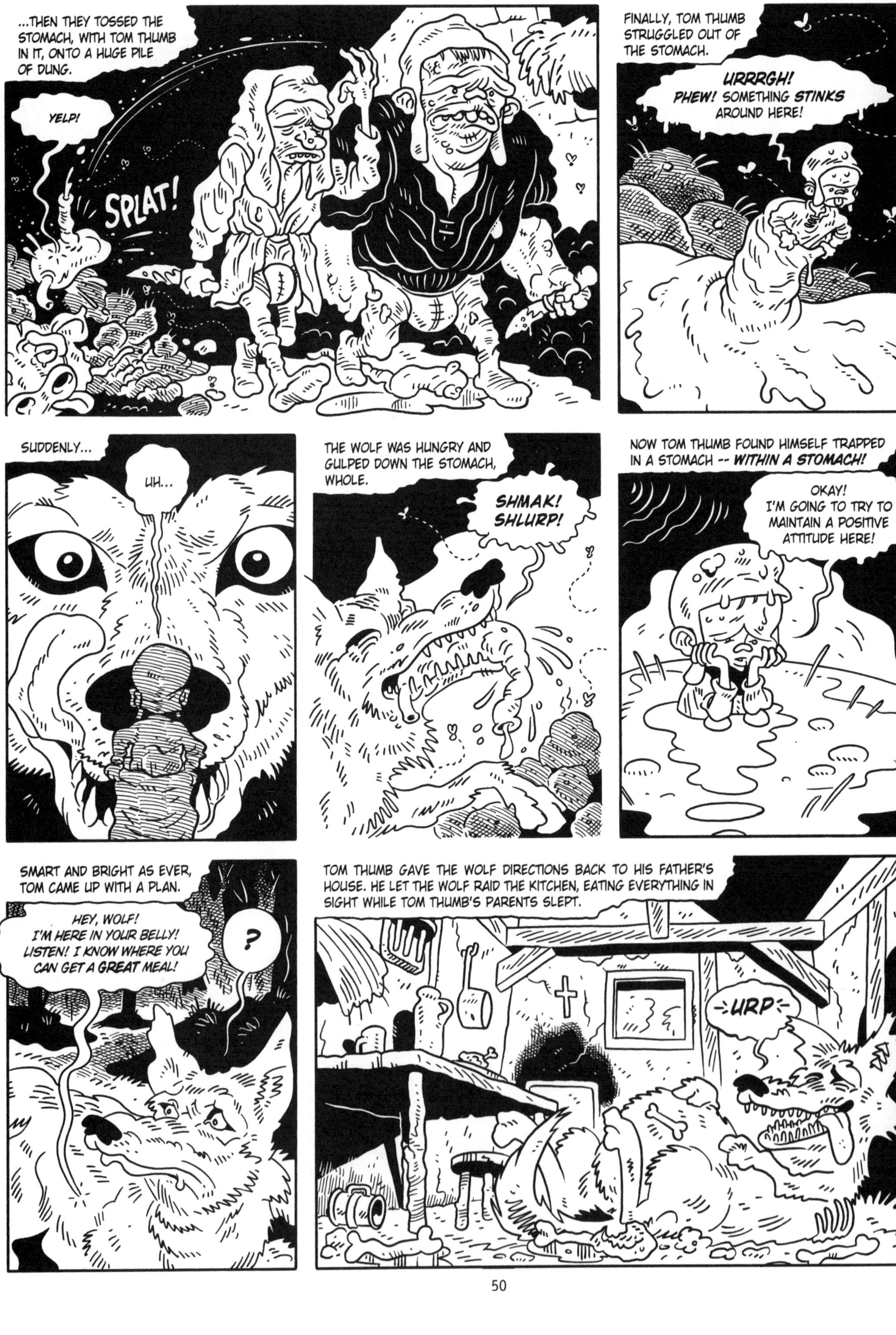
...THEN THEY TOSSED THE STOMACH, WITH TOM THUMB IN IT, ONTO A HUGE PILE OF DUNG.
YELP!
SPLAT!
FINALLY, TOM THUMB STRUGGLED OUT OF THE STOMACH.
URRRGH! PHEW! SOMETHING STINKS AROUND HERE!
SUDDENLY...
UH...
THE WOLF WAS HUNGRY AND GULPED DOWN THE STOMACH, WHOLE.
SHMAK! SHLURP!
NOW TOM THUMB FOUND HIMSELF TRAPPED IN A STOMACH -- WITHIN A STOMACH!
OKAY! I'M GOING TO TRY TO MAINTAIN A POSITIVE ATTITUDE HERE!
SMART AND BRIGHT AS EVER, TOM CAME UP WITH A PLAN.
HEY, WOLF! I'M HERE IN YOUR BELLY! LISTEN! I KNOW WHERE YOU CAN GET A GREAT MEAL!
?
TOM THUMB GAVE THE WOLF DIRECTIONS BACK TO HIS FATHER'S HOUSE. HE LET THE WOLF RAID THE KITCHEN, EATING EVERYTHING IN SIGHT WHILE TOM THUMB'S PARENTS SLEPT.
URP

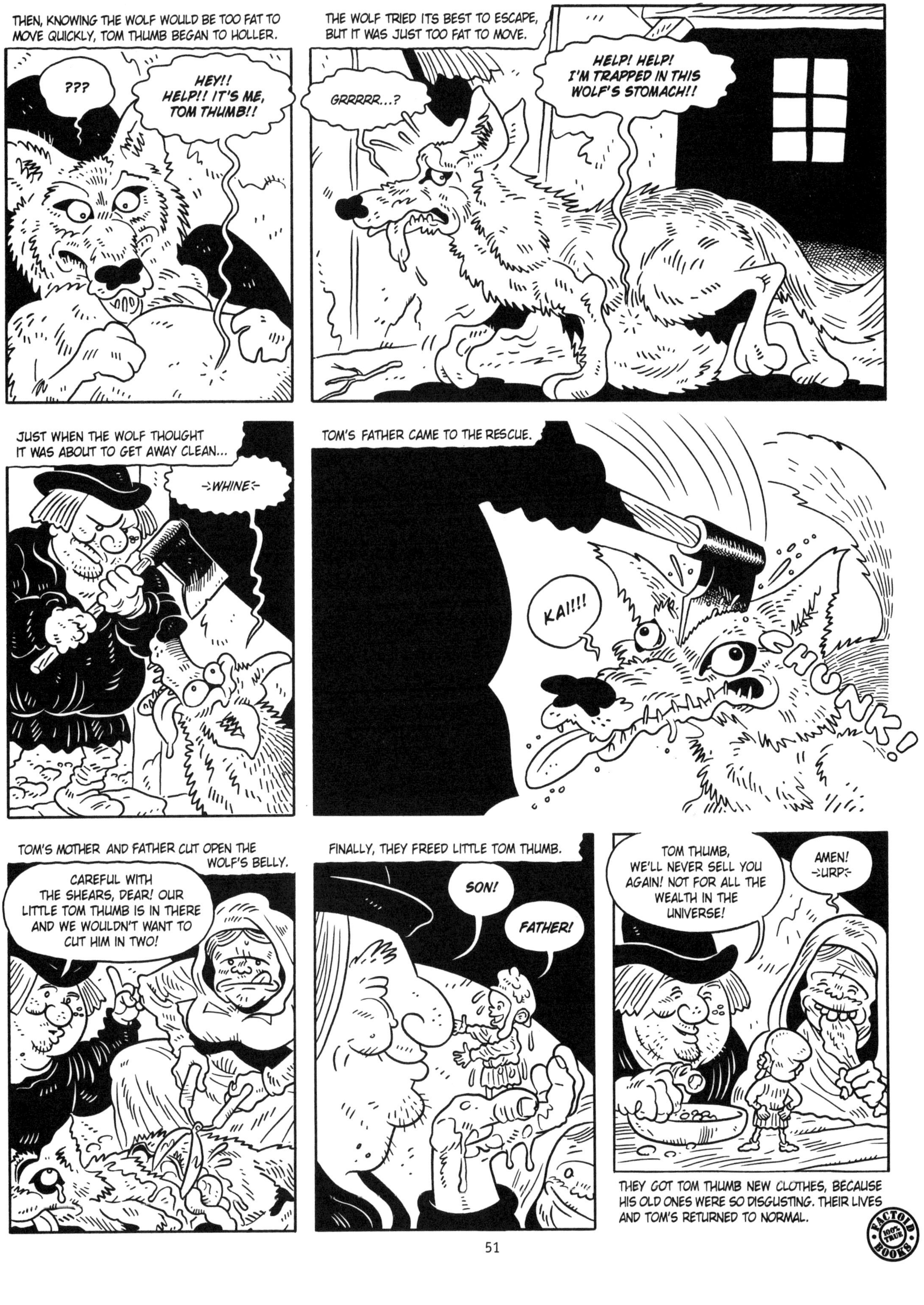

THEN, KNOWING THE WOLF WOULD BE TOO FAT TO MOVE QUICKLY, TOM THUMB BEGAN TO HOLLER.
???
HEY!! HELP!! IT'S ME, TOM THUMB!!
THE WOLF TRIED ITS BEST TO ESCAPE, BUT IT WAS JUST TOO FAT TO MOVE.
GRRRRR...?
HELP! HELP! I'M TRAPPED IN THIS WOLF'S STOMACH!!
JUST WHEN THE WOLF THOUGHT IT WAS ABOUT TO GET AWAY CLEAN...
WHINE
TOM'S FATHER CAME TO THE RESCUE.
KAI!!!
CHUNK!
TOM'S MOTHER AND FATHER CUT OPEN THE WOLF'S BELLY.
CAREFUL WITH THE SHEARS, DEAR! OUR LITTLE TOM THUMB IS IN THERE AND WE WOULDN'T WANT TO CUT HIM IN TWO!
FINALLY, THEY FREED LITTLE TOM THUMB.
SON!
FATHER!
TOM THUMB, WE'LL NEVER SELL YOU AGAIN! NOT FOR ALL THE WEALTH IN THE UNIVERSE!
AMEN! URP
THEY GOT TOM THUMB NEW CLOTHES, BECAUSE HIS OLD ONES WERE SO DISGUSTING. THEIR LIVES AND TOM'S RETURNED TO NORMAL.
FACTOID BOOKS 100% TRUE

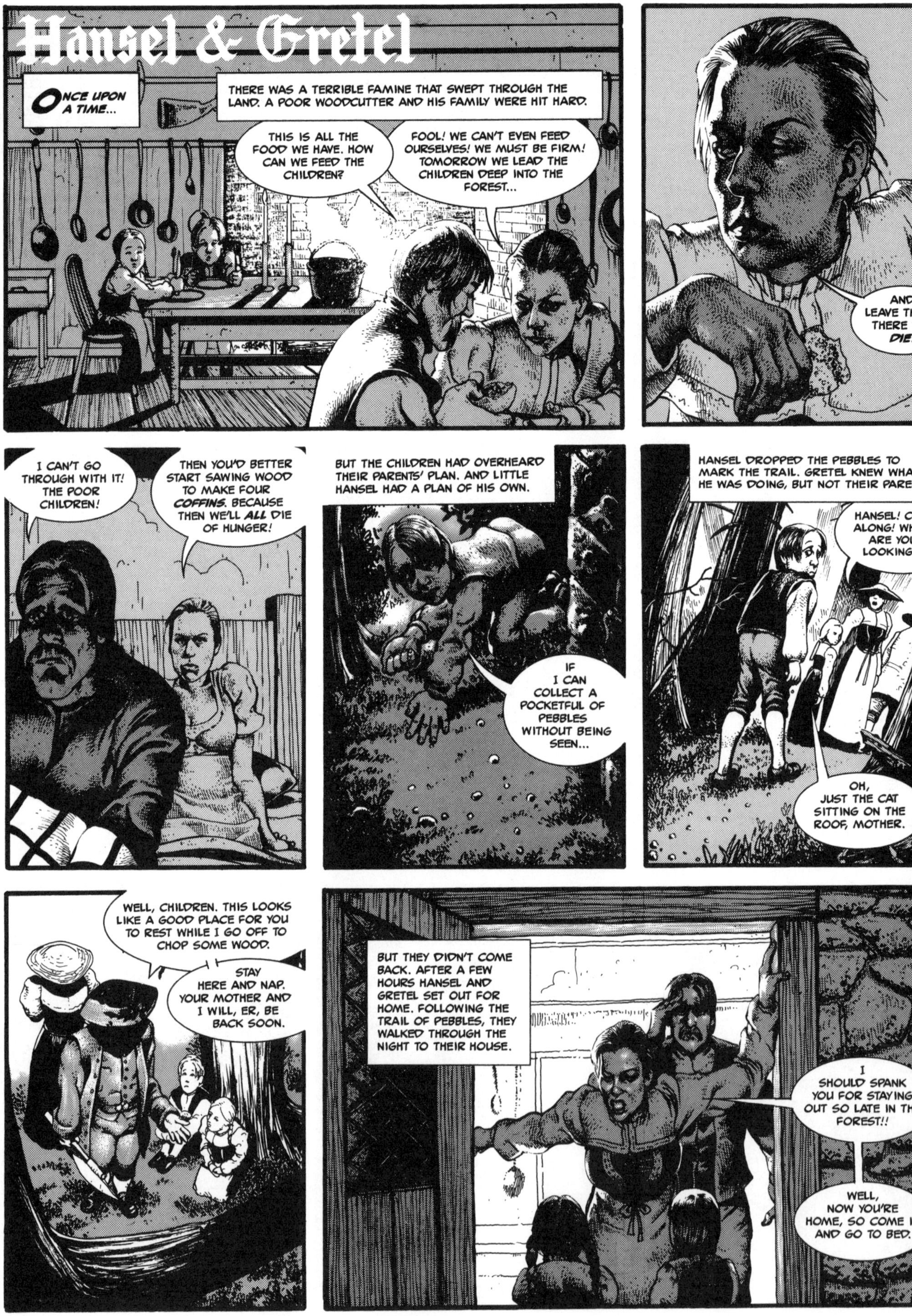
Hansel & Gretel
ONCE UPON A TIME...
THERE WAS A TERRIBLE FAMINE THAT SWEPT THROUGH THE LAND. A POOR WOODCUTTER AND HIS FAMILY WERE HIT HARD.
THIS IS ALL THE FOOD WE HAVE. HOW CAN WE FEED THE CHILDREN?
FOOL! WE CAN'T EVEN FEED OURSELVES! WE MUST BE FIRM! TOMORROW WE LEAD THE CHILDREN DEEP INTO THE FOREST...
AND LEAVE THEM THERE TO DIE.
I CAN'T GO THROUGH WITH IT! THE POOR CHILDREN!
THEN YOU'D BETTER START SAWING WOOD TO MAKE FOUR COFFINS. BECAUSE THEN WE'LL ALL DIE OF HUNGER!
BUT THE CHILDREN HAD OVERHEARD THEIR PARENTS' PLAN. AND LITTLE HANSEL HAD A PLAN OF HIS OWN.
IF I CAN COLLECT A POCKETFUL OF PEBBLES WITHOUT BEING SEEN...
HANSEL DROPPED THE PEBBLES TO MARK THE TRAIL. GRETEL KNEW WHAT HE WAS DOING, BUT NOT THEIR PARENTS.
HANSEL! COME ALONG! WHAT ARE YOU LOOKING AT?
OH, JUST THE CAT SITTING ON THE ROOF, MOTHER.
WELL, CHILDREN. THIS LOOKS LIKE A GOOD PLACE FOR YOU TO REST WHILE I GO OFF TO CHOP SOME WOOD.
STAY HERE AND NAP. YOUR MOTHER AND I WILL, ER, BE BACK SOON.
BUT THEY DIDN'T COME BACK. AFTER A FEW HOURS HANSEL AND GRETEL SET OUT FOR HOME. FOLLOWING THE TRAIL OF PEBBLES, THEY WALKED THROUGH THE NIGHT TO THEIR HOUSE.
I SHOULD SPANK YOU FOR STAYING OUT SO LATE IN THE FOREST!!
WELL, NOW YOU'RE HOME, SO COME IN AND GO TO BED.

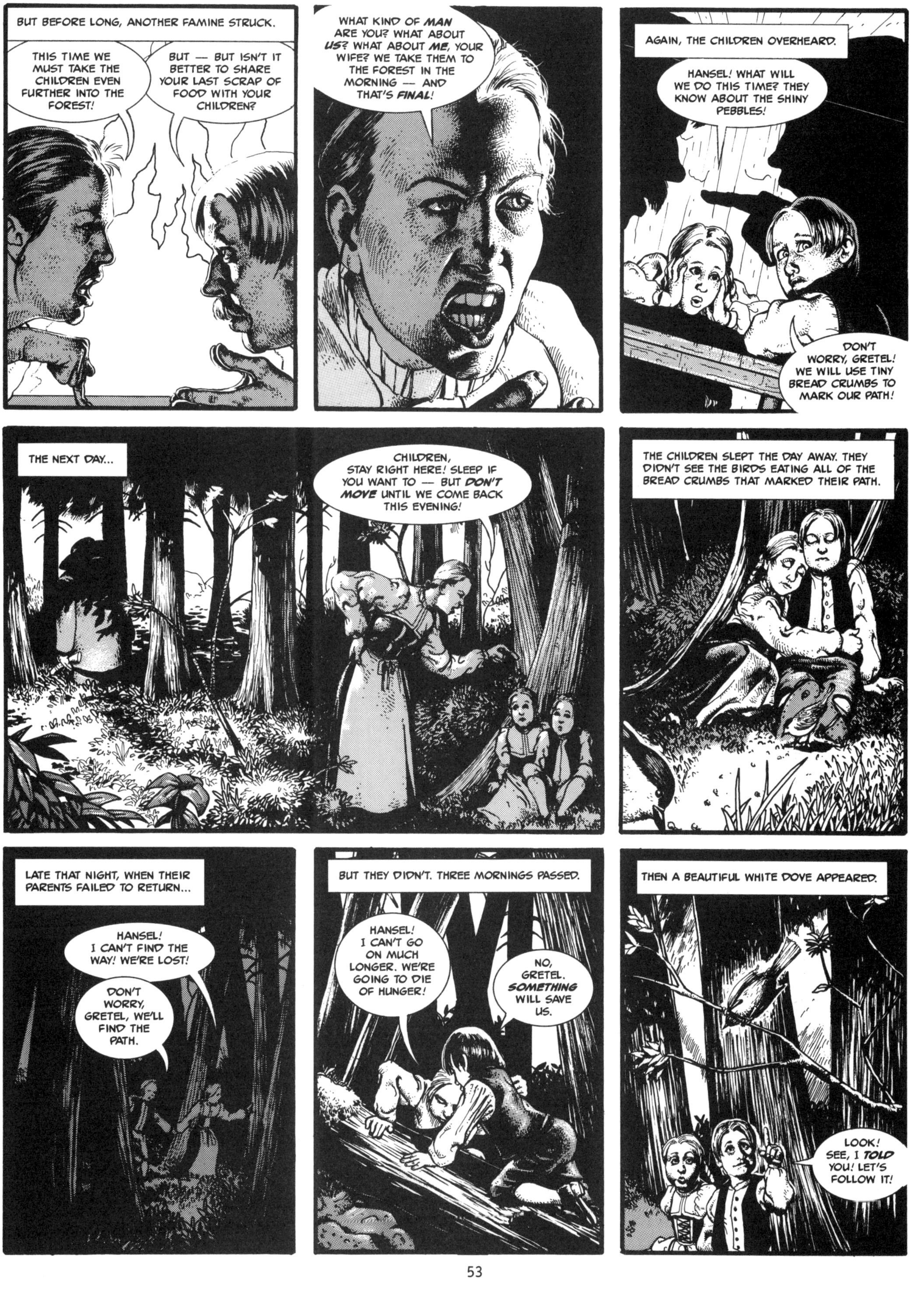
BUT BEFORE LONG, ANOTHER FAMINE STRUCK.
THIS TIME WE MUST TAKE THE CHILDREN EVEN FURTHER INTO THE FOREST!
BUT — BUT ISN'T IT BETTER TO SHARE YOUR LAST SCRAP OF FOOD WITH YOUR CHILDREN?
WHAT KIND OF MAN ARE YOU? WHAT ABOUT US? WHAT ABOUT ME, YOUR WIFE? WE TAKE THEM TO THE FOREST IN THE MORNING — AND THAT'S FINAL!
AGAIN, THE CHILDREN OVERHEARD.
HANSEL! WHAT WILL WE DO THIS TIME? THEY KNOW ABOUT THE SHINY PEBBLES!
DON'T WORRY, GRETEL! WE WILL USE TINY BREAD CRUMBS TO MARK OUR PATH!
THE NEXT DAY...
CHILDREN, STAY RIGHT HERE! SLEEP IF YOU WANT TO — BUT DON'T MOVE UNTIL WE COME BACK THIS EVENING!
THE CHILDREN SLEPT THE DAY AWAY. THEY DIDN'T SEE THE BIRDS EATING ALL OF THE BREAD CRUMBS THAT MARKED THEIR PATH.
LATE THAT NIGHT, WHEN THEIR PARENTS FAILED TO RETURN...
HANSEL! I CAN'T FIND THE WAY! WE'RE LOST!
DON'T WORRY, GRETEL, WE'LL FIND THE PATH.
BUT THEY DIDN'T. THREE MORNINGS PASSED.
HANSEL! I CAN'T GO ON MUCH LONGER. WE'RE GOING TO DIE OF HUNGER!
NO, GRETEL. SOMETHING WILL SAVE US.
THEN A BEAUTIFUL WHITE DOVE APPEARED.
LOOK! SEE, I TOLD YOU! LET'S FOLLOW IT!

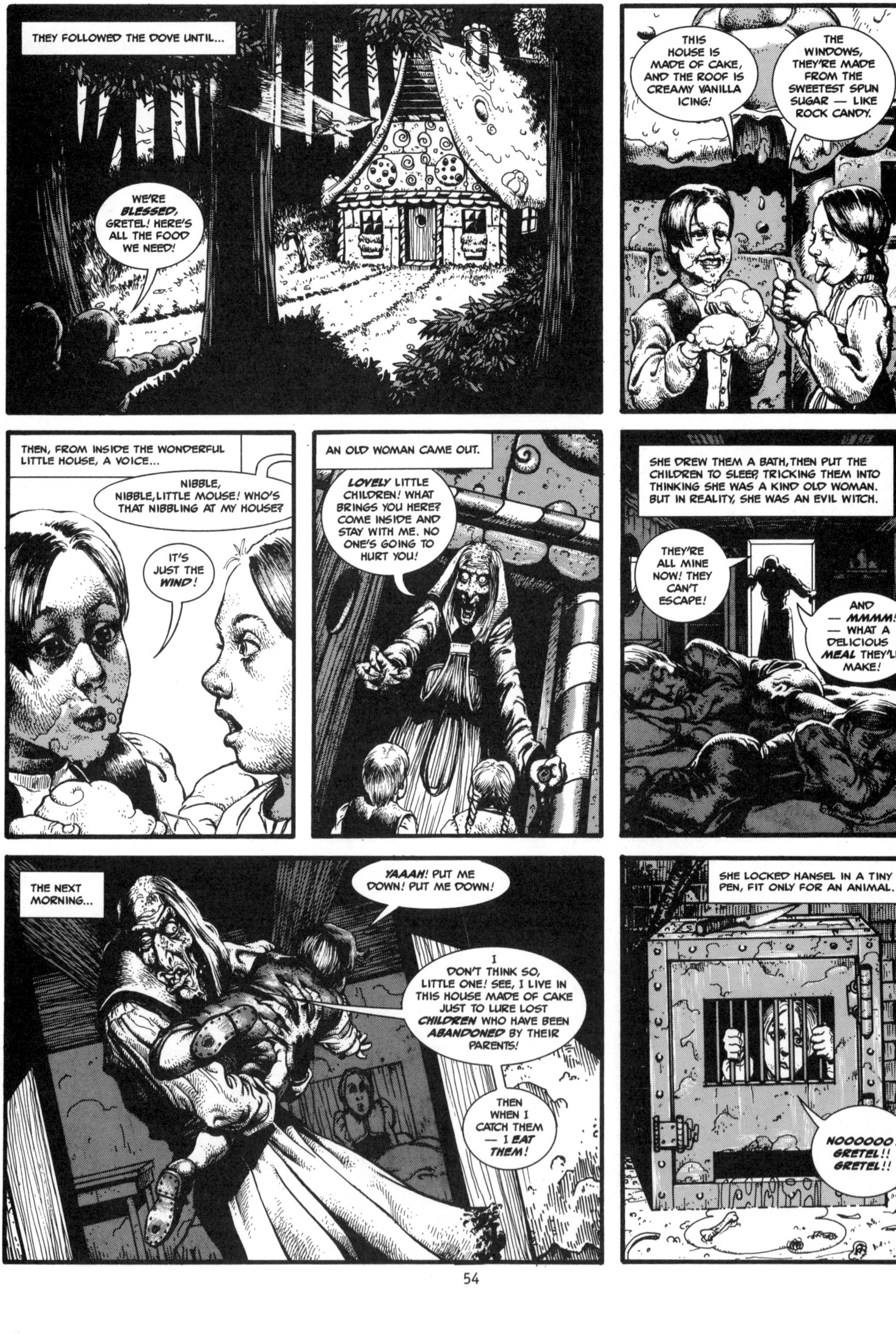
THEY FOLLOWED THE DOVE UNTIL...
WE'RE BLESSED, GRETEL! HERE'S ALL THE FOOD WE NEED!
THIS HOUSE IS MADE OF CAKE, AND THE ROOF IS CREAMY VANILLA ICING!
THE WINDOWS, THEY'RE MADE FROM THE SWEETEST SPUN SUGAR — LIKE ROCK CANDY.
THEN, FROM INSIDE THE WONDERFUL LITTLE HOUSE, A VOICE...
NIBBLE, NIBBLE, LITTLE MOUSE! WHO'S THAT NIBBLING AT MY HOUSE?
IT'S JUST THE WIND!
AN OLD WOMAN CAME OUT.
LOVELY LITTLE CHILDREN! WHAT BRINGS YOU HERE? COME INSIDE AND STAY WITH ME. NO ONE'S GOING TO HURT YOU!
SHE DREW THEM A BATH, THEN PUT THE CHILDREN TO SLEEP, TRICKING THEM INTO THINKING SHE WAS A KIND OLD WOMAN. BUT IN REALITY, SHE WAS AN EVIL WITCH.
THEY'RE ALL MINE NOW! THEY CAN'T ESCAPE!
AND — MMMM! — WHAT A DELICIOUS MEAL THEY'LL MAKE!
THE NEXT MORNING...
YAAAH! PUT ME DOWN! PUT ME DOWN!
I DON'T THINK SO, LITTLE ONE! SEE, I LIVE IN THIS HOUSE MADE OF CAKE JUST TO LURE LOST CHILDREN WHO HAVE BEEN ABANDONED BY THEIR PARENTS!
THEN WHEN I CATCH THEM — I EAT THEM!
SHE LOCKED HANSEL IN A TINY PEN, FIT ONLY FOR AN ANIMAL.
NOOOOOO! GRETEL!! GRETEL!!

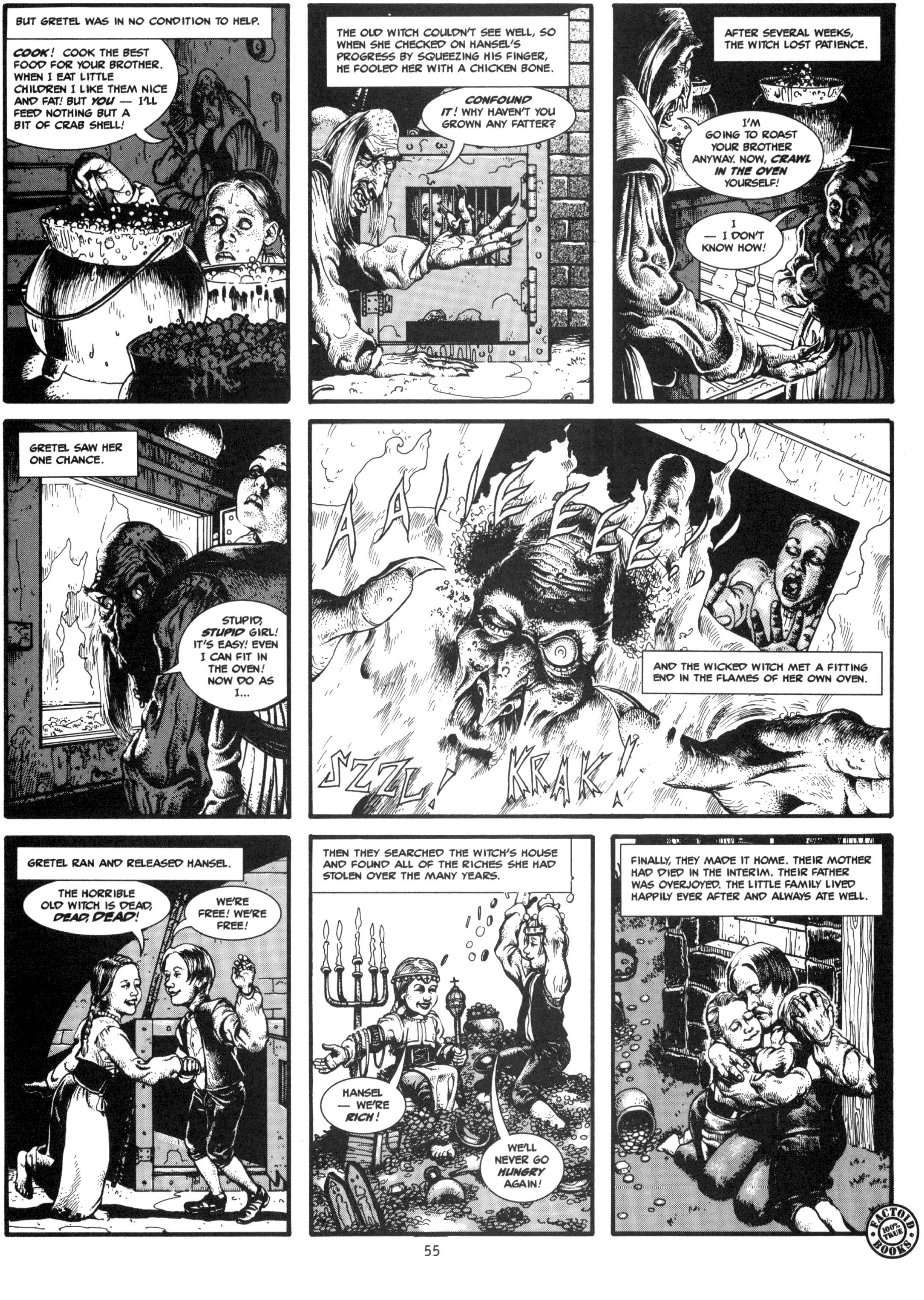

BUT GRETEL WAS IN NO CONDITION TO HELP.
COOK! COOK THE BEST FOOD FOR YOUR BROTHER. WHEN I EAT LITTLE CHILDREN I LIKE THEM NICE AND FAT! BUT YOU — I'LL FEED NOTHING BUT A BIT OF CRAB SHELL!
THE OLD WITCH COULDN'T SEE WELL, SO WHEN SHE CHECKED ON HANSEL'S PROGRESS BY SQUEEZING HIS FINGER, HE FOOLED HER WITH A CHICKEN BONE.
CONFOUND IT! WHY HAVEN'T YOU GROWN ANY FATTER?
AFTER SEVERAL WEEKS, THE WITCH LOST PATIENCE.
I'M GOING TO ROAST YOUR BROTHER ANYWAY. NOW, CRAWL IN THE OVEN YOURSELF!
I — I DON'T KNOW HOW!
GRETEL SAW HER ONE CHANCE.
STUPID, STUPID GIRL! IT'S EASY! EVEN I CAN FIT IN THE OVEN! NOW DO AS I...
AAIIEEEE!
AND THE WICKED WITCH MET A FITTING END IN THE FLAMES OF HER OWN OVEN.
SZZL! KRAK!
GRETEL RAN AND RELEASED HANSEL.
THE HORRIBLE OLD WITCH IS DEAD, DEAD, DEAD!
WE'RE FREE! WE'RE FREE!
THEN THEY SEARCHED THE WITCH'S HOUSE AND FOUND ALL OF THE RICHES SHE HAD STOLEN OVER THE MANY YEARS.
HANSEL — WE'RE RICH!
WE'LL NEVER GO HUNGRY AGAIN!
FINALLY, THEY MADE IT HOME. THEIR MOTHER HAD DIED IN THE INTERIM. THEIR FATHER WAS OVERJOYED. THE LITTLE FAMILY LIVED HAPPILY EVER AFTER AND ALWAYS ATE WELL.
FACTOID 100% TRUE BOOKS

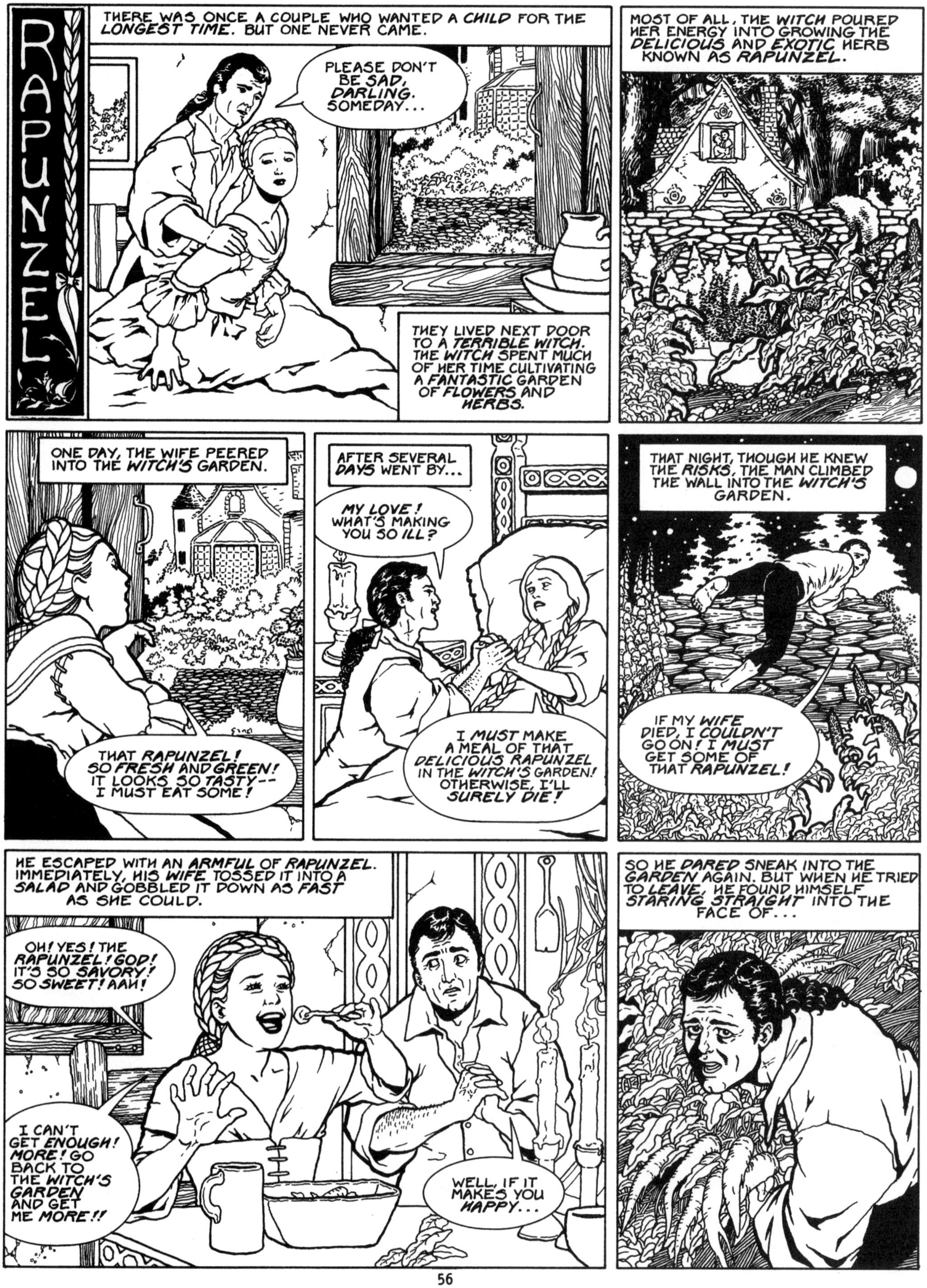
RAPUNZEL
THERE WAS ONCE A COUPLE WHO WANTED A CHILD FOR THE LONGEST TIME. BUT ONE NEVER CAME.
PLEASE DON'T BE SAD, DARLING. SOMEDAY...
THEY LIVED NEXT DOOR TO A TERRIBLE WITCH. THE WITCH SPENT MUCH OF HER TIME CULTIVATING A FANTASTIC GARDEN OF FLOWERS AND HERBS.
MOST OF ALL, THE WITCH POURED HER ENERGY INTO GROWING THE DELICIOUS AND EXOTIC HERB KNOWN AS RAPUNZEL.
ONE DAY, THE WIFE PEERED INTO THE WITCH'S GARDEN.
THAT RAPUNZEL! SO FRESH AND GREEN! IT LOOKS SO TASTY-- I MUST EAT SOME!
AFTER SEVERAL DAYS WENT BY...
MY LOVE! WHAT'S MAKING YOU SO ILL?
I MUST MAKE A MEAL OF THAT DELICIOUS RAPUNZEL IN THE WITCH'S GARDEN! OTHERWISE, I'LL SURELY DIE!
THAT NIGHT, THOUGH HE KNEW THE RISKS, THE MAN CLIMBED THE WALL INTO THE WITCH'S GARDEN.
IF MY WIFE DIED, I COULDN'T GO ON! I MUST GET SOME OF THAT RAPUNZEL!
HE ESCAPED WITH AN ARMFUL OF RAPUNZEL. IMMEDIATELY, HIS WIFE TOSSED IT INTO A SALAD AND GOBBLED IT DOWN AS FAST AS SHE COULD.
OH! YES! THE RAPUNZEL! GOD! IT'S SO SAVORY! SO SWEET! AAH!
I CAN'T GET ENOUGH! MORE! GO BACK TO THE WITCH'S GARDEN AND GET ME MORE!!
WELL, IF IT MAKES YOU HAPPY...
SO HE DARED SNEAK INTO THE GARDEN AGAIN. BUT WHEN HE TRIED TO LEAVE, HE FOUND HIMSELF STARING STRAIGHT INTO THE FACE OF...

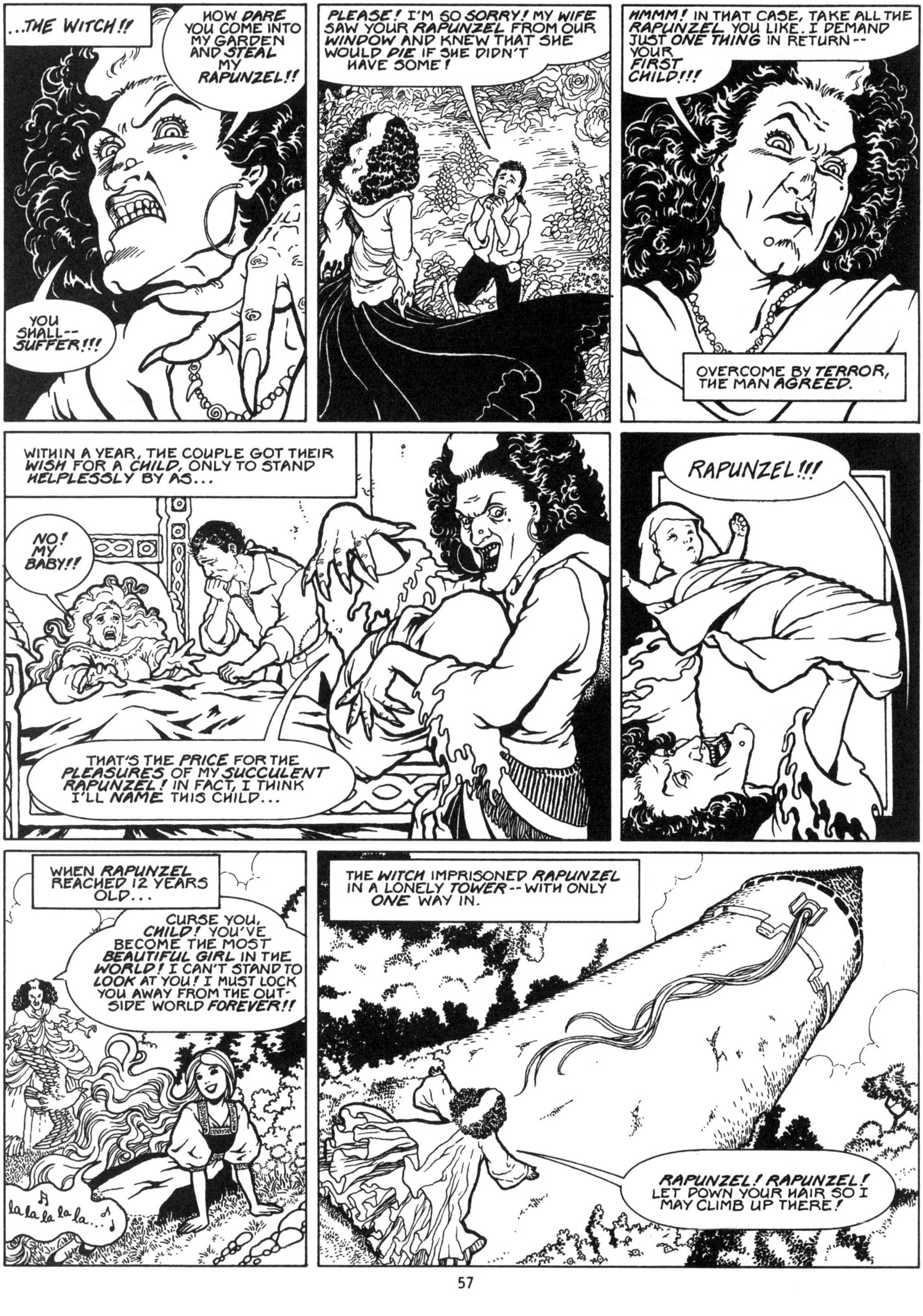
...THE WITCH!!
HOW DARE YOU COME INTO MY GARDEN AND STEAL MY RAPUNZEL!!
YOU SHALL-- SUFFER!!!
PLEASE! I'M SO SORRY! MY WIFE SAW YOUR RAPUNZEL FROM OUR WINDOW AND KNEW THAT SHE WOULD DIE IF SHE DIDN'T HAVE SOME!
HMMM! IN THAT CASE, TAKE ALL THE RAPUNZEL YOU LIKE. I DEMAND JUST ONE THING IN RETURN-- YOUR FIRST CHILD!!!
OVERCOME BY TERROR, THE MAN AGREED.
WITHIN A YEAR, THE COUPLE GOT THEIR WISH FOR A CHILD, ONLY TO STAND HELPLESSLY BY AS...
NO! MY BABY!!
THAT'S THE PRICE FOR THE PLEASURES OF MY SUCCULENT RAPUNZEL! IN FACT, I THINK I'LL NAME THIS CHILD...
RAPUNZEL!!!
WHEN RAPUNZEL REACHED 12 YEARS OLD...
CURSE YOU, CHILD! YOU'VE BECOME THE MOST BEAUTIFUL GIRL IN THE WORLD! I CAN'T STAND TO LOOK AT YOU! I MUST LOCK YOU AWAY FROM THE OUTSIDE WORLD FOREVER!!
la la la la la...
THE WITCH IMPRISONED RAPUNZEL IN A LONELY TOWER--WITH ONLY ONE WAY IN.
RAPUNZEL! RAPUNZEL! LET DOWN YOUR HAIR SO I MAY CLIMB UP THERE!

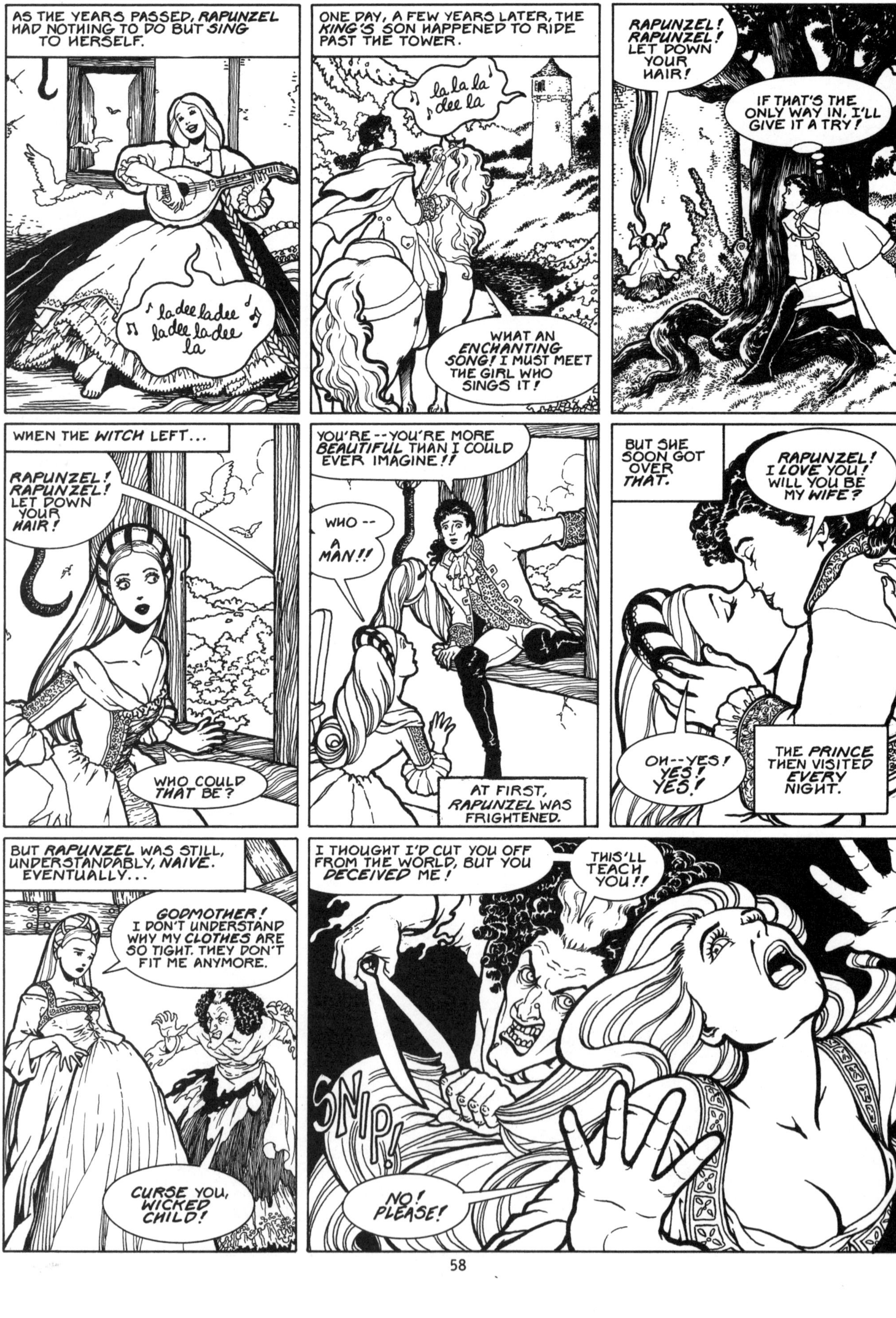
AS THE YEARS PASSED, RAPUNZEL HAD NOTHING TO DO BUT SING TO HERSELF.
la dee la dee la dee la dee la
ONE DAY, A FEW YEARS LATER, THE KING'S SON HAPPENED TO RIDE PAST THE TOWER.
la la la dee la
WHAT AN ENCHANTING SONG! I MUST MEET THE GIRL WHO SINGS IT!
RAPUNZEL! RAPUNZEL! LET DOWN YOUR HAIR!
IF THAT'S THE ONLY WAY IN, I'LL GIVE IT A TRY!
WHEN THE WITCH LEFT...
RAPUNZEL! RAPUNZEL! LET DOWN YOUR HAIR!
WHO COULD THAT BE?
YOU'RE --YOU'RE MORE BEAUTIFUL THAN I COULD EVER IMAGINE!!
WHO -- A MAN!!
AT FIRST, RAPUNZEL WAS FRIGHTENED.
BUT SHE SOON GOT OVER THAT.
RAPUNZEL! I LOVE YOU! WILL YOU BE MY WIFE?
OH--YES! YES! YES!
THE PRINCE THEN VISITED EVERY NIGHT.
BUT RAPUNZEL WAS STILL, UNDERSTANDABLY, NAIVE. EVENTUALLY...
GODMOTHER! I DON'T UNDERSTAND WHY MY CLOTHES ARE SO TIGHT. THEY DON'T FIT ME ANYMORE.
CURSE YOU, WICKED CHILD!
I THOUGHT I'D CUT YOU OFF FROM THE WORLD, BUT YOU DECEIVED ME!
THIS'LL TEACH YOU!!
SNIP!
NO! PLEASE!

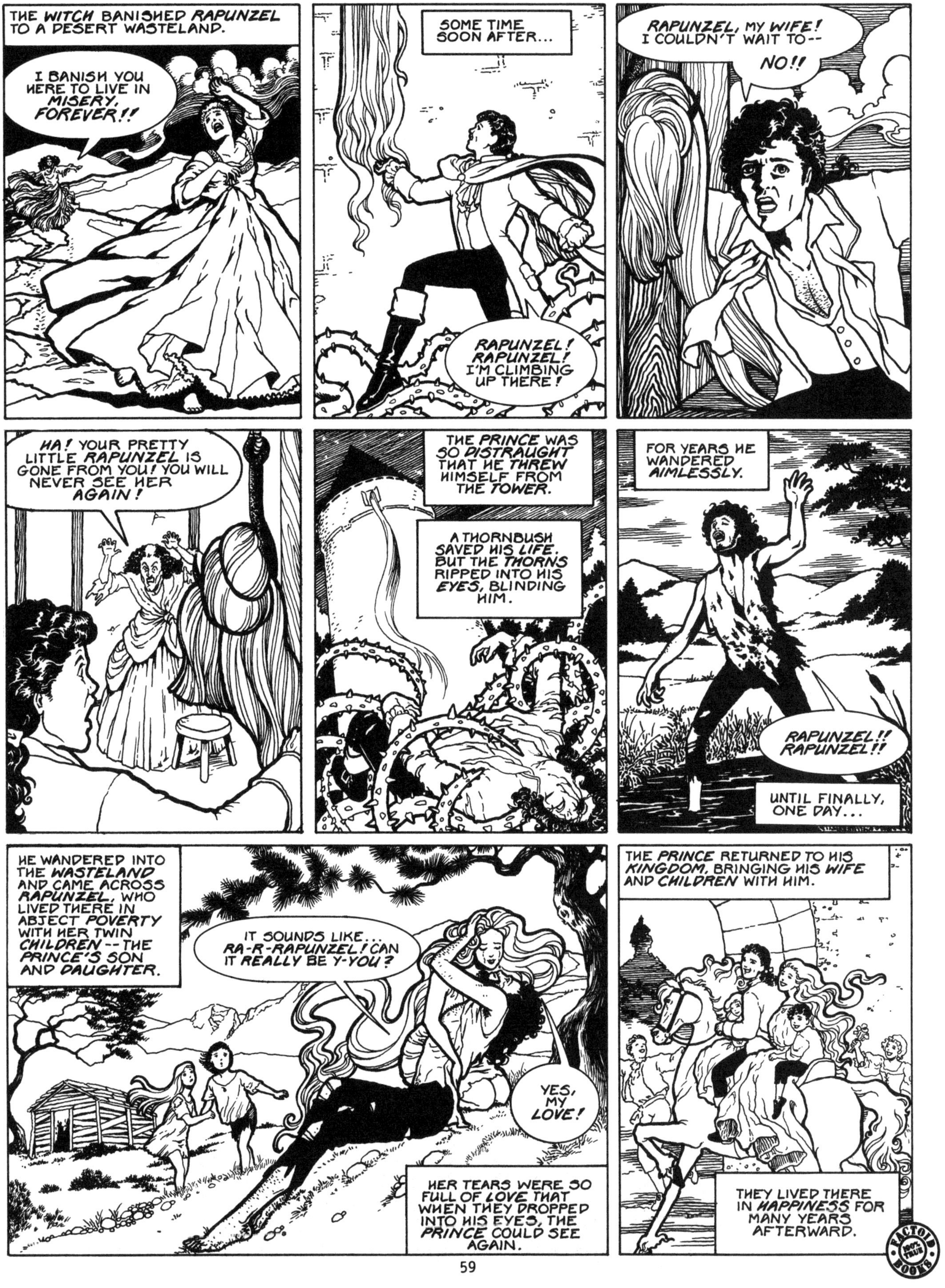

THE *WITCH* BANISHED *RAPUNZEL* TO A DESERT WASTELAND.
I BANISH YOU HERE TO LIVE IN *MISERY. FOREVER!!*
SOME TIME SOON AFTER...
RAPUNZEL! RAPUNZEL! I'M CLIMBING UP THERE!
RAPUNZEL, MY *WIFE!* I COULDN'T WAIT TO--
NO!!
HA! YOUR PRETTY LITTLE *RAPUNZEL* IS GONE FROM YOU! YOU WILL NEVER SEE HER *AGAIN!*
THE *PRINCE* WAS SO *DISTRAUGHT* THAT HE *THREW* HIMSELF FROM THE *TOWER*.
A THORNBUSH SAVED HIS *LIFE*. BUT THE *THORNS* RIPPED INTO HIS *EYES*, BLINDING HIM.
FOR YEARS HE WANDERED *AIMLESSLY*.
RAPUNZEL!! RAPUNZEL!!
UNTIL FINALLY, ONE DAY...
HE WANDERED INTO THE *WASTELAND* AND CAME ACROSS *RAPUNZEL*, WHO LIVED THERE IN ABJECT *POVERTY* WITH HER TWIN *CHILDREN* -- THE *PRINCE'S* SON AND *DAUGHTER*.
IT SOUNDS LIKE... *RA-R-RAPUNZEL!* CAN IT *REALLY* BE *Y-YOU?*
YES, MY *LOVE!*
HER TEARS WERE SO FULL OF *LOVE* THAT WHEN THEY DROPPED INTO HIS EYES, THE *PRINCE* COULD SEE AGAIN.
THE *PRINCE* RETURNED TO HIS *KINGDOM*, BRINGING HIS *WIFE* AND *CHILDREN* WITH HIM.
THEY LIVED THERE IN *HAPPINESS* FOR MANY YEARS AFTERWARD.

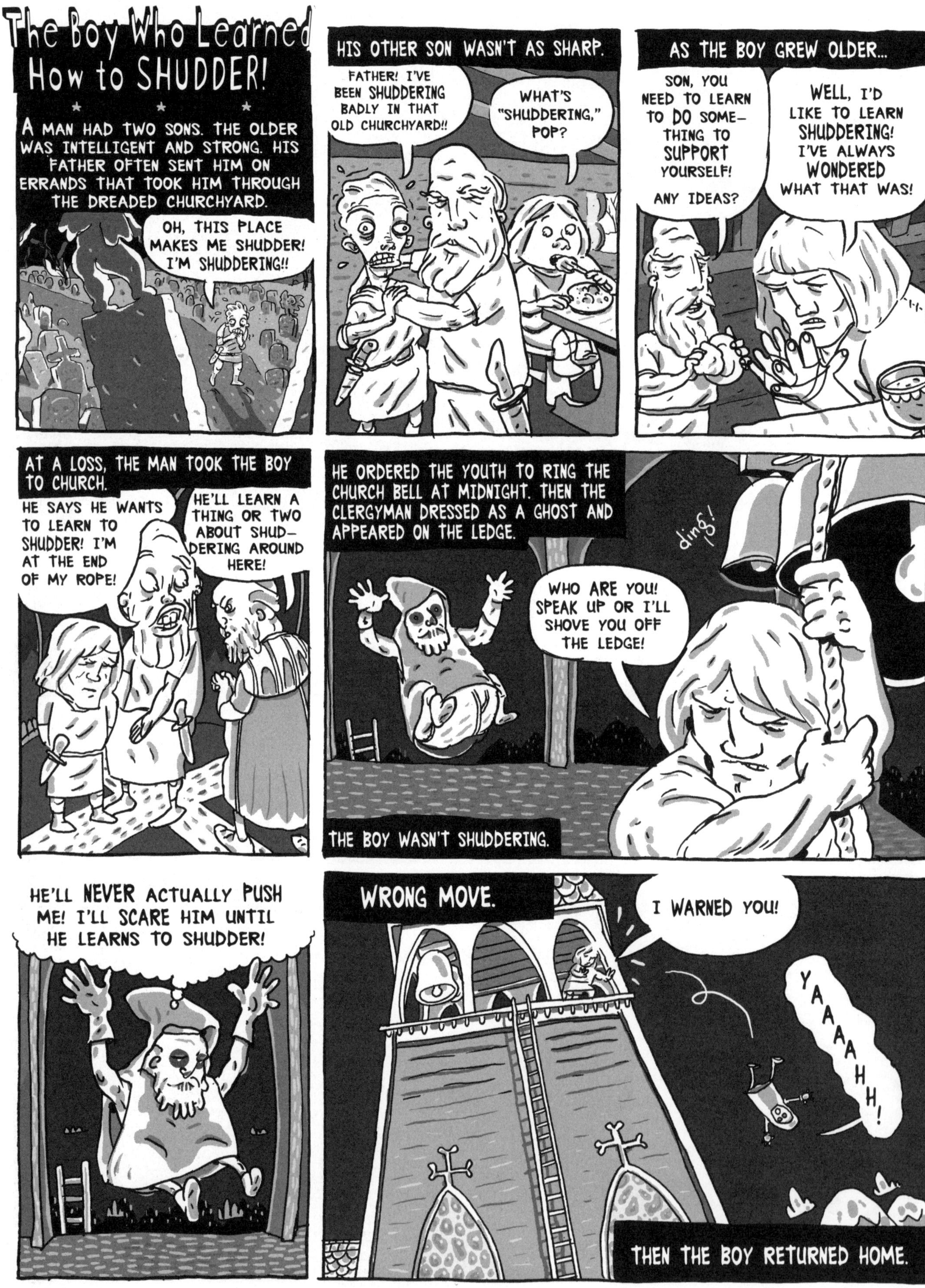

The Boy Who Learned How to SHUDDER!
A MAN HAD TWO SONS. THE OLDER WAS INTELLIGENT AND STRONG. HIS FATHER OFTEN SENT HIM ON ERRANDS THAT TOOK HIM THROUGH THE DREADED CHURCHYARD.
OH, THIS PLACE MAKES ME SHUDDER! I'M SHUDDERING!!
HIS OTHER SON WASN'T AS SHARP.
FATHER! I'VE BEEN SHUDDERING BADLY IN THAT OLD CHURCHYARD!!
WHAT'S "SHUDDERING," POP?
AS THE BOY GREW OLDER...
SON, YOU NEED TO LEARN TO DO SOMETHING TO SUPPORT YOURSELF! ANY IDEAS?
WELL, I'D LIKE TO LEARN SHUDDERING! I'VE ALWAYS WONDERED WHAT THAT WAS!
AT A LOSS, THE MAN TOOK THE BOY TO CHURCH.
HE SAYS HE WANTS TO LEARN TO SHUDDER! I'M AT THE END OF MY ROPE!
HE'LL LEARN A THING OR TWO ABOUT SHUDDERING AROUND HERE!
HE ORDERED THE YOUTH TO RING THE CHURCH BELL AT MIDNIGHT. THEN THE CLERGYMAN DRESSED AS A GHOST AND APPEARED ON THE LEDGE.
ding!
WHO ARE YOU! SPEAK UP OR I'LL SHOVE YOU OFF THE LEDGE!
THE BOY WASN'T SHUDDERING.
HE'LL NEVER ACTUALLY PUSH ME! I'LL SCARE HIM UNTIL HE LEARNS TO SHUDDER!
WRONG MOVE.
I WARNED YOU!
YAAAAHH!
THEN THE BOY RETURNED HOME.

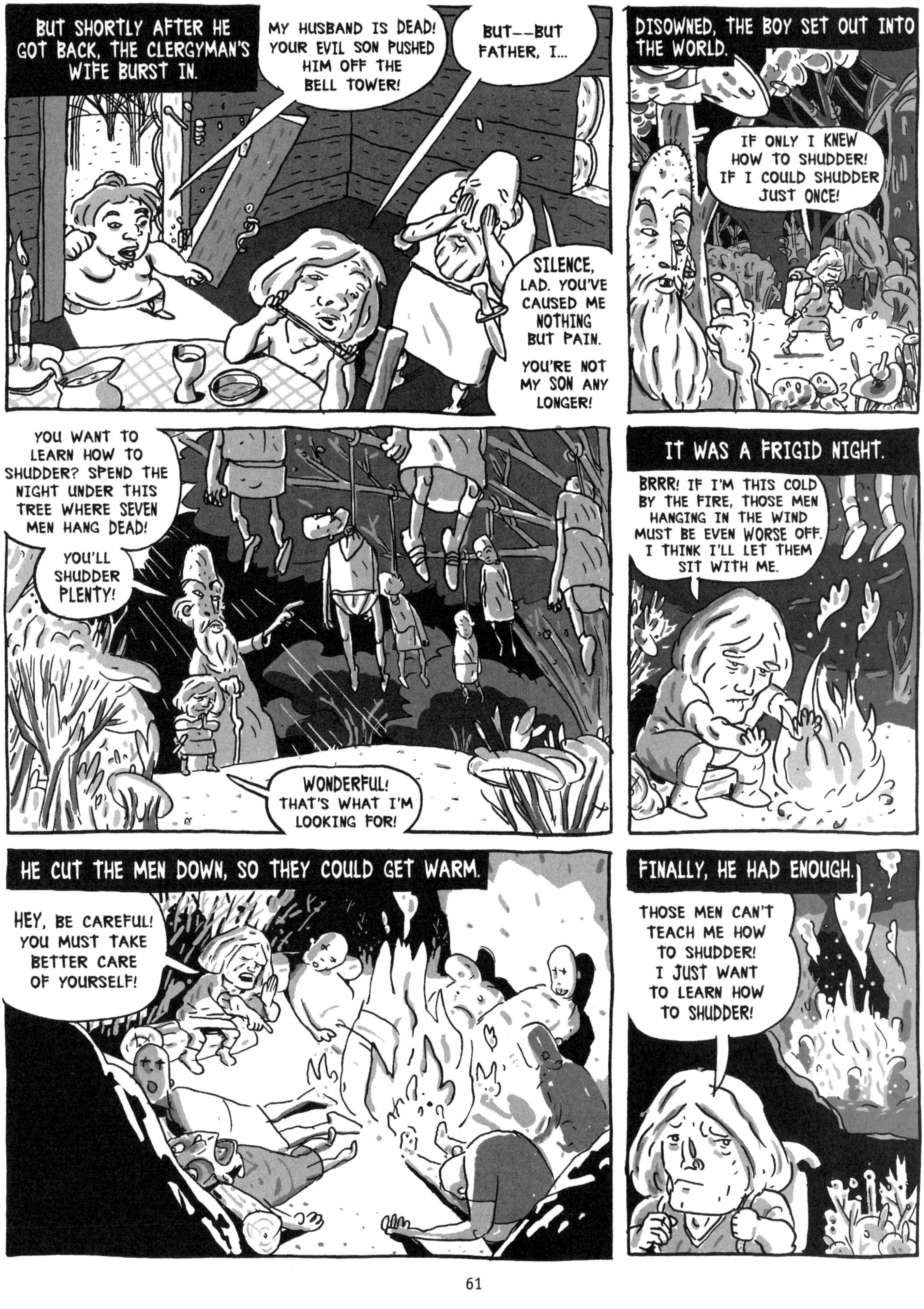

BUT SHORTLY AFTER HE GOT BACK, THE CLERGYMAN'S WIFE BURST IN.
MY HUSBAND IS DEAD! YOUR EVIL SON PUSHED HIM OFF THE BELL TOWER!
BUT--BUT FATHER, I...
SILENCE, LAD. YOU'VE CAUSED ME NOTHING BUT PAIN.
YOU'RE NOT MY SON ANY LONGER!
DISOWNED, THE BOY SET OUT INTO THE WORLD.
IF ONLY I KNEW HOW TO SHUDDER! IF I COULD SHUDDER JUST ONCE!
YOU WANT TO LEARN HOW TO SHUDDER? SPEND THE NIGHT UNDER THIS TREE WHERE SEVEN MEN HANG DEAD!
YOU'LL SHUDDER PLENTY!
WONDERFUL! THAT'S WHAT I'M LOOKING FOR!
IT WAS A FRIGID NIGHT.
BRRR! IF I'M THIS COLD BY THE FIRE, THOSE MEN HANGING IN THE WIND MUST BE EVEN WORSE OFF. I THINK I'LL LET THEM SIT WITH ME.
HE CUT THE MEN DOWN, SO THEY COULD GET WARM.
HEY, BE CAREFUL! YOU MUST TAKE BETTER CARE OF YOURSELF!
FINALLY, HE HAD ENOUGH.
THOSE MEN CAN'T TEACH ME HOW TO SHUDDER! I JUST WANT TO LEARN HOW TO SHUDDER!

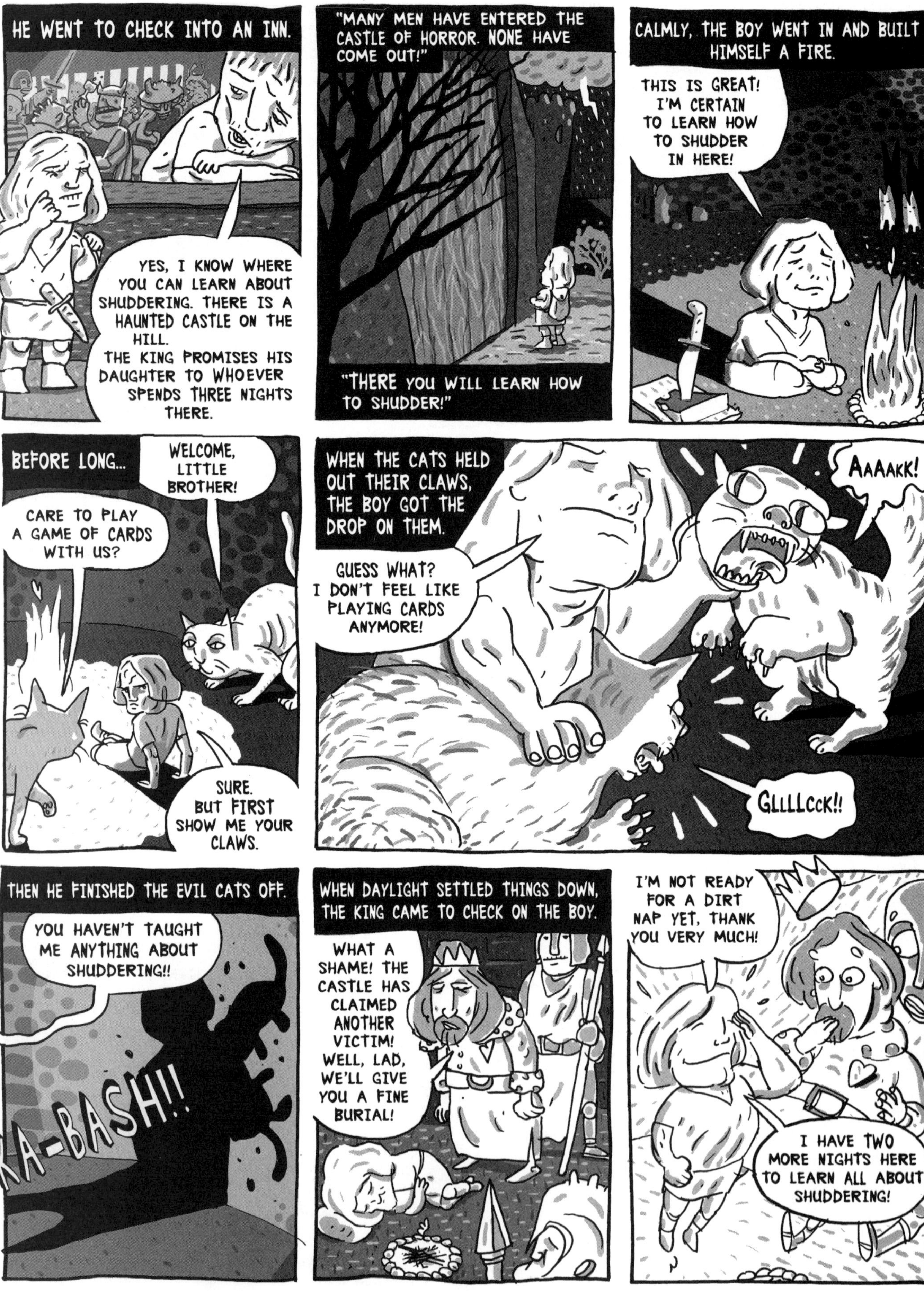

HE WENT TO CHECK INTO AN INN.
YES, I KNOW WHERE YOU CAN LEARN ABOUT SHUDDERING. THERE IS A HAUNTED CASTLE ON THE HILL. THE KING PROMISES HIS DAUGHTER TO WHOEVER SPENDS THREE NIGHTS THERE.
"MANY MEN HAVE ENTERED THE CASTLE OF HORROR. NONE HAVE COME OUT!"
"THERE YOU WILL LEARN HOW TO SHUDDER!"
CALMLY, THE BOY WENT IN AND BUILT HIMSELF A FIRE.
THIS IS GREAT! I'M CERTAIN TO LEARN HOW TO SHUDDER IN HERE!
BEFORE LONG...
WELCOME, LITTLE BROTHER!
CARE TO PLAY A GAME OF CARDS WITH US?
SURE. BUT FIRST SHOW ME YOUR CLAWS.
WHEN THE CATS HELD OUT THEIR CLAWS, THE BOY GOT THE DROP ON THEM.
GUESS WHAT? I DON'T FEEL LIKE PLAYING CARDS ANYMORE!
AAAAKK!
GLLLLCCK!!
THEN HE FINISHED THE EVIL CATS OFF.
YOU HAVEN'T TAUGHT ME ANYTHING ABOUT SHUDDERING!!
KA-BASH!!
WHEN DAYLIGHT SETTLED THINGS DOWN, THE KING CAME TO CHECK ON THE BOY.
WHAT A SHAME! THE CASTLE HAS CLAIMED ANOTHER VICTIM! WELL, LAD, WE'LL GIVE YOU A FINE BURIAL!
I'M NOT READY FOR A DIRT NAP YET, THANK YOU VERY MUCH!
I HAVE TWO MORE NIGHTS HERE TO LEARN ALL ABOUT SHUDDERING!

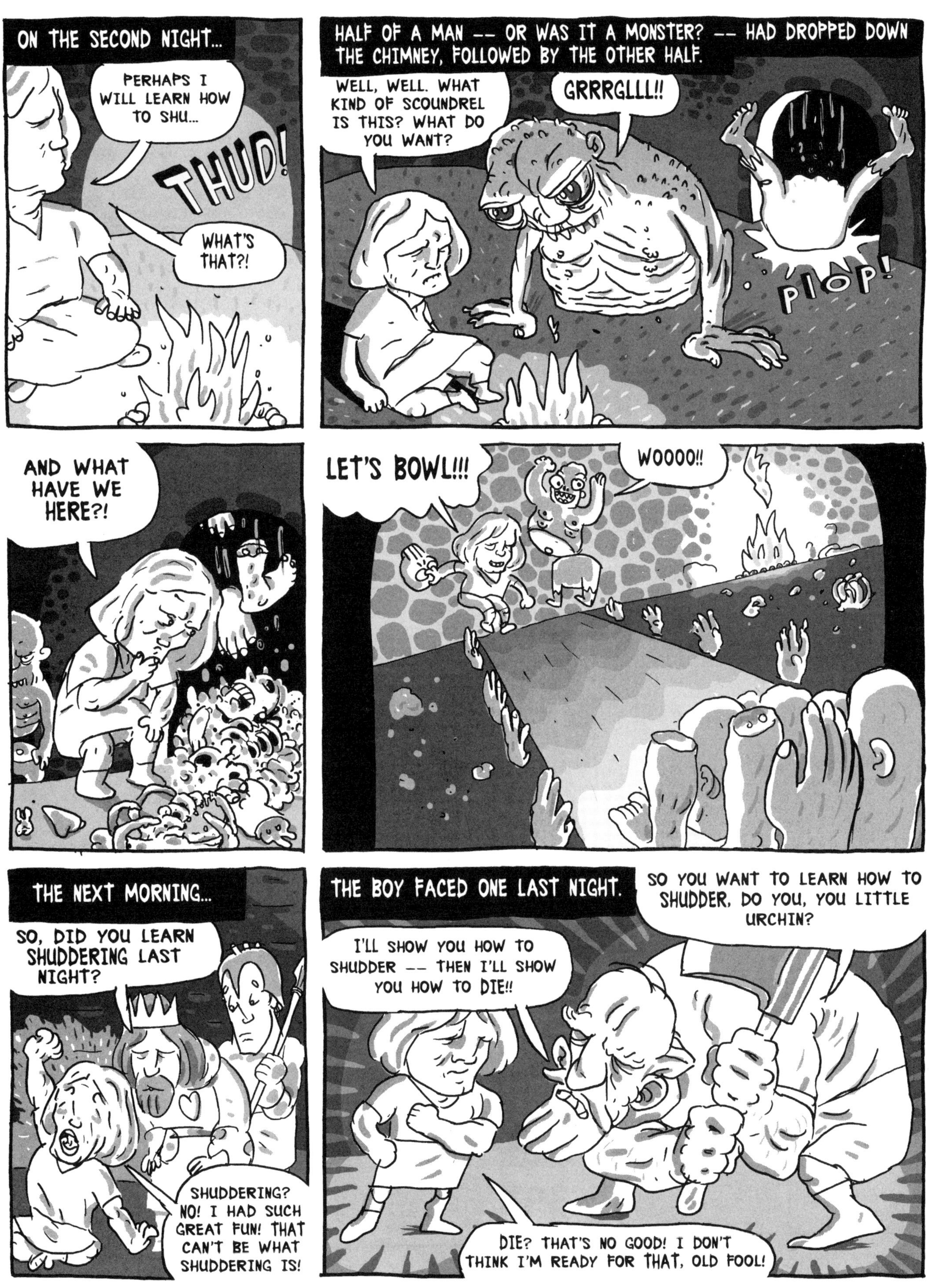
ON THE SECOND NIGHT...
PERHAPS I WILL LEARN HOW TO SHU...
THUD!
WHAT'S THAT?!
HALF OF A MAN -- OR WAS IT A MONSTER? -- HAD DROPPED DOWN THE CHIMNEY, FOLLOWED BY THE OTHER HALF.
WELL, WELL. WHAT KIND OF SCOUNDREL IS THIS? WHAT DO YOU WANT?
GRRRGLLL!!
PLOP!
AND WHAT HAVE WE HERE?!
LET'S BOWL!!!
WOOOO!!
THE NEXT MORNING...
SO, DID YOU LEARN SHUDDERING LAST NIGHT?
SHUDDERING? NO! I HAD SUCH GREAT FUN! THAT CAN'T BE WHAT SHUDDERING IS!
THE BOY FACED ONE LAST NIGHT.
SO YOU WANT TO LEARN HOW TO SHUDDER, DO YOU, YOU LITTLE URCHIN?
I'LL SHOW YOU HOW TO SHUDDER -- THEN I'LL SHOW YOU HOW TO DIE!!
DIE? THAT'S NO GOOD! I DON'T THINK I'M READY FOR THAT, OLD FOOL!

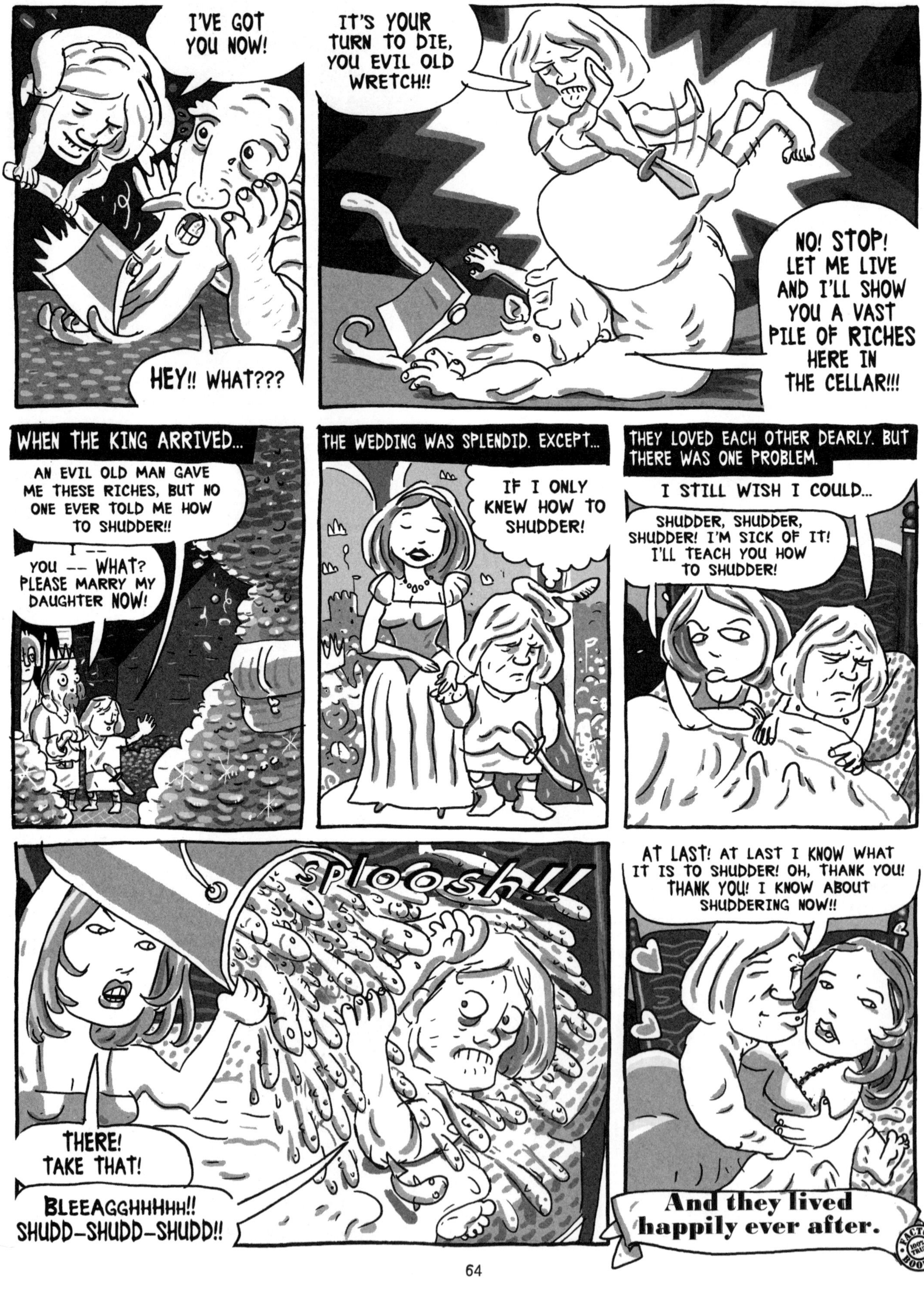
I'VE GOT YOU NOW!
HEY!! WHAT???
IT'S YOUR TURN TO DIE, YOU EVIL OLD WRETCH!!
NO! STOP! LET ME LIVE AND I'LL SHOW YOU A VAST PILE OF RICHES HERE IN THE CELLAR!!!
WHEN THE KING ARRIVED...
AN EVIL OLD MAN GAVE ME THESE RICHES, BUT NO ONE EVER TOLD ME HOW TO SHUDDER!!
I -- YOU -- WHAT? PLEASE MARRY MY DAUGHTER NOW!
THE WEDDING WAS SPLENDID. EXCEPT...
IF I ONLY KNEW HOW TO SHUDDER!
THEY LOVED EACH OTHER DEARLY. BUT THERE WAS ONE PROBLEM.
I STILL WISH I COULD...
SHUDDER, SHUDDER, SHUDDER! I'M SICK OF IT! I'LL TEACH YOU HOW TO SHUDDER!
sploosh!!
THERE! TAKE THAT!
BLEEAGGHHHHH!! SHUDD-SHUDD-SHUDD!!
AT LAST! AT LAST I KNOW WHAT IT IS TO SHUDDER! OH, THANK YOU! THANK YOU! I KNOW ABOUT SHUDDERING NOW!!
And they lived happily ever after.
FACTOID BOOKS 100% TRUE

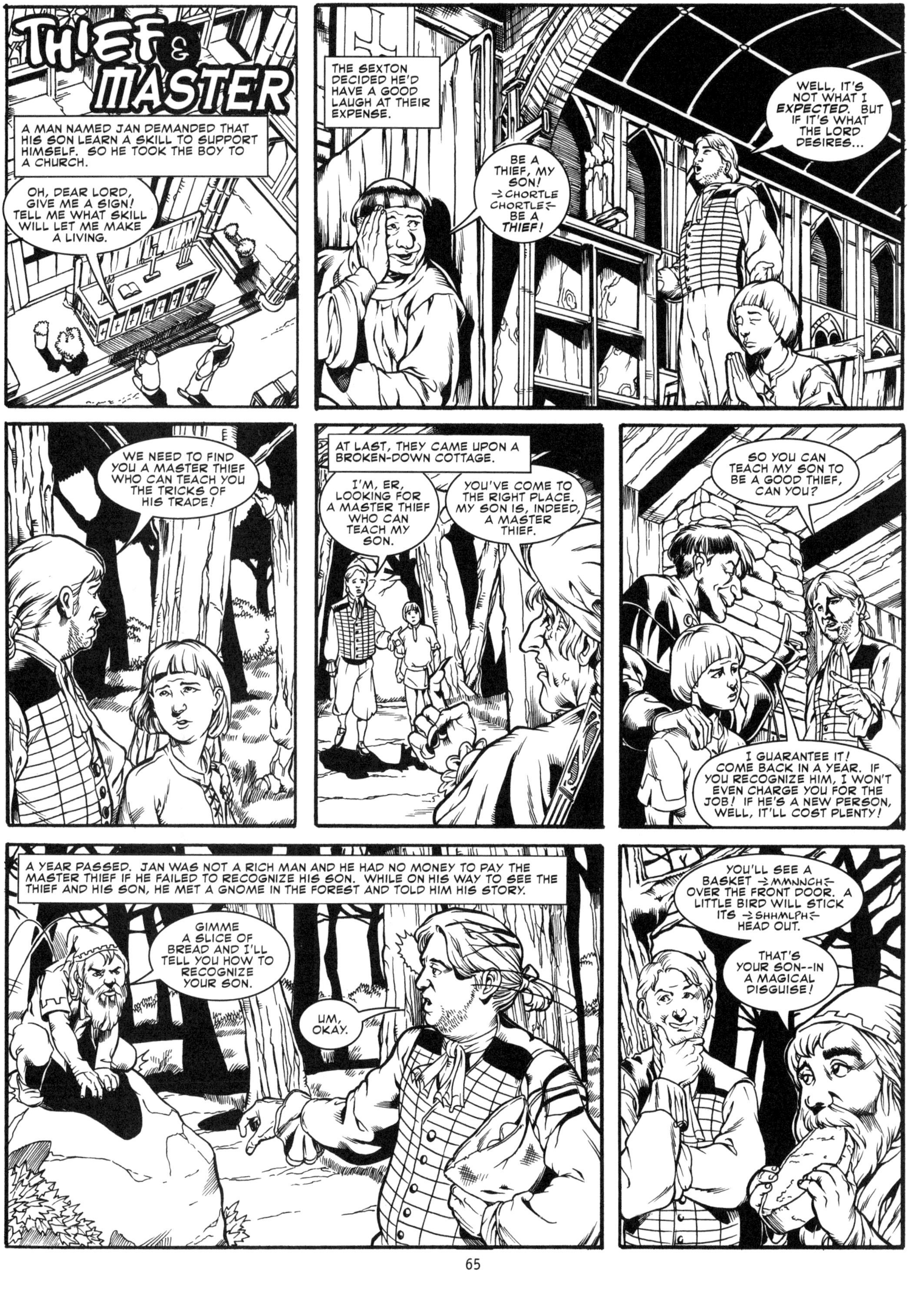
THIEF & MASTER
A MAN NAMED JAN DEMANDED THAT HIS SON LEARN A SKILL TO SUPPORT HIMSELF. SO HE TOOK THE BOY TO A CHURCH.
OH, DEAR LORD, GIVE ME A SIGN! TELL ME WHAT SKILL WILL LET ME MAKE A LIVING.
THE SEXTON DECIDED HE'D HAVE A GOOD LAUGH AT THEIR EXPENSE.
BE A THIEF, MY SON! CHORTLE CHORTLE BE A THIEF!
WELL, IT'S NOT WHAT I EXPECTED. BUT IF IT'S WHAT THE LORD DESIRES...
WE NEED TO FIND YOU A MASTER THIEF WHO CAN TEACH YOU THE TRICKS OF HIS TRADE!
AT LAST, THEY CAME UPON A BROKEN-DOWN COTTAGE.
I'M, ER, LOOKING FOR A MASTER THIEF WHO CAN TEACH MY SON.
YOU'VE COME TO THE RIGHT PLACE. MY SON IS, INDEED, A MASTER THIEF.
SO YOU CAN TEACH MY SON TO BE A GOOD THIEF, CAN YOU?
I GUARANTEE IT! COME BACK IN A YEAR. IF YOU RECOGNIZE HIM, I WON'T EVEN CHARGE YOU FOR THE JOB! IF HE'S A NEW PERSON, WELL, IT'LL COST PLENTY!
A YEAR PASSED. JAN WAS NOT A RICH MAN AND HE HAD NO MONEY TO PAY THE MASTER THIEF IF HE FAILED TO RECOGNIZE HIS SON. WHILE ON HIS WAY TO SEE THE THIEF AND HIS SON, HE MET A GNOME IN THE FOREST AND TOLD HIM HIS STORY.
GIMME A SLICE OF BREAD AND I'LL TELL YOU HOW TO RECOGNIZE YOUR SON.
UM, OKAY.
YOU'LL SEE A BASKET MMNNCH OVER THE FRONT DOOR. A LITTLE BIRD WILL STICK ITS SHHMLPH HEAD OUT.
THAT'S YOUR SON--IN A MAGICAL DISGUISE!

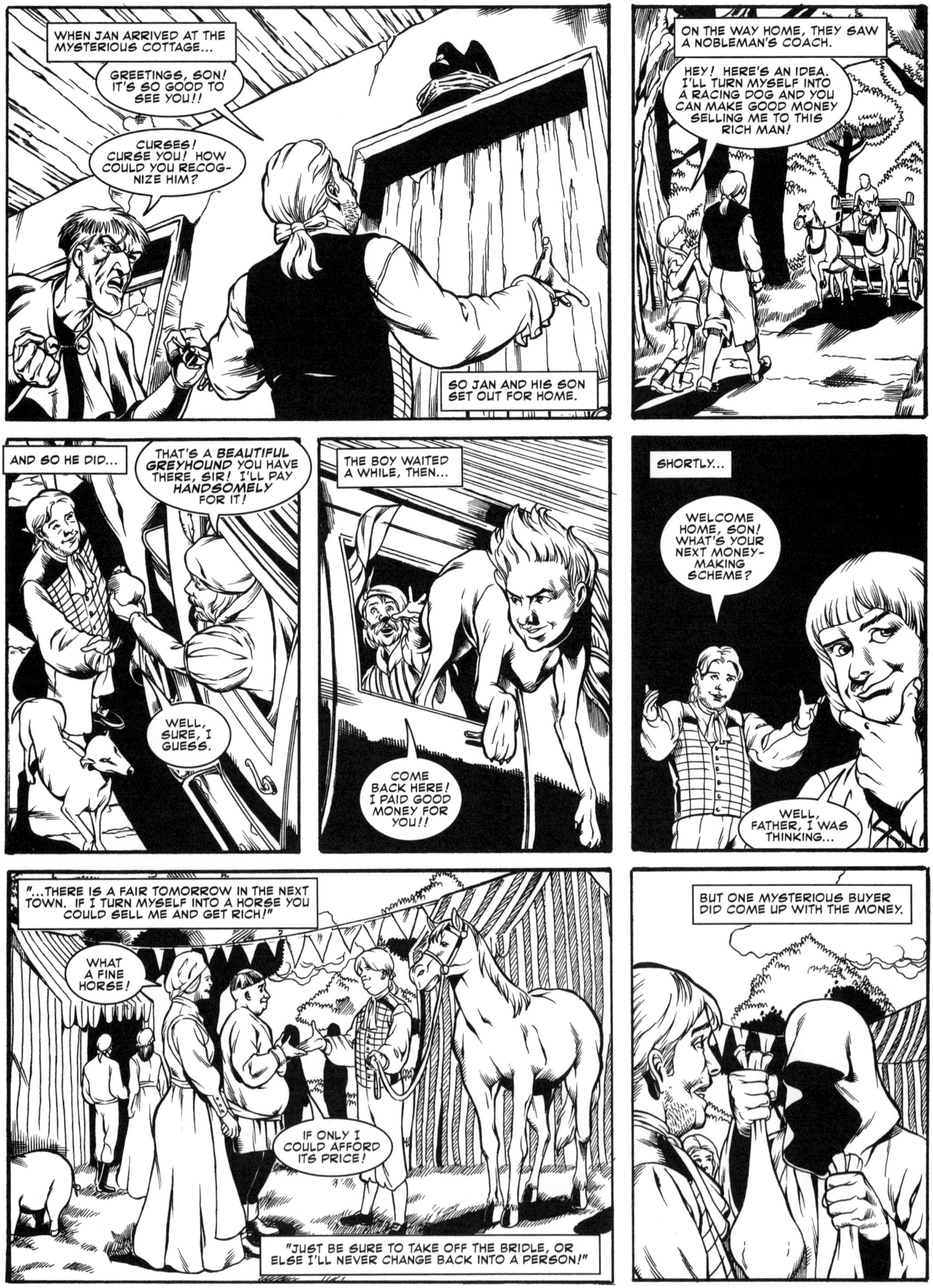
WHEN JAN ARRIVED AT THE MYSTERIOUS COTTAGE...
GREETINGS, SON! IT'S SO GOOD TO SEE YOU!!
CURSES! CURSE YOU! HOW COULD YOU RECOGNIZE HIM?
SO JAN AND HIS SON SET OUT FOR HOME.
ON THE WAY HOME, THEY SAW A NOBLEMAN'S COACH.
HEY! HERE'S AN IDEA. I'LL TURN MYSELF INTO A RACING DOG AND YOU CAN MAKE GOOD MONEY SELLING ME TO THIS RICH MAN!
AND SO HE DID...
THAT'S A BEAUTIFUL GREYHOUND YOU HAVE THERE, SIR! I'LL PAY HANDSOMELY FOR IT!
WELL, SURE, I GUESS.
THE BOY WAITED A WHILE, THEN...
COME BACK HERE! I PAID GOOD MONEY FOR YOU!!
SHORTLY...
WELCOME HOME, SON! WHAT'S YOUR NEXT MONEY-MAKING SCHEME?
WELL, FATHER, I WAS THINKING...
"...THERE IS A FAIR TOMORROW IN THE NEXT TOWN. IF I TURN MYSELF INTO A HORSE YOU COULD SELL ME AND GET RICH!"
WHAT A FINE HORSE!
IF ONLY I COULD AFFORD ITS PRICE!
"JUST BE SURE TO TAKE OFF THE BRIDLE, OR ELSE I'LL NEVER CHANGE BACK INTO A PERSON!"
BUT ONE MYSTERIOUS BUYER DID COME UP WITH THE MONEY.

IT WAS THE MASTER THIEF!

THOUGHT YOU COULD ESCAPE ME, EH?

AND JAN HAD BEEN SO OVERWHELMED BY THE MONEY HE'D MADE THAT HE FORGOT TO TAKE OFF THE BRIDLE!

SOME TIME LATER, A MAID CAME TO CLEAN THE STABLE.

HELP! TAKE MY BRIDLE OFF! I'M A PRISONER HERE!

A TALKING HORSE?

AS SOON AS THE BRIDLE WAS OFF, THE BOY CHANGED FROM A HORSE INTO A DOVE AND FLEW AWAY FOR A QUICK ESCAPE.

WHEN THE MASTER THIEF FOUND OUT...

WHAT?? WHY, YOU INCOMPETENT, SIMPERING...!!

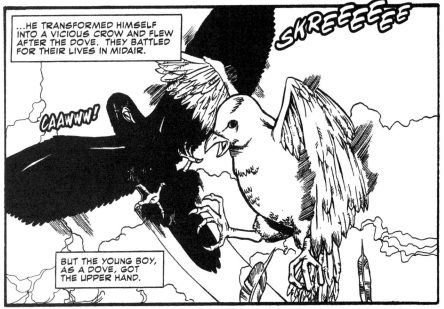

...HE TRANSFORMED HIMSELF INTO A VICIOUS CROW AND FLEW AFTER THE DOVE. THEY BATTLED FOR THEIR LIVES IN MIDAIR.

SKREEEEEE

CAAWWW!

BUT THE YOUNG BOY, AS A DOVE, GOT THE UPPER HAND.

ON THE GROUND, THE MASTER BECAME A ROOSTER, THINKING HE COULD OVER-POWER THE DOVE.

BUT THE BOY TURNED THE TABLES. HE BECAME A FOX--AND BIT THE ROOSTER'S HEAD CLEAN OFF!

CHOMPP!

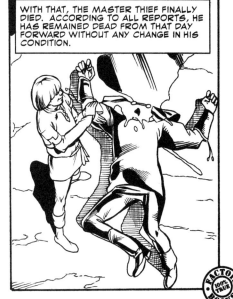

WITH THAT, THE MASTER THIEF FINALLY DIED. ACCORDING TO ALL REPORTS, HE HAS REMAINED DEAD FROM THAT DAY FORWARD WITHOUT ANY CHANGE IN HIS CONDITION.

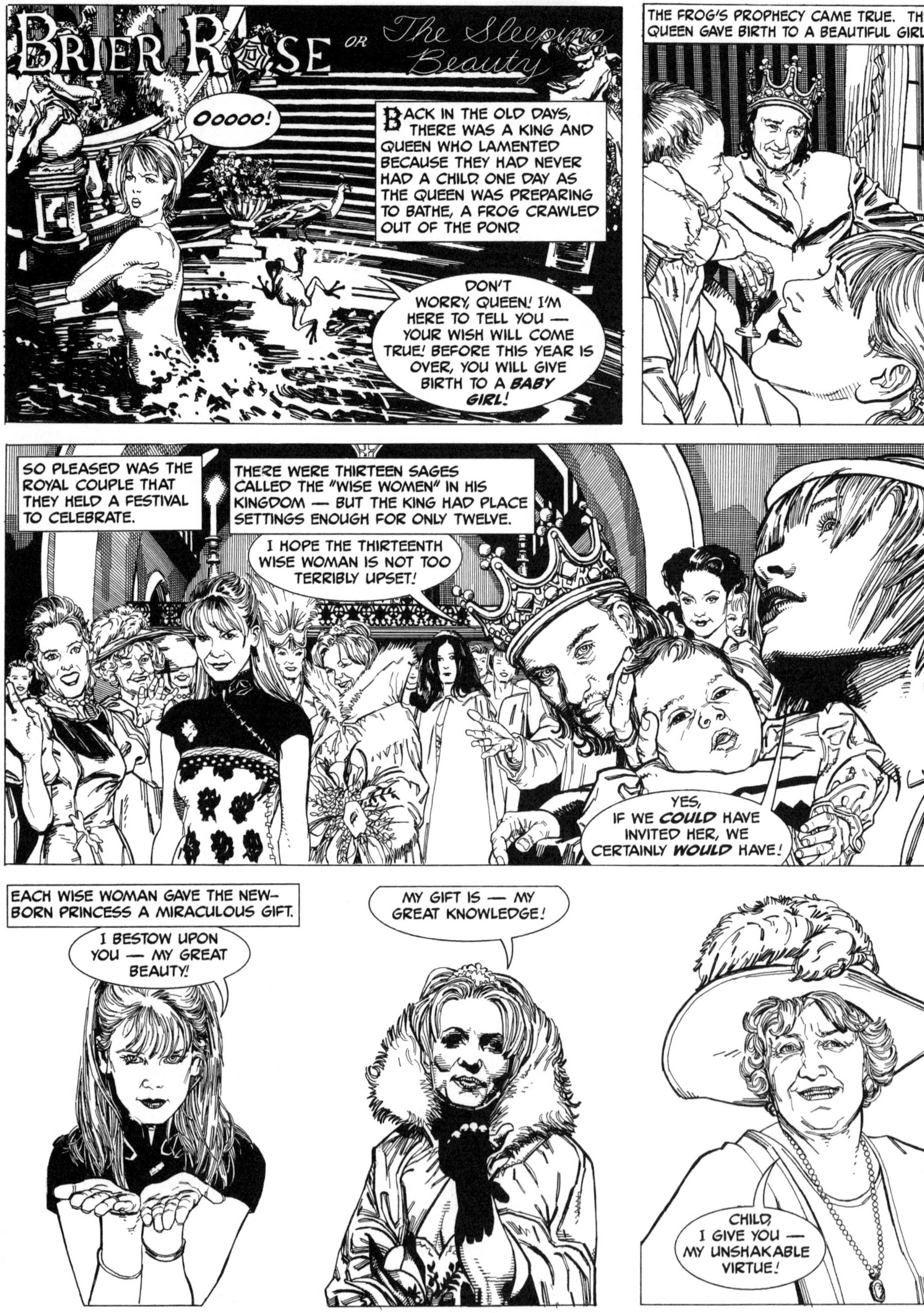
BRIER ROSE OR The Sleeping Beauty
OOOOO!
BACK IN THE OLD DAYS, THERE WAS A KING AND QUEEN WHO LAMENTED BECAUSE THEY HAD NEVER HAD A CHILD. ONE DAY AS THE QUEEN WAS PREPARING TO BATHE, A FROG CRAWLED OUT OF THE POND.
DON'T WORRY, QUEEN! I'M HERE TO TELL YOU — YOUR WISH WILL COME TRUE! BEFORE THIS YEAR IS OVER, YOU WILL GIVE BIRTH TO A BABY GIRL!
THE FROG'S PROPHECY CAME TRUE. THE QUEEN GAVE BIRTH TO A BEAUTIFUL GIRL.
SO PLEASED WAS THE ROYAL COUPLE THAT THEY HELD A FESTIVAL TO CELEBRATE.
THERE WERE THIRTEEN SAGES CALLED THE "WISE WOMEN" IN HIS KINGDOM — BUT THE KING HAD PLACE SETTINGS ENOUGH FOR ONLY TWELVE.
I HOPE THE THIRTEENTH WISE WOMAN IS NOT TOO TERRIBLY UPSET!
YES, IF WE COULD HAVE INVITED HER, WE CERTAINLY WOULD HAVE!
EACH WISE WOMAN GAVE THE NEW-BORN PRINCESS A MIRACULOUS GIFT.
I BESTOW UPON YOU — MY GREAT BEAUTY!
MY GIFT IS — MY GREAT KNOWLEDGE!
CHILD, I GIVE YOU — MY UNSHAKABLE VIRTUE!

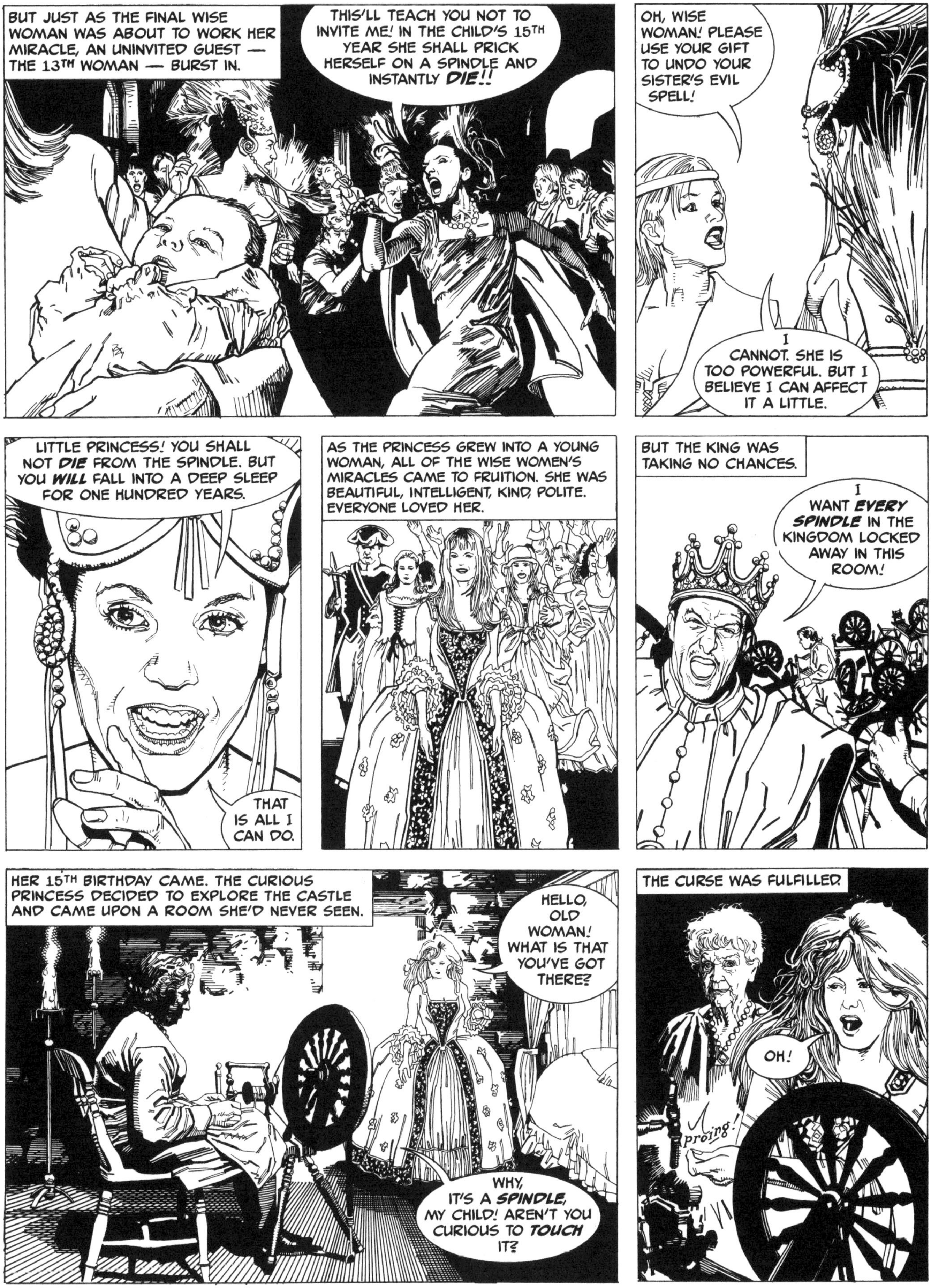

BUT JUST AS THE FINAL WISE WOMAN WAS ABOUT TO WORK HER MIRACLE, AN UNINVITED GUEST — THE 13TH WOMAN — BURST IN.
THIS'LL TEACH YOU NOT TO INVITE ME! IN THE CHILD'S 15TH YEAR SHE SHALL PRICK HERSELF ON A SPINDLE AND INSTANTLY DIE!!
OH, WISE WOMAN! PLEASE USE YOUR GIFT TO UNDO YOUR SISTER'S EVIL SPELL!
I CANNOT. SHE IS TOO POWERFUL. BUT I BELIEVE I CAN AFFECT IT A LITTLE.
LITTLE PRINCESS! YOU SHALL NOT DIE FROM THE SPINDLE. BUT YOU WILL FALL INTO A DEEP SLEEP FOR ONE HUNDRED YEARS.
THAT IS ALL I CAN DO.
AS THE PRINCESS GREW INTO A YOUNG WOMAN, ALL OF THE WISE WOMEN'S MIRACLES CAME TO FRUITION. SHE WAS BEAUTIFUL, INTELLIGENT, KIND, POLITE. EVERYONE LOVED HER.
BUT THE KING WAS TAKING NO CHANCES.
I WANT EVERY SPINDLE IN THE KINGDOM LOCKED AWAY IN THIS ROOM!
HER 15TH BIRTHDAY CAME. THE CURIOUS PRINCESS DECIDED TO EXPLORE THE CASTLE AND CAME UPON A ROOM SHE'D NEVER SEEN.
HELLO, OLD WOMAN! WHAT IS THAT YOU'VE GOT THERE?
WHY, IT'S A SPINDLE, MY CHILD! AREN'T YOU CURIOUS TO TOUCH IT?
THE CURSE WAS FULFILLED.
OH!
proing!

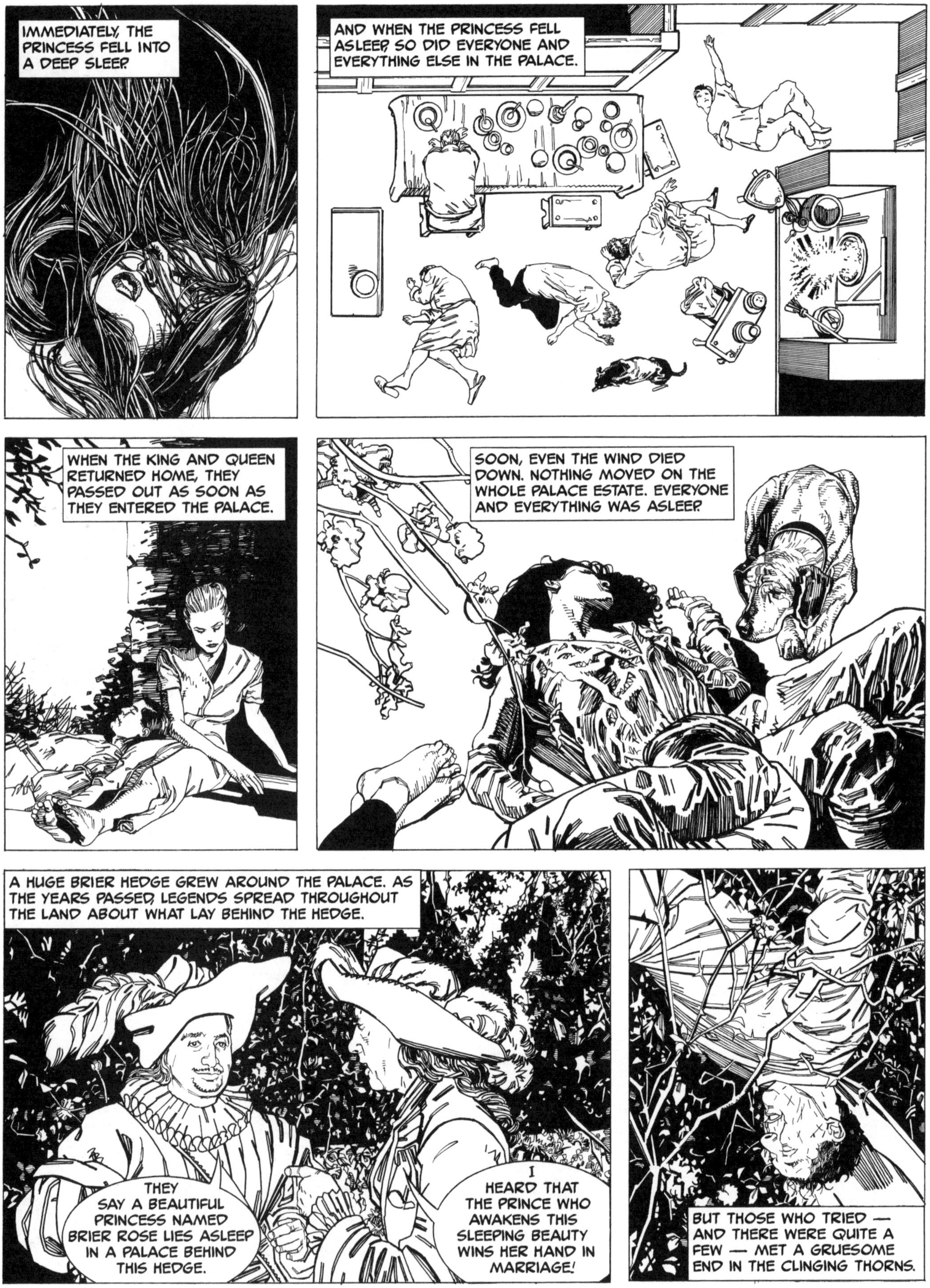
IMMEDIATELY, THE PRINCESS FELL INTO A DEEP SLEEP.
AND WHEN THE PRINCESS FELL ASLEEP, SO DID EVERYONE AND EVERYTHING ELSE IN THE PALACE.
WHEN THE KING AND QUEEN RETURNED HOME, THEY PASSED OUT AS SOON AS THEY ENTERED THE PALACE.
SOON, EVEN THE WIND DIED DOWN. NOTHING MOVED ON THE WHOLE PALACE ESTATE. EVERYONE AND EVERYTHING WAS ASLEEP.
A HUGE BRIER HEDGE GREW AROUND THE PALACE. AS THE YEARS PASSED, LEGENDS SPREAD THROUGHOUT THE LAND ABOUT WHAT LAY BEHIND THE HEDGE.
THEY SAY A BEAUTIFUL PRINCESS NAMED BRIER ROSE LIES ASLEEP IN A PALACE BEHIND THIS HEDGE.
I HEARD THAT THE PRINCE WHO AWAKENS THIS SLEEPING BEAUTY WINS HER HAND IN MARRIAGE!
BUT THOSE WHO TRIED — AND THERE WERE QUITE A FEW — MET A GRUESOME END IN THE CLINGING THORNS.

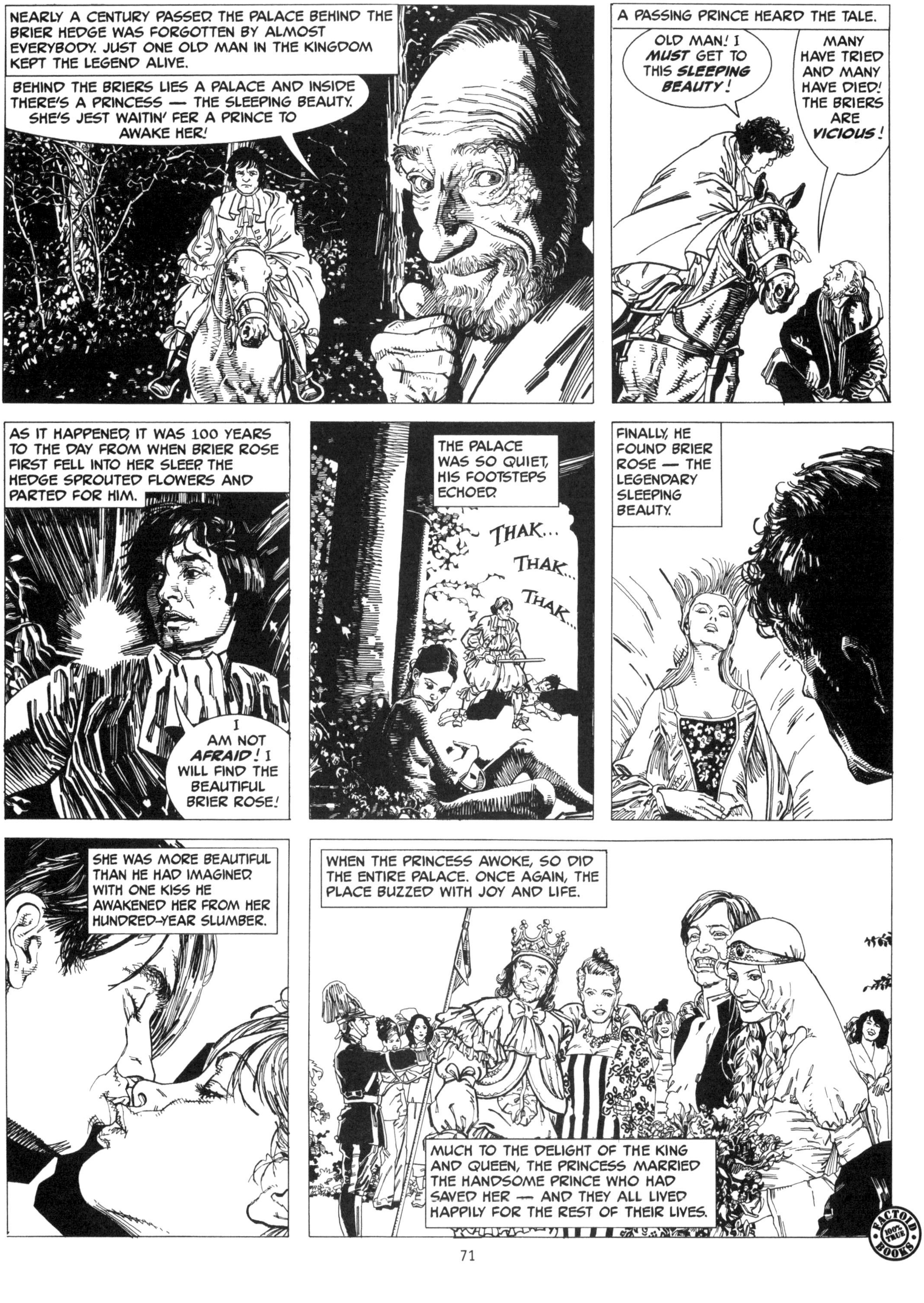
NEARLY A CENTURY PASSED. THE PALACE BEHIND THE BRIER HEDGE WAS FORGOTTEN BY ALMOST EVERYBODY. JUST ONE OLD MAN IN THE KINGDOM KEPT THE LEGEND ALIVE.
BEHIND THE BRIERS LIES A PALACE AND INSIDE THERE'S A PRINCESS — THE SLEEPING BEAUTY. SHE'S JEST WAITIN' FER A PRINCE TO AWAKE HER!
A PASSING PRINCE HEARD THE TALE.
OLD MAN! I MUST GET TO THIS SLEEPING BEAUTY!
MANY HAVE TRIED AND MANY HAVE DIED! THE BRIERS ARE VICIOUS!
AS IT HAPPENED, IT WAS 100 YEARS TO THE DAY FROM WHEN BRIER ROSE FIRST FELL INTO HER SLEEP. THE HEDGE SPROUTED FLOWERS AND PARTED FOR HIM.
I AM NOT AFRAID! I WILL FIND THE BEAUTIFUL BRIER ROSE!
THE PALACE WAS SO QUIET, HIS FOOTSTEPS ECHOED.
THAK...
THAK...
THAK...
FINALLY, HE FOUND BRIER ROSE — THE LEGENDARY SLEEPING BEAUTY.
SHE WAS MORE BEAUTIFUL THAN HE HAD IMAGINED. WITH ONE KISS HE AWAKENED HER FROM HER HUNDRED-YEAR SLUMBER.
WHEN THE PRINCESS AWOKE, SO DID THE ENTIRE PALACE. ONCE AGAIN, THE PLACE BUZZED WITH JOY AND LIFE.
MUCH TO THE DELIGHT OF THE KING AND QUEEN, THE PRINCESS MARRIED THE HANDSOME PRINCE WHO HAD SAVED HER — AND THEY ALL LIVED HAPPILY FOR THE REST OF THEIR LIVES.
FACTOID BOOKS 100% TRUE

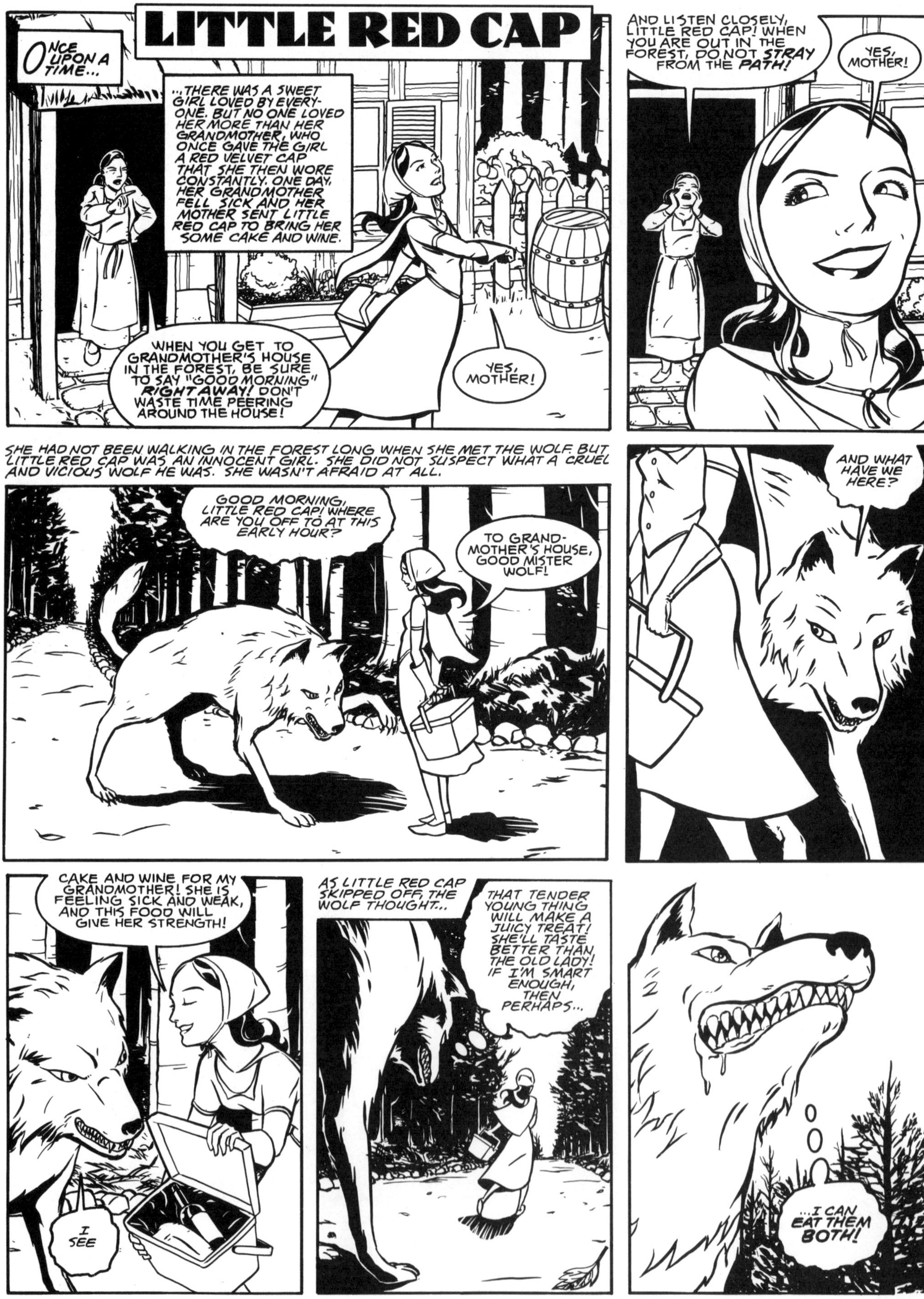
LITTLE RED CAP
ONCE UPON A TIME...
...THERE WAS A SWEET GIRL LOVED BY EVERY-ONE. BUT NO ONE LOVED HER MORE THAN HER GRANDMOTHER, WHO ONCE GAVE THE GIRL A RED VELVET CAP THAT SHE THEN WORE CONSTANTLY. ONE DAY, HER GRANDMOTHER FELL SICK AND HER MOTHER SENT LITTLE RED CAP TO BRING HER SOME CAKE AND WINE.
WHEN YOU GET TO GRANDMOTHER'S HOUSE IN THE FOREST, BE SURE TO SAY "GOOD MORNING" RIGHT AWAY! DON'T WASTE TIME PEERING AROUND THE HOUSE!
YES, MOTHER!
AND LISTEN CLOSELY, LITTLE RED CAP! WHEN YOU ARE OUT IN THE FOREST, DO NOT STRAY FROM THE PATH!
YES, MOTHER!
SHE HAD NOT BEEN WALKING IN THE FOREST LONG WHEN SHE MET THE WOLF. BUT LITTLE RED CAP WAS AN INNOCENT GIRL. SHE DID NOT SUSPECT WHAT A CRUEL AND VICIOUS WOLF HE WAS. SHE WASN'T AFRAID AT ALL.
GOOD MORNING, LITTLE RED CAP! WHERE ARE YOU OFF TO AT THIS EARLY HOUR?
TO GRAND-MOTHER'S HOUSE, GOOD MISTER WOLF!
AND WHAT HAVE WE HERE?
CAKE AND WINE FOR MY GRANDMOTHER! SHE IS FEELING SICK AND WEAK, AND THIS FOOD WILL GIVE HER STRENGTH!
I SEE
AS LITTLE RED CAP SKIPPED OFF, THE WOLF THOUGHT...
THAT TENDER YOUNG THING WILL MAKE A JUICY TREAT! SHE'LL TASTE BETTER THAN THE OLD LADY! IF I'M SMART ENOUGH, THEN PERHAPS...
...I CAN EAT THEM BOTH!

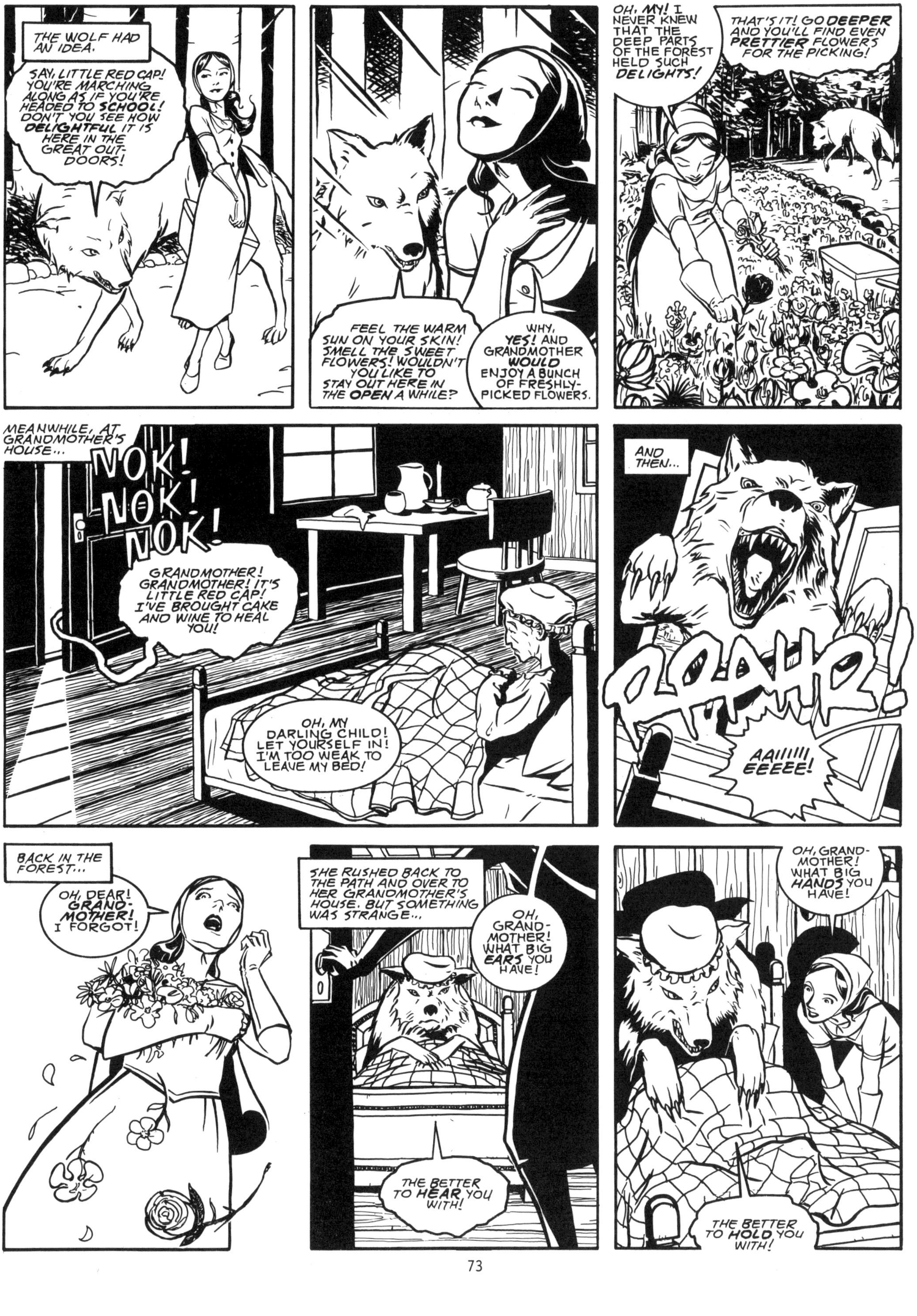

THE WOLF HAD AN IDEA.
SAY, LITTLE RED CAP! YOU'RE MARCHING ALONG AS IF YOU'RE HEADED TO SCHOOL! DON'T YOU SEE HOW DELIGHTFUL IT IS HERE IN THE GREAT OUT-DOORS!
FEEL THE WARM SUN ON YOUR SKIN! SMELL THE SWEET FLOWERS! WOULDN'T YOU LIKE TO STAY OUT HERE IN THE OPEN A WHILE?
WHY, YES! AND GRANDMOTHER WOULD ENJOY A BUNCH OF FRESHLY-PICKED FLOWERS.
OH, MY! I NEVER KNEW THAT THE DEEP PARTS OF THE FOREST HELD SUCH DELIGHTS!
THAT'S IT! GO DEEPER AND YOU'LL FIND EVEN PRETTIER FLOWERS FOR THE PICKING!
MEANWHILE, AT GRANDMOTHER'S HOUSE...
NOK! NOK! NOK!
GRANDMOTHER! GRANDMOTHER! IT'S LITTLE RED CAP! I'VE BROUGHT CAKE AND WINE TO HEAL YOU!
OH, MY DARLING CHILD! LET YOURSELF IN! I'M TOO WEAK TO LEAVE MY BED!
AND THEN...
ROAHR!
AAIIIII EEEEE!
BACK IN THE FOREST...
OH, DEAR! GRANDMOTHER! I FORGOT!
SHE RUSHED BACK TO THE PATH AND OVER TO HER GRANDMOTHER'S HOUSE. BUT SOMETHING WAS STRANGE...
OH, GRANDMOTHER! WHAT BIG EARS YOU HAVE!
THE BETTER TO HEAR YOU WITH!
OH, GRANDMOTHER! WHAT BIG HANDS YOU HAVE!
THE BETTER TO HOLD YOU WITH!

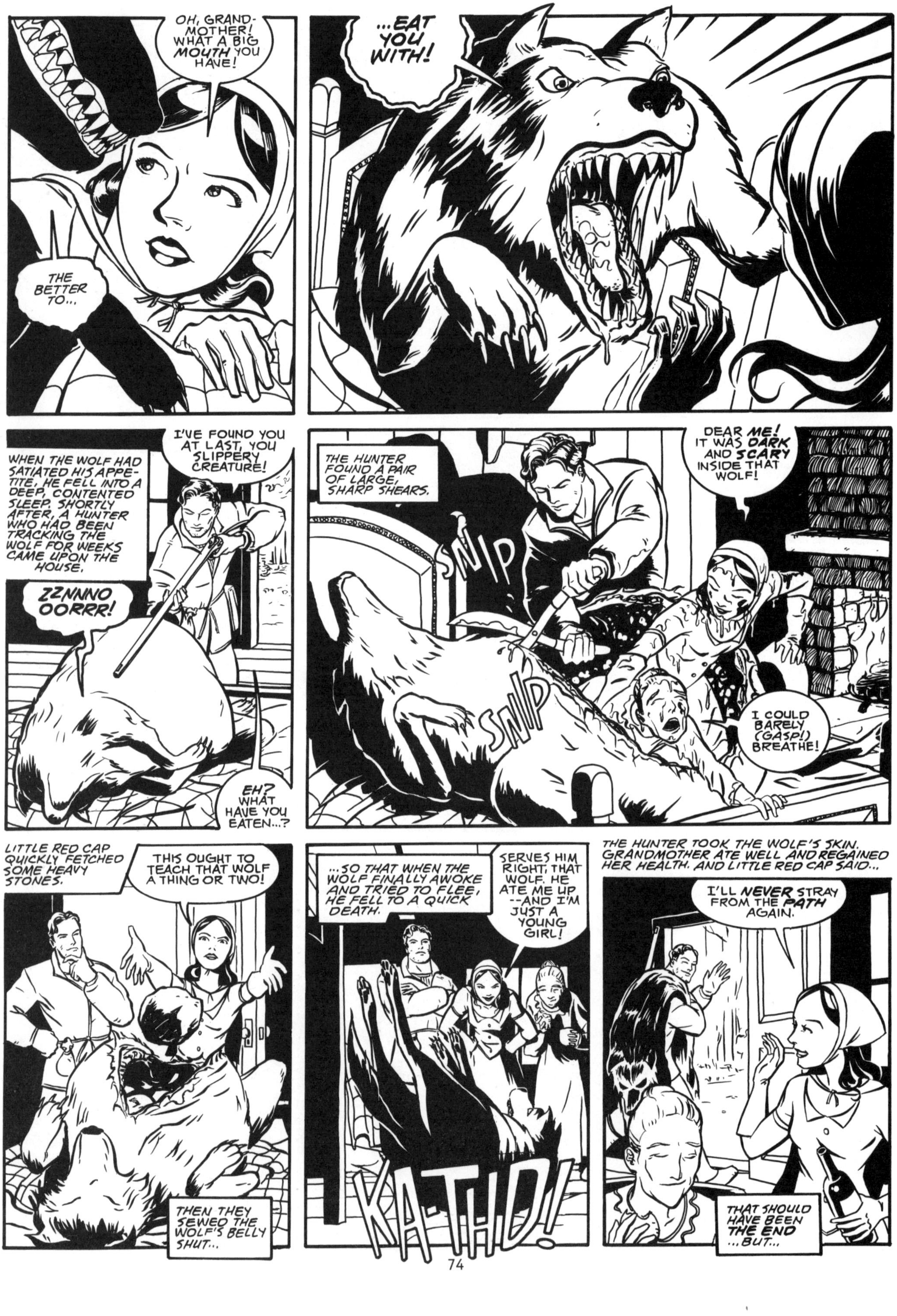

OH, GRAND-MOTHER! WHAT A BIG MOUTH YOU HAVE!
THE BETTER TO...
...EAT YOU WITH!
WHEN THE WOLF HAD SATIATED HIS APPETITE, HE FELL INTO A DEEP, CONTENTED SLEEP. SHORTLY AFTER, A HUNTER WHO HAD BEEN TRACKING THE WOLF FOR WEEKS CAME UPON THE HOUSE.
I'VE FOUND YOU AT LAST, YOU SLIPPERY CREATURE!
ZZNNNO OORRR!
EH? WHAT HAVE YOU EATEN...?
THE HUNTER FOUND A PAIR OF LARGE, SHARP SHEARS.
SNIP
SNIP
DEAR ME! IT WAS DARK AND SCARY INSIDE THAT WOLF!
I COULD BARELY (GASP!) BREATHE!
LITTLE RED CAP QUICKLY FETCHED SOME HEAVY STONES.
THIS OUGHT TO TEACH THAT WOLF A THING OR TWO!
THEN THEY SEWED THE WOLF'S BELLY SHUT...
...SO THAT WHEN THE WOLF FINALLY AWOKE AND TRIED TO FLEE, HE FELL TO A QUICK DEATH.
SERVES HIM RIGHT, THAT WOLF. HE ATE ME UP --AND I'M JUST A YOUNG GIRL!
KA-THD!
THE HUNTER TOOK THE WOLF'S SKIN. GRANDMOTHER ATE WELL AND REGAINED HER HEALTH. AND LITTLE RED CAP SAID...
I'LL NEVER STRAY FROM THE PATH AGAIN.
THAT SHOULD HAVE BEEN THE END ...BUT...

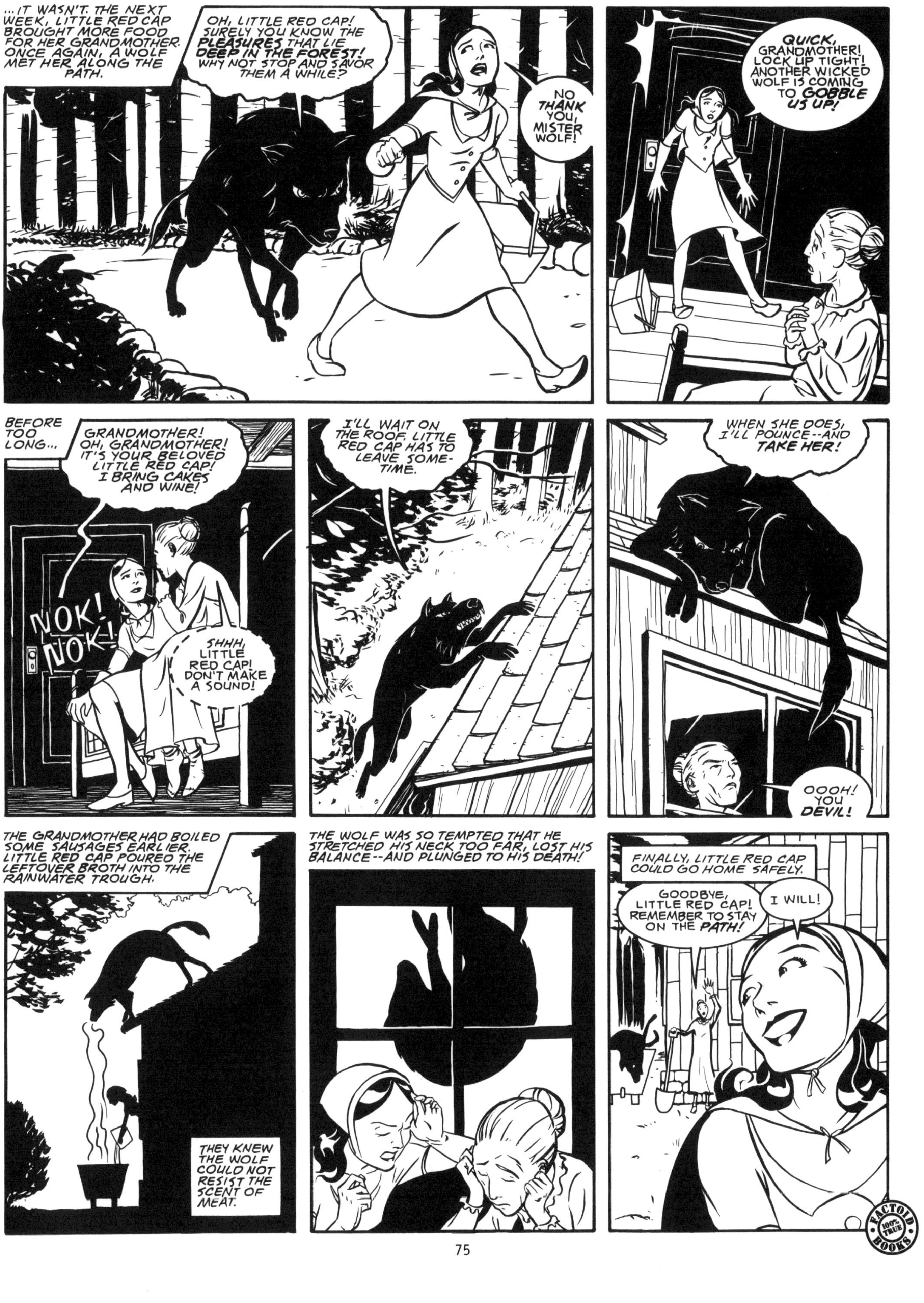
...IT WASN'T. THE NEXT WEEK, LITTLE RED CAP BROUGHT MORE FOOD FOR HER GRANDMOTHER. ONCE AGAIN, A WOLF MET HER ALONG THE PATH.
OH, LITTLE RED CAP! SURELY YOU KNOW THE PLEASURES THAT LIE DEEP IN THE FOREST! WHY NOT STOP AND SAVOR THEM A WHILE?
NO THANK YOU, MISTER WOLF!
QUICK, GRANDMOTHER! LOCK UP TIGHT! ANOTHER WICKED WOLF IS COMING TO GOBBLE US UP!
BEFORE TOO LONG...
GRANDMOTHER! OH, GRANDMOTHER! IT'S YOUR BELOVED LITTLE RED CAP! I BRING CAKES AND WINE!
NOK! NOK!
SHHH, LITTLE RED CAP! DON'T MAKE A SOUND!
I'LL WAIT ON THE ROOF. LITTLE RED CAP HAS TO LEAVE SOME-TIME.
WHEN SHE DOES, I'LL POUNCE--AND TAKE HER!
OOOH! YOU DEVIL!
THE GRANDMOTHER HAD BOILED SOME SAUSAGES EARLIER. LITTLE RED CAP POURED THE LEFTOVER BROTH INTO THE RAINWATER TROUGH.
THEY KNEW THE WOLF COULD NOT RESIST THE SCENT OF MEAT.
THE WOLF WAS SO TEMPTED THAT HE STRETCHED HIS NECK TOO FAR, LOST HIS BALANCE--AND PLUNGED TO HIS DEATH!
FINALLY, LITTLE RED CAP COULD GO HOME SAFELY.
GOODBYE, LITTLE RED CAP! REMEMBER TO STAY ON THE PATH!
I WILL!
FACTOID 100% TRUE BOOKS

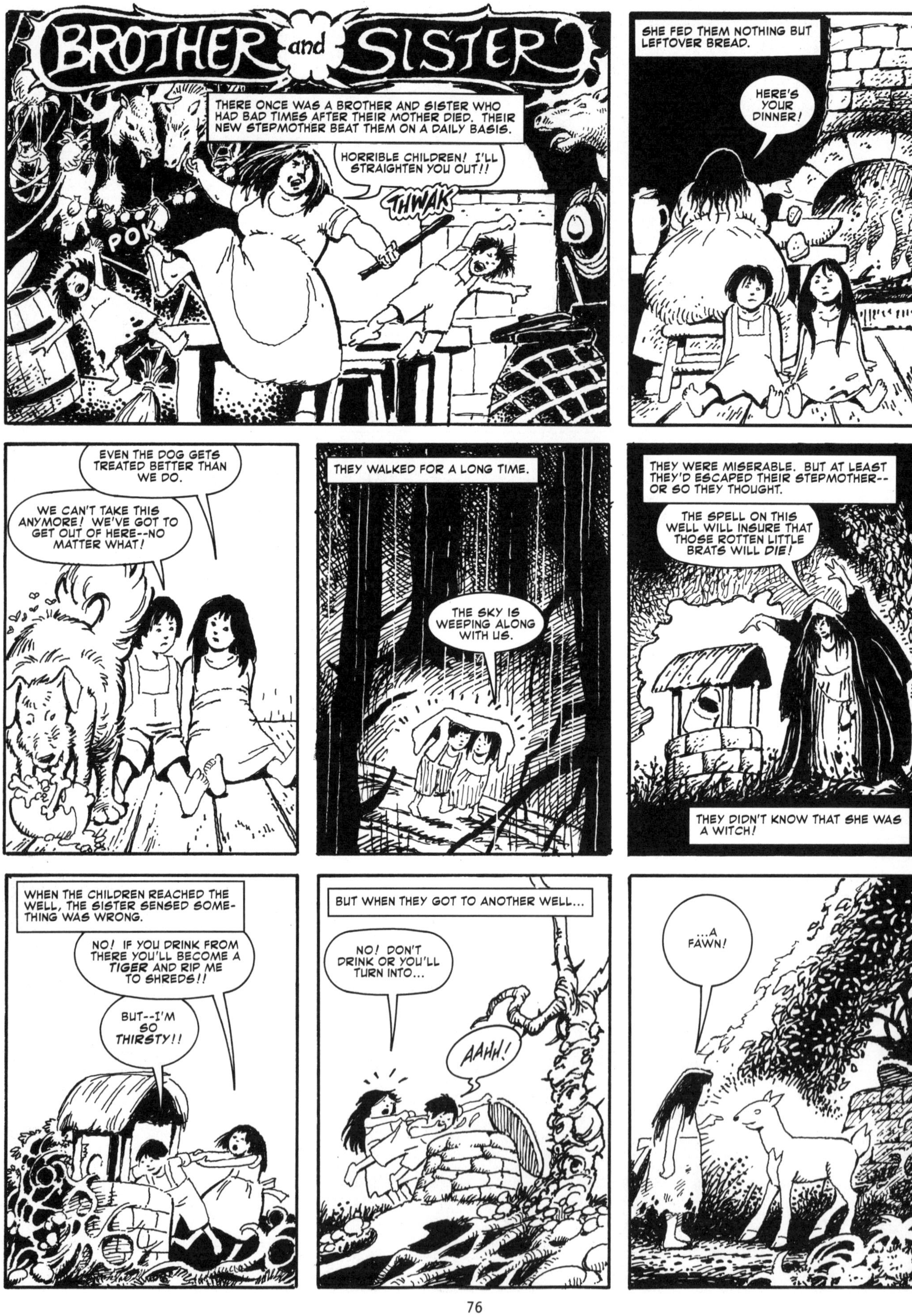
BROTHER and SISTER
THERE ONCE WAS A BROTHER AND SISTER WHO HAD BAD TIMES AFTER THEIR MOTHER DIED. THEIR NEW STEPMOTHER BEAT THEM ON A DAILY BASIS.
HORRIBLE CHILDREN! I'LL STRAIGHTEN YOU OUT!!
THWAK
POK
SHE FED THEM NOTHING BUT LEFTOVER BREAD.
HERE'S YOUR DINNER!
EVEN THE DOG GETS TREATED BETTER THAN WE DO.
WE CAN'T TAKE THIS ANYMORE! WE'VE GOT TO GET OUT OF HERE--NO MATTER WHAT!
THEY WALKED FOR A LONG TIME.
THE SKY IS WEEPING ALONG WITH US.
THEY WERE MISERABLE. BUT AT LEAST THEY'D ESCAPED THEIR STEPMOTHER--OR SO THEY THOUGHT.
THE SPELL ON THIS WELL WILL INSURE THAT THOSE ROTTEN LITTLE BRATS WILL DIE!
THEY DIDN'T KNOW THAT SHE WAS A WITCH!
WHEN THE CHILDREN REACHED THE WELL, THE SISTER SENSED SOMETHING WAS WRONG.
NO! IF YOU DRINK FROM THERE YOU'LL BECOME A TIGER AND RIP ME TO SHREDS!!
BUT--I'M SO THIRSTY!!
BUT WHEN THEY GOT TO ANOTHER WELL...
NO! DON'T DRINK OR YOU'LL TURN INTO...
AAHH!
...A FAWN!

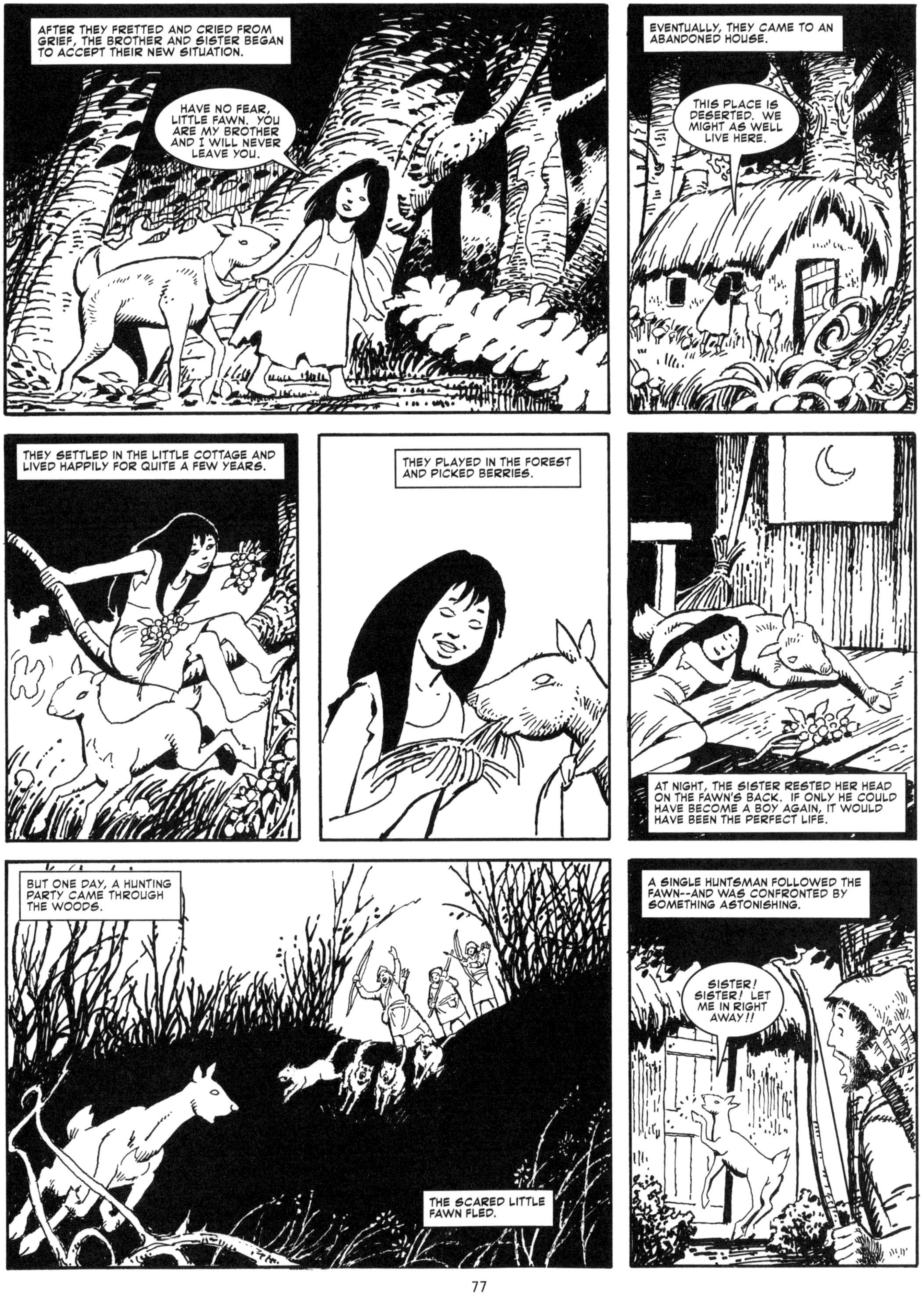
AFTER THEY FRETTED AND CRIED FROM GRIEF, THE BROTHER AND SISTER BEGAN TO ACCEPT THEIR NEW SITUATION.
HAVE NO FEAR, LITTLE FAWN. YOU ARE MY BROTHER AND I WILL NEVER LEAVE YOU.
EVENTUALLY, THEY CAME TO AN ABANDONED HOUSE.
THIS PLACE IS DESERTED. WE MIGHT AS WELL LIVE HERE.
THEY SETTLED IN THE LITTLE COTTAGE AND LIVED HAPPILY FOR QUITE A FEW YEARS.
THEY PLAYED IN THE FOREST AND PICKED BERRIES.
AT NIGHT, THE SISTER RESTED HER HEAD ON THE FAWN'S BACK. IF ONLY HE COULD HAVE BECOME A BOY AGAIN, IT WOULD HAVE BEEN THE PERFECT LIFE.
BUT ONE DAY, A HUNTING PARTY CAME THROUGH THE WOODS.
THE SCARED LITTLE FAWN FLED.
A SINGLE HUNTSMAN FOLLOWED THE FAWN--AND WAS CONFRONTED BY SOMETHING ASTONISHING.
SISTER! SISTER! LET ME IN RIGHT AWAY!!

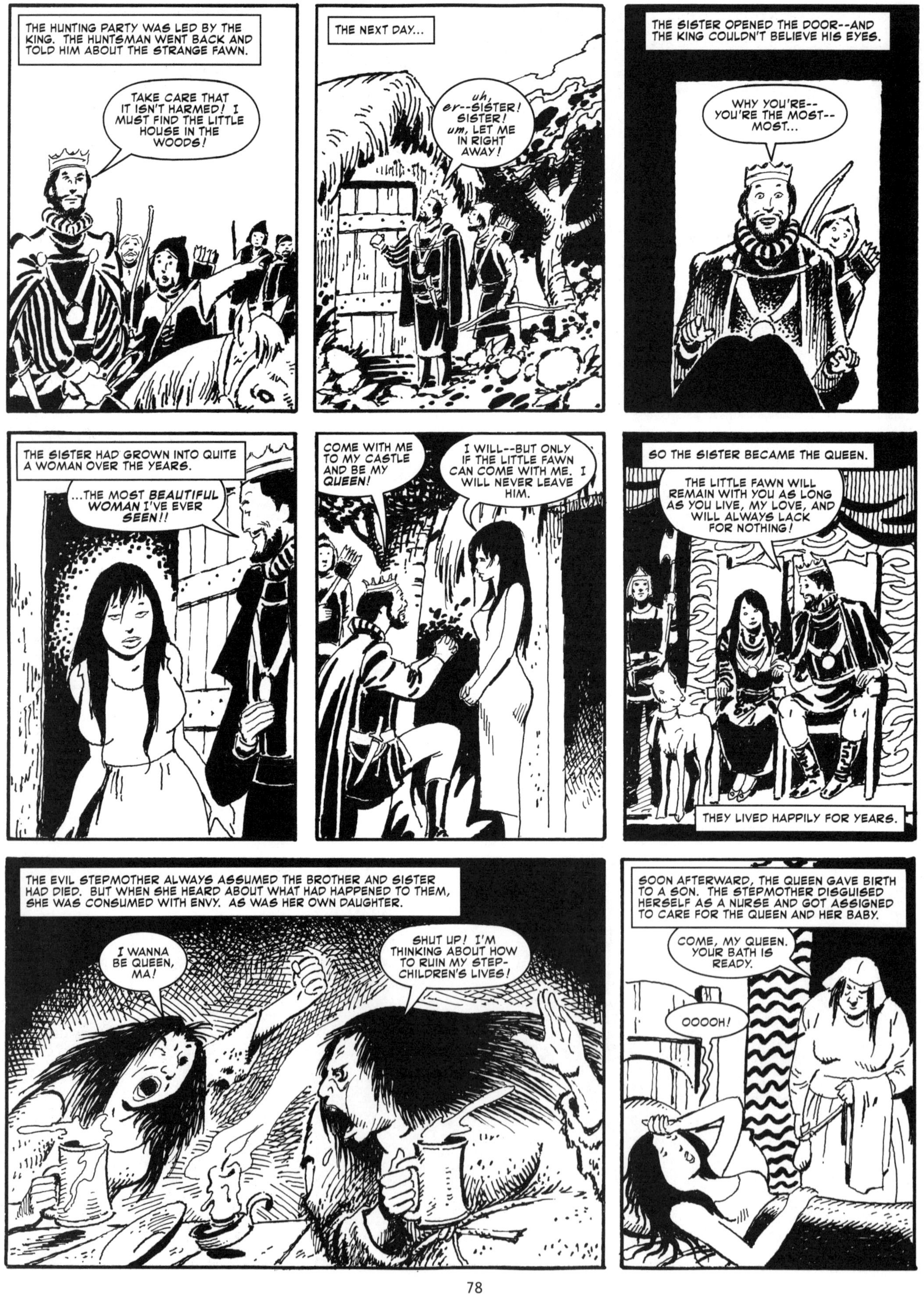
THE HUNTING PARTY WAS LED BY THE KING. THE HUNTSMAN WENT BACK AND TOLD HIM ABOUT THE STRANGE FAWN.
TAKE CARE THAT IT ISN'T HARMED! I MUST FIND THE LITTLE HOUSE IN THE WOODS!
THE NEXT DAY...
uh, er--SISTER! SISTER! um, LET ME IN RIGHT AWAY!
THE SISTER OPENED THE DOOR--AND THE KING COULDN'T BELIEVE HIS EYES.
WHY YOU'RE-- YOU'RE THE MOST-- MOST...
THE SISTER HAD GROWN INTO QUITE A WOMAN OVER THE YEARS.
...THE MOST BEAUTIFUL WOMAN I'VE EVER SEEN!!
COME WITH ME TO MY CASTLE AND BE MY QUEEN!
I WILL--BUT ONLY IF THE LITTLE FAWN CAN COME WITH ME. I WILL NEVER LEAVE HIM.
SO THE SISTER BECAME THE QUEEN.
THE LITTLE FAWN WILL REMAIN WITH YOU AS LONG AS YOU LIVE, MY LOVE, AND WILL ALWAYS LACK FOR NOTHING!
THEY LIVED HAPPILY FOR YEARS.
THE EVIL STEPMOTHER ALWAYS ASSUMED THE BROTHER AND SISTER HAD DIED. BUT WHEN SHE HEARD ABOUT WHAT HAD HAPPENED TO THEM, SHE WAS CONSUMED WITH ENVY. AS WAS HER OWN DAUGHTER.
I WANNA BE QUEEN, MA!
SHUT UP! I'M THINKING ABOUT HOW TO RUIN MY STEP-CHILDREN'S LIVES!
SOON AFTERWARD, THE QUEEN GAVE BIRTH TO A SON. THE STEPMOTHER DISGUISED HERSELF AS A NURSE AND GOT ASSIGNED TO CARE FOR THE QUEEN AND HER BABY.
COME, MY QUEEN. YOUR BATH IS READY.
OOOOH!

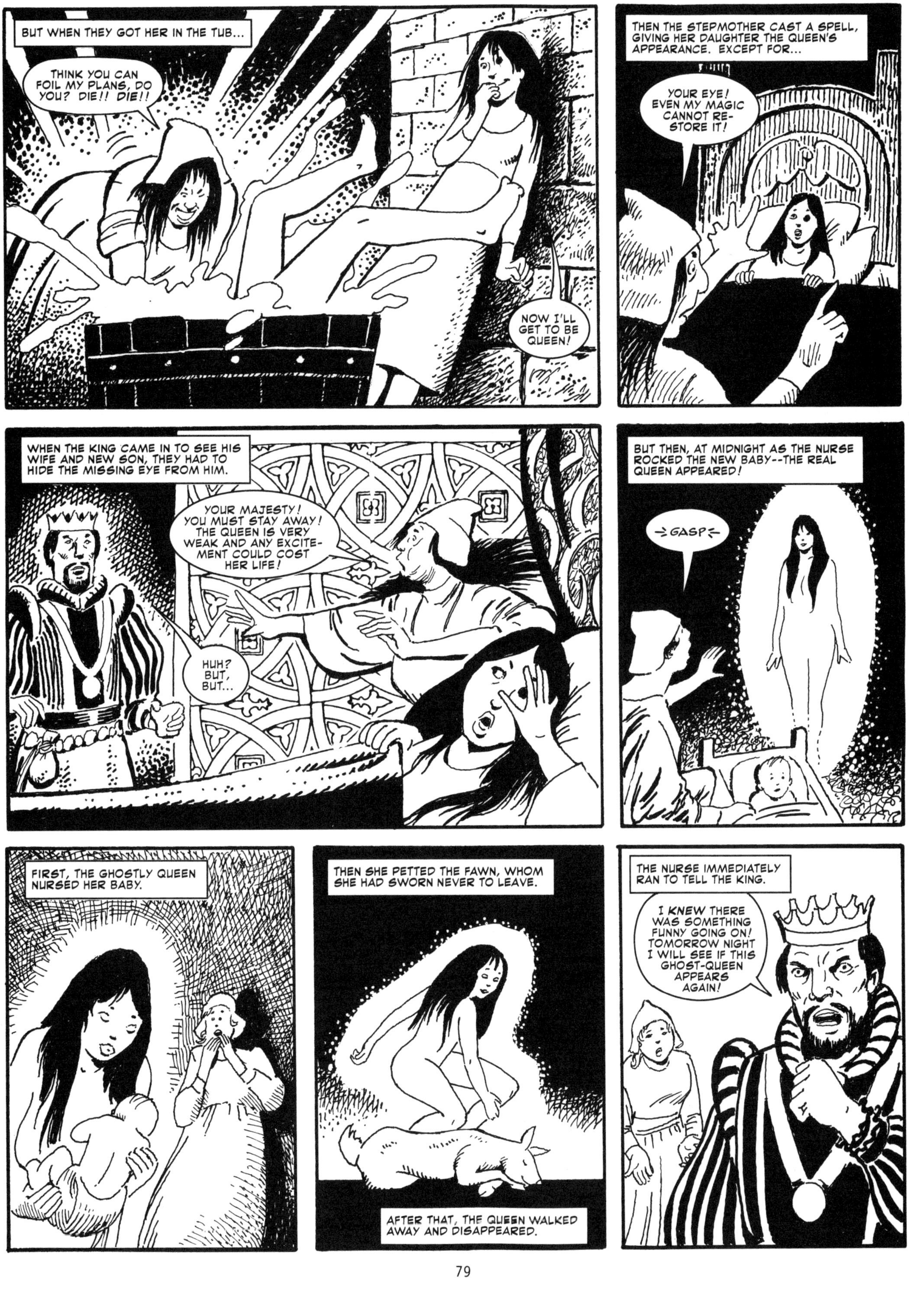
BUT WHEN THEY GOT HER IN THE TUB...
THINK YOU CAN FOIL MY PLANS, DO YOU? DIE!! DIE!!
NOW I'LL GET TO BE QUEEN!
THEN THE STEPMOTHER CAST A SPELL, GIVING HER DAUGHTER THE QUEEN'S APPEARANCE. EXCEPT FOR...
YOUR EYE! EVEN MY MAGIC CANNOT RE-STORE IT!
WHEN THE KING CAME IN TO SEE HIS WIFE AND NEW SON, THEY HAD TO HIDE THE MISSING EYE FROM HIM.
YOUR MAJESTY! YOU MUST STAY AWAY! THE QUEEN IS VERY WEAK AND ANY EXCITE-MENT COULD COST HER LIFE!
HUH? BUT, BUT...
BUT THEN, AT MIDNIGHT AS THE NURSE ROCKED THE NEW BABY--THE REAL QUEEN APPEARED!
GASP
FIRST, THE GHOSTLY QUEEN NURSED HER BABY.
THEN SHE PETTED THE FAWN, WHOM SHE HAD SWORN NEVER TO LEAVE.
AFTER THAT, THE QUEEN WALKED AWAY AND DISAPPEARED.
THE NURSE IMMEDIATELY RAN TO TELL THE KING.
I KNEW THERE WAS SOMETHING FUNNY GOING ON! TOMORROW NIGHT I WILL SEE IF THIS GHOST-QUEEN APPEARS AGAIN!

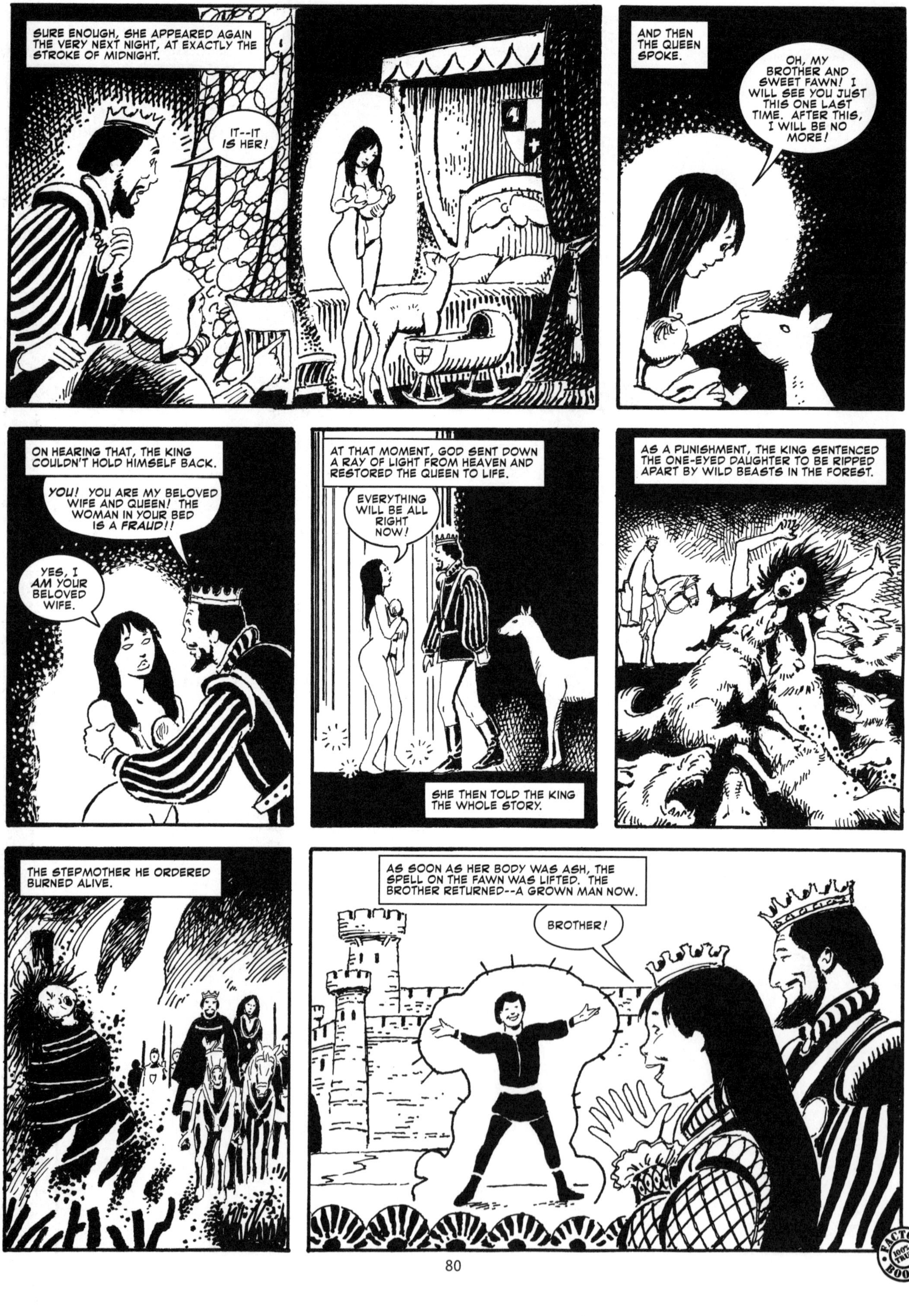

SURE ENOUGH, SHE APPEARED AGAIN THE VERY NEXT NIGHT, AT EXACTLY THE STROKE OF MIDNIGHT.
IT--IT IS HER!
AND THEN THE QUEEN SPOKE.
OH, MY BROTHER AND SWEET FAWN! I WILL SEE YOU JUST THIS ONE LAST TIME. AFTER THIS, I WILL BE NO MORE!
ON HEARING THAT, THE KING COULDN'T HOLD HIMSELF BACK.
YOU! YOU ARE MY BELOVED WIFE AND QUEEN! THE WOMAN IN YOUR BED IS A FRAUD!!
YES, I AM YOUR BELOVED WIFE.
AT THAT MOMENT, GOD SENT DOWN A RAY OF LIGHT FROM HEAVEN AND RESTORED THE QUEEN TO LIFE.
EVERYTHING WILL BE ALL RIGHT NOW!
SHE THEN TOLD THE KING THE WHOLE STORY.
AS A PUNISHMENT, THE KING SENTENCED THE ONE-EYED DAUGHTER TO BE RIPPED APART BY WILD BEASTS IN THE FOREST.
THE STEPMOTHER HE ORDERED BURNED ALIVE.
AS SOON AS HER BODY WAS ASH, THE SPELL ON THE FAWN WAS LIFTED. THE BROTHER RETURNED--A GROWN MAN NOW.
BROTHER!

CHAPTER THREE

NUPTIAL NIGHTMARES

" 'Til death do us part." You ain't kidding! There's nothing romantic about marriage in this genre of Grimms' tales. Pity the poor damsel approaching matrimony. Her betrothed is as likely to be a mass murderer — and one who makes Jeffrey Dahmer look like Cap'n Crunch — as Prince Charming. That's the miserable fate of the brides-to-be in "The Robber Bridegroom" or "Fitcher's Bird." If she's coerced to the matrimonial bed by an incestuous father, as in "Allerleirauh," at least she hasn't been eaten in a stew. There are stories in this category of perilous journeys to marriage that end well, some even with the words: "And they all lived happily ever after." The Grimm brothers were very likely interested in picking these stories to fit with their Christian religious beliefs which highlighted the sanctity of marriage. But they also presented a hope that despite the potential dangers of childhood and family, despite the psychotic spouses and lurid lovers out there, you still have a chance of growing up and finding a love that will veer away from that path of cruelty and brutality and into a more peaceful life.

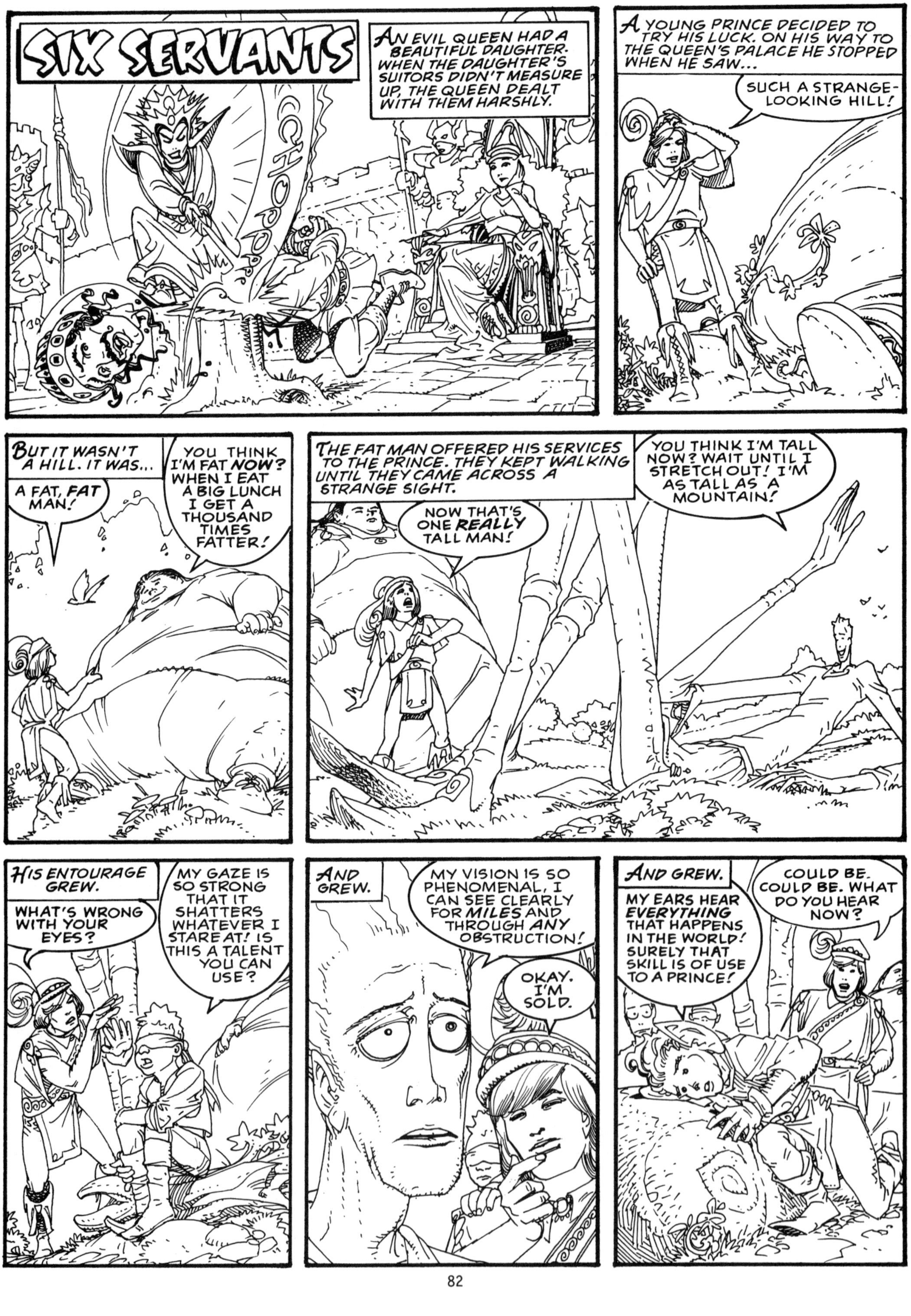
SIX SERVANTS
AN EVIL QUEEN HAD A BEAUTIFUL DAUGHTER. WHEN THE DAUGHTER'S SUITORS DIDN'T MEASURE UP, THE QUEEN DEALT WITH THEM HARSHLY.
A YOUNG PRINCE DECIDED TO TRY HIS LUCK. ON HIS WAY TO THE QUEEN'S PALACE HE STOPPED WHEN HE SAW...
SUCH A STRANGE-LOOKING HILL!
BUT IT WASN'T A HILL. IT WAS...
A FAT, FAT MAN!
YOU THINK I'M FAT NOW? WHEN I EAT A BIG LUNCH I GET A THOUSAND TIMES FATTER!
THE FAT MAN OFFERED HIS SERVICES TO THE PRINCE. THEY KEPT WALKING UNTIL THEY CAME ACROSS A STRANGE SIGHT.
NOW THAT'S ONE REALLY TALL MAN!
YOU THINK I'M TALL NOW? WAIT UNTIL I STRETCH OUT! I'M AS TALL AS A MOUNTAIN!
HIS ENTOURAGE GREW.
WHAT'S WRONG WITH YOUR EYES?
MY GAZE IS SO STRONG THAT IT SHATTERS WHATEVER I STARE AT! IS THIS A TALENT YOU CAN USE?
AND GREW.
MY VISION IS SO PHENOMENAL, I CAN SEE CLEARLY FOR MILES AND THROUGH ANY OBSTRUCTION!
OKAY. I'M SOLD.
AND GREW.
MY EARS HEAR EVERYTHING THAT HAPPENS IN THE WORLD! SURELY THAT SKILL IS OF USE TO A PRINCE!
COULD BE. COULD BE. WHAT DO YOU HEAR NOW?

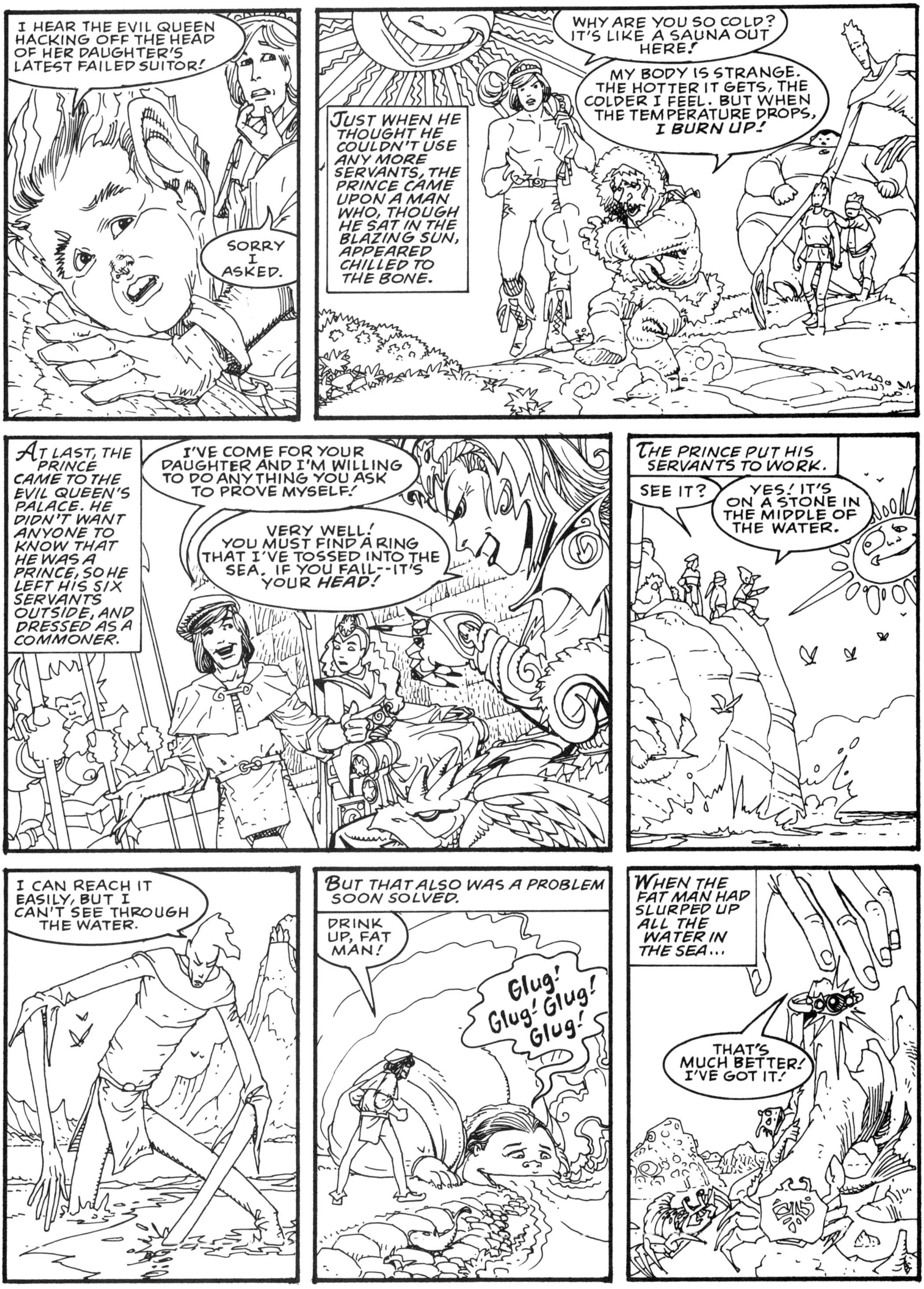
I HEAR THE EVIL QUEEN HACKING OFF THE HEAD OF HER DAUGHTER'S LATEST FAILED SUITOR!
SORRY I ASKED.
JUST WHEN HE THOUGHT HE COULDN'T USE ANY MORE SERVANTS, THE PRINCE CAME UPON A MAN WHO, THOUGH HE SAT IN THE BLAZING SUN, APPEARED CHILLED TO THE BONE.
WHY ARE YOU SO COLD? IT'S LIKE A SAUNA OUT HERE!
MY BODY IS STRANGE. THE HOTTER IT GETS, THE COLDER I FEEL. BUT WHEN THE TEMPERATURE DROPS, I BURN UP!
AT LAST, THE PRINCE CAME TO THE EVIL QUEEN'S PALACE. HE DIDN'T WANT ANYONE TO KNOW THAT HE WAS A PRINCE, SO HE LEFT HIS SIX SERVANTS OUTSIDE, AND DRESSED AS A COMMONER.
I'VE COME FOR YOUR DAUGHTER AND I'M WILLING TO DO ANYTHING YOU ASK TO PROVE MYSELF!
VERY WELL! YOU MUST FIND A RING THAT I'VE TOSSED INTO THE SEA. IF YOU FAIL--IT'S YOUR HEAD!
THE PRINCE PUT HIS SERVANTS TO WORK.
SEE IT?
YES! IT'S ON A STONE IN THE MIDDLE OF THE WATER.
I CAN REACH IT EASILY, BUT I CAN'T SEE THROUGH THE WATER.
BUT THAT ALSO WAS A PROBLEM SOON SOLVED.
DRINK UP, FAT MAN!
Glug! Glug! Glug! Glug!
WHEN THE FAT MAN HAD SLURPED UP ALL THE WATER IN THE SEA...
THAT'S MUCH BETTER! I'VE GOT IT!

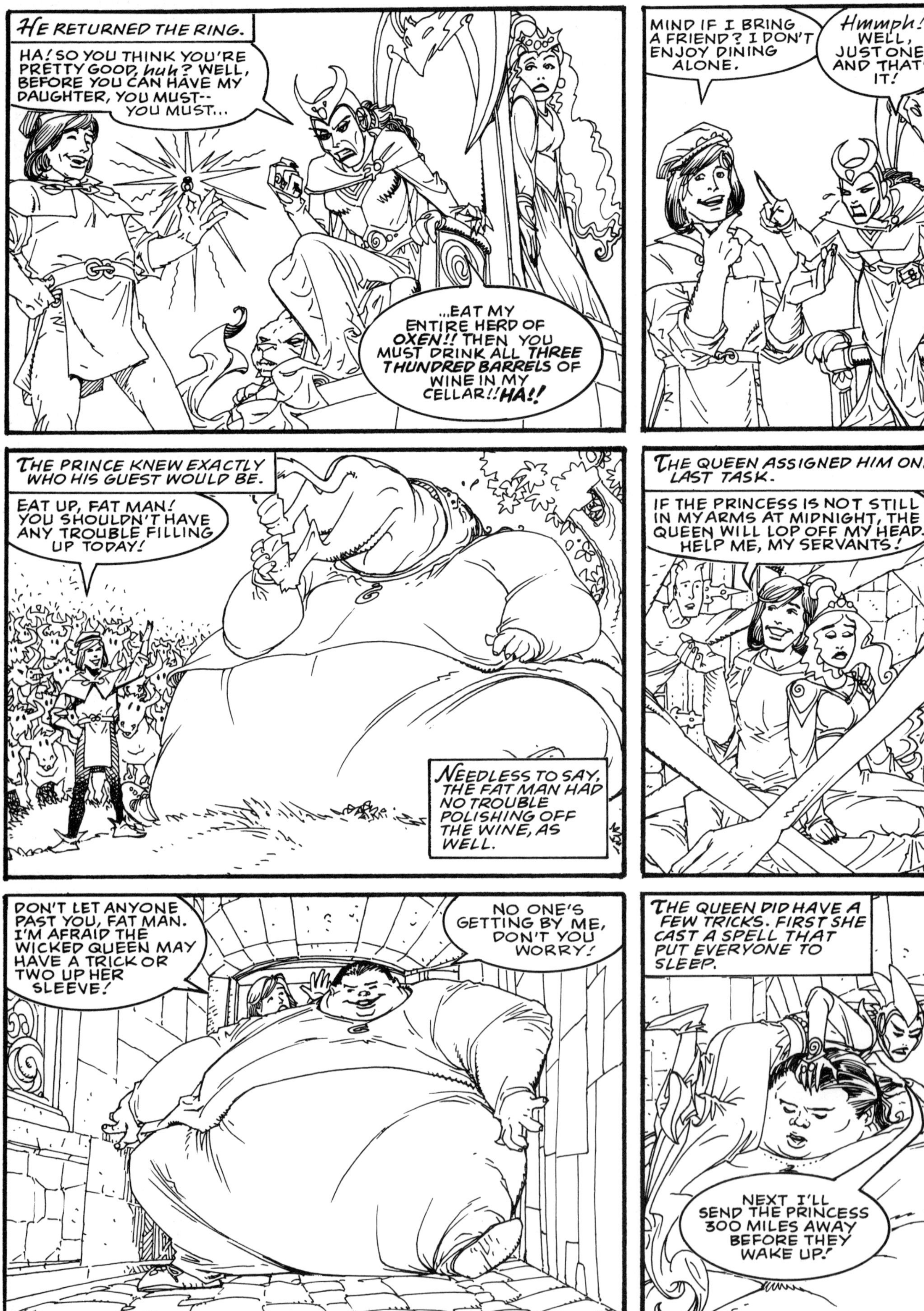
HE RETURNED THE RING.
HA! SO YOU THINK YOU'RE PRETTY GOOD, huh? WELL, BEFORE YOU CAN HAVE MY DAUGHTER, YOU MUST-- YOU MUST...
...EAT MY ENTIRE HERD OF OXEN!! THEN YOU MUST DRINK ALL THREE THUNDRED BARRELS OF WINE IN MY CELLAR!! HA!!
MIND IF I BRING A FRIEND? I DON'T ENJOY DINING ALONE.
Hmmph! WELL, JUST ONE AND THAT'S IT!
THE PRINCE KNEW EXACTLY WHO HIS GUEST WOULD BE.
EAT UP, FAT MAN! YOU SHOULDN'T HAVE ANY TROUBLE FILLING UP TODAY!
NEEDLESS TO SAY, THE FAT MAN HAD NO TROUBLE POLISHING OFF THE WINE, AS WELL.
THE QUEEN ASSIGNED HIM ONE LAST TASK.
IF THE PRINCESS IS NOT STILL IN MY ARMS AT MIDNIGHT, THE QUEEN WILL LOP OFF MY HEAD! HELP ME, MY SERVANTS!
DON'T LET ANYONE PAST YOU, FAT MAN. I'M AFRAID THE WICKED QUEEN MAY HAVE A TRICK OR TWO UP HER SLEEVE!
NO ONE'S GETTING BY ME, DON'T YOU WORRY!
THE QUEEN DID HAVE A FEW TRICKS. FIRST SHE CAST A SPELL THAT PUT EVERYONE TO SLEEP.
NEXT I'LL SEND THE PRINCESS 300 MILES AWAY BEFORE THEY WAKE UP!

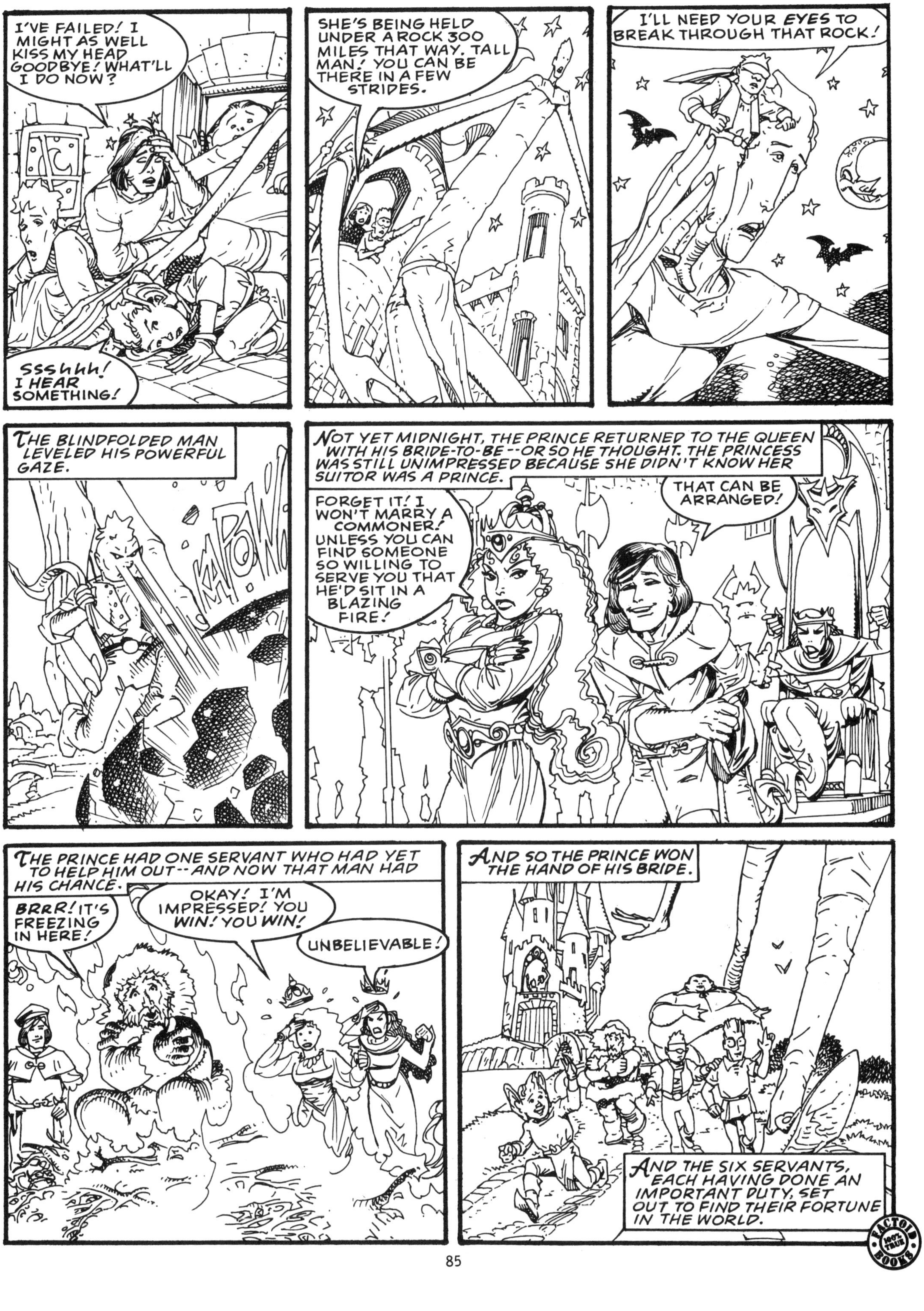

I'VE FAILED! I MIGHT AS WELL KISS MY HEAD GOODBYE! WHAT'LL I DO NOW?
SSSHHH! I HEAR SOMETHING!
SHE'S BEING HELD UNDER A ROCK 300 MILES THAT WAY. TALL MAN! YOU CAN BE THERE IN A FEW STRIDES.
I'LL NEED YOUR EYES TO BREAK THROUGH THAT ROCK!
THE BLINDFOLDED MAN LEVELED HIS POWERFUL GAZE.
KAPOW!
NOT YET MIDNIGHT, THE PRINCE RETURNED TO THE QUEEN WITH HIS BRIDE-TO-BE--OR SO HE THOUGHT. THE PRINCESS WAS STILL UNIMPRESSED BECAUSE SHE DIDN'T KNOW HER SUITOR WAS A PRINCE.
FORGET IT! I WON'T MARRY A COMMONER! UNLESS YOU CAN FIND SOMEONE SO WILLING TO SERVE YOU THAT HE'D SIT IN A BLAZING FIRE!
THAT CAN BE ARRANGED!
THE PRINCE HAD ONE SERVANT WHO HAD YET TO HELP HIM OUT--AND NOW THAT MAN HAD HIS CHANCE.
BRRR! IT'S FREEZING IN HERE!
OKAY! I'M IMPRESSED! YOU WIN! YOU WIN!
UNBELIEVABLE!
AND SO THE PRINCE WON THE HAND OF HIS BRIDE.
AND THE SIX SERVANTS, EACH HAVING DONE AN IMPORTANT DUTY, SET OUT TO FIND THEIR FORTUNE IN THE WORLD.

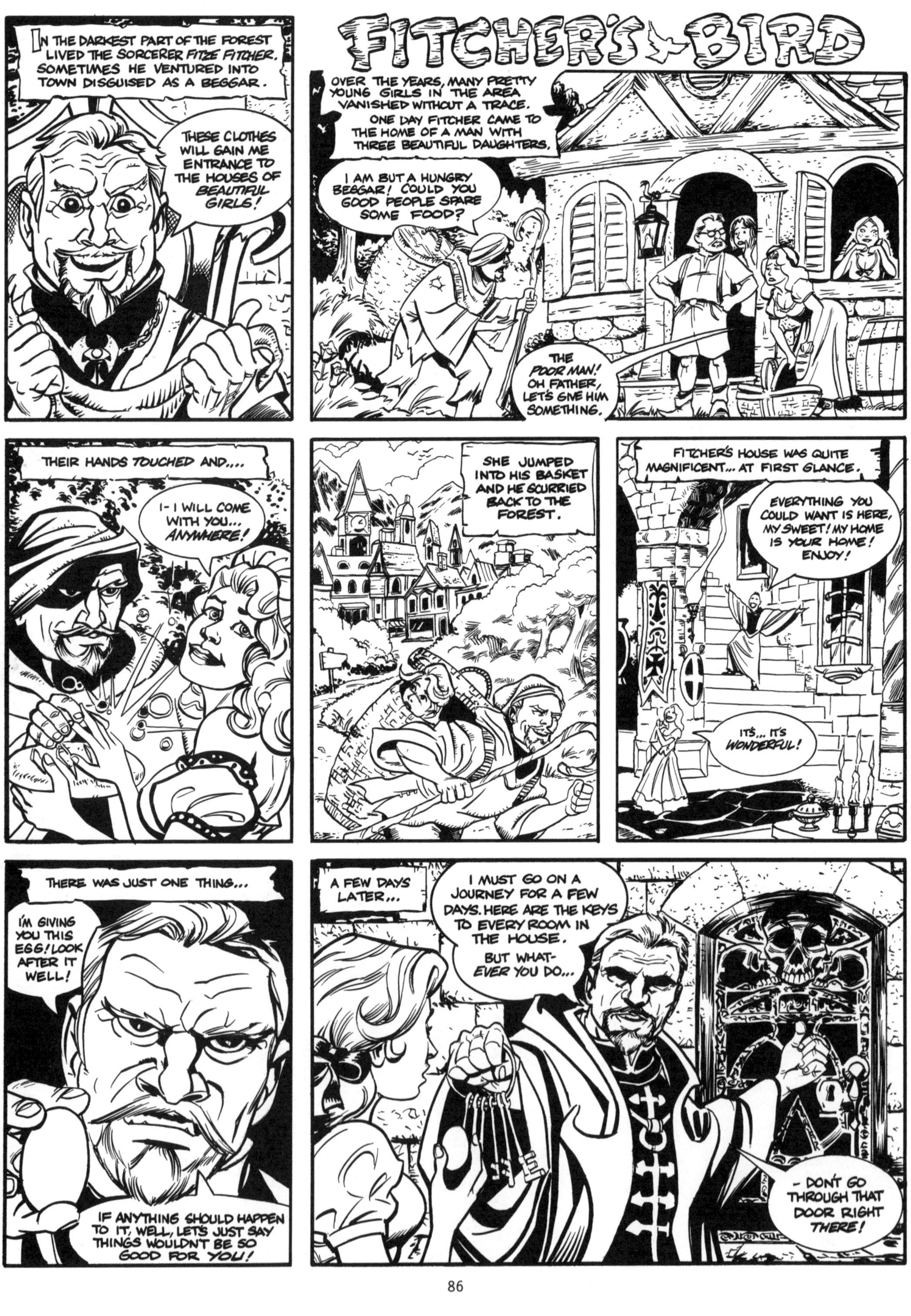

IN THE DARKEST PART OF THE FOREST LIVED THE SORCERER FITZE FITCHER. SOMETIMES HE VENTURED INTO TOWN DISGUISED AS A BEGGAR.
THESE CLOTHES WILL GAIN ME ENTRANCE TO THE HOUSES OF BEAUTIFUL GIRLS!
FITCHER'S BIRD
OVER THE YEARS, MANY PRETTY YOUNG GIRLS IN THE AREA VANISHED WITHOUT A TRACE.
ONE DAY FITCHER CAME TO THE HOME OF A MAN WITH THREE BEAUTIFUL DAUGHTERS.
I AM BUT A HUNGRY BEGGAR! COULD YOU GOOD PEOPLE SPARE SOME FOOD?
THE POOR MAN! OH FATHER, LET'S GIVE HIM SOMETHING.
THEIR HANDS TOUCHED AND....
I- I WILL COME WITH YOU... ANYWHERE!
SHE JUMPED INTO HIS BASKET AND HE SCURRIED BACK TO THE FOREST.
FITCHER'S HOUSE WAS QUITE MAGNIFICENT... AT FIRST GLANCE.
EVERYTHING YOU COULD WANT IS HERE, MY SWEET! MY HOME IS YOUR HOME! ENJOY!
IT'S... IT'S WONDERFUL!
THERE WAS JUST ONE THING...
I'M GIVING YOU THIS EGG! LOOK AFTER IT WELL!
IF ANYTHING SHOULD HAPPEN TO IT, WELL, LET'S JUST SAY THINGS WOULDN'T BE SO GOOD FOR YOU!
A FEW DAYS LATER...
I MUST GO ON A JOURNEY FOR A FEW DAYS. HERE ARE THE KEYS TO EVERY ROOM IN THE HOUSE.
BUT WHAT-EVER YOU DO...
- DON'T GO THROUGH THAT DOOR RIGHT THERE!

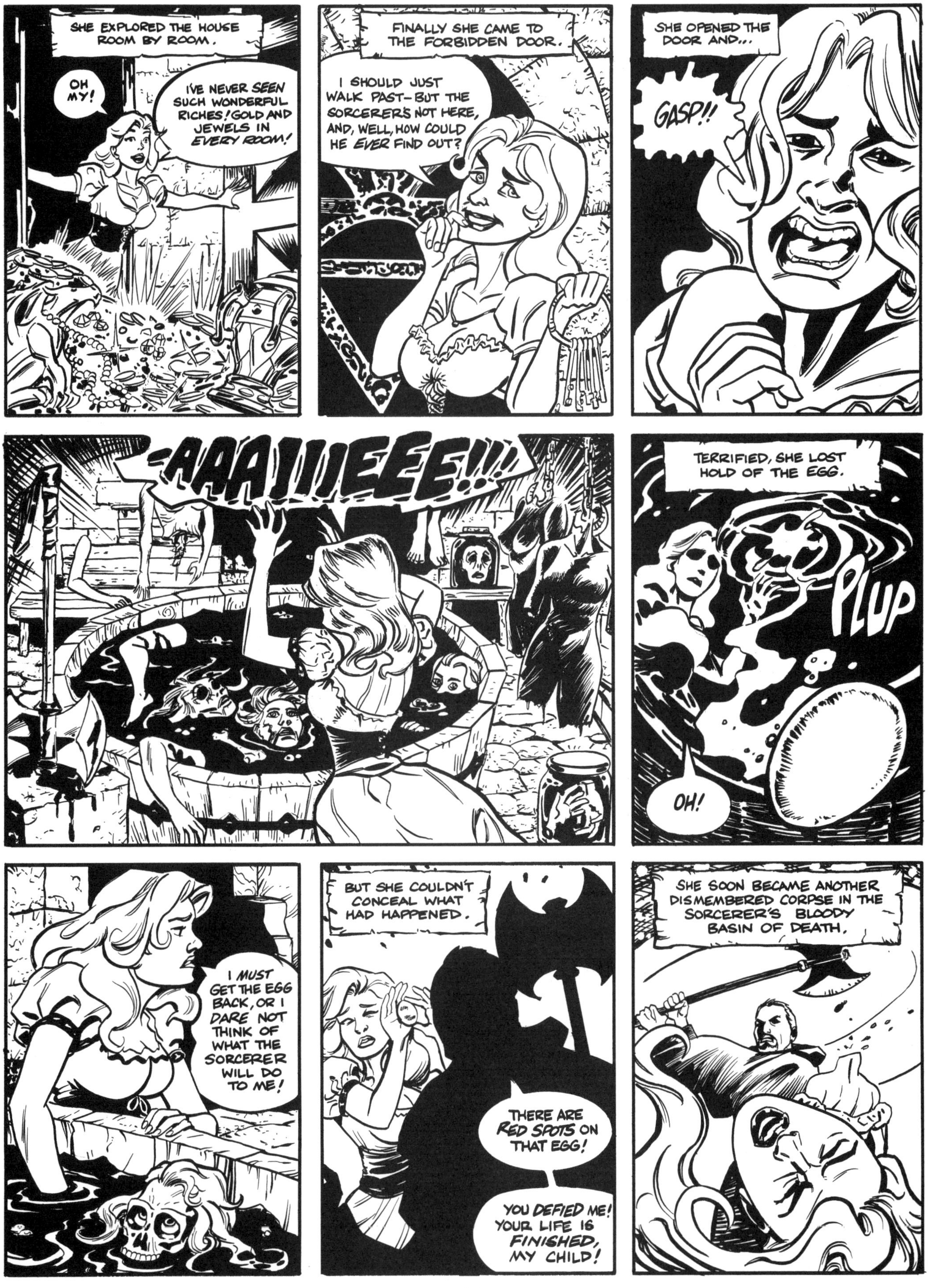
SHE EXPLORED THE HOUSE ROOM BY ROOM.
OH MY!
I'VE NEVER SEEN SUCH WONDERFUL RICHES! GOLD AND JEWELS IN EVERY ROOM!
FINALLY SHE CAME TO THE FORBIDDEN DOOR.
I SHOULD JUST WALK PAST—BUT THE SORCERER'S NOT HERE, AND, WELL, HOW COULD HE EVER FIND OUT?
SHE OPENED THE DOOR AND...
GASP!!
-AAAIIIEEEE!!!
TERRIFIED, SHE LOST HOLD OF THE EGG.
PLUP
OH!
I MUST GET THE EGG BACK, OR I DARE NOT THINK OF WHAT THE SORCERER WILL DO TO ME!
BUT SHE COULDN'T CONCEAL WHAT HAD HAPPENED.
THERE ARE RED SPOTS ON THAT EGG!
YOU DEFIED ME! YOUR LIFE IS FINISHED, MY CHILD!
SHE SOON BECAME ANOTHER DISMEMBERED CORPSE IN THE SORCERER'S BLOODY BASIN OF DEATH.

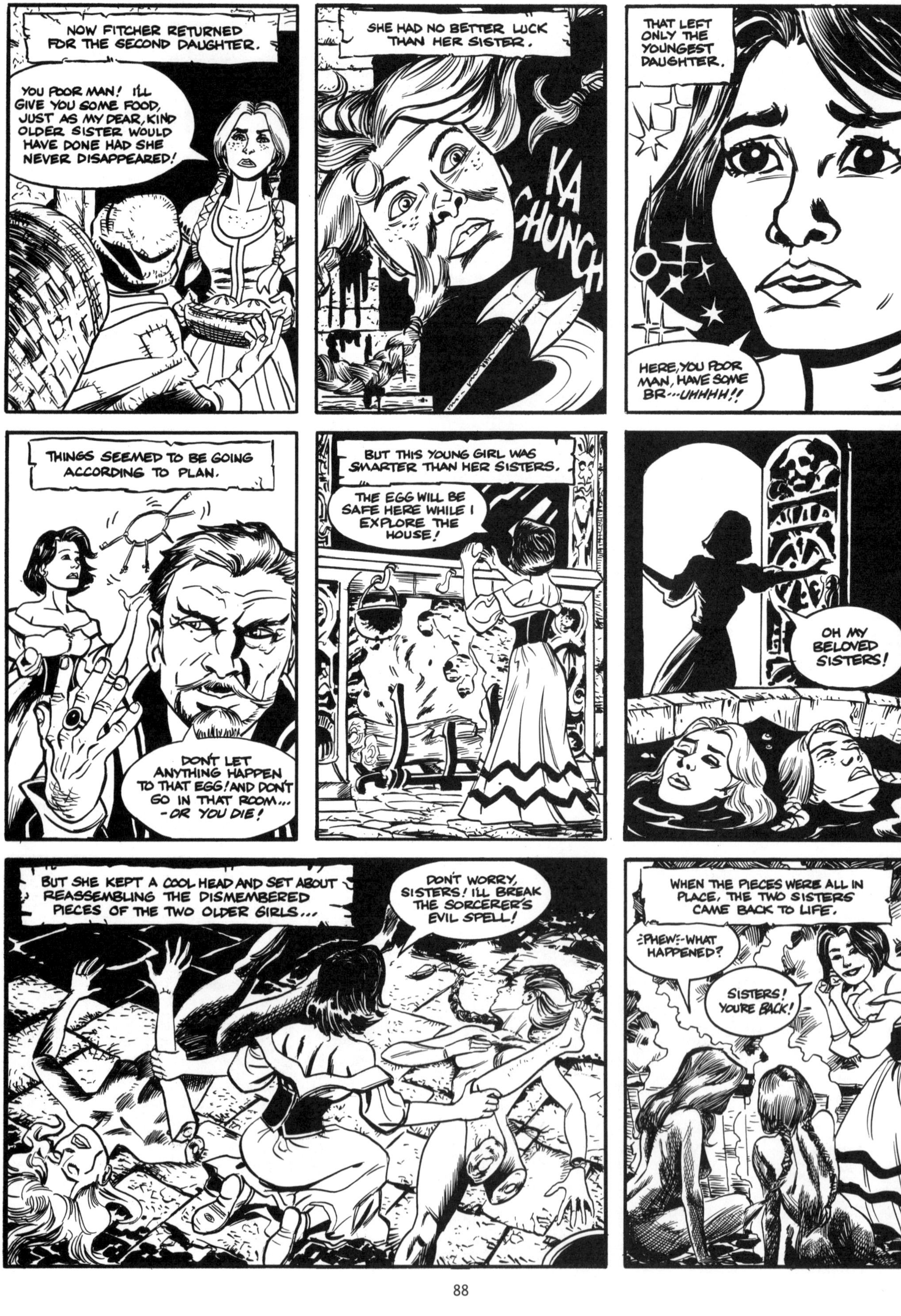
NOW FITCHER RETURNED FOR THE SECOND DAUGHTER.
YOU POOR MAN! I'LL GIVE YOU SOME FOOD, JUST AS MY DEAR, KIND OLDER SISTER WOULD HAVE DONE HAD SHE NEVER DISAPPEARED!
SHE HAD NO BETTER LUCK THAN HER SISTER.
KA CHUNCH
THAT LEFT ONLY THE YOUNGEST DAUGHTER.
HERE, YOU POOR MAN, HAVE SOME BR---UHHHH!!
THINGS SEEMED TO BE GOING ACCORDING TO PLAN.
DON'T LET ANYTHING HAPPEN TO THAT EGG! AND DON'T GO IN THAT ROOM... -OR YOU DIE!
BUT THIS YOUNG GIRL WAS SMARTER THAN HER SISTERS.
THE EGG WILL BE SAFE HERE WHILE I EXPLORE THE HOUSE!
OH MY BELOVED SISTERS!
BUT SHE KEPT A COOL HEAD AND SET ABOUT REASSEMBLING THE DISMEMBERED PIECES OF THE TWO OLDER GIRLS...
DON'T WORRY, SISTERS! I'LL BREAK THE SORCERER'S EVIL SPELL!
WHEN THE PIECES WERE ALL IN PLACE, THE TWO SISTERS CAME BACK TO LIFE.
=PHEW!=-WHAT HAPPENED?
SISTERS! YOU'RE BACK!

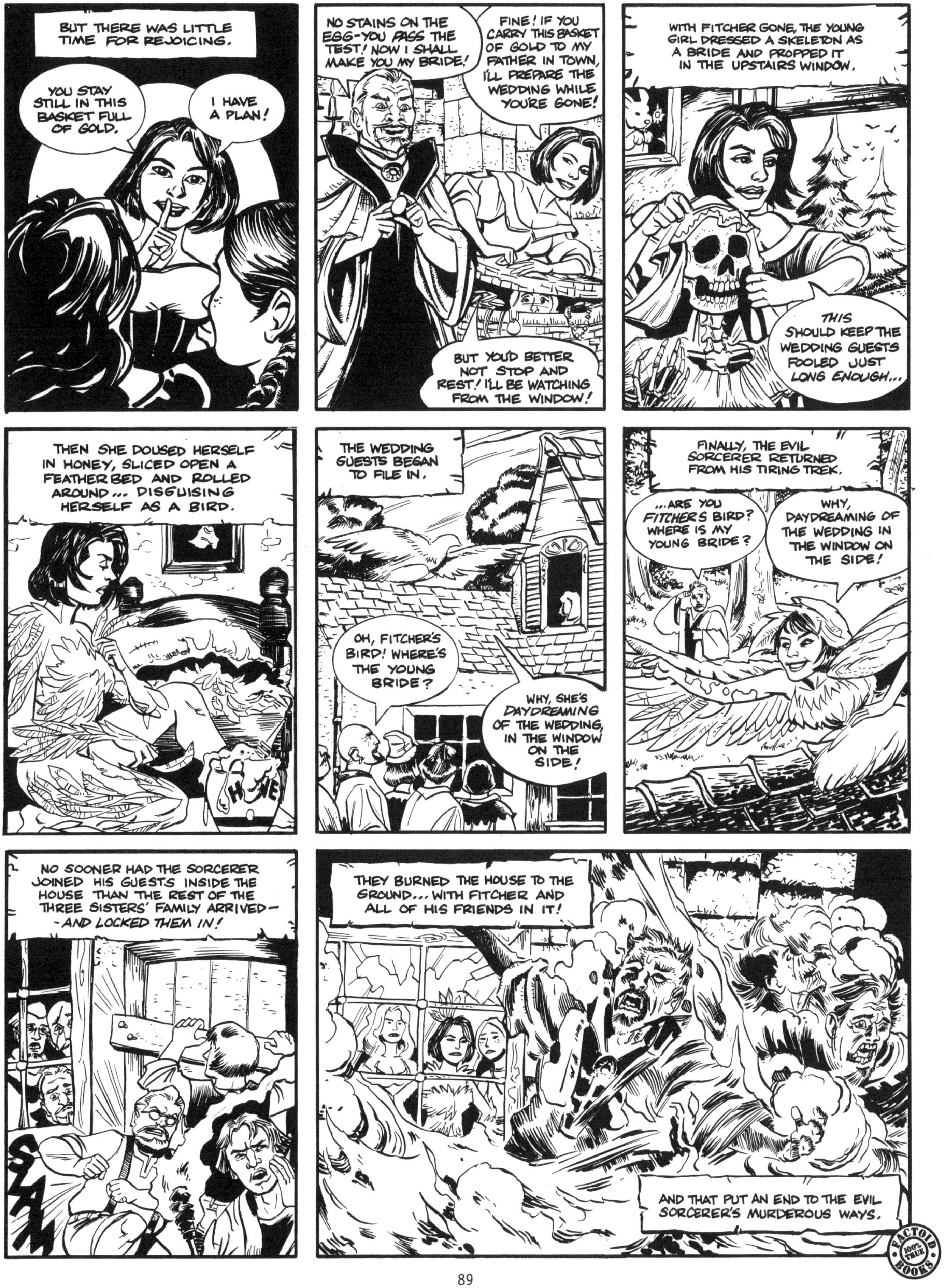

BUT THERE WAS LITTLE TIME FOR REJOICING.
YOU STAY STILL IN THIS BASKET FULL OF GOLD.
I HAVE A PLAN!
NO STAINS ON THE EGG-YOU PASS THE TEST! NOW I SHALL MAKE YOU MY BRIDE!
FINE! IF YOU CARRY THIS BASKET OF GOLD TO MY FATHER IN TOWN, I'LL PREPARE THE WEDDING WHILE YOU'RE GONE!
BUT YOU'D BETTER NOT STOP AND REST! I'LL BE WATCHING FROM THE WINDOW!
WITH FITCHER GONE, THE YOUNG GIRL DRESSED A SKELETON AS A BRIDE AND PROPPED IT IN THE UPSTAIRS WINDOW.
THIS SHOULD KEEP THE WEDDING GUESTS FOOLED JUST LONG ENOUGH...
THEN SHE DOUSED HERSELF IN HONEY, SLICED OPEN A FEATHER BED AND ROLLED AROUND... DISGUISING HERSELF AS A BIRD.
THE WEDDING GUESTS BEGAN TO FILE IN.
OH, FITCHER'S BIRD! WHERE'S THE YOUNG BRIDE?
WHY, SHE'S DAYDREAMING OF THE WEDDING, IN THE WINDOW ON THE SIDE!
FINALLY, THE EVIL SORCERER RETURNED FROM HIS TIRING TREK.
...ARE YOU FITCHER'S BIRD? WHERE IS MY YOUNG BRIDE?
WHY, DAYDREAMING OF THE WEDDING IN THE WINDOW ON THE SIDE!
NO SOONER HAD THE SORCERER JOINED HIS GUESTS INSIDE THE HOUSE THAN THE REST OF THE THREE SISTERS' FAMILY ARRIVED--AND LOCKED THEM IN!
SLAM
THEY BURNED THE HOUSE TO THE GROUND... WITH FITCHER AND ALL OF HIS FRIENDS IN IT!
AND THAT PUT AN END TO THE EVIL SORCERER'S MURDEROUS WAYS.
FACTOID 100% TRUE BOOKS

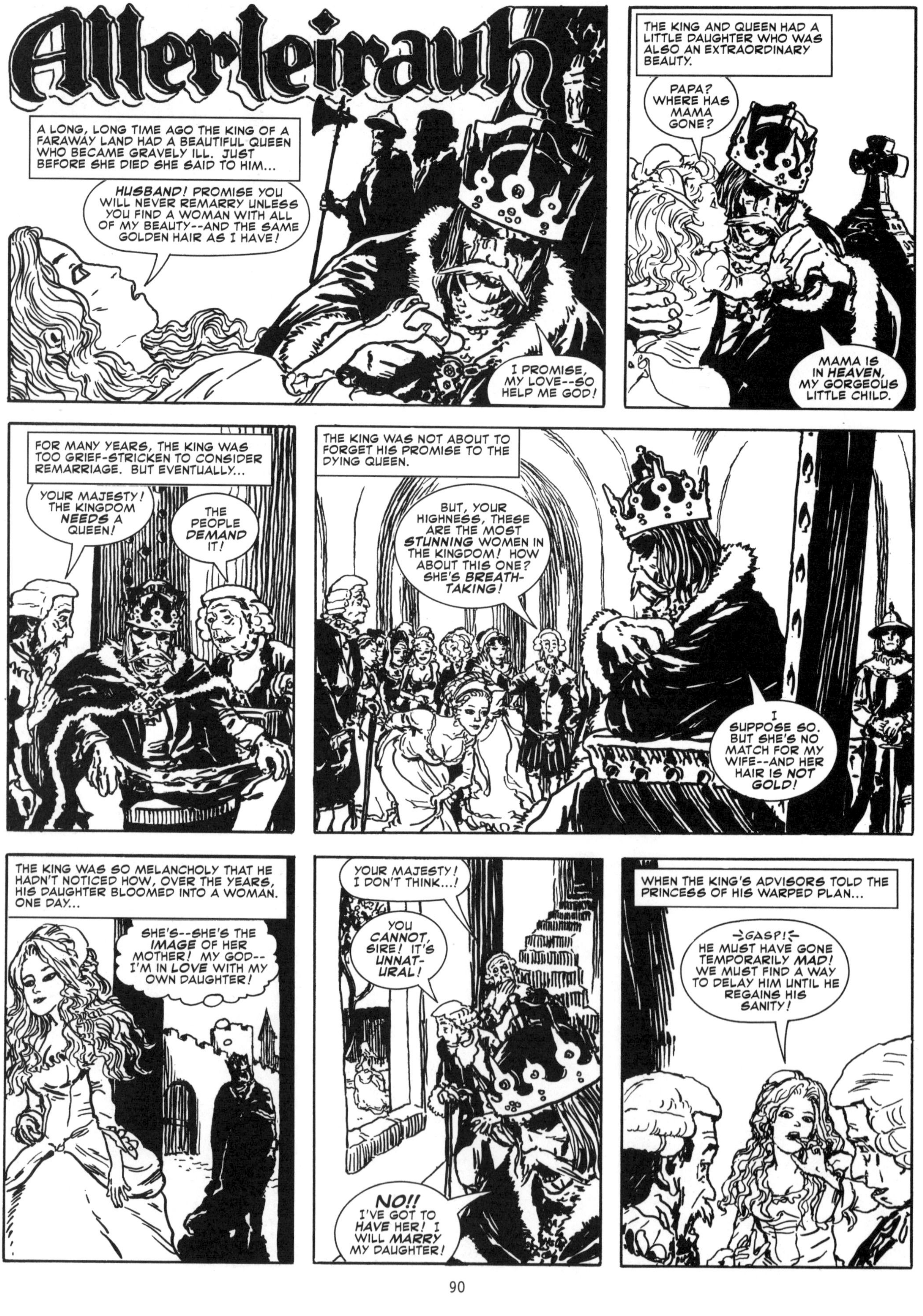
Allerleirauh
A LONG, LONG TIME AGO THE KING OF A FARAWAY LAND HAD A BEAUTIFUL QUEEN WHO BECAME GRAVELY ILL. JUST BEFORE SHE DIED SHE SAID TO HIM...
HUSBAND! PROMISE YOU WILL NEVER REMARRY UNLESS YOU FIND A WOMAN WITH ALL OF MY BEAUTY--AND THE SAME GOLDEN HAIR AS I HAVE!
I PROMISE, MY LOVE--SO HELP ME GOD!
THE KING AND QUEEN HAD A LITTLE DAUGHTER WHO WAS ALSO AN EXTRAORDINARY BEAUTY.
PAPA? WHERE HAS MAMA GONE?
MAMA IS IN HEAVEN, MY GORGEOUS LITTLE CHILD.
FOR MANY YEARS, THE KING WAS TOO GRIEF-STRICKEN TO CONSIDER REMARRIAGE. BUT EVENTUALLY...
YOUR MAJESTY! THE KINGDOM NEEDS A QUEEN!
THE PEOPLE DEMAND IT!
THE KING WAS NOT ABOUT TO FORGET HIS PROMISE TO THE DYING QUEEN.
BUT, YOUR HIGHNESS, THESE ARE THE MOST STUNNING WOMEN IN THE KINGDOM! HOW ABOUT THIS ONE? SHE'S BREATH-TAKING!
I SUPPOSE SO. BUT SHE'S NO MATCH FOR MY WIFE--AND HER HAIR IS NOT GOLD!
THE KING WAS SO MELANCHOLY THAT HE HADN'T NOTICED HOW, OVER THE YEARS, HIS DAUGHTER BLOOMED INTO A WOMAN. ONE DAY...
SHE'S--SHE'S THE IMAGE OF HER MOTHER! MY GOD--I'M IN LOVE WITH MY OWN DAUGHTER!
YOUR MAJESTY! I DON'T THINK...!
YOU CANNOT, SIRE! IT'S UNNAT-URAL!
NO!! I'VE GOT TO HAVE HER! I WILL MARRY MY DAUGHTER!
WHEN THE KING'S ADVISORS TOLD THE PRINCESS OF HIS WARPED PLAN...
GASP!
HE MUST HAVE GONE TEMPORARILY MAD! WE MUST FIND A WAY TO DELAY HIM UNTIL HE REGAINS HIS SANITY!

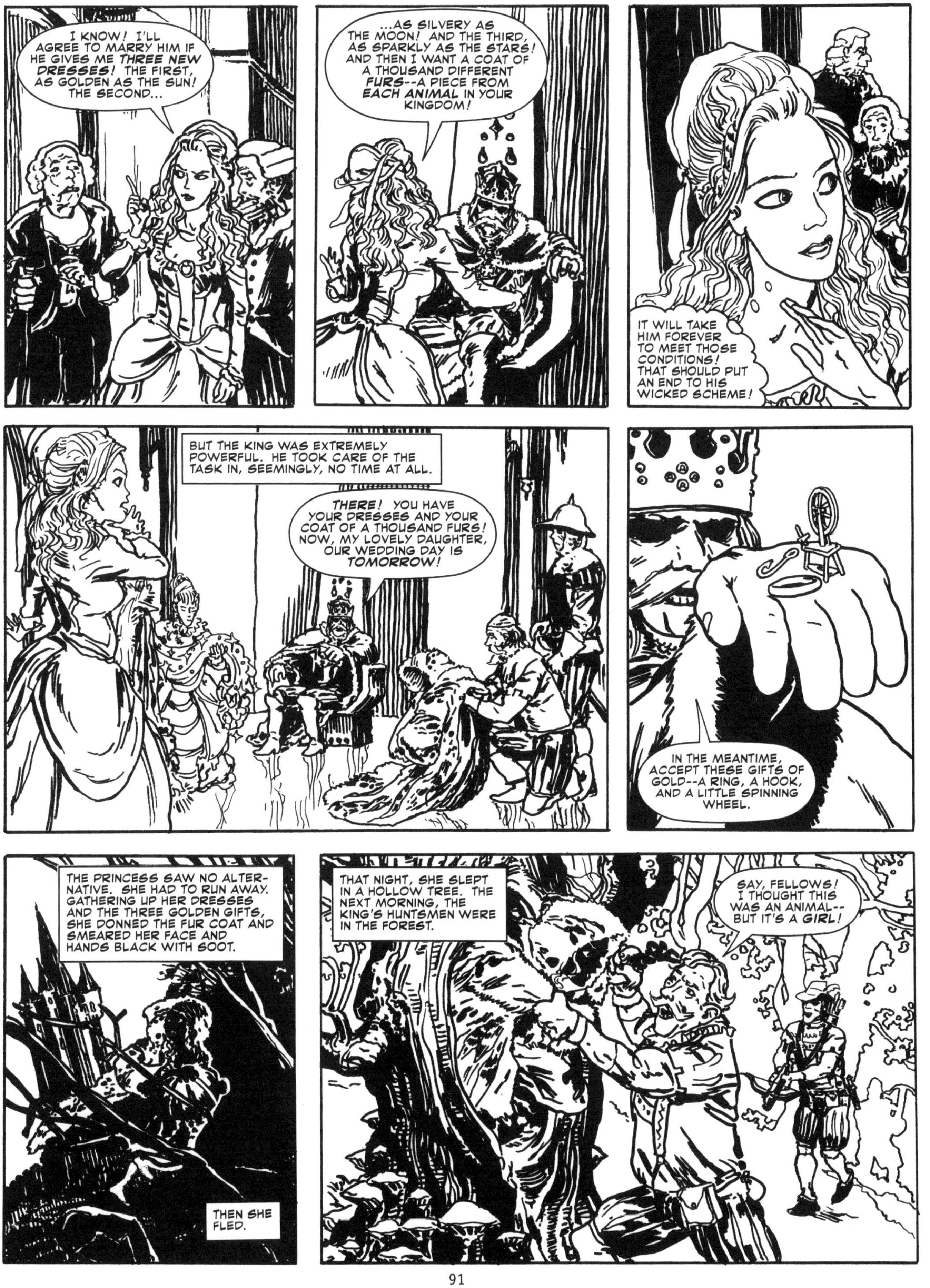
I KNOW! I'LL AGREE TO MARRY HIM IF HE GIVES ME THREE NEW DRESSES! THE FIRST, AS GOLDEN AS THE SUN! THE SECOND...
...AS SILVERY AS THE MOON! AND THE THIRD, AS SPARKLY AS THE STARS! AND THEN I WANT A COAT OF A THOUSAND DIFFERENT FURS--A PIECE FROM EACH ANIMAL IN YOUR KINGDOM!
IT WILL TAKE HIM FOREVER TO MEET THOSE CONDITIONS! THAT SHOULD PUT AN END TO HIS WICKED SCHEME!
BUT THE KING WAS EXTREMELY POWERFUL. HE TOOK CARE OF THE TASK IN, SEEMINGLY, NO TIME AT ALL.
THERE! YOU HAVE YOUR DRESSES AND YOUR COAT OF A THOUSAND FURS! NOW, MY LOVELY DAUGHTER, OUR WEDDING DAY IS TOMORROW!
IN THE MEANTIME, ACCEPT THESE GIFTS OF GOLD--A RING, A HOOK, AND A LITTLE SPINNING WHEEL.
THE PRINCESS SAW NO ALTERNATIVE. SHE HAD TO RUN AWAY. GATHERING UP HER DRESSES AND THE THREE GOLDEN GIFTS, SHE DONNED THE FUR COAT AND SMEARED HER FACE AND HANDS BLACK WITH SOOT.
THEN SHE FLED.
THAT NIGHT, SHE SLEPT IN A HOLLOW TREE. THE NEXT MORNING, THE KING'S HUNTSMEN WERE IN THE FOREST.
SAY, FELLOWS! I THOUGHT THIS WAS AN ANIMAL-- BUT IT'S A GIRL!

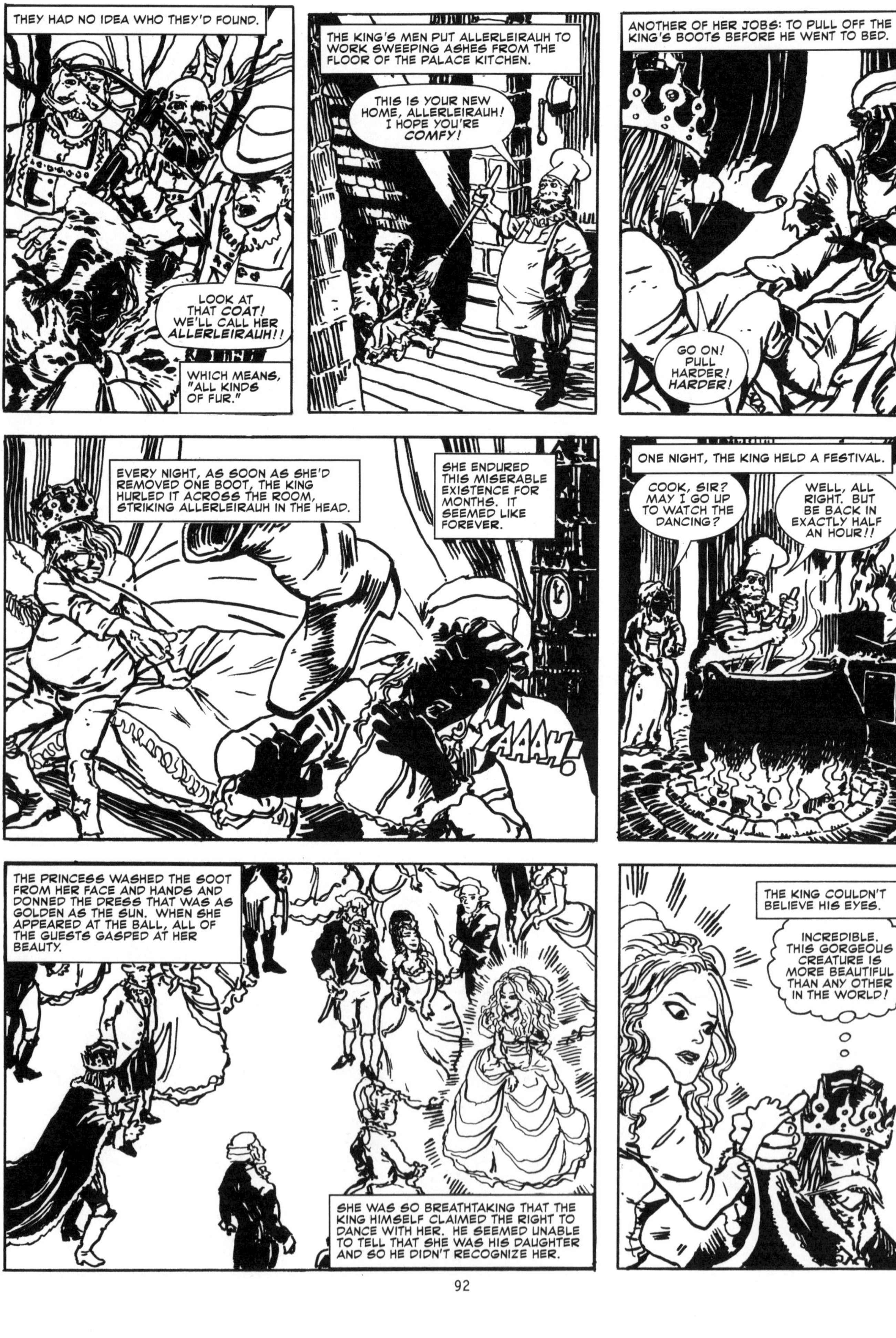
THEY HAD NO IDEA WHO THEY'D FOUND.
LOOK AT THAT COAT! WE'LL CALL HER ALLERLEIRAUH!!
WHICH MEANS, "ALL KINDS OF FUR."
THE KING'S MEN PUT ALLERLEIRAUH TO WORK SWEEPING ASHES FROM THE FLOOR OF THE PALACE KITCHEN.
THIS IS YOUR NEW HOME, ALLERLEIRAUH! I HOPE YOU'RE COMFY!
ANOTHER OF HER JOBS: TO PULL OFF THE KING'S BOOTS BEFORE HE WENT TO BED.
GO ON! PULL HARDER! HARDER!
EVERY NIGHT, AS SOON AS SHE'D REMOVED ONE BOOT, THE KING HURLED IT ACROSS THE ROOM, STRIKING ALLERLEIRAUH IN THE HEAD.
SHE ENDURED THIS MISERABLE EXISTENCE FOR MONTHS. IT SEEMED LIKE FOREVER.
YAAAH!
ONE NIGHT, THE KING HELD A FESTIVAL.
COOK, SIR? MAY I GO UP TO WATCH THE DANCING?
WELL, ALL RIGHT. BUT BE BACK IN EXACTLY HALF AN HOUR!!
THE PRINCESS WASHED THE SOOT FROM HER FACE AND HANDS AND DONNED THE DRESS THAT WAS AS GOLDEN AS THE SUN. WHEN SHE APPEARED AT THE BALL, ALL OF THE GUESTS GASPED AT HER BEAUTY.
SHE WAS SO BREATHTAKING THAT THE KING HIMSELF CLAIMED THE RIGHT TO DANCE WITH HER. HE SEEMED UNABLE TO TELL THAT SHE WAS HIS DAUGHTER AND SO HE DIDN'T RECOGNIZE HER.
THE KING COULDN'T BELIEVE HIS EYES.
INCREDIBLE. THIS GORGEOUS CREATURE IS MORE BEAUTIFUL THAN ANY OTHER IN THE WORLD!

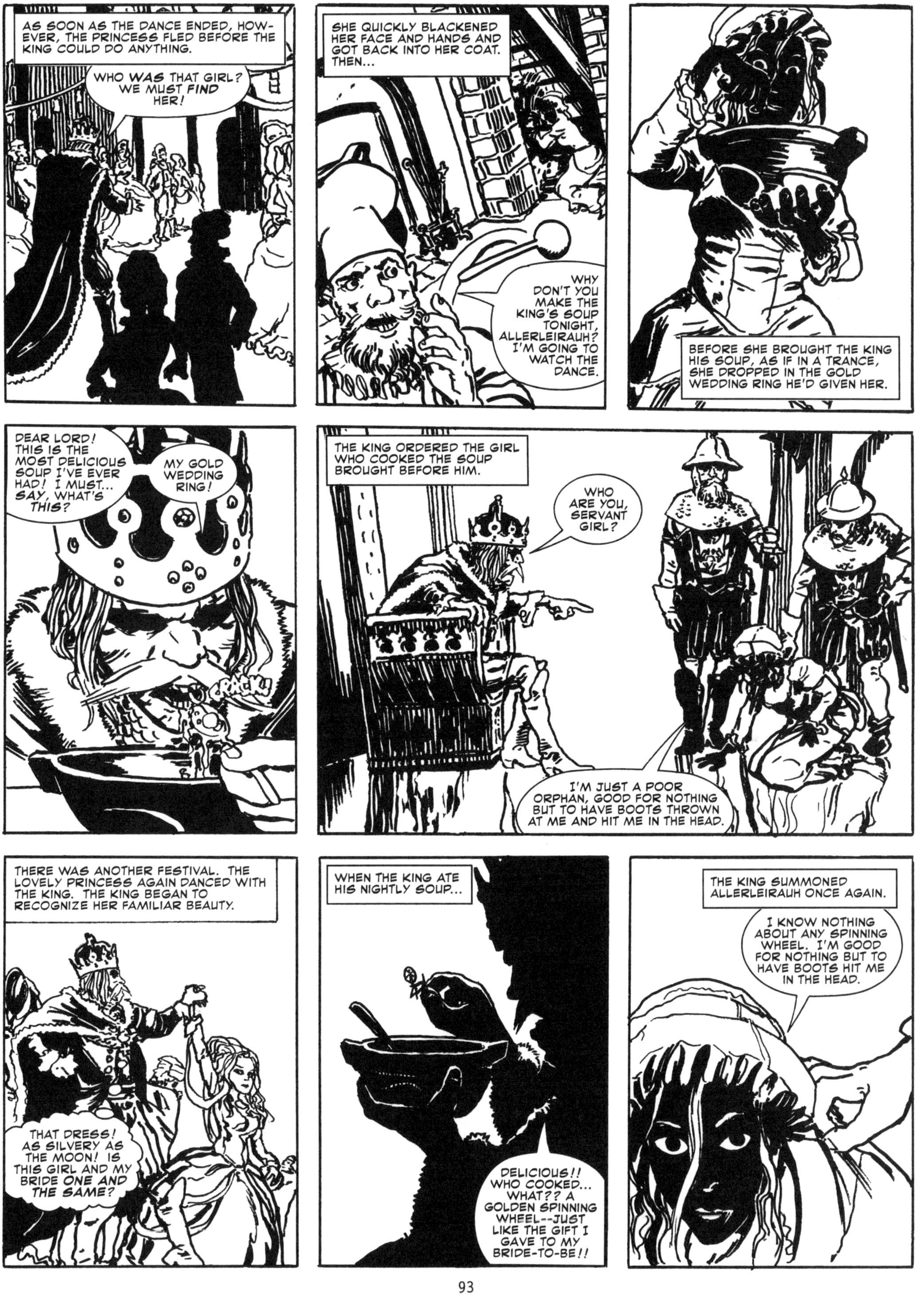
AS SOON AS THE DANCE ENDED, HOWEVER, THE PRINCESS FLED BEFORE THE KING COULD DO ANYTHING.
WHO *WAS* THAT GIRL? WE MUST *FIND* HER!
SHE QUICKLY BLACKENED HER FACE AND HANDS AND GOT BACK INTO HER COAT. THEN...
WHY DON'T YOU MAKE THE KING'S SOUP TONIGHT, ALLERLEIRAUH? I'M GOING TO WATCH THE DANCE.
BEFORE SHE BROUGHT THE KING HIS SOUP, AS IF IN A TRANCE, SHE DROPPED IN THE GOLD WEDDING RING HE'D GIVEN HER.
DEAR LORD! THIS IS THE MOST DELICIOUS SOUP I'VE EVER HAD! I MUST... *SAY*, WHAT'S *THIS*?
MY GOLD WEDDING RING!
THE KING ORDERED THE GIRL WHO COOKED THE SOUP BROUGHT BEFORE HIM.
WHO ARE YOU, SERVANT GIRL?
I'M JUST A POOR ORPHAN, GOOD FOR NOTHING BUT TO HAVE BOOTS THROWN AT ME AND HIT ME IN THE HEAD.
THERE WAS ANOTHER FESTIVAL. THE LOVELY PRINCESS AGAIN DANCED WITH THE KING. THE KING BEGAN TO RECOGNIZE HER FAMILIAR BEAUTY.
THAT DRESS! AS SILVERY AS THE MOON! IS THIS GIRL AND MY BRIDE *ONE AND THE SAME*?
WHEN THE KING ATE HIS NIGHTLY SOUP...
DELICIOUS!! WHO COOKED... WHAT?? A GOLDEN SPINNING WHEEL--JUST LIKE THE GIFT I GAVE TO MY BRIDE-TO-BE!!
THE KING SUMMONED ALLERLEIRAUH ONCE AGAIN.
I KNOW NOTHING ABOUT ANY SPINNING WHEEL. I'M GOOD FOR NOTHING BUT TO HAVE BOOTS HIT ME IN THE HEAD.

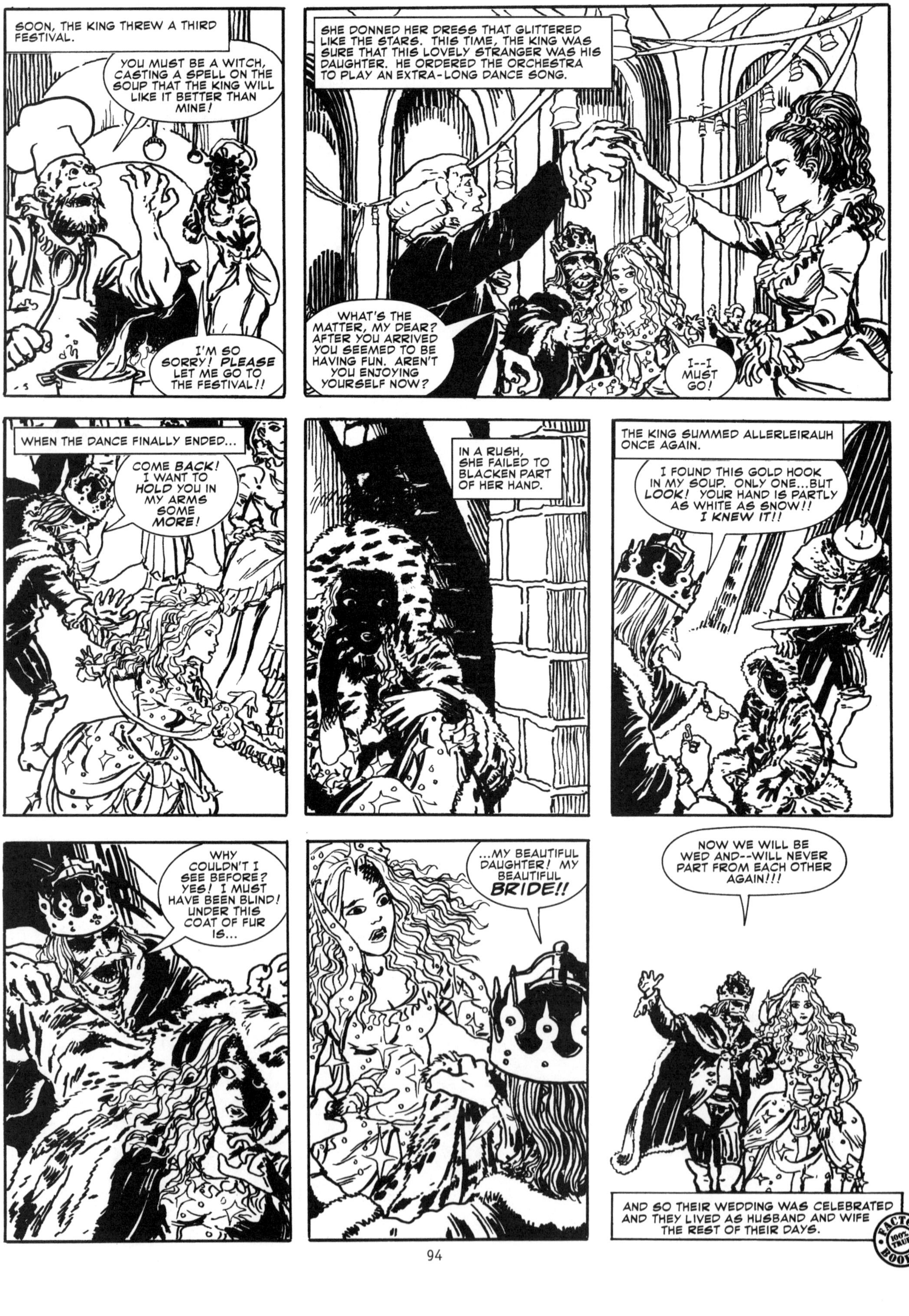
SOON, THE KING THREW A THIRD FESTIVAL.
YOU MUST BE A WITCH, CASTING A SPELL ON THE SOUP THAT THE KING WILL LIKE IT BETTER THAN MINE!
I'M SO SORRY! PLEASE LET ME GO TO THE FESTIVAL!!
SHE DONNED HER DRESS THAT GLITTERED LIKE THE STARS. THIS TIME, THE KING WAS SURE THAT THIS LOVELY STRANGER WAS HIS DAUGHTER. HE ORDERED THE ORCHESTRA TO PLAY AN EXTRA-LONG DANCE SONG.
WHAT'S THE MATTER, MY DEAR? AFTER YOU ARRIVED YOU SEEMED TO BE HAVING FUN. AREN'T YOU ENJOYING YOURSELF NOW?
I--I MUST GO!
WHEN THE DANCE FINALLY ENDED...
COME BACK! I WANT TO HOLD YOU IN MY ARMS SOME MORE!
IN A RUSH, SHE FAILED TO BLACKEN PART OF HER HAND.
THE KING SUMMED ALLERLEIRAUH ONCE AGAIN.
I FOUND THIS GOLD HOOK IN MY SOUP. ONLY ONE...BUT LOOK! YOUR HAND IS PARTLY AS WHITE AS SNOW!! I KNEW IT!!
WHY COULDN'T I SEE BEFORE? YES! I MUST HAVE BEEN BLIND! UNDER THIS COAT OF FUR IS...
...MY BEAUTIFUL DAUGHTER! MY BEAUTIFUL BRIDE!!
NOW WE WILL BE WED AND--WILL NEVER PART FROM EACH OTHER AGAIN!!!
AND SO THEIR WEDDING WAS CELEBRATED AND THEY LIVED AS HUSBAND AND WIFE THE REST OF THEIR DAYS.

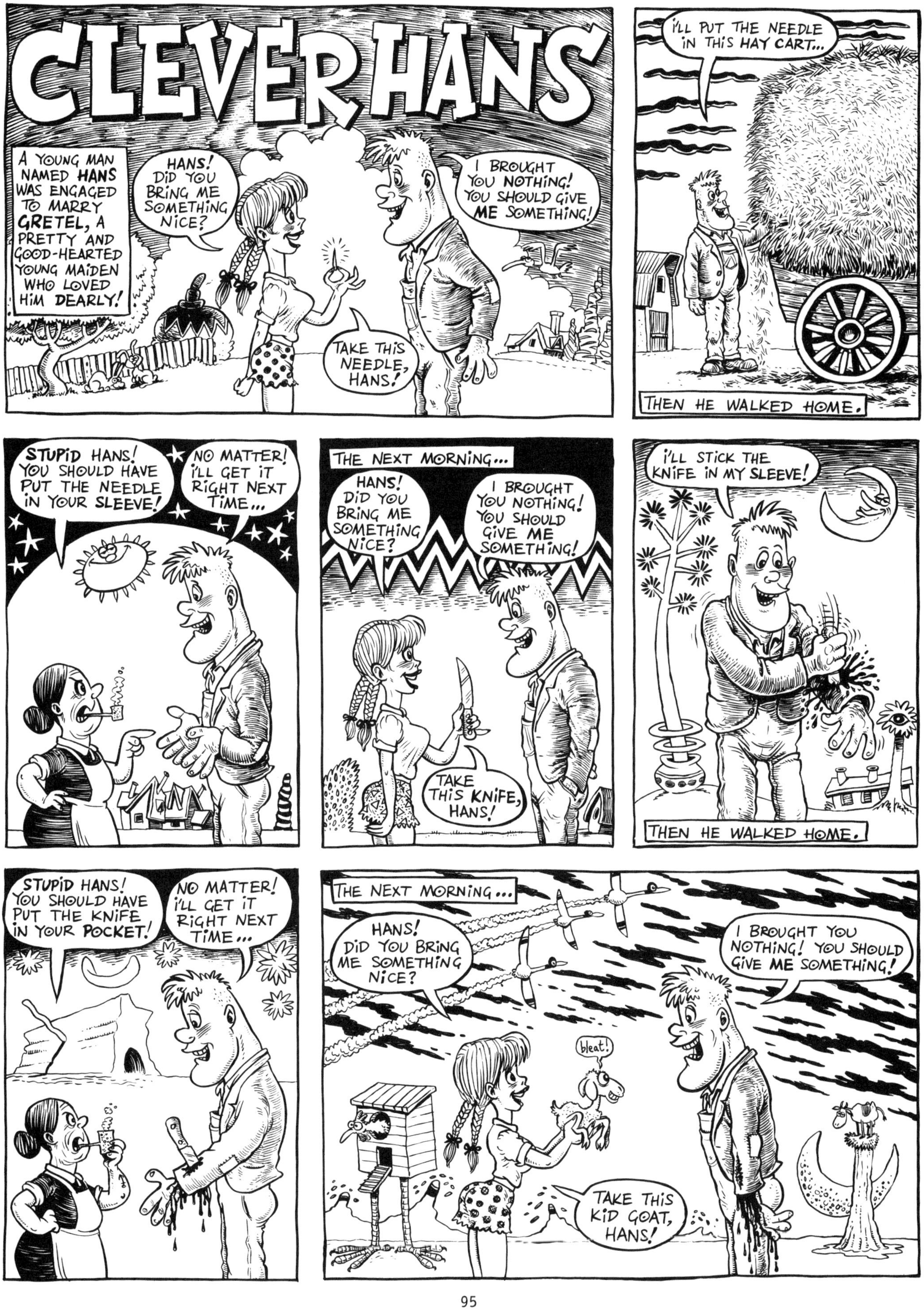
CLEVER HANS
A YOUNG MAN NAMED HANS WAS ENGAGED TO MARRY GRETEL, A PRETTY AND GOOD-HEARTED YOUNG MAIDEN WHO LOVED HIM DEARLY!
HANS! DID YOU BRING ME SOMETHING NICE?
I BROUGHT YOU NOTHING! YOU SHOULD GIVE ME SOMETHING!
TAKE THIS NEEDLE, HANS!
I'LL PUT THE NEEDLE IN THIS HAY CART...
THEN HE WALKED HOME.
STUPID HANS! YOU SHOULD HAVE PUT THE NEEDLE IN YOUR SLEEVE!
NO MATTER! I'LL GET IT RIGHT NEXT TIME...
THE NEXT MORNING...
HANS! DID YOU BRING ME SOMETHING NICE?
I BROUGHT YOU NOTHING! YOU SHOULD GIVE ME SOMETHING!
TAKE THIS KNIFE, HANS!
I'LL STICK THE KNIFE IN MY SLEEVE!
THEN HE WALKED HOME.
STUPID HANS! YOU SHOULD HAVE PUT THE KNIFE IN YOUR POCKET!
NO MATTER! I'LL GET IT RIGHT NEXT TIME...
THE NEXT MORNING...
HANS! DID YOU BRING ME SOMETHING NICE?
I BROUGHT YOU NOTHING! YOU SHOULD GIVE ME SOMETHING!
bleat!
TAKE THIS KID GOAT, HANS!

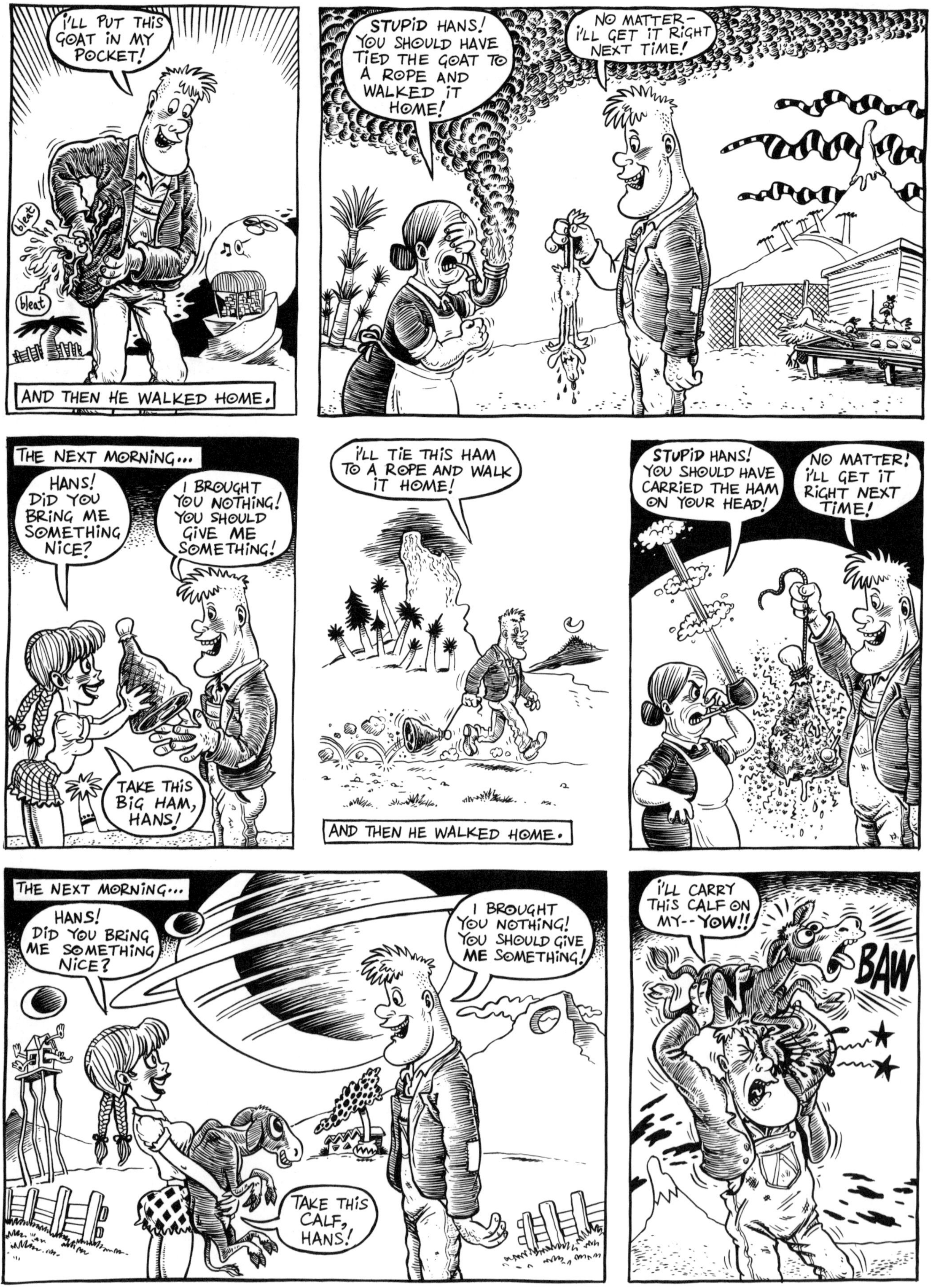

I'LL PUT THIS GOAT IN MY POCKET!
bleat
bleat
AND THEN HE WALKED HOME.
STUPID HANS! YOU SHOULD HAVE TIED THE GOAT TO A ROPE AND WALKED IT HOME!
NO MATTER- I'LL GET IT RIGHT NEXT TIME!
THE NEXT MORNING...
HANS! DID YOU BRING ME SOMETHING NICE?
I BROUGHT YOU NOTHING! YOU SHOULD GIVE ME SOMETHING!
TAKE THIS BIG HAM, HANS!
I'LL TIE THIS HAM TO A ROPE AND WALK IT HOME!
AND THEN HE WALKED HOME.
STUPID HANS! YOU SHOULD HAVE CARRIED THE HAM ON YOUR HEAD!
NO MATTER! I'LL GET IT RIGHT NEXT TIME!
THE NEXT MORNING...
HANS! DID YOU BRING ME SOMETHING NICE?
I BROUGHT YOU NOTHING! YOU SHOULD GIVE ME SOMETHING!
TAKE THIS CALF, HANS!
I'LL CARRY THIS CALF ON MY--YOW!!
BAW

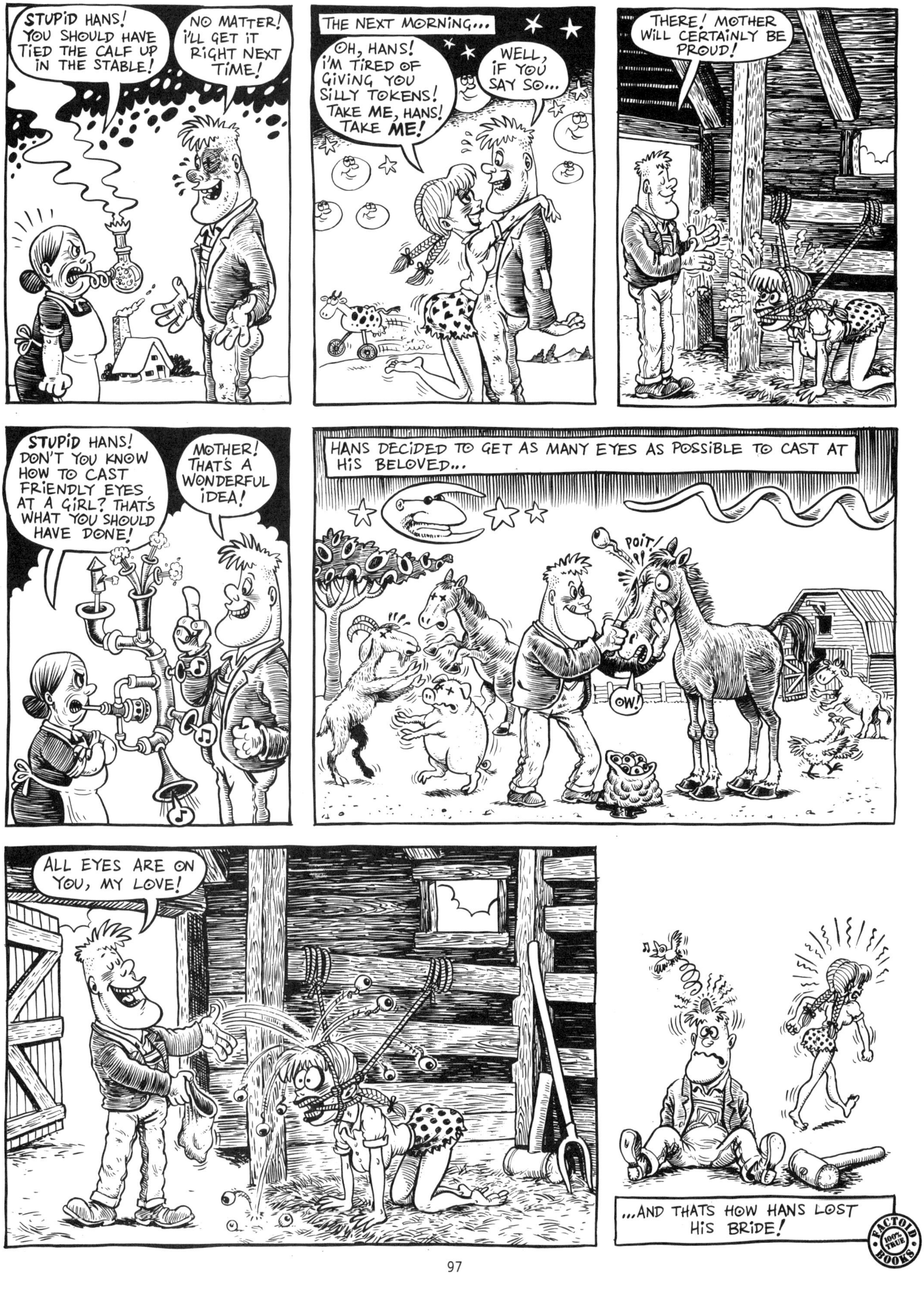
STUPID HANS! YOU SHOULD HAVE TIED THE CALF UP IN THE STABLE!
NO MATTER! I'LL GET IT RIGHT NEXT TIME!
THE NEXT MORNING...
OH, HANS! I'M TIRED OF GIVING YOU SILLY TOKENS! TAKE ME, HANS! TAKE ME!
WELL, IF YOU SAY SO...
THERE! MOTHER WILL CERTAINLY BE PROUD!
STUPID HANS! DON'T YOU KNOW HOW TO CAST FRIENDLY EYES AT A GIRL? THAT'S WHAT YOU SHOULD HAVE DONE!
MOTHER! THAT'S A WONDERFUL IDEA!
HANS DECIDED TO GET AS MANY EYES AS POSSIBLE TO CAST AT HIS BELOVED...
POIT!
OW!
ALL EYES ARE ON YOU, MY LOVE!
...AND THATS HOW HANS LOST HIS BRIDE!

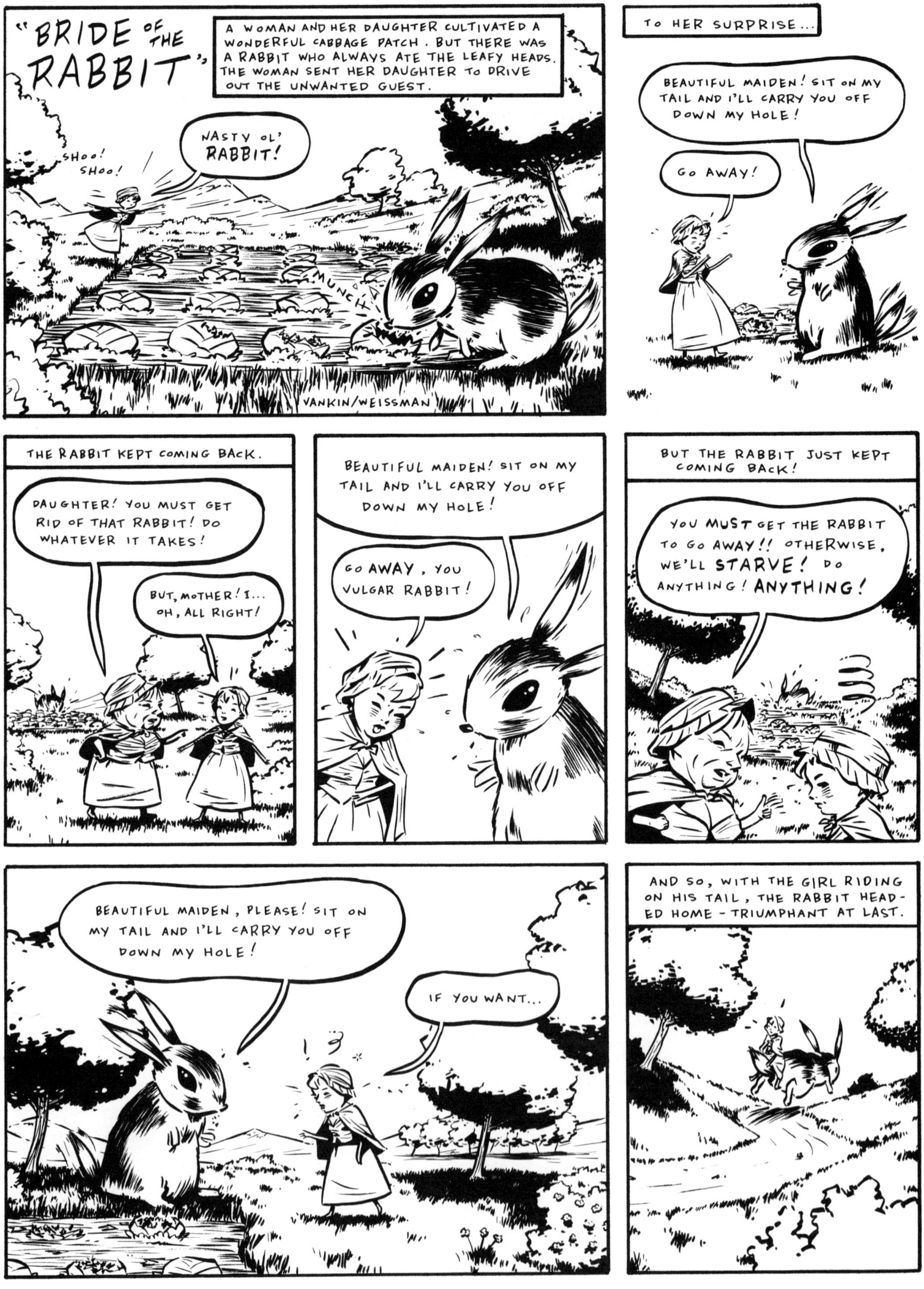
"BRIDE OF THE RABBIT"
A WOMAN AND HER DAUGHTER CULTIVATED A WONDERFUL CABBAGE PATCH. BUT THERE WAS A RABBIT WHO ALWAYS ATE THE LEAFY HEADS. THE WOMAN SENT HER DAUGHTER TO DRIVE OUT THE UNWANTED GUEST.
SHOO! SHOO!
NASTY OL' RABBIT!
MUNCH
VANKIN/WEISSMAN
TO HER SURPRISE...
BEAUTIFUL MAIDEN! SIT ON MY TAIL AND I'LL CARRY YOU OFF DOWN MY HOLE!
GO AWAY!
THE RABBIT KEPT COMING BACK.
DAUGHTER! YOU MUST GET RID OF THAT RABBIT! DO WHATEVER IT TAKES!
BUT, MOTHER! I... OH, ALL RIGHT!
BEAUTIFUL MAIDEN! SIT ON MY TAIL AND I'LL CARRY YOU OFF DOWN MY HOLE!
GO AWAY, YOU VULGAR RABBIT!
BUT THE RABBIT JUST KEPT COMING BACK!
YOU MUST GET THE RABBIT TO GO AWAY!! OTHERWISE, WE'LL STARVE! DO ANYTHING! ANYTHING!
BEAUTIFUL MAIDEN, PLEASE! SIT ON MY TAIL AND I'LL CARRY YOU OFF DOWN MY HOLE!
IF YOU WANT...
AND SO, WITH THE GIRL RIDING ON HIS TAIL, THE RABBIT HEADED HOME - TRIUMPHANT AT LAST.

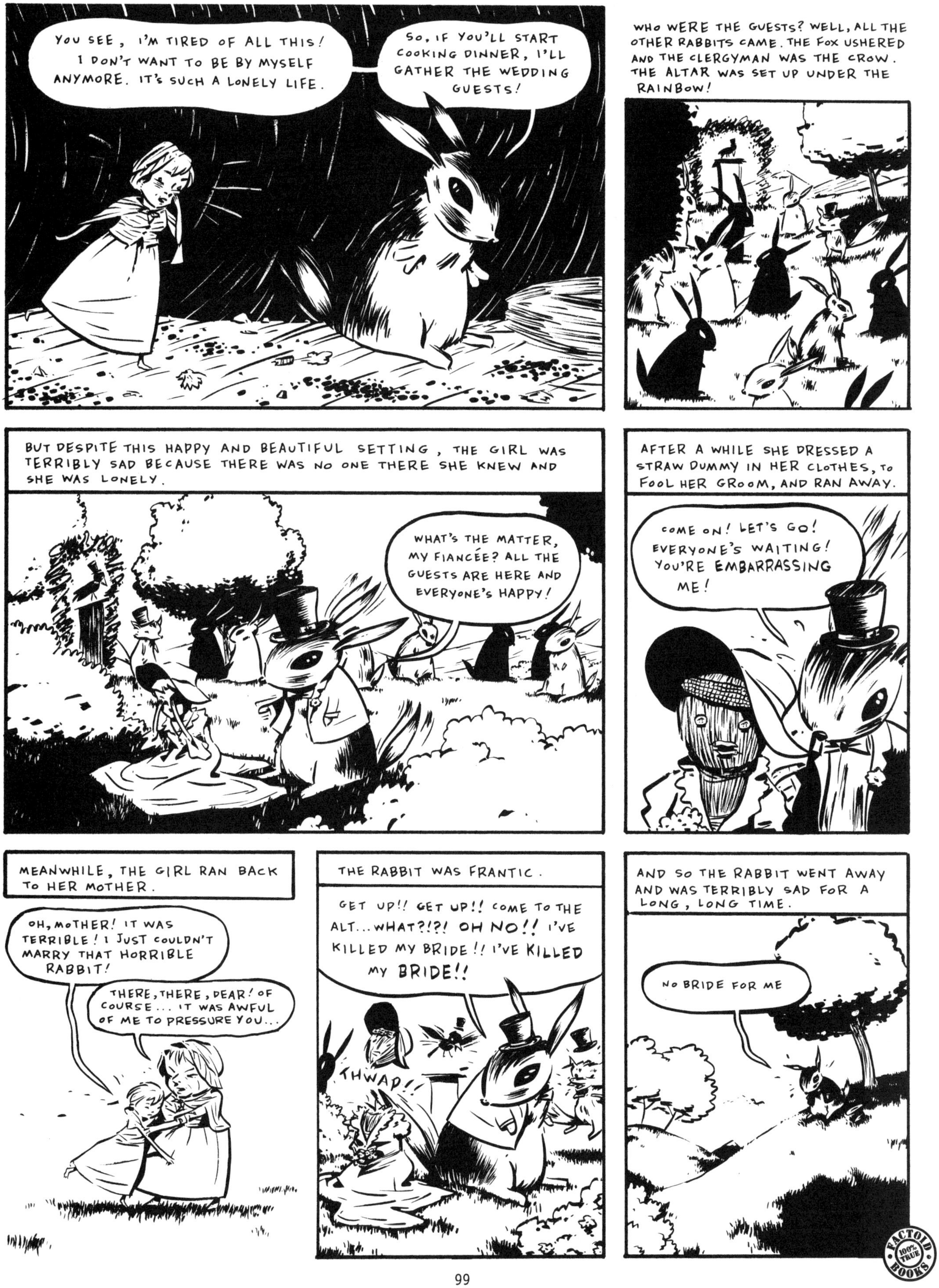

YOU SEE, I'M TIRED OF ALL THIS! I DON'T WANT TO BE BY MYSELF ANYMORE. IT'S SUCH A LONELY LIFE.
SO, IF YOU'LL START COOKING DINNER, I'LL GATHER THE WEDDING GUESTS!
WHO WERE THE GUESTS? WELL, ALL THE OTHER RABBITS CAME. THE FOX USHERED AND THE CLERGYMAN WAS THE CROW. THE ALTAR WAS SET UP UNDER THE RAINBOW!
BUT DESPITE THIS HAPPY AND BEAUTIFUL SETTING, THE GIRL WAS TERRIBLY SAD BECAUSE THERE WAS NO ONE THERE SHE KNEW AND SHE WAS LONELY.
WHAT'S THE MATTER, MY FIANCÉE? ALL THE GUESTS ARE HERE AND EVERYONE'S HAPPY!
AFTER A WHILE SHE DRESSED A STRAW DUMMY IN HER CLOTHES, TO FOOL HER GROOM, AND RAN AWAY.
COME ON! LET'S GO! EVERYONE'S WAITING! YOU'RE EMBARRASSING ME!
MEANWHILE, THE GIRL RAN BACK TO HER MOTHER.
OH, MOTHER! IT WAS TERRIBLE! I JUST COULDN'T MARRY THAT HORRIBLE RABBIT!
THERE, THERE, DEAR! OF COURSE... IT WAS AWFUL OF ME TO PRESSURE YOU...
THE RABBIT WAS FRANTIC.
GET UP!! GET UP!! COME TO THE ALT...WHAT?!?! OH NO!! I'VE KILLED MY BRIDE!! I'VE KILLED MY BRIDE!!
THWAP!!
AND SO THE RABBIT WENT AWAY AND WAS TERRIBLY SAD FOR A LONG, LONG TIME.
NO BRIDE FOR ME
FACTOID 100% TRUE BOOKS

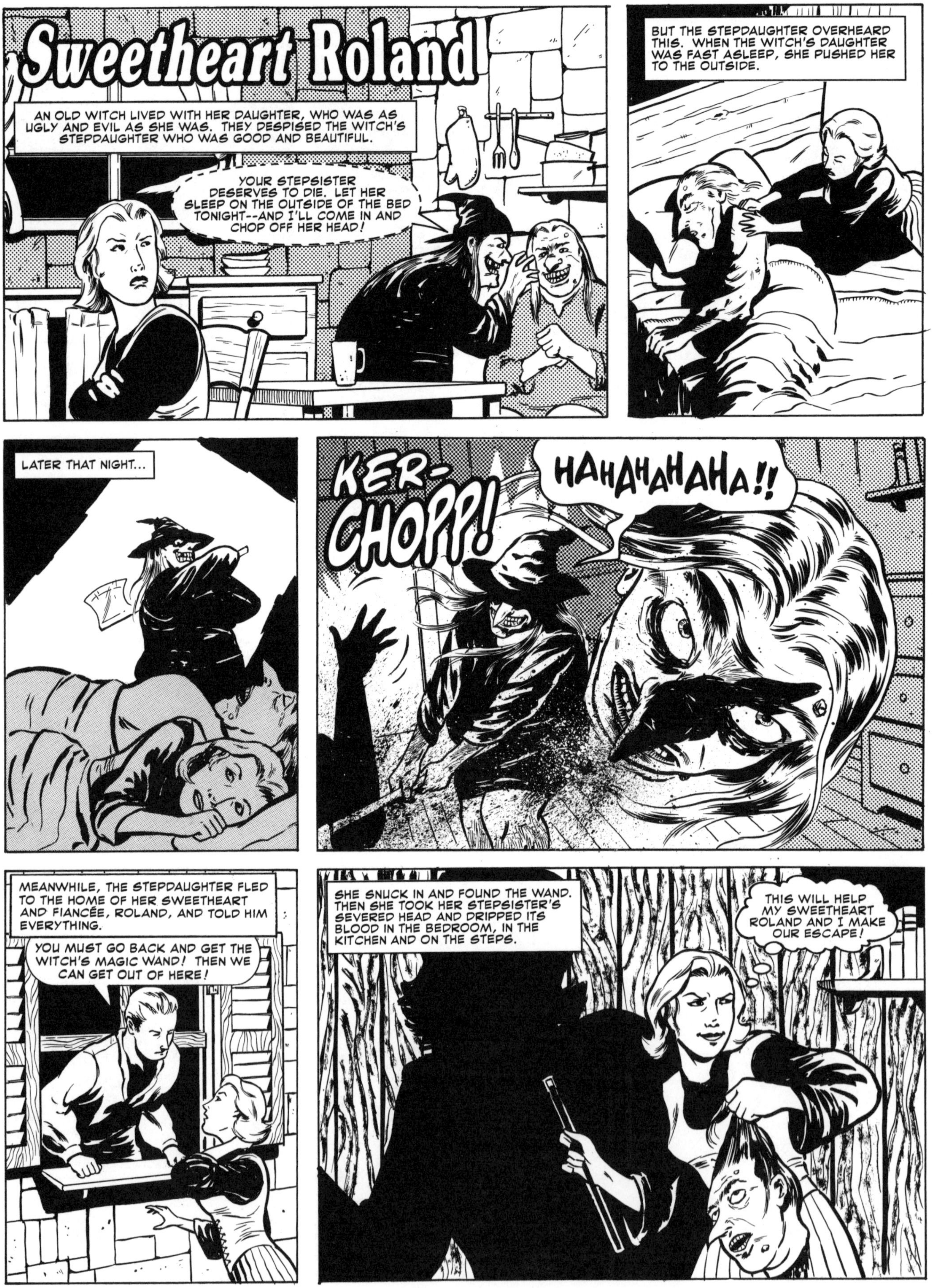
Sweetheart Roland
AN OLD WITCH LIVED WITH HER DAUGHTER, WHO WAS AS UGLY AND EVIL AS SHE WAS. THEY DESPISED THE WITCH'S STEPDAUGHTER WHO WAS GOOD AND BEAUTIFUL.
YOUR STEPSISTER DESERVES TO DIE. LET HER SLEEP ON THE OUTSIDE OF THE BED TONIGHT--AND I'LL COME IN AND CHOP OFF HER HEAD!
BUT THE STEPDAUGHTER OVERHEARD THIS. WHEN THE WITCH'S DAUGHTER WAS FAST ASLEEP, SHE PUSHED HER TO THE OUTSIDE.
LATER THAT NIGHT...
KER-CHOPP!
HAHAHAHAHA!!
MEANWHILE, THE STEPDAUGHTER FLED TO THE HOME OF HER SWEETHEART AND FIANCÉE, ROLAND, AND TOLD HIM EVERYTHING.
YOU MUST GO BACK AND GET THE WITCH'S MAGIC WAND! THEN WE CAN GET OUT OF HERE!
SHE SNUCK IN AND FOUND THE WAND. THEN SHE TOOK HER STEPSISTER'S SEVERED HEAD AND DRIPPED ITS BLOOD IN THE BEDROOM, IN THE KITCHEN AND ON THE STEPS.
THIS WILL HELP MY SWEETHEART ROLAND AND I MAKE OUR ESCAPE!

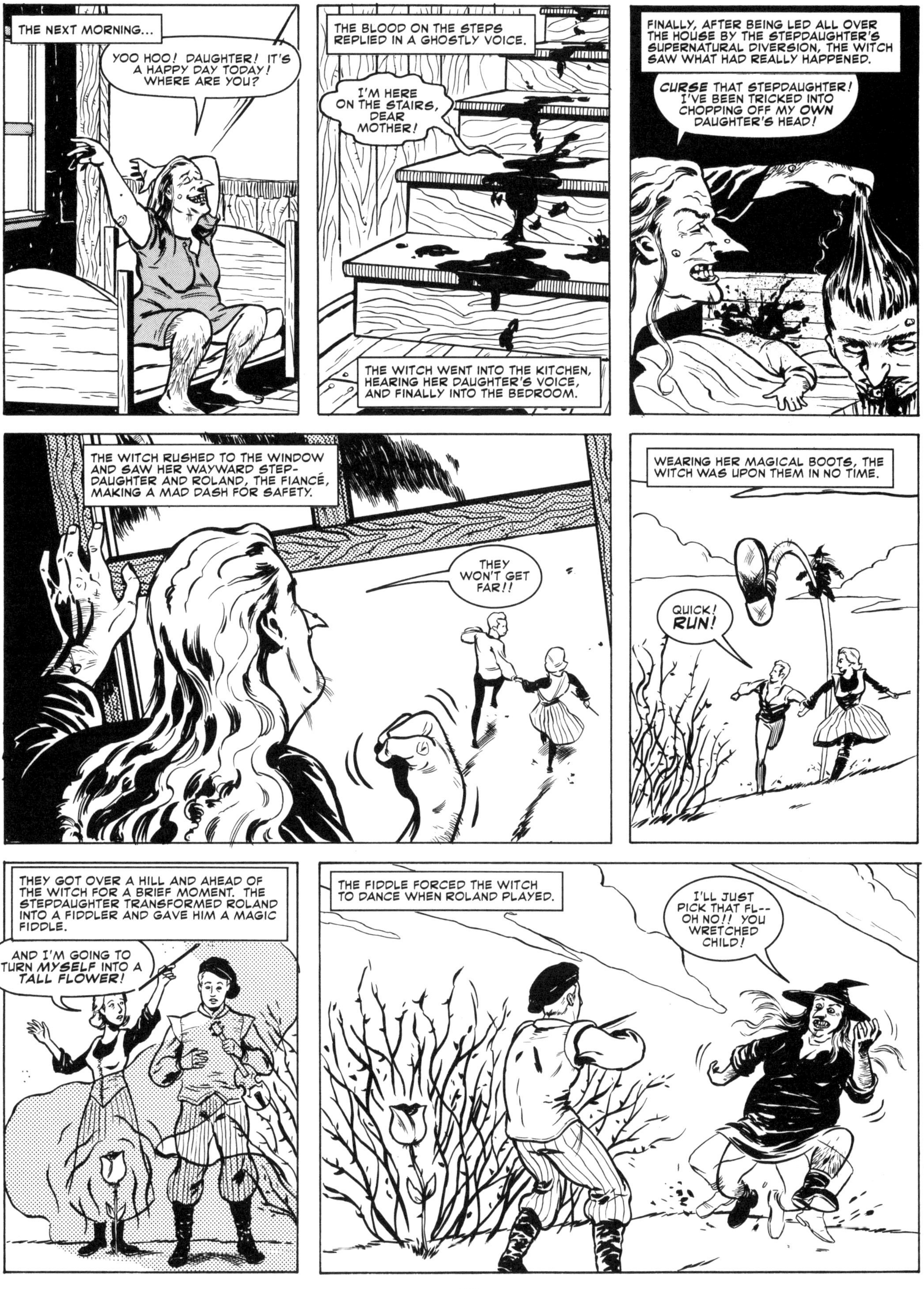
THE NEXT MORNING...
YOO HOO! DAUGHTER! IT'S A HAPPY DAY TODAY! WHERE ARE YOU?
THE BLOOD ON THE STEPS REPLIED IN A GHOSTLY VOICE.
I'M HERE ON THE STAIRS, DEAR MOTHER!
THE WITCH WENT INTO THE KITCHEN, HEARING HER DAUGHTER'S VOICE, AND FINALLY INTO THE BEDROOM.
FINALLY, AFTER BEING LED ALL OVER THE HOUSE BY THE STEPDAUGHTER'S SUPERNATURAL DIVERSION, THE WITCH SAW WHAT HAD REALLY HAPPENED.
CURSE THAT STEPDAUGHTER! I'VE BEEN TRICKED INTO CHOPPING OFF MY OWN DAUGHTER'S HEAD!
THE WITCH RUSHED TO THE WINDOW AND SAW HER WAYWARD STEP-DAUGHTER AND ROLAND, THE FIANCÉ, MAKING A MAD DASH FOR SAFETY.
THEY WON'T GET FAR!!
WEARING HER MAGICAL BOOTS, THE WITCH WAS UPON THEM IN NO TIME.
QUICK! RUN!
THEY GOT OVER A HILL AND AHEAD OF THE WITCH FOR A BRIEF MOMENT. THE STEPDAUGHTER TRANSFORMED ROLAND INTO A FIDDLER AND GAVE HIM A MAGIC FIDDLE.
AND I'M GOING TO TURN MYSELF INTO A TALL FLOWER!
THE FIDDLE FORCED THE WITCH TO DANCE WHEN ROLAND PLAYED.
I'LL JUST PICK THAT FL-- OH NO!! YOU WRETCHED CHILD!

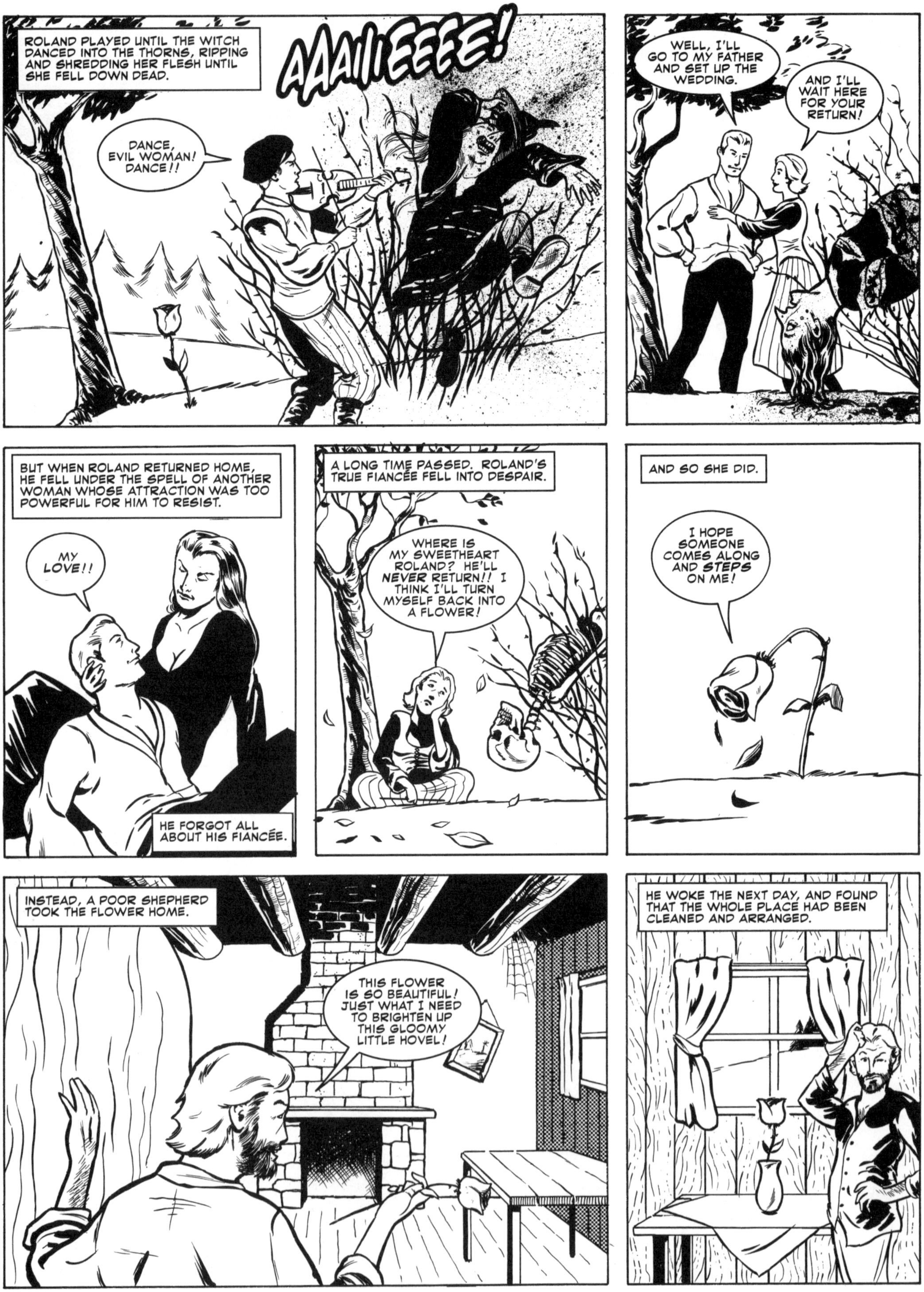
ROLAND PLAYED UNTIL THE WITCH DANCED INTO THE THORNS, RIPPING AND SHREDDING HER FLESH UNTIL SHE FELL DOWN DEAD.
AAAIIIEEEE!
DANCE, EVIL WOMAN! DANCE!!
WELL, I'LL GO TO MY FATHER AND SET UP THE WEDDING.
AND I'LL WAIT HERE FOR YOUR RETURN!
BUT WHEN ROLAND RETURNED HOME, HE FELL UNDER THE SPELL OF ANOTHER WOMAN WHOSE ATTRACTION WAS TOO POWERFUL FOR HIM TO RESIST.
MY LOVE!!
HE FORGOT ALL ABOUT HIS FIANCÉE.
A LONG TIME PASSED. ROLAND'S TRUE FIANCÉE FELL INTO DESPAIR.
WHERE IS MY SWEETHEART ROLAND? HE'LL NEVER RETURN!! I THINK I'LL TURN MYSELF BACK INTO A FLOWER!
AND SO SHE DID.
I HOPE SOMEONE COMES ALONG AND STEPS ON ME!
INSTEAD, A POOR SHEPHERD TOOK THE FLOWER HOME.
THIS FLOWER IS SO BEAUTIFUL! JUST WHAT I NEED TO BRIGHTEN UP THIS GLOOMY LITTLE HOVEL!
HE WOKE THE NEXT DAY, AND FOUND THAT THE WHOLE PLACE HAD BEEN CLEANED AND ARRANGED.

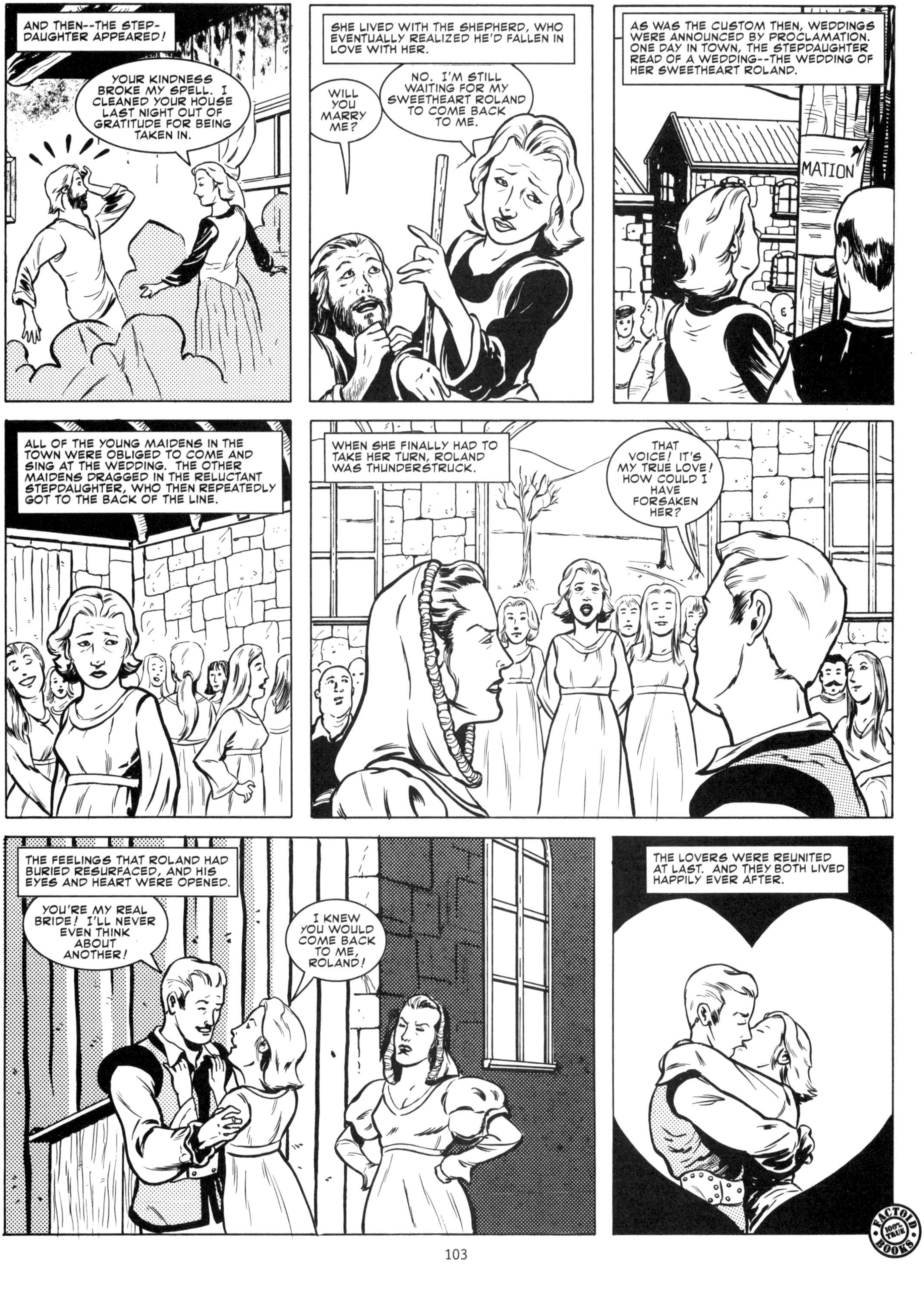
AND THEN--THE STEP-DAUGHTER APPEARED!
YOUR KINDNESS BROKE MY SPELL. I CLEANED YOUR HOUSE LAST NIGHT OUT OF GRATITUDE FOR BEING TAKEN IN.
SHE LIVED WITH THE SHEPHERD, WHO EVENTUALLY REALIZED HE'D FALLEN IN LOVE WITH HER.
WILL YOU MARRY ME?
NO. I'M STILL WAITING FOR MY SWEETHEART ROLAND TO COME BACK TO ME.
AS WAS THE CUSTOM THEN, WEDDINGS WERE ANNOUNCED BY PROCLAMATION. ONE DAY IN TOWN, THE STEPDAUGHTER READ OF A WEDDING--THE WEDDING OF HER SWEETHEART ROLAND.
MATION
ALL OF THE YOUNG MAIDENS IN THE TOWN WERE OBLIGED TO COME AND SING AT THE WEDDING. THE OTHER MAIDENS DRAGGED IN THE RELUCTANT STEPDAUGHTER, WHO THEN REPEATEDLY GOT TO THE BACK OF THE LINE.
WHEN SHE FINALLY HAD TO TAKE HER TURN, ROLAND WAS THUNDERSTRUCK.
THAT VOICE! IT'S MY TRUE LOVE! HOW COULD I HAVE FORSAKEN HER?
THE FEELINGS THAT ROLAND HAD BURIED RESURFACED, AND HIS EYES AND HEART WERE OPENED.
YOU'RE MY REAL BRIDE! I'LL NEVER EVEN THINK ABOUT ANOTHER!
I KNEW YOU WOULD COME BACK TO ME, ROLAND!
THE LOVERS WERE REUNITED AT LAST. AND THEY BOTH LIVED HAPPILY EVER AFTER.
FACTOID BOOKS 100% TRUE

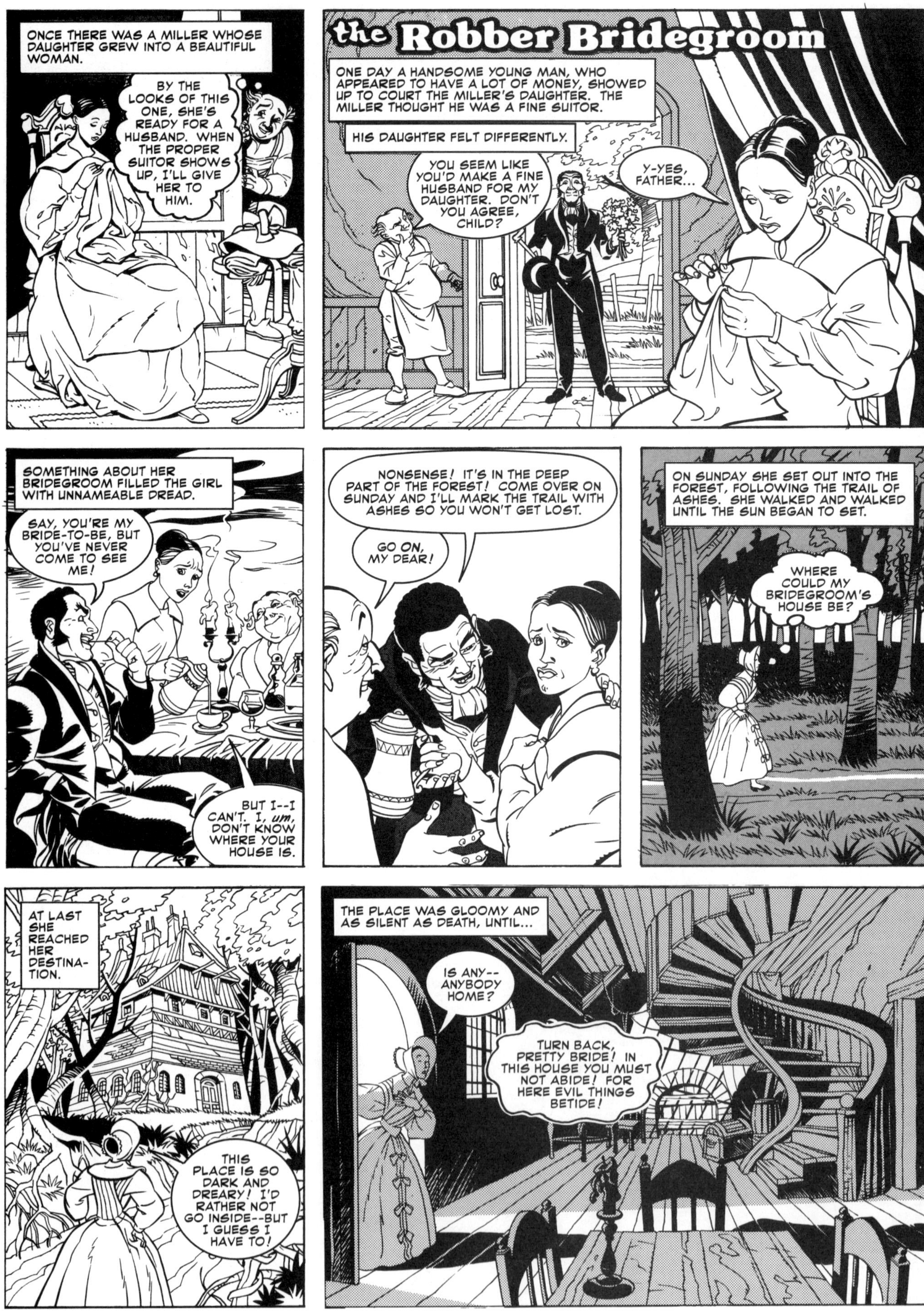

ONCE THERE WAS A MILLER WHOSE DAUGHTER GREW INTO A BEAUTIFUL WOMAN.
BY THE LOOKS OF THIS ONE, SHE'S READY FOR A HUSBAND. WHEN THE PROPER SUITOR SHOWS UP, I'LL GIVE HER TO HIM.
the Robber Bridegroom
ONE DAY A HANDSOME YOUNG MAN, WHO APPEARED TO HAVE A LOT OF MONEY, SHOWED UP TO COURT THE MILLER'S DAUGHTER. THE MILLER THOUGHT HE WAS A FINE SUITOR.
HIS DAUGHTER FELT DIFFERENTLY.
YOU SEEM LIKE YOU'D MAKE A FINE HUSBAND FOR MY DAUGHTER. DON'T YOU AGREE, CHILD?
Y-YES, FATHER...
SOMETHING ABOUT HER BRIDEGROOM FILLED THE GIRL WITH UNNAMEABLE DREAD.
SAY, YOU'RE MY BRIDE-TO-BE, BUT YOU'VE NEVER COME TO SEE ME!
BUT I--I CAN'T. I, *um*, DON'T KNOW WHERE YOUR HOUSE IS.
NONSENSE! IT'S IN THE DEEP PART OF THE FOREST! COME OVER ON SUNDAY AND I'LL MARK THE TRAIL WITH ASHES SO YOU WON'T GET LOST.
GO ON, MY DEAR!
ON SUNDAY SHE SET OUT INTO THE FOREST, FOLLOWING THE TRAIL OF ASHES. SHE WALKED AND WALKED UNTIL THE SUN BEGAN TO SET.
WHERE COULD MY BRIDEGROOM'S HOUSE BE?
AT LAST SHE REACHED HER DESTINATION.
THIS PLACE IS SO DARK AND DREARY! I'D RATHER NOT GO INSIDE--BUT I GUESS I HAVE TO!
THE PLACE WAS GLOOMY AND AS SILENT AS DEATH, UNTIL...
IS ANY--ANYBODY HOME?
TURN BACK, PRETTY BRIDE! IN THIS HOUSE YOU MUST NOT ABIDE! FOR HERE EVIL THINGS BETIDE!

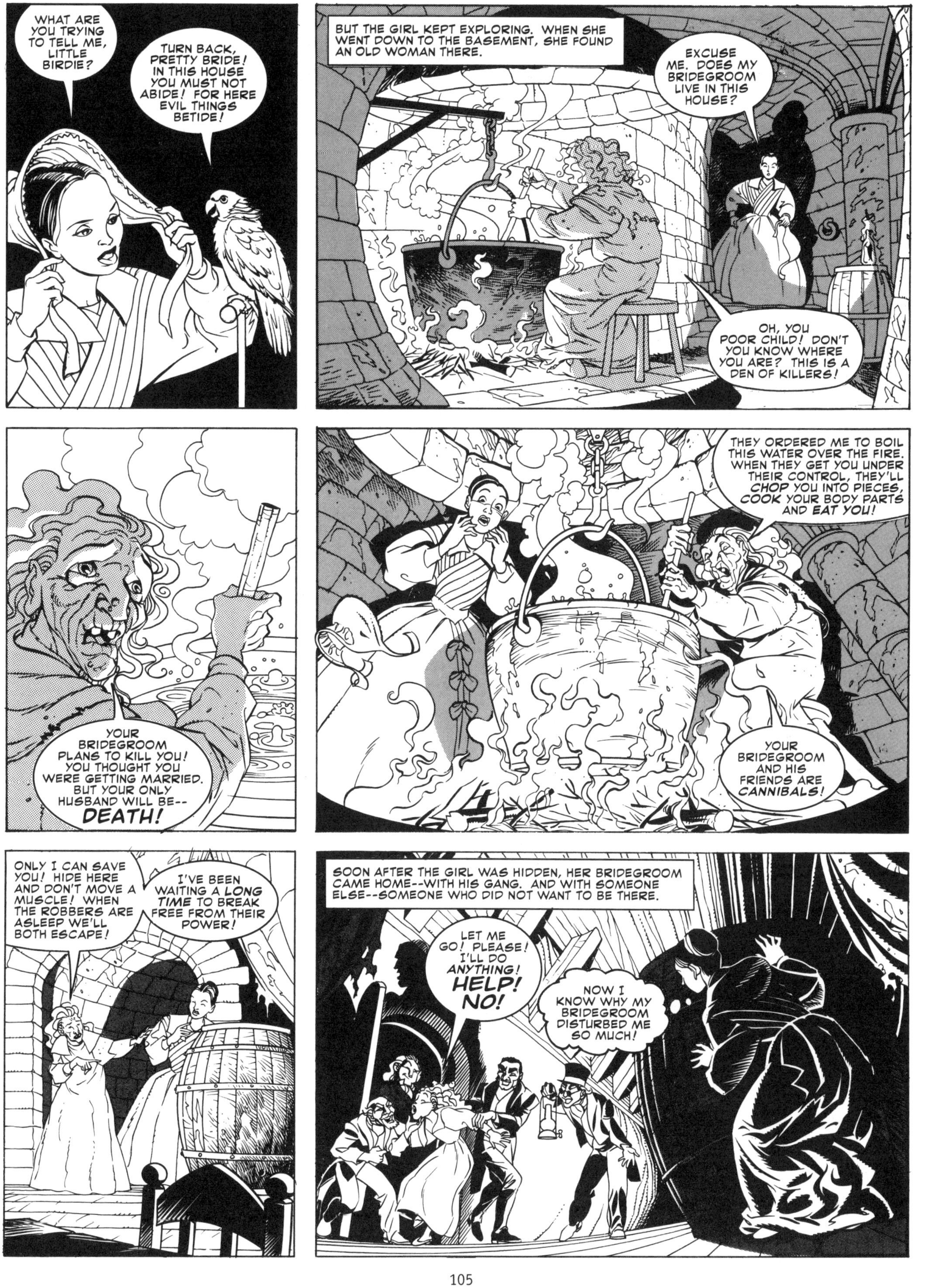
WHAT ARE YOU TRYING TO TELL ME, LITTLE BIRDIE?
TURN BACK, PRETTY BRIDE! IN THIS HOUSE YOU MUST NOT ABIDE! FOR HERE EVIL THINGS BETIDE!
BUT THE GIRL KEPT EXPLORING. WHEN SHE WENT DOWN TO THE BASEMENT, SHE FOUND AN OLD WOMAN THERE.
EXCUSE ME. DOES MY BRIDEGROOM LIVE IN THIS HOUSE?
OH, YOU POOR CHILD! DON'T YOU KNOW WHERE YOU ARE? THIS IS A DEN OF KILLERS!
YOUR BRIDEGROOM PLANS TO KILL YOU! YOU THOUGHT YOU WERE GETTING MARRIED. BUT YOUR ONLY HUSBAND WILL BE-- DEATH!
THEY ORDERED ME TO BOIL THIS WATER OVER THE FIRE. WHEN THEY GET YOU UNDER THEIR CONTROL, THEY'LL CHOP YOU INTO PIECES, COOK YOUR BODY PARTS AND EAT YOU!
YOUR BRIDEGROOM AND HIS FRIENDS ARE CANNIBALS!
ONLY I CAN SAVE YOU! HIDE HERE AND DON'T MOVE A MUSCLE! WHEN THE ROBBERS ARE ASLEEP WE'LL BOTH ESCAPE!
I'VE BEEN WAITING A LONG TIME TO BREAK FREE FROM THEIR POWER!
SOON AFTER THE GIRL WAS HIDDEN, HER BRIDEGROOM CAME HOME--WITH HIS GANG. AND WITH SOMEONE ELSE--SOMEONE WHO DID NOT WANT TO BE THERE.
LET ME GO! PLEASE! I'LL DO ANYTHING! HELP! NO!
NOW I KNOW WHY MY BRIDEGROOM DISTURBED ME SO MUCH!

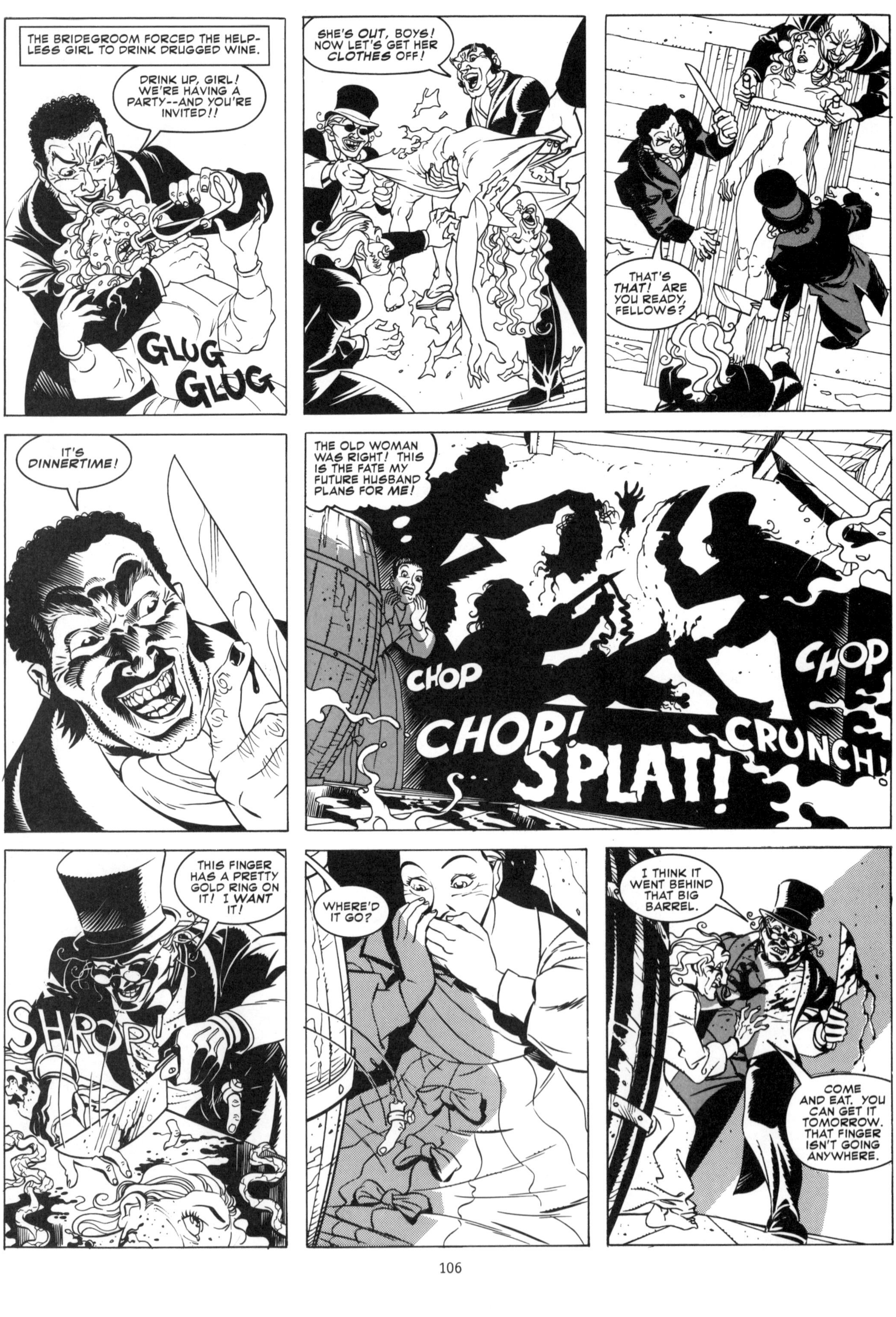
THE BRIDEGROOM FORCED THE HELPLESS GIRL TO DRINK DRUGGED WINE.
DRINK UP, GIRL! WE'RE HAVING A PARTY--AND YOU'RE INVITED!!
GLUG GLUG
SHE'S OUT, BOYS! NOW LET'S GET HER CLOTHES OFF!
THAT'S THAT! ARE YOU READY, FELLOWS?
IT'S DINNERTIME!
THE OLD WOMAN WAS RIGHT! THIS IS THE FATE MY FUTURE HUSBAND PLANS FOR ME!
CHOP
CHOP
CHOP!
SPLAT!
CRUNCH!
THIS FINGER HAS A PRETTY GOLD RING ON IT! I WANT IT!
SHROP!
WHERE'D IT GO?
I THINK IT WENT BEHIND THAT BIG BARREL.
COME AND EAT. YOU CAN GET IT TOMORROW. THAT FINGER ISN'T GOING ANYWHERE.

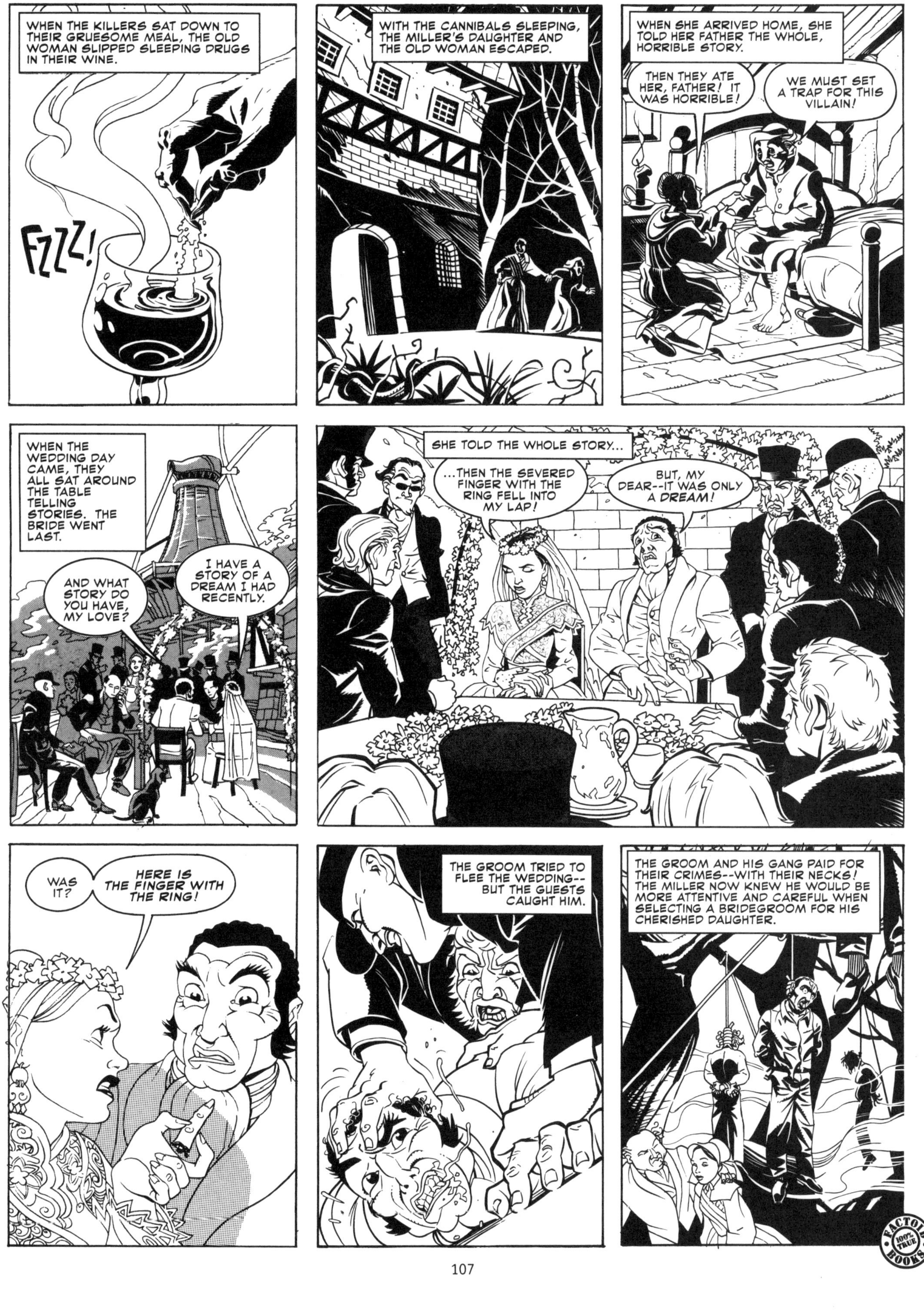

WHEN THE KILLERS SAT DOWN TO THEIR GRUESOME MEAL, THE OLD WOMAN SLIPPED SLEEPING DRUGS IN THEIR WINE.
FZZZ!
WITH THE CANNIBALS SLEEPING, THE MILLER'S DAUGHTER AND THE OLD WOMAN ESCAPED.
WHEN SHE ARRIVED HOME, SHE TOLD HER FATHER THE WHOLE, HORRIBLE STORY.
THEN THEY ATE HER, FATHER! IT WAS HORRIBLE!
WE MUST SET A TRAP FOR THIS VILLAIN!
WHEN THE WEDDING DAY CAME, THEY ALL SAT AROUND THE TABLE TELLING STORIES. THE BRIDE WENT LAST.
AND WHAT STORY DO YOU HAVE, MY LOVE?
I HAVE A STORY OF A DREAM I HAD RECENTLY.
SHE TOLD THE WHOLE STORY...
...THEN THE SEVERED FINGER WITH THE RING FELL INTO MY LAP!
BUT, MY DEAR--IT WAS ONLY A DREAM!
WAS IT?
HERE IS THE FINGER WITH THE RING!
THE GROOM TRIED TO FLEE THE WEDDING-- BUT THE GUESTS CAUGHT HIM.
THE GROOM AND HIS GANG PAID FOR THEIR CRIMES--WITH THEIR NECKS! THE MILLER NOW KNEW HE WOULD BE MORE ATTENTIVE AND CAREFUL WHEN SELECTING A BRIDEGROOM FOR HIS CHERISHED DAUGHTER.

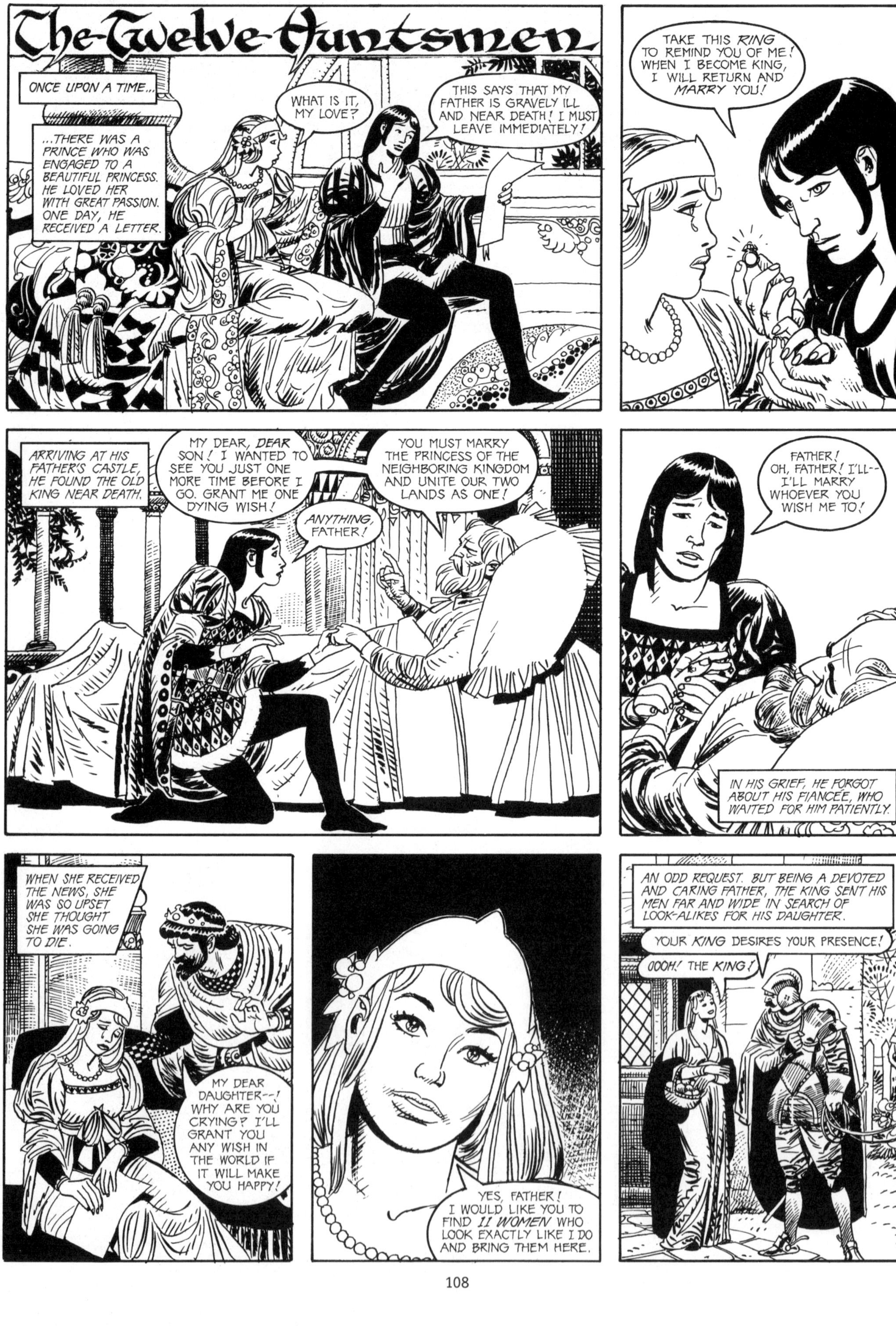
The Twelve Huntsmen
ONCE UPON A TIME...
...THERE WAS A PRINCE WHO WAS ENGAGED TO A BEAUTIFUL PRINCESS. HE LOVED HER WITH GREAT PASSION. ONE DAY, HE RECEIVED A LETTER.
WHAT IS IT, MY LOVE?
THIS SAYS THAT MY FATHER IS GRAVELY ILL AND NEAR DEATH! I MUST LEAVE IMMEDIATELY!
TAKE THIS RING TO REMIND YOU OF ME! WHEN I BECOME KING, I WILL RETURN AND MARRY YOU!
ARRIVING AT HIS FATHER'S CASTLE, HE FOUND THE OLD KING NEAR DEATH.
MY DEAR, DEAR SON! I WANTED TO SEE YOU JUST ONE MORE TIME BEFORE I GO. GRANT ME ONE DYING WISH!
ANYTHING, FATHER!
YOU MUST MARRY THE PRINCESS OF THE NEIGHBORING KINGDOM AND UNITE OUR TWO LANDS AS ONE!
FATHER! OH, FATHER! I'LL-- I'LL MARRY WHOEVER YOU WISH ME TO!
IN HIS GRIEF, HE FORGOT ABOUT HIS FIANCEE, WHO WAITED FOR HIM PATIENTLY.
WHEN SHE RECEIVED THE NEWS, SHE WAS SO UPSET SHE THOUGHT SHE WAS GOING TO DIE.
MY DEAR DAUGHTER--! WHY ARE YOU CRYING? I'LL GRANT YOU ANY WISH IN THE WORLD IF IT WILL MAKE YOU HAPPY!
YES, FATHER! I WOULD LIKE YOU TO FIND 11 WOMEN WHO LOOK EXACTLY LIKE I DO AND BRING THEM HERE.
AN ODD REQUEST. BUT BEING A DEVOTED AND CARING FATHER, THE KING SENT HIS MEN FAR AND WIDE IN SEARCH OF LOOK-ALIKES FOR HIS DAUGHTER.
YOUR KING DESIRES YOUR PRESENCE!
OOOH! THE KING!

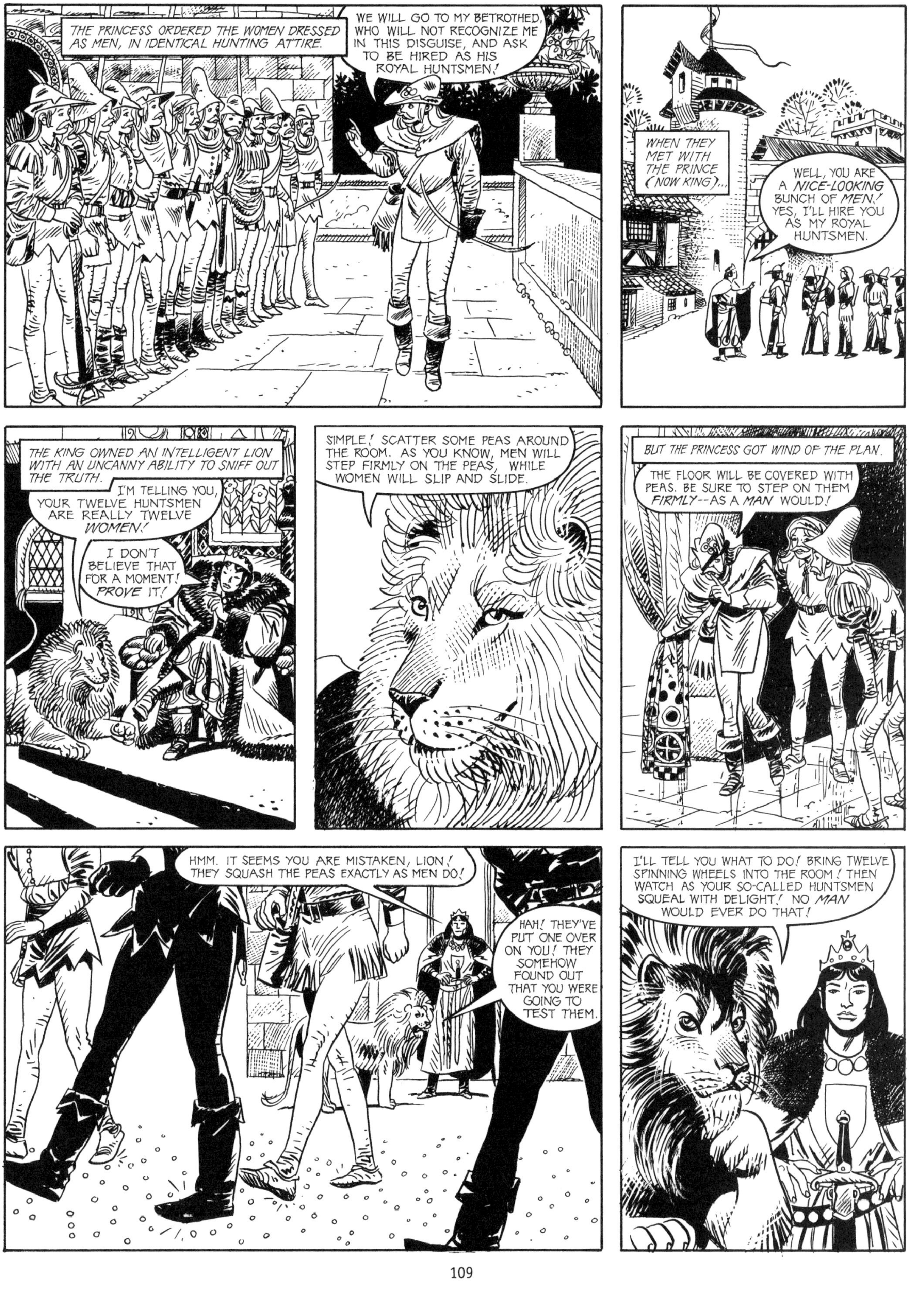
THE PRINCESS ORDERED THE WOMEN DRESSED AS MEN, IN IDENTICAL HUNTING ATTIRE.
WE WILL GO TO MY BETROTHED, WHO WILL NOT RECOGNIZE ME IN THIS DISGUISE, AND ASK TO BE HIRED AS HIS ROYAL HUNTSMEN!
WHEN THEY MET WITH THE PRINCE (NOW KING)...
WELL, YOU ARE A NICE-LOOKING BUNCH OF MEN! YES, I'LL HIRE YOU AS MY ROYAL HUNTSMEN.
THE KING OWNED AN INTELLIGENT LION WITH AN UNCANNY ABILITY TO SNIFF OUT THE TRUTH.
I'M TELLING YOU, YOUR TWELVE HUNTSMEN ARE REALLY TWELVE WOMEN!
I DON'T BELIEVE THAT FOR A MOMENT! PROVE IT!
SIMPLE! SCATTER SOME PEAS AROUND THE ROOM. AS YOU KNOW, MEN WILL STEP FIRMLY ON THE PEAS, WHILE WOMEN WILL SLIP AND SLIDE.
BUT THE PRINCESS GOT WIND OF THE PLAN.
THE FLOOR WILL BE COVERED WITH PEAS. BE SURE TO STEP ON THEM FIRMLY--AS A MAN WOULD!
HMM. IT SEEMS YOU ARE MISTAKEN, LION! THEY SQUASH THE PEAS EXACTLY AS MEN DO!
HAH! THEY'VE PUT ONE OVER ON YOU! THEY SOMEHOW FOUND OUT THAT YOU WERE GOING TO TEST THEM.
I'LL TELL YOU WHAT TO DO! BRING TWELVE SPINNING WHEELS INTO THE ROOM! THEN WATCH AS YOUR SO-CALLED HUNTSMEN SQUEAL WITH DELIGHT! NO MAN WOULD EVER DO THAT!

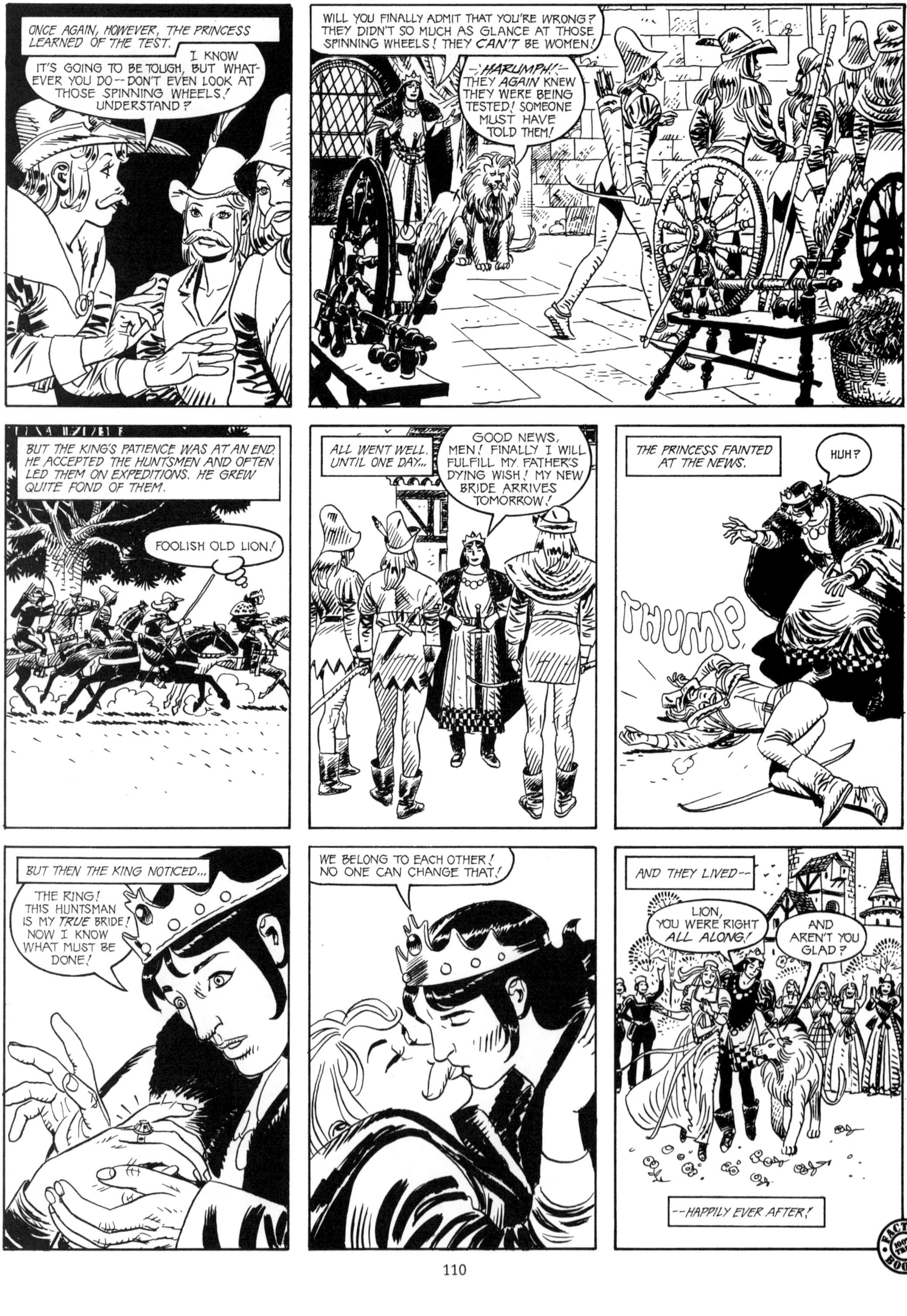
ONCE AGAIN, HOWEVER, THE PRINCESS LEARNED OF THE TEST.
I KNOW IT'S GOING TO BE TOUGH, BUT WHATEVER YOU DO-- DON'T EVEN LOOK AT THOSE SPINNING WHEELS! UNDERSTAND?
WILL YOU FINALLY ADMIT THAT YOU'RE WRONG? THEY DIDN'T SO MUCH AS GLANCE AT THOSE SPINNING WHEELS! THEY CAN'T BE WOMEN!
-HARUMPH!- THEY AGAIN KNEW THEY WERE BEING TESTED! SOMEONE MUST HAVE TOLD THEM!
BUT THE KING'S PATIENCE WAS AT AN END. HE ACCEPTED THE HUNTSMEN AND OFTEN LED THEM ON EXPEDITIONS. HE GREW QUITE FOND OF THEM.
FOOLISH OLD LION!
ALL WENT WELL, UNTIL ONE DAY...
GOOD NEWS, MEN! FINALLY I WILL FULFILL MY FATHER'S DYING WISH! MY NEW BRIDE ARRIVES TOMORROW!
THE PRINCESS FAINTED AT THE NEWS.
HUH?
THUMP
BUT THEN THE KING NOTICED...
THE RING! THIS HUNTSMAN IS MY TRUE BRIDE! NOW I KNOW WHAT MUST BE DONE!
WE BELONG TO EACH OTHER! NO ONE CAN CHANGE THAT!
AND THEY LIVED--
LION, YOU WERE RIGHT ALL ALONG!
AND AREN'T YOU GLAD?
--HAPPILY EVER AFTER!

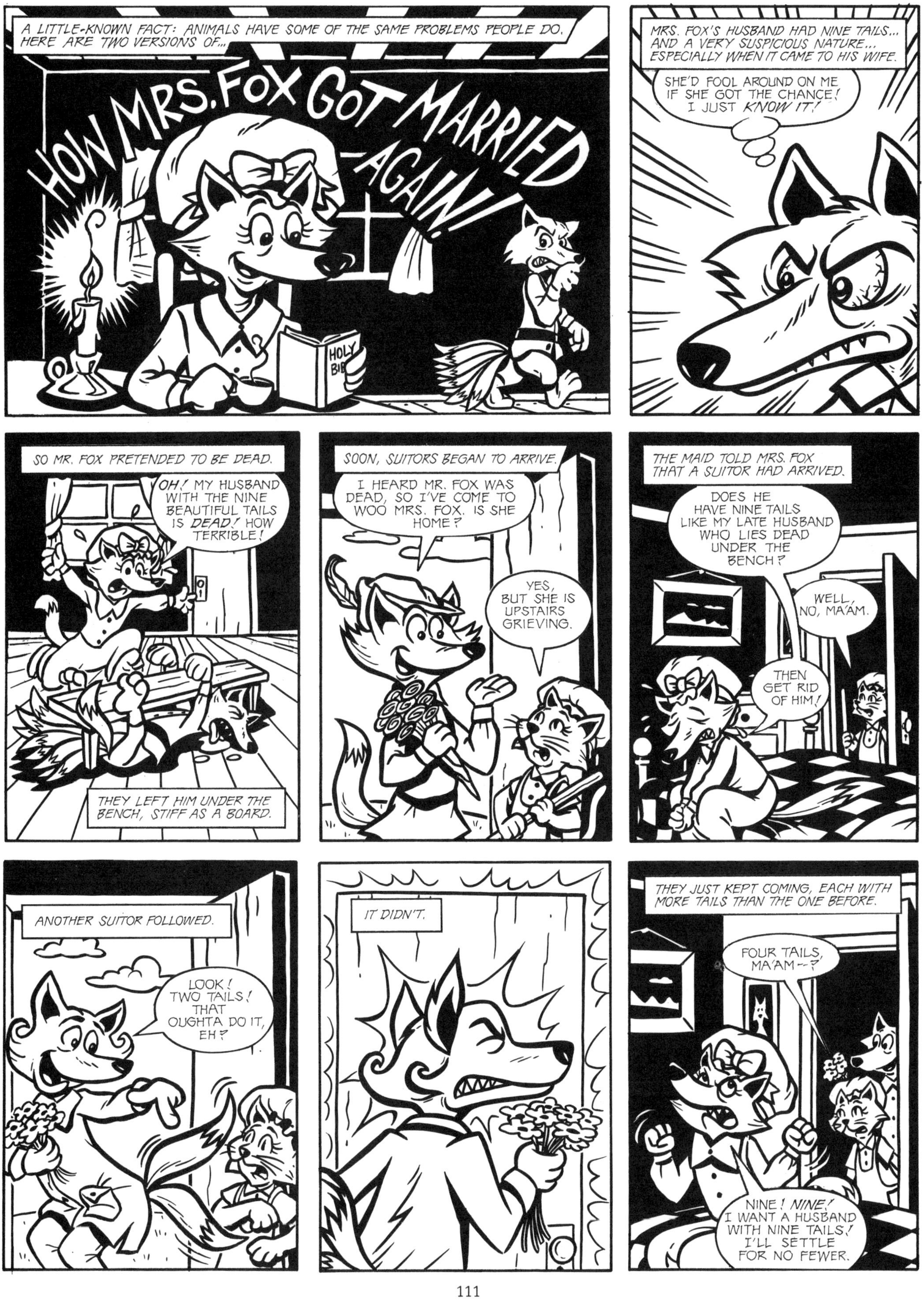
A LITTLE-KNOWN FACT: ANIMALS HAVE SOME OF THE SAME PROBLEMS PEOPLE DO. HERE ARE TWO VERSIONS OF...
HOW MRS. FOX GOT MARRIED AGAIN!
HOLY BIB
MRS. FOX'S HUSBAND HAD NINE TAILS... AND A VERY SUSPICIOUS NATURE... ESPECIALLY WHEN IT CAME TO HIS WIFE.
SHE'D FOOL AROUND ON ME IF SHE GOT THE CHANCE! I JUST KNOW IT!
SO MR. FOX PRETENDED TO BE DEAD.
OH! MY HUSBAND WITH THE NINE BEAUTIFUL TAILS IS DEAD! HOW TERRIBLE!
THEY LEFT HIM UNDER THE BENCH, STIFF AS A BOARD.
SOON, SUITORS BEGAN TO ARRIVE.
I HEARD MR. FOX WAS DEAD, SO I'VE COME TO WOO MRS. FOX. IS SHE HOME?
YES, BUT SHE IS UPSTAIRS GRIEVING.
THE MAID TOLD MRS. FOX THAT A SUITOR HAD ARRIVED.
DOES HE HAVE NINE TAILS LIKE MY LATE HUSBAND WHO LIES DEAD UNDER THE BENCH?
WELL, NO, MA'AM.
THEN GET RID OF HIM!
ANOTHER SUITOR FOLLOWED.
LOOK! TWO TAILS! THAT OUGHTA DO IT, EH?
IT DIDN'T.
THEY JUST KEPT COMING, EACH WITH MORE TAILS THAN THE ONE BEFORE.
FOUR TAILS, MA'AM--?
NINE! NINE! I WANT A HUSBAND WITH NINE TAILS! I'LL SETTLE FOR NO FEWER.

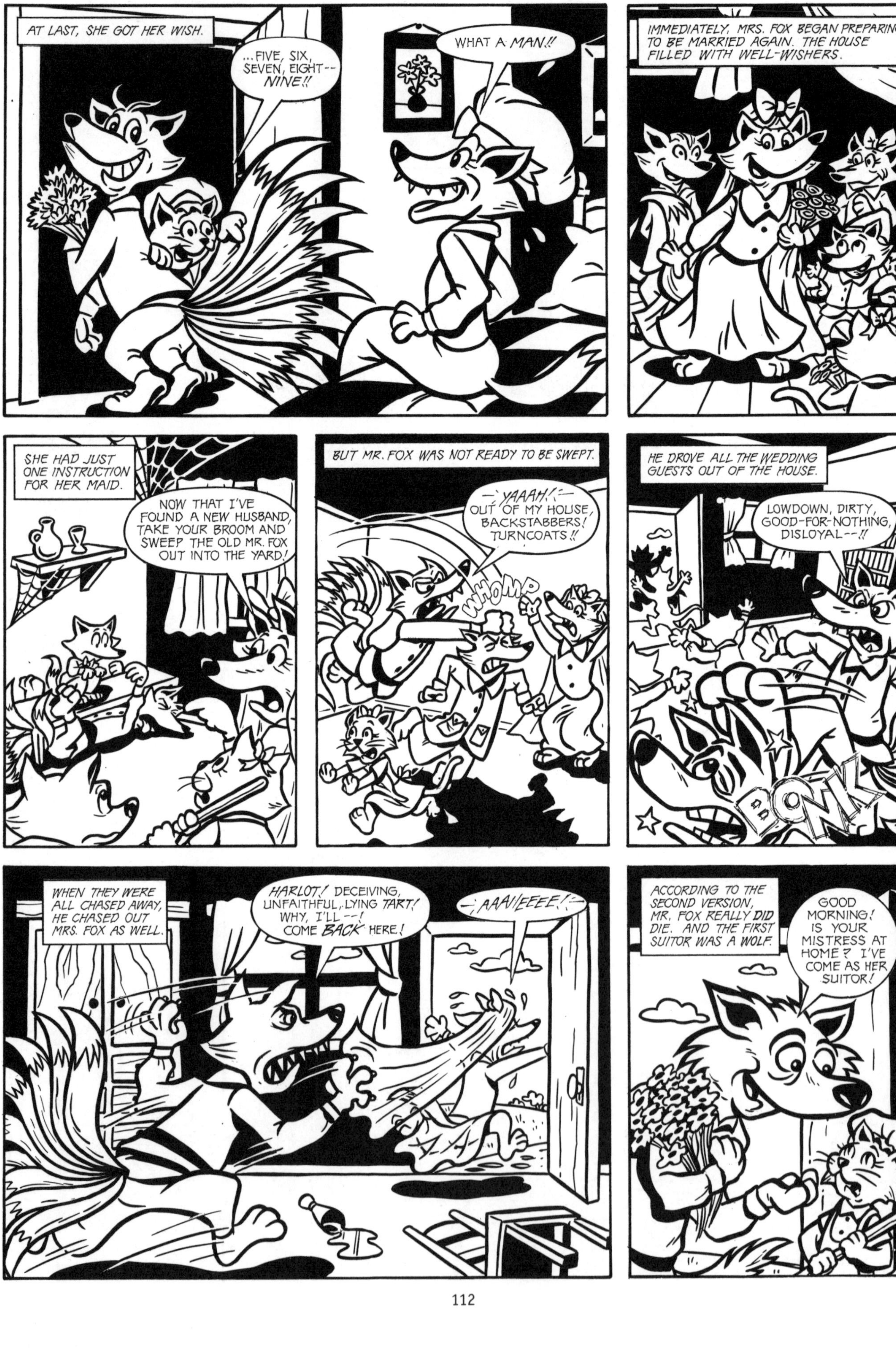
AT LAST, SHE GOT HER WISH.
...FIVE, SIX, SEVEN, EIGHT-- NINE!!
WHAT A MAN!!
IMMEDIATELY, MRS. FOX BEGAN PREPARING TO BE MARRIED AGAIN. THE HOUSE FILLED WITH WELL-WISHERS.
SHE HAD JUST ONE INSTRUCTION FOR HER MAID.
NOW THAT I'VE FOUND A NEW HUSBAND, TAKE YOUR BROOM AND SWEEP THE OLD MR. FOX OUT INTO THE YARD!
BUT MR. FOX WAS NOT READY TO BE SWEPT.
-YAAAH!- OUT OF MY HOUSE, BACKSTABBERS! TURNCOATS!!
WHOMP
HE DROVE ALL THE WEDDING GUESTS OUT OF THE HOUSE.
LOWDOWN, DIRTY, GOOD-FOR-NOTHING, DISLOYAL--!!
BONK
WHEN THEY WERE ALL CHASED AWAY, HE CHASED OUT MRS. FOX AS WELL.
HARLOT! DECEIVING, UNFAITHFUL, LYING TART! WHY, I'LL--! COME BACK HERE!
-AAAIIEEEE!-
ACCORDING TO THE SECOND VERSION, MR. FOX REALLY DID DIE. AND THE FIRST SUITOR WAS A WOLF.
GOOD MORNING! IS YOUR MISTRESS AT HOME? I'VE COME AS HER SUITOR!

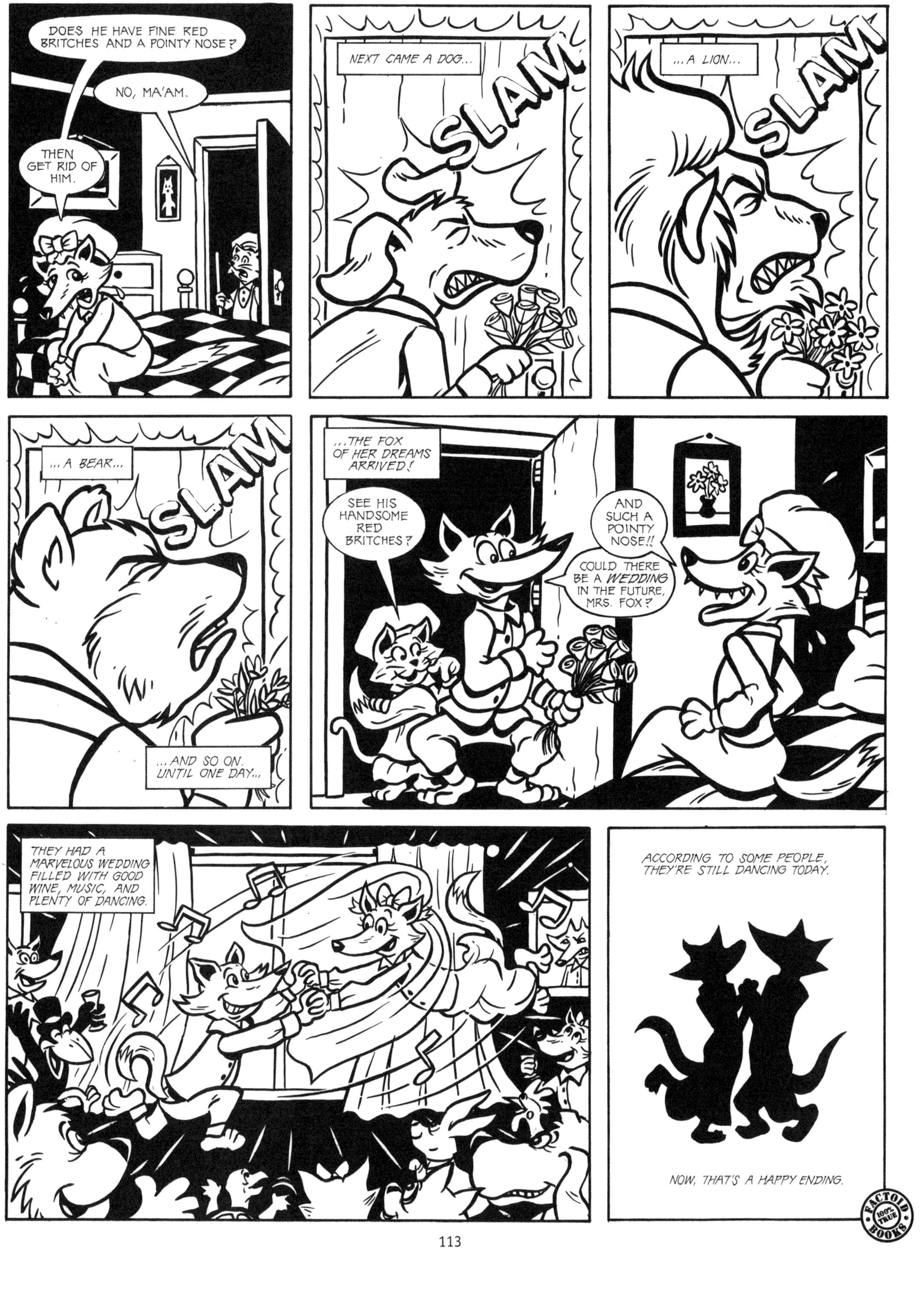
DOES HE HAVE FINE RED BRITCHES AND A POINTY NOSE?
NO, MA'AM.
THEN GET RID OF HIM.
NEXT CAME A DOG...
SLAM
...A LION...
SLAM
...A BEAR...
SLAM
...AND SO ON. UNTIL ONE DAY...
...THE FOX OF HER DREAMS ARRIVED!
SEE HIS HANDSOME RED BRITCHES?
AND SUCH A POINTY NOSE!!
COULD THERE BE A WEDDING IN THE FUTURE, MRS. FOX?
THEY HAD A MARVELOUS WEDDING FILLED WITH GOOD WINE, MUSIC, AND PLENTY OF DANCING.
ACCORDING TO SOME PEOPLE, THEY'RE STILL DANCING TODAY.
NOW, THAT'S A HAPPY ENDING.
FACTOID BOOKS 100% TRUE

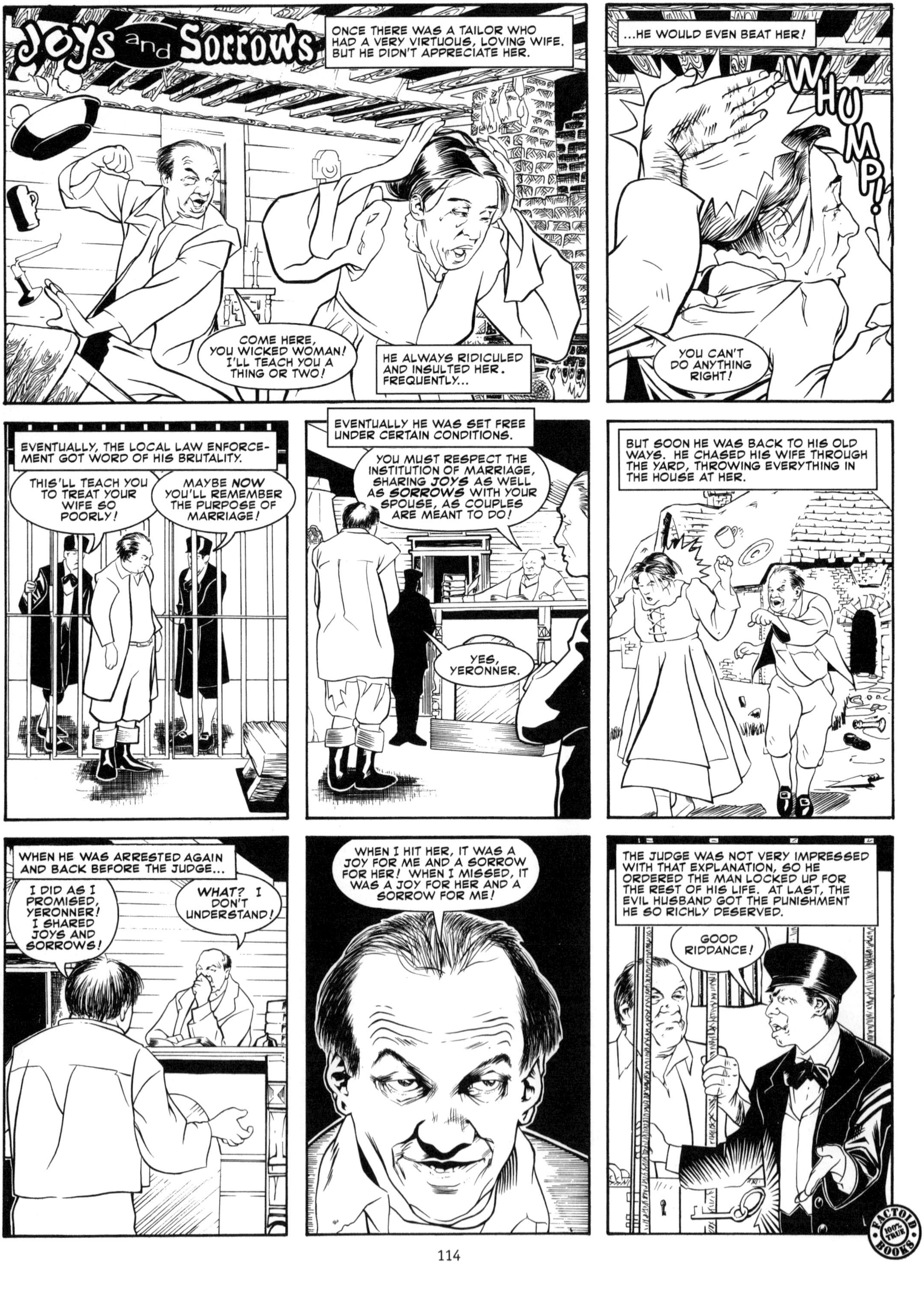

JOYS and SORROWS
ONCE THERE WAS A TAILOR WHO HAD A VERY VIRTUOUS, LOVING WIFE. BUT HE DIDN'T APPRECIATE HER.
COME HERE, YOU WICKED WOMAN! I'LL TEACH YOU A THING OR TWO!
HE ALWAYS RIDICULED AND INSULTED HER. FREQUENTLY...
...HE WOULD EVEN BEAT HER!
WHUMP!
YOU CAN'T DO ANYTHING RIGHT!
EVENTUALLY, THE LOCAL LAW ENFORCEMENT GOT WORD OF HIS BRUTALITY.
THIS'LL TEACH YOU TO TREAT YOUR WIFE SO POORLY!
MAYBE NOW YOU'LL REMEMBER THE PURPOSE OF MARRIAGE!
EVENTUALLY HE WAS SET FREE UNDER CERTAIN CONDITIONS.
YOU MUST RESPECT THE INSTITUTION OF MARRIAGE, SHARING JOYS AS WELL AS SORROWS WITH YOUR SPOUSE, AS COUPLES ARE MEANT TO DO!
YES, YERONNER.
BUT SOON HE WAS BACK TO HIS OLD WAYS. HE CHASED HIS WIFE THROUGH THE YARD, THROWING EVERYTHING IN THE HOUSE AT HER.
WHEN HE WAS ARRESTED AGAIN AND BACK BEFORE THE JUDGE...
I DID AS I PROMISED, YERONNER! I SHARED JOYS AND SORROWS!
WHAT? I DON'T UNDERSTAND!
WHEN I HIT HER, IT WAS A JOY FOR ME AND A SORROW FOR HER! WHEN I MISSED, IT WAS A JOY FOR HER AND A SORROW FOR ME!
THE JUDGE WAS NOT VERY IMPRESSED WITH THAT EXPLANATION, SO HE ORDERED THE MAN LOCKED UP FOR THE REST OF HIS LIFE. AT LAST, THE EVIL HUSBAND GOT THE PUNISHMENT HE SO RICHLY DESERVED.
GOOD RIDDANCE!
FACTOID BOOKS 100% TRUE

CHAPTER FOUR

MAGICAL STRANGERS

Good fortune often emanates from strange sources. Bad luck, too. One thing is for sure: in Grimms' tales, the stranger, that mystical being from outside the family, outside the village, outside the human race, can really make a mess of things. Once you come in contact with a powerful being beyond the ordinary there is no turning back. You've got a whole new life — whether you want one or not. There are stories of gnomes and elves, friendly bears and cantankerous frogs, which find a modern-era echo in today's tales of aliens and angels which dominates so much of the entertainment media's output lately. The Other, with a capital O, can destroy you or make your dreams come true. You could keep to yourself, but if you never talk to strangers you'll never get a chance to get whatever it is that you truly desire.

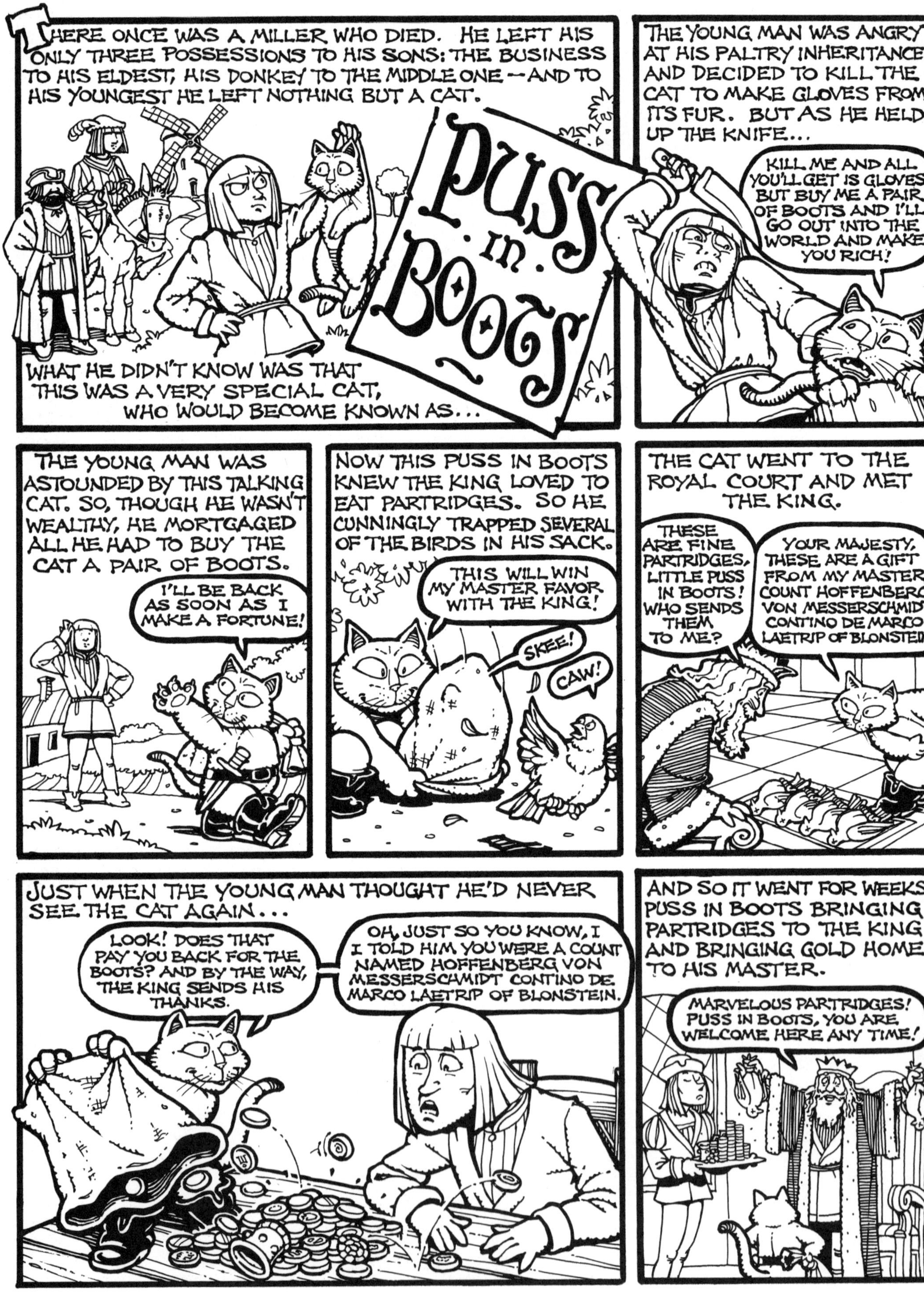
THERE ONCE WAS A MILLER WHO DIED. HE LEFT HIS ONLY THREE POSSESSIONS TO HIS SONS: THE BUSINESS TO HIS ELDEST, HIS DONKEY TO THE MIDDLE ONE -- AND TO HIS YOUNGEST HE LEFT NOTHING BUT A CAT.
WHAT HE DIDN'T KNOW WAS THAT THIS WAS A VERY SPECIAL CAT, WHO WOULD BECOME KNOWN AS...
PUSS in BOOTS
THE YOUNG MAN WAS ANGRY AT HIS PALTRY INHERITANCE AND DECIDED TO KILL THE CAT TO MAKE GLOVES FROM ITS FUR. BUT AS HE HELD UP THE KNIFE...
KILL ME AND ALL YOU'LL GET IS GLOVES! BUT BUY ME A PAIR OF BOOTS AND I'LL GO OUT INTO THE WORLD AND MAKE YOU RICH!
THE YOUNG MAN WAS ASTOUNDED BY THIS TALKING CAT. SO, THOUGH HE WASN'T WEALTHY, HE MORTGAGED ALL HE HAD TO BUY THE CAT A PAIR OF BOOTS.
I'LL BE BACK AS SOON AS I MAKE A FORTUNE!
NOW THIS PUSS IN BOOTS KNEW THE KING LOVED TO EAT PARTRIDGES. SO HE CUNNINGLY TRAPPED SEVERAL OF THE BIRDS IN HIS SACK.
THIS WILL WIN MY MASTER FAVOR WITH THE KING!
SKEE!
CAW!
THE CAT WENT TO THE ROYAL COURT AND MET THE KING.
THESE ARE FINE PARTRIDGES, LITTLE PUSS IN BOOTS! WHO SENDS THEM TO ME?
YOUR MAJESTY, THESE ARE A GIFT FROM MY MASTER, COUNT HOFFENBERG VON MESSERSCHMIDT CONTINO DE MARCO LAETRIP OF BLONSTEIN.
JUST WHEN THE YOUNG MAN THOUGHT HE'D NEVER SEE THE CAT AGAIN...
LOOK! DOES THAT PAY YOU BACK FOR THE BOOTS? AND BY THE WAY, THE KING SENDS HIS THANKS.
OH, JUST SO YOU KNOW, I I TOLD HIM YOU WERE A COUNT NAMED HOFFENBERG VON MESSERSCHMIDT CONTINO DE MARCO LAETRIP OF BLONSTEIN.
AND SO IT WENT FOR WEEKS, PUSS IN BOOTS BRINGING PARTRIDGES TO THE KING AND BRINGING GOLD HOME TO HIS MASTER.
MARVELOUS PARTRIDGES! PUSS IN BOOTS, YOU ARE WELCOME HERE ANY TIME!

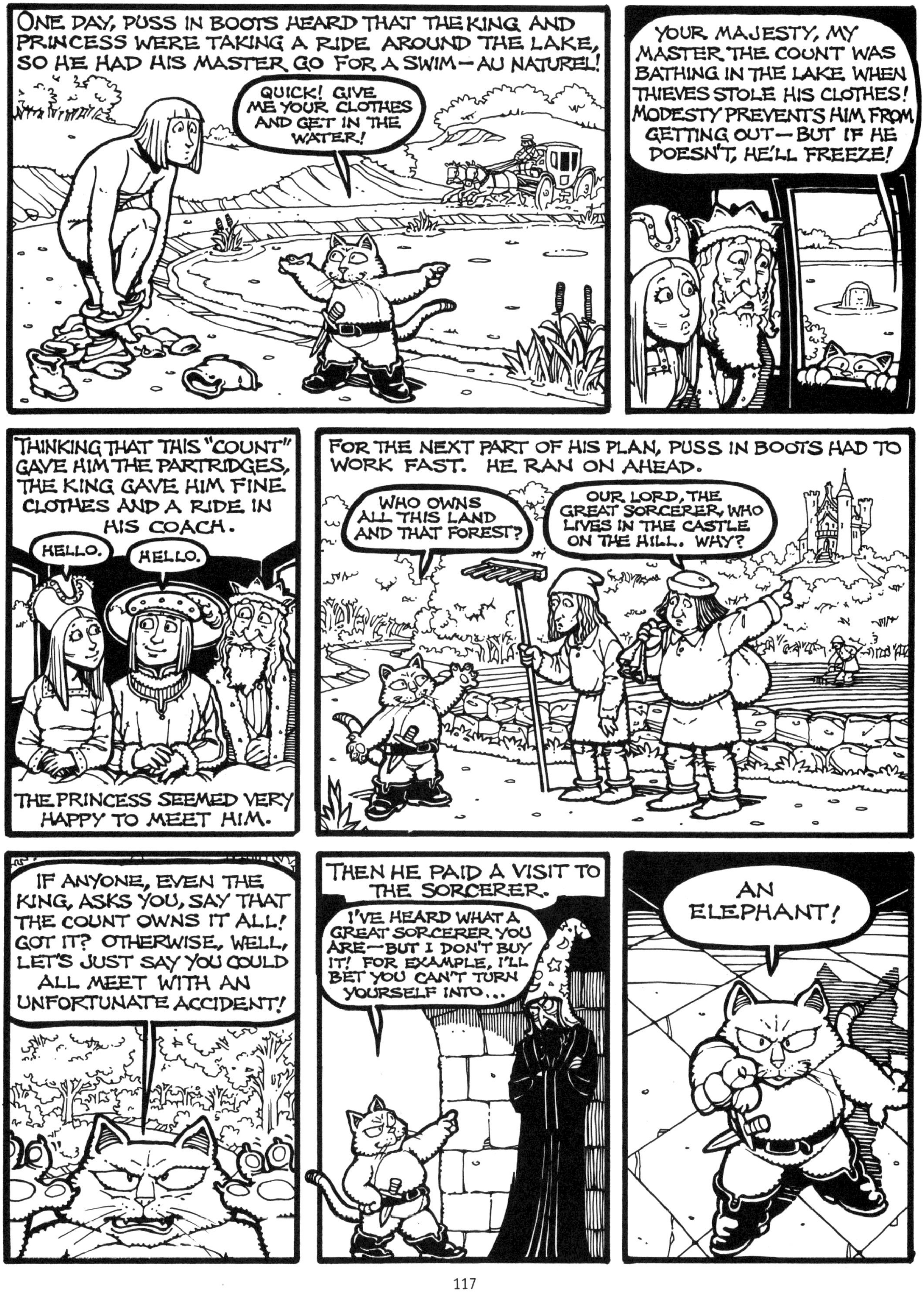
ONE DAY, PUSS IN BOOTS HEARD THAT THE KING AND PRINCESS WERE TAKING A RIDE AROUND THE LAKE, SO HE HAD HIS MASTER GO FOR A SWIM—AU NATUREL!
QUICK! GIVE ME YOUR CLOTHES AND GET IN THE WATER!
YOUR MAJESTY, MY MASTER THE COUNT WAS BATHING IN THE LAKE WHEN THIEVES STOLE HIS CLOTHES! MODESTY PREVENTS HIM FROM GETTING OUT—BUT IF HE DOESN'T, HE'LL FREEZE!
THINKING THAT THIS "COUNT" GAVE HIM THE PARTRIDGES, THE KING GAVE HIM FINE CLOTHES AND A RIDE IN HIS COACH.
HELLO.
HELLO.
THE PRINCESS SEEMED VERY HAPPY TO MEET HIM.
FOR THE NEXT PART OF HIS PLAN, PUSS IN BOOTS HAD TO WORK FAST. HE RAN ON AHEAD.
WHO OWNS ALL THIS LAND AND THAT FOREST?
OUR LORD, THE GREAT SORCERER, WHO LIVES IN THE CASTLE ON THE HILL. WHY?
IF ANYONE, EVEN THE KING, ASKS YOU, SAY THAT THE COUNT OWNS IT ALL! GOT IT? OTHERWISE, WELL, LET'S JUST SAY YOU COULD ALL MEET WITH AN UNFORTUNATE ACCIDENT!
THEN HE PAID A VISIT TO THE SORCERER.
I'VE HEARD WHAT A GREAT SORCERER YOU ARE—BUT I DON'T BUY IT! FOR EXAMPLE, I'LL BET YOU CAN'T TURN YOURSELF INTO...
AN ELEPHANT!

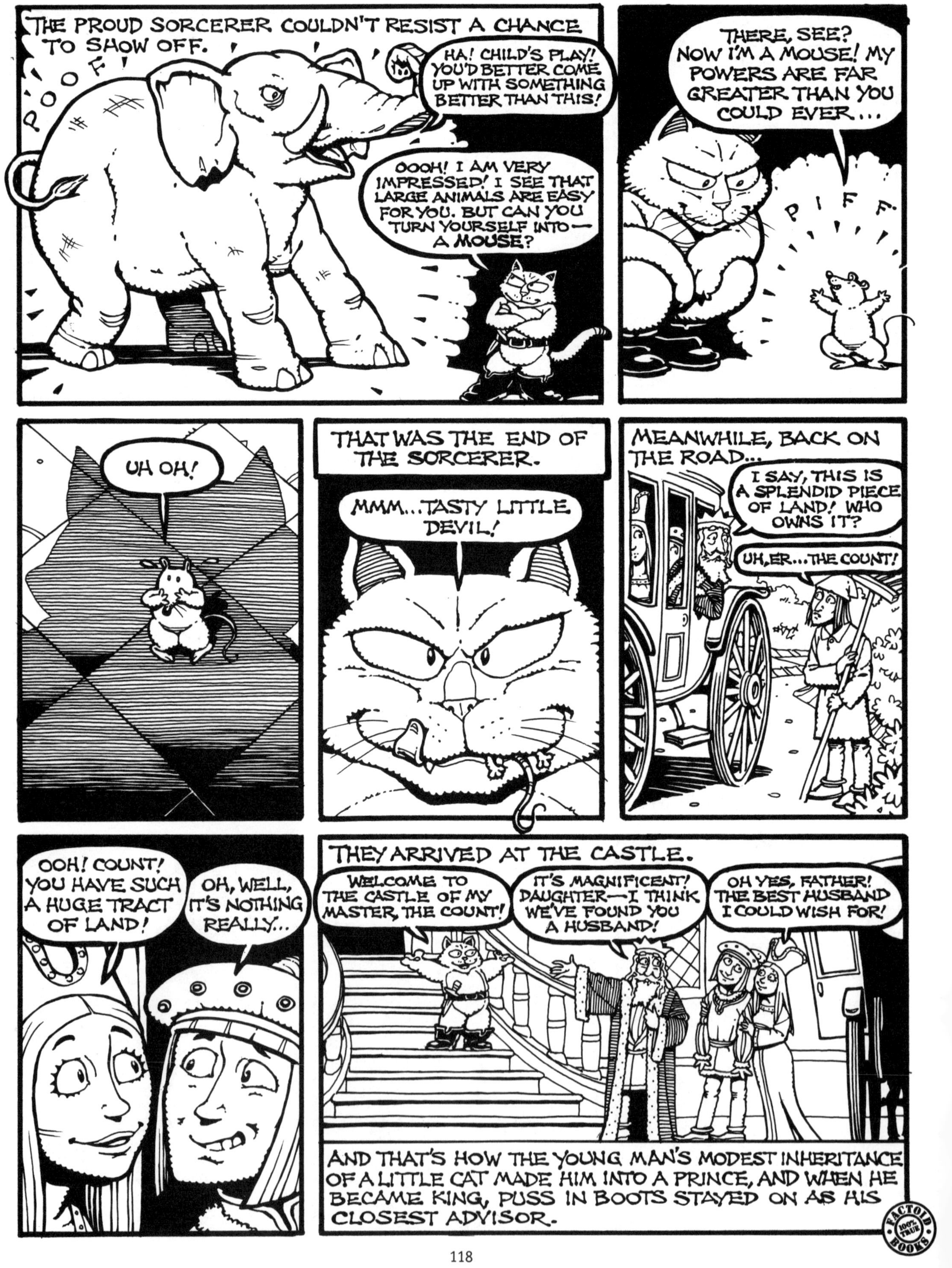
THE PROUD SORCERER COULDN'T RESIST A CHANCE TO SHOW OFF.
POOF!
HA! CHILD'S PLAY! YOU'D BETTER COME UP WITH SOMETHING BETTER THAN THIS!
OOOH! I AM VERY IMPRESSED! I SEE THAT LARGE ANIMALS ARE EASY FOR YOU. BUT CAN YOU TURN YOURSELF INTO— A MOUSE?
THERE, SEE? NOW I'M A MOUSE! MY POWERS ARE FAR GREATER THAN YOU COULD EVER...
PIFF.
UH OH!
THAT WAS THE END OF THE SORCERER.
MMM...TASTY LITTLE DEVIL!
MEANWHILE, BACK ON THE ROAD...
I SAY, THIS IS A SPLENDID PIECE OF LAND! WHO OWNS IT?
UH, ER...THE COUNT!
OOH! COUNT! YOU HAVE SUCH A HUGE TRACT OF LAND!
OH, WELL, IT'S NOTHING REALLY...
THEY ARRIVED AT THE CASTLE.
WELCOME TO THE CASTLE OF MY MASTER, THE COUNT!
IT'S MAGNIFICENT! DAUGHTER—I THINK WE'VE FOUND YOU A HUSBAND!
OH YES, FATHER! THE BEST HUSBAND I COULD WISH FOR!
AND THAT'S HOW THE YOUNG MAN'S MODEST INHERITANCE OF A LITTLE CAT MADE HIM INTO A PRINCE, AND WHEN HE BECAME KING, PUSS IN BOOTS STAYED ON AS HIS CLOSEST ADVISOR.
FACTOID BOOKS 100% TRUE

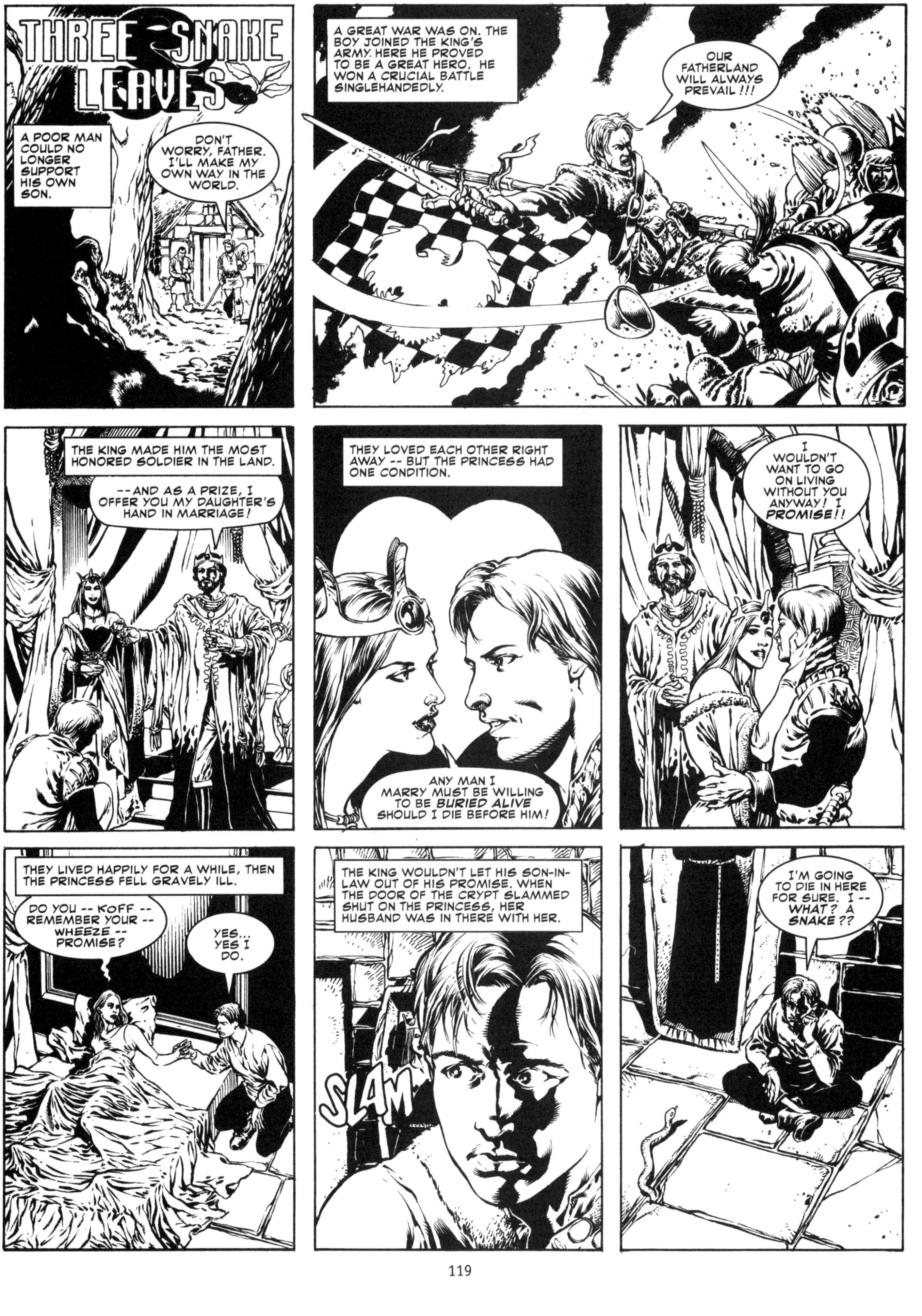
THREE SNAKE LEAVES
A POOR MAN COULD NO LONGER SUPPORT HIS OWN SON.
DON'T WORRY, FATHER. I'LL MAKE MY OWN WAY IN THE WORLD.
A GREAT WAR WAS ON. THE BOY JOINED THE KING'S ARMY. HERE HE PROVED TO BE A GREAT HERO. HE WON A CRUCIAL BATTLE SINGLEHANDEDLY.
OUR FATHERLAND WILL ALWAYS PREVAIL!!!
THE KING MADE HIM THE MOST HONORED SOLDIER IN THE LAND.
--AND AS A PRIZE, I OFFER YOU MY DAUGHTER'S HAND IN MARRIAGE!
THEY LOVED EACH OTHER RIGHT AWAY -- BUT THE PRINCESS HAD ONE CONDITION.
ANY MAN I MARRY MUST BE WILLING TO BE BURIED ALIVE SHOULD I DIE BEFORE HIM!
I WOULDN'T WANT TO GO ON LIVING WITHOUT YOU ANYWAY! I PROMISE!!
THEY LIVED HAPPILY FOR A WHILE, THEN THE PRINCESS FELL GRAVELY ILL.
DO YOU -- KOFF -- REMEMBER YOUR -- WHEEZE -- PROMISE?
YES... YES I DO.
THE KING WOULDN'T LET HIS SON-IN-LAW OUT OF HIS PROMISE. WHEN THE DOOR OF THE CRYPT SLAMMED SHUT ON THE PRINCESS, HER HUSBAND WAS IN THERE WITH HER.
SLAM
I'M GOING TO DIE IN HERE FOR SURE. I -- WHAT? A SNAKE??

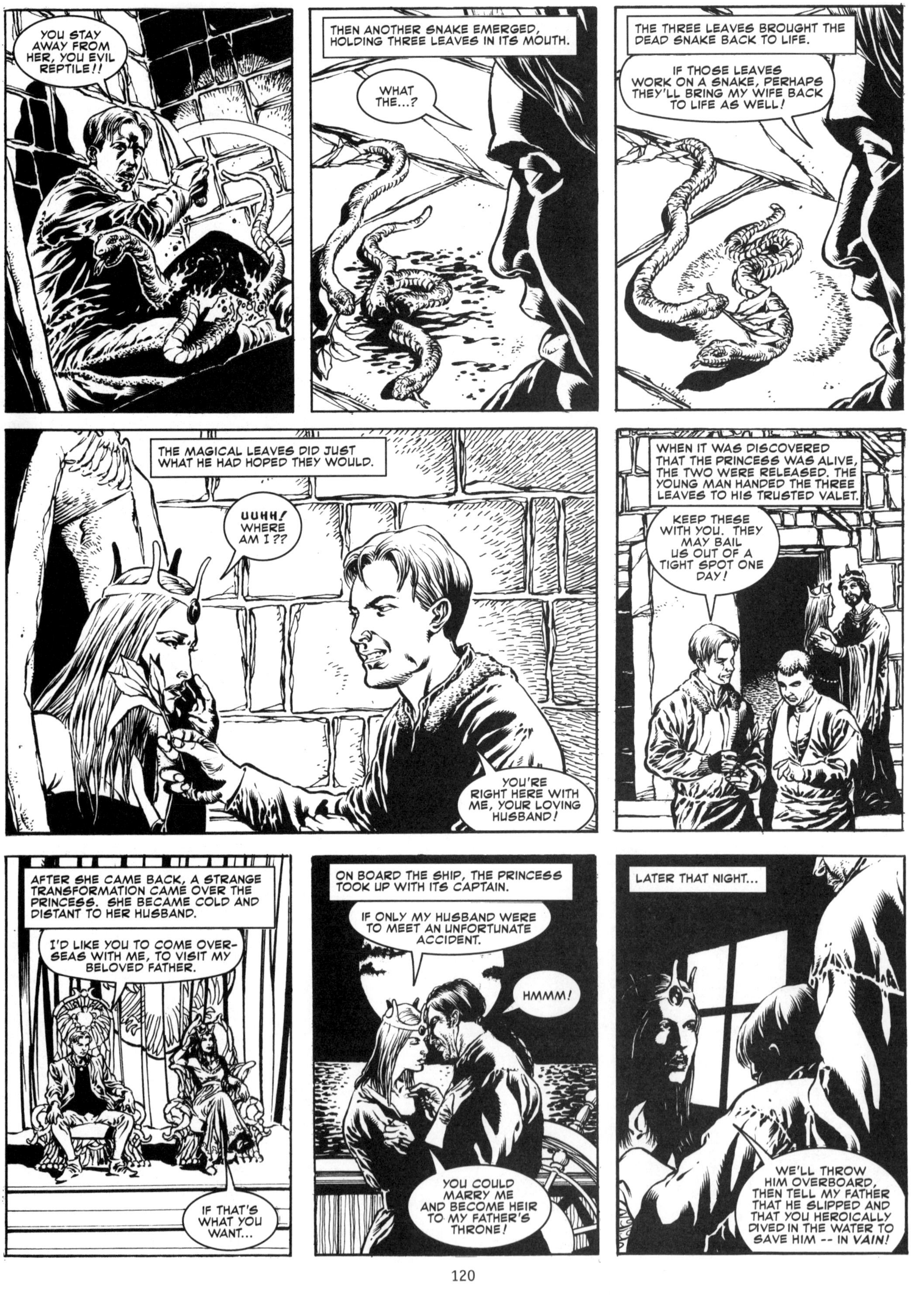
YOU STAY AWAY FROM HER, YOU EVIL REPTILE!!
THEN ANOTHER SNAKE EMERGED, HOLDING THREE LEAVES IN ITS MOUTH.
WHAT THE...?
THE THREE LEAVES BROUGHT THE DEAD SNAKE BACK TO LIFE.
IF THOSE LEAVES WORK ON A SNAKE, PERHAPS THEY'LL BRING MY WIFE BACK TO LIFE AS WELL!
THE MAGICAL LEAVES DID JUST WHAT HE HAD HOPED THEY WOULD.
UUHH! WHERE AM I??
YOU'RE RIGHT HERE WITH ME, YOUR LOVING HUSBAND!
WHEN IT WAS DISCOVERED THAT THE PRINCESS WAS ALIVE, THE TWO WERE RELEASED. THE YOUNG MAN HANDED THE THREE LEAVES TO HIS TRUSTED VALET.
KEEP THESE WITH YOU. THEY MAY BAIL US OUT OF A TIGHT SPOT ONE DAY!
AFTER SHE CAME BACK, A STRANGE TRANSFORMATION CAME OVER THE PRINCESS. SHE BECAME COLD AND DISTANT TO HER HUSBAND.
I'D LIKE YOU TO COME OVERSEAS WITH ME, TO VISIT MY BELOVED FATHER.
IF THAT'S WHAT YOU WANT...
ON BOARD THE SHIP, THE PRINCESS TOOK UP WITH ITS CAPTAIN.
IF ONLY MY HUSBAND WERE TO MEET AN UNFORTUNATE ACCIDENT.
HMMM!
YOU COULD MARRY ME AND BECOME HEIR TO MY FATHER'S THRONE!
LATER THAT NIGHT...
WE'LL THROW HIM OVERBOARD, THEN TELL MY FATHER THAT HE SLIPPED AND THAT YOU HEROICALLY DIVED IN THE WATER TO SAVE HIM -- IN VAIN!

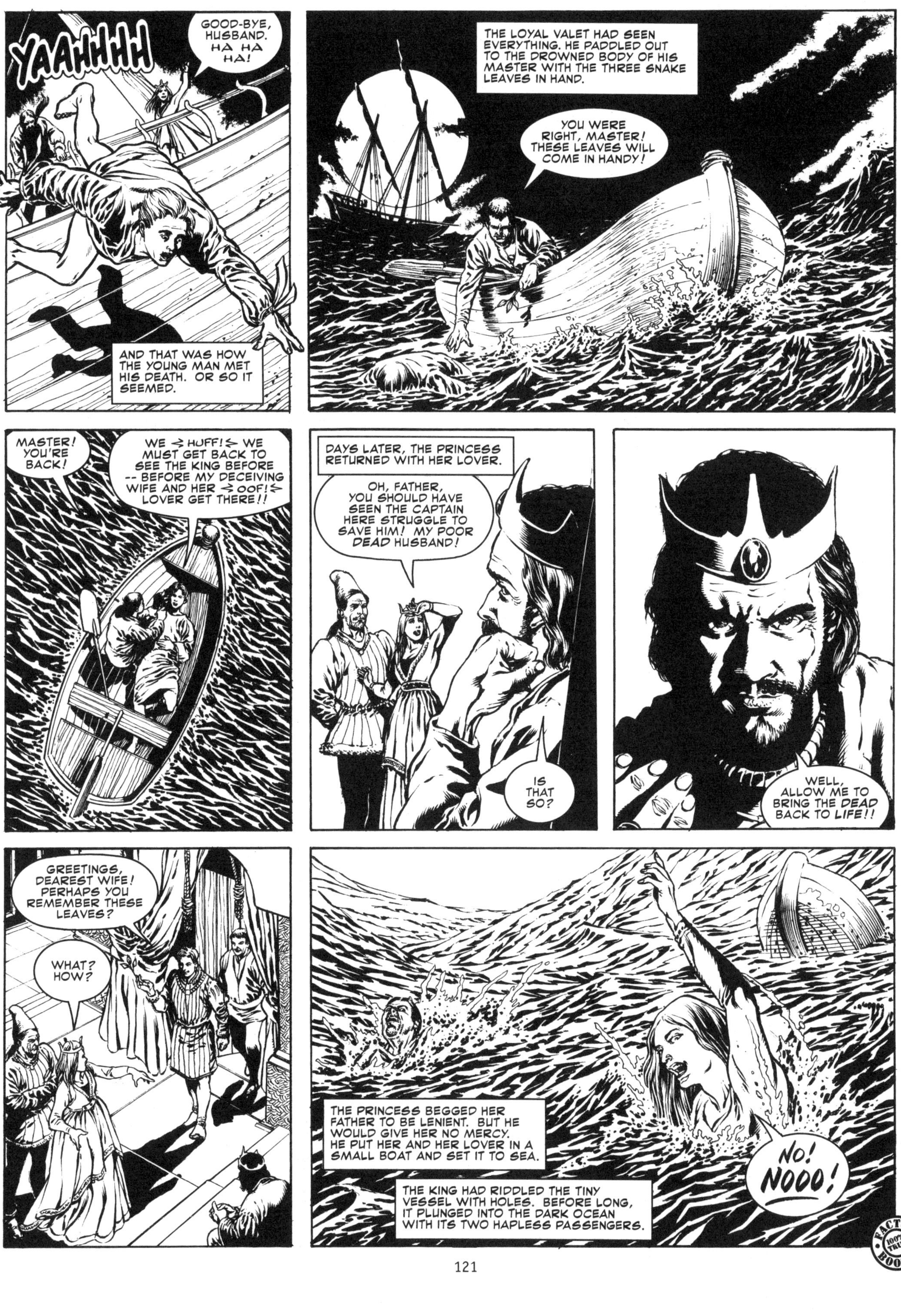

YAAHHHH
GOOD-BYE, HUSBAND. HA HA HA!
AND THAT WAS HOW THE YOUNG MAN MET HIS DEATH. OR SO IT SEEMED.
THE LOYAL VALET HAD SEEN EVERYTHING. HE PADDLED OUT TO THE DROWNED BODY OF HIS MASTER WITH THE THREE SNAKE LEAVES IN HAND.
YOU WERE RIGHT, MASTER! THESE LEAVES WILL COME IN HANDY!
MASTER! YOU'RE BACK!
WE ≥HUFF!≤ WE MUST GET BACK TO SEE THE KING BEFORE -- BEFORE MY DECEIVING WIFE AND HER ≥OOF!≤ LOVER GET THERE!!
DAYS LATER, THE PRINCESS RETURNED WITH HER LOVER.
OH, FATHER, YOU SHOULD HAVE SEEN THE CAPTAIN HERE STRUGGLE TO SAVE HIM! MY POOR DEAD HUSBAND!
IS THAT SO?
WELL, ALLOW ME TO BRING THE DEAD BACK TO LIFE!!
GREETINGS, DEAREST WIFE! PERHAPS YOU REMEMBER THESE LEAVES?
WHAT? HOW?
THE PRINCESS BEGGED HER FATHER TO BE LENIENT. BUT HE WOULD GIVE HER NO MERCY. HE PUT HER AND HER LOVER IN A SMALL BOAT AND SET IT TO SEA.
THE KING HAD RIDDLED THE TINY VESSEL WITH HOLES. BEFORE LONG, IT PLUNGED INTO THE DARK OCEAN WITH ITS TWO HAPLESS PASSENGERS.
NO! NOOO!
FACTOID BOOKS 100% TRUE

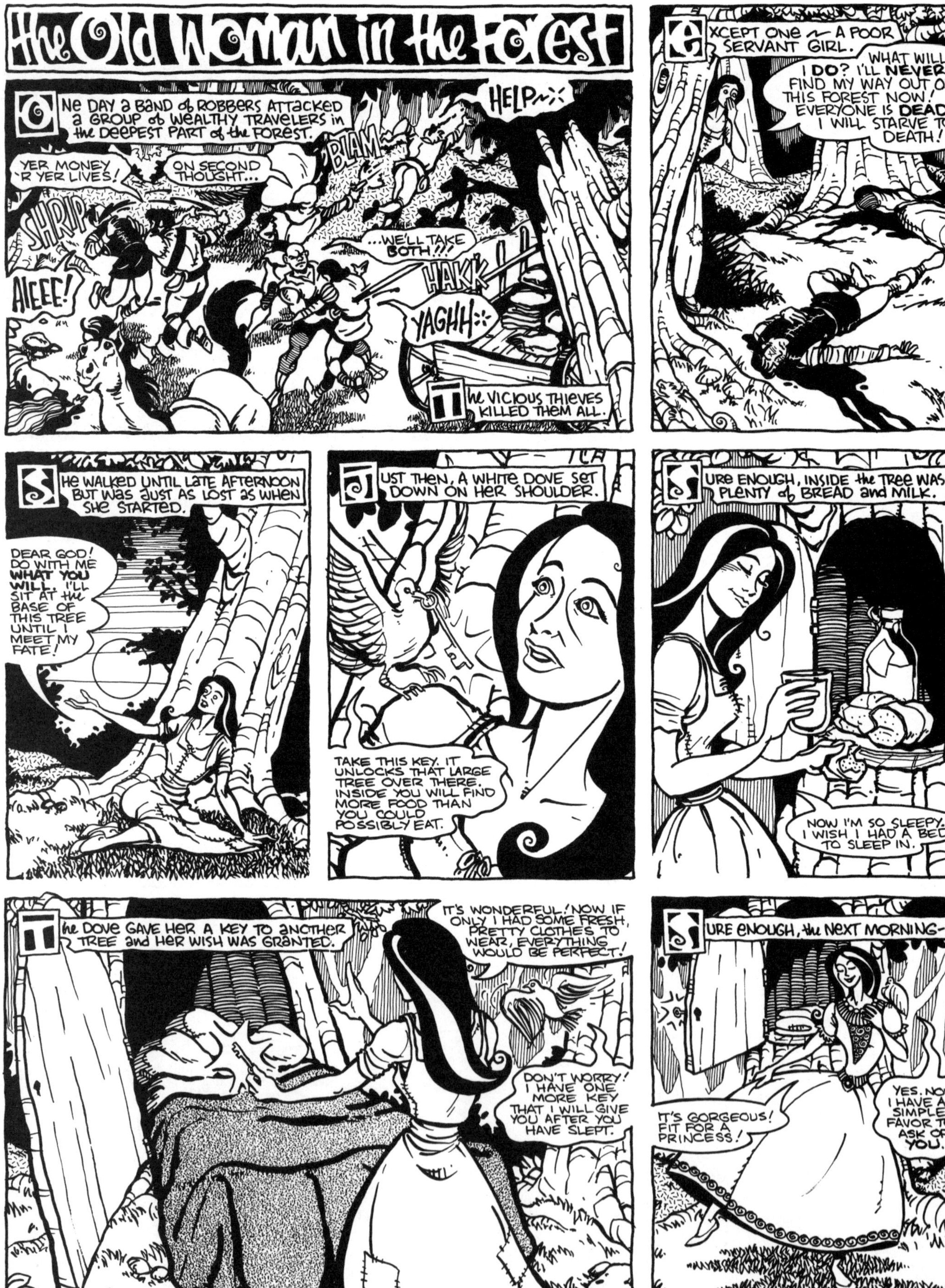
The Old Woman in the Forest
One day a band of robbers attacked a group of wealthy travelers in the deepest part of the forest.
HELP~!
YER MONEY 'R YER LIVES!
ON SECOND THOUGHT...
BLAM
SHRIP
...WE'LL TAKE BOTH!!!
HAKK
AIEEE!
YAGHH
The vicious thieves killed them all.
Except one — a poor servant girl.
WHAT WILL I DO? I'LL NEVER FIND MY WAY OUT OF THIS FOREST NOW! EVERYONE IS DEAD! I WILL STARVE TO DEATH!
She walked until late afternoon but was just as lost as when she started.
DEAR GOD! DO WITH ME WHAT YOU WILL. I'LL SIT AT THE BASE OF THIS TREE UNTIL I MEET MY FATE!
Just then, a white dove set down on her shoulder.
TAKE THIS KEY. IT UNLOCKS THAT LARGE TREE OVER THERE. INSIDE YOU WILL FIND MORE FOOD THAN YOU COULD POSSIBLY EAT.
Sure enough, inside the tree was plenty of bread and milk.
NOW I'M SO SLEEPY. I WISH I HAD A BED TO SLEEP IN.
The dove gave her a key to another tree and her wish was granted.
IT'S WONDERFUL! NOW IF ONLY I HAD SOME FRESH, PRETTY CLOTHES TO WEAR, EVERYTHING WOULD BE PERFECT!
DON'T WORRY! I HAVE ONE MORE KEY THAT I WILL GIVE YOU AFTER YOU HAVE SLEPT.
Sure enough, the next morning-
IT'S GORGEOUS! FIT FOR A PRINCESS!
YES. NOW I HAVE A SIMPLE FAVOR TO ASK OF YOU.

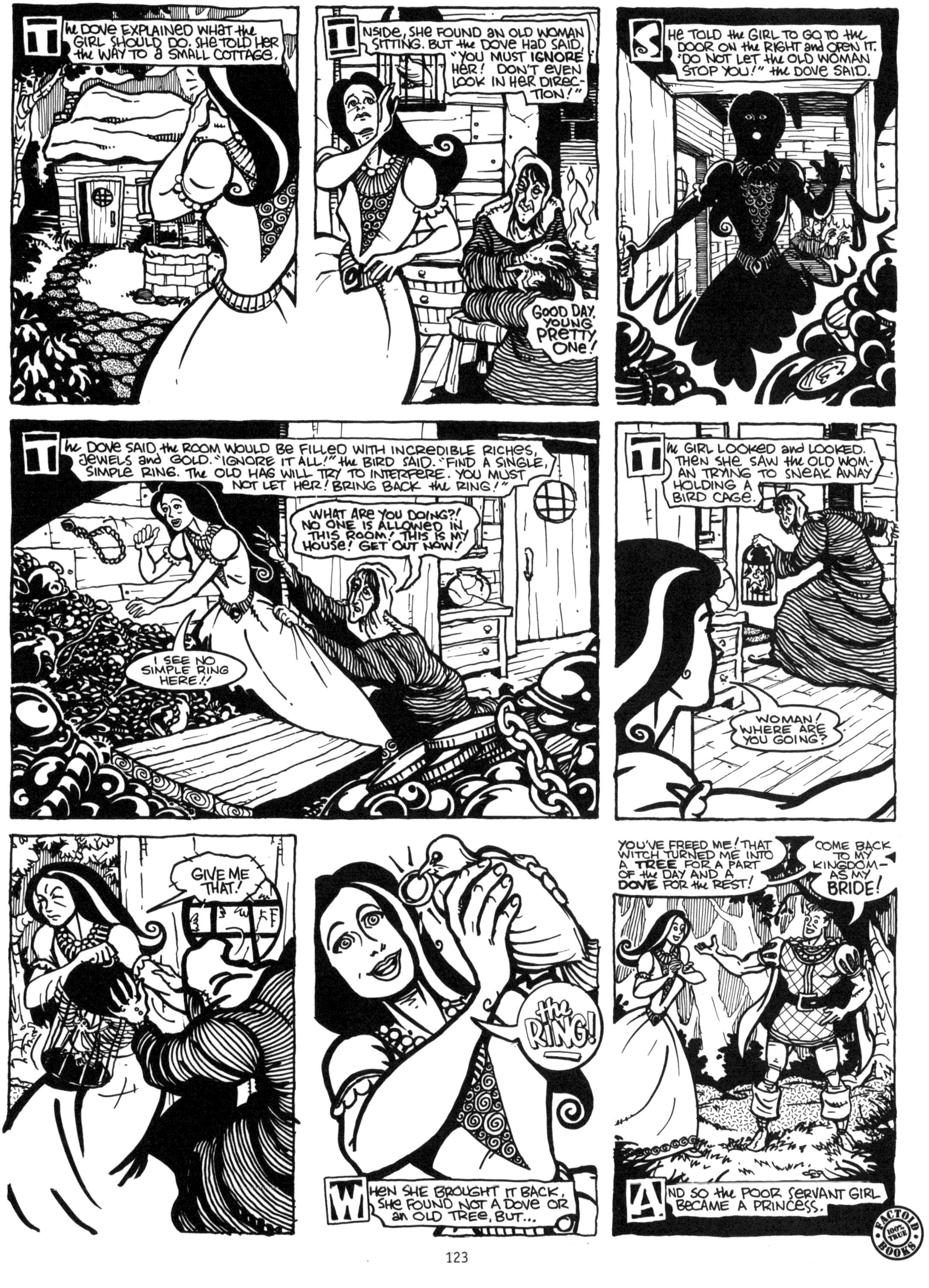
THE DOVE EXPLAINED WHAT THE GIRL SHOULD DO. SHE TOLD HER THE WAY TO A SMALL COTTAGE.
INSIDE, SHE FOUND AN OLD WOMAN SITTING. BUT THE DOVE HAD SAID, "YOU MUST IGNORE HER! DON'T EVEN LOOK IN HER DIRECTION!"
GOOD DAY, YOUNG PRETTY ONE!
SHE TOLD THE GIRL TO GO TO THE DOOR ON THE RIGHT AND OPEN IT. "DO NOT LET THE OLD WOMAN STOP YOU!" THE DOVE SAID.
THE DOVE SAID THE ROOM WOULD BE FILLED WITH INCREDIBLE RICHES, JEWELS AND GOLD. "IGNORE IT ALL!" THE BIRD SAID. "FIND A SINGLE, SIMPLE RING. THE OLD HAG WILL TRY TO INTERFERE. YOU MUST NOT LET HER! BRING BACK THE RING!"
WHAT ARE YOU DOING?! NO ONE IS ALLOWED IN THIS ROOM! THIS IS MY HOUSE! GET OUT NOW!
I SEE NO SIMPLE RING HERE!!
THE GIRL LOOKED AND LOOKED. THEN SHE SAW THE OLD WOMAN TRYING TO SNEAK AWAY HOLDING A BIRD CAGE.
WOMAN! WHERE ARE YOU GOING?
GIVE ME THAT!
THE RING!
WHEN SHE BROUGHT IT BACK, SHE FOUND NOT A DOVE OR AN OLD TREE, BUT...
YOU'VE FREED ME! THAT WITCH TURNED ME INTO A TREE FOR A PART OF THE DAY AND A DOVE FOR THE REST!
COME BACK TO MY KINGDOM— AS MY BRIDE!
AND SO THE POOR SERVANT GIRL BECAME A PRINCESS.

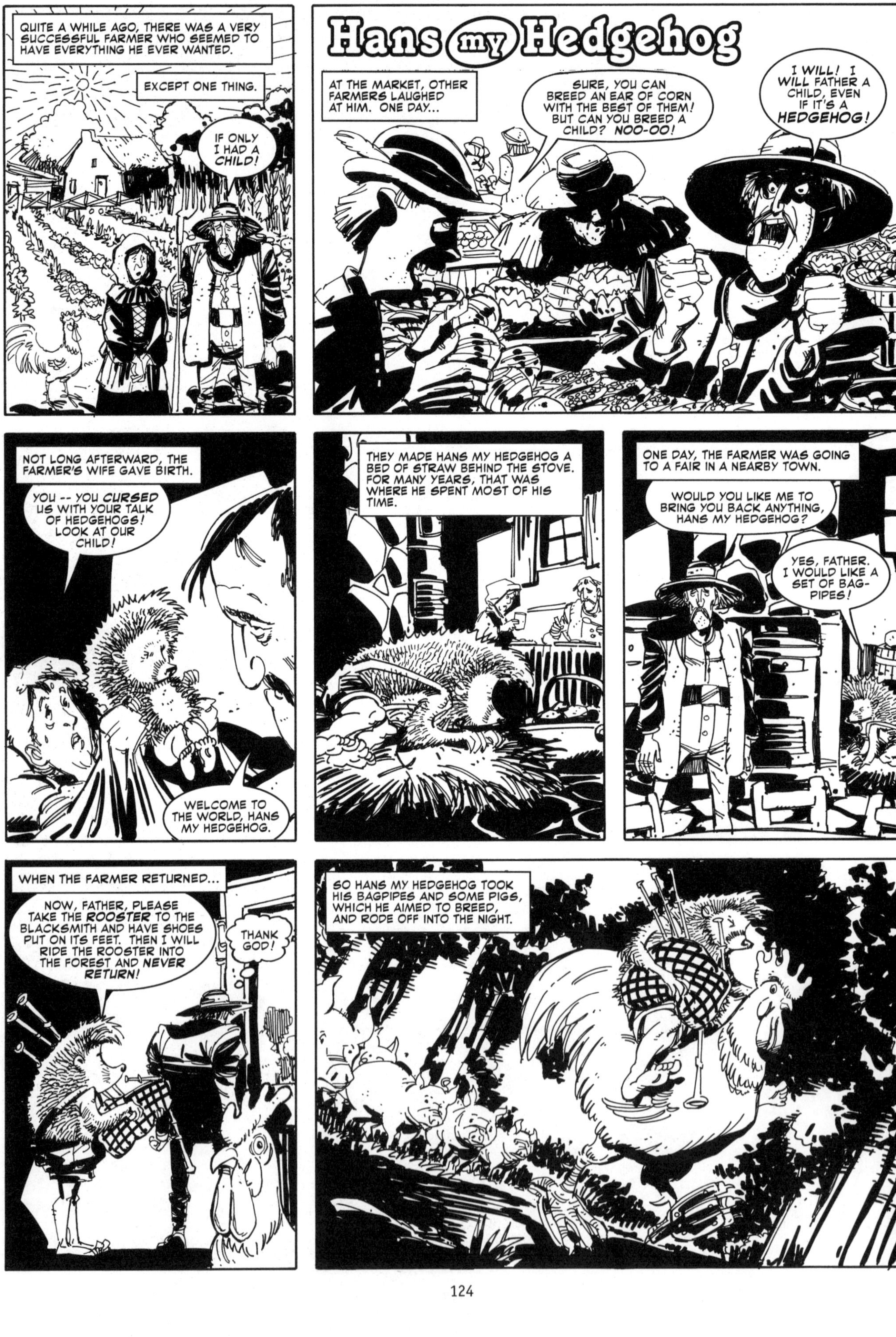

QUITE A WHILE AGO, THERE WAS A VERY SUCCESSFUL FARMER WHO SEEMED TO HAVE EVERYTHING HE EVER WANTED.
EXCEPT ONE THING.
IF ONLY I HAD A CHILD!
Hans my Hedgehog
AT THE MARKET, OTHER FARMERS LAUGHED AT HIM. ONE DAY...
SURE, YOU CAN BREED AN EAR OF CORN WITH THE BEST OF THEM! BUT CAN YOU BREED A CHILD? NOO-OO!
I WILL! I WILL FATHER A CHILD, EVEN IF IT'S A HEDGEHOG!
NOT LONG AFTERWARD, THE FARMER'S WIFE GAVE BIRTH.
YOU -- YOU CURSED US WITH YOUR TALK OF HEDGEHOGS! LOOK AT OUR CHILD!
WELCOME TO THE WORLD, HANS MY HEDGEHOG.
THEY MADE HANS MY HEDGEHOG A BED OF STRAW BEHIND THE STOVE. FOR MANY YEARS, THAT WAS WHERE HE SPENT MOST OF HIS TIME.
ONE DAY, THE FARMER WAS GOING TO A FAIR IN A NEARBY TOWN.
WOULD YOU LIKE ME TO BRING YOU BACK ANYTHING, HANS MY HEDGEHOG?
YES, FATHER. I WOULD LIKE A SET OF BAG-PIPES!
WHEN THE FARMER RETURNED...
NOW, FATHER, PLEASE TAKE THE ROOSTER TO THE BLACKSMITH AND HAVE SHOES PUT ON ITS FEET. THEN I WILL RIDE THE ROOSTER INTO THE FOREST AND NEVER RETURN!
THANK GOD!
SO HANS MY HEDGEHOG TOOK HIS BAGPIPES AND SOME PIGS, WHICH HE AIMED TO BREED, AND RODE OFF INTO THE NIGHT.

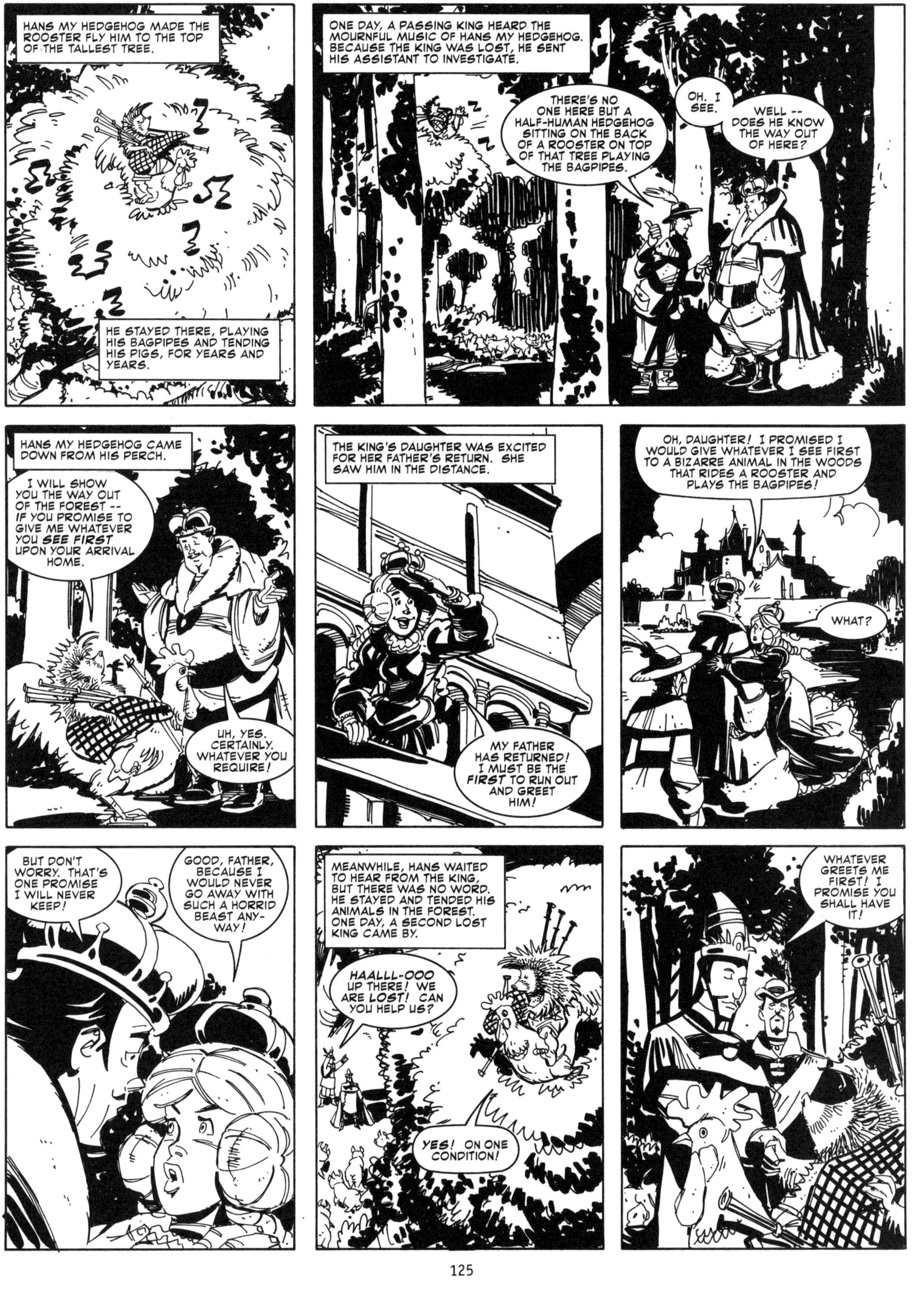
HANS MY HEDGEHOG MADE THE ROOSTER FLY HIM TO THE TOP OF THE TALLEST TREE.
HE STAYED THERE, PLAYING HIS BAGPIPES AND TENDING HIS PIGS, FOR YEARS AND YEARS.
ONE DAY, A PASSING KING HEARD THE MOURNFUL MUSIC OF HANS MY HEDGEHOG. BECAUSE THE KING WAS LOST, HE SENT HIS ASSISTANT TO INVESTIGATE.
THERE'S NO ONE HERE BUT A HALF-HUMAN HEDGEHOG SITTING ON THE BACK OF A ROOSTER ON TOP OF THAT TREE PLAYING THE BAGPIPES.
OH. I SEE.
WELL -- DOES HE KNOW THE WAY OUT OF HERE?
HANS MY HEDGEHOG CAME DOWN FROM HIS PERCH.
I WILL SHOW YOU THE WAY OUT OF THE FOREST -- *IF* YOU PROMISE TO GIVE ME WHATEVER YOU *SEE FIRST* UPON YOUR ARRIVAL HOME.
UH, YES. CERTAINLY. WHATEVER YOU REQUIRE!
THE KING'S DAUGHTER WAS EXCITED FOR HER FATHER'S RETURN. SHE SAW HIM IN THE DISTANCE.
MY FATHER HAS RETURNED! I MUST BE THE *FIRST* TO RUN OUT AND GREET HIM!
OH, DAUGHTER! I PROMISED I WOULD GIVE WHATEVER I SEE FIRST TO A BIZARRE ANIMAL IN THE WOODS THAT RIDES A ROOSTER AND PLAYS THE BAGPIPES!
WHAT?
BUT DON'T WORRY. THAT'S ONE PROMISE I WILL NEVER KEEP!
GOOD, FATHER, BECAUSE I WOULD NEVER GO AWAY WITH SUCH A HORRID BEAST ANY-WAY!
MEANWHILE, HANS WAITED TO HEAR FROM THE KING, BUT THERE WAS NO WORD. HE STAYED AND TENDED HIS ANIMALS IN THE FOREST. ONE DAY, A SECOND LOST KING CAME BY.
HAALLL-OOO UP THERE! WE ARE *LOST*! CAN YOU HELP US?
YES! ON ONE CONDITION!
WHATEVER GREETS ME FIRST! I PROMISE YOU SHALL HAVE IT!

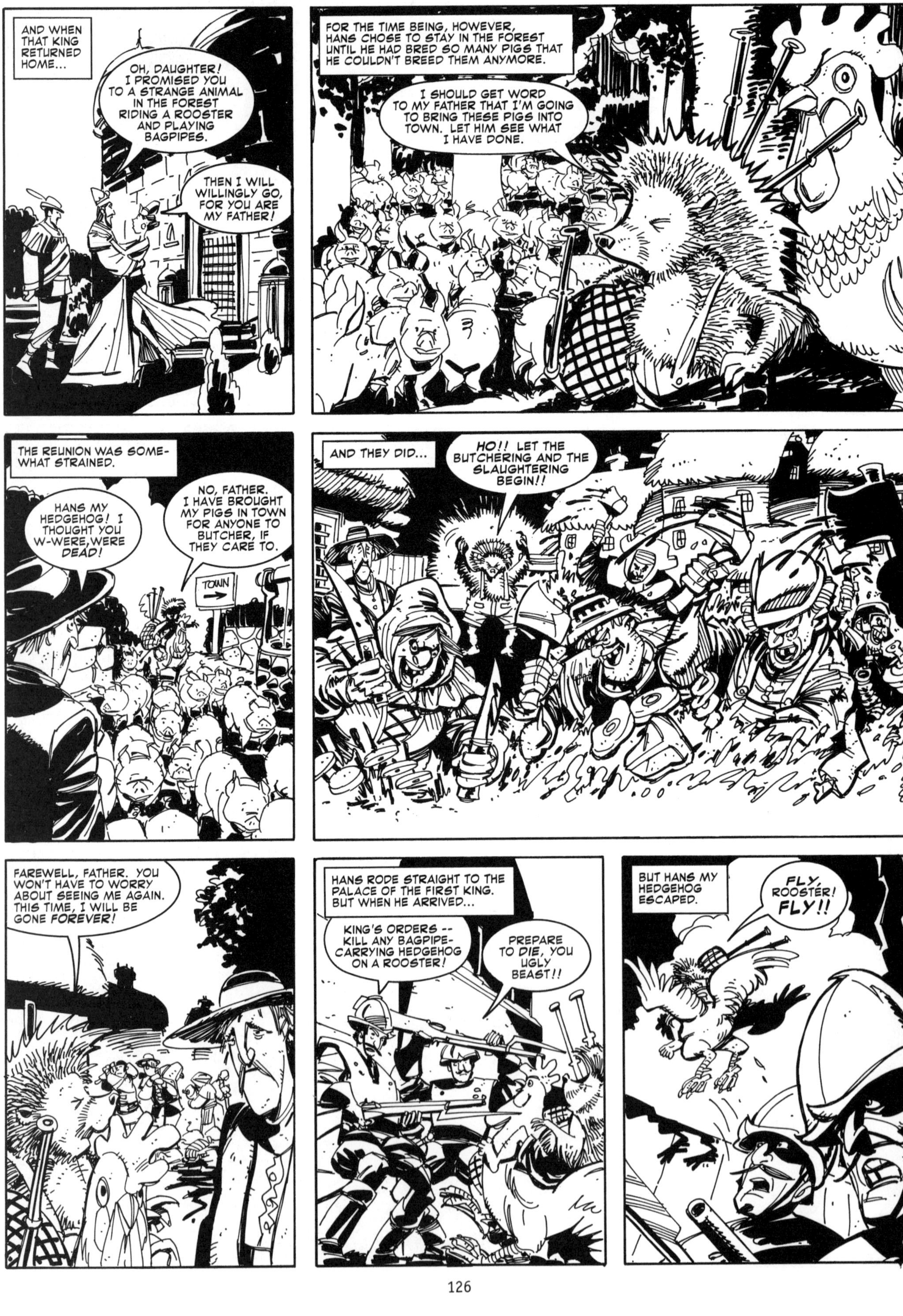

AND WHEN THAT KING RETURNED HOME...
OH, DAUGHTER! I PROMISED YOU TO A STRANGE ANIMAL IN THE FOREST RIDING A ROOSTER AND PLAYING BAGPIPES.
THEN I WILL WILLINGLY GO, FOR YOU ARE MY FATHER!
FOR THE TIME BEING, HOWEVER, HANS CHOSE TO STAY IN THE FOREST UNTIL HE HAD BRED SO MANY PIGS THAT HE COULDN'T BREED THEM ANYMORE.
I SHOULD GET WORD TO MY FATHER THAT I'M GOING TO BRING THESE PIGS INTO TOWN. LET HIM SEE WHAT I HAVE DONE.
THE REUNION WAS SOME-WHAT STRAINED.
HANS MY HEDGEHOG! I THOUGHT YOU W-WERE, WERE DEAD!
NO, FATHER. I HAVE BROUGHT MY PIGS IN TOWN FOR ANYONE TO BUTCHER, IF THEY CARE TO.
TOWN
AND THEY DID...
HO!! LET THE BUTCHERING AND THE SLAUGHTERING BEGIN!!
FAREWELL, FATHER. YOU WON'T HAVE TO WORRY ABOUT SEEING ME AGAIN. THIS TIME, I WILL BE GONE FOREVER!
HANS RODE STRAIGHT TO THE PALACE OF THE FIRST KING. BUT WHEN HE ARRIVED...
KING'S ORDERS -- KILL ANY BAGPIPE-CARRYING HEDGEHOG ON A ROOSTER!
PREPARE TO DIE, YOU UGLY BEAST!!
BUT HANS MY HEDGEHOG ESCAPED.
FLY, ROOSTER! FLY!!

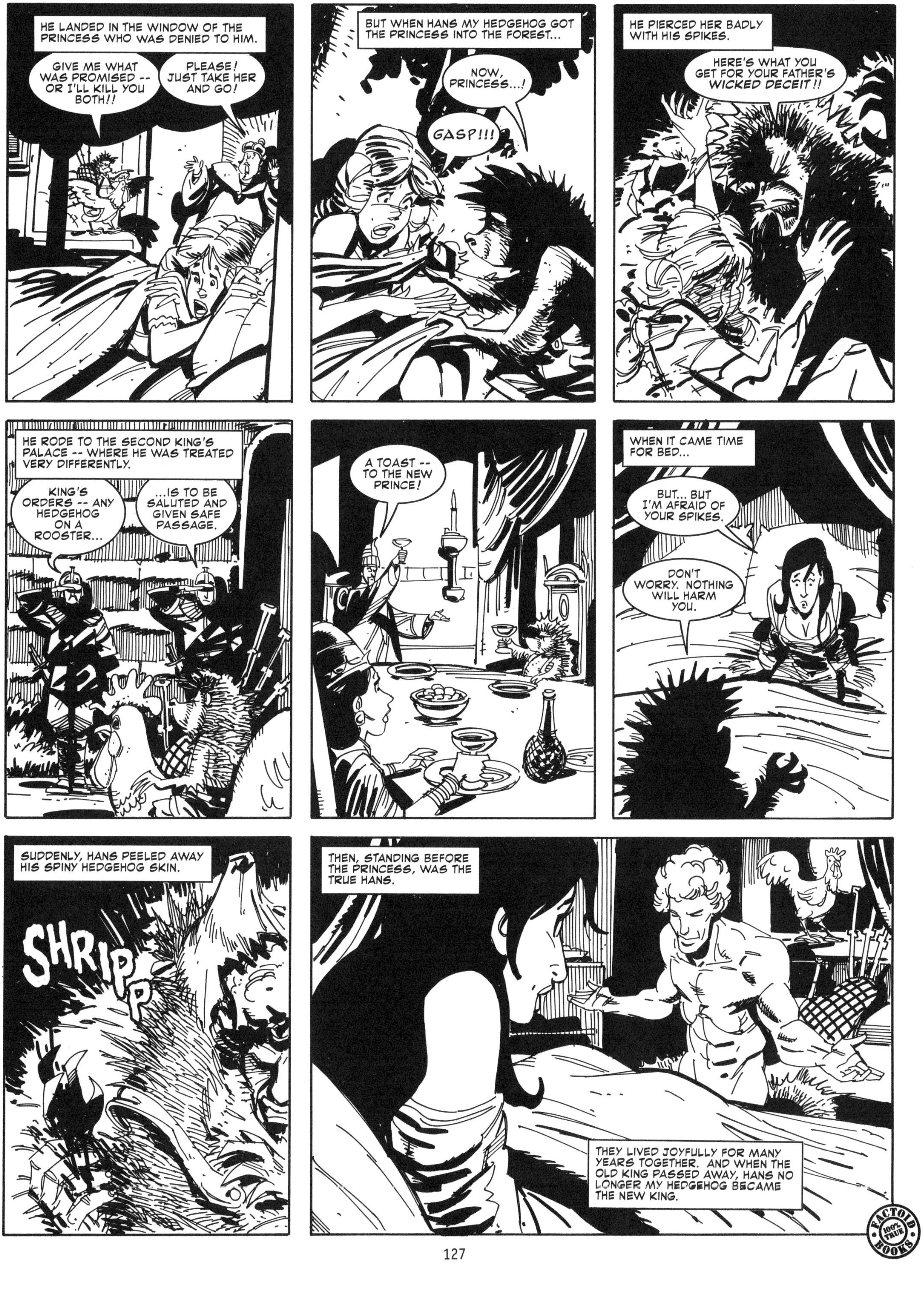
HE LANDED IN THE WINDOW OF THE PRINCESS WHO WAS DENIED TO HIM.
GIVE ME WHAT WAS PROMISED -- OR I'LL KILL YOU BOTH!!
PLEASE! JUST TAKE HER AND GO!
BUT WHEN HANS MY HEDGEHOG GOT THE PRINCESS INTO THE FOREST...
NOW, PRINCESS...!
GASP!!!
HE PIERCED HER BADLY WITH HIS SPIKES.
HERE'S WHAT YOU GET FOR YOUR FATHER'S WICKED DECEIT!!
HE RODE TO THE SECOND KING'S PALACE -- WHERE HE WAS TREATED VERY DIFFERENTLY.
KING'S ORDERS -- ANY HEDGEHOG ON A ROOSTER...
...IS TO BE SALUTED AND GIVEN SAFE PASSAGE.
A TOAST -- TO THE NEW PRINCE!
WHEN IT CAME TIME FOR BED...
BUT... BUT I'M AFRAID OF YOUR SPIKES.
DON'T WORRY. NOTHING WILL HARM YOU.
SUDDENLY, HANS PEELED AWAY HIS SPINY HEDGEHOG SKIN.
SHRIPP
THEN, STANDING BEFORE THE PRINCESS, WAS THE TRUE HANS.
THEY LIVED JOYFULLY FOR MANY YEARS TOGETHER. AND WHEN THE OLD KING PASSED AWAY, HANS NO LONGER MY HEDGEHOG BECAME THE NEW KING.

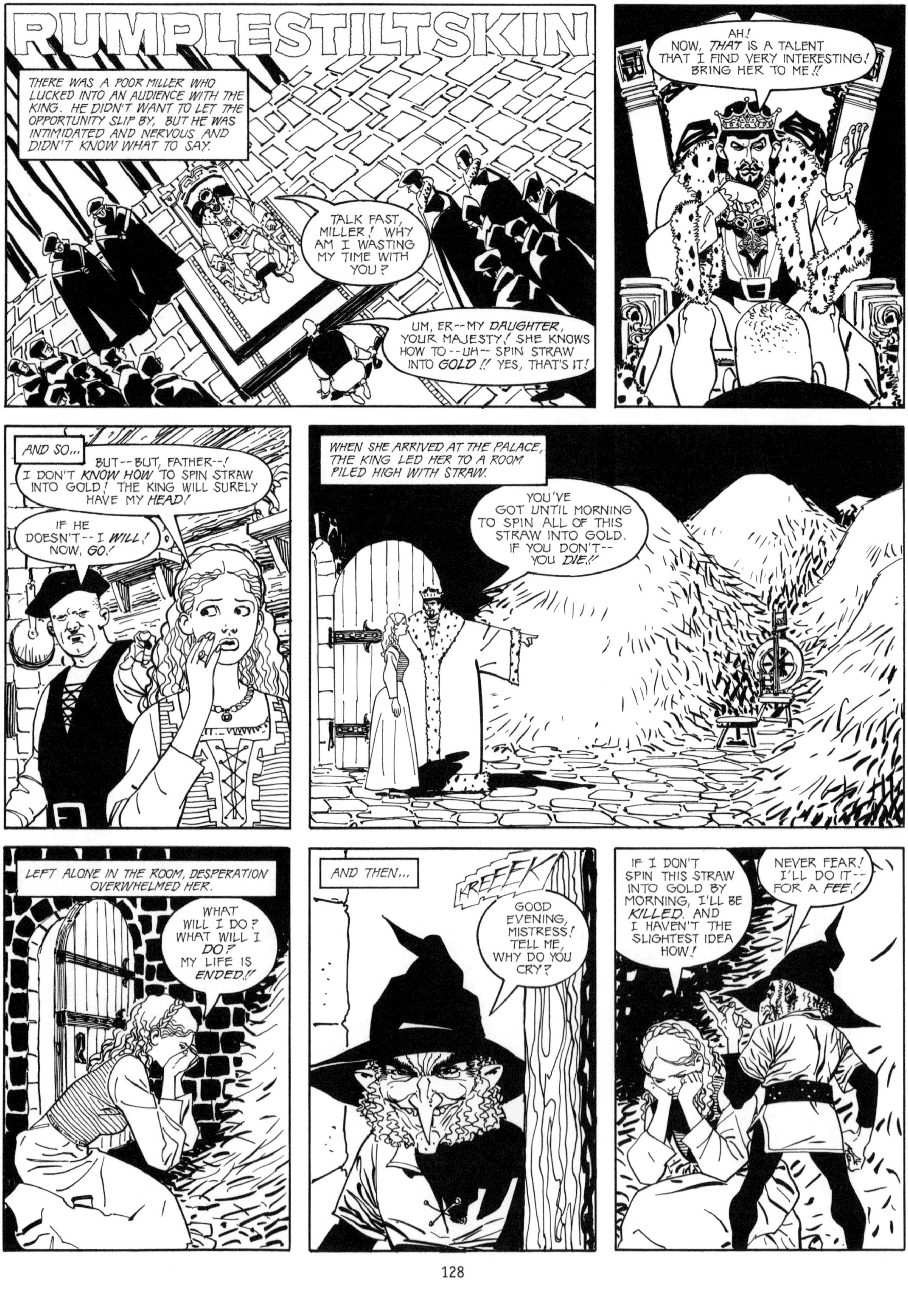
RUMPLESTILTSKIN
THERE WAS A POOR MILLER WHO LUCKED INTO AN AUDIENCE WITH THE KING. HE DIDN'T WANT TO LET THE OPPORTUNITY SLIP BY, BUT HE WAS INTIMIDATED AND NERVOUS AND DIDN'T KNOW WHAT TO SAY.
TALK FAST, MILLER! WHY AM I WASTING MY TIME WITH YOU?
UM, ER--MY DAUGHTER, YOUR MAJESTY! SHE KNOWS HOW TO--UH--SPIN STRAW INTO GOLD!! YES, THAT'S IT!
AH! NOW, THAT IS A TALENT THAT I FIND VERY INTERESTING! BRING HER TO ME!!
AND SO...
BUT--BUT, FATHER--! I DON'T KNOW HOW TO SPIN STRAW INTO GOLD! THE KING WILL SURELY HAVE MY HEAD!
IF HE DOESN'T--I WILL! NOW, GO!
WHEN SHE ARRIVED AT THE PALACE, THE KING LED HER TO A ROOM PILED HIGH WITH STRAW.
YOU'VE GOT UNTIL MORNING TO SPIN ALL OF THIS STRAW INTO GOLD. IF YOU DON'T--YOU DIE!!
LEFT ALONE IN THE ROOM, DESPERATION OVERWHELMED HER.
WHAT WILL I DO? WHAT WILL I DO? MY LIFE IS ENDED!!
AND THEN...
KREEEEK
GOOD EVENING, MISTRESS! TELL ME, WHY DO YOU CRY?
IF I DON'T SPIN THIS STRAW INTO GOLD BY MORNING, I'LL BE KILLED. AND I HAVEN'T THE SLIGHTEST IDEA HOW!
NEVER FEAR! I'LL DO IT--FOR A FEE!

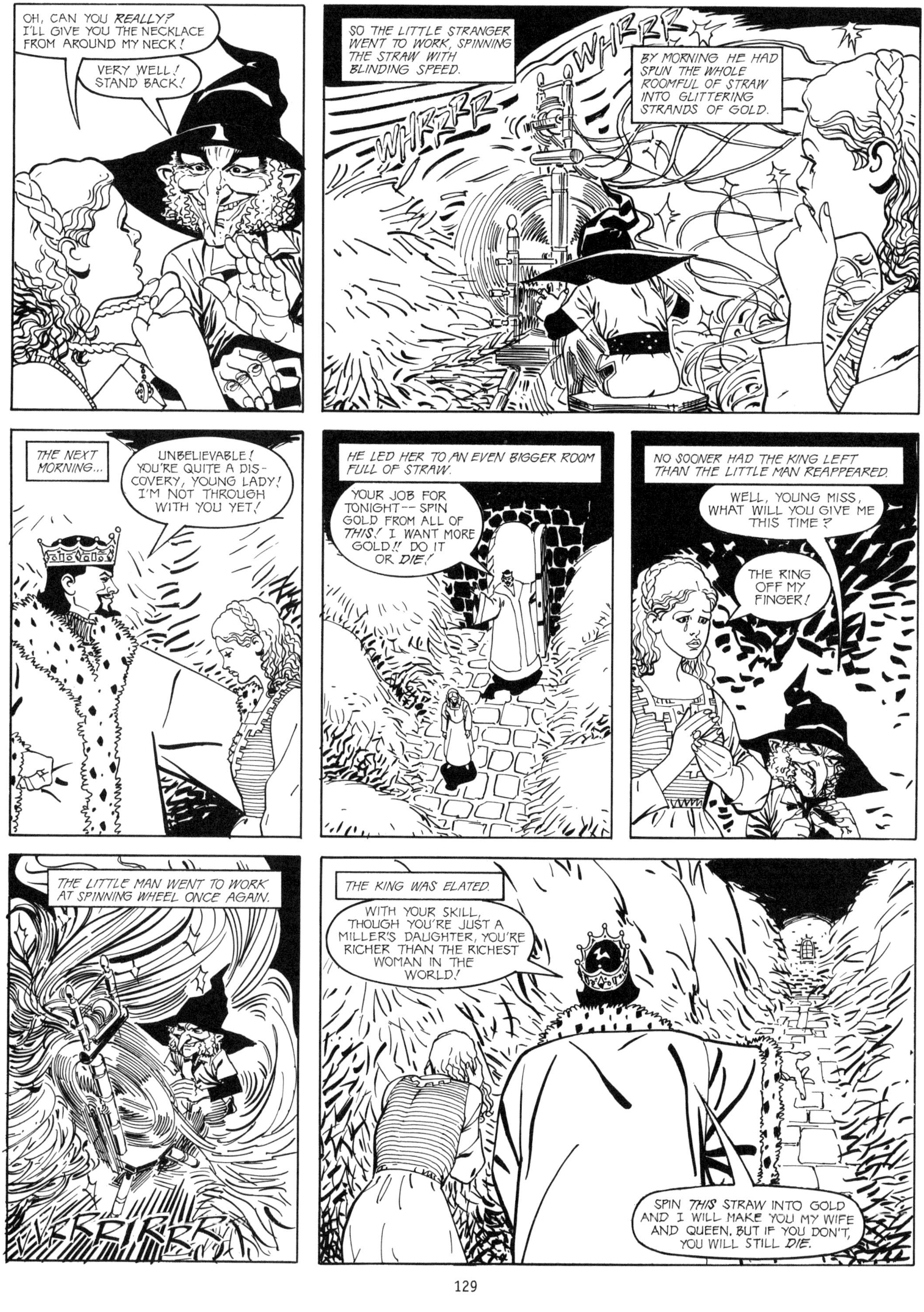
OH, CAN YOU REALLY? I'LL GIVE YOU THE NECKLACE FROM AROUND MY NECK!
VERY WELL! STAND BACK!
SO THE LITTLE STRANGER WENT TO WORK, SPINNING THE STRAW WITH BLINDING SPEED.
WHRRRR
WHRRRR
BY MORNING HE HAD SPUN THE WHOLE ROOMFUL OF STRAW INTO GLITTERING STRANDS OF GOLD.
THE NEXT MORNING...
UNBELIEVABLE! YOU'RE QUITE A DISCOVERY, YOUNG LADY! I'M NOT THROUGH WITH YOU YET!
HE LED HER TO AN EVEN BIGGER ROOM FULL OF STRAW.
YOUR JOB FOR TONIGHT-- SPIN GOLD FROM ALL OF THIS! I WANT MORE GOLD!! DO IT OR DIE!
NO SOONER HAD THE KING LEFT THAN THE LITTLE MAN REAPPEARED.
WELL, YOUNG MISS, WHAT WILL YOU GIVE ME THIS TIME?
THE RING OFF MY FINGER!
THE LITTLE MAN WENT TO WORK AT SPINNING WHEEL ONCE AGAIN.
VRRRIRRR!
THE KING WAS ELATED.
WITH YOUR SKILL, THOUGH YOU'RE JUST A MILLER'S DAUGHTER, YOU'RE RICHER THAN THE RICHEST WOMAN IN THE WORLD!
SPIN THIS STRAW INTO GOLD AND I WILL MAKE YOU MY WIFE AND QUEEN. BUT IF YOU DON'T, YOU WILL STILL DIE.

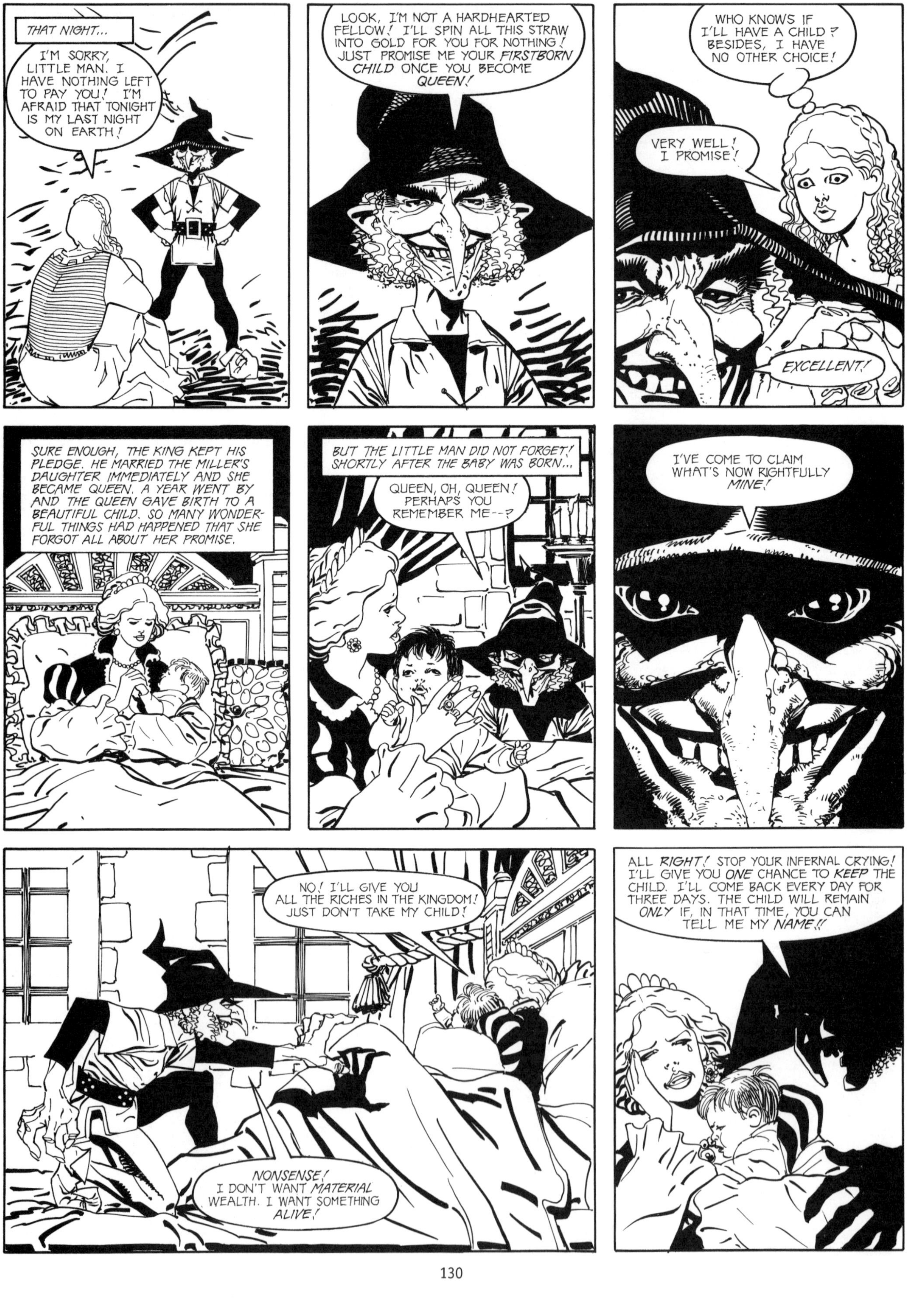
THAT NIGHT...
I'M SORRY, LITTLE MAN. I HAVE NOTHING LEFT TO PAY YOU! I'M AFRAID THAT TONIGHT IS MY LAST NIGHT ON EARTH!
LOOK, I'M NOT A HARDHEARTED FELLOW! I'LL SPIN ALL THIS STRAW INTO GOLD FOR YOU FOR NOTHING! JUST PROMISE ME YOUR FIRSTBORN CHILD ONCE YOU BECOME QUEEN!
WHO KNOWS IF I'LL HAVE A CHILD? BESIDES, I HAVE NO OTHER CHOICE!
VERY WELL! I PROMISE!
EXCELLENT!
SURE ENOUGH, THE KING KEPT HIS PLEDGE. HE MARRIED THE MILLER'S DAUGHTER IMMEDIATELY AND SHE BECAME QUEEN. A YEAR WENT BY AND THE QUEEN GAVE BIRTH TO A BEAUTIFUL CHILD. SO MANY WONDERFUL THINGS HAD HAPPENED THAT SHE FORGOT ALL ABOUT HER PROMISE.
BUT THE LITTLE MAN DID NOT FORGET! SHORTLY AFTER THE BABY WAS BORN...
QUEEN, OH, QUEEN! PERHAPS YOU REMEMBER ME--?
I'VE COME TO CLAIM WHAT'S NOW RIGHTFULLY MINE!
NO! I'LL GIVE YOU ALL THE RICHES IN THE KINGDOM! JUST DON'T TAKE MY CHILD!
NONSENSE! I DON'T WANT MATERIAL WEALTH. I WANT SOMETHING ALIVE!
ALL RIGHT! STOP YOUR INFERNAL CRYING! I'LL GIVE YOU ONE CHANCE TO KEEP THE CHILD. I'LL COME BACK EVERY DAY FOR THREE DAYS. THE CHILD WILL REMAIN ONLY IF, IN THAT TIME, YOU CAN TELL ME MY NAME!!

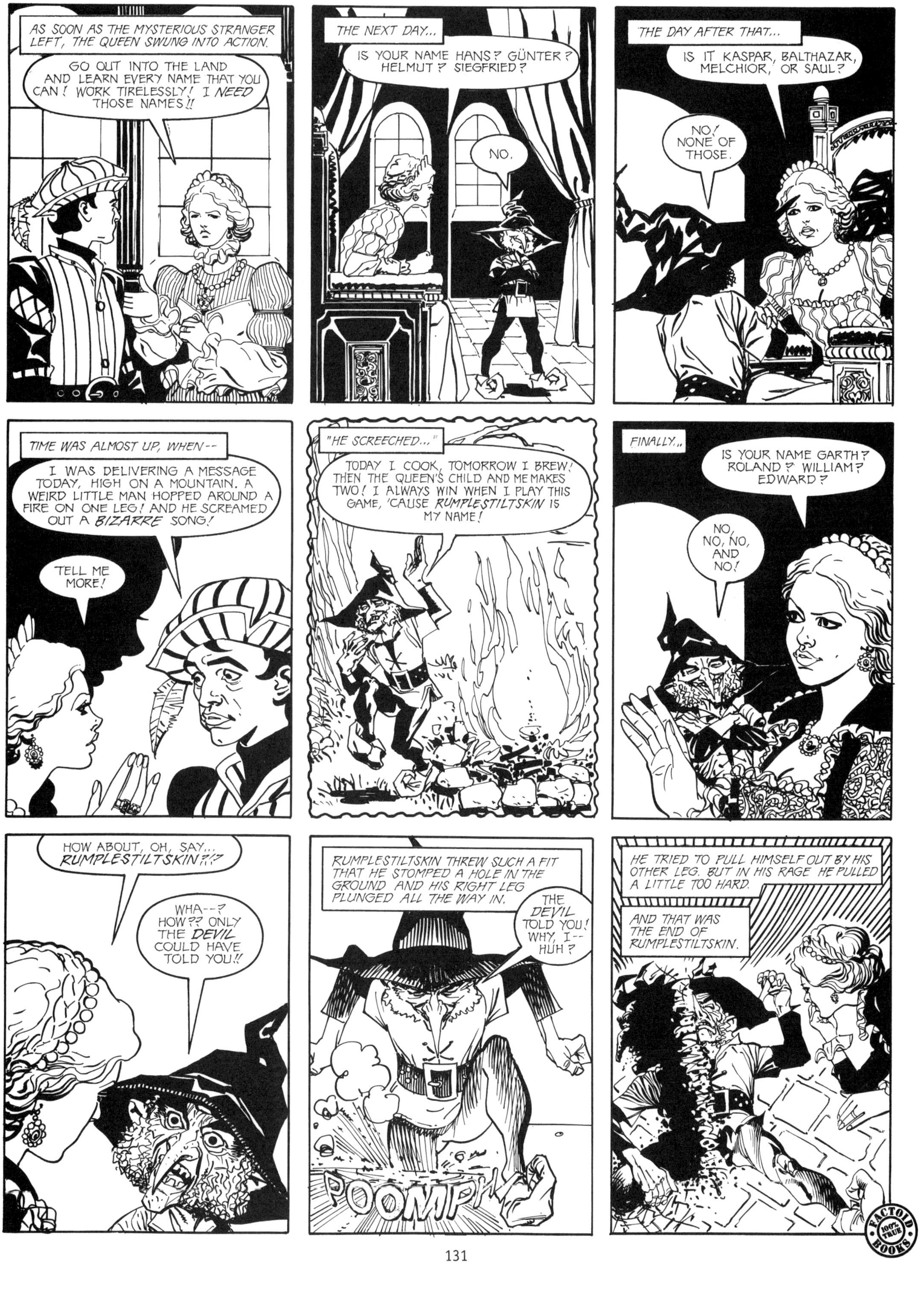

AS SOON AS THE MYSTERIOUS STRANGER LEFT, THE QUEEN SWUNG INTO ACTION.
GO OUT INTO THE LAND AND LEARN EVERY NAME THAT YOU CAN! WORK TIRELESSLY! I NEED THOSE NAMES!!
THE NEXT DAY...
IS YOUR NAME HANS? GÜNTER? HELMUT? SIEGFRIED?
NO.
THE DAY AFTER THAT...
IS IT KASPAR, BALTHAZAR, MELCHIOR, OR SAUL?
NO! NONE OF THOSE.
TIME WAS ALMOST UP, WHEN--
I WAS DELIVERING A MESSAGE TODAY, HIGH ON A MOUNTAIN. A WEIRD LITTLE MAN HOPPED AROUND A FIRE ON ONE LEG! AND HE SCREAMED OUT A BIZARRE SONG!
TELL ME MORE!
"HE SCREECHED..."
TODAY I COOK, TOMORROW I BREW! THEN THE QUEEN'S CHILD AND ME MAKES TWO! I ALWAYS WIN WHEN I PLAY THIS GAME, 'CAUSE RUMPLESTILTSKIN IS MY NAME!
FINALLY...
IS YOUR NAME GARTH? ROLAND? WILLIAM? EDWARD?
NO, NO, NO, AND NO!
HOW ABOUT, OH, SAY... RUMPLESTILTSKIN?!?
WHA--? HOW?? ONLY THE DEVIL COULD HAVE TOLD YOU!!
RUMPLESTILTSKIN THREW SUCH A FIT THAT HE STOMPED A HOLE IN THE GROUND AND HIS RIGHT LEG PLUNGED ALL THE WAY IN.
THE DEVIL TOLD YOU! WHY, I-- HUH?
POOMPH
HE TRIED TO PULL HIMSELF OUT BY HIS OTHER LEG. BUT IN HIS RAGE HE PULLED A LITTLE TOO HARD.
AND THAT WAS THE END OF RUMPLESTILTSKIN.

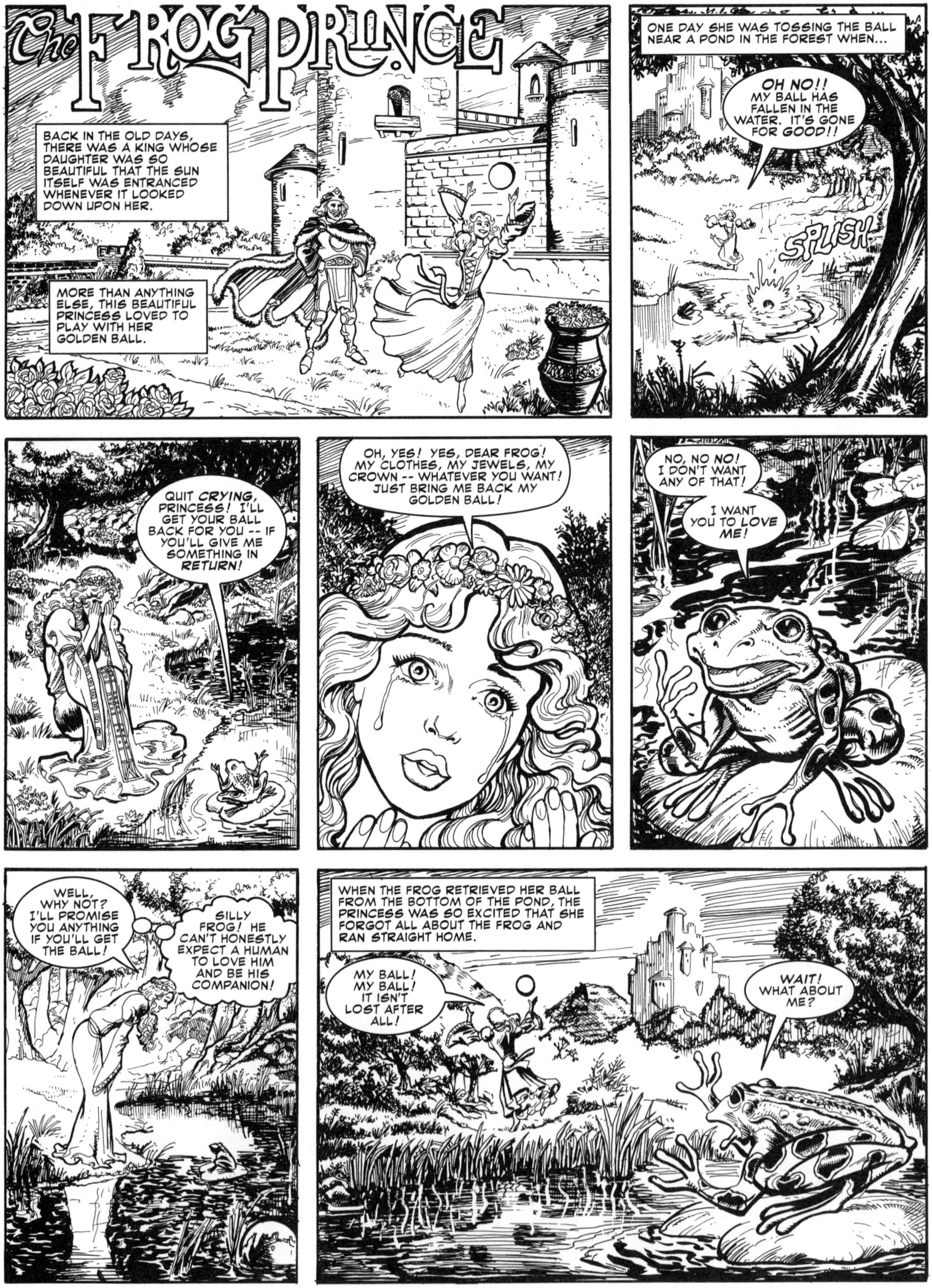
The FROG PRINCE
BACK IN THE OLD DAYS, THERE WAS A KING WHOSE DAUGHTER WAS SO BEAUTIFUL THAT THE SUN ITSELF WAS ENTRANCED WHENEVER IT LOOKED DOWN UPON HER.
MORE THAN ANYTHING ELSE, THIS BEAUTIFUL PRINCESS LOVED TO PLAY WITH HER GOLDEN BALL.
ONE DAY SHE WAS TOSSING THE BALL NEAR A POND IN THE FOREST WHEN...
OH NO!! MY BALL HAS FALLEN IN THE WATER. IT'S GONE FOR GOOD!!
SPLISH
QUIT CRYING, PRINCESS! I'LL GET YOUR BALL BACK FOR YOU -- IF YOU'LL GIVE ME SOMETHING IN RETURN!
OH, YES! YES, DEAR FROG! MY CLOTHES, MY JEWELS, MY CROWN -- WHATEVER YOU WANT! JUST BRING ME BACK MY GOLDEN BALL!
NO, NO NO! I DON'T WANT ANY OF THAT!
I WANT YOU TO LOVE ME!
WELL, WHY NOT? I'LL PROMISE YOU ANYTHING IF YOU'LL GET THE BALL!
SILLY FROG! HE CAN'T HONESTLY EXPECT A HUMAN TO LOVE HIM AND BE HIS COMPANION!
WHEN THE FROG RETRIEVED HER BALL FROM THE BOTTOM OF THE POND, THE PRINCESS WAS SO EXCITED THAT SHE FORGOT ALL ABOUT THE FROG AND RAN STRAIGHT HOME.
MY BALL! MY BALL! IT ISN'T LOST AFTER ALL!
WAIT! WHAT ABOUT ME?

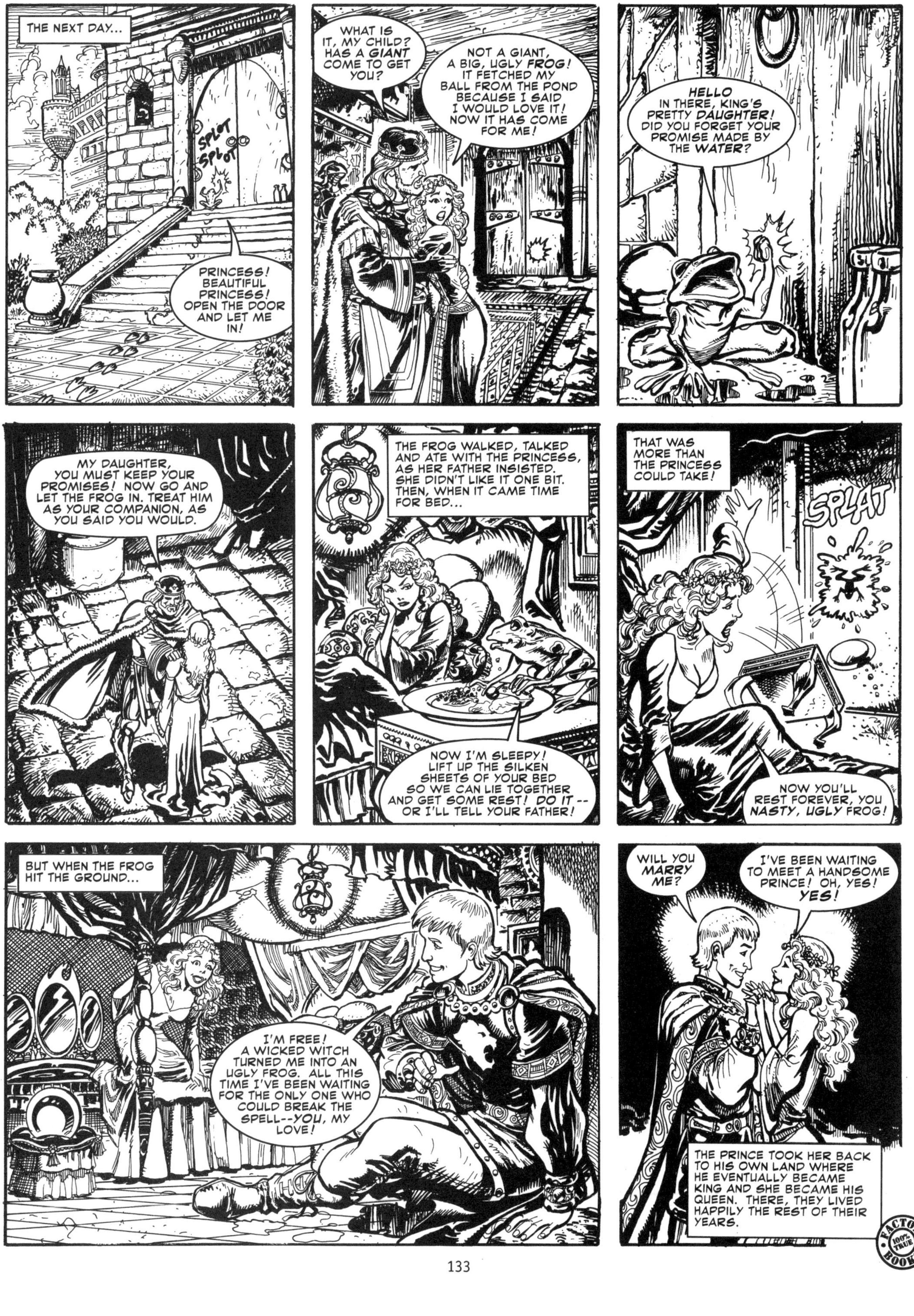

THE NEXT DAY...
SPLOT SPLOT
PRINCESS! BEAUTIFUL PRINCESS! OPEN THE DOOR AND LET ME IN!
WHAT IS IT, MY CHILD? HAS A GIANT COME TO GET YOU?
NOT A GIANT, A BIG, UGLY FROG! IT FETCHED MY BALL FROM THE POND BECAUSE I SAID I WOULD LOVE IT! NOW IT HAS COME FOR ME!
HELLO IN THERE, KING'S PRETTY DAUGHTER! DID YOU FORGET YOUR PROMISE MADE BY THE WATER?
MY DAUGHTER, YOU MUST KEEP YOUR PROMISES! NOW GO AND LET THE FROG IN. TREAT HIM AS YOUR COMPANION, AS YOU SAID YOU WOULD.
THE FROG WALKED, TALKED AND ATE WITH THE PRINCESS, AS HER FATHER INSISTED. SHE DIDN'T LIKE IT ONE BIT. THEN, WHEN IT CAME TIME FOR BED...
NOW I'M SLEEPY! LIFT UP THE SILKEN SHEETS OF YOUR BED SO WE CAN LIE TOGETHER AND GET SOME REST! DO IT -- OR I'LL TELL YOUR FATHER!
THAT WAS MORE THAN THE PRINCESS COULD TAKE!
SPLAT
NOW YOU'LL REST FOREVER, YOU NASTY, UGLY FROG!
BUT WHEN THE FROG HIT THE GROUND...
I'M FREE! A WICKED WITCH TURNED ME INTO AN UGLY FROG. ALL THIS TIME I'VE BEEN WAITING FOR THE ONLY ONE WHO COULD BREAK THE SPELL--YOU, MY LOVE!
WILL YOU MARRY ME?
I'VE BEEN WAITING TO MEET A HANDSOME PRINCE! OH, YES! YES!
THE PRINCE TOOK HER BACK TO HIS OWN LAND WHERE HE EVENTUALLY BECAME KING AND SHE BECAME HIS QUEEN. THERE, THEY LIVED HAPPILY THE REST OF THEIR YEARS.

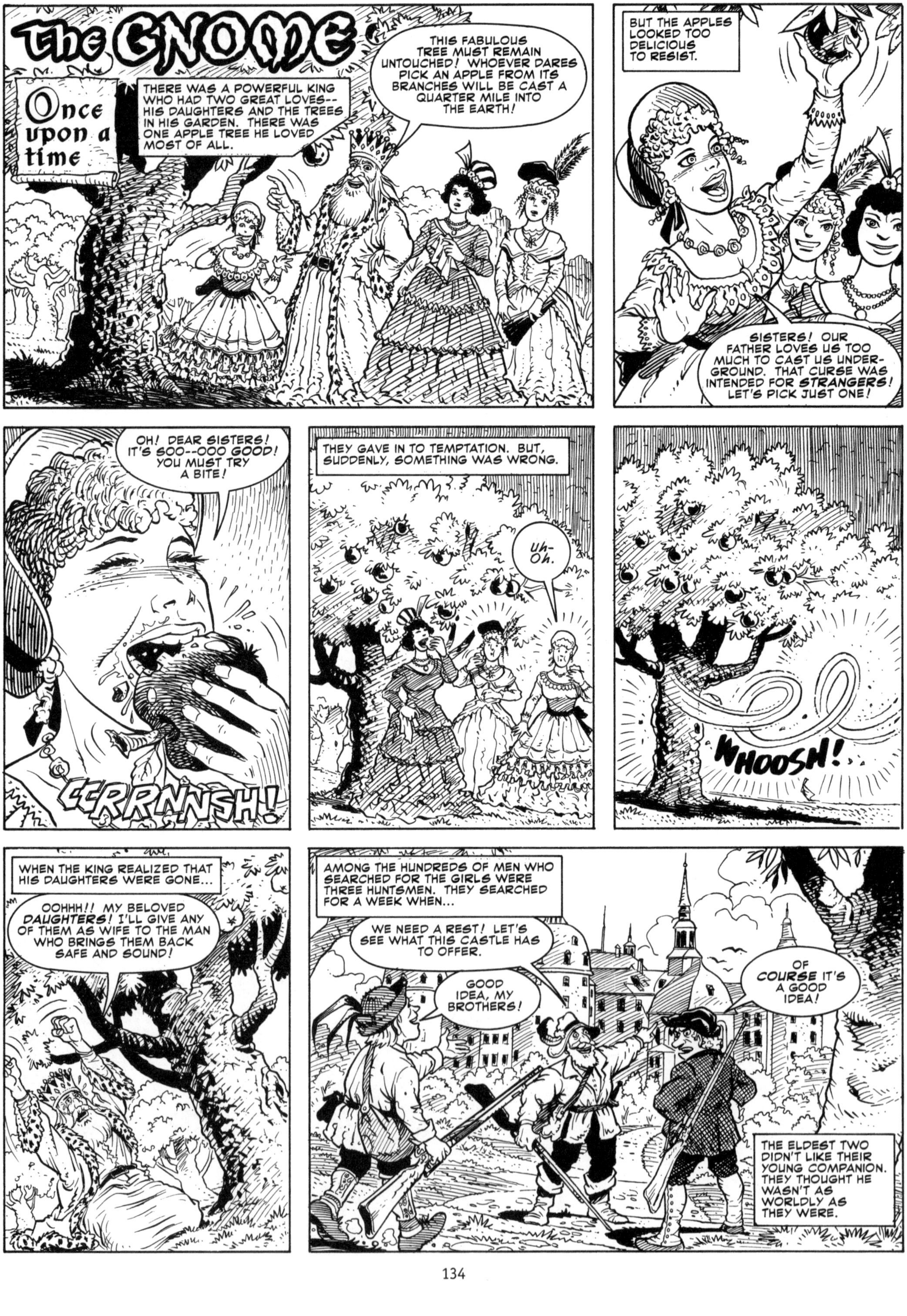
The GNOME
Once upon a time
THERE WAS A POWERFUL KING WHO HAD TWO GREAT LOVES-- HIS DAUGHTERS AND THE TREES IN HIS GARDEN. THERE WAS ONE APPLE TREE HE LOVED MOST OF ALL.
THIS FABULOUS TREE MUST REMAIN UNTOUCHED! WHOEVER DARES PICK AN APPLE FROM ITS BRANCHES WILL BE CAST A QUARTER MILE INTO THE EARTH!
BUT THE APPLES LOOKED TOO DELICIOUS TO RESIST.
SISTERS! OUR FATHER LOVES US TOO MUCH TO CAST US UNDERGROUND. THAT CURSE WAS INTENDED FOR STRANGERS! LET'S PICK JUST ONE!
OH! DEAR SISTERS! IT'S SOO--OOO GOOD! YOU MUST TRY A BITE!
CCRRNNSH!
THEY GAVE IN TO TEMPTATION. BUT, SUDDENLY, SOMETHING WAS WRONG.
Uh-Oh.
WHOOSH!
WHEN THE KING REALIZED THAT HIS DAUGHTERS WERE GONE...
OOHHH!! MY BELOVED DAUGHTERS! I'LL GIVE ANY OF THEM AS WIFE TO THE MAN WHO BRINGS THEM BACK SAFE AND SOUND!
AMONG THE HUNDREDS OF MEN WHO SEARCHED FOR THE GIRLS WERE THREE HUNTSMEN. THEY SEARCHED FOR A WEEK WHEN...
WE NEED A REST! LET'S SEE WHAT THIS CASTLE HAS TO OFFER.
GOOD IDEA, MY BROTHERS!
OF COURSE IT'S A GOOD IDEA!
THE ELDEST TWO DIDN'T LIKE THEIR YOUNG COMPANION. THEY THOUGHT HE WASN'T AS WORLDLY AS THEY WERE.

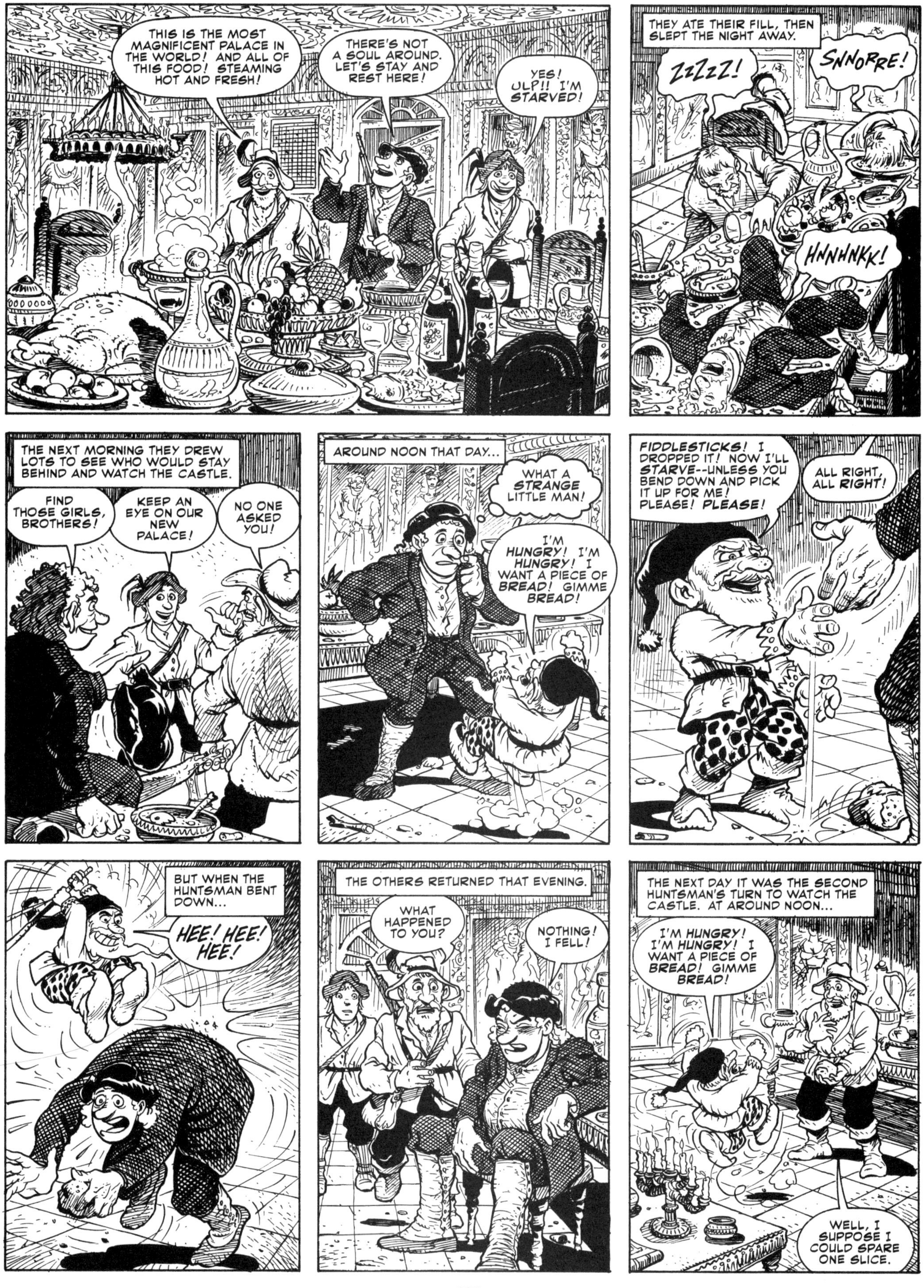

THIS IS THE MOST MAGNIFICENT PALACE IN THE WORLD! AND ALL OF THIS FOOD! STEAMING HOT AND FRESH!
THERE'S NOT A SOUL AROUND. LET'S STAY AND REST HERE!
YES! ULP!! I'M STARVED!
THEY ATE THEIR FILL, THEN SLEPT THE NIGHT AWAY.
ZZZZZ!
SNNORRE!
HNNHNKK!
THE NEXT MORNING THEY DREW LOTS TO SEE WHO WOULD STAY BEHIND AND WATCH THE CASTLE.
FIND THOSE GIRLS, BROTHERS!
KEEP AN EYE ON OUR NEW PALACE!
NO ONE ASKED YOU!
AROUND NOON THAT DAY...
WHAT A STRANGE LITTLE MAN!
I'M HUNGRY! I'M HUNGRY! I WANT A PIECE OF BREAD! GIMME BREAD!
FIDDLESTICKS! I DROPPED IT! NOW I'LL STARVE--UNLESS YOU BEND DOWN AND PICK IT UP FOR ME! PLEASE! PLEASE!
ALL RIGHT, ALL RIGHT!
BUT WHEN THE HUNTSMAN BENT DOWN...
HEE! HEE! HEE!
THE OTHERS RETURNED THAT EVENING.
WHAT HAPPENED TO YOU?
NOTHING! I FELL!
THE NEXT DAY IT WAS THE SECOND HUNTSMAN'S TURN TO WATCH THE CASTLE. AT AROUND NOON...
I'M HUNGRY! I'M HUNGRY! I WANT A PIECE OF BREAD! GIMME BREAD!
WELL, I SUPPOSE I COULD SPARE ONE SLICE.

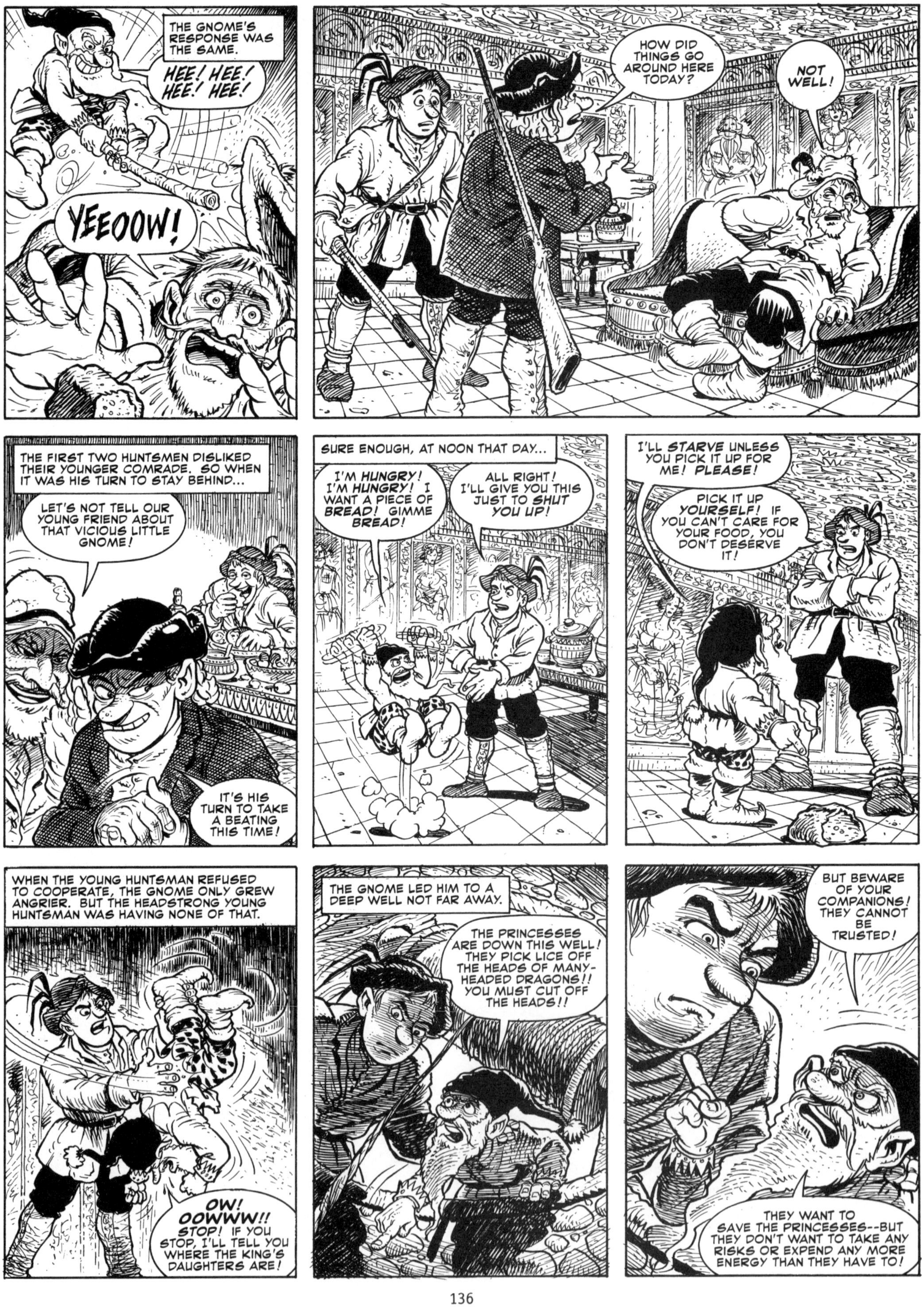

THE GNOME'S RESPONSE WAS THE SAME.
HEE! HEE! HEE! HEE!
YEEOOW!
HOW DID THINGS GO AROUND HERE TODAY?
NOT WELL!
THE FIRST TWO HUNTSMEN DISLIKED THEIR YOUNGER COMRADE. SO WHEN IT WAS HIS TURN TO STAY BEHIND...
LET'S NOT TELL OUR YOUNG FRIEND ABOUT THAT VICIOUS LITTLE GNOME!
IT'S HIS TURN TO TAKE A BEATING THIS TIME!
SURE ENOUGH, AT NOON THAT DAY...
I'M HUNGRY! I'M HUNGRY! I WANT A PIECE OF BREAD! GIMME BREAD!
ALL RIGHT! I'LL GIVE YOU THIS JUST TO SHUT YOU UP!
I'LL STARVE UNLESS YOU PICK IT UP FOR ME! PLEASE!
PICK IT UP YOURSELF! IF YOU CAN'T CARE FOR YOUR FOOD, YOU DON'T DESERVE IT!
WHEN THE YOUNG HUNTSMAN REFUSED TO COOPERATE, THE GNOME ONLY GREW ANGRIER. BUT THE HEADSTRONG YOUNG HUNTSMAN WAS HAVING NONE OF THAT.
OW! OOWWW!! STOP! IF YOU STOP, I'LL TELL YOU WHERE THE KING'S DAUGHTERS ARE!
THE GNOME LED HIM TO A DEEP WELL NOT FAR AWAY.
THE PRINCESSES ARE DOWN THIS WELL! THEY PICK LICE OFF THE HEADS OF MANY-HEADED DRAGONS!! YOU MUST CUT OFF THE HEADS!!
BUT BEWARE OF YOUR COMPANIONS! THEY CANNOT BE TRUSTED!
THEY WANT TO SAVE THE PRINCESSES--BUT THEY DON'T WANT TO TAKE ANY RISKS OR EXPEND ANY MORE ENERGY THAN THEY HAVE TO!

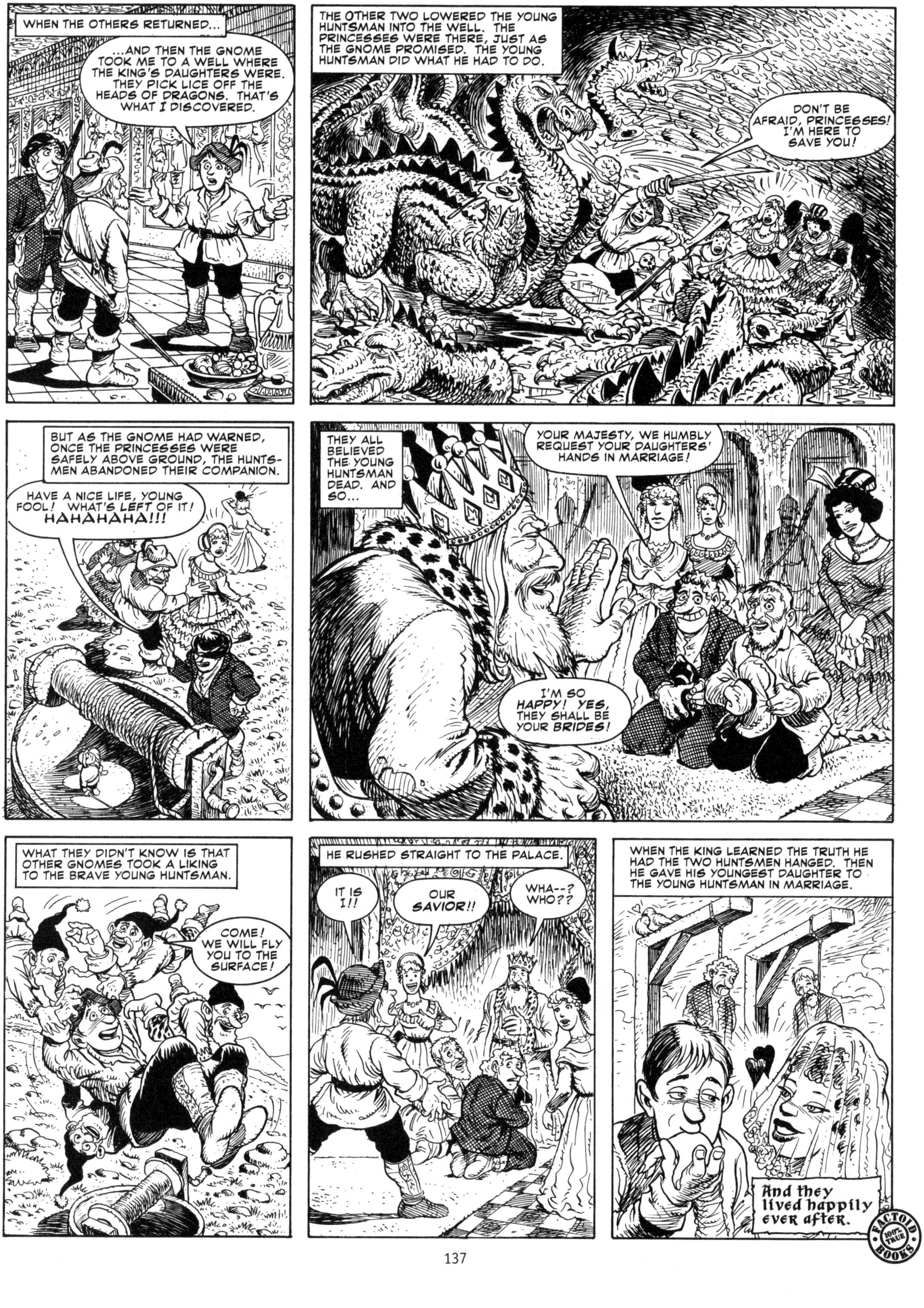
WHEN THE OTHERS RETURNED...
...AND THEN THE GNOME TOOK ME TO A WELL WHERE THE KING'S DAUGHTERS WERE. THEY PICK LICE OFF THE HEADS OF DRAGONS. THAT'S WHAT I DISCOVERED.
THE OTHER TWO LOWERED THE YOUNG HUNTSMAN INTO THE WELL. THE PRINCESSES WERE THERE, JUST AS THE GNOME PROMISED. THE YOUNG HUNTSMAN DID WHAT HE HAD TO DO.
DON'T BE AFRAID, PRINCESSES! I'M HERE TO SAVE YOU!
BUT AS THE GNOME HAD WARNED, ONCE THE PRINCESSES WERE SAFELY ABOVE GROUND, THE HUNTSMEN ABANDONED THEIR COMPANION.
HAVE A NICE LIFE, YOUNG FOOL! WHAT'S LEFT OF IT! HAHAHAHA!!!
THEY ALL BELIEVED THE YOUNG HUNTSMAN DEAD. AND SO...
YOUR MAJESTY, WE HUMBLY REQUEST YOUR DAUGHTERS' HANDS IN MARRIAGE!
I'M SO HAPPY! YES, THEY SHALL BE YOUR BRIDES!
WHAT THEY DIDN'T KNOW IS THAT OTHER GNOMES TOOK A LIKING TO THE BRAVE YOUNG HUNTSMAN.
COME! WE WILL FLY YOU TO THE SURFACE!
HE RUSHED STRAIGHT TO THE PALACE.
IT IS I!!
OUR SAVIOR!!
WHA--? WHO??
WHEN THE KING LEARNED THE TRUTH HE HAD THE TWO HUNTSMEN HANGED. THEN HE GAVE HIS YOUNGEST DAUGHTER TO THE YOUNG HUNTSMAN IN MARRIAGE.
And they lived happily ever after.
FACTOID BOOKS 100% TRUE

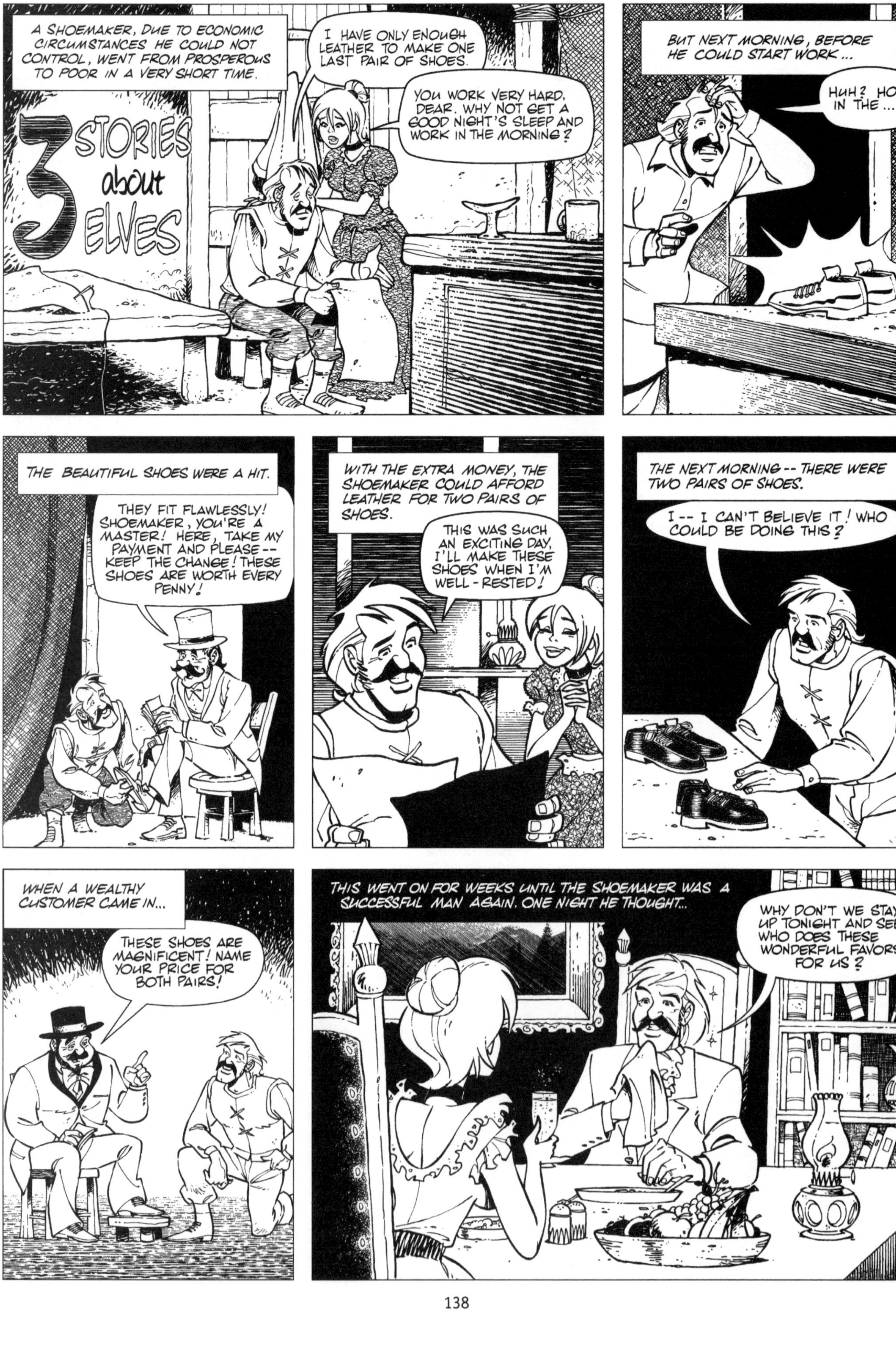
A SHOEMAKER, DUE TO ECONOMIC CIRCUMSTANCES HE COULD NOT CONTROL, WENT FROM PROSPEROUS TO POOR IN A VERY SHORT TIME.
3 STORIES about ELVES
I HAVE ONLY ENOUGH LEATHER TO MAKE ONE LAST PAIR OF SHOES.
YOU WORK VERY HARD, DEAR. WHY NOT GET A GOOD NIGHT'S SLEEP AND WORK IN THE MORNING?
BUT NEXT MORNING, BEFORE HE COULD START WORK...
HUH? HOW IN THE...?
THE BEAUTIFUL SHOES WERE A HIT.
THEY FIT FLAWLESSLY! SHOEMAKER, YOU'RE A MASTER! HERE, TAKE MY PAYMENT AND PLEASE -- KEEP THE CHANGE! THESE SHOES ARE WORTH EVERY PENNY!
WITH THE EXTRA MONEY, THE SHOEMAKER COULD AFFORD LEATHER FOR TWO PAIRS OF SHOES.
THIS WAS SUCH AN EXCITING DAY, I'LL MAKE THESE SHOES WHEN I'M WELL-RESTED!
THE NEXT MORNING -- THERE WERE TWO PAIRS OF SHOES.
I -- I CAN'T BELIEVE IT! WHO COULD BE DOING THIS?
WHEN A WEALTHY CUSTOMER CAME IN...
THESE SHOES ARE MAGNIFICENT! NAME YOUR PRICE FOR BOTH PAIRS!
THIS WENT ON FOR WEEKS UNTIL THE SHOEMAKER WAS A SUCCESSFUL MAN AGAIN. ONE NIGHT HE THOUGHT...
WHY DON'T WE STAY UP TONIGHT AND SEE WHO DOES THESE WONDERFUL FAVORS FOR US?

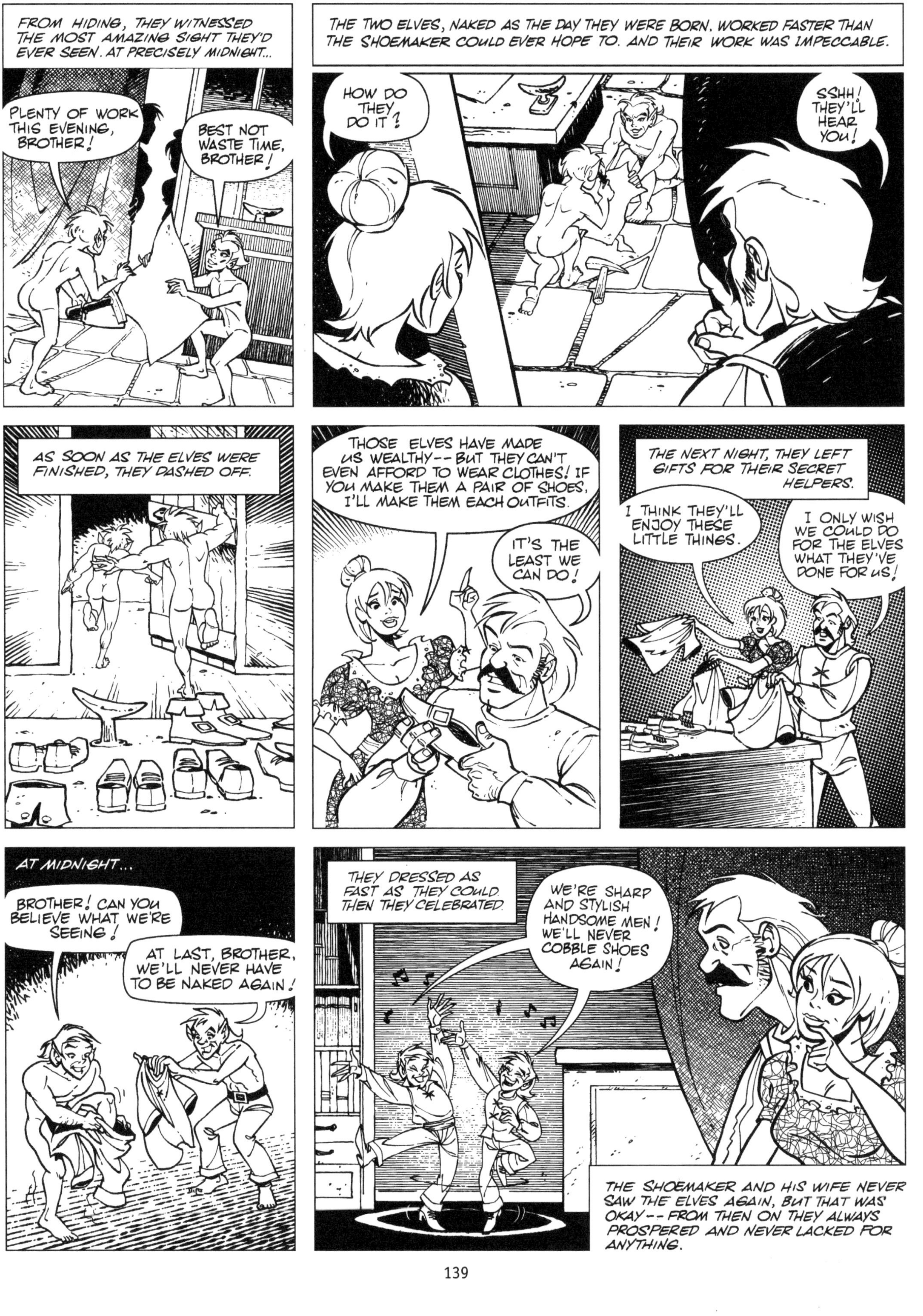
FROM HIDING, THEY WITNESSED THE MOST AMAZING SIGHT THEY'D EVER SEEN. AT PRECISELY MIDNIGHT...
PLENTY OF WORK THIS EVENING, BROTHER!
BEST NOT WASTE TIME, BROTHER!
THE TWO ELVES, NAKED AS THE DAY THEY WERE BORN, WORKED FASTER THAN THE SHOEMAKER COULD EVER HOPE TO. AND THEIR WORK WAS IMPECCABLE.
HOW DO THEY DO IT?
SSHH! THEY'LL HEAR YOU!
AS SOON AS THE ELVES WERE FINISHED, THEY DASHED OFF.
THOSE ELVES HAVE MADE US WEALTHY-- BUT THEY CAN'T EVEN AFFORD TO WEAR CLOTHES! IF YOU MAKE THEM A PAIR OF SHOES, I'LL MAKE THEM EACH OUTFITS.
IT'S THE LEAST WE CAN DO!
THE NEXT NIGHT, THEY LEFT GIFTS FOR THEIR SECRET HELPERS.
I THINK THEY'LL ENJOY THESE LITTLE THINGS.
I ONLY WISH WE COULD DO FOR THE ELVES WHAT THEY'VE DONE FOR US!
AT MIDNIGHT...
BROTHER! CAN YOU BELIEVE WHAT WE'RE SEEING!
AT LAST, BROTHER, WE'LL NEVER HAVE TO BE NAKED AGAIN!
THEY DRESSED AS FAST AS THEY COULD. THEN THEY CELEBRATED.
WE'RE SHARP AND STYLISH HANDSOME MEN! WE'LL NEVER COBBLE SHOES AGAIN!
THE SHOEMAKER AND HIS WIFE NEVER SAW THE ELVES AGAIN, BUT THAT WAS OKAY-- FROM THEN ON THEY ALWAYS PROSPERED AND NEVER LACKED FOR ANYTHING.

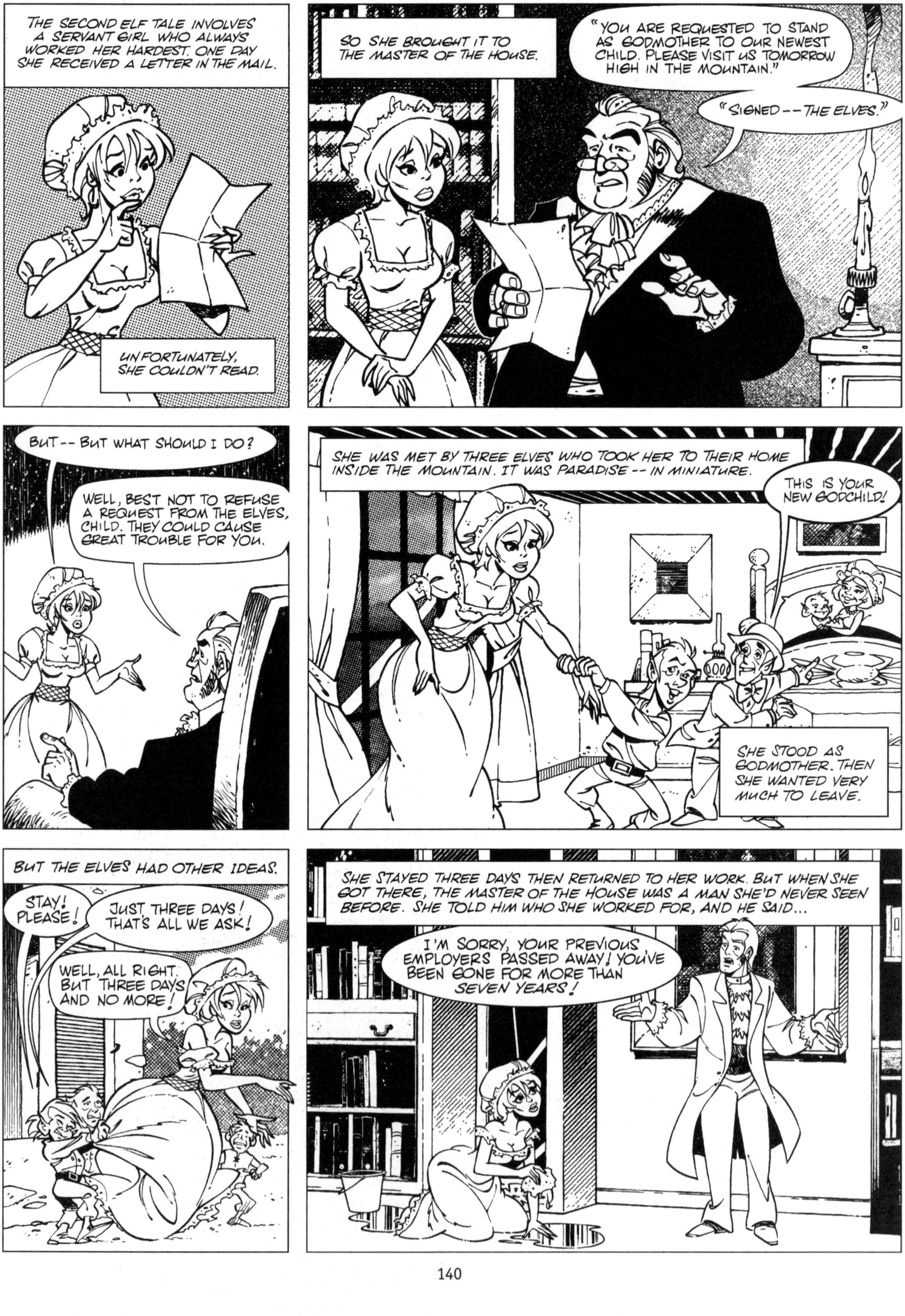
THE SECOND ELF TALE INVOLVES A SERVANT GIRL WHO ALWAYS WORKED HER HARDEST. ONE DAY SHE RECEIVED A LETTER IN THE MAIL.
UNFORTUNATELY, SHE COULDN'T READ.
SO SHE BROUGHT IT TO THE MASTER OF THE HOUSE.
"YOU ARE REQUESTED TO STAND AS GODMOTHER TO OUR NEWEST CHILD. PLEASE VISIT US TOMORROW HIGH IN THE MOUNTAIN."
"SIGNED -- THE ELVES."
BUT -- BUT WHAT SHOULD I DO?
WELL, BEST NOT TO REFUSE A REQUEST FROM THE ELVES, CHILD. THEY COULD CAUSE GREAT TROUBLE FOR YOU.
SHE WAS MET BY THREE ELVES WHO TOOK HER TO THEIR HOME INSIDE THE MOUNTAIN. IT WAS PARADISE -- IN MINIATURE.
THIS IS YOUR NEW GODCHILD!
SHE STOOD AS GODMOTHER. THEN SHE WANTED VERY MUCH TO LEAVE.
BUT THE ELVES HAD OTHER IDEAS.
STAY! PLEASE!
JUST THREE DAYS! THAT'S ALL WE ASK!
WELL, ALL RIGHT. BUT THREE DAYS AND NO MORE!
SHE STAYED THREE DAYS THEN RETURNED TO HER WORK. BUT WHEN SHE GOT THERE, THE MASTER OF THE HOUSE WAS A MAN SHE'D NEVER SEEN BEFORE. SHE TOLD HIM WHO SHE WORKED FOR, AND HE SAID...
I'M SORRY, YOUR PREVIOUS EMPLOYERS PASSED AWAY! YOU'VE BEEN GONE FOR MORE THAN SEVEN YEARS!

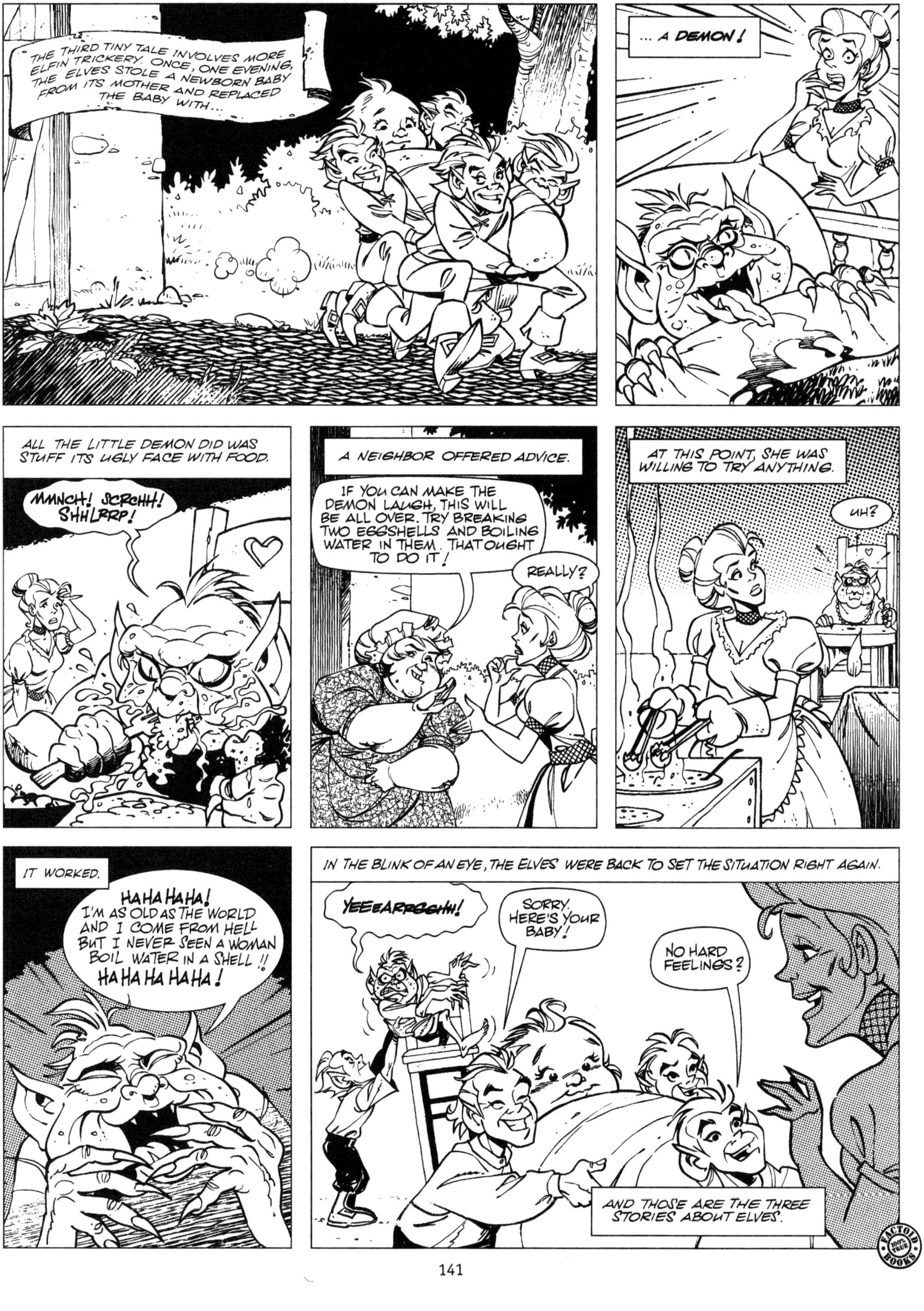
THE THIRD TINY TALE INVOLVES MORE ELFIN TRICKERY. ONCE, ONE EVENING, THE ELVES STOLE A NEWBORN BABY FROM ITS MOTHER AND REPLACED THE BABY WITH...
... A DEMON!
ALL THE LITTLE DEMON DID WAS STUFF ITS UGLY FACE WITH FOOD.
MMNCH! SCRCHH! SHHLRRP!
A NEIGHBOR OFFERED ADVICE.
IF YOU CAN MAKE THE DEMON LAUGH, THIS WILL BE ALL OVER. TRY BREAKING TWO EGGSHELLS AND BOILING WATER IN THEM. THAT OUGHT TO DO IT!
REALLY?
AT THIS POINT, SHE WAS WILLING TO TRY ANYTHING.
UH?
IT WORKED.
HAHAHAHA! I'M AS OLD AS THE WORLD AND I COME FROM HELL BUT I NEVER SEEN A WOMAN BOIL WATER IN A SHELL !! HA HA HA HA HA!
IN THE BLINK OF AN EYE, THE ELVES WERE BACK TO SET THE SITUATION RIGHT AGAIN.
YEEEARRGGHH!
SORRY. HERE'S YOUR BABY!
NO HARD FEELINGS?
AND THOSE ARE THE THREE STORIES ABOUT ELVES.
FACTOID BOOKS 100% TRUE

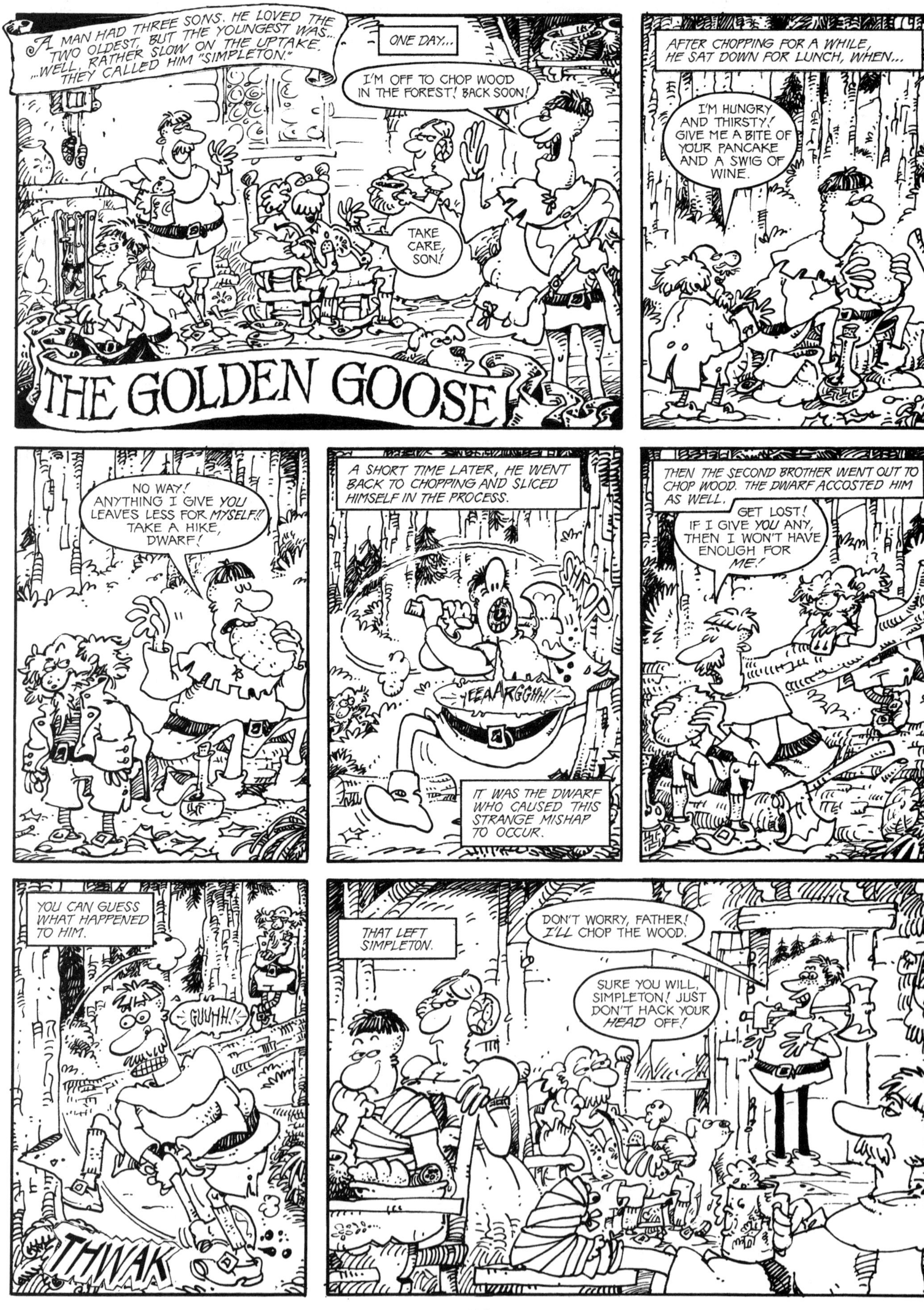
A MAN HAD THREE SONS. HE LOVED THE TWO OLDEST, BUT THE YOUNGEST WAS... ...WELL, RATHER SLOW ON THE UPTAKE. THEY CALLED HIM "SIMPLETON."
THE GOLDEN GOOSE
ONE DAY...
I'M OFF TO CHOP WOOD IN THE FOREST! BACK SOON!
TAKE CARE, SON!
AFTER CHOPPING FOR A WHILE, HE SAT DOWN FOR LUNCH, WHEN...
I'M HUNGRY AND THIRSTY! GIVE ME A BITE OF YOUR PANCAKE AND A SWIG OF WINE.
NO WAY! ANYTHING I GIVE YOU LEAVES LESS FOR MYSELF!! TAKE A HIKE, DWARF!
A SHORT TIME LATER, HE WENT BACK TO CHOPPING AND SLICED HIMSELF IN THE PROCESS.
YEEAARGGHH!
IT WAS THE DWARF WHO CAUSED THIS STRANGE MISHAP TO OCCUR.
THEN THE SECOND BROTHER WENT OUT TO CHOP WOOD. THE DWARF ACCOSTED HIM AS WELL.
GET LOST! IF I GIVE YOU ANY, THEN I WON'T HAVE ENOUGH FOR ME!
YOU CAN GUESS WHAT HAPPENED TO HIM.
GUUHH!
THWAK
THAT LEFT SIMPLETON.
DON'T WORRY, FATHER! I'LL CHOP THE WOOD.
SURE YOU WILL, SIMPLETON! JUST DON'T HACK YOUR HEAD OFF!

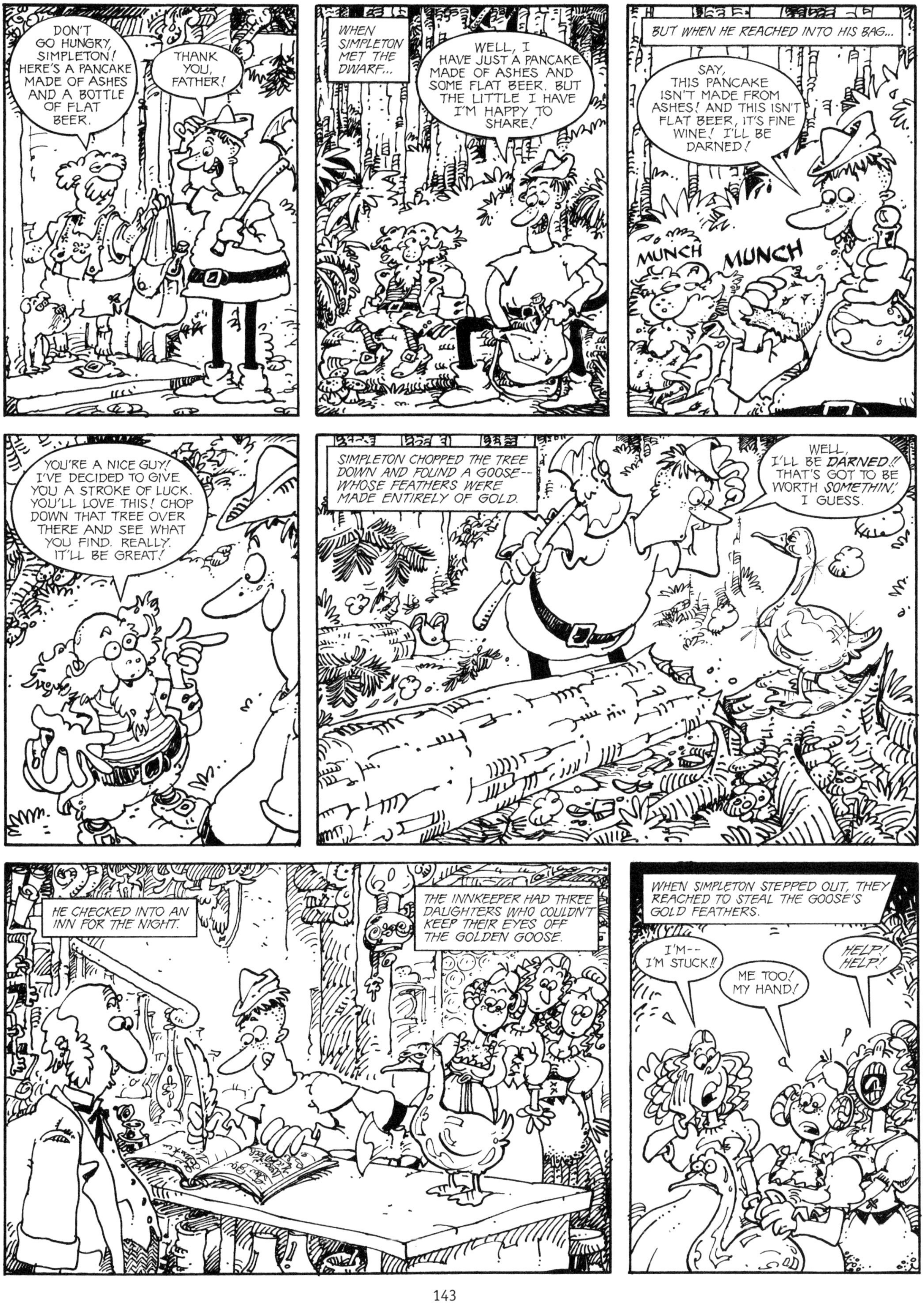
DON'T GO HUNGRY, SIMPLETON! HERE'S A PANCAKE MADE OF ASHES AND A BOTTLE OF FLAT BEER.
THANK YOU, FATHER!
WHEN SIMPLETON MET THE DWARF...
WELL, I HAVE JUST A PANCAKE MADE OF ASHES AND SOME FLAT BEER. BUT THE LITTLE I HAVE I'M HAPPY TO SHARE!
BUT WHEN HE REACHED INTO HIS BAG...
SAY, THIS PANCAKE ISN'T MADE FROM ASHES! AND THIS ISN'T FLAT BEER, IT'S FINE WINE! I'LL BE DARNED!
MUNCH
MUNCH
YOU'RE A NICE GUY! I'VE DECIDED TO GIVE YOU A STROKE OF LUCK. YOU'LL LOVE THIS! CHOP DOWN THAT TREE OVER THERE AND SEE WHAT YOU FIND. REALLY. IT'LL BE GREAT!
SIMPLETON CHOPPED THE TREE DOWN AND FOUND A GOOSE-- WHOSE FEATHERS WERE MADE ENTIRELY OF GOLD.
WELL, I'LL BE DARNED!! THAT'S GOT TO BE WORTH SOMETHIN', I GUESS.
HE CHECKED INTO AN INN FOR THE NIGHT.
THE INNKEEPER HAD THREE DAUGHTERS WHO COULDN'T KEEP THEIR EYES OFF THE GOLDEN GOOSE.
WHEN SIMPLETON STEPPED OUT, THEY REACHED TO STEAL THE GOOSE'S GOLD FEATHERS.
I'M-- I'M STUCK!!
ME TOO! MY HAND!
HELP! HELP!

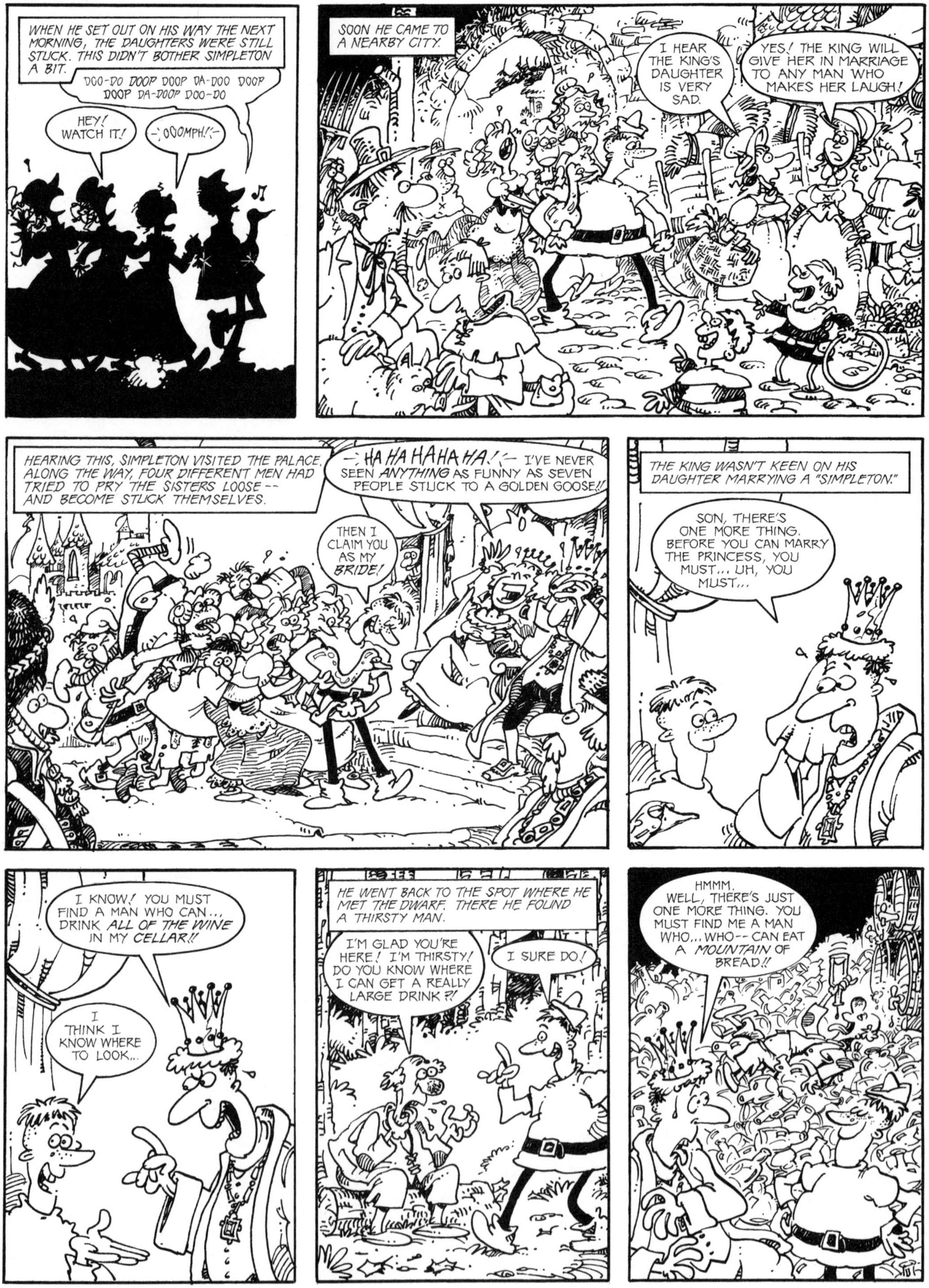
WHEN HE SET OUT ON HIS WAY THE NEXT MORNING, THE DAUGHTERS WERE STILL STUCK. THIS DIDN'T BOTHER SIMPLETON A BIT.
DOO-DO DOOP DOOP DA-DOO DOOP DOOP DA-DOOP DOO-DO
HEY! WATCH IT!
OOOMPH!
SOON HE CAME TO A NEARBY CITY.
I HEAR THE KING'S DAUGHTER IS VERY SAD.
YES! THE KING WILL GIVE HER IN MARRIAGE TO ANY MAN WHO MAKES HER LAUGH!
HEARING THIS, SIMPLETON VISITED THE PALACE. ALONG THE WAY, FOUR DIFFERENT MEN HAD TRIED TO PRY THE SISTERS LOOSE -- AND BECOME STUCK THEMSELVES.
HA HA HAHAHA HA! I'VE NEVER SEEN ANYTHING AS FUNNY AS SEVEN PEOPLE STUCK TO A GOLDEN GOOSE!!
THEN I CLAIM YOU AS MY BRIDE!
THE KING WASN'T KEEN ON HIS DAUGHTER MARRYING A "SIMPLETON."
SON, THERE'S ONE MORE THING. BEFORE YOU CAN MARRY THE PRINCESS, YOU MUST... UH, YOU MUST...
I KNOW! YOU MUST FIND A MAN WHO CAN... DRINK ALL OF THE WINE IN MY CELLAR!!
I THINK I KNOW WHERE TO LOOK...
HE WENT BACK TO THE SPOT WHERE HE MET THE DWARF. THERE HE FOUND A THIRSTY MAN.
I'M GLAD YOU'RE HERE! I'M THIRSTY! DO YOU KNOW WHERE I CAN GET A REALLY LARGE DRINK?!
I SURE DO!
HMMM. WELL, THERE'S JUST ONE MORE THING. YOU MUST FIND ME A MAN WHO... WHO-- CAN EAT A MOUNTAIN OF BREAD!!

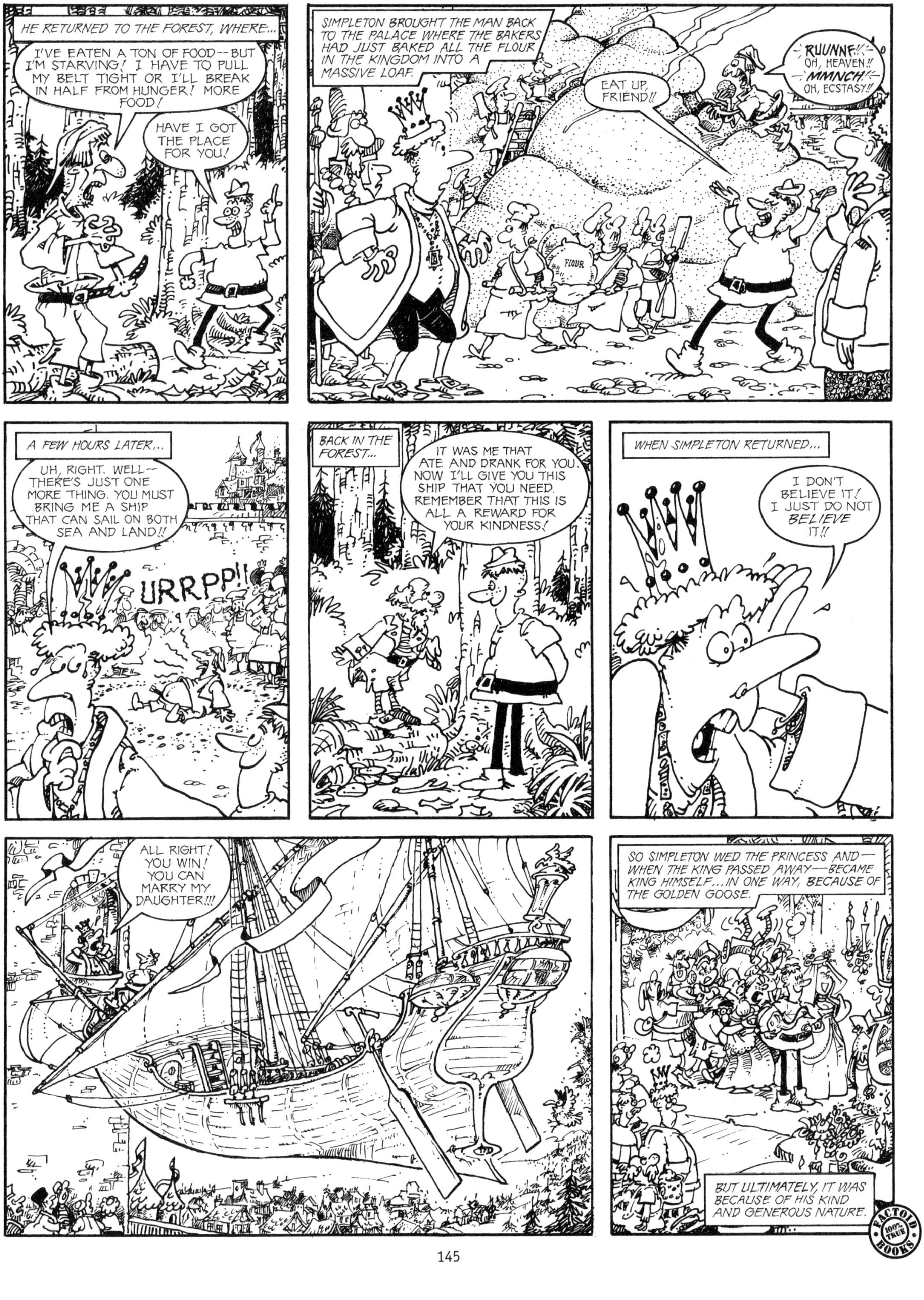
HE RETURNED TO THE FOREST, WHERE...
I'VE EATEN A TON OF FOOD--BUT I'M STARVING! I HAVE TO PULL MY BELT TIGHT OR I'LL BREAK IN HALF FROM HUNGER! MORE FOOD!
HAVE I GOT THE PLACE FOR YOU!
SIMPLETON BROUGHT THE MAN BACK TO THE PALACE WHERE THE BAKERS HAD JUST BAKED ALL THE FLOUR IN THE KINGDOM INTO A MASSIVE LOAF.
EAT UP, FRIEND!!
RUUNNF!! OH, HEAVEN!! MMNCH!! OH, ECSTASY!!
FLOUR
A FEW HOURS LATER...
UH, RIGHT. WELL-- THERE'S JUST ONE MORE THING. YOU MUST BRING ME A SHIP THAT CAN SAIL ON BOTH SEA AND LAND!!
URRPP!!
BACK IN THE FOREST...
IT WAS ME THAT ATE AND DRANK FOR YOU. NOW I'LL GIVE YOU THIS SHIP THAT YOU NEED. REMEMBER THAT THIS IS ALL A REWARD FOR YOUR KINDNESS!
WHEN SIMPLETON RETURNED...
I DON'T BELIEVE IT! I JUST DO NOT BELIEVE IT!!
ALL RIGHT! YOU WIN! YOU CAN MARRY MY DAUGHTER!!!
SO SIMPLETON WED THE PRINCESS AND—WHEN THE KING PASSED AWAY—BECAME KING HIMSELF...IN ONE WAY, BECAUSE OF THE GOLDEN GOOSE.
BUT ULTIMATELY, IT WAS BECAUSE OF HIS KIND AND GENEROUS NATURE.
FACTOID BOOKS 100% TRUE

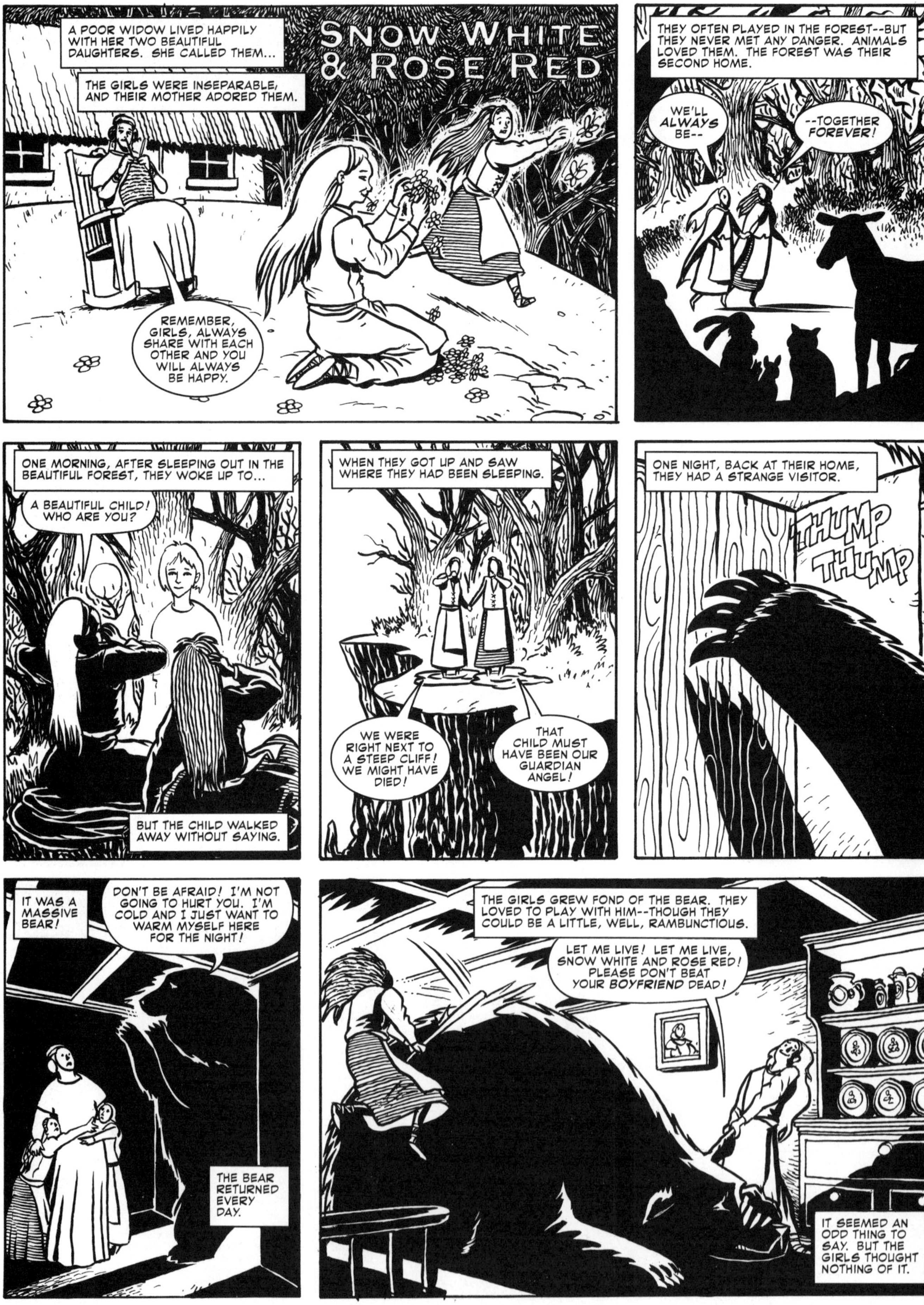
A POOR WIDOW LIVED HAPPILY WITH HER TWO BEAUTIFUL DAUGHTERS. SHE CALLED THEM...
SNOW WHITE & ROSE RED
THE GIRLS WERE INSEPARABLE, AND THEIR MOTHER ADORED THEM.
REMEMBER, GIRLS, ALWAYS SHARE WITH EACH OTHER AND YOU WILL ALWAYS BE HAPPY.
THEY OFTEN PLAYED IN THE FOREST--BUT THEY NEVER MET ANY DANGER. ANIMALS LOVED THEM. THE FOREST WAS THEIR SECOND HOME.
WE'LL ALWAYS BE--
--TOGETHER FOREVER!
ONE MORNING, AFTER SLEEPING OUT IN THE BEAUTIFUL FOREST, THEY WOKE UP TO...
A BEAUTIFUL CHILD! WHO ARE YOU?
BUT THE CHILD WALKED AWAY WITHOUT SAYING.
WHEN THEY GOT UP AND SAW WHERE THEY HAD BEEN SLEEPING.
WE WERE RIGHT NEXT TO A STEEP CLIFF! WE MIGHT HAVE DIED!
THAT CHILD MUST HAVE BEEN OUR GUARDIAN ANGEL!
ONE NIGHT, BACK AT THEIR HOME, THEY HAD A STRANGE VISITOR.
THUMP THUMP
IT WAS A MASSIVE BEAR!
DON'T BE AFRAID! I'M NOT GOING TO HURT YOU. I'M COLD AND I JUST WANT TO WARM MYSELF HERE FOR THE NIGHT!
THE BEAR RETURNED EVERY DAY.
THE GIRLS GREW FOND OF THE BEAR. THEY LOVED TO PLAY WITH HIM--THOUGH THEY COULD BE A LITTLE, WELL, RAMBUNCTIOUS.
LET ME LIVE! LET ME LIVE, SNOW WHITE AND ROSE RED! PLEASE DON'T BEAT YOUR BOYFRIEND DEAD!
IT SEEMED AN ODD THING TO SAY. BUT THE GIRLS THOUGHT NOTHING OF IT.

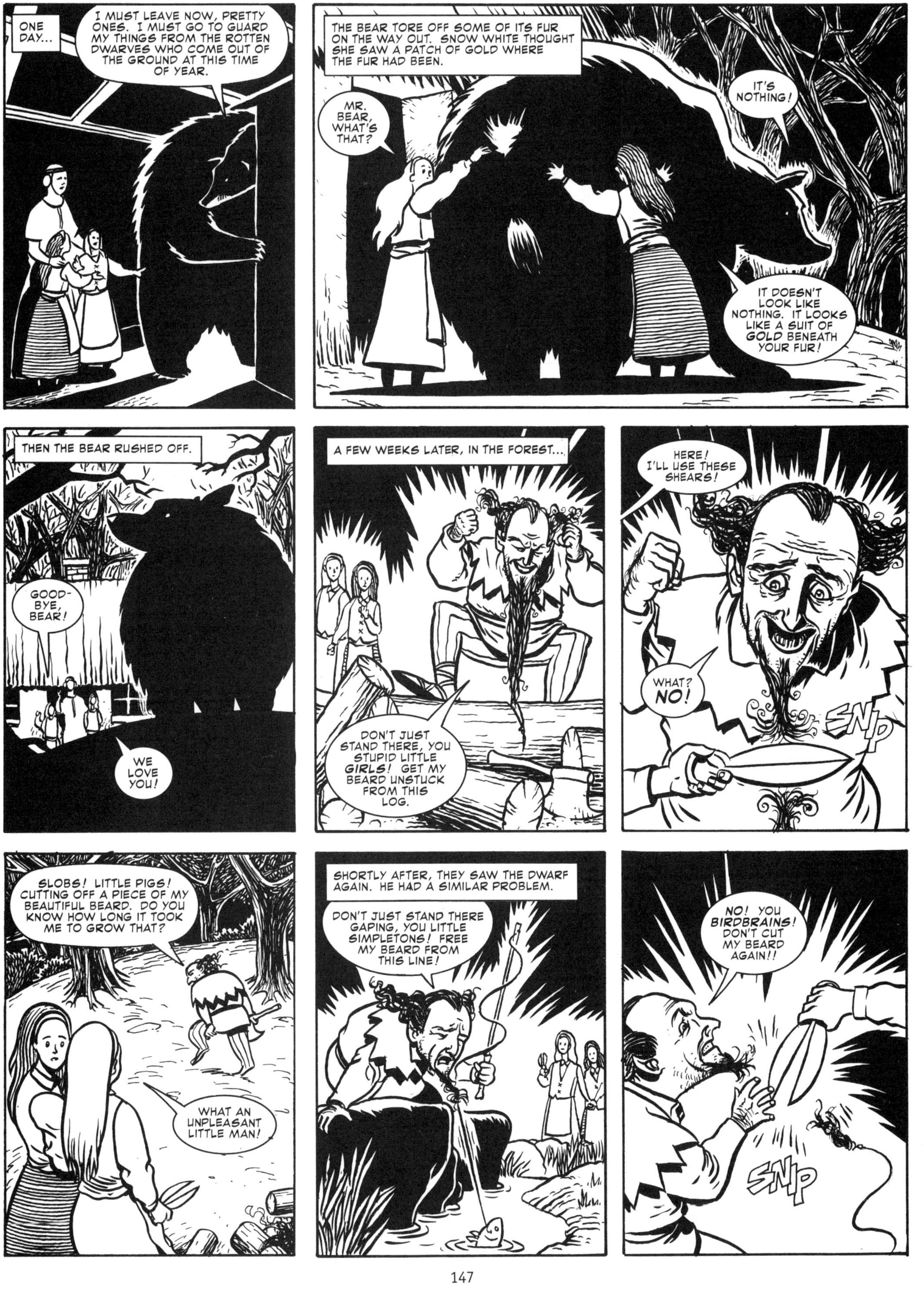

ONE DAY...
I MUST LEAVE NOW, PRETTY ONES. I MUST GO TO GUARD MY THINGS FROM THE ROTTEN DWARVES WHO COME OUT OF THE GROUND AT THIS TIME OF YEAR.
THE BEAR TORE OFF SOME OF ITS FUR ON THE WAY OUT. SNOW WHITE THOUGHT SHE SAW A PATCH OF GOLD WHERE THE FUR HAD BEEN.
MR. BEAR, WHAT'S THAT?
IT'S NOTHING!
IT DOESN'T LOOK LIKE NOTHING. IT LOOKS LIKE A SUIT OF GOLD BENEATH YOUR FUR!
THEN THE BEAR RUSHED OFF.
GOOD-BYE, BEAR!
WE LOVE YOU!
A FEW WEEKS LATER, IN THE FOREST...
DON'T JUST STAND THERE, YOU STUPID LITTLE GIRLS! GET MY BEARD UNSTUCK FROM THIS LOG.
HERE! I'LL USE THESE SHEARS!
WHAT? NO!
SNIP
SLOBS! LITTLE PIGS! CUTTING OFF A PIECE OF MY BEAUTIFUL BEARD. DO YOU KNOW HOW LONG IT TOOK ME TO GROW THAT?
WHAT AN UNPLEASANT LITTLE MAN!
SHORTLY AFTER, THEY SAW THE DWARF AGAIN. HE HAD A SIMILAR PROBLEM.
DON'T JUST STAND THERE GAPING, YOU LITTLE SIMPLETONS! FREE MY BEARD FROM THIS LINE!
NO! YOU BIRDBRAINS! DON'T CUT MY BEARD AGAIN!!
SNIP

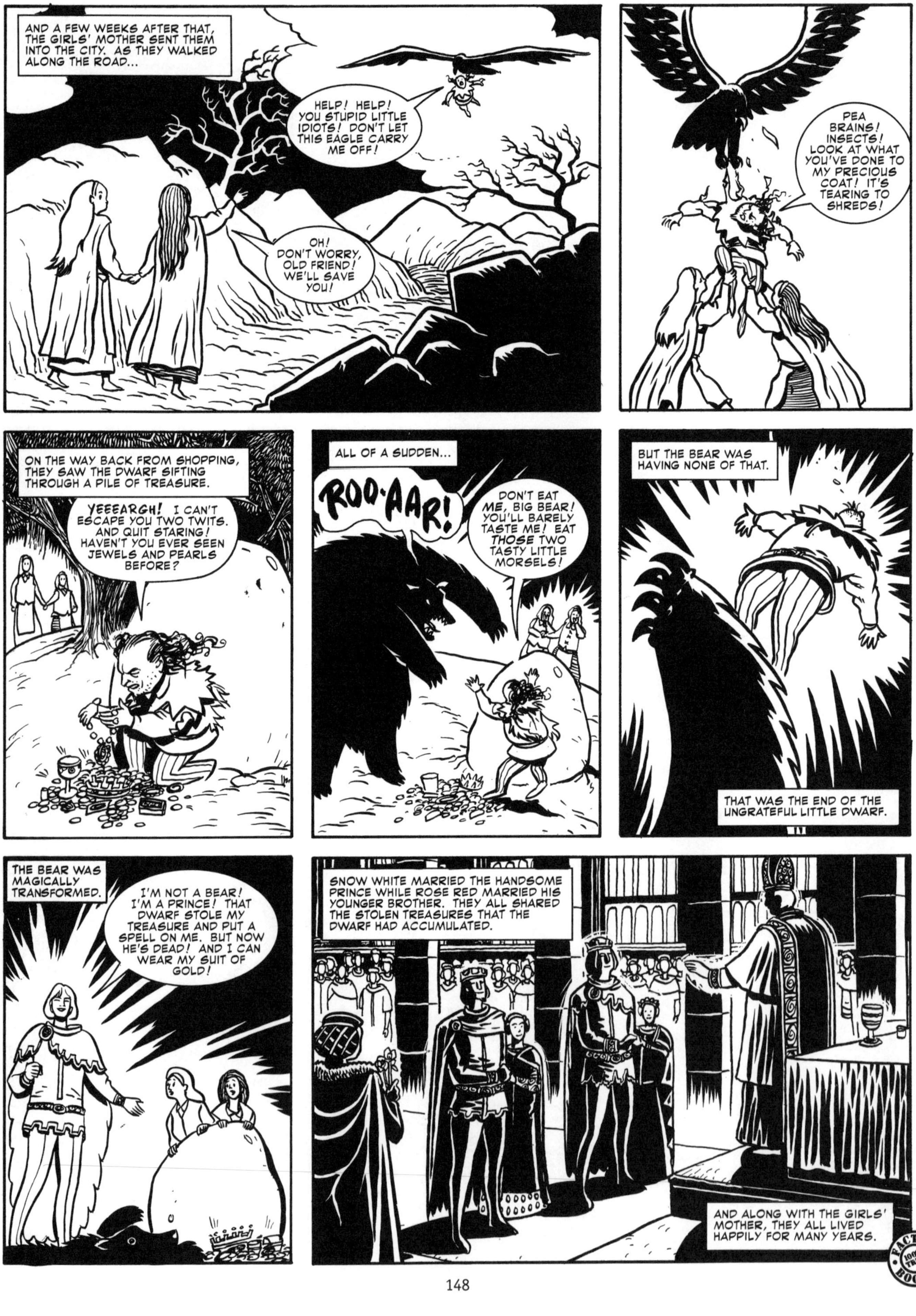

AND A FEW WEEKS AFTER THAT, THE GIRLS' MOTHER SENT THEM INTO THE CITY. AS THEY WALKED ALONG THE ROAD...
HELP! HELP! YOU STUPID LITTLE IDIOTS! DON'T LET THIS EAGLE CARRY ME OFF!
OH! DON'T WORRY, OLD FRIEND! WE'LL SAVE YOU!
PEA BRAINS! INSECTS! LOOK AT WHAT YOU'VE DONE TO MY PRECIOUS COAT! IT'S TEARING TO SHREDS!
ON THE WAY BACK FROM SHOPPING, THEY SAW THE DWARF SIFTING THROUGH A PILE OF TREASURE.
YEEEARGH! I CAN'T ESCAPE YOU TWO TWITS. AND QUIT STARING! HAVEN'T YOU EVER SEEN JEWELS AND PEARLS BEFORE?
ALL OF A SUDDEN...
ROO-AAR!
DON'T EAT ME, BIG BEAR! YOU'LL BARELY TASTE ME! EAT THOSE TWO TASTY LITTLE MORSELS!
BUT THE BEAR WAS HAVING NONE OF THAT.
THAT WAS THE END OF THE UNGRATEFUL LITTLE DWARF.
THE BEAR WAS MAGICALLY TRANSFORMED.
I'M NOT A BEAR! I'M A PRINCE! THAT DWARF STOLE MY TREASURE AND PUT A SPELL ON ME. BUT NOW HE'S DEAD! AND I CAN WEAR MY SUIT OF GOLD!
SNOW WHITE MARRIED THE HANDSOME PRINCE WHILE ROSE RED MARRIED HIS YOUNGER BROTHER. THEY ALL SHARED THE STOLEN TREASURES THAT THE DWARF HAD ACCUMULATED.
AND ALONG WITH THE GIRLS' MOTHER, THEY ALL LIVED HAPPILY FOR MANY YEARS.

FACTOID BOOKS 100% TRUE

CHAPTER FIVE

LESSONS LEARNED — THE HARD WAY

Despite the horror, gore, death and human misery that makes Grimms' fairy tales such enjoyable diversions for young and old alike, the real purpose of the Grimm brothers' stories was to teach lessons about life. But that education often comes with a heavy price tag. For example, in "Three Army Surgeons," three doctors hack off parts of their bodies just to show that they can put them back on. Eventually, it turns out that they CAN'T. Arrogance is certainly a vice, but dismemberment seems a bit of a high cost to learn a simple lesson. In the stories that follow, learning is never an easy process. A whack on the hand from a ruler-wielding nun would seem a welcome relief for these sorry souls who sometimes endured death — or worse — to glean a little moral instruction. The real lesson we take from these tales of terror: better to read them than to live them.

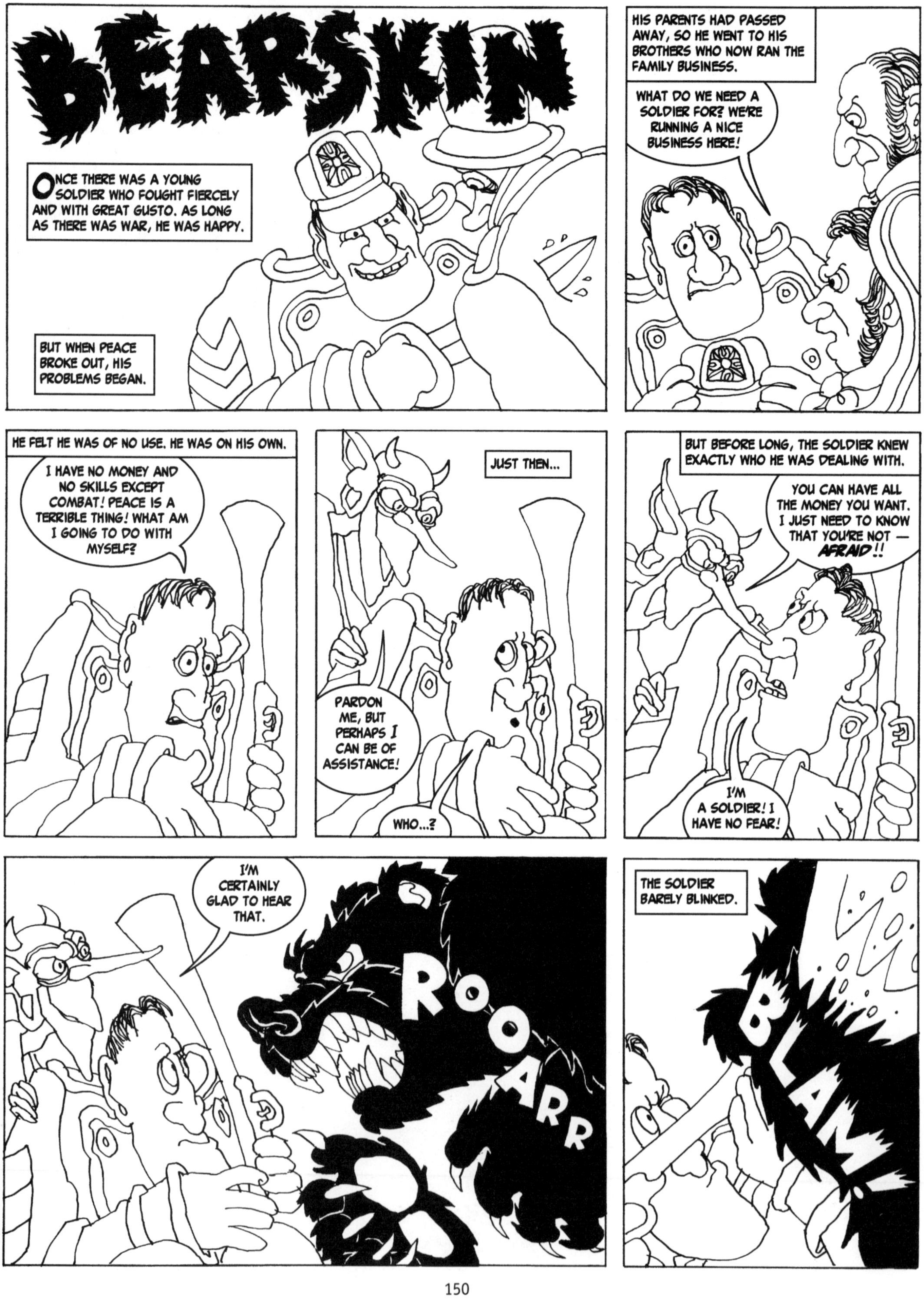

BEARSKIN
ONCE THERE WAS A YOUNG SOLDIER WHO FOUGHT FIERCELY AND WITH GREAT GUSTO. AS LONG AS THERE WAS WAR, HE WAS HAPPY.
BUT WHEN PEACE BROKE OUT, HIS PROBLEMS BEGAN.
HIS PARENTS HAD PASSED AWAY, SO HE WENT TO HIS BROTHERS WHO NOW RAN THE FAMILY BUSINESS.
WHAT DO WE NEED A SOLDIER FOR? WE'RE RUNNING A NICE BUSINESS HERE!
HE FELT HE WAS OF NO USE. HE WAS ON HIS OWN.
I HAVE NO MONEY AND NO SKILLS EXCEPT COMBAT! PEACE IS A TERRIBLE THING! WHAT AM I GOING TO DO WITH MYSELF?
JUST THEN...
PARDON ME, BUT PERHAPS I CAN BE OF ASSISTANCE!
WHO...?
BUT BEFORE LONG, THE SOLDIER KNEW EXACTLY WHO HE WAS DEALING WITH.
YOU CAN HAVE ALL THE MONEY YOU WANT. I JUST NEED TO KNOW THAT YOU'RE NOT — AFRAID!!
I'M A SOLDIER! I HAVE NO FEAR!
I'M CERTAINLY GLAD TO HEAR THAT.
ROOOARR
THE SOLDIER BARELY BLINKED.
BLAM!

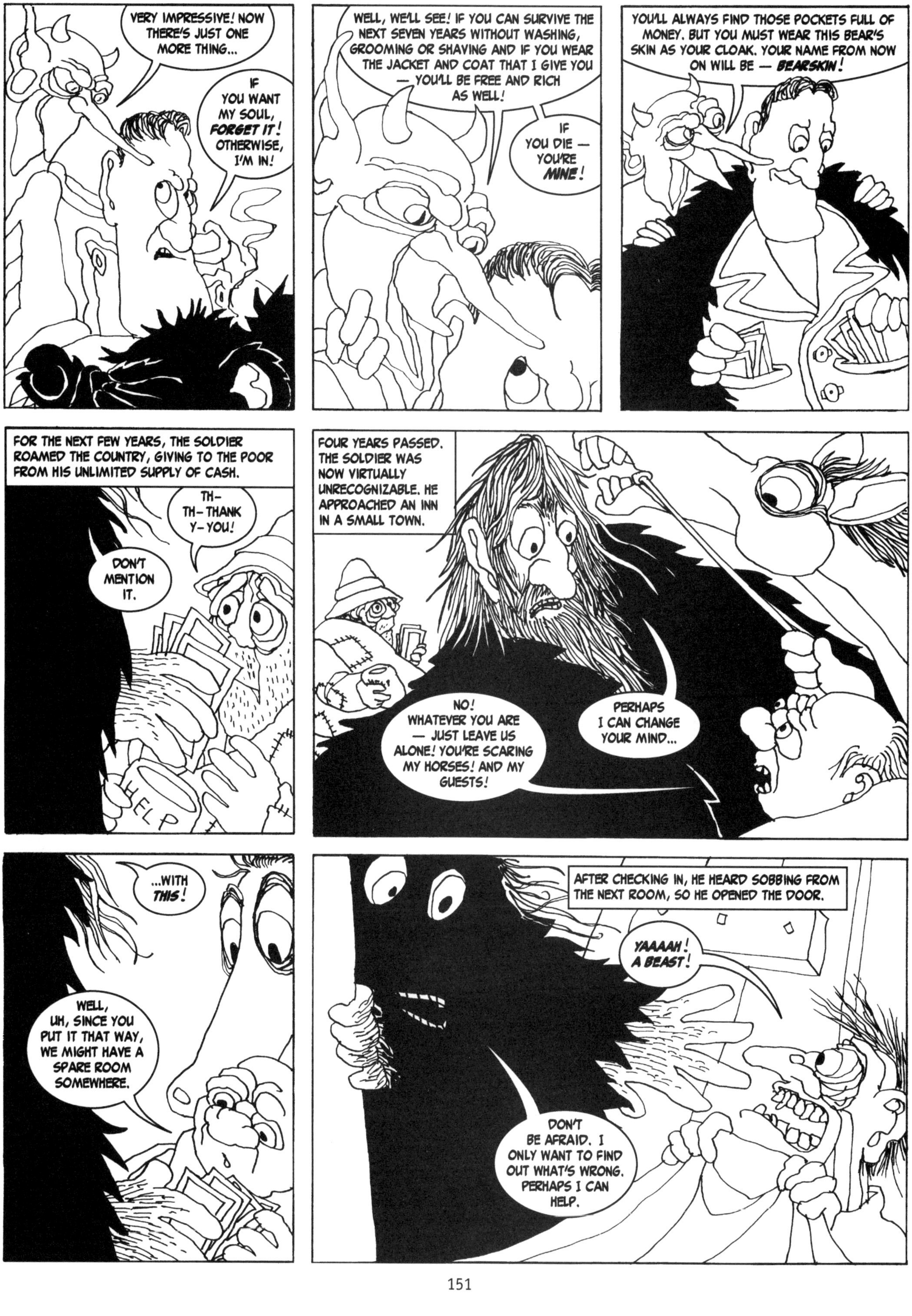
VERY IMPRESSIVE! NOW THERE'S JUST ONE MORE THING...
IF YOU WANT MY SOUL, FORGET IT! OTHERWISE, I'M IN!
WELL, WE'LL SEE! IF YOU CAN SURVIVE THE NEXT SEVEN YEARS WITHOUT WASHING, GROOMING OR SHAVING AND IF YOU WEAR THE JACKET AND COAT THAT I GIVE YOU — YOU'LL BE FREE AND RICH AS WELL!
IF YOU DIE — YOU'RE MINE!
YOU'LL ALWAYS FIND THOSE POCKETS FULL OF MONEY. BUT YOU MUST WEAR THIS BEAR'S SKIN AS YOUR CLOAK. YOUR NAME FROM NOW ON WILL BE — BEARSKIN!
FOR THE NEXT FEW YEARS, THE SOLDIER ROAMED THE COUNTRY, GIVING TO THE POOR FROM HIS UNLIMITED SUPPLY OF CASH.
TH- TH-THANK Y-YOU!
DON'T MENTION IT.
HELP
FOUR YEARS PASSED. THE SOLDIER WAS NOW VIRTUALLY UNRECOGNIZABLE. HE APPROACHED AN INN IN A SMALL TOWN.
NO! WHATEVER YOU ARE — JUST LEAVE US ALONE! YOU'RE SCARING MY HORSES! AND MY GUESTS!
PERHAPS I CAN CHANGE YOUR MIND...
...WITH THIS!
WELL, UH, SINCE YOU PUT IT THAT WAY, WE MIGHT HAVE A SPARE ROOM SOMEWHERE.
AFTER CHECKING IN, HE HEARD SOBBING FROM THE NEXT ROOM, SO HE OPENED THE DOOR.
YAAAAH! A BEAST!
DON'T BE AFRAID. I ONLY WANT TO FIND OUT WHAT'S WRONG. PERHAPS I CAN HELP.

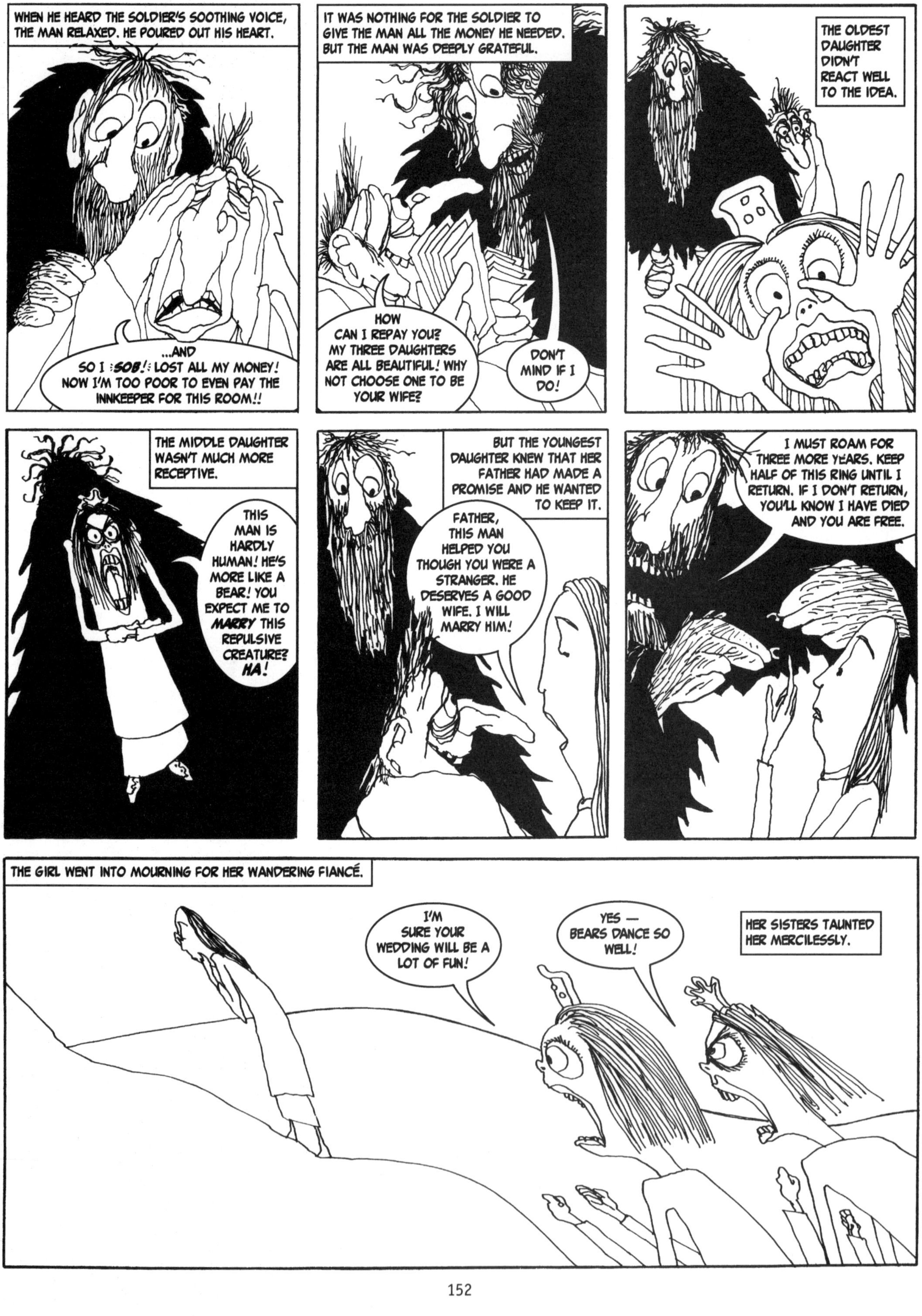
WHEN HE HEARD THE SOLDIER'S SOOTHING VOICE, THE MAN RELAXED. HE POURED OUT HIS HEART.
...AND SO I SOB! LOST ALL MY MONEY! NOW I'M TOO POOR TO EVEN PAY THE INNKEEPER FOR THIS ROOM!!
IT WAS NOTHING FOR THE SOLDIER TO GIVE THE MAN ALL THE MONEY HE NEEDED. BUT THE MAN WAS DEEPLY GRATEFUL.
HOW CAN I REPAY YOU? MY THREE DAUGHTERS ARE ALL BEAUTIFUL! WHY NOT CHOOSE ONE TO BE YOUR WIFE?
DON'T MIND IF I DO!
THE OLDEST DAUGHTER DIDN'T REACT WELL TO THE IDEA.
THE MIDDLE DAUGHTER WASN'T MUCH MORE RECEPTIVE.
THIS MAN IS HARDLY HUMAN! HE'S MORE LIKE A BEAR! YOU EXPECT ME TO MARRY THIS REPULSIVE CREATURE? HA!
BUT THE YOUNGEST DAUGHTER KNEW THAT HER FATHER HAD MADE A PROMISE AND HE WANTED TO KEEP IT.
FATHER, THIS MAN HELPED YOU THOUGH YOU WERE A STRANGER. HE DESERVES A GOOD WIFE. I WILL MARRY HIM!
I MUST ROAM FOR THREE MORE YEARS. KEEP HALF OF THIS RING UNTIL I RETURN. IF I DON'T RETURN, YOU'LL KNOW I HAVE DIED AND YOU ARE FREE.
THE GIRL WENT INTO MOURNING FOR HER WANDERING FIANCÉ.
I'M SURE YOUR WEDDING WILL BE A LOT OF FUN!
YES — BEARS DANCE SO WELL!
HER SISTERS TAUNTED HER MERCILESSLY.

AT LONG LAST, THE SEVEN YEARS WERE UP.

WELL, I'VE BEATEN YOU. I SURVIVED. NOW YOU HAVE TO CLEAN ME UP!!

VERY WELL. I ALWAYS HONOR MY AGREEMENTS. BUT I ALWAYS GET *MINE* IN THE END.

SEVERAL HOURS LATER...

SAY, I'M NOT SUCH A BAD-LOOKING GUY AFTER ALL!

HE BOUGHT A WHITE CARRIAGE AND EXPENSIVE CLOTHES. WHEN HE RETURNED, NO ONE RECOGNIZED HIM.

HE'S SO HANDSOME! PERHAPS HE'S HERE TO FIND A BRIDE!

OR MAYBE TWO BRIDES!

DO YOU HAVE YOUR HALF OF THE RING, MY BETROTHED?

OH! IT'S YOU, MY FIANCÉ! YOU'RE ALIVE!

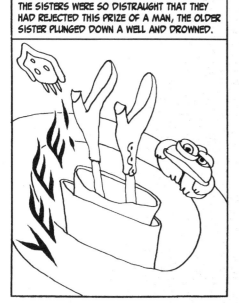

THE SISTERS WERE SO DISTRAUGHT THAT THEY HAD REJECTED THIS PRIZE OF A MAN, THE OLDER SISTER PLUNGED DOWN A WELL AND DROWNED.

THE OTHER SISTER HANGED HERSELF FROM A NEARBY TREE.

A FEW MONTHS LATER...

WHAT DO *YOU* WANT?

JUST TO THANK YOU. I LOST *YOUR* SOUL — BUT CLAIMED TWO IN RETURN. NOW *THAT'S* A GOOD DEAL!

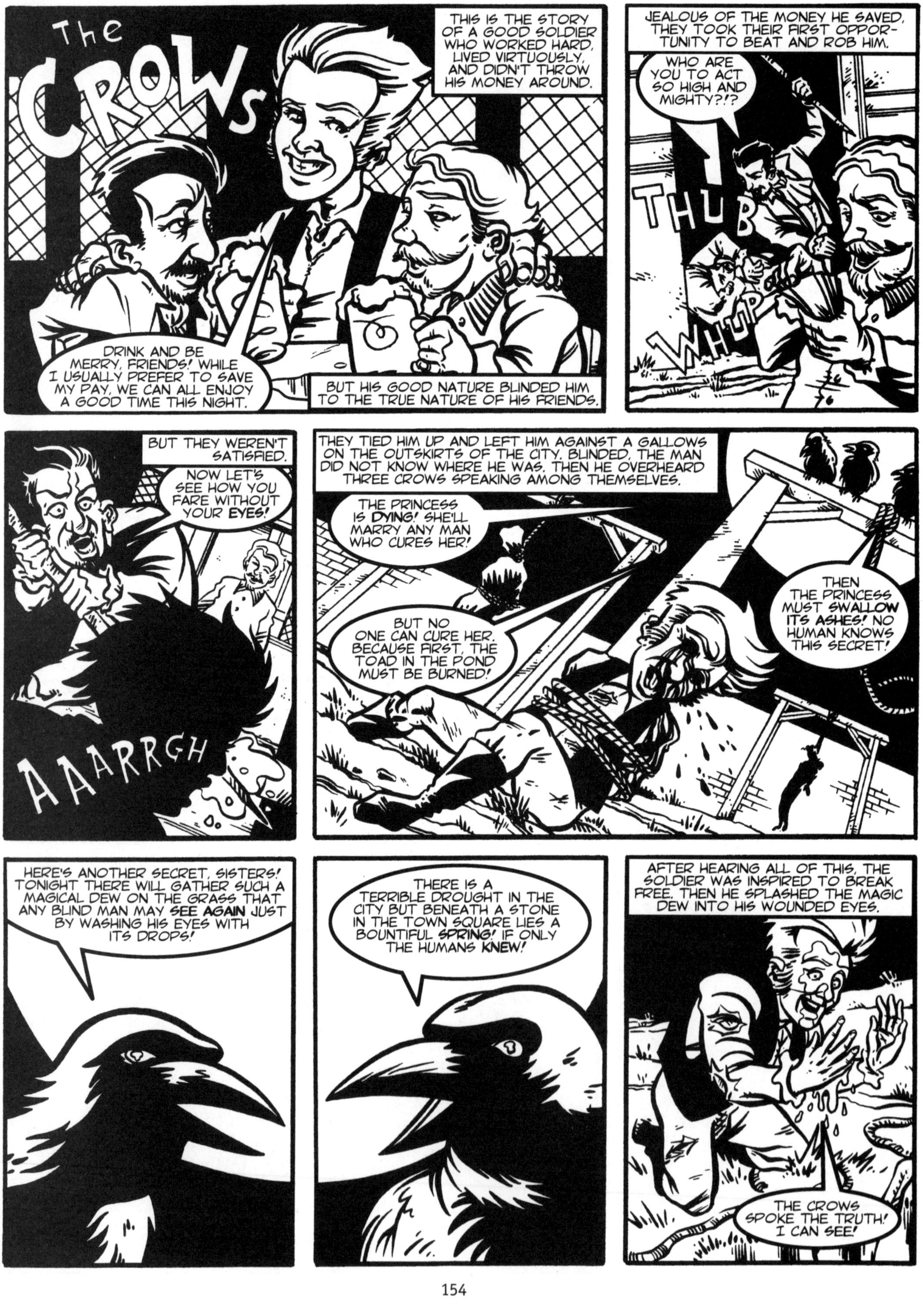
The CROWS
THIS IS THE STORY OF A GOOD SOLDIER WHO WORKED HARD, LIVED VIRTUOUSLY, AND DIDN'T THROW HIS MONEY AROUND.
DRINK AND BE MERRY, FRIENDS! WHILE I USUALLY PREFER TO SAVE MY PAY, WE CAN ALL ENJOY A GOOD TIME THIS NIGHT.
BUT HIS GOOD NATURE BLINDED HIM TO THE TRUE NATURE OF HIS FRIENDS.
JEALOUS OF THE MONEY HE SAVED, THEY TOOK THEIR FIRST OPPORTUNITY TO BEAT AND ROB HIM.
WHO ARE YOU TO ACT SO HIGH AND MIGHTY?!?
THUB
WHUP
BUT THEY WEREN'T SATISFIED.
NOW LET'S SEE HOW YOU FARE WITHOUT YOUR **EYES**!
AAARRGH
THEY TIED HIM UP AND LEFT HIM AGAINST A GALLOWS ON THE OUTSKIRTS OF THE CITY. BLINDED, THE MAN DID NOT KNOW WHERE HE WAS. THEN HE OVERHEARD THREE CROWS SPEAKING AMONG THEMSELVES.
THE PRINCESS IS **DYING**! SHE'LL MARRY ANY MAN WHO CURES HER!
BUT NO ONE CAN CURE HER, BECAUSE FIRST, THE TOAD IN THE POND MUST BE BURNED!
THEN THE PRINCESS MUST **SWALLOW ITS ASHES**! NO HUMAN KNOWS THIS SECRET!
HERE'S ANOTHER SECRET, SISTERS! TONIGHT THERE WILL GATHER SUCH A MAGICAL DEW ON THE GRASS THAT ANY BLIND MAN MAY **SEE AGAIN** JUST BY WASHING HIS EYES WITH ITS DROPS!
THERE IS A TERRIBLE DROUGHT IN THE CITY BUT BENEATH A STONE IN THE TOWN SQUARE LIES A BOUNTIFUL **SPRING**! IF ONLY THE HUMANS **KNEW**!
AFTER HEARING ALL OF THIS, THE SOLDIER WAS INSPIRED TO BREAK FREE. THEN HE SPLASHED THE MAGIC DEW INTO HIS WOUNDED EYES.
THE CROWS SPOKE THE TRUTH! I CAN SEE!

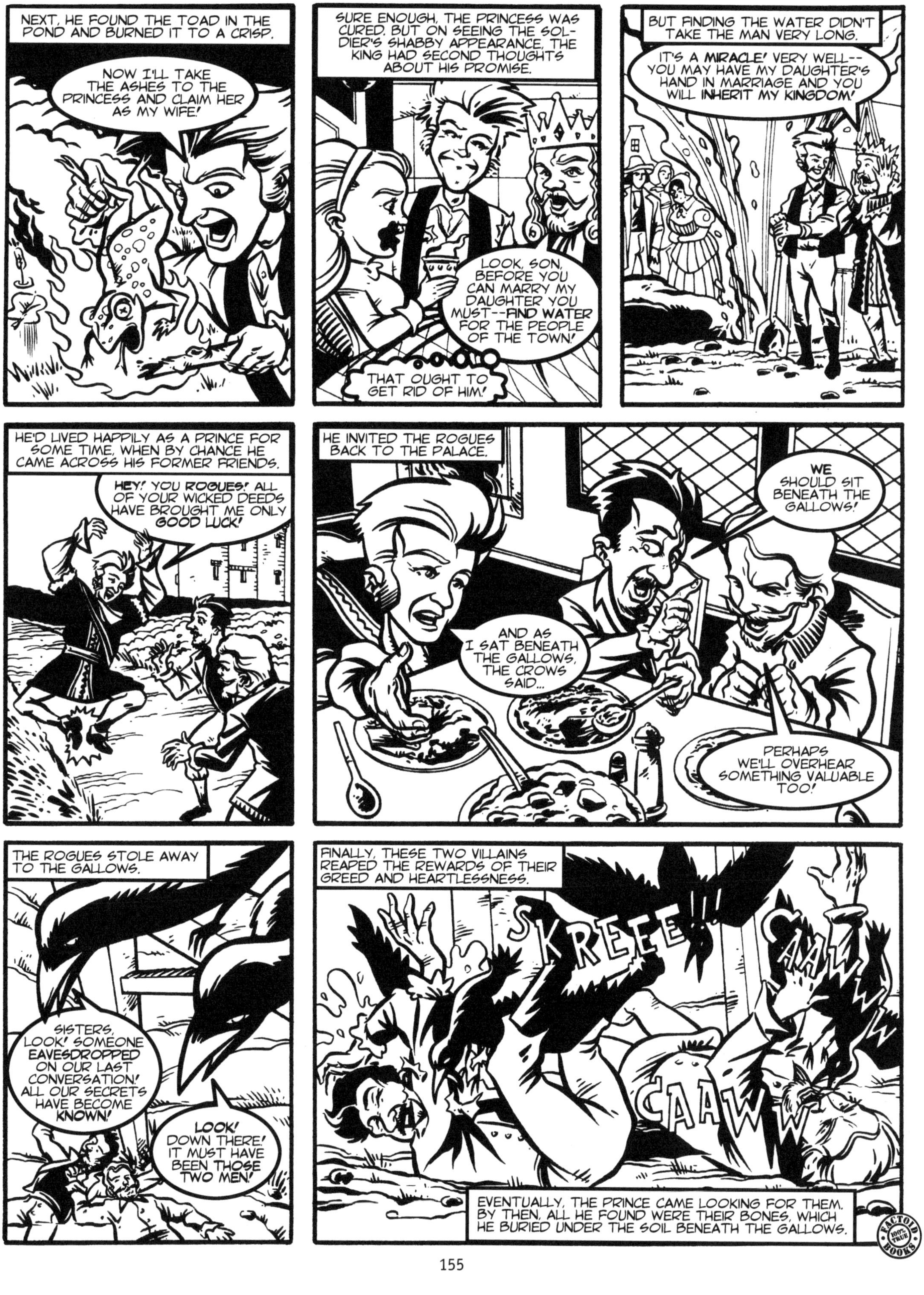
NEXT, HE FOUND THE TOAD IN THE POND AND BURNED IT TO A CRISP.
NOW I'LL TAKE THE ASHES TO THE PRINCESS AND CLAIM HER AS MY WIFE!
SURE ENOUGH, THE PRINCESS WAS CURED. BUT ON SEEING THE SOLDIER'S SHABBY APPEARANCE, THE KING HAD SECOND THOUGHTS ABOUT HIS PROMISE.
LOOK, SON, BEFORE YOU CAN MARRY MY DAUGHTER YOU MUST--FIND WATER FOR THE PEOPLE OF THE TOWN!
THAT OUGHT TO GET RID OF HIM!
BUT FINDING THE WATER DIDN'T TAKE THE MAN VERY LONG.
IT'S A MIRACLE! VERY WELL--YOU MAY HAVE MY DAUGHTER'S HAND IN MARRIAGE AND YOU WILL INHERIT MY KINGDOM!
HE'D LIVED HAPPILY AS A PRINCE FOR SOME TIME, WHEN BY CHANCE HE CAME ACROSS HIS FORMER FRIENDS.
HEY! YOU ROGUES! ALL OF YOUR WICKED DEEDS HAVE BROUGHT ME ONLY GOOD LUCK!
HE INVITED THE ROGUES BACK TO THE PALACE.
AND AS I SAT BENEATH THE GALLOWS, THE CROWS SAID...
WE SHOULD SIT BENEATH THE GALLOWS!
PERHAPS WE'LL OVERHEAR SOMETHING VALUABLE TOO!
THE ROGUES STOLE AWAY TO THE GALLOWS.
SISTERS, LOOK! SOMEONE EAVESDROPPED ON OUR LAST CONVERSATION! ALL OUR SECRETS HAVE BECOME KNOWN!
LOOK! DOWN THERE! IT MUST HAVE BEEN THOSE TWO MEN!
FINALLY, THESE TWO VILLAINS REAPED THE REWARDS OF THEIR GREED AND HEARTLESSNESS.
SKREEE!!
CAAW
CAAWW
EVENTUALLY, THE PRINCE CAME LOOKING FOR THEM. BY THEN, ALL HE FOUND WERE THEIR BONES, WHICH HE BURIED UNDER THE SOIL BENEATH THE GALLOWS.

THE DEVIL'S SMELLY BROTHER

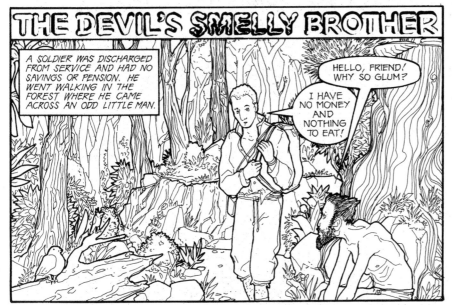

A SOLDIER WAS DISCHARGED FROM SERVICE AND HAD NO SAVINGS OR PENSION. HE WENT WALKING IN THE FOREST WHERE HE CAME ACROSS AN ODD LITTLE MAN.

HELLO, FRIEND! WHY SO GLUM?

I HAVE NO MONEY AND NOTHING TO EAT!

WHAT THE SOLDIER DIDN'T KNOW WAS THAT THIS MAN WAS REALLY-- THE DEVIL!

WHY NOT COME WORK FOR ME?! I'LL SEE THAT YOU'VE GOT EVERYTHING YOU NEED FOR THE REST OF YOUR LIFE!

ALL I ASK IS SEVEN YEARS. OH, AND DURING THAT TIME YOU MAY NOT WASH, SHAVE, COMB YOUR HAIR, CUT YOUR NAILS, OR RUB YOUR EYES.

WELL, OKAY.

HELL

THE DEVIL LED THE SOLDIER DOWN TO HELL.

YOUR JOB IS TO STOKE THE FIRES UNDERNEATH MY KETTLES, BECAUSE THAT'S WHERE I BOIL THE DAMNED SOULS. AND KEEP YOUR AREA CLEAN. THIS PLACE IS BEGINNING TO LOOK LIKE HELL.

NO SWEAT.

JUST ONE THING... NEVER LOOK INSIDE THESE KETTLES! OTHERWISE-- WELL, USE YOUR IMAGINATION!

BUT AFTER SOME TIME PASSED...

JUST ONE LITTLE PEEK COULDN'T HURT...

IN THE FIRST KETTLE... WAS THE SOLDIER'S OLD SERGEANT!

HA! YOU PIECE OF--! YOU USED TO PUSH ME AROUND, BUT LOOK AT YOU NOW! I'LL TEACH YOU!

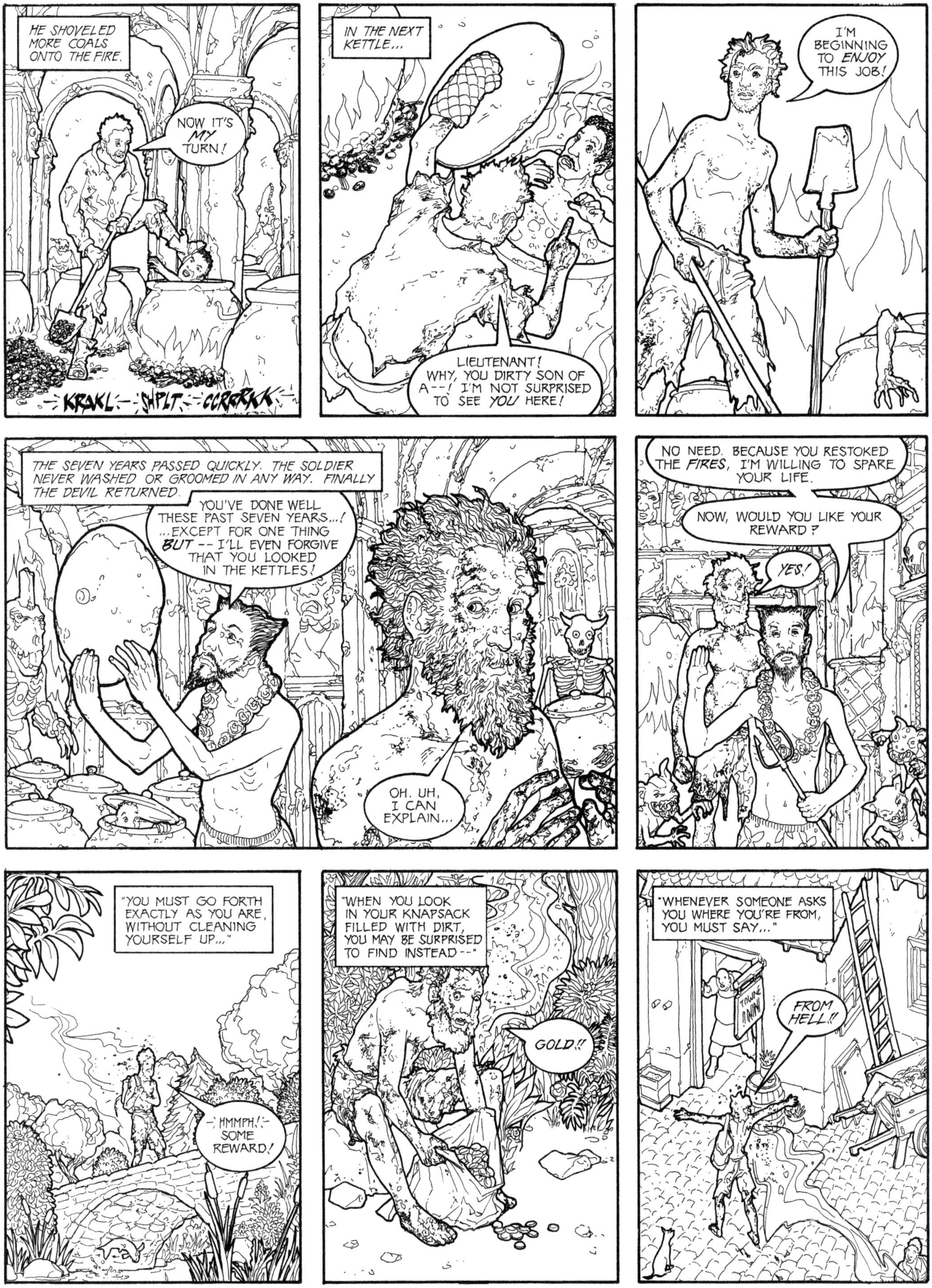
HE SHOVELED MORE COALS ONTO THE FIRE.
NOW IT'S MY TURN!
KRAKL SHPLT CCRRRKK
IN THE NEXT KETTLE...
LIEUTENANT! WHY, YOU DIRTY SON OF A--! I'M NOT SURPRISED TO SEE YOU HERE!
I'M BEGINNING TO ENJOY THIS JOB!
THE SEVEN YEARS PASSED QUICKLY. THE SOLDIER NEVER WASHED OR GROOMED IN ANY WAY. FINALLY THE DEVIL RETURNED.
YOU'VE DONE WELL THESE PAST SEVEN YEARS...! ...EXCEPT FOR ONE THING BUT -- I'LL EVEN FORGIVE THAT YOU LOOKED IN THE KETTLES!
OH. UH, I CAN EXPLAIN...
NO NEED. BECAUSE YOU RESTOKED THE FIRES, I'M WILLING TO SPARE YOUR LIFE.
NOW, WOULD YOU LIKE YOUR REWARD?
YES!
"YOU MUST GO FORTH EXACTLY AS YOU ARE, WITHOUT CLEANING YOURSELF UP..."
HMMPH! SOME REWARD!
"WHEN YOU LOOK IN YOUR KNAPSACK FILLED WITH DIRT, YOU MAY BE SURPRISED TO FIND INSTEAD--"
GOLD!!
"WHENEVER SOMEONE ASKS YOU WHERE YOU'RE FROM, YOU MUST SAY..."
TOWNE INN
FROM HELL!!

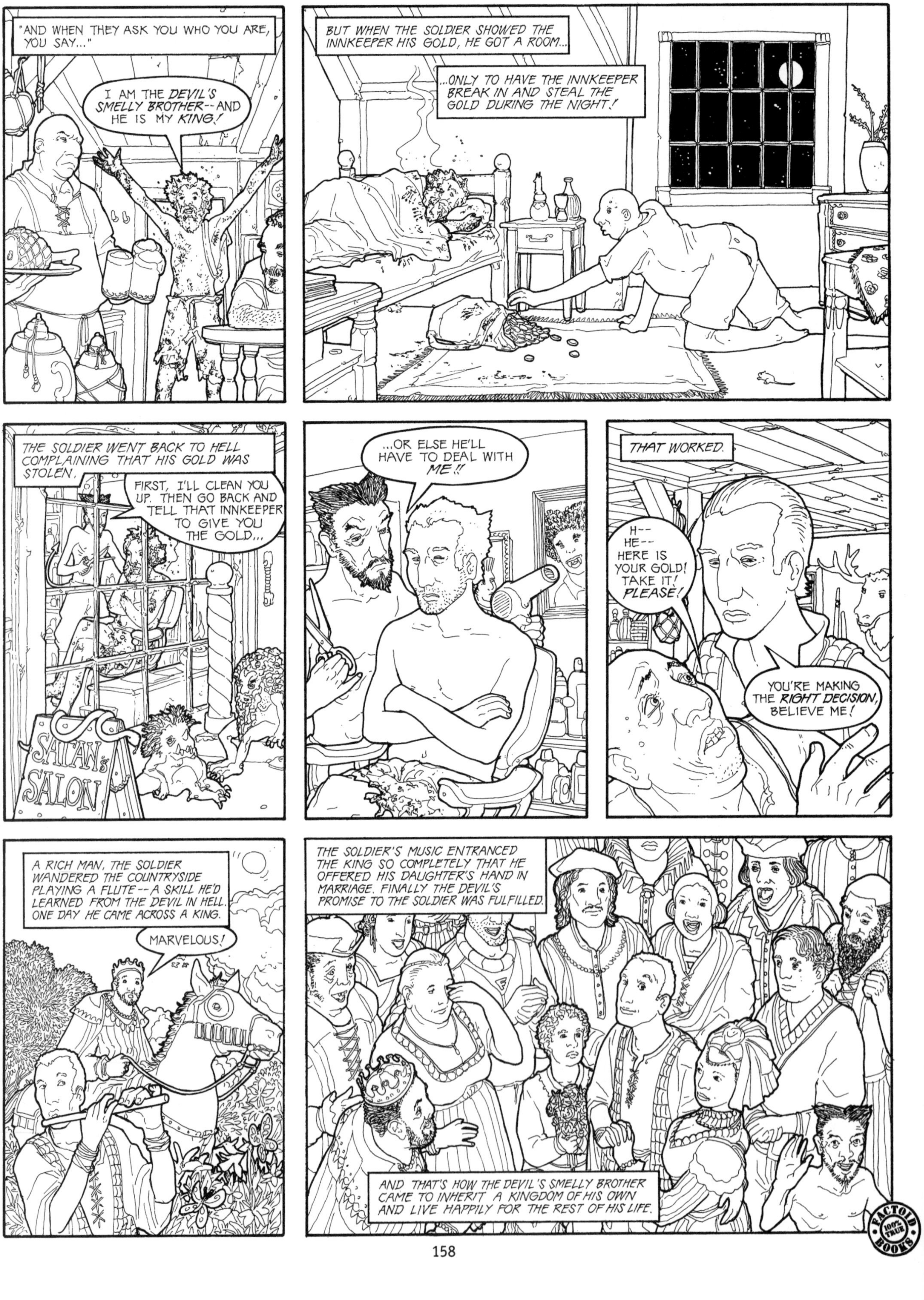
"AND WHEN THEY ASK YOU WHO YOU ARE, YOU SAY..."
I AM THE DEVIL'S SMELLY BROTHER--AND HE IS MY KING!
BUT WHEN THE SOLDIER SHOWED THE INNKEEPER HIS GOLD, HE GOT A ROOM...
...ONLY TO HAVE THE INNKEEPER BREAK IN AND STEAL THE GOLD DURING THE NIGHT!
THE SOLDIER WENT BACK TO HELL COMPLAINING THAT HIS GOLD WAS STOLEN.
FIRST, I'LL CLEAN YOU UP. THEN GO BACK AND TELL THAT INNKEEPER TO GIVE YOU THE GOLD...
SATAN'S SALON
...OR ELSE HE'LL HAVE TO DEAL WITH ME!!
THAT WORKED.
H-- HE-- HERE IS YOUR GOLD! TAKE IT! PLEASE!
YOU'RE MAKING THE RIGHT DECISION, BELIEVE ME!
A RICH MAN, THE SOLDIER WANDERED THE COUNTRYSIDE PLAYING A FLUTE--A SKILL HE'D LEARNED FROM THE DEVIL IN HELL. ONE DAY HE CAME ACROSS A KING.
MARVELOUS!
THE SOLDIER'S MUSIC ENTRANCED THE KING SO COMPLETELY THAT HE OFFERED HIS DAUGHTER'S HAND IN MARRIAGE. FINALLY THE DEVIL'S PROMISE TO THE SOLDIER WAS FULFILLED.
AND THAT'S HOW THE DEVIL'S SMELLY BROTHER CAME TO INHERIT A KINGDOM OF HIS OWN AND LIVE HAPPILY FOR THE REST OF HIS LIFE.

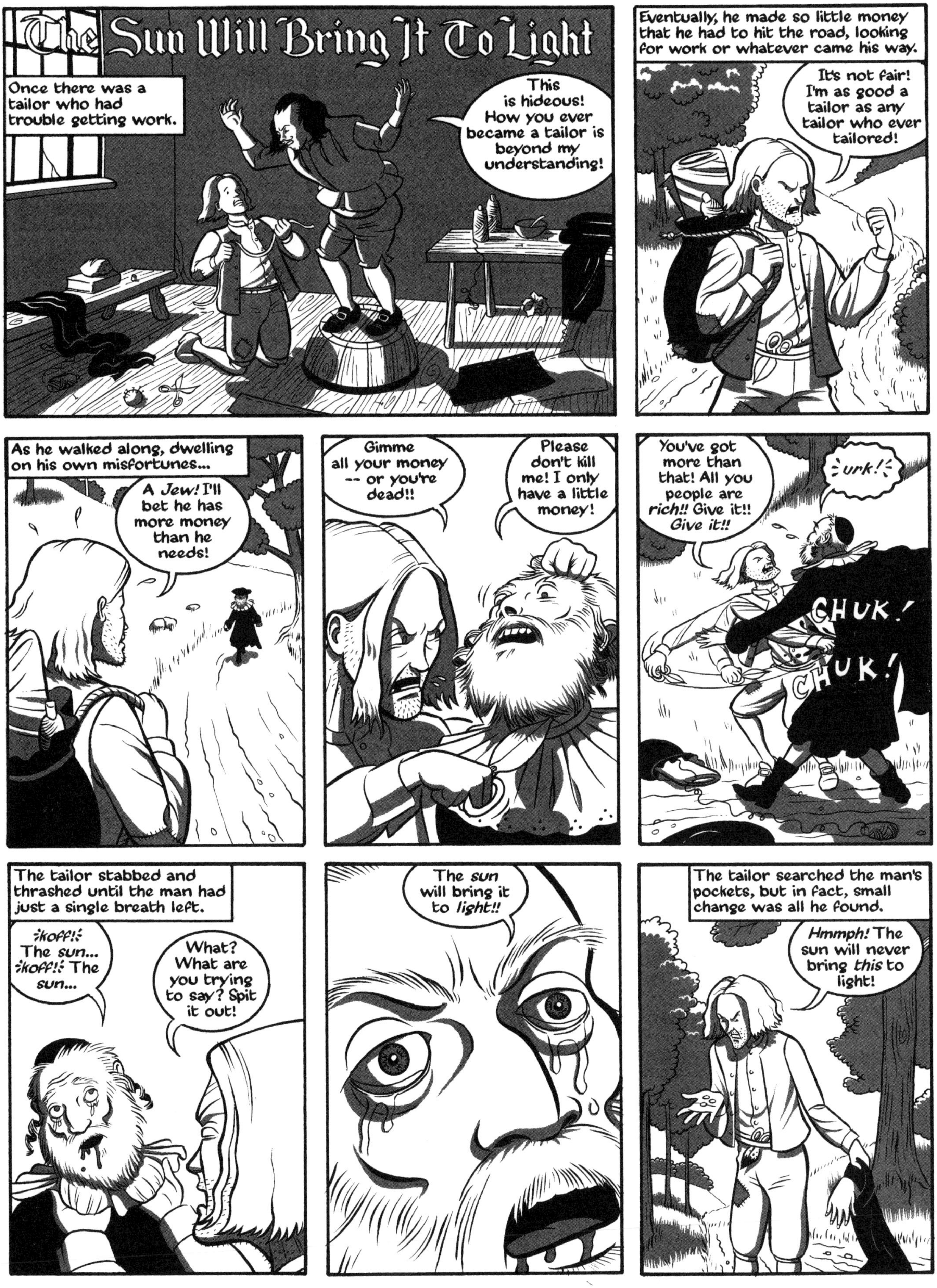
The Sun Will Bring It To Light
Once there was a tailor who had trouble getting work.
This is hideous! How you ever became a tailor is beyond my understanding!
Eventually, he made so little money that he had to hit the road, looking for work or whatever came his way.
It's not fair! I'm as good a tailor as any tailor who ever tailored!
As he walked along, dwelling on his own misfortunes...
A Jew! I'll bet he has more money than he needs!
Gimme all your money -- or you're dead!!
Please don't kill me! I only have a little money!
You've got more than that! All you people are rich!! Give it!! Give it!!
urk!
CHUK!
CHUK!
The tailor stabbed and thrashed until the man had just a single breath left.
koff! The sun... koff! The sun...
What? What are you trying to say? Spit it out!
The sun will bring it to light!!
The tailor searched the man's pockets, but in fact, small change was all he found.
Hmmph! The sun will never bring this to light!

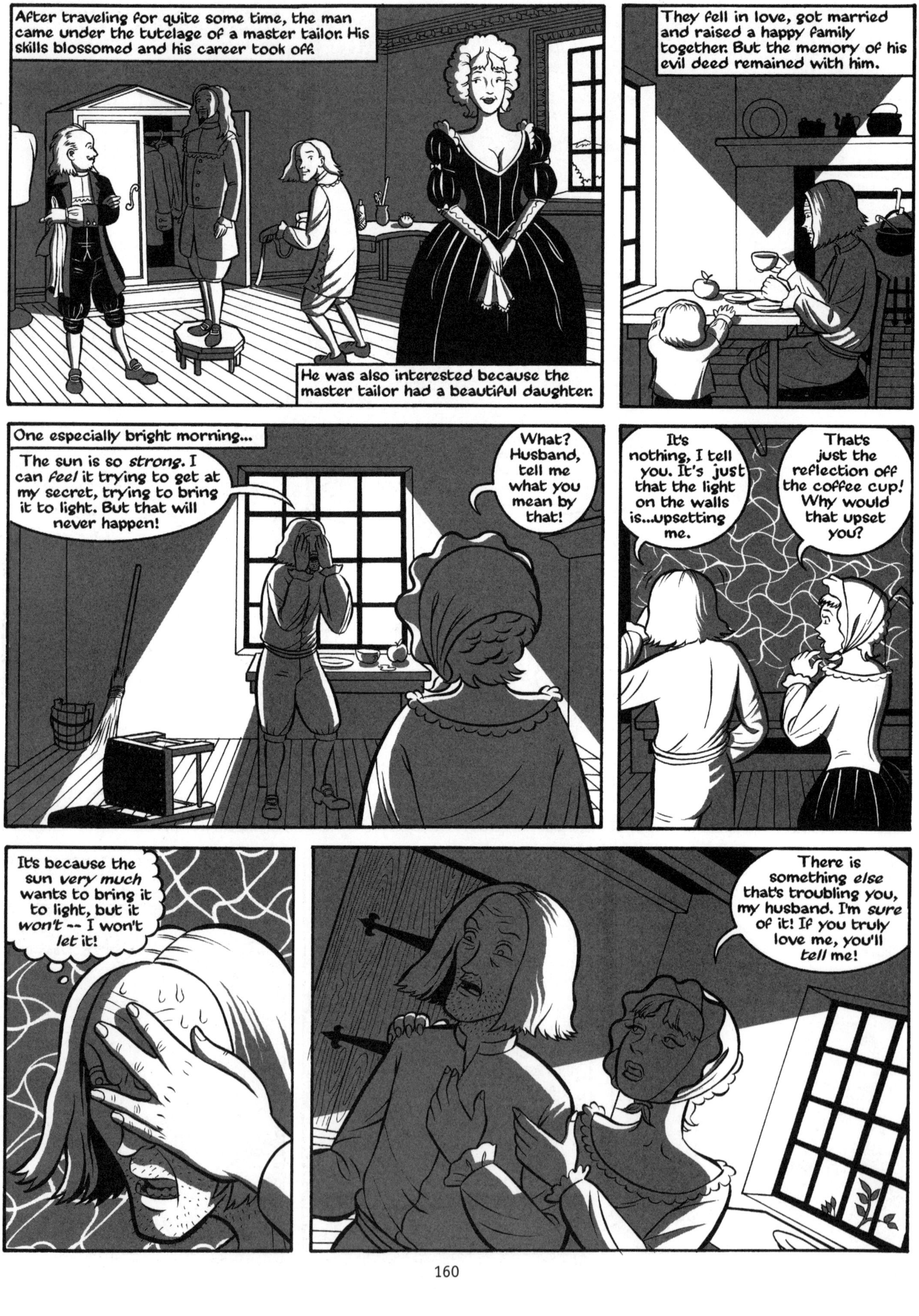
After traveling for quite some time, the man came under the tutelage of a master tailor. His skills blossomed and his career took off.
He was also interested because the master tailor had a beautiful daughter.
They fell in love, got married and raised a happy family together. But the memory of his evil deed remained with him.
One especially bright morning...
The sun is so *strong*. I can *feel* it trying to get at my secret, trying to bring it to light. But that will never happen!
What? Husband, tell me what you mean by that!
It's nothing, I tell you. It's just that the light on the walls is...upsetting me.
That's just the reflection off the coffee cup! Why would that upset you?
It's because the sun *very much* wants to bring it to light, but it *won't* -- I won't *let* it!
There is something *else* that's troubling you, my husband. I'm *sure* of it! If you truly love me, you'll *tell* me!

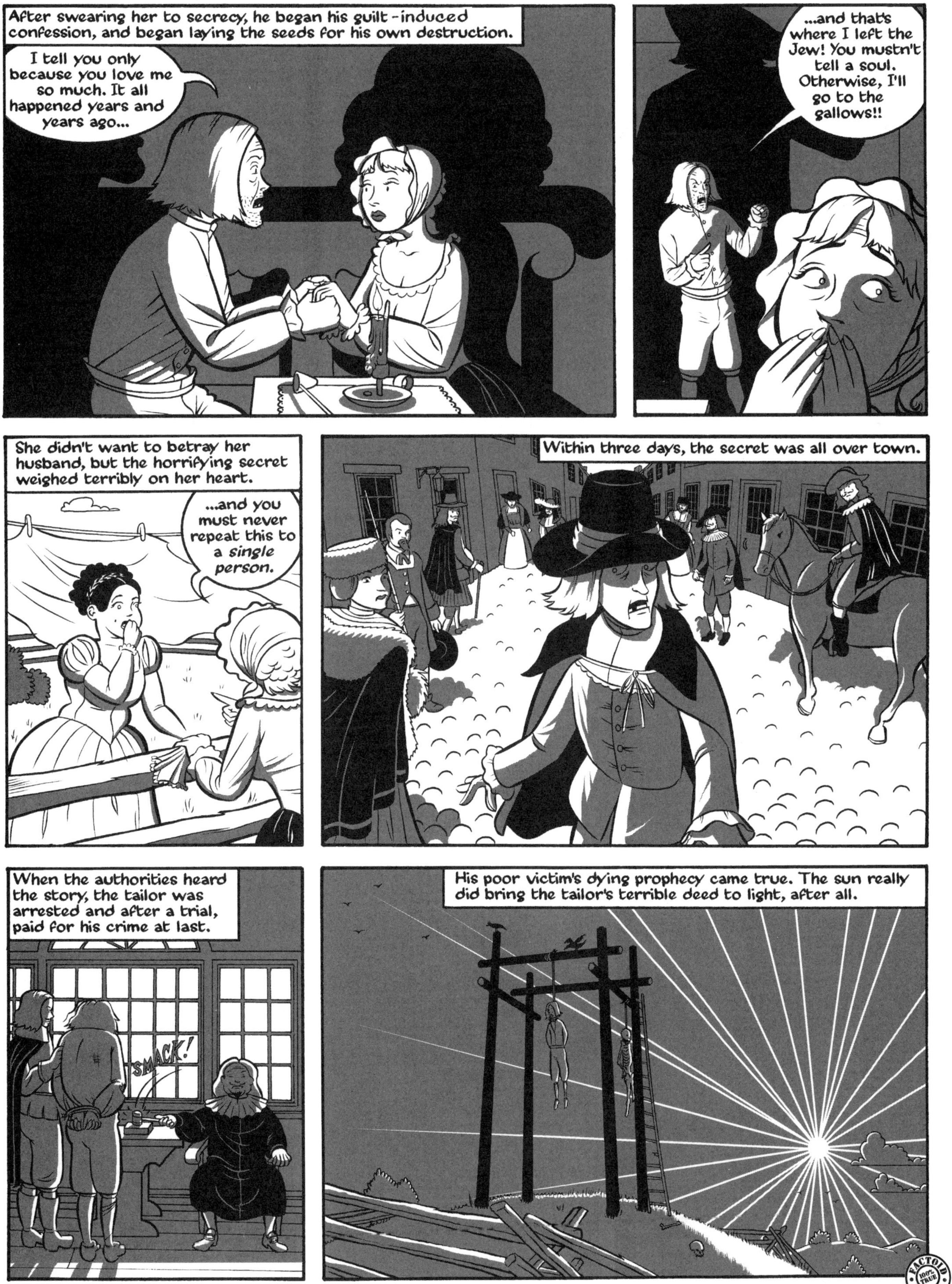
After swearing her to secrecy, he began his guilt-induced confession, and began laying the seeds for his own destruction.
I tell you only because you love me so much. It all happened years and years ago...
...and that's where I left the Jew! You mustn't tell a soul. Otherwise, I'll go to the gallows!!
She didn't want to betray her husband, but the horrifying secret weighed terribly on her heart.
...and you must never repeat this to a *single person.*
Within three days, the secret was all over town.
When the authorities heard the story, the tailor was arrested and after a trial, paid for his crime at last.
SMACK!
His poor victim's dying prophecy came true. The sun really did bring the tailor's terrible deed to light, after all.

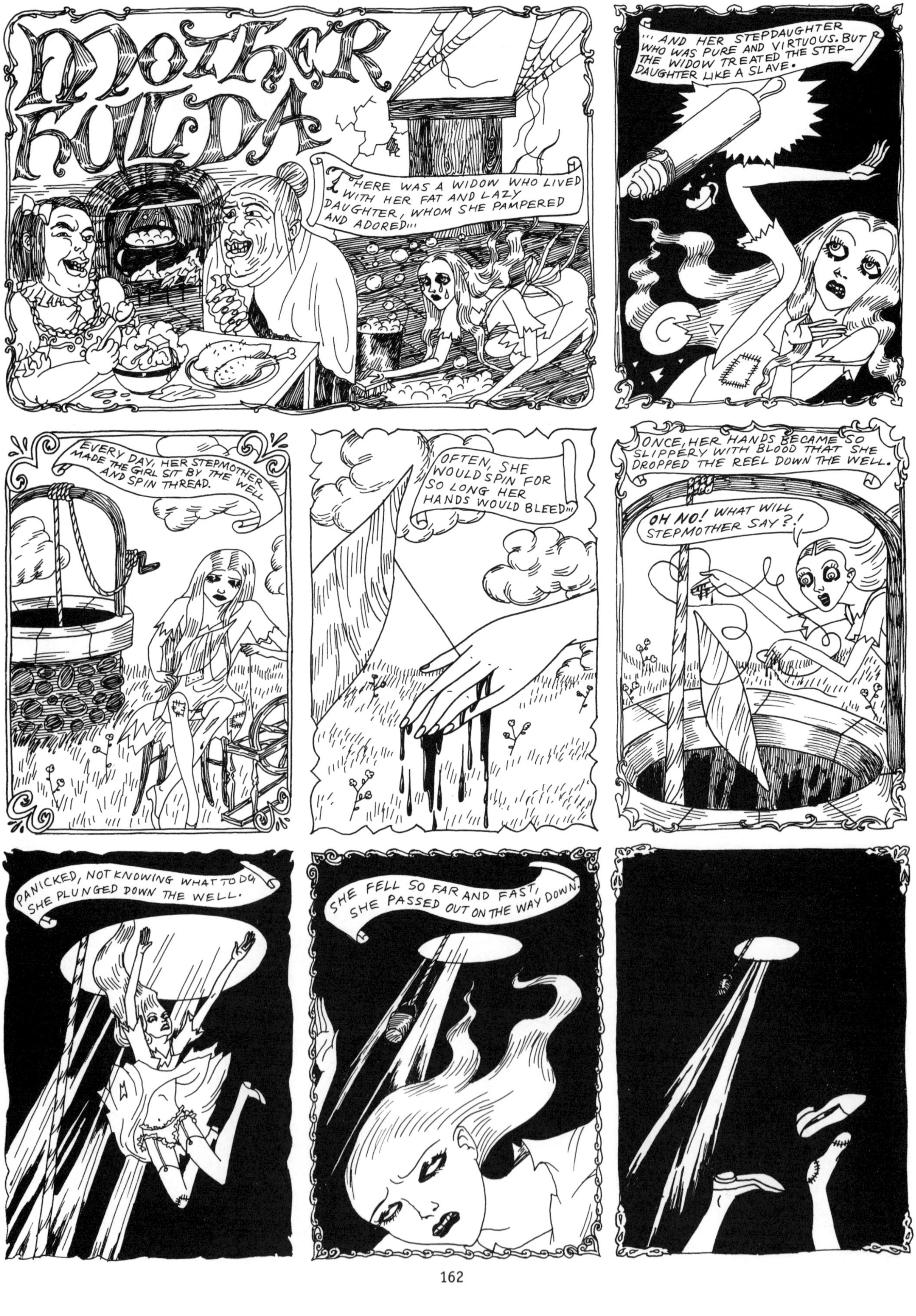
Mother Hulda
THERE WAS A WIDOW WHO LIVED WITH HER FAT AND LAZY DAUGHTER, WHOM SHE PAMPERED AND ADORED...
...AND HER STEPDAUGHTER WHO WAS PURE AND VIRTUOUS. BUT THE WIDOW TREATED THE STEP-DAUGHTER LIKE A SLAVE.
EVERY DAY, HER STEPMOTHER MADE THE GIRL SIT BY THE WELL AND SPIN THREAD.
OFTEN, SHE WOULD SPIN FOR SO LONG HER HANDS WOULD BLEED...
ONCE, HER HANDS BECAME SO SLIPPERY WITH BLOOD THAT SHE DROPPED THE REEL DOWN THE WELL.
OH NO! WHAT WILL STEPMOTHER SAY?!
PANICKED, NOT KNOWING WHAT TO DO, SHE PLUNGED DOWN THE WELL.
SHE FELL SO FAR AND FAST, SHE PASSED OUT ON THE WAY DOWN.

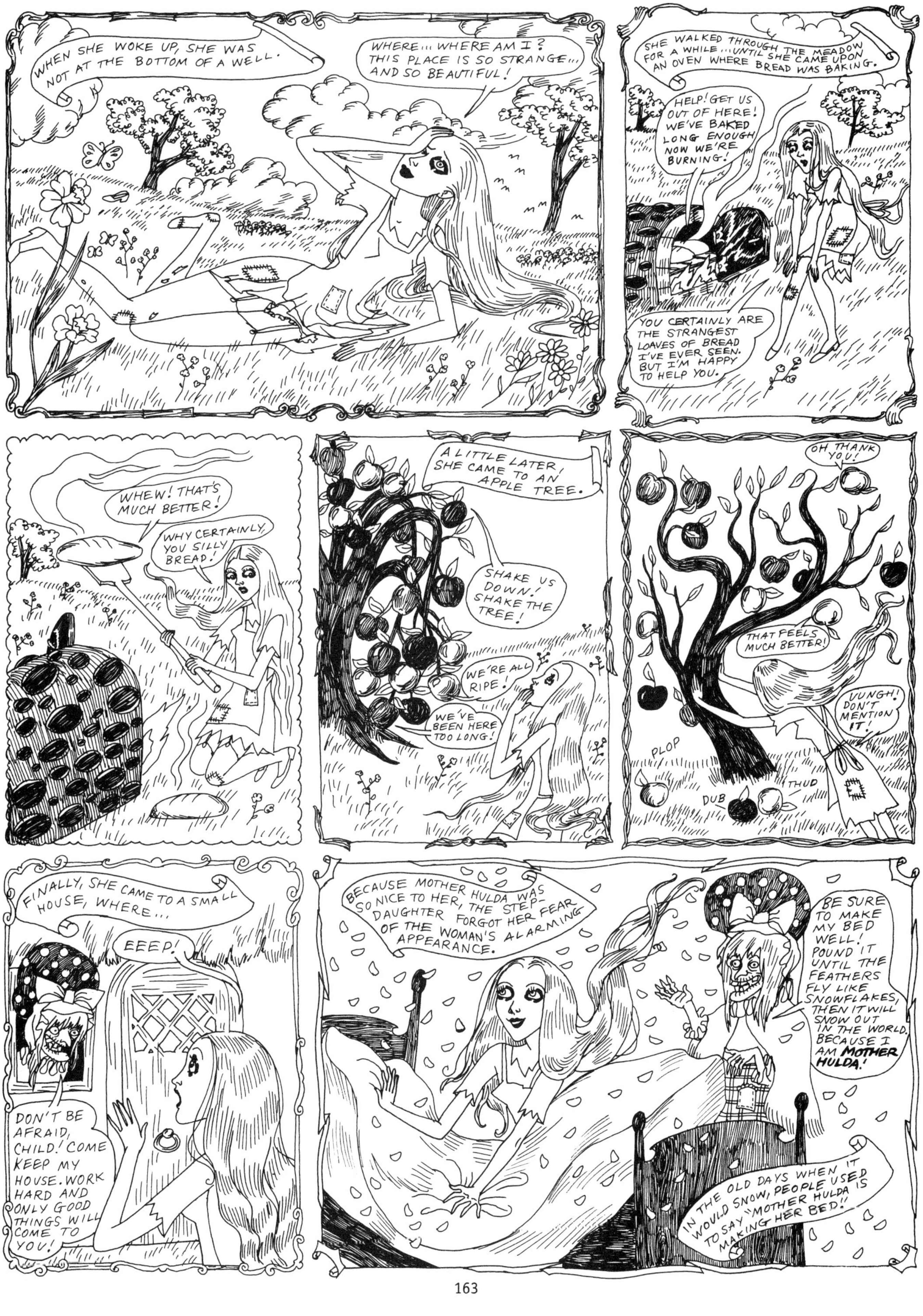
WHEN SHE WOKE UP, SHE WAS NOT AT THE BOTTOM OF A WELL.
WHERE... WHERE AM I? THIS PLACE IS SO STRANGE... AND SO BEAUTIFUL!
SHE WALKED THROUGH THE MEADOW FOR A WHILE... UNTIL SHE CAME UPON AN OVEN WHERE BREAD WAS BAKING.
HELP! GET US OUT OF HERE! WE'VE BAKED LONG ENOUGH NOW WE'RE BURNING!
YOU CERTAINLY ARE THE STRANGEST LOAVES OF BREAD I'VE EVER SEEN. BUT I'M HAPPY TO HELP YOU.
WHEW! THAT'S MUCH BETTER!
WHY CERTAINLY, YOU SILLY BREAD!
A LITTLE LATER, SHE CAME TO AN APPLE TREE.
SHAKE US DOWN! SHAKE THE TREE!
WE'RE ALL RIPE!
WE'VE BEEN HERE TOO LONG!
OH THANK YOU!
THAT FEELS MUCH BETTER!
VUNGH! DON'T MENTION IT!
PLOP
DUB
THUD
FINALLY, SHE CAME TO A SMALL HOUSE, WHERE...
EEEP!
DON'T BE AFRAID, CHILD! COME KEEP MY HOUSE. WORK HARD AND ONLY GOOD THINGS WILL COME TO YOU!
BECAUSE MOTHER HULDA WAS SO NICE TO HER, THE STEP-DAUGHTER FORGOT HER FEAR OF THE WOMAN'S ALARMING APPEARANCE.
BE SURE TO MAKE MY BED WELL! POUND IT UNTIL THE FEATHERS FLY LIKE SNOWFLAKES, THEN IT WILL SNOW OUT IN THE WORLD. BECAUSE I AM MOTHER HULDA!
IN THE OLD DAYS WHEN IT WOULD SNOW, PEOPLE USED TO SAY "MOTHER HULDA IS MAKING HER BED!"

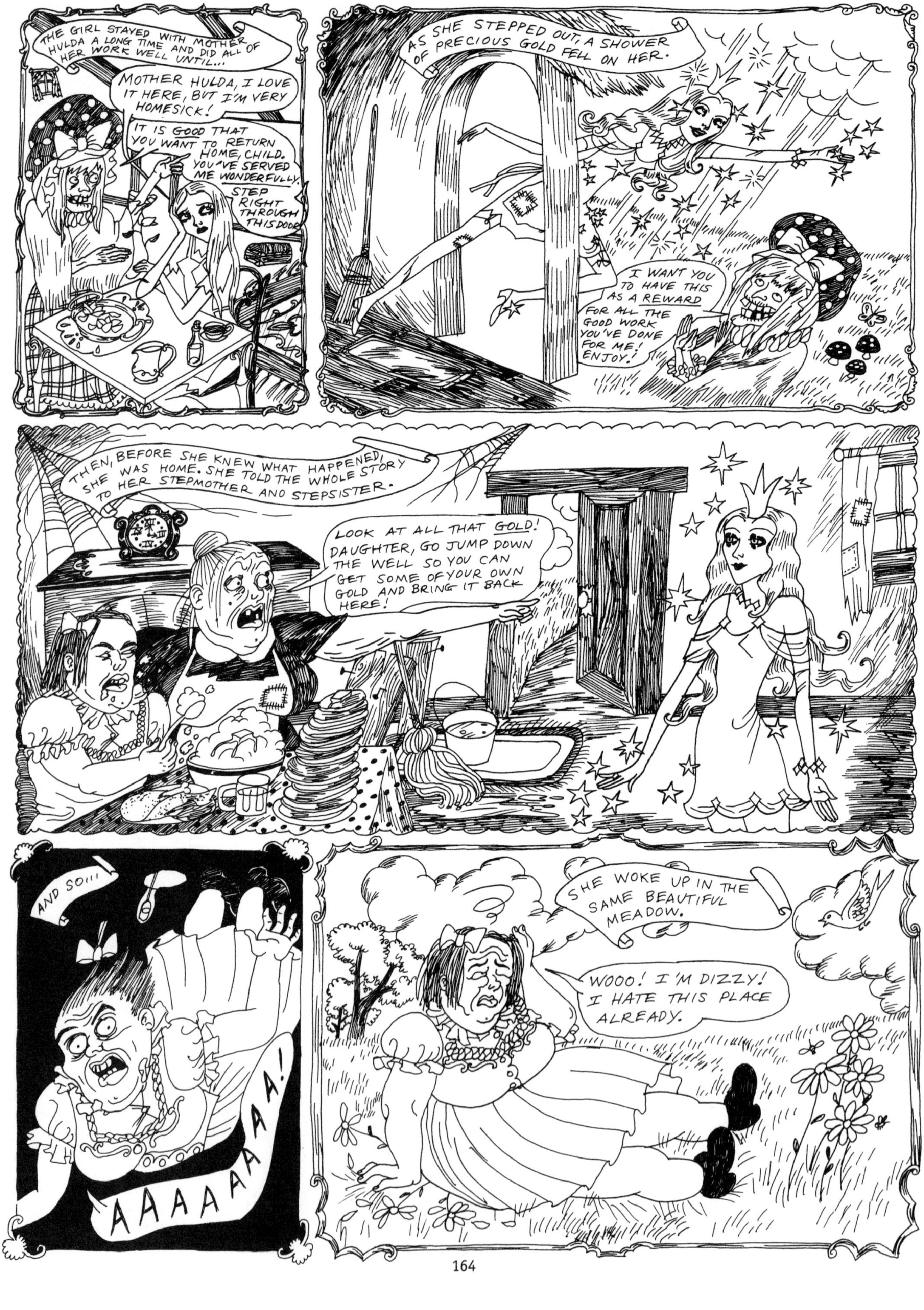
THE GIRL STAYED WITH MOTHER HULDA A LONG TIME AND DID ALL OF HER WORK WELL UNTIL...
MOTHER HULDA, I LOVE IT HERE, BUT I'M VERY HOMESICK!
IT IS GOOD THAT YOU WANT TO RETURN HOME, CHILD. YOU'VE SERVED ME WONDERFULLY. STEP RIGHT THROUGH THIS DOOR.
AS SHE STEPPED OUT, A SHOWER OF PRECIOUS GOLD FELL ON HER.
I WANT YOU TO HAVE THIS AS A REWARD FOR ALL THE GOOD WORK YOU'VE DONE FOR ME! ENJOY!
THEN, BEFORE SHE KNEW WHAT HAPPENED, SHE WAS HOME. SHE TOLD THE WHOLE STORY TO HER STEPMOTHER AND STEPSISTER.
LOOK AT ALL THAT GOLD! DAUGHTER, GO JUMP DOWN THE WELL SO YOU CAN GET SOME OF YOUR OWN GOLD AND BRING IT BACK HERE!
AND SO...
AAAAAAAA!
SHE WOKE UP IN THE SAME BEAUTIFUL MEADOW.
WOOO! I'M DIZZY! I HATE THIS PLACE ALREADY.

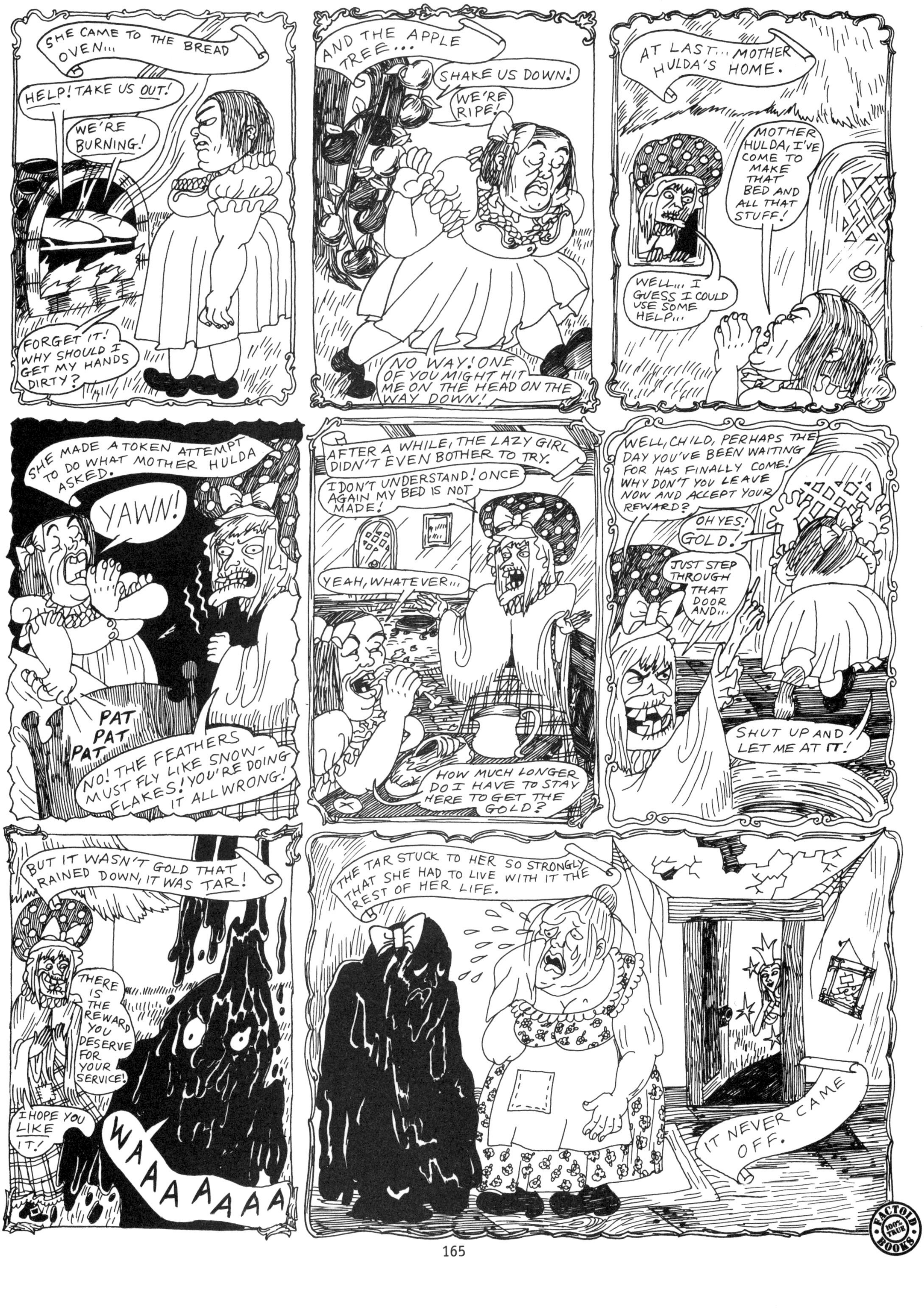

SHE CAME TO THE BREAD OVEN...
HELP! TAKE US OUT!
WE'RE BURNING!
FORGET IT! WHY SHOULD I GET MY HANDS DIRTY?
AND THE APPLE TREE...
SHAKE US DOWN!
WE'RE RIPE!
NO WAY! ONE OF YOU MIGHT HIT ME ON THE HEAD ON THE WAY DOWN!
AT LAST... MOTHER HULDA'S HOME.
MOTHER HULDA, I'VE COME TO MAKE THAT BED AND ALL THAT STUFF!
WELL... I GUESS I COULD USE SOME HELP...
SHE MADE A TOKEN ATTEMPT TO DO WHAT MOTHER HULDA ASKED.
YAWN!
PAT PAT PAT
NO! THE FEATHERS MUST FLY LIKE SNOW-FLAKES! YOU'RE DOING IT ALL WRONG!
AFTER A WHILE, THE LAZY GIRL DIDN'T EVEN BOTHER TO TRY.
I DON'T UNDERSTAND! ONCE AGAIN MY BED IS NOT MADE!
YEAH, WHATEVER...
HOW MUCH LONGER DO I HAVE TO STAY HERE TO GET THE GOLD?
WELL, CHILD, PERHAPS THE DAY YOU'VE BEEN WAITING FOR HAS FINALLY COME! WHY DON'T YOU LEAVE NOW AND ACCEPT YOUR REWARD?
OH YES! GOLD!
JUST STEP THROUGH THAT DOOR AND...
SHUT UP AND LET ME AT IT!
BUT IT WASN'T GOLD THAT RAINED DOWN, IT WAS TAR!
THERE IS THE REWARD YOU DESERVE FOR YOUR SERVICE!
I HOPE YOU LIKE IT!
WAAAAAAAA
THE TAR STUCK TO HER SO STRONGLY THAT SHE HAD TO LIVE WITH IT THE REST OF HER LIFE.
IT NEVER CAME OFF.
FACTOID BOOKS 100% TRUE

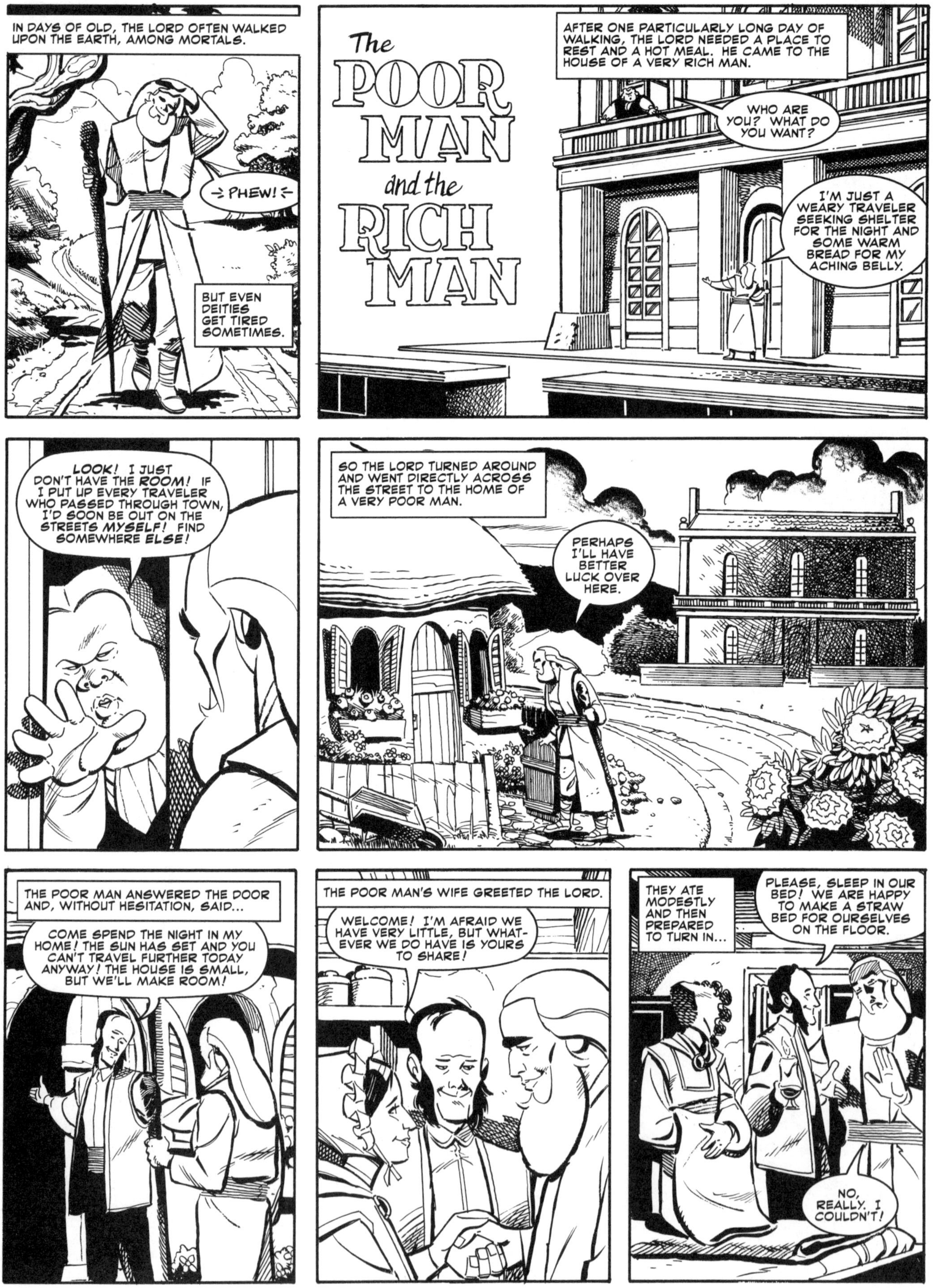
IN DAYS OF OLD, THE LORD OFTEN WALKED UPON THE EARTH, AMONG MORTALS.
PHEW!
BUT EVEN DEITIES GET TIRED SOMETIMES.
The POOR MAN and the RICH MAN
AFTER ONE PARTICULARLY LONG DAY OF WALKING, THE LORD NEEDED A PLACE TO REST AND A HOT MEAL. HE CAME TO THE HOUSE OF A VERY RICH MAN.
WHO ARE YOU? WHAT DO YOU WANT?
I'M JUST A WEARY TRAVELER SEEKING SHELTER FOR THE NIGHT AND SOME WARM BREAD FOR MY ACHING BELLY.
LOOK! I JUST DON'T HAVE THE ROOM! IF I PUT UP EVERY TRAVELER WHO PASSED THROUGH TOWN, I'D SOON BE OUT ON THE STREETS MYSELF! FIND SOMEWHERE ELSE!
SO THE LORD TURNED AROUND AND WENT DIRECTLY ACROSS THE STREET TO THE HOME OF A VERY POOR MAN.
PERHAPS I'LL HAVE BETTER LUCK OVER HERE.
THE POOR MAN ANSWERED THE DOOR AND, WITHOUT HESITATION, SAID...
COME SPEND THE NIGHT IN MY HOME! THE SUN HAS SET AND YOU CAN'T TRAVEL FURTHER TODAY ANYWAY! THE HOUSE IS SMALL, BUT WE'LL MAKE ROOM!
THE POOR MAN'S WIFE GREETED THE LORD.
WELCOME! I'M AFRAID WE HAVE VERY LITTLE, BUT WHAT-EVER WE DO HAVE IS YOURS TO SHARE!
THEY ATE MODESTLY AND THEN PREPARED TO TURN IN...
PLEASE, SLEEP IN OUR BED! WE ARE HAPPY TO MAKE A STRAW BED FOR OURSELVES ON THE FLOOR.
NO, REALLY. I COULDN'T!

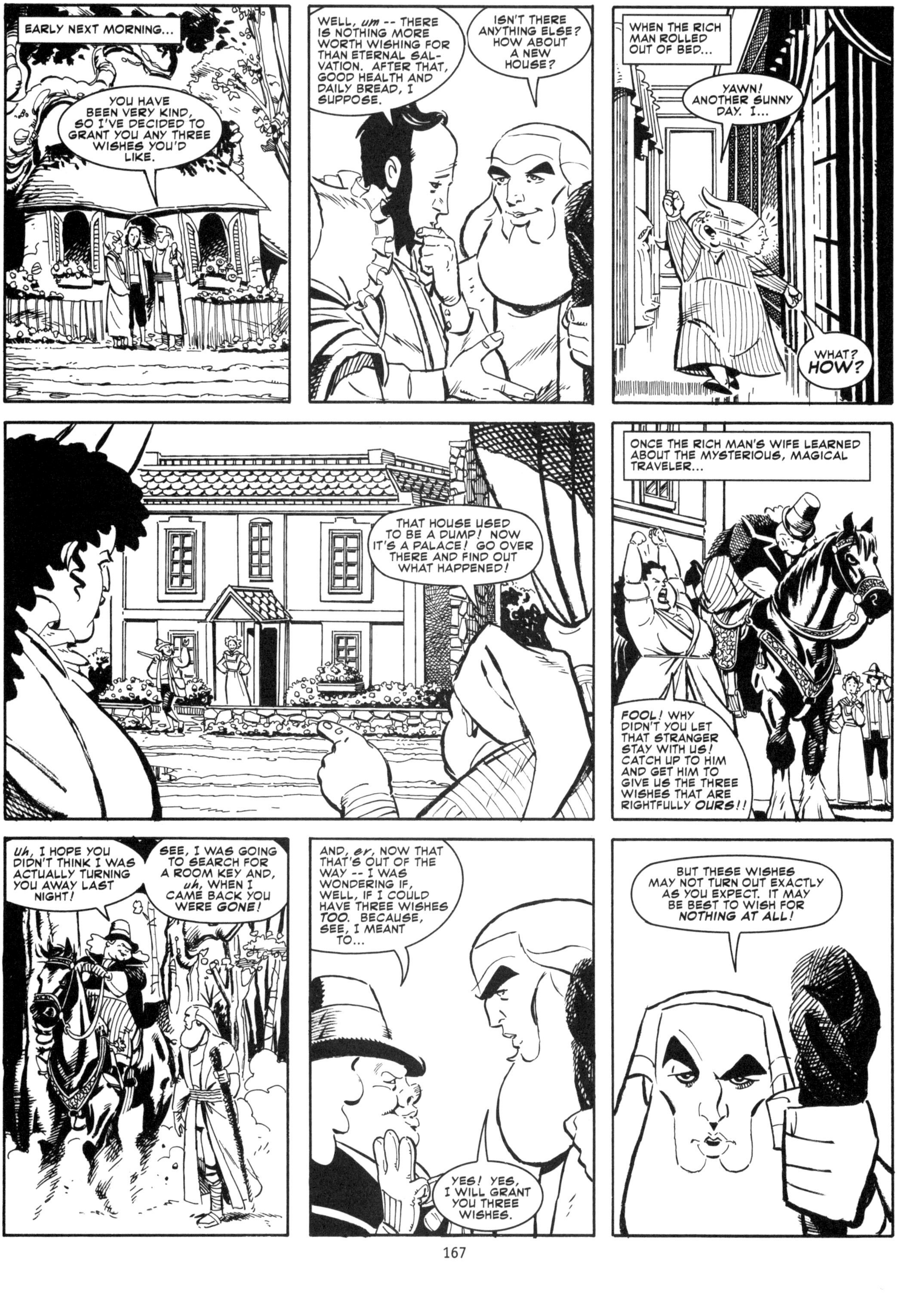
EARLY NEXT MORNING...
YOU HAVE BEEN VERY KIND, SO I'VE DECIDED TO GRANT YOU ANY THREE WISHES YOU'D LIKE.
WELL, um -- THERE IS NOTHING MORE WORTH WISHING FOR THAN ETERNAL SAL-VATION. AFTER THAT, GOOD HEALTH AND DAILY BREAD, I SUPPOSE.
ISN'T THERE ANYTHING ELSE? HOW ABOUT A NEW HOUSE?
WHEN THE RICH MAN ROLLED OUT OF BED...
YAWN! ANOTHER SUNNY DAY. I...
WHAT? HOW?
THAT HOUSE USED TO BE A DUMP! NOW IT'S A PALACE! GO OVER THERE AND FIND OUT WHAT HAPPENED!
ONCE THE RICH MAN'S WIFE LEARNED ABOUT THE MYSTERIOUS, MAGICAL TRAVELER...
FOOL! WHY DIDN'T YOU LET THAT STRANGER STAY WITH US! CATCH UP TO HIM AND GET HIM TO GIVE US THE THREE WISHES THAT ARE RIGHTFULLY OURS!!
uh, I HOPE YOU DIDN'T THINK I WAS ACTUALLY TURNING YOU AWAY LAST NIGHT!
SEE, I WAS GOING TO SEARCH FOR A ROOM KEY AND, uh, WHEN I CAME BACK YOU WERE GONE!
AND, er, NOW THAT THAT'S OUT OF THE WAY -- I WAS WONDERING IF, WELL, IF I COULD HAVE THREE WISHES TOO. BECAUSE, SEE, I MEANT TO...
YES! YES, I WILL GRANT YOU THREE WISHES.
BUT THESE WISHES MAY NOT TURN OUT EXACTLY AS YOU EXPECT. IT MAY BE BEST TO WISH FOR NOTHING AT ALL!

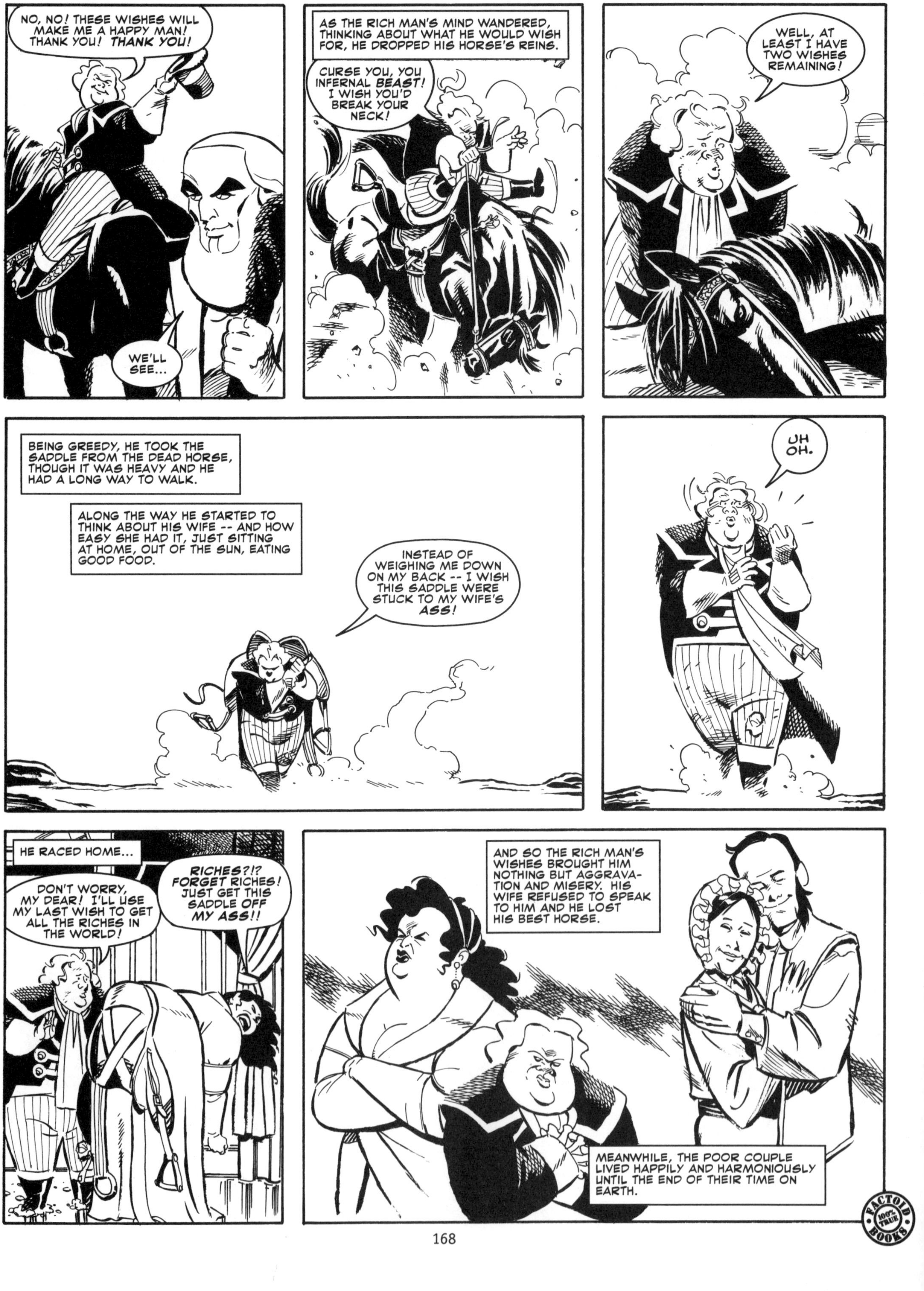
NO, NO! THESE WISHES WILL MAKE ME A HAPPY MAN! THANK YOU! THANK YOU!
WE'LL SEE...
AS THE RICH MAN'S MIND WANDERED, THINKING ABOUT WHAT HE WOULD WISH FOR, HE DROPPED HIS HORSE'S REINS.
CURSE YOU, YOU INFERNAL BEAST! I WISH YOU'D BREAK YOUR NECK!
WELL, AT LEAST I HAVE TWO WISHES REMAINING!
BEING GREEDY, HE TOOK THE SADDLE FROM THE DEAD HORSE, THOUGH IT WAS HEAVY AND HE HAD A LONG WAY TO WALK.
ALONG THE WAY HE STARTED TO THINK ABOUT HIS WIFE -- AND HOW EASY SHE HAD IT, JUST SITTING AT HOME, OUT OF THE SUN, EATING GOOD FOOD.
INSTEAD OF WEIGHING ME DOWN ON MY BACK -- I WISH THIS SADDLE WERE STUCK TO MY WIFE'S ASS!
UH OH.
HE RACED HOME...
DON'T WORRY, MY DEAR! I'LL USE MY LAST WISH TO GET ALL THE RICHES IN THE WORLD!
RICHES?!? FORGET RICHES! JUST GET THIS SADDLE OFF MY ASS!!
AND SO THE RICH MAN'S WISHES BROUGHT HIM NOTHING BUT AGGRAVATION AND MISERY. HIS WIFE REFUSED TO SPEAK TO HIM AND HE LOST HIS BEST HORSE.
MEANWHILE, THE POOR COUPLE LIVED HAPPILY AND HARMONIOUSLY UNTIL THE END OF THEIR TIME ON EARTH.
FACTOID BOOKS 100% TRUE

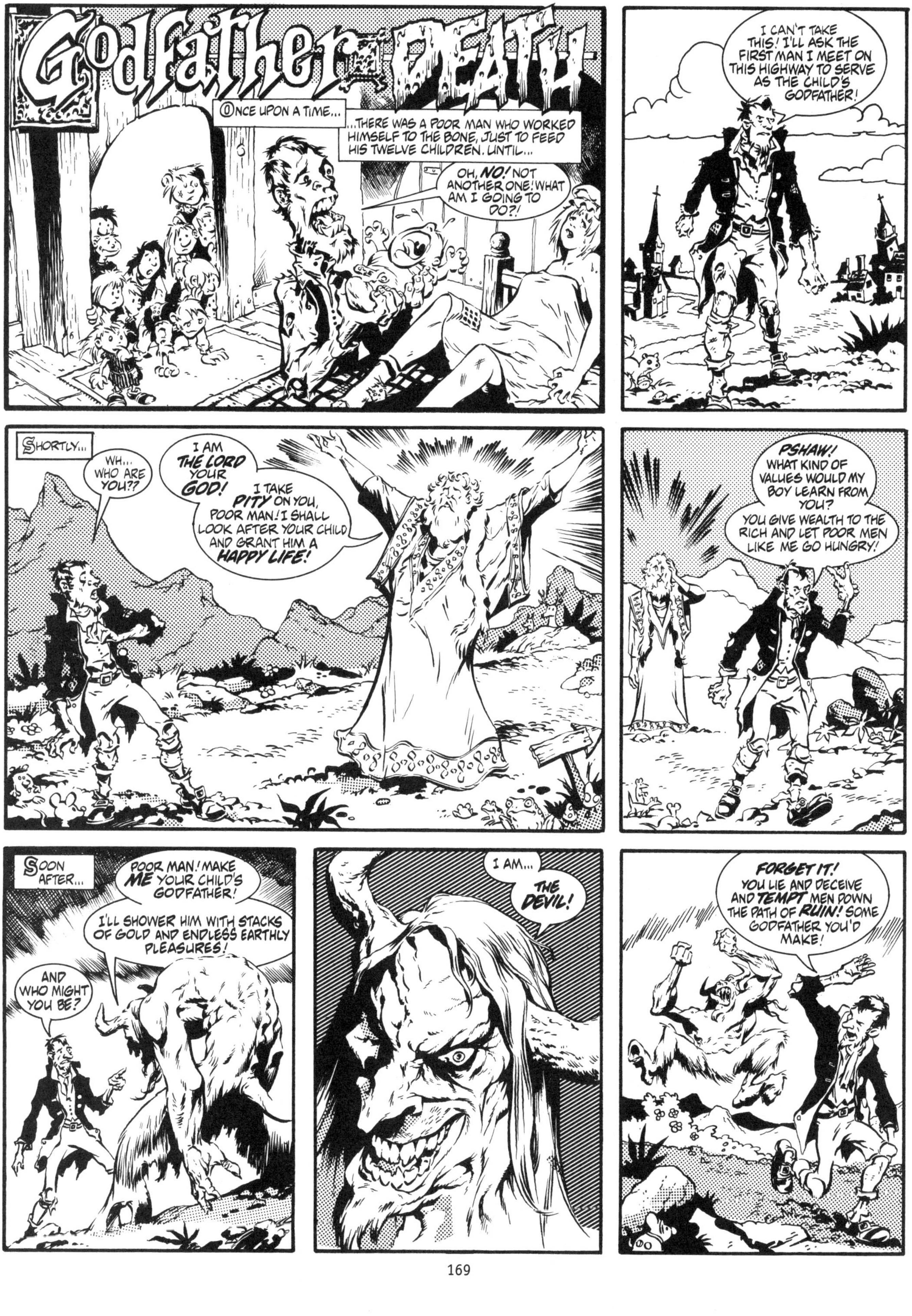

Godfather Death
Once upon a time...
...there was a poor man who worked himself to the bone, just to feed his twelve children. Until...
Oh, NO! Not another one! What am I going to do?!
I can't take this! I'll ask the first man I meet on this highway to serve as the child's godfather!
Shortly...
Wh... who are you??
I am THE LORD YOUR GOD!
I take PITY on you, poor man! I shall look after your child and grant him a HAPPY LIFE!
PSHAW! What kind of values would my boy learn from you? You give wealth to the rich and let poor men like me go hungry!
Soon after...
Poor man! Make ME your child's godfather!
I'll shower him with stacks of gold and endless earthly pleasures!
And who might you be?
I am... THE DEVIL!
FORGET IT! You lie and deceive and TEMPT men down the path of RUIN! Some godfather you'd make!

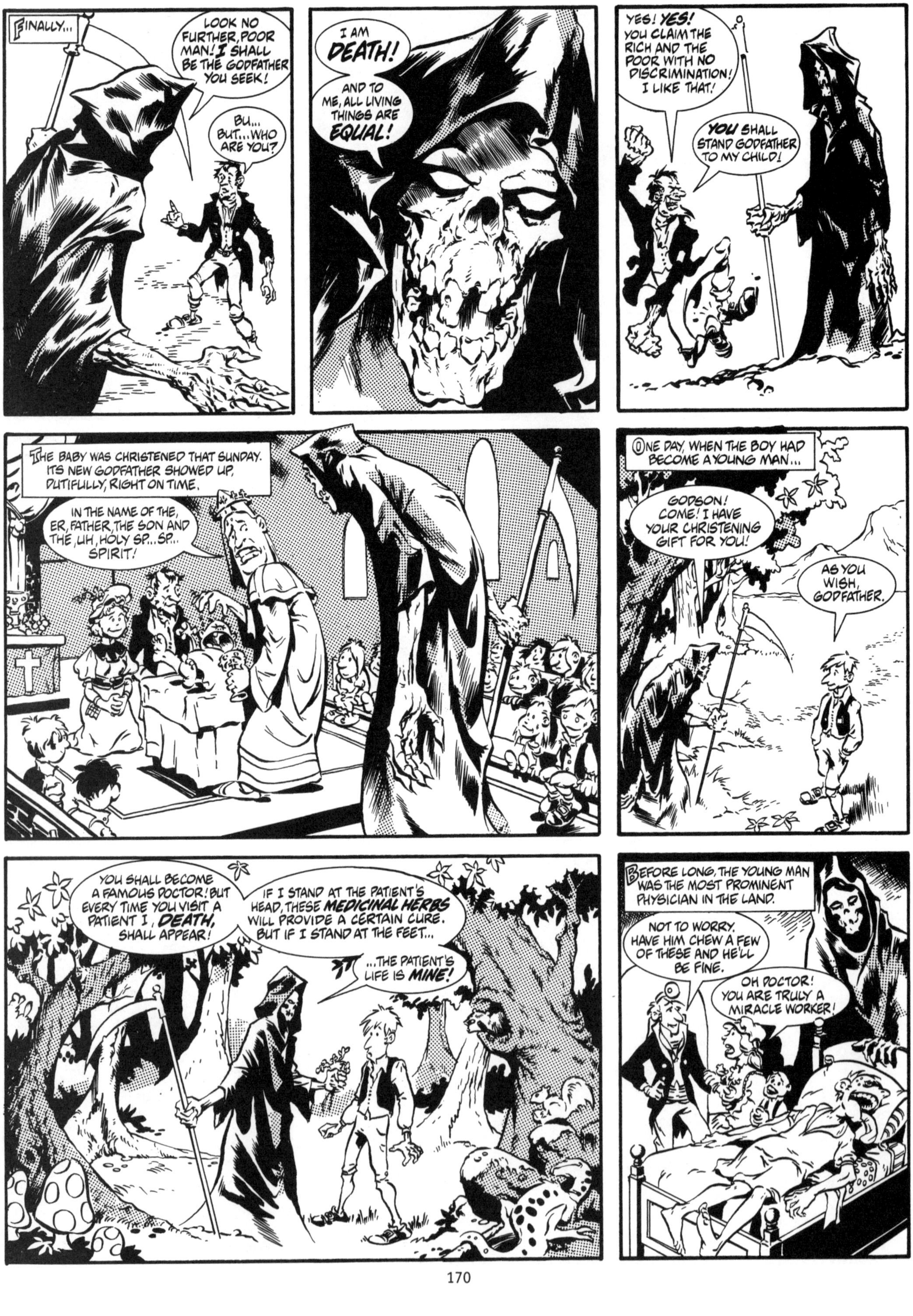
FINALLY...
LOOK NO FURTHER, POOR MAN! I SHALL BE THE GODFATHER YOU SEEK!
BU... BUT... WHO ARE YOU?
I AM DEATH!
AND TO ME, ALL LIVING THINGS ARE EQUAL!
YES! YES! YOU CLAIM THE RICH AND THE POOR WITH NO DISCRIMINATION! I LIKE THAT!
YOU SHALL STAND GODFATHER TO MY CHILD!
THE BABY WAS CHRISTENED THAT SUNDAY. ITS NEW GODFATHER SHOWED UP, DUTIFULLY, RIGHT ON TIME.
IN THE NAME OF THE, ER, FATHER, THE SON AND THE, UH, HOLY SP...SP... SPIRIT!
ONE DAY, WHEN THE BOY HAD BECOME A YOUNG MAN...
GODSON! COME! I HAVE YOUR CHRISTENING GIFT FOR YOU!
AS YOU WISH, GODFATHER.
YOU SHALL BECOME A FAMOUS DOCTOR! BUT EVERY TIME YOU VISIT A PATIENT I, DEATH, SHALL APPEAR!
IF I STAND AT THE PATIENT'S HEAD, THESE MEDICINAL HERBS WILL PROVIDE A CERTAIN CURE. BUT IF I STAND AT THE FEET...
...THE PATIENT'S LIFE IS MINE!
BEFORE LONG, THE YOUNG MAN WAS THE MOST PROMINENT PHYSICIAN IN THE LAND.
NOT TO WORRY. HAVE HIM CHEW A FEW OF THESE AND HE'LL BE FINE.
OH DOCTOR! YOU ARE TRULY A MIRACLE WORKER!

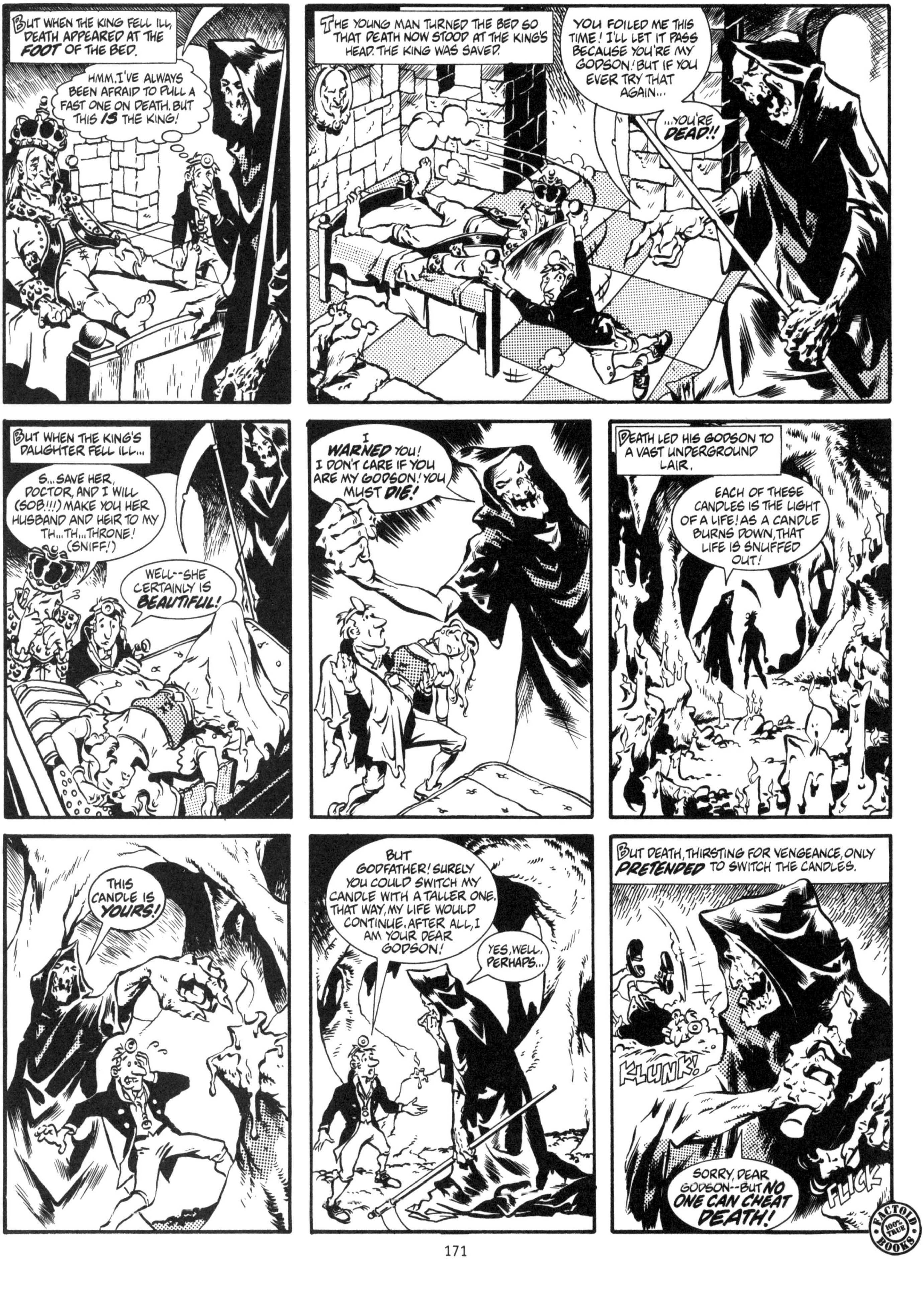
BUT WHEN THE KING FELL ILL, DEATH APPEARED AT THE FOOT OF THE BED.
HMM. I'VE ALWAYS BEEN AFRAID TO PULL A FAST ONE ON DEATH. BUT THIS IS THE KING!
THE YOUNG MAN TURNED THE BED SO THAT DEATH NOW STOOD AT THE KING'S HEAD. THE KING WAS SAVED.
YOU FOILED ME THIS TIME! I'LL LET IT PASS BECAUSE YOU'RE MY GODSON! BUT IF YOU EVER TRY THAT AGAIN...
...YOU'RE DEAD!!
BUT WHEN THE KING'S DAUGHTER FELL ILL...
S...SAVE HER, DOCTOR, AND I WILL (SOB!!!) MAKE YOU HER HUSBAND AND HEIR TO MY TH...TH...THRONE! (SNIFF!)
WELL--SHE CERTAINLY IS BEAUTIFUL!
I WARNED YOU! I DON'T CARE IF YOU ARE MY GODSON! YOU MUST DIE!
DEATH LED HIS GODSON TO A VAST UNDERGROUND LAIR.
EACH OF THESE CANDLES IS THE LIGHT OF A LIFE! AS A CANDLE BURNS DOWN, THAT LIFE IS SNUFFED OUT!
THIS CANDLE IS YOURS!
BUT GODFATHER! SURELY YOU COULD SWITCH MY CANDLE WITH A TALLER ONE. THAT WAY, MY LIFE WOULD CONTINUE. AFTER ALL, I AM YOUR DEAR GODSON!
YES, WELL, PERHAPS...
BUT DEATH, THIRSTING FOR VENGEANCE, ONLY PRETENDED TO SWITCH THE CANDLES.
KLUNK!
SORRY, DEAR GODSON--BUT NO ONE CAN CHEAT DEATH!
FLICK

DOG AND SPARROW

A FRIENDLY DOG WAS MISTREATED BY HIS CRUEL MASTER.

Get your OWN food! You can STARVE for all I care!

THE DOG LEFT HOME -- THOUGH HE HAD NOWHERE TO GO. ALONG THE WAY HE MET A SPARROW.

Say, Brother Dog, why the glum face?

My master starves me.

I'm so hungry

THE SPARROW TOOK THE DOG TO A BUTCHER SHOP.

Don't worry, friend

I'll see to it that you're well fed!

AFTER A FEW MORE PIECES OF MEAT AND BREAD THEY WENT FOR A WALK OUT OF TOWN.

How ya doing, Buddy? Feel better now?

Much better. You're a true friend, Sparrow

IT WAS A WARM SUMMER DAY, SO THE DOG SETTLED IN FOR A SNOOZE AND DREAMED ABOUT HIS NEW FRIEND.

NEITHER OF THEM SAW THE WAGON HEADED STRAIGHT FOR THE DOG.

I have two barrels of wine to deliver--

I'll be on time no matter what gets in my way!

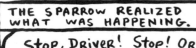

THE SPARROW REALIZED WHAT WAS HAPPENING.

Stop, Driver! Stop! Or you'll be sorry! I'm warning you!

HA!!

What can YOU do to harm me??

I'll make you a poor man! You'd better stop NOW!

You can't do anything to make me poor!

Now get lost!

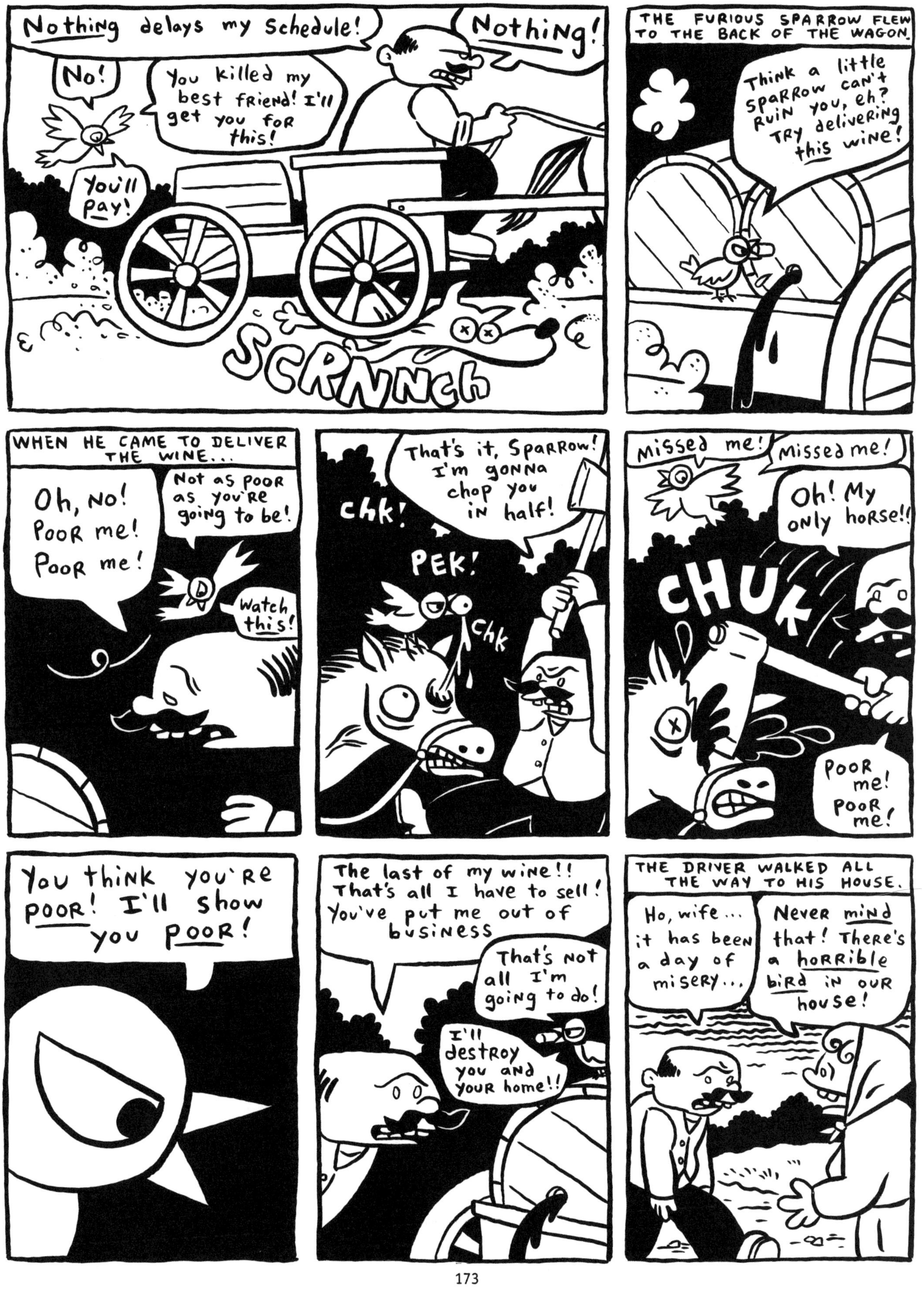

Nothing delays my schedule!
Nothing!
No!
You killed my best friend! I'll get you for this!
You'll pay!
SCRNNCH
THE FURIOUS SPARROW FLEW TO THE BACK OF THE WAGON.
Think a little sparrow can't ruin you, eh? Try delivering this wine!
WHEN HE CAME TO DELIVER THE WINE...
Oh, No! Poor me! Poor me!
Not as poor as you're going to be!
Watch this!
That's it, Sparrow! I'm gonna chop you in half!
CHK!
PEK!
CHK
Missed me!
Missed me!
Oh! My only horse!!
CHUK
Poor me! Poor me!
You think you're poor! I'll show you poor!
The last of my wine!! That's all I have to sell! You've put me out of business
That's not all I'm going to do!
I'll destroy you and your home!!
THE DRIVER WALKED ALL THE WAY TO HIS HOUSE.
Ho, wife... it has been a day of misery...
Never mind that! There's a horrible bird in our house!

THE SPARROW HAD BROUGHT HUNDREDS OF HIS FRIENDS-- AND EATEN EVERYTHING IN THE PLACE!

Now I have No money and No food!

I'm not finished with you yet!

You killed my friend-- and that will cost you your life!!

ALL THE MAN COULD DO WAS SIT AND BROOD. BUT THE SPARROW WOULDN'T LET UP.

I hope you're saying your prayers, murderer! I'm going to make you pay with your life!

AT LAST, THE MAN COULD TAKE NO MORE.

I'll Stop this torment Right now!

SHHMASSH

You'll pay! You'll pay!

THIS TIME THE SPARROW WENT TOO FAR-- OR SO IT SEEMED.

You'll pay!

I've got you! And this time-- I'm going to swallow you whole!!

You'll pay!

HE TRIED TO FORCE THE SPARROW INTO HIS MOUTH, BUT THE LITTLE BIRD REFUSED TO GO.

AAAAAARRRR

This is it!

It's all over for you

THE DRIVER'S WIFE CAME TO THE RESCUE!

Stand still, Husband! I'll kill that bird and save you!

NNPPPHHH! NNNPPHH!!

HA! HA! Missed me! Missed me!

Too bad about your dog-killing husband!

CRSMASH

THE BIRD FLEW UP AND AWAY.

THE DEATH OF HIS FRIEND WAS FINALLY AVENGED.

FACTOID BOOKS

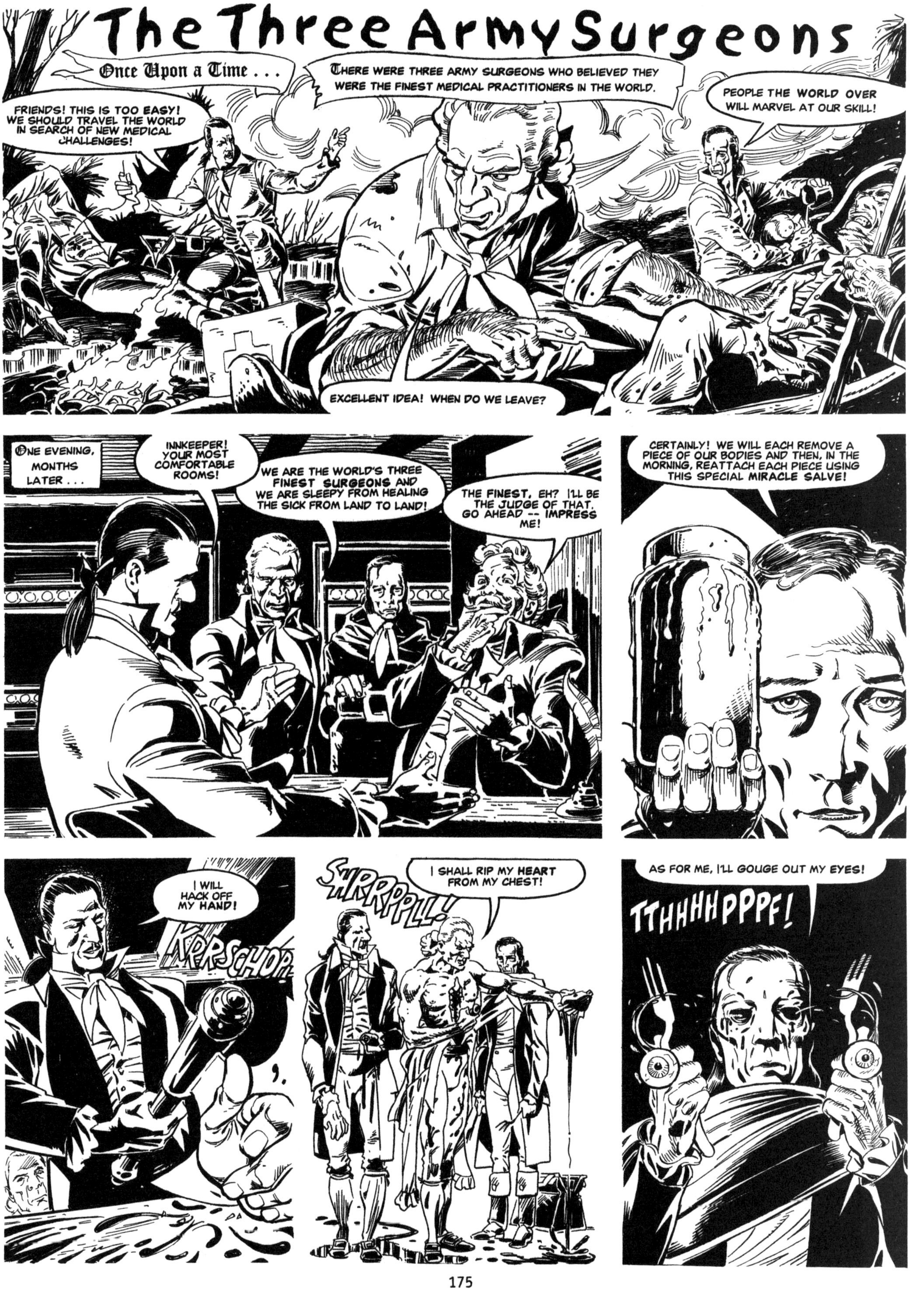
The Three Army Surgeons
Once Upon a Time . . .
There were three army surgeons who believed they were the finest medical practitioners in the world.
FRIENDS! THIS IS TOO EASY! WE SHOULD TRAVEL THE WORLD IN SEARCH OF NEW MEDICAL CHALLENGES!
PEOPLE THE WORLD OVER WILL MARVEL AT OUR SKILL!
EXCELLENT IDEA! WHEN DO WE LEAVE?
ONE EVENING, MONTHS LATER . . .
INNKEEPER! YOUR MOST COMFORTABLE ROOMS!
WE ARE THE WORLD'S THREE FINEST SURGEONS AND WE ARE SLEEPY FROM HEALING THE SICK FROM LAND TO LAND!
THE FINEST, EH? I'LL BE THE JUDGE OF THAT. GO AHEAD -- IMPRESS ME!
CERTAINLY! WE WILL EACH REMOVE A PIECE OF OUR BODIES AND THEN, IN THE MORNING, REATTACH EACH PIECE USING THIS SPECIAL MIRACLE SALVE!
I WILL HACK OFF MY HAND!
KRRSCHOP!
SHRRPPLL!
I SHALL RIP MY HEART FROM MY CHEST!
AS FOR ME, I'LL GOUGE OUT MY EYES!
TTHHHHPPPF!

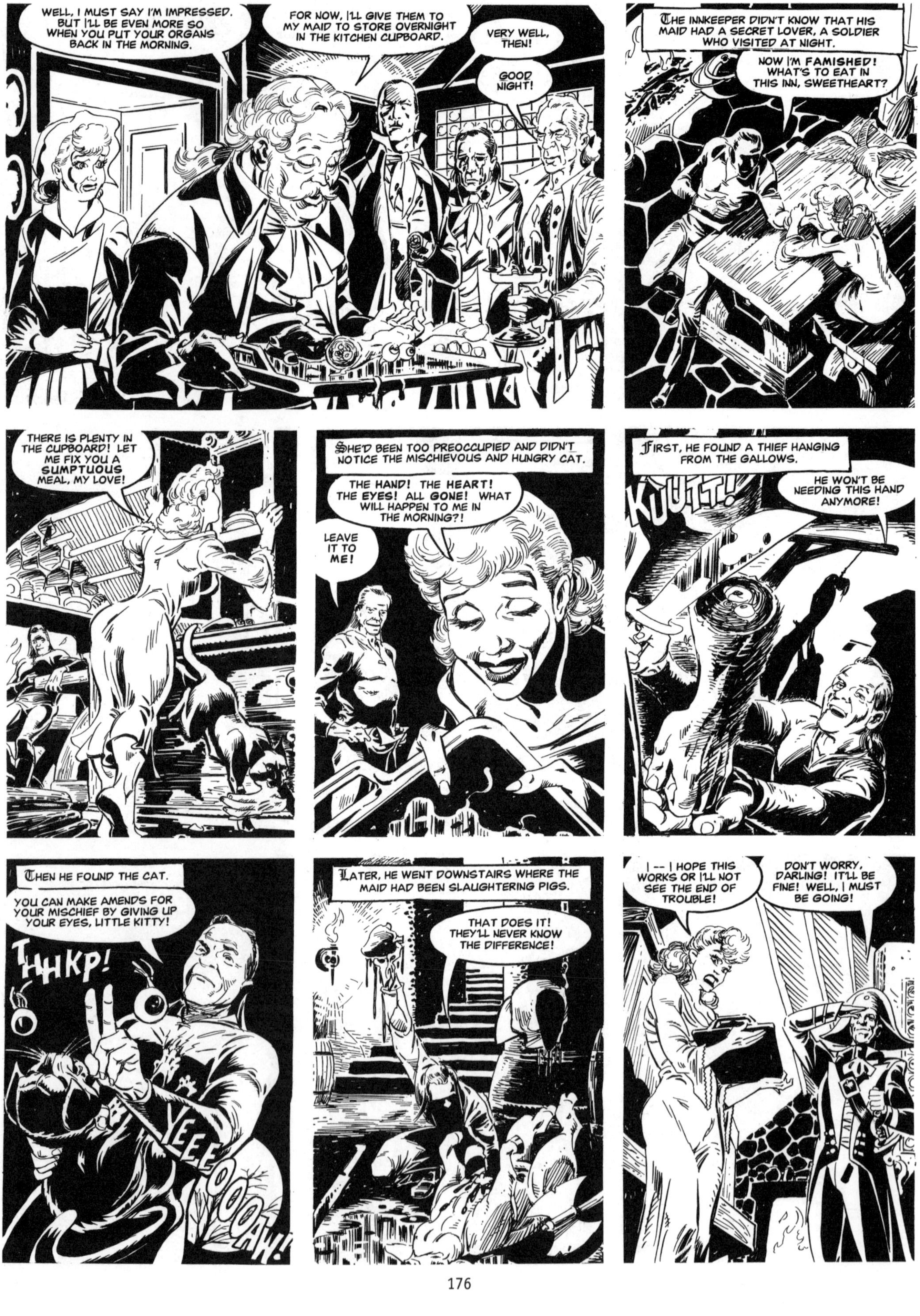
WELL, I MUST SAY I'M IMPRESSED. BUT I'LL BE EVEN MORE SO WHEN YOU PUT YOUR ORGANS BACK IN THE MORNING.
FOR NOW, I'LL GIVE THEM TO MY MAID TO STORE OVERNIGHT IN THE KITCHEN CUPBOARD.
VERY WELL, THEN!
GOOD NIGHT!
THE INNKEEPER DIDN'T KNOW THAT HIS MAID HAD A SECRET LOVER, A SOLDIER WHO VISITED AT NIGHT.
NOW I'M FAMISHED! WHAT'S TO EAT IN THIS INN, SWEETHEART?
THERE IS PLENTY IN THE CUPBOARD! LET ME FIX YOU A SUMPTUOUS MEAL, MY LOVE!
SHE'D BEEN TOO PREOCCUPIED AND DIDN'T NOTICE THE MISCHIEVOUS AND HUNGRY CAT.
THE HAND! THE HEART! THE EYES! ALL GONE! WHAT WILL HAPPEN TO ME IN THE MORNING?!
LEAVE IT TO ME!
FIRST, HE FOUND A THIEF HANGING FROM THE GALLOWS.
KUUTT!
HE WON'T BE NEEDING THIS HAND ANYMORE!
THEN HE FOUND THE CAT.
YOU CAN MAKE AMENDS FOR YOUR MISCHIEF BY GIVING UP YOUR EYES, LITTLE KITTY!
THHKP!
YEEEOOOAH!
LATER, HE WENT DOWNSTAIRS WHERE THE MAID HAD BEEN SLAUGHTERING PIGS.
THAT DOES IT! THEY'LL NEVER KNOW THE DIFFERENCE!
I -- I HOPE THIS WORKS OR I'LL NOT SEE THE END OF TROUBLE!
DON'T WORRY, DARLING! IT'LL BE FINE! WELL, I MUST BE GOING!

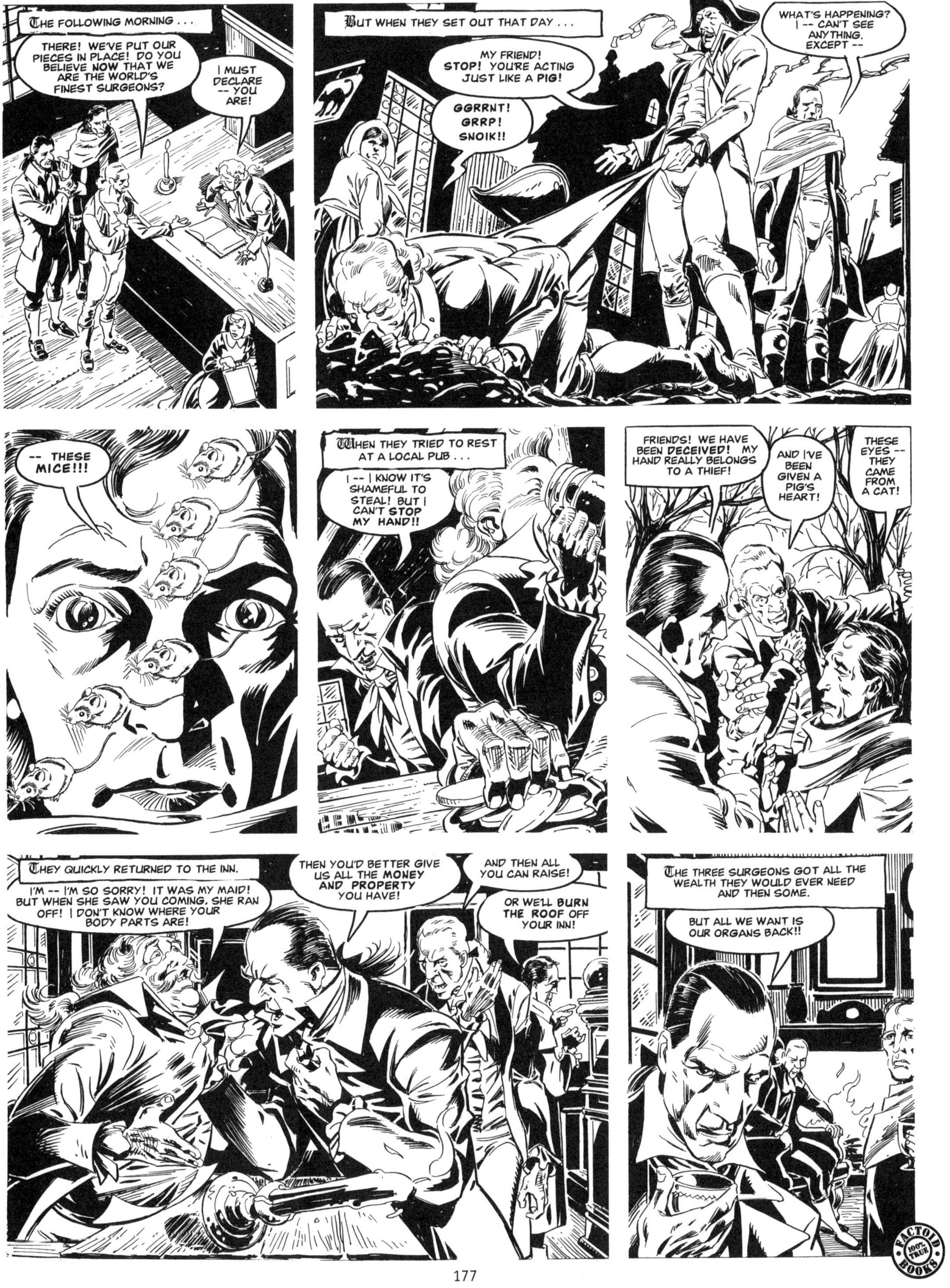
THE FOLLOWING MORNING . . .
THERE! WE'VE PUT OUR PIECES IN PLACE! DO YOU BELIEVE NOW THAT WE ARE THE WORLD'S FINEST SURGEONS?
I MUST DECLARE -- YOU ARE!
BUT WHEN THEY SET OUT THAT DAY . . .
MY FRIEND! STOP! YOU'RE ACTING JUST LIKE A PIG!
GGRRNT! GRRP! SNOIK!!
WHAT'S HAPPENING? I -- CAN'T SEE ANYTHING. EXCEPT --
-- THESE MICE!!!
WHEN THEY TRIED TO REST AT A LOCAL PUB . . .
I -- I KNOW IT'S SHAMEFUL TO STEAL! BUT I CAN'T STOP MY HAND!!
FRIENDS! WE HAVE BEEN DECEIVED! MY HAND REALLY BELONGS TO A THIEF!
AND I'VE BEEN GIVEN A PIG'S HEART!
THESE EYES -- THEY CAME FROM A CAT!
THEY QUICKLY RETURNED TO THE INN.
I'M -- I'M SO SORRY! IT WAS MY MAID! BUT WHEN SHE SAW YOU COMING, SHE RAN OFF! I DON'T KNOW WHERE YOUR BODY PARTS ARE!
THEN YOU'D BETTER GIVE US ALL THE MONEY AND PROPERTY YOU HAVE!
AND THEN ALL YOU CAN RAISE!
OR WE'LL BURN THE ROOF OFF YOUR INN!
THE THREE SURGEONS GOT ALL THE WEALTH THEY WOULD EVER NEED AND THEN SOME.
BUT ALL WE WANT IS OUR ORGANS BACK!!
FACTOID BOOKS 100% TRUE

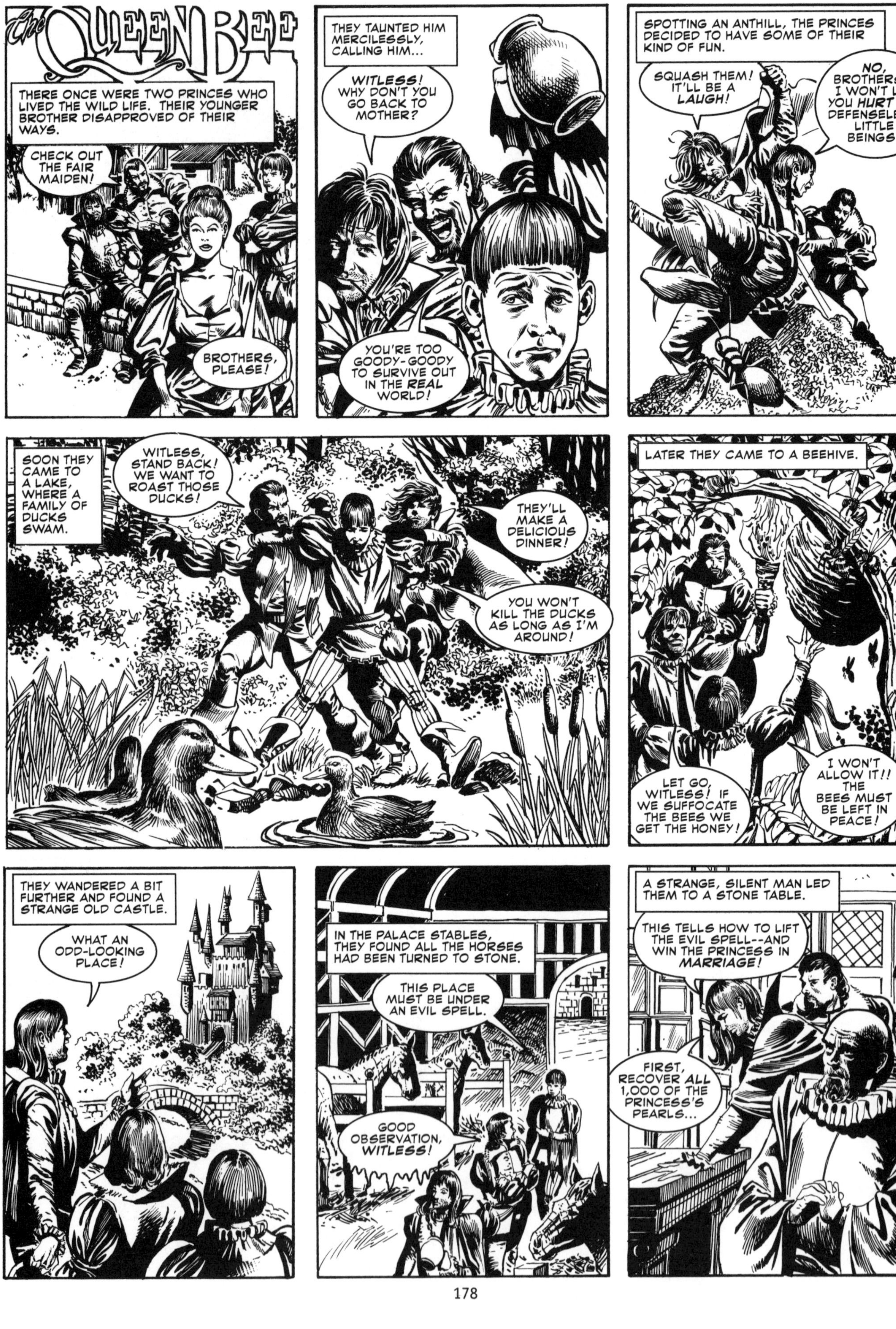

The QUEEN BEE
THERE ONCE WERE TWO PRINCES WHO LIVED THE WILD LIFE. THEIR YOUNGER BROTHER DISAPPROVED OF THEIR WAYS.
CHECK OUT THE FAIR MAIDEN!
BROTHERS, PLEASE!
THEY TAUNTED HIM MERCILESSLY, CALLING HIM...
WITLESS! WHY DON'T YOU GO BACK TO MOTHER?
YOU'RE TOO GOODY-GOODY TO SURVIVE OUT IN THE REAL WORLD!
SPOTTING AN ANTHILL, THE PRINCES DECIDED TO HAVE SOME OF THEIR KIND OF FUN.
SQUASH THEM! IT'LL BE A LAUGH!
NO, BROTHERS!! I WON'T LET YOU HURT THE DEFENSELESS LITTLE BEINGS!
SOON THEY CAME TO A LAKE, WHERE A FAMILY OF DUCKS SWAM.
WITLESS, STAND BACK! WE WANT TO ROAST THOSE DUCKS!
THEY'LL MAKE A DELICIOUS DINNER!
YOU WON'T KILL THE DUCKS AS LONG AS I'M AROUND!
LATER THEY CAME TO A BEEHIVE.
LET GO, WITLESS! IF WE SUFFOCATE THE BEES WE GET THE HONEY!
I WON'T ALLOW IT!! THE BEES MUST BE LEFT IN PEACE!
THEY WANDERED A BIT FURTHER AND FOUND A STRANGE OLD CASTLE.
WHAT AN ODD-LOOKING PLACE!
IN THE PALACE STABLES, THEY FOUND ALL THE HORSES HAD BEEN TURNED TO STONE.
THIS PLACE MUST BE UNDER AN EVIL SPELL.
GOOD OBSERVATION, WITLESS!
A STRANGE, SILENT MAN LED THEM TO A STONE TABLE.
THIS TELLS HOW TO LIFT THE EVIL SPELL--AND WIN THE PRINCESS IN MARRIAGE!
FIRST, RECOVER ALL 1,000 OF THE PRINCESS'S PEARLS...

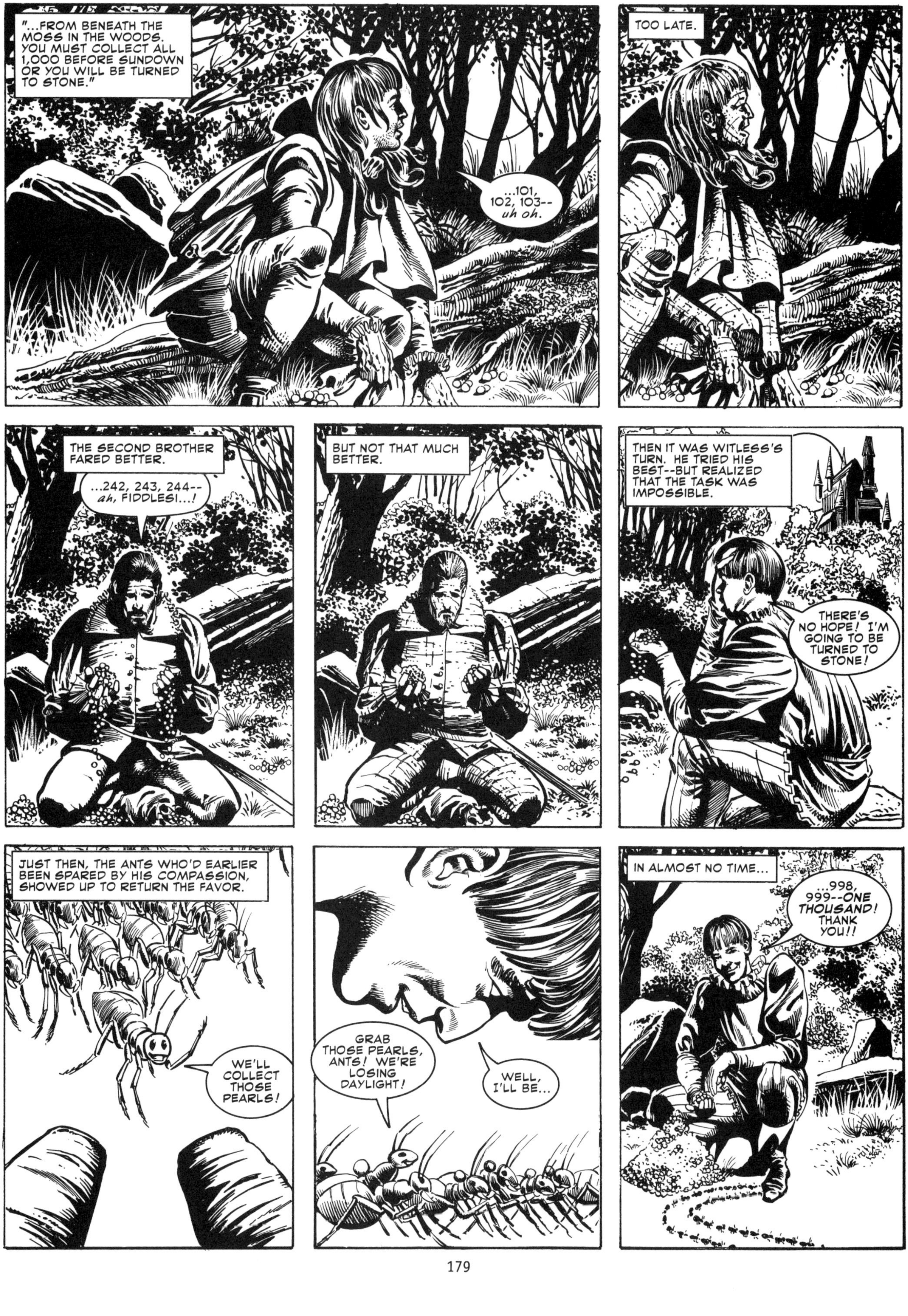
"...FROM BENEATH THE MOSS IN THE WOODS. YOU MUST COLLECT ALL 1,000 BEFORE SUNDOWN OR YOU WILL BE TURNED TO STONE."
...101, 102, 103-- uh oh.
TOO LATE.
THE SECOND BROTHER FARED BETTER.
...242, 243, 244-- ah, FIDDLES!...!
BUT NOT THAT MUCH BETTER.
THEN IT WAS WITLESS'S TURN. HE TRIED HIS BEST--BUT REALIZED THAT THE TASK WAS IMPOSSIBLE.
THERE'S NO HOPE! I'M GOING TO BE TURNED TO STONE!
JUST THEN, THE ANTS WHO'D EARLIER BEEN SPARED BY HIS COMPASSION, SHOWED UP TO RETURN THE FAVOR.
WE'LL COLLECT THOSE PEARLS!
GRAB THOSE PEARLS, ANTS! WE'RE LOSING DAYLIGHT!
WELL, I'LL BE...
IN ALMOST NO TIME...
...998, 999--ONE THOUSAND! THANK YOU!!

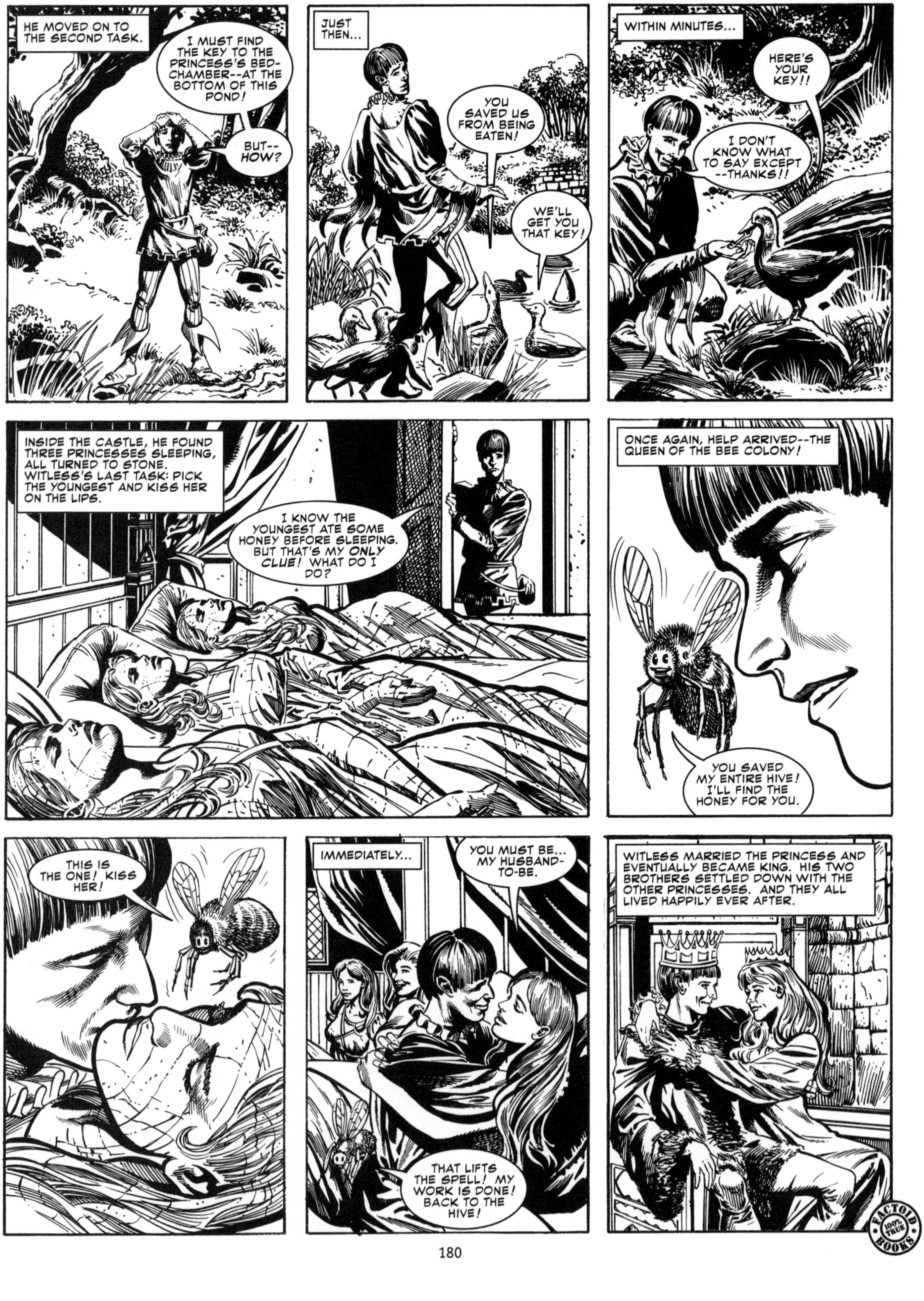
HE MOVED ON TO THE SECOND TASK.
I MUST FIND THE KEY TO THE PRINCESS'S BED-CHAMBER--AT THE BOTTOM OF THIS POND!
BUT-- HOW?
JUST THEN...
YOU SAVED US FROM BEING EATEN!
WE'LL GET YOU THAT KEY!
WITHIN MINUTES...
HERE'S YOUR KEY!!
I DON'T KNOW WHAT TO SAY EXCEPT --THANKS!!
INSIDE THE CASTLE, HE FOUND THREE PRINCESSES SLEEPING, ALL TURNED TO STONE. WITLESS'S LAST TASK: PICK THE YOUNGEST AND KISS HER ON THE LIPS.
I KNOW THE YOUNGEST ATE SOME HONEY BEFORE SLEEPING. BUT THAT'S MY ONLY CLUE! WHAT DO I DO?
ONCE AGAIN, HELP ARRIVED--THE QUEEN OF THE BEE COLONY!
YOU SAVED MY ENTIRE HIVE! I'LL FIND THE HONEY FOR YOU.
THIS IS THE ONE! KISS HER!
IMMEDIATELY...
YOU MUST BE... MY HUSBAND-TO-BE.
THAT LIFTS THE SPELL! MY WORK IS DONE! BACK TO THE HIVE!
WITLESS MARRIED THE PRINCESS AND EVENTUALLY BECAME KING. HIS TWO BROTHERS SETTLED DOWN WITH THE OTHER PRINCESSES. AND THEY ALL LIVED HAPPILY EVER AFTER.
FACTOID BOOKS 100% TRUE

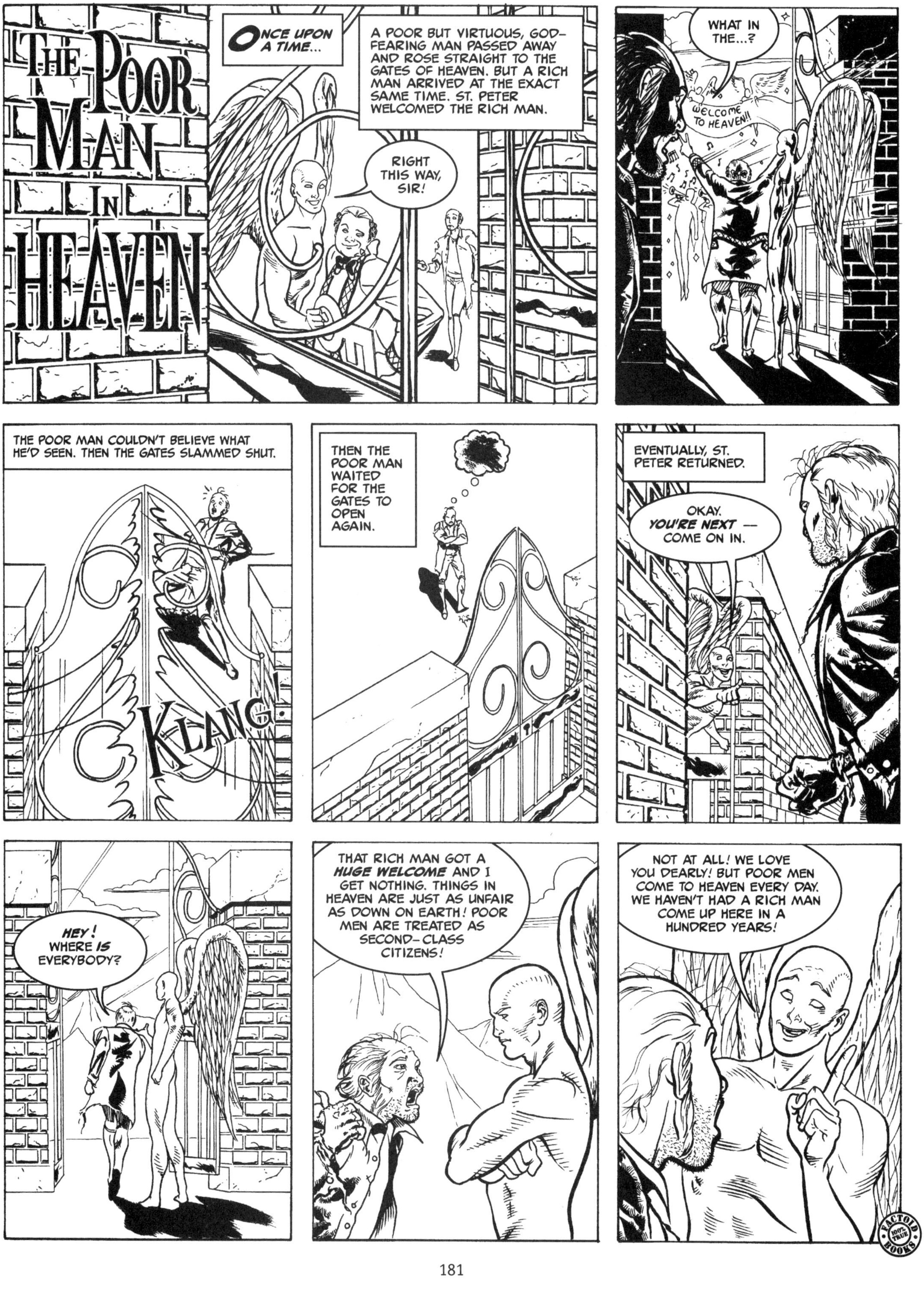
THE POOR MAN IN HEAVEN
ONCE UPON A TIME...
A POOR BUT VIRTUOUS, GOD-FEARING MAN PASSED AWAY AND ROSE STRAIGHT TO THE GATES OF HEAVEN. BUT A RICH MAN ARRIVED AT THE EXACT SAME TIME. ST. PETER WELCOMED THE RICH MAN.
RIGHT THIS WAY, SIR!
WHAT IN THE...?
WELCOME TO HEAVEN!!
THE POOR MAN COULDN'T BELIEVE WHAT HE'D SEEN. THEN THE GATES SLAMMED SHUT.
KLANG!
THEN THE POOR MAN WAITED FOR THE GATES TO OPEN AGAIN.
EVENTUALLY, ST. PETER RETURNED.
OKAY. YOU'RE NEXT — COME ON IN.
HEY! WHERE IS EVERYBODY?
THAT RICH MAN GOT A HUGE WELCOME AND I GET NOTHING. THINGS IN HEAVEN ARE JUST AS UNFAIR AS DOWN ON EARTH! POOR MEN ARE TREATED AS SECOND-CLASS CITIZENS!
NOT AT ALL! WE LOVE YOU DEARLY! BUT POOR MEN COME TO HEAVEN EVERY DAY. WE HAVEN'T HAD A RICH MAN COME UP HERE IN A HUNDRED YEARS!
FACTOID BOOKS 100% TRUE

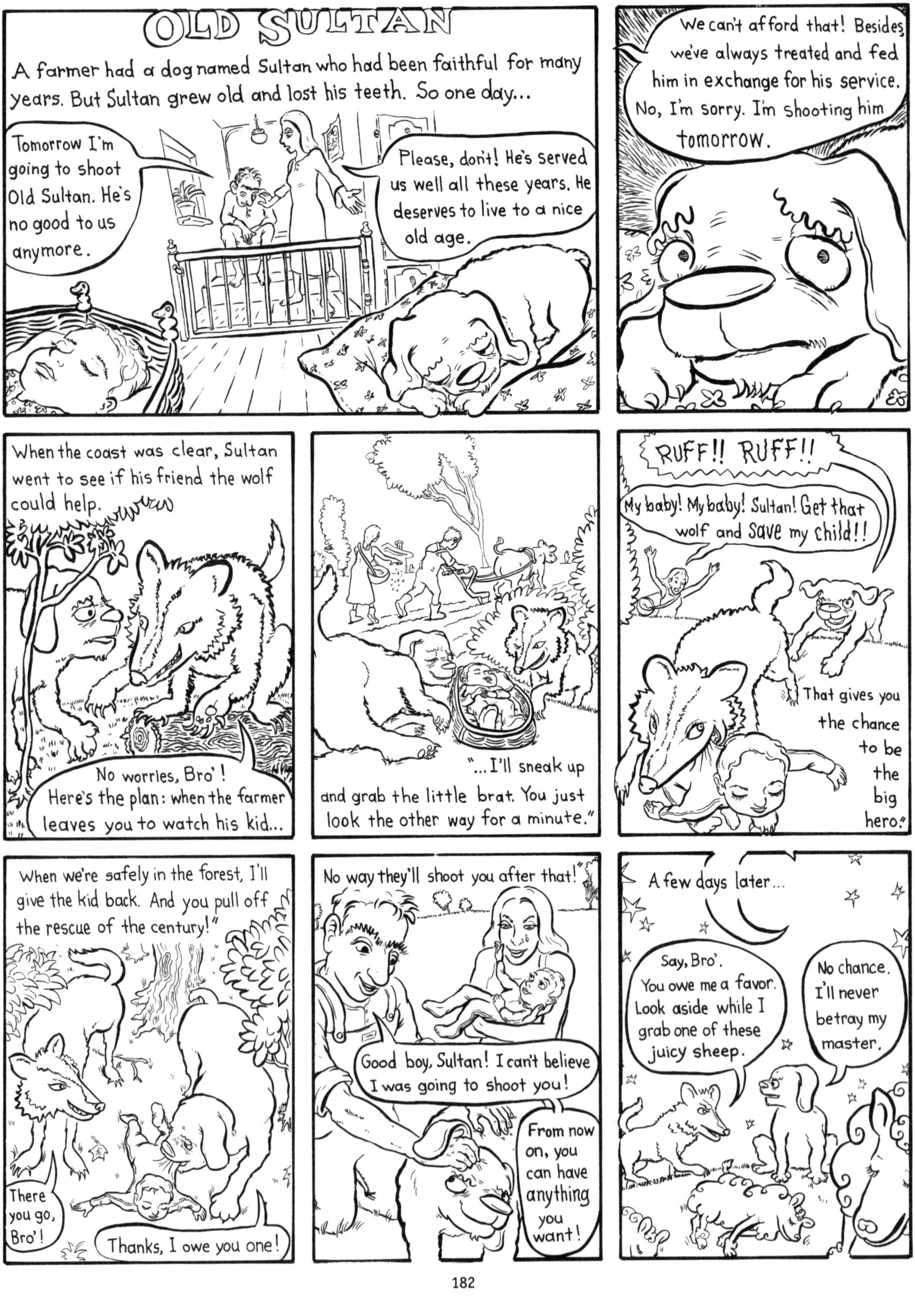
OLD SULTAN
A farmer had a dog named Sultan who had been faithful for many years. But Sultan grew old and lost his teeth. So one day...
Tomorrow I'm going to shoot Old Sultan. He's no good to us anymore.
Please, don't! He's served us well all these years. He deserves to live to a nice old age.
We can't afford that! Besides, we've always treated and fed him in exchange for his service. No, I'm sorry. I'm shooting him tomorrow.
When the coast was clear, Sultan went to see if his friend the wolf could help.
No worries, Bro'! Here's the plan: when the farmer leaves you to watch his kid...
"...I'll sneak up and grab the little brat. You just look the other way for a minute."
RUFF!! RUFF!!
My baby! My baby! Sultan! Get that wolf and save my child!!
That gives you the chance to be the big hero."
When we're safely in the forest, I'll give the kid back. And you pull off the rescue of the century!"
There you go, Bro'!
Thanks, I owe you one!
No way they'll shoot you after that!"
Good boy, Sultan! I can't believe I was going to shoot you!
From now on, you can have anything you want!
A few days later...
Say, Bro'. You owe me a favor. Look aside while I grab one of these juicy sheep.
No chance. I'll never betray my master.

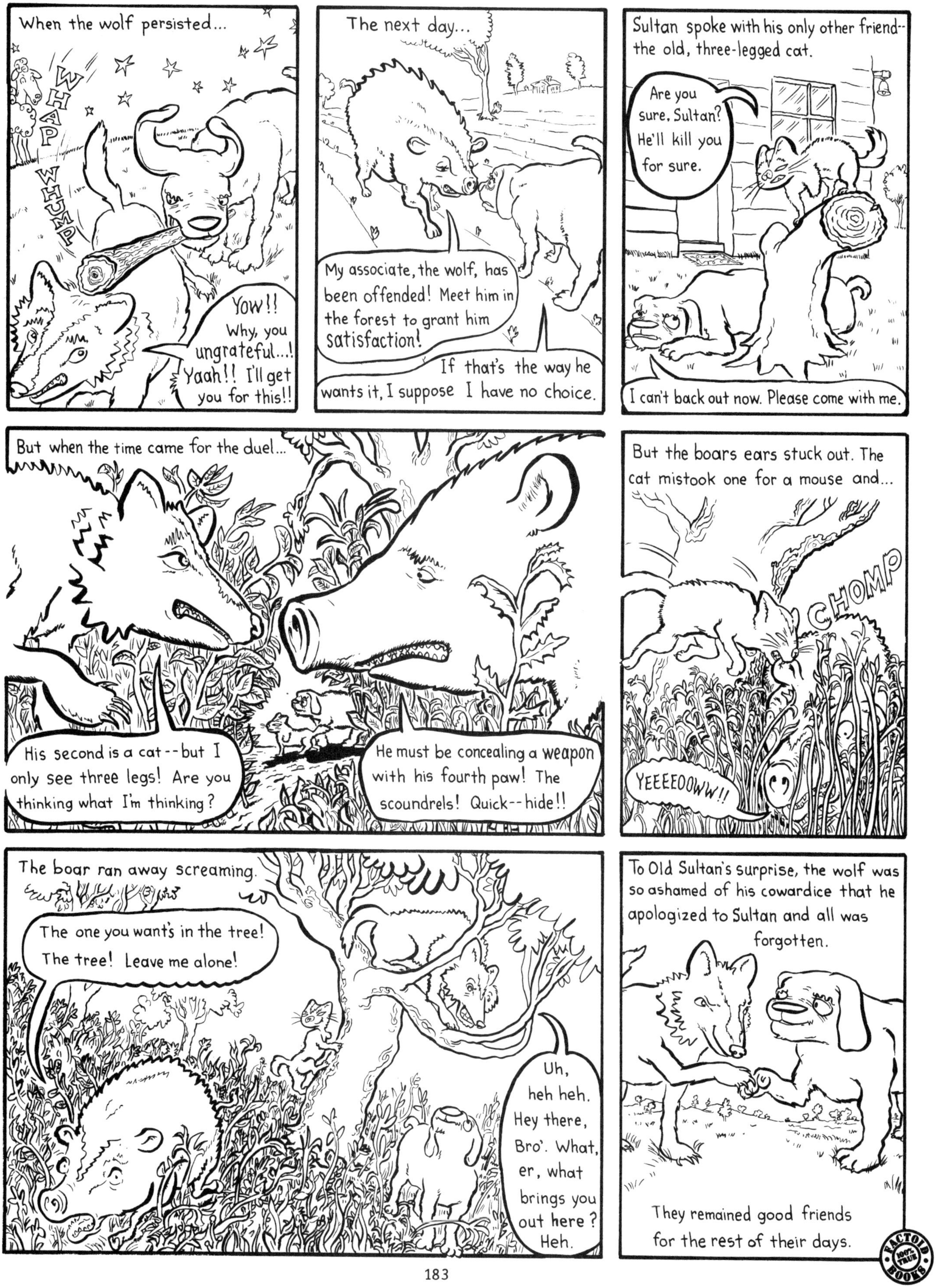
When the wolf persisted...
WHAP
WHUMP
Yow!! Why, you ungrateful...! Yaah!! I'll get you for this!!
The next day...
My associate, the wolf, has been offended! Meet him in the forest to grant him satisfaction!
If that's the way he wants it, I suppose I have no choice.
Sultan spoke with his only other friend--the old, three-legged cat.
Are you sure, Sultan? He'll kill you for sure.
I can't back out now. Please come with me.
But when the time came for the duel...
His second is a cat--but I only see three legs! Are you thinking what I'm thinking?
He must be concealing a weapon with his fourth paw! The scoundrels! Quick--hide!!
But the boars ears stuck out. The cat mistook one for a mouse and...
CHOMP
YEEEEOOWW!!
The boar ran away screaming.
The one you want's in the tree! The tree! Leave me alone!
Uh, heh heh. Hey there, Bro'. What, er, what brings you out here? Heh.
To Old Sultan's surprise, the wolf was so ashamed of his cowardice that he apologized to Sultan and all was forgotten.
They remained good friends for the rest of their days.

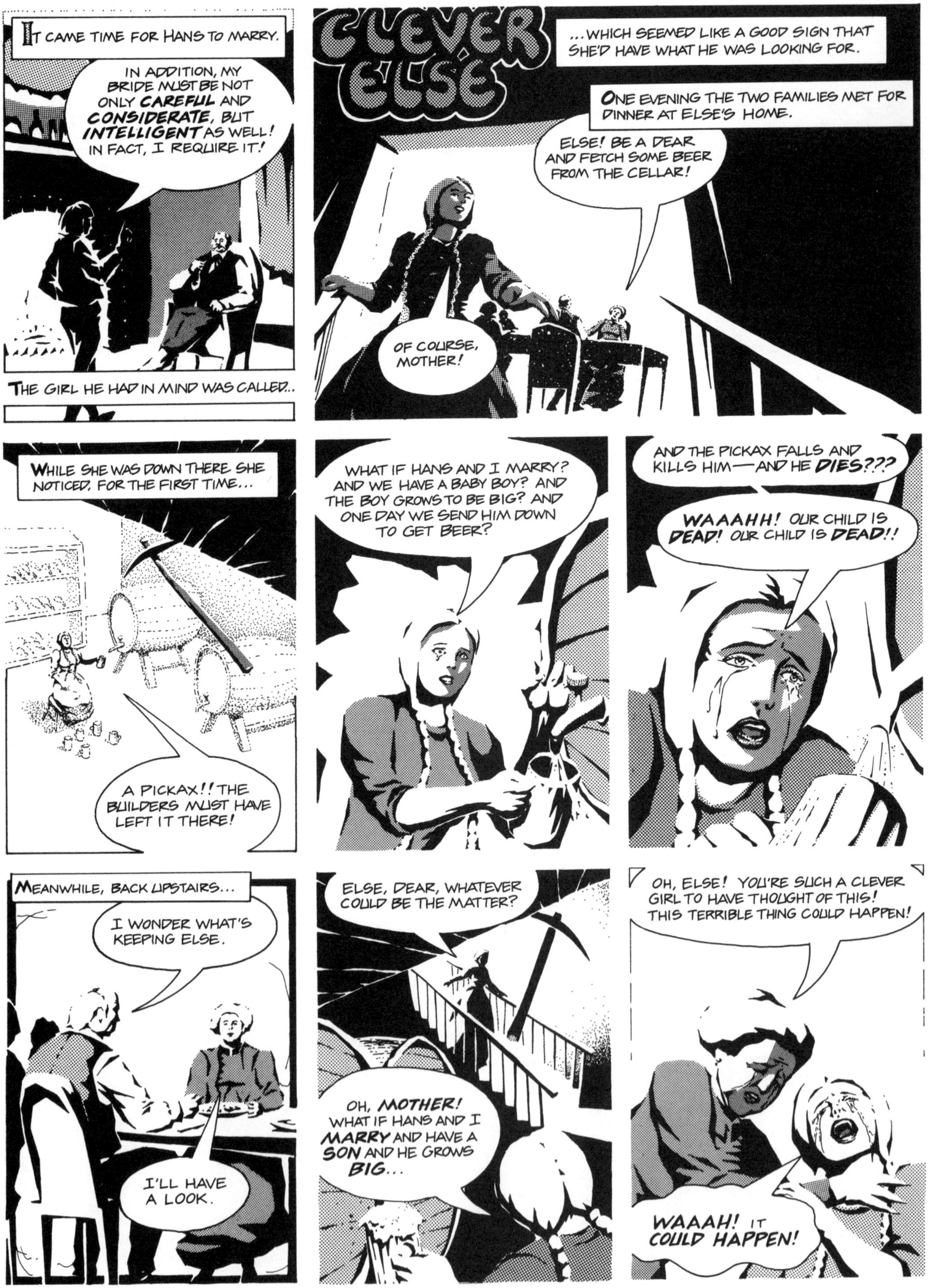

IT CAME TIME FOR HANS TO MARRY.
IN ADDITION, MY BRIDE MUST BE NOT ONLY CAREFUL AND CONSIDERATE, BUT INTELLIGENT AS WELL! IN FACT, I REQUIRE IT!
THE GIRL HE HAD IN MIND WAS CALLED...
CLEVER ELSE
...WHICH SEEMED LIKE A GOOD SIGN THAT SHE'D HAVE WHAT HE WAS LOOKING FOR.
ONE EVENING THE TWO FAMILIES MET FOR DINNER AT ELSE'S HOME.
ELSE! BE A DEAR AND FETCH SOME BEER FROM THE CELLAR!
OF COURSE, MOTHER!
WHILE SHE WAS DOWN THERE SHE NOTICED, FOR THE FIRST TIME...
A PICKAX!! THE BUILDERS MUST HAVE LEFT IT THERE!
WHAT IF HANS AND I MARRY? AND WE HAVE A BABY BOY? AND THE BOY GROWS TO BE BIG? AND ONE DAY WE SEND HIM DOWN TO GET BEER?
AND THE PICKAX FALLS AND KILLS HIM—AND HE DIES???
WAAAHH! OUR CHILD IS DEAD! OUR CHILD IS DEAD!!
MEANWHILE, BACK UPSTAIRS...
I WONDER WHAT'S KEEPING ELSE.
I'LL HAVE A LOOK.
ELSE, DEAR, WHATEVER COULD BE THE MATTER?
OH, MOTHER! WHAT IF HANS AND I MARRY AND HAVE A SON AND HE GROWS BIG...
OH, ELSE! YOU'RE SUCH A CLEVER GIRL TO HAVE THOUGHT OF THIS! THIS TERRIBLE THING COULD HAPPEN!
WAAAH! IT COULD HAPPEN!

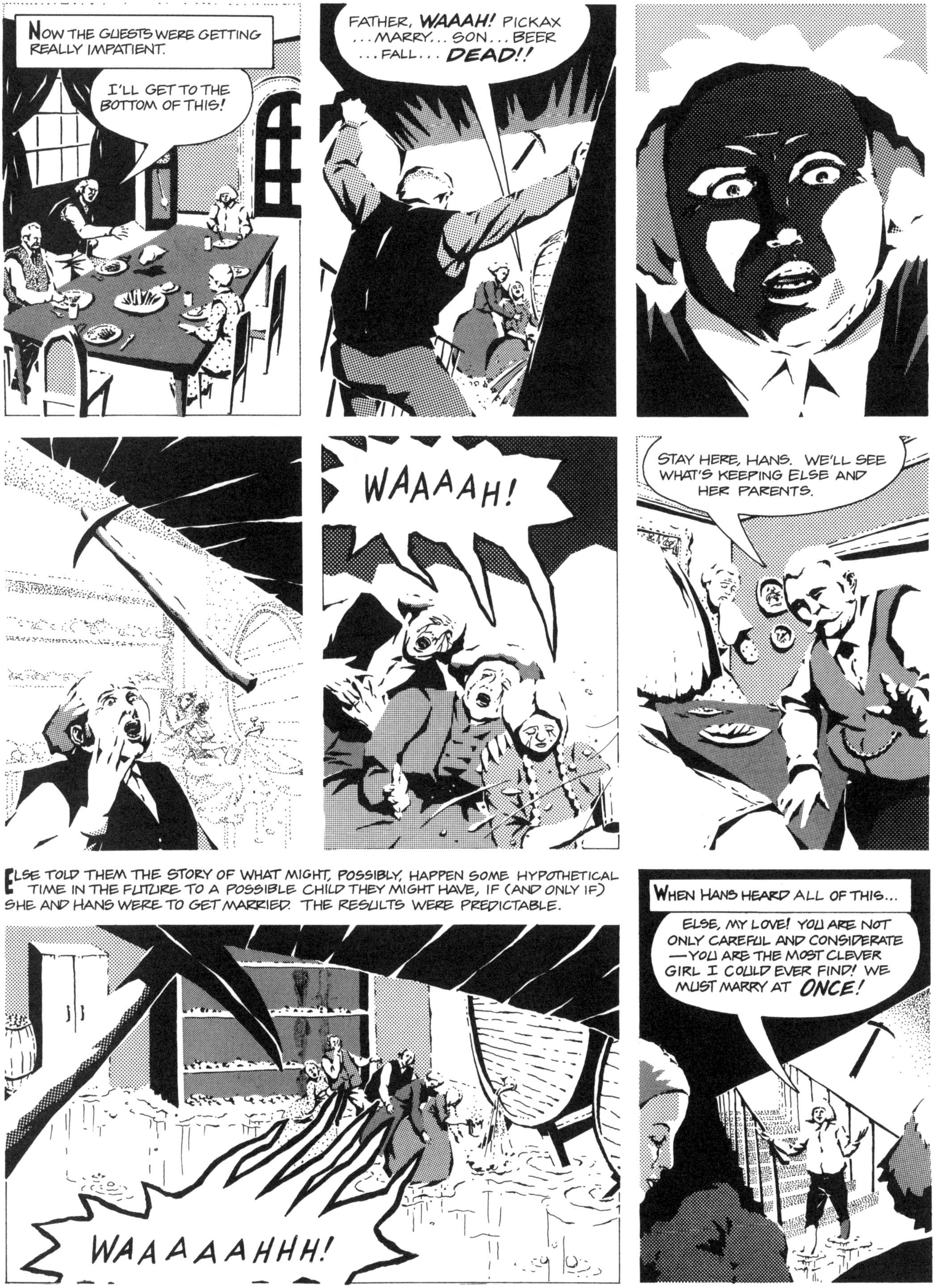
NOW THE GUESTS WERE GETTING REALLY IMPATIENT.
I'LL GET TO THE BOTTOM OF THIS!
FATHER, WAAAH! PICKAX ... MARRY... SON... BEER ... FALL... DEAD!!
WAAAAH!
STAY HERE, HANS. WE'LL SEE WHAT'S KEEPING ELSE AND HER PARENTS.
ELSE TOLD THEM THE STORY OF WHAT MIGHT, POSSIBLY, HAPPEN SOME HYPOTHETICAL TIME IN THE FUTURE TO A POSSIBLE CHILD THEY MIGHT HAVE, IF (AND ONLY IF) SHE AND HANS WERE TO GET MARRIED. THE RESULTS WERE PREDICTABLE.
WAAAAAAHHH!
WHEN HANS HEARD ALL OF THIS...
ELSE, MY LOVE! YOU ARE NOT ONLY CAREFUL AND CONSIDERATE—YOU ARE THE MOST CLEVER GIRL I COULD EVER FIND! WE MUST MARRY AT ONCE!

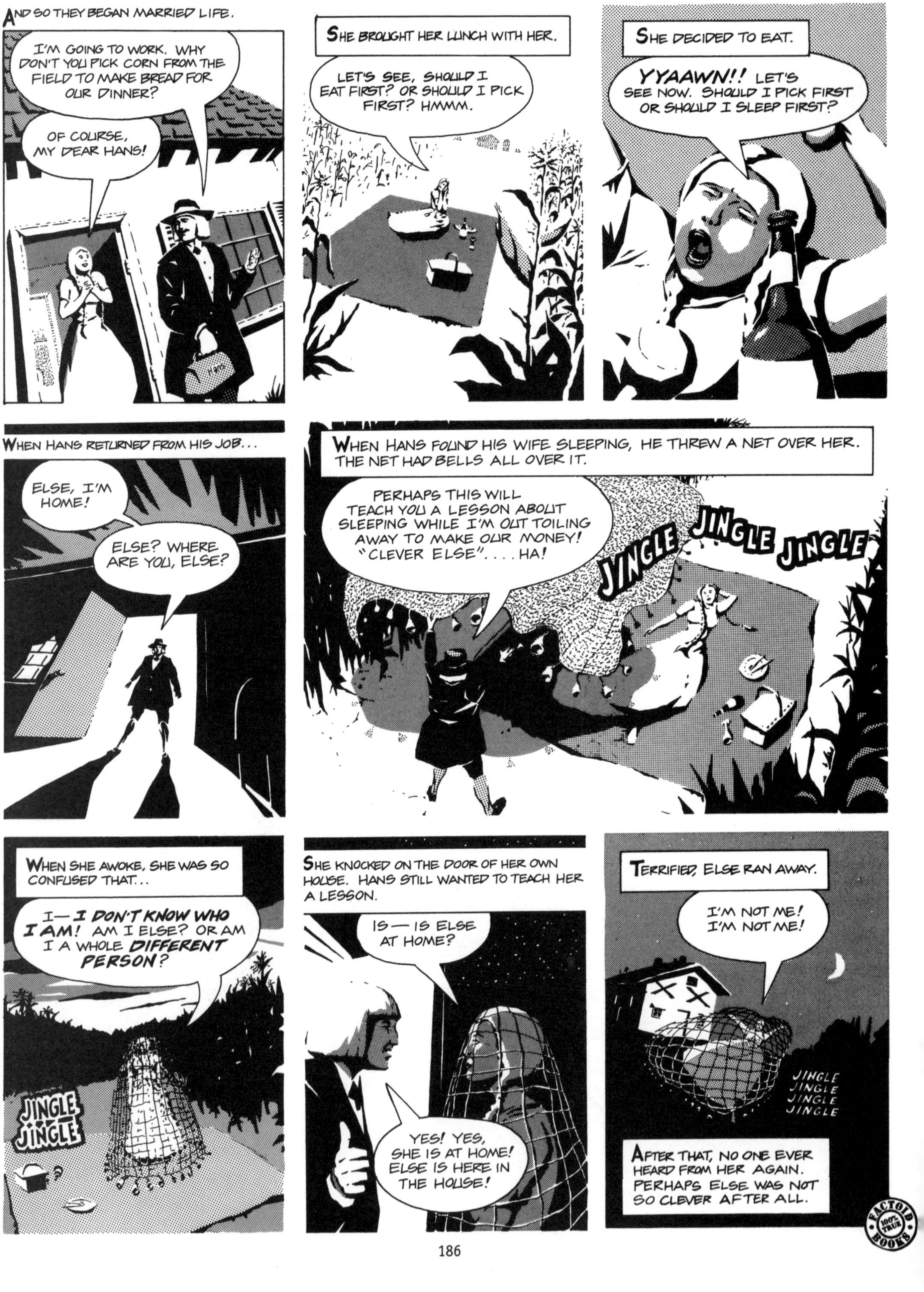
AND SO THEY BEGAN MARRIED LIFE.
I'M GOING TO WORK. WHY DON'T YOU PICK CORN FROM THE FIELD TO MAKE BREAD FOR OUR DINNER?
OF COURSE, MY DEAR HANS!
SHE BROUGHT HER LUNCH WITH HER.
LET'S SEE, SHOULD I EAT FIRST? OR SHOULD I PICK FIRST? HMMM.
SHE DECIDED TO EAT.
YYAAWN!! LET'S SEE NOW. SHOULD I PICK FIRST OR SHOULD I SLEEP FIRST?
WHEN HANS RETURNED FROM HIS JOB...
ELSE, I'M HOME!
ELSE? WHERE ARE YOU, ELSE?
WHEN HANS FOUND HIS WIFE SLEEPING, HE THREW A NET OVER HER. THE NET HAD BELLS ALL OVER IT.
PERHAPS THIS WILL TEACH YOU A LESSON ABOUT SLEEPING WHILE I'M OUT TOILING AWAY TO MAKE OUR MONEY! "CLEVER ELSE"....HA!
JINGLE JINGLE JINGLE
WHEN SHE AWOKE, SHE WAS SO CONFUSED THAT...
I— I DON'T KNOW WHO I AM! AM I ELSE? OR AM I A WHOLE DIFFERENT PERSON?
JINGLE JINGLE
SHE KNOCKED ON THE DOOR OF HER OWN HOUSE. HANS STILL WANTED TO TEACH HER A LESSON.
IS — IS ELSE AT HOME?
YES! YES, SHE IS AT HOME! ELSE IS HERE IN THE HOUSE!
TERRIFIED, ELSE RAN AWAY.
I'M NOT ME! I'M NOT ME!
JINGLE JINGLE JINGLE JINGLE
AFTER THAT, NO ONE EVER HEARD FROM HER AGAIN. PERHAPS ELSE WAS NOT SO CLEVER AFTER ALL.
FACTOID 100% TRUE BOOKS

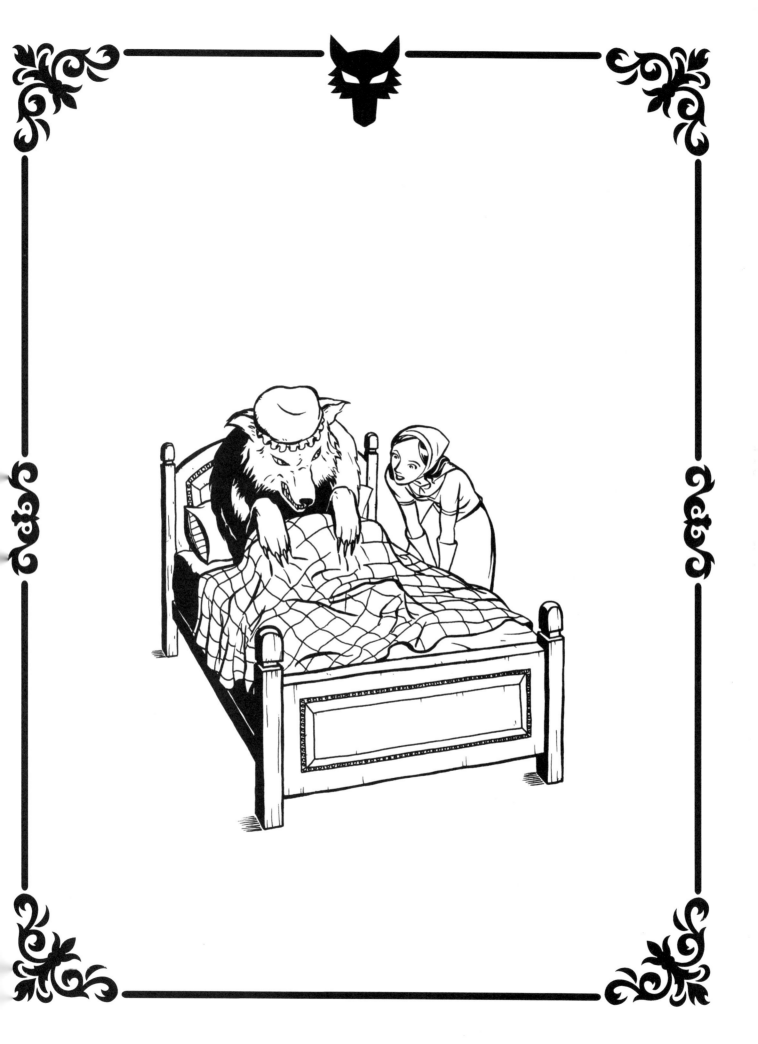

BIOGRAPHIES

WRITER

JONATHAN VANKIN

Jonathan Vankin has worked his sorcery on such earlier Big Books as *The Big Book of Bad* and *The Big Book of Scandal*. He has also conjured a charming collection of wondrous stories known as *The 70 Greatest Conspiracies of All Time*. He dwells in a faraway kingdom known as Los Angeles, where he lives in a magical palace with the most beautiful fairy tale princess in all the land, his wife Debbie.

ARTISTS

CHARLES ADLARD

Charles has drawn *The X-Files* comic for Topps, various comics for Acclaim, *Superman* for DC, as well as many others. (Page 18)

BILL ALGER

Former child televangelist and current liquor-soused vagrant, Bill Alger draws kids' comics for a childless society. (Page 111)

SERGIO ARAGONÉS

Sergio is the creator of the award-winning comic *Groo*. His comics and illustrations have appeared in *MAD*, and most recently in *Sergio Aragonés' Louder Than Words* from Dark Horse Comics and in *Fanboy*, written by Mark Evanier, from DC Comics. (Page 142)

GREGORY BENTON

Gregory's cartooning wonderment has appeared in *Details, High Times*, and in his own comic book *Hummingbird*. (Page 60)

JOSÉ MARÍA BEROY

Beroy has done illustrations for magazines, books, cinema and other media. He would like to make a living solely by drawing comics. For now, he'll just have to live with being as handsome as Antonio Banderas. (Page 104)

NICK BERTOZZI

Nick is very adept at drawing nipple rings and inebriated barflies. Find out for yourself in the self-published *Incredible Drinkin' Buddies* and his new book *Tranquilizer*. (Page 38)

RICK BURCHETT

Rick drew *Batman: Gotham Adventures*, will draw two upcoming *Legends of the Dark Knight* issues, and is doing a new miniseries for DC/Vertigo. (Page 166)

JOHN CEBOLLERO

John recently underwent surgery to correct the slight aberrations in his skull (it was shaped like a toy piano). He may lose some of his classical musician friends, but dammit, at least he's got a skull like a man. (Page 52)

CLIFF CHIANG

Cliff has been working steadily in comics for the past 20 years. This is his first published work after the unfortunate legal entanglements surrounding his daily strip "Jeffrey Cartwright, Teen Sleuth" in the '70s. He is currently working on a fictional autobiography. (Page 72)

JOE CHIAPPETTA

Joe is the Xeric Award-winning cartoonist of *Silly Daddy* (also nominated for a Harvey and an Ignatz Award) which features him, his eight-year-old daughter, and his new bride. (Page 182)

SCOTT COHN

When he's not busy making money for "the Man," Scott likes to work on his strip "Hem'n'Haw" for *Action Planet*. He also likes to drink. (Page 181)

MICHAEL COLLINS

Mike took up comics after realizing that, as a flabby white guy from Britain, he would never achieve his ambitions: to become president of the U.S.A. and/or one of Diana Ross's Supremes. (Page 132)

DAME DARCY

This Grand Dame of the Neo-Victorians is a comics creator, singer, filmmaker, animator, banjo player (and much, much more). She is best known for her long-running comic *Meatcake* and her Manhattan cable TV show "Turn of the Century." (Page 162)

ADAM DEKRAKER

Adam drew *WildCATS: Wild Times* and the upcoming *Pandora* both from WildStorm. (Page 40)

VINCENT DEPORTER

Vince draws cartoons in Belgium, France, and the U.S. including "Fourmidables," in the magazine *Spirou*, and "Roméo," which has appeared in *Maxi* for over 12 years. He has recently done Superman illustrations for DC's licensing department. (Page 138)

COLLEEN DORAN

Colleen is the writer, artist, and creator of the series *A Distant Soil*. She worked on *Sandman* and drew the graphic novel *Wonder Woman: The Once and Future Story* for DC. (Page 56)

D'ISRAELI D'EMON DRAUGHTSMAN

D'Israeli lives in Sheffield with his mummy and the nice kitty, who is back after a short break. He colors most of the British *2000 AD* comic, is the love-slave of a celebrated female small-press artist, and draws his own comic, *D'Adventures of I.S.R.A.E.L.I.* (Page 146)

RANDY DuBURKE

Randy's work for DC Comics includes covers of *Animal Man, Darkstars, Ms. Tree, and The Shadow*. He drew the story "Big Shot" for the DC/Vertigo anthology *Gangland*, as well as *Hunter's Heart*, a Paradox Graphic Mystery. (Page 30)

HUNT EMERSON

Hunt Emerson lurks 100 feet in the air, in sight of the New Hindu Temple on Soho Road. At night, the dome is lit from below in blue light. (Page 95)

JIM FERN

Jim started as an inker on various Marvel titles in 1983. He began pencilling in 1987, and has drawn *L.E.G.I.O.N '90, Detective Comics, Adventures of Superman,* and the *Scarlett* series for DC. (Page 128)

BOB FINGERMAN

When Bob isn't drawing weird stuff for Paradox, he's illustrating his comic *Minimum Wage* from Fantagraphics. Which you should buy and read. Because it makes Bob all cuddly inside when you do. He might even hug you and say, "Mommy, kiss the baby!" (Page 47)

SETH FISHER

Trudging onward, Seth's never-ending mission to fill blank pages with little black lines continues. Look for his art in *Happydale: Devils in the Desert*, published by DC/Vertigo. His homepage on the Web keeps the world updated on his every scribble. When will it ever end? (Page 156)

ALFONSO FONT

Font studied fine arts and drawing in Barcelona and decided to become a comic-book author. He has won several awards, among them the Critic Award (Barcelona, 1979), the 1984 Readers Award (Barcelona, 1981), and the Yellow Kid Award (Rome, 1996). (Page 108)

JAMES FRANCIS
James Francis walks among us... (Page 100)

GEORGE FREEMAN
George started in comics drawing *Captain Canuck*. He has worked for Marvel and DC for many years pencilling and inking. He lives in Canada with his wife, colorist Laurie Smith, and their two cats. (Page 8)

RICK GEARY
Rick is an occasional contributor to *MAD*. His last graphic novel is *The Borden Tragedy* and his latest is *The Fatal Bullet*, a study of the assassination of President James A. Garfield, both published by NBM. He also publishes a line of unusual postcards. (Page 116)

DEAN HASPIEL
Dino's comix have appeared in *Billy Dogma, Keyhole, Top Shelf, Non, Minimum Wage,* and *SPX*. Coming soon: *The Y2-401-Special-K Problem: a Billy Dogma Experience*. (Page 154)

KARL HEITMUELLER, JR.
Karl's past and present strips include "S'tan & Social Grace," "Aka Thunderstorm," and "The Retail Adventures of Kalli & Rex." Karl is indebted to a woman named "Pix" for her help with this story. (Page 122)

SHEPHERD HENDRIX
Shep has spent many years dancing with the big boys (DC, Dark Horse, Milestone, and Kitchen Sink). He recently inked *Clone Corps* for Reverie Comics. (Page 28)

JAMAL YASEEM IGLE
Jamal likes comics. He likes comics a lot. And occasionally, he gets to draw a few (like *Race Against Time* from Dark Angel Productions). (Page 65)

CHRIS JORDAN
Chris is an illustrator whose credits include *Discover, Disney Adventures, Family Fun,* and *Allure*. He is also working on *Babyhead Magazine* to be published by Slave Labor Graphics. All this without pants. (Page 25)

JAMES KOCHALKA
James has had numerous books published by Alternative Comics, Top Shelf, Highwater Books, Blackeye, and Slave Labor, including *Tiny Bubbles* and *Magic Boy and Girlfriend*. He was nominated for two Harvey Awards and won the coveted Ignatz Award. (Page 172)

ALAN KUPPERBERG
Since 1971, New Yorker Alan Kupperberg has drawn *Justice League, Firestorm, Warlord,* et cetera for DC Comics, and *Spider-Man, Thor, The Avengers, Captain America,* and others for Marvel. (Page 175)

ROGER LANGRIDGE
Frozen in a block of ice since World War II, Roger Langridge has recently been revived to carry on the cause of bringing more good comics into the world. (Page 34)

STEVE LEIALOHA
Steve has been drawing and inking comics for twenty-five years, including many major books for Marvel and DC. He recently inked *Chronos* for DC and *Nevada* for DC/Vertigo, and is drawing the upcoming miniseries *Sandman Presents: Petrefax* for DC/Vertigo. (Page 82)

JASON LITTLE
Xeric-winner Jason Little is the author of *Jack's Luck Runs Out* and the forthcoming *Shutterbug Follies*, the first collection of his weekly strip *Bee*. (Page 159)

STEVE MANNION
Steve Mannion was raised among his people, the Mannionites, in the wilds of New Jersey known as the Pine Barrens. No matter how much love he spreads through the world, some still think he is the Jersey Devil. (Page 169)

TAYYAR OZKAN
Tayyar's collection *Caveman: Evolution Heck* was published by NBM in the U.S. and to popular and critical acclaim in France. His *Caveman* comic, started in 1998, is published regularly. Tayyar also drew *La Pacifica*, a Paradox Graphic Mystery written by Joel Rose and Amos Poe, published by Paradox Press. (Page 134)

JEFF PARKER
There is much that your scientists still do not fully understand about how Parker draws the way he does. (Page 86)

MIKE PERKINS
Mike enjoyed working on *The Big Book of Grimm*. He even managed to get two free meals out of it. (Page 119)

RICHARD PIERS RAYNER
Richard was the Russ Manning Award-winner for Most Promising Newcomer in 1989 and has illustrated *Dr. Fate, L.E.G.I.O.N. '90, Swamp Thing* and *Hellblazer*. He also drew *Road to Perdition*, a graphic novel in the Paradox Graphic Mystery line, written by Max Allan Collins. (Page 68)

HARVEY RICHARDS
Harvey is making his freelance debut here. He's worked as an intern and production artist at Milestone and Acclaim Comics and is currently an assistant editor at DC Comics. He thanks his family and his wife Monica for all their support. (Page 114)

DAVID ROACH
David started drawing professionally ten years ago for *2000 AD*, eventually doing a long run on the Judge Anderson series. He has drawn *Star Wars* and *Aliens* comics for Dark Horse and various Batman titles for DC Comics. (Page 178)

WM. MARSHALL ROGERS
—was born at the beginning of the half-century and is still alive. (Page 13)

JAMES ROMBERGER
James Romberger's sleazy horror is on view in *Flinch* from Vertigo, and most of the rest of the Big Book series, also from Paradox Press. (Page 90)

CHRISTOPHER SCHENCK
Chris drew *Tarzan: Primeval* for Dark Horse, and *Amber: The Guns of Avalon* for DC/Byron Preiss. (Page 22)

JOE STATON
Joe has worked for Marvel on *The Incredible Hulk* and for DC illustrating *Superman, Batman, Plastic Man, Green Lantern,* and many others. Joe illustrated *Family Man*, a graphic novel in the Paradox Mystery line written by Jerome Charyn. (Page 124)

ALEC STEVENS
Alec Stevens has illustrated for *The New York Times Book Review, The New Yorker,* and many other publications. He recently contributed to *Proverbs & Parables*, a Christian comics anthology published by New Creation. (Page 184)

TOM SUTTON
Tom has drawn comics for many years, including various horror comics in the '70s and '80s, and many stories for the Big Book series in the '90s. We have sent the bio that Tom originally submitted to be placed in a listing of personal ads under "Variations." (Page 76)

CHARLES VESS
Charles has done paintings, illustrations, and comics for many years, including *Stardust* with Neil Gaiman for DC/Vertigo and *The Book of Ballads and Sagas* for his own Green Man Press. His next project is with Jeff Smith, which will be a prequel to the comic *Bone* called *Rose*. (Page 42)

STEVEN WEISSMAN
Steven Weissman has been in the business for almost five years. If nothing else, he'll be remembered for creating "Li'l Bloody" and the other cartoon characters in *Yikes* comic books. (Page 98)

GAHAN WILSON
Gahan's cartoons have appeared in *Playboy, The New Yorker, Gourmet, Punch, Paris Match,* and many others. He has had sixteen collections of his cartoons published. He is also the author of *The Big Book of Freaks* from Paradox Press. (Page 150)

BIBLIOGRAPHY

Grimm, Jacob and Wilhelm. *The Complete Fairy Tales of the Brothers Grimm*. Jack Zipes, trans. John B. Gruelle, illus. New York: Bantam, 1987.

--. *The Complete Grimm's Fairy Tales. 1944*. Margaret Hunt and James Stern, trans. Joseph Campbell, afterword. New York: Pantheon Books, 1972.

--. *German Popular Stories*. Edgar Taylor, ed. London: John Camden Hotten, Piccadilly, 1868.

--. *Household Stories*. 1886. Lucy Crane, trans. Walter Crane, illus. New York: Dover, 1963.

--. *The Juniper Tree and Other Tales from Grimm*. Lore Segal and Randall Jarrell, trans. Maurice Sendak, illus. New York: Farrar, Strauss and Giroux, 1973.

Grimm's Grimmest. Tracy Arah Dockray, illus. San Francisco, CA: Chronicle, 1997.

COPYRIGHT INFORMATION

THE LIBRARY OF BIG BOOKS:

THE BIG BOOK OF BAD
THE BEST of the WORST of EVERYTHING!
BY JONATHAN VANKIN and over 50 top comics writers and artists

IT'S ALL GOOD!

THE BIG BOOK OF HOAXES
TRUE TALES OF THE GREATEST LIES EVER TOLD!

BIG LIES THE WHOLE WORLD BELIEVED!

THE BIG BOOK OF LITTLE CRIMINALS
67 TRUE TALES OF THE WORLD'S MOST INCOMPETENT JAILBIRDS!

LITTLE MEN. BIG SCHEMES. TOUGH LUCK.

THE BIG BOOK OF THE UNEXPLAINED
ALLEGEDLY TRUE TALES OF PARANORMAL PHENOMENA!
BY DOUG MOENCH and OVER 40 of the WORLD'S TOP COMICS ARTISTS!

STRANGE PHENOMENA REVEALED!

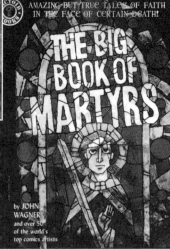

THE BIG BOOK OF MARTYRS
AMAZING BUT TRUE TALES OF FAITH IN THE FACE OF CERTAIN DEATH!
by JOHN WAGNER and over 50 of the world's top comics artists

TRUE TALES OF THE ULTIMATE SACRIFICE!

THE BIG BOOK OF THUGS
TOUGH-AS-NAILS TRUE TALES OF THE WORLD'S BADDEST MOBS, GANGS, AND NE'ER-DO-WELLS!
BY JOEL ROSE AND 57 OF THE WORLD'S TOP COMIC ARTISTS

YOU WANT TOUGH? WE GOT TOUGH!